ISBN 978-0-9844596-2-9
Church Love: Fire Works
Book Three in the Seasons in Savannah Series

Copyright © 2010 Shantae A. Charles
www.shantaecharles.com, www.godideasllc.com

Published by- GOD Ideas, LLC.

Scripture Quotations are taken from the King James Version of the Bible and are put into modern-day vernacular, context and application.

This is a work of fiction. Names, characters, places, and incidents are products of the author's imagination, the author's own personal experience, or are used fictitiously and are not to be construed as real. While the author was inspired in part by actual events, the characters are not distantly inspired by any individual known or unknown to the author. Any resemblance to actual events, locales, business establishments, organizations, or persons, living or dead, is entirely coincidental.

The author makes no apology for how the very **REAL** presence of God in this work of fiction may impact the reader's spiritual life.

Printed in the United States of America
First Printing 2010
10 9 8 7 6 5 4 3 2 1

Edited by Anita Wholuba; Cover Design: ROC Studios International, Inc.

Church Love:

Fire Works

Book Three in the Seasons in Savannah Series

Shantae A. Charles

Published by
GOD Ideas, LLC

Author's Commission and Foreword

"The Spirit of the Lord is upon me; because the Lord hath anointed me to preach good tidings unto the meek; he hath sent me to bind up the brokenhearted, to proclaim liberty to the captives, and the opening of the prison to them that are bound; to proclaim the acceptable year of the Lord. " - Isaiah 61:1-2

If you opened up this novel or inadvertently turned to this page as you were browsing through, **know that this is no accident.** This novel is in your hands **for a reason.** At this very moment, you are helping me to fulfill the call and commission of God for my life and you are walking into a greater understanding of God's will for the relationships in your life.

I count it an honor that God would place His Spirit upon me to pen words of hope, life, peace, joy, and deliverance in which I believe come from straight from His heart to yours. God has sent me to deliver some good news: Church Love is not a fictional concept. Whether you believe it or not, God has a community of believers who are waiting to receive you, who will be there to nurture you, and who will hold you accountable for your actions and speak the truth in love.

God wants to heal your broken heart and give you a reason to smile again, to laugh again, and to trust Him to work out every situation in your life. He wants to liberate you from the captivity of un-forgiveness, disappointment, bitterness, pessimism, cynicism, and grief. He wants you to love Him freely and not be afraid to receive His love and the love of other believers, especially as the love of the world waxes colder and grows more unnatural in their affections. God wants to refresh your heart and restore the principles of godly relationships among believers.

Though you may be saved, salvation is not the ending point but a starting point. God wants to ignite within you a fresh fire, fire that works out the Word of God in you to give you a passion to live on purpose, in purpose, for purpose, and through purpose to the glory of His son Jesus. I have written under the unction of the Holy Spirit and pray that you will glean the very real principles told through this parabolic novel. Join me on this journey as I venture once more into the heart of Savannah, GA where a community of believers awaits us.

Church Love....*Real* Characters....*Real* Issues....**God** Answers by Fire.

Shantae A. Charles
Author/Teacher

God's Foreword

"It is with great pleasure that I introduce Myself and reveal Myself in a more intimate way to you through this literary work. You were created for My glory and for My pleasure before the foundation of the world. For some, this is the beginning of our love affair. For others, this is yet another life changing encounter. May you seek Me and search for Me with all your heart. I will be found of you. I will strengthen you and empower you. You can rest in My love for I will never leave you nor forsake you. I desire to pour out My heart to you and lead you in the way that is true. Yield your will, thoughts, and desires to Me and you will not be disappointed. Believe in Me and you will never be put to shame. I desire your best always and forever.

I loved you before you ever knew Me. Don't think my love is predicated on what you can do; I loved you before I created you. While you were still a thought, loved you; before you could conceive to do wrong, I loved you. I have engraved you in the palm of my hand so that as I judge, I am reminded that you are mine and I am yours. You are apart of the rhythm of My heart. I feel when you are missing, when you have been drawn away. Return to Me, your first love and I will receive you; I will heal you; I will return the years that have been stolen from you. Remember, no one can hold you or love you like Me. Forever rest in My love and My love will forever rest in you.

The Everlasting Lover of your Soul,

(YHWH) Father, Son, and Holy Spirit

Dedication

To the wonderful married couples
who have deeply impacted
and influenced my life holistically
as I have continued this writing ministry.

To Pastors
(Especially Gerald & Judy Mandrell)
Who feed the flock of God
with knowledge and understanding.

To my husband
Robert
my daily inspiration
for godliness
and Church Love.

To my parents
Willie and Mary
who sacrificed
Some of their own dreams
Choosing the responsibility of
Birthing me rather than aborting me.

To singles everywhere
Who are living holy lives
Seeking God
and are **not afraid**
to acknowledge
It is not good for man to be alone.

To my **'adoptive children'** who
Started out as students
But became living examples
of success.
Keep making me proud!

Prologue

It feels good to be home, Seth thought to himself. Though he had enjoyed doing the work of the Lord in Ecuador immensely, he knew that the real work was just beginning. As he stepped off the plane, he was hit with a wave of nostalgia. *Home, sweet home*, he murmured again, wondering when he had grown to love the city of Savannah.

"Hey, Seth,"

Seth turned to the rowdy crowd, surprised that someone was calling his name. Correction; his brothers were calling his name. It was a most welcome sight. There before him stood some of the most courageous men he'd ever had the privilege of knowing: Josiah Edward Worth III, Shemiah Isaiah Newman, Nicholas and Giovanni Cartellini, Kevin Thomas, and Enrique Estrada. As he approached them, they stood, each man a giant in his own right, with huge grins on their faces. Enrique was the first to give him a bone crushing bear hug.

"Good to have you back, man." Josiah whacked him on the back, others joining in, a chorus of well-wishing pouring over him.

"Good to be back. The mission work went well. We were able to build a school, a church, dig several wells, and build a new home for the pastor there. How've things been stateside?" he looked to his friends expectantly. He had done some soul searching about what he planned to do once he landed stateside. He was no longer in denial. Time away had forced him to come to a searing reality: he was in love with a feisty, humorous, beautiful woman. Whether she loved him back was yet to be determined.

"We've definitely missed your presence around here. It's been mad crazy with all the press surrounding the kidnapping, but hopefully things will settle down soon." Josiah admitted.

"Not likely," Kevin joked, "with two of the hottest weddings of the summer about to take place!" they all teased Shemiah.

As they assisted Seth with his luggage and made their way outside, he couldn't help the nagging feeling that all was not as it should be.

"How's Aliya doing?"

Everyone stopped in their tracks, looking at each other, no one wanting to speak first.

"Well, don't all speak at once," Seth laughed unsteadily.

"We thought that you two could catch up tomorrow night at your welcome back dinner." Shemiah spoke up.

"My *what*?" Seth looked clueless.

"The dinner your brother is hosting on your behalf. You can thank him when you see him." Josiah grinned.

Seth stood transfixed, a million thoughts flooding his mind. *I'm not ready for this.*

Ready or not, it's time.

1

"Hold still for one more minute, Ms. Robinson," Aliya Peyton balanced the task of giving directions and holding straight pins between her lips. "You've got a great figure. How do you stay in shape?"

Marilyn turned her head as she stood on Aliya's pedestal in her boutique. "My fiancé chases me quite often." She joked.

"I can't *believe* I missed your engagement announcement." Aliya shook her head ruefully. "Savannah is still bubbling over. I think her excitement escalates daily." Aliya chuckled.

"She's got a long way to go before she tops her father. The man has been at my office every single day this week. It's going to be nearly *impossible* to keep him from seeing me before the ceremony." Marilyn grimaced.

Aliya helped Marilyn down from the pedestal. "I don't think the man will be able to help himself. You're going to be a gorgeous bride, Marilyn."

Marilyn blushed at the compliment. "I can't believe it's nearly June already. Time flies by so fast."

Isn't that the truth? It's been three months since my kidnapping and recovery and I'm still trying to get my bearings. "July eighth is the big day, right?" Aliya worked to pin Marilyn with ease.

"Yes." Marilyn buttoned her blazer. "Are you going to be able to attend the wedding? I know you all have to get ready to leave town as well."

Aliya gave her a chiding glance. "Do you think I'd miss a chance to see you walk down the aisle in a Divine Design Original? No way! Besides, I feel so honored to be apart of such a special occasion."

Marilyn hugged her. "I'm glad you're *alive* to be apart of such a special occasion." She set Aliya apart to look at her. "You, young lady, are a walking testimony to the goodness and mercy of God. Look at you. No one could even tell just by looking at you what you've endured."

Aliya smiled. "God's a miracle worker."

Just then, the doorbell jostled overhead. Aliya stuck her head out of her dressing area. "Be with you in a minute."

"No rush. Take your time." Jamar allowed the door to swing behind him as he took a stroll around her shop.

Aliya braced herself for what she knew was bound to turn into an argument. "I'll have your dress ready within two weeks for your fitting." She informed Marilyn walking past Jamar.

"Thank you so much, Aliya. You don't know how much this means to me." Marilyn hugged her. "You take care of yourself and don't overdo it. I know you're trying to make up for lost time, but take it one day at a time, okay?"

Aliya accepted the advice grudgingly. "Okay." She waved goodbye. Then she turned to face Jamar. "What can I do for you?"

You and Seth can put an end to this standoff, Jamar thought to himself. "Nothing really; I'm on break. I just thought I'd come over and say hello."

And pick my brains concerning your brother. "How very thoughtful of you." she said, letting her sarcasm ring loud and clear.

"And invite you to a celebratory dinner for Seth tomorrow evening." Jamar steeled himself for her response.

"He's back from Ecuador?" Aliya cringed at the thought of facing him now. The last time she saw Seth, they hadn't parted on good terms. Augusta however couldn't help but sing his praises. *If you dare try to avoid him, I'm going to throw you over my shoulder and drop you off on his doorstep.* Aliya remembered the declaration quite vividly.

"He just got back this morning. He's in the process of tying up some loose ends with the ministry." Jamar had been left in charge of Fresh Fire as an interim minister until Seth's mission trip was completed and he was ready to relinquish his duties. *I am definitely not pastoral material.*

"I see." Aliya had heard all about his sudden departure shortly before she'd awakened. She had been surprised to hear that Seth had been one of her most avid visitors outside of her immediate family. That revelation had somehow lessened her fears about Seth. *What must have gone through his mind during those months that I lay comatose? I'm sure he must have had second thoughts about us.* The very fact that it had been a month and he had not bothered to contact her at all perturbed her. *Was he just playing the role of a caring minister or was he concerned about me?* They were all good questions with no answers; at least not at the moment. "Well, let me check my schedule and I'll get back with you."

Jamar's eyes narrowed. *So it's going to be like that?* He spotted her appointment book open on the counter and decided to check it out for himself. Turning the page, he thumbed down to the eighth day. "According to your planner, you don't have anything on your agenda for tomorrow night at eight."

Guilty as charged. Aliya flipped the planner closed. "I don't keep my personal plans in the company planner."

Jamar eyed her suspiciously. "Well, why don't you break out your personal planner then? I'd like a definite answer from you."

Do I look like a woman who owns a personal planner? "I can't give you a definite answer right now." Aliya stood toe to toe, hands on her hips daring him to ask her why.

Jamar could see that Aliya's defenses were up. *Way up.* "Fine, I'll drop by around closing time if I don't hear from you by phone." He strode to the door.

"Closing time is fine." At least it would bide her some time. She needed time to sort out her emotions. She knew her feelings for Seth had not changed but she wasn't so sure about his feelings for her. *I've never been sure how he felt about me and I certainly don't want to find out in public.*

Jamar was out the door before she could change her mind. He had seen the indecision in her eyes. He would wait until round two to persuade her further. *If she thinks she's going to weasel out of this engagement, she's got another thing coming.*

"Are you going to eat that? Because I'm starving," Rodia pointed to the French fries on Nadia's plate.

"I'm not really that hungry." Nadia mentioned. She'd just received another hate letter slipped into her locker. It was the third one this week. She hadn't bothered to tell Rodia knowing that it would only make for two angry twins.

"How did your physics test go?" Rodia dipped her fry into a mound of ketchup.

"I think I aced it. Two students got caught cheating, though; took off ten minutes of our test time." Nadia scanned the lunchroom, her mind on other things.

"Don't you just hate that? Why does everybody have to suffer for the few?" Rodia finished off the fries.

"Get your prom tickets! Today is the last day!" the student council rep walked through the lunch tables flashing unsold tickets.

"Date or no date, I still think you should go." Rodia told her twin.

"How would that look-a junior showing up at a senior prom alone? No way. You couldn't pay me for the embarrassment." Nadia looked behind her at two cheerleaders buying tickets. Then she saw him. Brett Hamilton was coming her way. She hopped up quickly grabbing her bags.

"Where are you going? Rodia's questioning glance turned to a knowing glare.

"I've got to grab my homework for History class from my locker before the bell rings." Nadia swung her backpack over her shoulder. "Meet me outside the gym after school." She trotted off.

You can't run away forever. Rodia shook her head as Brett Hamilton made his way down the table giving high fives and waving to his female admirers. Rodia was hoping he would wave and keep right on moving. Instead, he sat down across from her.

"What's up, Rodia?" It was not lost on Brett that Nadia had once again run in the opposite direction. But today, hopefully, he would figure out why.

"Nothing much," Rodia looked around. For some reason, all eyes were on her. *I'm going to get you Nadia.*

"So, what's up with your sister?" Brett eyed Rodia who seemed hesitant to speak.

"She's fine." Rodia smiled wanly. "She's real busy: exam week and all."

"I just finished my last one fifth period." Brett admitted. "But besides exams, I'm just a little concerned."

"Concerned?" Rodia leaned over for this. "Why?"

"Well, she hasn't talked to me in months. I try to wave at her in practice but she just ignores me." Brett's exasperation was evident. "Every time I try to approach her, she walks off in the other direction."

"It takes Nadia a little more time than most to get over her anger." Rodia assured him.

"Is she upset with me?" Brett pointed to his chest.

Rodia looked at him as if that was obvious. "She is *beyond* upset with you."

Brett looked confused. "But we haven't talked in months. I've been trying to talk to her about the letter she wrote."

"You mean the letter she wishes she'd *never* written?"

"What was wrong with it? I thought it was sweet." Brett still had the letter. In fact, he read it over daily.

"Where have you *been*? It was all over school for weeks that my sister almost got into a fight about that letter. Some cheerleader told her that you were already taken and to pretty much back off." Rodia was surprised to see the look of anger on Brett's face. "Apparently word got out somehow that she had written you a letter."

Brett's brows furrowed together. "I didn't tell *anyone* about her letter. I would *never* do that to Nadia." Then he thought about it. "But I know who *would*." Brett's mind flashed back to a brief moment in the locker room months ago. He'd been reading the letter when his best friend had snatched it from him. He'd made some smart comment and handed it back. "I think I can straighten this all out if you can get her to talk to me."

Rodia shook her head regretfully. "It's not likely." Then an idea came to mind. "Wait-- what are you doing around three today?"

"I was just going to hang out with my boys and play some ball." But that wasn't important. What mattered to him right now was clearing his name and asking Nadia to the prom.

"Well, I don't know how she would react but we usually help my mom out around her shop and we get there around two-thirty after we pick up our little sister. I figure you could give us about thirty minutes before you stop in for a haircut." Rodia wiggled her eyebrows.

"A haircut; you don't think she's going to find that a bit odd?" Brett gave her an unbelieving stare.

"Whether it's odd or not, at least you'll have her attention. We don't leave the shop until my mom calls it quits for the day." Rodia notified him. *She's going to have a fit.* Rodia was only trying to help Brett out because he seemed genuinely interested in her sister. And she believed he was telling the truth.

"I'll be there at three then. Hopefully we can straighten out this whole mess and she'll accept my invitation to the prom." Brett stood then as the bell sounded.

"You're going to ask her to the prom?" Rodia was excited at the news.

"I've been trying to ask her for months now." He pulled out the tickets. "I guess I was a little too confident." He grinned sheepishly pulling out another ticket. "And this one's for you."

"Me?" Rodia took the ticket with shaky hands. "You really should have saved your money, Brett." She wasn't even planning on going.

"Oh, I didn't buy it. My friend over there did." he pointed to a tall, slender guy with a goatee, a cocoa tan and buzz cut. "He's a bit shy and since I was headed in this direction I thought I would pass on the message."

Rodia's mouth fell open. *Xavier Roberts?* "You're kidding right?" Rodia didn't run with the in-crowd but she was familiar with all the senior celebrities. And he was one of them. His break-up two months ago with his girlfriend he had been dating since his freshman year was headline news yet she noticed that he hadn't jumped into a relationship on the rebound. He was the power forward and star player for the basketball team. He was also someone Rodia had secretly admired since her sophomore year for his diligence in sports and academics. *I must be dreaming.* "Xavier Roberts; with me at Prom,"

What is her problem? Brett thought. "He asked me who I thought would be a nice girl to escort to the prom and I immediately thought about you. I think it would be great if we could all go together, provided your sister says yes. But even if she doesn't, I know you'd have a great time with Xavier. He's a world-class gentleman and I realize now that I can't say that about all my friends." He thought about the friend whose neck he was going to wring after school for interfering with his relationship with Nadia.

So, it's just an issue of him not wanting to go alone. Cool. I can handle that. I can just go, act polite, keep my feelings to myself and think of it as a friendly favor. I'll be fine. "I'll have to ask my mom first. I don't have a thing to wear since I hadn't planned on going so that means I'll have to go out shopping this weekend if she says yes."

"So translation is yes if your mom approves?" Brett smiled at Rodia's frazzled starry-eyed look. *She's got it bad.*

"Exactly," Brett and Rodia walked to their classes.
"How about I have him swing by your mom's shop this afternoon as well?" Brett knew he would have to warn Rodia about wearing her heart on her sleeve. Her eyes were dancing with excitement.

"Cool." Rodia bounced off toward her class. "See you then."

"Rodia," Brett called after her.

Rodia turned around in the middle of the hallway.

"Your heart reads like a Times Square billboard." Brett waved and stepped into his last class for the day.

Rodia gasped. *I never was too good at hiding my emotions. I'd better get it together before next Friday.*

Tatyanna paced back and forth in front of Augusta's office door. *How long do they need to deliberate?* Tatyanna could not believe their client was giving them such a hard time. She'd submitted seven different design proposals and all of them had been rejected. *We can't lose this account, Lord. We need to recoup our losses.*

"Standing at her door isn't going to make it open any sooner," Jamar reminded her from the counter.

Tatyanna glared at him. "Though you love to give it, we didn't hire you for your advice. Are you done typing that proposal yet?"

Jamar walked from around the receptionist desk. "Got it right here," He placed it in her outstretched hands giving a bow.

"If you were a little younger I'd put you over my knee and spank you." Tatyanna glared.

"If *you* were a little younger, Kevin would have himself some competition." Jamar dodged out of the way of Tatyanna's blow.

"Don't try to call me old on the sly." Tatyanna threatened him with her fists.

Jamar hurried back toward the reception desk. "It's okay Tatyanna. Growing old is a natural part of life."

"Keep it up and you're going to be a natural part of that desk." Tatyanna warned.

"Touchy, touchy," Jamar snickered as the door to Alpha, Inc. swung opened to reveal a frazzled employee.

"Are you okay, Ginny?" Tatyanna looked down at the five foot five petite brunette woman. Ginevieve Dubois had worked for Alpha, Inc. for the past five years and still she seemed no more acclimated to graphic design than when she first began.

"I'm just extremely overheated. I tell you. Louisiana was kinder to me than this city." Ginny fanned herself rapidly.

"Are you done delivering the local orders for today?" Tatyanna helped her to a seat.

"Yeah, I guess I should have just waited until after lunch. The air condition went out in the van again." Ginny threw her head back in relief.

"Alright Southern Belle, you got five minutes. But after that, back to work." Jamar teased her.

"I am *not* a Southern Belle, Jamar. An' I do not appreciate your calling me that." Ginny's steel tone echoed in the lobby.

Alright, you two, cut it out." Tatyanna warned them just in time as Augusta walked out of her office followed by their latest client.

"I'm sure we'll find something suitable to your tastes," Augusta walked the gentleman out the door. As soon as he turned the corner she closed her door leaning against it to address her staff. "That account is not worth the headache, Tatyanna."

"Tell me about it," Tatyanna agreed. "He simply can't make up his mind."

"He wants seven more designs." Augusta winced, as she knew what was coming.

"Seven *more*," Tatyanna threw up her hands. "Ginny, you can have this account if you want it. It would be a great addition to your portfolio."

"Nope; you know our motto. A project started is a project finished. You start it, you finish it." Ginny rose up from the sofa then.

"Drats," Tatyanna murmured under her breath.

"Drats indeed," Augusta smiled at her partner.

2

I need to hold off on the cheesecake until after the wedding, Savannah thought to herself. Her fuchsia nails perused the menu at Savannah's Taste as she awaited her soon to be mother-in law.

"Are you ready to order, Miss?" Her waiter interrupted her thoughts.

"Yes, I'm going to go ahead and order," Savannah ordered refreshment and was relieved to see her mother-in-law walk through the doors. She stood to greet her but her smile left completely as she saw the gentleman who followed behind her. Her stomach twisted into knots.

Indina Newman saw the pained expression on Savannah's face immediately. "Savannah, dear, are you alright?"

"I'm fine." Savannah managed to croak out as she took her seat once more. *Lysander Townsend? What on earth is he doing here, and with Indina for that matter?*

Indina sat down and motioned for her guest to be seated as well. "Don't just stand there, Lysander; Have a seat."

I can't believe this, Lysander thought to himself as he sat down stoically.

Indina looked from Savannah's distressed face to her nephew's angry expression. "You two know each other?"

They both began at the same time, and then stopped.
"You go first," Lysander offered.

Savannah squirmed in her seat then. "Lysander and I dated briefly during my sophomore year of college."

Indina's brow rose. "How brief?'
"One week," Lysander ground out. "Nothing beyond that," he assured her. *It was certainly not for my lack of trying.*

Indina didn't know how to respond.
"*Nothing* happened between us, Indina," Savannah assured her, feeling annoyed that her past was being put on the spot. *Thank God nothing happened.* Savannah had found out afterward that she been the object of a longstanding bet between immature fraternity men. She'd told Lysander exactly what she thought of him. It had been pretty easy to dodge him on campus after that. She had never expected to see him again. Now he was having lunch with her.

"I'm sure your cousin will be happy to hear that." Indina looked to Lysander, an expression of relief on her face.

"You're Shemiah's *cousin*?" Savannah was about to go into cardiac arrest at the revelation. *How could two men who were so different be related to one another?*

"Yes, Savannah, Shemiah and I are cousins," Lysander smiled at the look of terror on her face. *It serves her right.* When Lysander had heard that his cousin was getting married, he was the first one to congratulate him—until he heard the bride's name: Savannah Charles. He had been compelled to join Indina today to see if it was the one and the same. He was not disappointed. His eyes poured over her shamelessly. *She looks lovelier than she did eight years ago.* Gone was the girlish figure. Savannah was definitely *a* woman and it infuriated him. He had really liked Savannah back then and the sad truth was he'd never fallen so hard for anyone since then. It had started out as a bet, but in the end he was the one who'd gotten the sour end of the deal. *Get over it! She's marrying your cousin for God's sake!* Lysander ignored his conscience.

Savannah thought she was going to be ill. "You're his cousin: great. What are you doing *here*?"

Indina could tell that the whole situation was distressing to Savannah but at the moment, it couldn't be helped. "Lysander is in town for dual purposes. He's here acting as our family attorney as well as checking on a partnership with another attorney in town."

Savannah was confused. "Why do we need a family attorney?"
Indina looked to Lysander for explanation. "Lysander, would you care to shed more light on why you're here?"

This was the part that gave him great pleasure. "I handle all the legal affairs for the Townsend and Newman family members. I'm here to witness the prenuptial agreement and answer any questions you may have before you sign." *Because you will sign, or there will be no wedding.* He was sure of that. Shemiah was a man in love, and it was no wonder: he'd fallen for the intoxicating Savannah; but he was not stupid. Lysander had to give him credit there.

"Shemiah and I never discussed a prenuptial. We both agreed that what's mine is his and what's his is mine," Savannah glared at Lysander.

"That's a very sweet sentiment, but as the attorney for this family, it would be unwise of me not to recommend this course of action. All Newman and Townsend men have prenuptial agreements. Shemiah would not be the first." Lysander's explanation was so logical. "Not to mention the fact that Shemiah is the one who stands to lose if you do not keep your vow of matrimony." *And if it is up to me, you may not get that far.*

Savannah could not believe what she was hearing. "Is this what you wanted to meet with me about?" She looked Indina in the eye.

Indina faltered. "This was apart of it. Look, Savannah. This isn't a question of whether or not you love my son. It's simply a family tradition. I myself signed a prenuptial before I married Isaiah. It hasn't diminished our relationship at all."
Savannah looked at the papers in front of her. "I understand your point of

15

view, Mrs. Newman, but for me these papers are a slap in the face to fidelity. Signing a prenuptial agreement, in my opinion, says that I believe my marriage has the potential for divorce."

"So are you saying you won't sign?" Lysander pressed her.

"I've already stated how I feel, Mr. Townsend." Savannah added the formality to make it clear she was not going to be boxed into a corner.

"I see. If you do sign, you stand to lose a lot more than if you chose not to sign." Lysander ground out. "Because you have nothing to bring to the table in this relationship, isn't that right?"

Savannah swallowed her bitter retort. "I have what is important, Mr. Townsend; faith, trust, integrity, purity, and holy intent. But, what would you know about any of those qualities since after eight years you are still so *obviously* lacking in them?" She stood then. "I have to get back to work."

Indina stood as well touching Savannah's arm. "I didn't mean to upset you, Savannah. But we had to deal with this sooner or later." She handed her the agreement. "Think about it. Pray about it. And let the Lord lead your decision. I'm sure it won't matter to Shemiah either way, but I did want you to know what would be expected of you."

Savannah needed to get away before she burst into tears right on the spot. "I'll call you this evening. I would rather we met alone."

"That's perfectly understandable." Indina assured her. "But don't avoid Lysander, Savannah. Whatever you two need to settle, you need to settle it *before* August eighth." She cautioned.

Savannah understood exactly what she meant. She nodded in understanding. *In just thirty minutes my love life has been turned upside down.* As Savannah walked out of the restaurant she flipped on her cell. There was no use trying to deny it. It would be hard to counsel anyone today when she was in need of counseling.

Indina sat down to order her lunch with Lysander. "Would you care to tell me what's going on between you and my son's fiancé? Her question was stated in a casual manner, but she meant business.

Lysander folded his hands together. "I was in love with her. She dumped me. End of story."

Indina glared at him over her menu. "Apparently it's not the end of the story, Lysander. The girl looked as though she was going to faint at the sight of you." She put her menu down. "I need details."

"My dating her started off as a bet between some of my frat brothers. Everyone knew of Savannah as the hard-working, good-looking, 'religious' sister. Anyway, as part of my initiation, I had to go out with her and see if she would give in to temptation so to speak."

Indina looked appalled. *"Lysander. You didn't. "*

"Hey, I'm not proud of what I did, but it was a part of getting in. Anyway, after the second date, I didn't want to play by the rules anymore because I really began to like her. I confessed to my frat that I was really interested in her and that I wanted to get out of the dare. They refused. I continued to date her ignoring the bet. When my frat brothers saw that I was serious about her, they told her she was a stupid bet and that I was just playing her to get what I really wanted. She came to my dorm room ranting and raving about my being a womanizing dog. I never saw her on campus after that."

Indina could imagine Savannah aflame with righteous indignation. "So what made you come today, Lysander? You had to have had a suspicion that she was the same woman."

Lysander didn't answer.

"Lysander, you can't *possibly* be infatuated with her after all this time." Indina stated.

"What if I am?" Lysander questioned her.

Indina did not want to even imagine the consequences of that statement. "She's engaged to your cousin whom happens to be *my* son. I for one am not going to tolerate the notion. From the looks of things you are as distasteful to Savannah now as you were then." Indina pointed out.

"That's because she doesn't know the truth about what really happened." Lysander countered.

"And you believe that eight years later she's going to believe your side of the story? Hardly," Indina was convinced her nephew had lost his mind. "So what are you going to tell my son? Hey Shemiah, you know the girl you plan to marry? Well, I saw her first and if you don't mind, I want to stir up an old flame one month before you get married? Lysander, you are asking for World War three here!"

"I believe its Savannah's decision entirely. I agree with you that eight years is a long time. But believe it or not, when I saw her today, my feelings for her only *intensified*. Savannah is Shemiah's fiancée- *not* his wife. Everyone would do well to remember that," Lysander took a sip of his lemonade leaving Indina to stare after him in disbelief.

"These projections look great, Shemiah." Josiah closed the portfolio and handed it back to him.

"Thanks. I wanted to turn it in before the wedding. The last thing I want to be thinking about come August is next year's revenue projections." Shemiah grinned from ear to ear.

Josiah laughed at his best friend. "I hear you on that. How are the plans going?"

Shemiah straightened up a bit. "The reception details are all ironed out. As you know I'll be taking the company plane and Enrique's jet. That puts us at a total of around fifty guests. I've got to fly down next month to finalize some details with the caterers."

"And how are the counseling sessions going with my father?" Josiah had heard nothing but good things from the Elder Worth concerning Savannah and Shemiah's participation.

"I'm glad Savannah and I have taken the time to get to know each other. I know I went in kicking and screaming, but I thank God she was able to talk me into it. It's refreshing to know that we have common interests. We both want to raise a family though not right away. Did you know she's been taking cooking lessons from her grandmothers?"

"That's great. I'll have to scratch fire extinguisher off my shopping list." Josiah kidded.

"Even if she burned every dinner, I'd still love her." Shemiah declared.

"I'll make sure to include that in my wedding toast." Josiah promised. "And where is the lovely bride to be?"

"She was having lunch with my mother today. I imagine she's back at work now. I plan to stop by and surprise her." Shemiah stood then.

"Well, don't let me keep you then. Don't forget the men's barbecue at Seth's this Saturday." Josiah reminded him.

Shemiah slapped his forehead. "I almost forgot. We need an extra grill, right?"

"Yep," Josiah nodded.

"Why are we having this on the beach again?" Shemiah couldn't remember if Josiah gave a reason or not.

"My wife is having the Women's sleepover at our beach house. I want to be close by in case she needs me." Josiah said innocently.

"Uh Huh; Sure; you mean in case you get tired of hanging with us singles, you can sneak on over there. That's pretty low, Siah." Shemiah grinned.

"Hey, a man's got to do what a man's got to do." He wiggled his eyebrows.

"How do you expect to see her? You know all men are barred." It was the one condition Shemiah hated about those women's fellowships.

"All men are barred from the beach house *not* the beach." Josiah amended.

"You know, you're a whole lot smarter than you look?" Shemiah managed to escape the paperweight thrown in his direction.

Josiah shook his head at his office door. *What a smart aleck.*

Though his jet had touched down only this morning, Enrique was already back to work in more ways than one.

The Venice heat had only deepened his tanned complexion. His usually close-cropped ebony hair had grown unruly making him look more like a renegade than a respectable businessman. Having discarded his tailored suit for casual slacks and a linen shirt, he stood with Kevin Thomas reviewing the site plans for his new headquarters. Nicholas stood behind him while Giovanni visually scanned the property.

He'd been determined to start his construction even during the trial. He would show no weakness or indecision to his foes. EAE Design Group was not going to surrender to organized crime in any way.

"You've got a great piece of property here." Kevin commented off hand.

"You've made good use of the property." Enrique complimented Kevin. "I'm pleased with the design and your attention to detail. Everything seems to be right on schedule."

"I saw your press conference today. You did well." Kevin knew the kidnapping was a very touchy subject these days. "I hope things will get back to normal for you."

Enrique gave a short laugh. "Hardly; I just had to realize that the life I live could never be seen as normal; those who risk knowing me, also risk being in danger. It's as simple and as complicated as that." It had been hard to come to grips with that truth but it was necessary.

"Have you seen Aliya yet?" Kevin knew from Tatyanna that she harbored no animosity or ill will toward Enrique for what happened. As for Augusta, well, no one was sure.

"I'm going to have to arrange a private meeting. The press is just lying in wait for our 'reunion'. I know she and Augusta have had more press than they can take. I don't want to add to it." He'd read all about Augusta's barrage with the press: *The Billionaire's Sweetie*. He was absolutely sure she didn't take too kindly to the nickname though he thought it suited her entirely. She had remained silent on their relationship of which he was strangely grateful and annoyed at the same time. *Don't I mean anything to you, Augusta?* She had not returned any of his calls or his emails. She was retreating from their relationship again but Enrique was not going to allow it.

"I know you've just got back in town, but the men are having a barbecue at Seth's beach house on Saturday. From what I understand, the women are meeting at Josiah's beach house. Maybe you could arrange to talk to her then. I could relay the message for you." Kevin offered.

"That would be fine. Call me Friday morning to let me know if she's agreeable to the meeting. I know she's been skittish about meeting anyone, including Seth. I have other plans as far as Augusta is concerned." Enrique turned to Giovanni. "Has Mr. Bolivar contacted you yet?"

"He should be contacting us any moment now."

"Good. I want a full report. Her reaction, her expression, her words," Enrique handed Kevin his next installment. "Thank you Kevin for all your hard work. I know sometimes it was difficult to get a hold of me in Venice, but I'll be more available now that I'm in town."

"Good to have you back." Kevin gripped his hand and grinned. "I'm sure there are more pressing matters you need to attend to."

"My thoughts exactly," Enrique agreed heartily.

3

"Five! Six! Seven! Eight! That's a rap folks!" Rosalynn picked up her water bottle and slung her towel over her shoulder as she sat down on the gym bleachers to catch her breath. She took a long swig of water before she sat her bottle upright.

"You did great, Roz," Carlton gave his sister a pat on the back as he sat down next to her.

"I'll take a one-to-one any day." Rosalynn informed him. Since they'd started combining church groups together for their Lunch Power Fitness Program the classes were overflowing their capacity. Carlton was training Rosalynn to take over as he split the workload.

"I didn't expect this level of success, but we're doing so well, I'm considering dropping some of our private clients." Carlton confessed.

Rosalynn stopped drinking her water bottle midair.

Carlton laughed at her expression of disbelief. "I'm going to recommend my older clients take the senior class we started. I think some of them can use the interaction and it would lessen their rates by coming with a group."

Rosalynn grinned. "So you're not the ruthless businessman I thought you were all these years. My brother *does* have a heart."

Carlton put his finger to his lips. "Don't blow my cover." He pulled Roz to her feet. "I've got to get going. I've got a two o'clock today. Will you be fine locking up here?' He tossed her the keys. Pastor Marks had volunteered his church gym for the workout sessions in exchange for a free membership.

Rosalynn rolled her eyes. "I'm a big girl. I think I can handle it."

Carlton grinned. "You know you can't say that anymore. You're so thin, you're libel to be picked up and carted off."

Rosalynn punched him playfully. "Judo and kickboxing have both taught me a lot."

Carlton laughed. "I guess I better remember that. It's your turn to cook tonight and takeout *doesn't* count."

"I'll remember that the next time you order pizza," Rosalynn called out.

She looked forward to Saturday night with the ladies. Her only responsibility was to bring the movies. Speaking of dinner, she smiled to herself as she thought about the call that came from Venice on Monday evening.

I owe you dinner. It had been a pleasant surprise for her that Nicholas Cartellini had even been thinking about their last conversation. He'd told her they would be arriving in the States sometime this week. Here it was Thursday and she had not heard anything else; although she couldn't blame him for not calling again; Carlton had nearly hit the roof when he found out who was on the line. After a shouting match that no doubt their entire neighborhood was now privy to, he'd grudgingly agreed to the fact that she was capable of making her own decisions and that one dinner date was not cause for hysteria or cardiac arrest.

Rosalynn was still trying to convince herself of the same thing. She couldn't shake the fact that Nicholas's voice held the promise of something far greater than a casual dinner between two adults.

As Rosalynn walked past the wall length mirror on her way out of the gym, she paused for a moment. *Wow. I really am a size six.* Rosalynn hadn't been trying to lose more weight. Instead she'd concentrated the past three months on toning and conditioning.

She had grown to love her new lifestyle and her new wardrobe and she felt better about herself not because she was thinner but because she now realized that whether she was a size six or a size sixteen, she was fearfully and wonderfully made by God and no one had the right to make her feel otherwise.

Being overweight Rosalynn had many critics but she soon found out that being thinner didn't exempt you from criticism either.

Don't you think you're overdoing it?
Girl, you've lost some of your best assets.
Enjoy it while it lasts.
Rosalynn was wise enough to know that with her change came the responsibility to maintain that change. *Lord, help me to maintain this change.*

"I'm sorry Mr. Newman. Savannah's gone for the afternoon. She cancelled all of her appointments for the rest of the day."

Shemiah sat outside S.P.I.C.Y. (Second Chance Preparatory School for Inner City Youth) in his SUV. "Alright, then," He couldn't fathom why Savannah was not at work. She loved conferencing. It was all she had talked about during their Sunday brunch the past week.

"Oh, and Mr. Newman,"
"Yes?"

"Her secretary said that she sounded a bit distressed." The assistant principal offered.

"Thank you." Shemiah snapped his cell phone shut. *That makes me feel wonderful. My fiancé is upset and I can't find her.* What was more telling was that she had not turned to him in her distress.

"She doesn't feel as if she can turn to you with what she is facing."

What's going on?

"Be quick to hear, slow to speak, slow to wrath." Shemiah knew the Lord spoke that scripture on very few occasions in his life. It could only mean that something explosive was around the corner. And this time it had to do with Savannah. He started his SUV his mind made up to drive off in search of Savannah when his cell phone rang.

"Hello."

"Shemiah, glad I could reach you," his mother's breathless reply rolled over him in apprehension.

"Where's Savannah?" his tone was terse.

"She went back to work. Listen, there's something--"

"I'm right outside her school and she's not here." Shemiah's voice was rising.

"She's not?" Indina had stepped into the ladies room to call her son.

"No. She cancelled all her appointments for the rest of the day. She didn't even tell her secretary where she was going. What happened today? I thought you two were meeting about the wedding plans." Shemiah was anxious to get moving.

"We didn't quite get to that part." Indina admitted. "Shemiah, there are some things you need to know about and deal with and I need to see you in person to talk about them. Lysander came down with me."

"Lysander?" Shemiah didn't see what the big deal was. "That's great that he was able to escort you down here."

Indina sighed resignedly. "Shemiah, it appears that Savannah and Lysander know each other."

Shemiah's grip tightened on the steering wheel. "Go on."

"They dated briefly in college. It appears that your cousin still has feelings for her."

If Shemiah had been holding a tin can it would have been pulverized at that very moment. "Does Savannah?"

"It's clear that she doesn't hold him in high regard but he claims that will change when he explains their break up was a misunderstanding." Indina knew it was coming.

"Misunderstanding my foot; she's *my* fiancée! Did you explain that to him?" Shemiah pulled onto the road.

"He understands *far* too well the difference between fiancée and wife. He feels its Savannah's decision to make. Not yours."

"Any *other* disastrous thing I should know about?" Shemiah sped toward Richmond.

"Your grandfather sent Lysander along to talk about the prenuptial agreement." Indina prepared her eardrums.

"What gives him the *right* to meddle in my personal life?" Shemiah was ready to explode.

"Shemiah, you knew it was going to come up sooner or later. Your grandfather is an extremely stubborn man. I explained to Savannah that it was entirely her choice to sign or not." Indina was unflinching on this particular subject. "But Lysander did make a good point."

"And what was that pray tell?"

"If Savannah doesn't sign the prenuptial, she stands to gain more than *half* of our family holdings."

"There was a very good reason why I didn't mention a prenuptial agreement."

"Why?"

"Because I love her and I'm not planning for divorce!" Shemiah released the pressure on the gas. "Did she sign it?"

"No."

"Thank God." *I love that woman!*

"But I did give it to her to look over and consider."

Shemiah shook his head. *Someone should have warned me about meddling in-laws.* "I should have eloped."

"Shemiah," Indina gasped.

"If I would have known my engagement was giving my family members time to wreck my wedding I most *certainly* would have. Tell Lysander to stay away from my fiancé." Shemiah ended the call and focused his attentions on reaching Savannah's home.

Marco Bolivar stepped hesitantly across the threshold of Divine Designs Boutique. *Lord, I hope the twins are in a good mood today.* He had known Aliya and Augusta for some time now and when it came to delivering flowers or any other such gifts some days the twins rewarded the messenger. Other days they shot the messenger. Neither twin lacked admirers. Today's package came from a faithful client of his.

"Is anyone in?"

Aliya was just walking out of her office when her eyes caught sight of the beautiful bouquet. She'd grown accustomed to receiving gifts after her recovery. She couldn't believe they were still coming. "Are those for me?"

Marco set the vase down proudly. "Yes, as a matter of fact."

Aliya pulled out the card and read it to herself.

I'm glad you're doing well. I look forward to a great big hug.

                                        Enrique

"He's back in town?" Aliya got excited. *Now Augusta can stop moping around.*

"You don't watch television? He was on at lunchtime. He had a press conference early this morning. But this is not the only package from him. The other is for your sister." Marco presented the other box to Aliya. "He asked that you deliver it on his behalf."

Aliya took the brown package from Marco reading the label. "Oh my goodness," Aliya started squealing.

"I take it this is good news?" Marco questioned her.

Aliya stopped mid-squeal. "Are you *kidding*? No man buys New York Jewelers *anything* if he's not serious." Aliya grabbed her keys to lock up.

"Where are you going?" Marco followed behind Aliya.

"I'm going to see my twin sister faint!" Aliya laughed giddily.

Marco remembered that he had similar instructions. "I guess I'll follow along, then."

Seth Davis stood at his window watching the strange happenings at Divine Designs.

Why can't I just bring myself to go over there and approach her? He berated himself for his cowardice.

He'd been afraid that he'd never get a chance to tell her how he felt when she was comatose. He'd had plenty of time to mull over the thought of Aliya being his wife and he'd come to grips with it. If he thought she lacked strength, tenacity or endurance she'd proved him wrong on all counts.

Even during her recovery, he'd heard about how she'd gone to the children's wing of the hospital and cheered up the little patients there.

She's not the shallow one in this relationship. He'd only been thinking about the image of a pastor's wife: Someone with refined manners and tastes. A woman, who said the right things, did the right things, wore the right clothes, and had the right connections.

Lord, what's the best way to approach her?

"Tell her you were wrong about her. Tell her you judged her on appearances. Most importantly tell her you love her for who she is not for what she can become."

Seth sat down to write what the Lord said.

"I didn't say write it down. I said tell her. I'll present the opportunity."

Augusta, Jamar, Tatyanna, and Ginevieve were still talking in the lobby when Aliya burst in.

"Should I call the cops?" Jamar picked up the telephone.

"Put the phone down, boy." Tatyanna glared at him.

"Liya, you just gave us all a heart attack. What's wrong?" Ginevieve questioned her.

"I have a delivery to make." Aliya presented Augusta with the package.

Marco watched anxiously.

"Who's this from?" Augusta read the label.

"As if you need to guess," Tatyanna looked to Augusta. "Well, don't keep us waiting. Open it."

Augusta's heart beat wildly. "I don't know if I should with all these on looking spectators,"

"Open it!" They all said in unison.

"Okay!" Augusta carefully opened the package. Inside was a white box with red lettering. She placed it on the receptionist counter opening it.

"Wow." The hushed sound came from her watching audience.

It was a beautiful velvet heart with a sterling silver clasp. She opened it. "Oh my: I can't accept this." Inside the velvet heart was a diamond-studded heart on a chain. Next to it laid a diamond-studded key. There was a card as well. She pulled it out and read it to herself.

You not only have my heart, but the key as well. When you are ready, it will always be open to you.

Love, Enrique

Augusta felt the warmth of those words wrap around her. She smiled. She picked up the chain and looked at the heart. It had a keyhole. She took the diamond-studded key and fit inside the heart. It opened. On one side was an engraved message. *I love you Augusta. I Corinthians 13:7.* On the other side was a picture of Enrique. "Can someone grab my bible for me?" It was going to be difficult for her to read the scripture through tears, but read it she would.

"What are we reading?" Aliya was already flipping through the scriptures.

"First Corinthians thirteen, verses seven and eight."

"Here goes: Love bears all things, believeth all things, hopes all things, and endures all things." Aliya closed the Book. "'I'd say that would just about cover your relationship with Enrique."

Augusta put the necklace back into the velvet box and closed it, embarrassed that she'd let herself get carried away. "Alright staff. There's been enough entertainment at my expense. Let's get back to work." She sniffled.

Marco Bolivar headed back to his shop mystified by Augusta's reaction.

"Have you made any decision yet?" Jamar questioned Aliya on her way out.

Aliya shrugged her shoulders. "I guess if Augusta can soften up a bit to take gifts from Enrique, I can bring myself to have dinner with Seth."

Jamar restrained his enthusiasm. "Great. Eight o'clock sharp at the beach house."

"Should I bring a gift?" Aliya thought to ask.

"Your presence will do." Jamar went back to work on his latest assignment.

"Dressy or casual wear?" Aliya tapped her foot.

"Dressy but comfortable," Jamar kept typing.

"Is there such a thing?"

"If there isn't, I'm sure you'll design it." Jamar glanced at her with a wry smile.

"I bet Seth wants to throttle you daily." Aliya joked.

"You have no idea how close to the truth you are." Jamar's rich laughter filled the lobby.

"Aliya, don't you have a business to run?" Augusta could be heard through her door.

"Of course I do!" Aliya snapped.

"Great. Then get to it!" Augusta thundered.

Aliya made a face at the door. "She's just mad that we saw her get sappy, that's all." She whispered to Jamar.

"I heard that!" Augusta roared.

Aliya escaped then. Rounding the corner, she could still hear Jamar's peals of laughter.

4

Naomi Watts was busy writing down her patient's current vitals when she heard the news update of her best friend's arrival back to the United States. She looked up then to hear the rehash of the early news.

"And in our local news, Enrique Estrada, CEO of EAE Design Group made his first public appearance today since the notorious attempt of Lorenzo Bataglioni to bring his company down through organized crime. Sources say that Mr. Estrada had been arraigned to testify in Venice in connection with the kidnapping attempt of his close friend Aliya Peyton. Mr. Estrada spoke confidently about the future of his company and he fervently declared that negotiations with terrorism of any kind could never be an option. I know many Americans share his sentiments. Back to you, Frank..."

Naomi stood, her eyes transfixed on the screen. That was exactly how Dr. Jones found her.

"Someone you know?" Dr. Jones interrupted her mental musing.
Naomi turned to face him. "Yes. He's a close friend of mine. You met him briefly once."

Dr. Jones wiggled his eyebrows. "How close are we talking about?"

Naomi punched him playfully. "Not *that* close; we grew up together."

Dr. Jones gave her a knowing look. "So are you telling me that a beautiful young lady such as yourself hasn't caught the attention of anyone?"

Naomi flushed at the compliment. "I didn't say that." She looked back at the screen as Enrique shook hands with the mayor. Nicholas and Giovanni stood close by.

Trey decided he would close the subject for now. He had other business to discuss. "Are you up for dinner tonight?"

"Sure." Naomi completed her chart and placed it back on the front of the patient' bed. "You cook?"

"How does lemon and garlic chicken, tabouli, and asparagus sound?"

Naomi rolled the menu around in her head. "Hmmm... sounds fancy." She looked at him with suspicion. "Why do I sense that I'm not the object of the invitation?"

"I just need you to talk Aurielle into having dinner with us." Dr. Jones could see the hesitation in her eyes. "It seems as if our paths never cross these days. I have reason to believe she's avoiding me though I can't prove it." Naomi still wasn't budging. "Please, Naomi. I need you help."

Naomi grinned. *It's good to see a man sweat every now and then.* "Throw in cheesecake for dessert and you've got a deal."

Dr. Jones sighed. "You drive a hard bargain."

"Negotiation is the name of the game." Naomi giggled.

"What if she says no?" Dr. Jones knew Aurielle could be strong-willed.

"I'm going to make her an offer she can't refuse." Naomi followed Dr. Jones down the hallway to the elevator.

"I'm counting on you, Naomi." Dr. Jones was serious then. "I'm leaving here in the next hour so if you hear anything let me know."

Naomi looked at her watch. It was nearing two. "Trey, you've got to stop doing this to yourself. You've worked overtime this entire week. How do you expect to convince Aurielle that you have time for a relationship if you're always here?"

The elevator doors opened. Trey stepped out looking back. "When I'm here, Naomi, it gives me no time to think about the relationship that continues to elude me." He waved as the doors closed leaving Naomi with her own thoughts.

Touché; how well I can identify with those words. Except that it didn't matter what she was doing, images of Giovanni Cartellini seemed to flash across her mind at the most inopportune times. Seeing him spread across the television screen today didn't help. His dark boys hid his expressive eyes. His grim expression hid the playful smile she'd seen from time to time. *Why am I thinking about him? I've got more important things to focus on.*

The past few months she'd been a mixture of emotions. And being unemotional was something Naomi prided herself on. She had given up the opportunity to begin a relationship with Giovanni just to be on the safe side only to discover that no one was safe. Aliya's kidnapping had brought to stark reality the dangers involved with being apart of Enrique Estrada's life.

It could have been me. By virtue of the fact that she and Enrique were close friends someone very well could have used her to satisfy their personal vendetta. She tortured herself wondering if she had done the right thing by rejecting Giovanni. She was coming to realize that everything involved risk. *If I don't risk telling Giovanni how I feel about him I may regret it for the rest of my life.* She also knew that there would be no return to the comfort of her well-ordered lifestyle. She wanted to let go of her apprehensions but she needed a little help.

Lord, I am terrified of being in a relationship with someone whose life has the potential to be snuffed out without warning.

"I have not given you the Spirit of fear but of power, love and a sound mind. Perfect love casts out all fear. He that dwells in the secret place of the Most High shall abide under the shadow of the Almighty. Don't be afraid of terror that flies by night nor arrows that fly by day. Don't be afraid of pestilence that walks in darkness or of destruction that happens at noonday. A thousand may fall at your

side and ten thousand at your right hand; but it shall not come close to you. As you make the Lord your refuge and your habitation, no evil shall befall you. No plague will come near your home. Trust me to keep you from falling. Trust me to protect what you care for."

Naomi walked out of the elevator in a daze. She'd heard the voice of God speak within her heart, but not with such force or such clarity. It was if He had given the okay. *Strange, but I feel lighter. Like something has been lifted from my shoulders.* Naomi had heard some of those passages of scriptures before but she'd never really applied them. *I never really believed them,* she confessed to herself. And she knew it was time. It was high time to mix the Word with her faith.

Nadia ran with the flow of traffic towards the girl's locker room. *Thank God finals are over.* It had been a long week and it still wasn't over. *Friday will be a piece of cake.* The majority of the seniors would be leaving early Friday morning for their senior trip. The halls would be devoid of slackers and those who were falling prey to 'senioritis'. *And I won't have to focus on dodging Brett.* She was having a pretty good afternoon until she reached her gym locker. Sprayed in black spray paint on the royal blue locker were all kinds of foul names.

Nadia sat down on the bench. *Why is this happening to me? All I did was write one stupid letter.* She hadn't bothered to talk to her mother to tell her what had happened since she'd written that letter. She knew her mother's temper was a lot greater than her own. Columbia Newcomb ranting and raving in the principal's office would not add to her popularity. She'd threatened physical damage to her twin if she didn't keep silent about the near fight she'd gotten into. There hadn't been any more confrontations. Instead the girls that had it in for her had taken things to another level altogether. Now with the damage done to school property she knew she was in over her head.

She opened her locker and nearly gasped in pain. She pulled out her cheerleading outfit or what was left of it. The cheerleading outfit she'd paid for with her own money. It was completely shredded. Added to injury there were feminine products glued to the garment. Nadia bit back a cry stuffing the garment back into her locker. She grabbed her book bag and ran out to the field ignoring the peals of laughter from some of the varsity cheerleaders.

"Nadia," Brett called out. He was talking with some of his teammates when he saw her take off past him like a streak of lightning. Her face had a look of shock. Something was wrong. He excused himself and took off after her.

Nadia kept running until she made it to her car. Rodia was already waiting for her. "Get in."

Rodia knew better than to ask her what was wrong. Nadia had the look of murder written across her features. She hopped in.

Nadia pulled off just as Brett reached the gate. She looked in her rearview mirror at the obviously miffed teenager who was banging his fist on the gate. She took a few deep breaths.

"Are you ready to share?" Rodia ventured.

"Someone broke into my gym locker and shredded my cheerleading uniform and decorated it with feminine products."

"*What?*" Rodia had heard of some pretty bad senior pranks but that was taking it too far. "Did you report it?'

"Tomorrow," Nadia tried to keep her focus on the road.

"What if it's gone?" Rodia tried to reason.

"It won't be. They spray painted the outside of my locker as well with profanity."

Rodia turned to look at her twin. "These senior pranks have got to stop."

Nadia rolled her eyes. "This isn't a senior *prank*, Rodia. It's about Brett. They want me to stay away from him."

"But you haven't spoken to him in months," Rodia insisted.

"*I* know that." Nadia breathed a sigh of regret. "This is not the first time this has happened." Nadia explained about the hate letters being slipped into her locker.

"Why didn't you *tell* me?" Rodia was a little hurt by Nadia's secrecy. They had always told each other everything.

"I didn't think it was serious. I thought I could handle it. Take care of the situation myself," Nadia admitted.

"Do you still have the letters?"

"Yeah," Nadia had been holding back tears long enough. "I can't believe they destroyed my uniform."

"Nadi, I'm so sorry this is happening." Rodia could find no other words then.

"I didn't want to bring mom into this either. She's going to think it's all her fault for making me write that letter." Nadia sniffed. "Why would anyone go to such lengths to make a point?"

"Maybe because they know what Brett told me today," Rodia knew she was treading on dangerous ground. *She's going to hit the fan anyway. I may as well get it over with.*

"You talked to Brett?" Nadia glared at her in disbelief.

"During lunch today; it was quite enlightening."

Nadia wished she were gripping her sister's neck rather than the steering wheel. "How so," she was nearly shaking with anger.

"He wants to talk to you about how sweet he thought your letter was. He also said that he didn't intentionally show the letter to anyone else. He wants to explain what happened." Rodia omitted the prom date. She would let Brett do the asking.

Nadia was silent.

"Don't you get it, Nadia? Brett likes *you*. That's why you're receiving hate letters. That's why people are spray painting your locker. You are a *threat*, Nadia Newcomb." Rodia smiled triumphantly. "They can't *stand* the fact that Brett is not interested in dating one of the 'in crowd' so they're doing their best to intimidate you, to force you to back off. My question to *you* is-- have they succeeded?" Rodia challenged her twin.

Nadia laughed. "Have you ever thought about being a talk-show psychologist? You seem to have everyone figured out."

Rodia was glad to see something had pulled Nadia out of her woe-is-me mode. "You didn't answer my question."

"I am a Newcomb. Newcombs *do not* back down." Nadia's steely expression was more dramatics than belief.

"Enough said." Rodia grinned from ear to ear. She knew that Nadia was going to get her opportunity to make good on her words sooner than she thought.

Aurielle Foqua' was on her way to her next assignment when her cell phone rang.

"Net Worth, Inc. Computer Tech Specialist speaking: how can I help you?" Aurielle entered the hotel in the downtown district. It was one of their contracted customers.

"Such formality; I'm impressed," Naomi teased.

Aurielle smiled when she heard her former roommate's voice. "What's up?" She headed upstairs with the assistant manager of the hotel.

"Dinner at eight," Naomi offered.

Aurielle knew Naomi better than that. "Where and with whom?"

"With Dr. Jones and I at his place," Naomi added.

"No." Aurielle walked into the hotel room and thanked the assistant manager. She pulled the computer desk out from the wall.

"Why not," Naomi countered.

"He's a doctor. I'm a computer technician. What do we have in common?" Aurielle wanted to see what she would pull out of that.

"You both love to repair operating systems. Yours is electrical and his is organic." Naomi didn't know where that came from.

"Good comeback, but not sufficient," Aurielle had to give her that. "Besides the man is rarely home."

"Ah, so you noticed." Naomi giggled.

"You are incorrigible. Look, Dr. Jones is a really nice, *handsome*, respectable, *dream* guy, but he's way over my head," Aurielle gave her lame excuse.

"Aurielle, I'm going to give you two choices. Choice number one is dinner. Choice number two is a full page single's ad with your picture." Naomi dropped the bomb.

"Oh come on, Naomi! That isn't fair." Aurielle wined.

"I have my sources, Aurielle. *Don't* make me use them," Naomi warned her.

"If I agree, what's in it for me?" Aurielle set the desk aright after replacing a computer cable.

"For you: Why, a date with one of the most eligible bachelors in Savannah. You can't convince me that you aren't interested." Naomi challenged her.

"If I agree to this so-called date, then you have to agree to a date as well." Aurielle sat Indian style on the floor. "You can bring Giovanni. I hear he's back in town."

Naomi swallowed at the name. "As if he's going to ask me; besides that, he's probably on twenty-four hour call given the circumstances."

"Who said anything about *him* asking you? You *are* best friends with the boss and all. I think he can manage for a few hours with three bodyguards."

Naomi forgot that two other agents had been added to Enrique's entourage for the time being. "Aurielle, I am *not* asking Giovanni to dinner."

"Why not," a very familiar masculine voice wondered aloud.

Naomi nearly dropped the phone. She turned around to face the very man she'd been speaking of. He seemed to be taking up all the space in the room.

"Naomi? Naomi?"

Naomi spoke then. "I'll call you back."

Aurielle looked at her cell phone in puzzlement. She straightened herself up, thankful that Shemiah allowed her to wear jeans on the job and headed downstairs. *She better call me back.*

Aurielle was not interested in tracking down every issue of the morning paper.

"Hi." Naomi chewed on her lower lip. *How much had he heard?*

"Hello." Giovanni slowly drank in the sight of Naomi Watts. Even in her drab nurse's uniform she was still lovely. He noticed she had lightened her dark tresses with a chestnut color. Unfortunately for the moment they were restrained and coiled into a bun at the nape of her neck. "How are you?"

"I'm fine. I didn't expect to see you." Naomi hung up the receiver that was still in her hands.

"Enrique is here getting a checkup. He's been experiencing some discomfort in his shoulder still." Giovanni wondered if she was going to give any explanation of her outburst over the phone.

"Oh, I see." Naomi stood there twiddling her fingers behind her back.

"So, are you going to tell me why you won't ask me to dinner?" Giovanni folded his arms.

Naomi's chin went up. "I didn't think it would be proper for a lady to do the inviting."

Giovanni allowed a slow smile to splay across his features. "And if I were to invite you to dinner, would you agree to go?"

"Yes." Naomi surprised herself with the answer.

Giovanni had to stop himself from staring open-mouthed. "Naomi, would you have dinner with me tonight?"

"I am already having dinner with Aurielle and Dr. Thomas but I was asked to bring a guest." Naomi witnessed several emotions play across Giovanni's face.

"Why would you need an escort?" *Dr. Jones should be enough.*

"It's a long story. Dr. Jones wants to have dinner with Aurielle and he asked me to come along. The only way she'll agree to go is if I don't come alone." Naomi paraphrased.

Giovanni was flooded with relief. *So she's not seeing him.* That revelation hit him squarely in the chest. *All this time I thought... it doesn't matter now.* "So, basically we're chaperoning."

"Pretty much," Naomi tried to remain casual about the whole thing.

"Who's going to chaperone us?" Giovanni grinned from ear to ear. Naomi swallowed as he came closer. "We're not really going out on date. It's just a dinner."

"I'm glad you can distinguish between the two. And since everyone here seems to be making demands here, I'll agree to accompany you to this dinner if you'll agree to a *real* date." Giovanni was leaning against the counter his eyes searching hers.

"Done," Naomi was sure that if she said anything else, she was a goner.

"I'll pick you up at your place." Giovanni stood then.

"Seven forty-five." Naomi agreed, exhaling slowly. *There's no turning back now.*

"Is this guy bothering you?" Enrique chuckled at the heated glances between his bodyguard and his best female friend.

"Enrique!" Naomi turned and gave him a hug being mindful of his shoulder.

"How are you, chica?" Enrique knew not to comment on her flushed appearance.

"Good. Glad to see you back in town. I saw a little bit of your press conference today." Naomi was careful to avert her eyes away from Giovanni's smoldering ones.

"I'm glad to be back. This shoulder has been the bane of my existence." Enrique stretched his arm out.

Naomi smiled cheekily. "There's nothing like a good war wound to tug on the heart strings of a particular lady."

"Hey, that's what I'm counting on." Enrique kidded. He motioned his other bodyguards to join them. "This is Fabian and Fabritza Ciccone. They are going to be with me for a while until things die down a little more."

Nadia shook hands with Fabian and Fabritza who looked at her with disdain. "I'm Naomi Watts."

"Naomi is a close friend of mine." Enrique told the Ciccones. "I know you will treat her as such." His eyes settled on Fabritza.

Naomi could tell she'd obviously ruffled the woman's feathers but she wasn't sure how.

"It's good to see you, Naomi." Nicholas gave her a brief hug.
"You too, Nicholas," Naomi was genuinely glad to see him. He wasn't his usually stoic self. "I'd love to stay and talk but I've got to get back on post. Enrique, I'll catch up with you."

"Seven-forty five," Giovanni reminded her.

Naomi nodded and off she went. *How could I forget?*

5

Mariella Estrada threw back her head to enjoy the warmth of the sun beating down upon her head. She'd opted for a patio table without the covering of an umbrella to enjoy her late lunch. The temperature was the only thing about Savannah that reminded her of Costa Rica. She looked forward to school in the fall but she pined for her old lifestyle. In Costa Rica she hadn't had to worry about making a good impression.

Three different companies had already turned her down today alone. *Not enough experience, too much experience. We're not taking any more applicants.* Still there was one more place she wanted to try. She looked down at the circled classified ad. It was a private law firm that was looking for a secretary.

Anything would be better than admitting defeat to my cousin. She knew Enrique would gloat over the fact if she had to sign on with EAE Design Group because no one else would hire her. *I need to do this on my own.* The interviews were from three to five. She looked down at her watch. *Two fifteen.* She would enjoy the view for a few more minutes. Then she would head on over to the interview.

"Enjoying the view?" Pastor Marks looked in the direction that his son had become so enamored with.

"Huh?" Noelle focused his attention back towards his father. He'd agreed to meet him for a late lunch to discuss his involvement in the Single's Retreat to be held Fourth of July weekend.

"If you're that intrigued, why don't you go introduce yourself?" Pastor Marks had rarely seen his son not take advantage of an opportunity to meet a beautiful woman. "You haven't heard a thing I've said for the past five minutes."

"She's a deadly combination, dad." Noelle glanced back at Mariella.

"What's that?" Pastor Marks hid his mirth.
"She's foreign, young, and beautiful." Noelle schooled his father. "She's probably a college student fresh off the plane."

Pastor Marks was curious to know what his son's 'ideal' woman was. "So what isn't a deadly combination?"

"They all are in some respect. She's just not relationship material. I need a mature woman; someone who's twenty-five to thirty-five, a woman who's financially independent and established in her career. Noelle took pride in knowing what he wanted. "No offense dad but I don't want to wind up being taken advantage of by some sweet, young, thing," Noelle referred to his mother of whom he felt no remorse for. She was currently going through her second divorce.

"Watch your mouth. I wasn't taken advantage of. We were two consenting adults." Pastor Marks was not going to allow his son to rehash old memories. "You can't judge every woman you meet based on what happened between your mother and me."

"Why are you *defending* her? She was a gold digger. You supported her and gave her the world. What did she do with it? She tried to take you to the cleaners. Thanks, but no thanks," Noelle motioned for a waiter to refill his drink.

Pastor Marks shook his head. *Lord, I see my son needs to be broken. Do what you do best.*

Mariella tried not to notice the gentleman that sat a few tables up from where she was sitting. But it was rather difficult. At first she thought he was enjoying the sights. But then she realized his gaze was fixed on one thing in particular-her.

Mariella was not the least bit shy but his continual gaze had made her somewhat uncomfortable; especially since it had accompanied a frown. *He'd be such a handsome man if he didn't have a scowl on his face.* She discreetly perused him with her eyes. *He's got great taste. Well groomed, in shape; definitely a businessman of some sort; probably in his late twenties, early thirties.* It was obvious he was out with a relative since the man who joined him bore a striking resemblance. *A family man,* Mariella went back to scanning the classifieds. *I'm supposed to be looking for a job not a man.*

Mariella looked up once more and this time she was caught. Her eyes seemed to lock with the gentleman's. Judging from his glare, Mariella knew he expected her to break eye contact first. Obviously he did not know Mariella. She sipped her lemonade.

"One day you're going to make a great wife for him."
Mariella sputtered sending a spray of lemonade all over the bodice of her dress. She coughed violently. *God, don't be ridiculous.*

"All you alright, Miss?" her waiter hurried over to her table.
Mariella nodded quickly managing to croak out, "Water." She gratefully thanked the waiter for the water. She used a napkin to work on the damage done to her dress. *Just great; I've been in the sun too long. I must be hallucinating.*

"I'm touched. No one has ever gotten choked up about me before," against his better judgment, Noelle Marks had made his way over to see if the 'dangerous combination' was alright.

Mariella pretended not to notice his presence, gathering up her things. *Of all the egotistical- If I ignore him, he'll go away.* She walked around her table in the opposite direction. Noelle stood in her way.

"Are you in a hurry?"

"I've got an appointment." She brushed past him. "Excuse me."

Noelle was caught off guard by the fragrant scent she left in her wake. *She's beautiful at point blank range.* "I'm Noelle and you are?"

Mariella looked over her shoulder. "Leaving," Mariella quickened her pace moving in between the other pedestrians allowing her to get lost in the traffic.

Noelle stood staring after the young lady a little perturbed by the whole incident. For a moment their eyes had finally met and Noelle had felt something pass between them.

"That deadly, huh," Pastor Marks spoke behind his son.

Noelle turned to face his father. "Don't start."

John could tell his son was more annoyed with his being attracted to the young lady than he was that she'd disappeared. He held up his hands in surrender. "Hey, I was just making an observation."

"It's a good thing she wasn't interested. She would have been nothing but trouble." He looked at his watch. I've got to get back to the office. I've got those interviews at three."

"Are we still on for dinner?" Pastor Marks had missed having dinner with his son since he'd found his own place.

"Of course; I'll try not to stay too late at the office." Noelle had to be mindful of the time. His father was discovering how much of a workaholic he was. Now his time was split between his caseloads and finding a competent interior designer for his home.

"I want to see you no later than six." John knew that if he didn't give him a time frame, Noelle wouldn't make it to his house until close to midnight.

"I'll do my best." Noelle saluted his father and headed toward his car.

"Mom, Dee is at it again." Rodia warned Columbia as she shampooed the hair of a client.

Columbia was applying relaxer to another client's hair when she looked up to see Delia coloring in her salon magazine. "Dee, put that back!"

Delia closed the magazine with a sullen expression.

"Nadia, give Dee some copy paper from the computer." She called out.

Nadia came from the break room. "I'm printing my research paper. Can it wait?" she stomped toward Dee and grabbed her by the arm, yanking her up. "Come with me."

Dee squirmed beneath her sister's grip. "No, Mommy says I can play out here!"

"You're getting in the way," Nadia scolded her.

"Leave her be, Nadia. Just bring the paper out here." Columbia pulled off her gloves and took a swig of her cola as she waited for the relaxer to process. *Calgon, take me away.* She was more than ready for a vacation. Seth Davis, the world's greatest pastor as she often referred to him as, had paid for her to go on the Singles Retreat to Montego Bay, Jamaica for the fourth of July weekend.

The trip was a combined effort of Fresh Fire, Second Chance, and New Life Ministries. Columbia was excited about leaving the United States for the first time in her life but she was also excited that John Marks had decided to go as well.

Except for his Saturday visits to her shop, she had rarely seen him. When his member Aliya Peyton had been kidnapped and subsequently hospitalized thereafter, he'd spent a great deal of time seeing to her and the needs of her family as well as ministering to his members words of hope and healing.

Columbia had decided to postpone any plans for a relationship between them. He had to see to the needs of his flock. She had been gifted with the responsibility of Administrative assistant to Jamar Davis, her Pastor's brother. Seth had been called out of the country on a mission trip to Ecuador. There had been no time to cultivate a relationship.

Then through nothing short of a miracle, God had seen fit to restore Aliya Peyton to full health. Columbia had paid her a visit at the hospital relieved to see that the woman her pastor cared deeply about was on the road to recovery. *This retreat will do everyone some good*, she thought to herself.

Her one concern was that Nadia, Rodia, and Delia would be left with each other for the weekend without her intervention. It was also the weekend of the prom. Nadia hadn't spoken to her about it since she'd written that letter to Brett Hamilton. That was months ago.

"Nadia," Columbia decided it was time to address the subject.

"Yes?" Nadia was on her way to get the computer paper.

"What ever happened with that letter you wrote to Brett?" Columbia walked her client over to her sink.

Nadia and Rodia looked at each other.

"Mom, I don't think this is a good time to talk about it." Nadia wrung her hands.

"I think it is." Columbia positioned her client at the sink and turned on the water.

"The Single's Retreat is next Thursday. I don't want you calling me in Montego Bay asking for permission to go to the prom. The answer will be no. Did you write the letter?"

"Yes."

"And what happened?"

"Somehow word got around about it. Some girls confronted me and told me to stay away from Brett."

Columbia stopped spraying her client's hair. "Did they threaten you?"

"They've been putting hate letters in her locker. They spray painted her gym locker with profanity and they ripped her cheerleading uniform to shreds." Rodia interjected.

Nadia rolled her eyes. "Thanks, Rodia. Anything *else* you want to add?"

"Brett really does like her. He thought the letter was sweet. Oh, and he'll be here any minute now." Rodia checked on the clients that were sitting under the hairdryers.

"What!" Nadia's screeching voice echoed in the little shop.

Columbia was just about to let Nadia have it for not telling her about what was going on at school when Brett Hamilton pushed open her shop door.

"Afternoon, Miss Newcomb." Brett scanned the shop. He noticed there was no barber on duty. *I guess I better come up with another reason for being here.*

"Hello Brett. What brings you by?" Columbia pasted on a smile. *He's got some guts coming here.* She noticed Nadia had disappeared.

He motioned to his friend to come forward. "This is my friend Xavier Roberts."

Columbia shook the young man's trembling hand. "Nice to meet you, ma'am," Brett spoke confidently.

She looked to Rodia who had a look of false innocence on her face. *So she's the mastermind.*

Brett cleared his throat. "Xavier and I are here this afternoon because we wanted to know if you would give us the privilege of taking your daughters to the prom."

"I think Xavier can speak for himself," Columbia stared up at the young man.

"Yes ma'am," Xavier straightened up. "I would like to take Rodia to the prom with your permission."

Columbia walked her client to an empty dryer and situated her. "Before I give either one of you an answer, I have some questions for Brett."

Brett remained standing while Xavier took a seat.

"Mr. Hamilton, did you know my daughter was being harassed because of you?" Columbia came to stand toe to toe, eyeball to eyeball with him.

"I just found out today. I had no idea," Brett admitted.

"Did you know that just today someone slashed her uniform to shreds and spray painted her locker?" Rodia interjected.

Brett's expression grew volatile. "They did *what*?"

"Someone obviously doesn't like the idea of the two of you together. You have any idea who that might be?" Rodia was standing next to her mother.

"I have an idea." Brett assured them. "Miss Newcomb, I really like Nadia. I haven't asked anyone else to prom and if she says no, I'll go alone. Some of my stupid teammates saw me reading the letter that she wrote. I've already confronted them."

"I think you need to confront the cheerleaders, mainly Serena Quintana. I think she's behind all of it." Rodia added.

"*I'm* going to be confronting everyone involved come tomorrow morning." Columbia declared.

"All of the seniors will be gone on the senior trip. It may be a good time to talk with our principal. I'll see what I can find out while we are gone. Is there anything else you want to ask me?" Brett was open to any suggestion.

"What time would you have her home from the prom?" Columbia saw the look of shock register on his face.

"Eleven thirty." Brett's own curfew was one o'clock but he wouldn't push his luck.

"I think she can handle twelve thirty as long as Rodia is attending as well." Columbia looked to Rodia.

"I'll be attending." Rodia looked to Xavier who smiled shyly. *I'm going to be scared out of my wits but I'll be there.*

"Nadia, come on out here!" Columbia decided she had let her hide long enough. It was time to face the music.

Nadia walked out front slowly. She stood with her sister. *I'm going to throttle her good when mom leaves for Jamaica.*

Brett began first. "Nadia, I just want to tell you that I'm sorry about what's been going on. I guess it is my fault for liking you but I'm not apologizing for that."

"Thanks for caring." Nadia didn't know what else to say.

"Now that I have your mother's permission, would you go to prom with me?" Brett could see the uncertainty in her eyes.

"After all that's happened, do you think that would be *wise*?" Nadia wasn't intimidated but she was certain the vandalism would only cease for a time.

"I'm not going to let some stupid jocks dictate who I can date. Are you?" Brett challenged her.

Nadia looked to her mother. "He said the 'd' word, mom."

Columbia thought about it for a moment. "You know I am not ready for you to start dating on a regular basis. One date; prom night only; we'll talk about the rest when I get back."

Brett was confused. "Nadia's not allowed to have a boyfriend?"

"Neither am I." Rodia added.

"Not at this time, no," Columbia noticed the forlorn expressions of both teenage boys.

Brett knew there was nothing he could say to convince Columbia to change her mind. "I guess I'll just have to pray for a miracle."

Columbia laughed at him. "You may want to include fasting with that."

He's got some nerve. Columbia hated to admit it, but she was beginning to admire Brett Hamilton. Then she turned her attention to Xavier. "Mr. Roberts, are *you* a Christian?"

"Yes, I am." Xavier stood then, towering over everyone in the room.

"Where do you attend church?" Columbia was curious to know.

"I attend Second Chance Ministries with my father," Xavier spoke softly.

"That's a very good ministry. Our church is going to be combining some of our fellowships with you all. Maybe you'll get a chance to see Rodia more often." Columbia threw in. "Are your parents divorced?"

"My mom passed away when I was in middle school." Xavier grew sad even now. A drunk driver had snuffed out his mother's life.

"I'm sorry to hear that." Columbia truly was sorry. She couldn't imagine what her children would do without her there. "What does your father do for a living?"

"He runs a Bed and Breakfast; Southern Charm," Xavier was glad that his father had decided to keep the business going. It was something that reminded him of his mother.

"I've heard good things about it." Columbia had seen an article concerning the Bed and Breakfast.

"He and my mom opened it together. I'm just glad he decided to keep the business going. At one time he thought about selling it." Xavier revealed.

"What about your parents, Brett?" Columbia decided she might as well interrogate them while she had the opportunity.

"They have their own real estate company." Brett knew the moment he said that, Columbia would have no trouble identifying his parents.

"Hamilton Realty; they've got that snazzy commercial, right?" Columbia was hard pressed *not* to remember Bryant and Anastasia Hamilton. In so many words they'd expressed to her that she didn't meet their "criteria" for home ownership in one of Savannah's more exclusive neighborhoods. *But that's water under the bridge.* Columbia had surpassed her own expectations where finances were concerned. She hoped the Hamiltons had changed since then.

"Yeah, Snazzy," Brett was a little embarrassed by the commercial. It painted the picture that his family only catered to the wealthy and elite of society.

Columbia turned to Nadia. "Well, are you going to the prom or not?"

Nadia's mouth was wide open. She thought for sure he mother was going to say something about the Hamiltons. Apparently she was going to hold her tongue until a later date. "Yes."

"Hello. Can I remind everyone here of something?" Rodia swung several pairs of heated hot curlers around.

"What?" Columbia lifted the blow dryers off of her client's heads.

"That I don't have a dress." Rodia proceeded to press the young woman's hair that sat before her.

"You and Nadia can go shopping tomorrow after school. Drop Delia off with me. I want you home by ten." Columbia had forgotten that Rodia had not planned to go. It would be good for them to experience their first date together.

Nadia couldn't believe it. *I'm going to prom.*

Brett looked down at his watch. It was after three. "I'd love to stay and talk, but I've got to get Xavier home. We've got to get packed for the senior trip."

"Have fun." Rodia chirped as the teenagers headed out.

"See you on Monday." Brett waved to Nadia.

Watch your back. Nadia wanted to tell him. "Same here," She tried to sound nonchalant. She felt anything but.

Columbia had managed to be fairly civil until Brett and Xavier departed. Then she turned to face Nadia. "I want to know why I'm just finding out today that you're being harassed at school."

Mariella Estrada sat in the waiting area for her turn to be interviewed. There were three other applicants along with her; an Asian male that looked as though he was interviewing for a restaurant job, an older African-American woman who looked more suited to be a school master, and a younger African-American woman who seemed to fit the bill. *Who am I kidding?*

Mariella surveyed her surroundings. She could tell it was a fairly new law practice. *Everything* smelled new. It was so new as a matter of fact the owner had yet to place a sign on the door stating the name of the practice. The classified ad had read simply: *Private law office seeks experienced secretary- Personal interviews only. Call for directions.* Mariella had called only to hear automated instructions on how to reach the law office.

Instead of thinking about how she could convince her interviewer that she had the skills necessary to be a hired as a secretary, her mind was focused on how the waiting area could be rearranged to be more inviting.

A petite blond exited the office with a look of satisfaction on her face.

She probably got the job. They're probably going to announce they don't need any more applicants.

"Next!"

Mariella jumped at the voice. *I guess there's still a chance.*

The Asian man went into the office closing the door behind him. Mariella breathed a sigh of relief. *Please, God. I know we don't talk much, but I really need a job.* Mariella wasn't expecting an answer.

It was a good thing God was expecting her to pray.

6

Enrique reclined in his SUV, a slow grin spreading from ear to ear. "What's so funny?" Giovanni eyed him suspiciously. "Go ahead and say it."

Nicholas smirked, peering at Giovanni and Enrique in the backseat. *If he doesn't say anything, I'll be the first.*

"I see you've got a hot date planned for this evening," Enrique teased him.

Giovanni glared at his twin who seemed to be enjoying the moment a little too much for his tastes. "I know I don't normally ask for the evening off."

"Try never." Enrique interjected.

"Okay. I've never asked for the evening off outside of what we've agreed on, but I figured with Fabritza and Fabian still on post, it could be arranged." Giovanni reasoned. "I would only be gone for a few hours."

"Fabian and Fabritza have gone to make hotel arrangements for their time here. As soon as they return, you're free to leave for the evening." Nicholas announced.

"Why thank you for being so *generous*," Giovanni's sarcasm was evident.

Enrique decided to intervene before it got ugly. "Any word yet from Carlton on when we can begin our training?"

Nicholas was the first to respond. "I can check on that today if you'd like." *And pay a visit to Rosalynn.* He was looking forward to seeing her.

"You could kill two birds with one stone, couldn't you?" Giovanni teased him knowing full well his brother was going to do more than check out their workout schedule.

"You better be glad I'm driving right now." He gave Giovanni a menacing glare in the rearview mirror.

"Save all that male aggression for the men's fellowship on Saturday. I think Seth has some touch football planned," Enrique chuckled. He could already picture the two brothers covered in sand.

"Saturday's a long way off, boss." Nicholas complained.

"I suggest you save all your energy. You're going to need it." Giovanni challenged him.

"You're on." Nicholas loved a challenge. "It'll be like old times."

"I'm a bit older and stronger now. It's not going to be easy trying to make me eat dirt." Giovanni warned him.

"Maybe I shouldn't have suggested touch football." Enrique thought aloud.

"Touch football is great. Nic deserves what's coming to him." Giovanni grinned mischievously.

Enrique shook his head at the antics of the two men. Saturday was going to prove to be quite entertaining.

Aurielle had almost reached Net Worth, Inc. when Naomi called her.

"Everything's set."

Aurielle recognized Naomi's voice. "So you've got an escort?"

"Yep," Naomi grinned mischievously.

"Who is it?" Aurielle was curious to know whom Naomi had picked out on such short notice.

"Giovanni Cartellini. He just happened to be standing behind me as we were talking earlier." Naomi mentioned.

"I bet you almost had a fit," Aurielle laughed out loud.

"It definitely goes on record as one of my most embarrassing moments." Naomi admitted. "And now that I've been humiliated there's no way you're getting out of this dinner. Eight sharp, No excuses."

"Fine," Aurielle pouted.

"And don't come looking like a construction worker." Naomi knew Aurielle had been trying a more bohemian look in lieu of her previous brazen look.

"Only if you don't come dressed like a nun." Aurielle shot back playfully.

Whereas Aurielle's wardrobe was in need of a conservative makeover, Naomi's needed to be jazzed up a bit.

"How about my uniform," Naomi kidded. She decided it wouldn't be wise to mention that most of her dresses still had the tags on them.

"No work clothes of any kind."

"Deal; Do I have to wear accessories?" Naomi teased.

"Am I going to have to come over and make sure you don't commit fashion suicide?' Aurielle threatened.

"I think I can manage." Naomi tried to appease her.

"And no black," Aurielle added. "Think bright. Think bold. Think-"

"I get the point," Naomi chuckled.

"Alright then, see you at eight."

Naomi stared at her receiver in amazement. Every now and then it still surprised her how much her relationship with Aurielle had changed. *From enemies to comrades; what a difference salvation makes.* She knew that if it had not been for Jesus, there would still be a wall of distrust between them. But forgiveness and love had brought down that barrier and Naomi was thankful for it.

Naomi was glad that she wasn't the only one who could notice the changes taking place in her friend. Naomi hoped that Aurielle would allow Dr. Jones access into her life. She needed to experience a godly friendship with the opposite sex as much as she needed a friendship with her own gender.

She must first see me as a friend before she'll accept anything else, Dr. Jones had said as he'd departed for the day. Naomi had taken those words to heart. She thought about her relationship with Enrique Estrada. It had been easy to joke around and laugh with him mainly because they had developed a friendship. Theirs was an ease born over time.

The only way she was going to get over the awkward stage with Giovanni would be to work on cultivating a friendship with him. *First I have to work on thinking straight when I'm around the man.* Naomi knew if she weren't careful, she would find herself giving too much too soon. *We should develop a friendship first.* She determined those words would be her mantra tonight.

"Next!" The stern voice was becoming familiar to Mariella. The last interview seemed as if it had taken an eternity.

Well, this is it. Mariella thought to herself. She scanned her appearance. The lemonade stain was almost unnoticeable. *Well, almost.* She pushed open the heavy ornate door.

Noelle Marks sat at his computer logging in his last applicant's information. "I'll be with you in just a moment. Have a seat." He'd already decided he was going to hire his last applicant. Fresh out of law school, Tehinnah Adams would be the perfect addition to his firm. The young African-American woman had an impressive record. She exuded the confidence Noelle knew would be necessary in his field. She would serve as his secretary until she passed the Bar. Then she would take on a dual role as his assistant. Now all he had to do was get through this interview.

"Thank you." Mariella sat down, her eyes roaming the walls. If the walls could talk, the man before her seemed to have a pretty impressive reputation.

Noelle Marks stood then, turning to face his interviewee with an outstretched hand. "I'm-"

Mariella was glad she was still in the seated position. *You!* She couldn't even say a word.

"What are you doing here?" Noelle hadn't intended to sound so harsh but given the circumstances he couldn't help it.

If I give the slightest inclination that I am affected by this it will just make things worse. But she was affected. She was trembling. "I'm here for an interview... Mr. Marks." She handed him a resume, eying his desk plate.

Noelle still couldn't believe the fireball he'd met mere hours ago was sitting in front of him. He perused the resume as he took his seat. "Very pretty," he mused aloud.

"Pardon me?" Mariella folded her hands in front of her.

"Your name," He read over her resume. *Just as I thought: Foreign, young and beautiful. The last name sounds familiar.*

Mariella hated the ensuing silence. But she would grin and bear it. After a few minutes, Noelle handed her back the resume. "So you are a student here at SCAD?"

"Yes. I'll be studying Graphic Design and Interior Design in the fall." Mariella was looking forward to starting her classes.

"Why aren't you looking for a job in your related field?" Noelle wondered aloud.

"I don't have enough experience as I've been told more times than I can count." Mariella admitted.

Noelle found himself wanting to help her. "Do you have any of your work with you?" he ventured.

"As a matter of fact I do," Mariella reached into her brief bag and pulled out her small portfolio. "This is some sample work I was doing back home."

Noelle took his time going over her pieces. *These are actually pretty good.* His eye rested on a photograph of her and a slightly older man. "I know him." Then it clicked. "Are you related to Enrique Estrada of EAE Design Group?"

I'm busted. "He's my cousin." Mariella said with a straight face.
Noelle closed the portfolio and handed it back to her. "Why are you here? I'm sure he's got plenty of positions lined up for you."

Mariella could hear that pompous tone rising within him. "I'm trying to prove that I'm capable of getting a job on my own."

Noelle couldn't believe he'd almost felt sorry for her. "You don't *need* to prove yourself, Miss Estrada."

Mariella's eyes flashed. "I'm here for an interview, not a counseling session, Mr. Marks."

Noelle held his tongue. "You're right." He picked up her resume once more. "Judging from your resume, you have very little secretarial skills. You are under qualified for the job that I advertised for." Noelle's mind was stirring. He didn't know why he was going to make this offer to such an infuriating woman but he couldn't shake the feeling that it was not a coincidence that she was in his office.

Mariella began to pack up her things. *He's just saying that because he thinks I'm spoiled and that I have other options available.*

"But there is a job that I haven't advertised for and I think you'd be perfect for it." Noelle baited her.

Mariella stilled, glaring at him.
Noelle continued. "It would only be temporary work."

Mariella sat stiffly. "Go on."

"I've just recently acquired a home. I just fired my interior designer and I'm in the market for a new one." Noelle saw her eyes light up. He wouldn't think right now about why that brought him pleasure.

"You'd hire *me* to do your interior design?" Mariella was flabbergasted. The opportunity would give her experience and add to her portfolio as well.

She's right. I must be out of my mind to invite this kind of trouble. "If you're not interested, I understand. I mean, we haven't exactly gotten off on the right foot," Noelle acknowledged.

"Are you *kidding*? Of *course* I'm interested." Mariella wanted to make that clear. "When can I start?"

Noelle sat transfixed by how animated Mariella was becoming. He would have to add to his previous description: *Young, foreign, beautiful, and passionate.* "I can give you a tour tomorrow. We can go over what my expectations are. I can draw up a contract for you concerning your salary. I know we're coming up to the Fourth of July weekend. I'll be out of town so you can take next week to look it over and think about it."

Mariella chewed on her lip. "There's just one problem. I don't have a car."

Noelle thought for a moment. "If you decide to take the job, I could pick you up mornings and drop you off at the house. I can leave the office by five to pick you up and take you home. If there are days when you need to search out something in town, I can send my secretary to assist you."

"You mean the secretary you hired *earlier* today?" Mariella gave him a knowing look.

"The one and the same," Noelle grinned sheepishly.

"Where is your home located?" Mariella thought to ask. *The man is dangerous when he smiles.*

"Richmond Hill." Noelle opened his desk drawer and pulled out some photos. "It's a quaint neighborhood. I've talked with the neighbors so they know it's going to be pretty noisy for the next couple of months."

"I live out that way." Mariella knew where the neighborhood was that he spoke. "Maybe my roommate could drop me off at the house tomorrow morning."

"Whatever works for you," Noelle had decided to spend the night at his father's. He would drive out to Richmond Hill in the morning. "Is seven good?"

"Seven should be fine." She took one of his business cards. "If there is a problem, I'll call you." Mariella couldn't believe the turn of events. *I have a job.*

"Don't hesitate to do so. My cell number is probably the most reliable way to get in touch." Noelle pointed out.

"Okay." Mariella tucked the card into her bag.

They shook hands.

"I apologize for earlier today."

"You wanted to be on time for *my* interview. How can I be upset?" Noelle joked. "Besides, we both got what we wanted. You wanted a job. I wanted an introduction. I guess God decided the timing was all off."

Mariella smile faltered. *God.* Then her memory was jogged. *Oh no.*

"Oh, yes."

She ignored the voice. "It was just a coincidence that we ran into each other."

"I don't believe in coincidences. God is too smart for that. *Nothing* happens by coincidence. You are in my life for a reason, Miss Estrada." Noelle spoke confidently.

Oh, if you only knew. Mariella walked toward the door. *But thank God you don't.* "And that reason is to ensure that your home looks good enough to grace the cover of any magazine."

Noelle followed her to the door. "Are you a believer, Miss Estrada?"

Mariella turned to face him then. "I'm a Christian if that's what you mean."

"That's good to know. It'll make our working relationship flow a little smoother." Noelle was not ashamed of the Gospel and he didn't intend to tiptoe around the subject either.

"Right, Well, I'll see you in the morning." Mariella pasted on a smile and hurried out of his office.

Noelle stood looking at the closed door. *Did I say something wrong?*

Augusta Peyton picked up the velvet box she'd avoided looking at since lunchtime. She opened it once more, taking out the card. She read it once more.

You not only have my heart, but the key as well. When you are ready, it will always be open to you.

"I guess it's all or nothing." Augusta spoke to herself. She pulled out the chain letting it slide through her fingers. She brushed her hair to one side. Opening the clasp she lifted the chain up to her neck and secured it. She tucked the chain in under her blouse. She wanted Enrique to be the first to see it.

She was reading over his words when her phone rang. "Alpha, Inc. Augusta Peyton here,"

"Miss Peyton? Your test results are in. You're more than welcome to come in before six to discuss them."

Augusta's stomach knotted. "Alright, I'm on my way now."

The silence on the other end of the line was deafening.

No matter what, I'm going to believe the report of the Lord. At her word, God sent his angels to work on her behalf.

7

Savannah was a little surprised to hear her doorbell ringing mid-afternoon. Her surprise turned to apprehension when she looked through the peephole to see who was on the other side. *I guess there's no use avoiding this.* Savannah was thankful that Shemiah hadn't showed up earlier. She'd been too distressed to even think straight. She opened the door hesitantly, a slight smile managing to grace her features.

"Hi."

"Hi yourself," Shemiah noticed the scratchiness in Savannah's voice. "Mind if I come in?"

Savannah ushered him in, leading him out to the breakfast room. *Lord, give me what to say.*

Shemiah seated himself across from her at the table. He gently took her hands in his. *Lord, give me what to say.* "Savannah, look at me."

Savannah had been staring at their hands linked together. She looked up into his eyes then.

"I love you, Savannah. Nothing that anyone can say or *do* will change that fact." Shemiah felt it was important that she hear that before he said anything else.

"I love you, too. I just don't want to cause tension between you and your family." Savannah had been toiling with her thoughts for the past few hours.

"Savannah, our relationship is more important to me than my family's opinion. You are the gift that God has given to me. I'll give up my right to inherit if it means losing you." Shemiah's features were etched in determination. "I don't want you signing a prenuptial agreement."

Savannah was confused then. "You *don't*?"

"I spoke with my mother earlier. I had not had a chance to talk with her about it. I know it's a tradition in our family but it's one that I intended to break. As for Lysander, we will deal with him together. I don't want him harassing you."

Savannah felt relieved then. "I can't possibly see how you two come from the same gene pool."

Shemiah grinned ruefully. "Neither can I; He truly is a unique individual." He touched Savannah's cheek. "We've always gotten along, but if his presence unsettles you, I will take him off the guest list."

Savannah shook her head. "I have to deal with him head on. If we are going to be family, then we have to face the good and the bad."

Shemiah brought her hands to his lips. "I agree. I'm only considering my cousin's safety. I'm not going to stand idly by if Lysander decides to overstep his bounds."

Savannah had never seen Shemiah in a state of anger. She was sure she didn't want to see it. "Remember to let God do His part. I think part of Lysander's problem is that he doesn't know the Lord."

"Quite the contrary, My Sweet: My mother's brother, his father, is a Pastor. Lysander grew up with the Gospel. He decided to go his own way just as I was coming into the faith. He always thought me weak for 'buying into the 'white man's religion' as he put it." Shemiah's eyes were filled with regret for his cousin's life choices.

Savannah's eyes filled with understanding. *He still sees me as a conquest because of my beliefs. He was never able to persuade me to give in.* Savannah understood the impact of that thought. In a very twisted way, Lysander Townsend was still trying to prove to himself that there was nothing to the God of the Bible. *Lord, make yourself real to Lysander.* "It seems as though your cousin is kicking against the pricks and sooner or later he's going to get knocked off his high horse."

"I hope it doesn't come to that." Shemiah stood then, pulling Savannah up with him. "But enough talk about Lysander." He pulled her close then. "Since you've taken the rest of the day off, what would you say to a nice boat ride on River Street?"

"That sounds ideal." Savannah rested her head upon his chest, embracing the strength and security she found there.

"We could take a leisure walk afterwards and visit some of the shops portside. That would bide us some time before dinner at your mom's." Shemiah offered knowing Savannah wasn't exactly overjoyed at the thought of seeing Lysander twice in one day.

Savannah was thankful that the rest of the family would be in attendance at the dinner. She was pretty confident that Lysander wouldn't do anything to sully his reputation publicly. She looked up at her fiancée then. "Have I told you how much I love you?"

"You have but I never get tired of hearing you say it." He grinned.

"Thank you for coming over to rescue me from me." Savannah confessed. "I just had to get away after the lunch today."

Shemiah knew just how much of an escape artist Savannah could be. This was why he had not hesitated in coming after her. "I was only fulfilling my duty as your knight to rescue my damsel in distress."

"The damsel is officially de-stressed," Savannah chuckled. "Now let's get moving."

"Urrgh," Aliya groaned aloud in frustration at the Single's Retreat roster. "If I get one more addition to this list, I'm going to scream."

"I guess you'd better get ready to scream then." Ginny spoke at the front door of Aliya's shop.

Aliya turned to face her, rolling her eyes in frustration. "Who is it *now*?"

Ginevieve Dubois grimaced as she handed Aliya two checks. "Well, apparently Jamar has been making quick friends around these parts. He's talked the florist into going on the trip."

Aliya stared in open-mouthed shock. "Marco?"

Ginny smiled. "Umm hmm," Ginny had made it no secret that she held the South American heartthrob in admiration.

Aliya laughed. "Oh, Ginny, I *know* you must be excited."

"Excited isn't a good enough word," Ginny flushed with color.

"Don't wear your heart on your sleeve." Aliya warned her.

Ginny shooed the comment away. "Even if I did, he wouldn't notice. The man eats, sleeps, and breathes that flower shop."

"Apparently not if he's going to take off for a few days." Aliya reminded her. "I don't think he's *ever* been closed for any holiday come to think of it." She said thoughtfully. "Who's the other person?"

"Tatyanna got a surprise today. Her little sister just graduated from law school recently. She's decided to move here to Savannah. Tatyanna wanted to present her with a surprise of her own and give her an opportunity to meet everyone." Ginny explained.

"I'm sure she's excited about having family in the area now. What's her name?"

"Tehinnah Adams. She's a sassy young lady. She stopped by earlier. She was on her way to a job interview."

"Well, I guess I can take these two. But no more," Aliya placed the checks in with the rest of the monies for the trip. "My father is going to strangle me by the time I get to Montego Bay if I keep faxing him more room changes."

Ginny grimaced. She did not want to be in Aliya's shoes at this point. It was only a matter of days before they were scheduled to leave. "When is our next meeting for the trip?"

"I e-mailed everyone today. We will meet tomorrow at 5:30 at Elder Worth's home. It is imperative that *everyone* be there." Aliya stressed. "If not for Enrique's generosity, many of us would be paying exorbitant fees for plane tickets due to last minute planning."

"I'll make sure Marco knows about the meeting." Ginny waited for Aliya to write down Elder Worth's address.

"Thanks Ginny. You've been very helpful this past month." Ginny had worked with Aliya on coordinating the rooms and prices and corresponding with those who had signed up for the Single's trip.

"No problem." Ginny started to leave then turned around. "Aliya,"

"Yes?" Aliya looked more than a tad frazzled.

"You make sure *you* enjoy this retreat. You need it more than any of us." Ginny admonished her.

"I'll try." Aliya didn't want to tell her how hard it was going to be to concentrate on relaxing with Seth Davis on the trip. *That's easier said than done.*

Augusta had been twiddling her fingers nervously for the past half hour when Dr. Evelyn Turner walked through the door from her private office. Augusta stood to receive the doctor.

"Miss Peyton." Dr. Turner ushered her into her sparsely furnished office.

Augusta felt her stomach tightening into knots at the woman's cool demeanor. She sat down across from her folding her hands in her lap with the utmost calm.

Dr. Turner opened up her file. "How are you doing today?"

"I'm doing fine." Augusta tried to keep the strain out of her voice but she was growing rather impatient. *Why is she taking so long?*

Dr. Turner closed her file and set it down on her desk. Her eyes met Augusta's with all seriousness. "I have some good news for you but I also have some other news that you may not have expected to hear. Which would you rather deal with first?"

"I'll take the good news." Augusta was without hesitation in her decision.

"Alright then, it appears that there should be no reason at this point why you shouldn't be able to bear children in the future."

Augusta's eyes watered then. "Thank you Jesus." She lifted her hands in praise to God.

"However, we have found some small fibroid tumors that sit near your ovaries." Dr. Turner thought it best to tell her while she yet rejoiced.

Augusta's eyes widened. "What does that mean?"

"They are not malignant, but you do need to have surgery as soon as possible to remove them. You said you have a twin as well?" Dr. Turner inquired.

"Yes. But what does she have to do with this?" Augusta knew a little about fibroid tumors.

"Fibroid tumors are not a hereditary thing, but being that you two are twins, it would be a good idea for your sister to have an exam done as well. I can set you up for surgery after the holidays and I can schedule your sister for an exam at that time. How does that sound to you?"

Augusta's mind was reeling with the information. "I guess it would be fine. I want to take care of this as soon as possible." She had intended to keep her visit between herself and Naomi. Now she would have to tell Aliya.

Dr. Turner stood then. "I know it isn't the best news, but it could be far worse. We've had women who've had to have their uterus removed completely due to fibroid tumors. Yours will be a minor outpatient surgery," She assured her. "If you will see my receptionist on the way out, she'll set up your exact time for surgery."

Augusta shook hands with Dr. Turner. "Thank you for working me into your schedule, Dr. Turner."

"Not a problem." The doctor smiled warmly. "You've got friends in the natural and the spiritual it seems."

Augusta smiled back. "Most definitely," she agreed.

Marco Angelo Arion Bolivar was preparing his flower arrangements for Friday when his phone rang. *If I've said it once, I've said it twice. All orders must come in before five.* If one more customer called him begging to place an order for Friday, he was going to scream. He picked up the phone hesitantly.

"Hello?"

"Mr. Bolivar? Frank Costanello here; your agent, remember?"

Marco hadn't heard from his literary agent in close to six months. He hadn't paid him in three. "You still consider me your client?" Marco had tried to put his attempt at writing behind him. Every time he thought about writing, he had only to take out his twenty-one rejection letters and read over them. It was a strong dose of reality. *I had best stick to what I am good at,* he had told himself.

"Of course I do. Although, you still have an outstanding bill with me, I have good news."

"What sort of news? If it is another writing symposium, I am not interested. Hobnobbing with successful authors doesn't guarantee my success."

"What about an interview with a major publishing house that is interested in your novel?" Frank knew he'd gotten his attention then.

Marco dropped the vase that was in his hand. "What did you say?"

"Let me put it plainly for you, Mr. Bolivar. They're offering you a one and a half million dollar book deal along with a three year contract."

Marco stepped past the broken glass. "And you told them I wish to remain anonymous?"

"Mr. Bolivar, with your looks and charisma, you could become an overnight phenomenon."

"But that was not the deal. I need the anonymity so that I can maintain the life that I now lead. I am not interested in press nor am I interested in book signings. Have you made these things clear?" Marco pressed his agent.

"I have, but I seriously think you should reconsider," Frank advised.

"Thanks, but no thanks. The money will help me expand my business here in Savannah." Marco was adamant.

Frank could see he would not be persuaded at least for the time being.

"So, your pseudonym is going to be?"

"Carmo Arion." Marco wanted to retain some of his personality while remaining anonymous.

"Very well, then. I've set up the meeting for after the holidays. You're going to have to close shop for a week or so. Their offices are in Oregon." Mr. Costanello informed him.

"That's fine." Marco wanted to jump up and down but he heard his bell ringing out front. "Fax me the rest of the details. I think I've got a customer." He hung up and hurried out to the front counter only to lay eyes on a familiar face.

"Afternoon, Miss Dubois. What can I do for you?" Marco queried.

Ginevieve sighed within. *Do you really want me to answer that question?* She shook her head trying to get rid of her traitorous thought. "I just came by to inform you that the meeting for the Single's Retreat will be held tomorrow at five thirty. Here's the address." She handed him a slip with typed directions.

Marco stared at her as if she'd grown three heads. "I'm sorry. I don't know what you are talking about. Is this some kind of how you say, joking?"

Ginny flushed beneath his stare. "No. Jamar gave me a check today and he asked me to place you on the list."

Marco thought back to a conversation he'd had weeks ago with Alpha Incorporated's new employee. He remembered the young man mentioning something about a trip. He'd merely responded by saying that a vacation would be nice. "He placed me on the list? I remember talking to him. I told him a vacation would be nice, but I did not tell him I was *going*. I have a business to run."

As if we don't? "Mr. Bolivar, if you don't mind my saying, don't you think you need a vacation?" Ginny winced as she saw a distinct flare in his nostrils.

"And you presume to tell me when to take one? Or are you accusing me of being a how you say in America, a workhorse?"

"I believe it would be workaholic, Mr. Bolivar." Ginny corrected him.

Marco shrugged off the comment. "Whatever the term, I am not. Anyway, it was a nice offer from Mr. Davis, but you can tell him to keep his money."

"But I'm afraid there are no refunds." Ginny tried to persuade him.

"That is not my problem." Marco folded his arms glaring at her. His rude demeanor equally perturbed Ginny. *And to think I actually liked him! How rude!* "Well, I shall tell Mr. Davis that you declined his offer." *And you declined ungraciously, at that.*

"Great. You save me the trouble of doing so myself." Marco stared at the flustered executive who looked ready to explode though she held back. *Too much of a lady,* he smiled to himself. If it had been any of his hot-tempered sisters, they would be throwing things at him by now for his impertinence.

Behind her bookish personality he believed Ginevieve Dubois to be a very feisty woman. As she stood there at a loss for words for his insolent behavior Marco took the opportunity to peruse the woman before him. *Petite but shapely, windswept strawberry blonde hair; Cerulean blue orbs that overpower her rose petal lips and pert nose. Delicate skin that betrays her every emotion; She would make an interesting character should I decide to write the sequel to my novel.* Marco immediately discarded the notion. But there was one notion that he couldn't dismiss and that was the fact that as many flowers as he'd delivered in the city, no one had seen fit to send her any. *But maybe I can remedy that.* It was amazing how much a man could take in through a matter of moments. But that was all that was needed for Marco to retain in mind the memory of the sweet if bookish Ginevieve Dubois.

"Very well, enjoy your afternoon." Ginny turned on her heels dismissing the look of interest she saw in the eyes of Marco Angelo Bolivar. *I must have taken leave of my senses. The man is obviously absorbed in his own self-importance. The sooner I stop thinking about him the better.*

Rosalynn had stopped home for a few minutes to freshen up for her last church workout session. She'd no more settled down with a salad and a smoothie when her doorbell rang. She hopped up to answer, thinking it was a delivery of replacement parts for one of their machines. It was quite another delivery altogether.

"Hi."

"Hello." Rosalynn swallowed. She shifted from side to side. She had not intended to be dressed for her encounter with Nicholas Giovanni in an oversized sweatshirt, tights, and rainbow colored leg warmers. *I bet my face matches a few of these colors right now.* She stepped aside. "Come on in."

Nicholas followed her to the kitchen and joined her at the counter. "I hope I haven't come at a bad time."

There's no way I can eat right now. Rosalynn sealed up her container of salad. "You're fine. I just had a break in my schedule. I've got one more class for the evening at six." She sat down on a stool.

"How have you been?" Nicholas turned himself to face her. Rosalynn was overjoyed at his presence yet apprehensive about his proximity. "I've been good. Things are going well with the classes and the clients. Things are going great at church and the choir is learning new songs and Shemiah is doing a wonderful job and Savannah too and--"

"I've missed you, Rosalynn." Nicholas said simply.

Rosalynn exhaled. "Really," she wanted to believe him.

"Really; Would Sunday evening be a good time for dinner?" Nicholas suggested.

Rosalynn rolled the day around in her mind. "I think Sunday would be okay."

Nicholas smiled in delight. "Eight o'clock sound reasonable?"

Rosalynn shook her head. "Reasonable? Yes."

"I figure it will give your brother some time to allow the steam to cool off," Nicholas joked.

Rosalynn agreed. "He's not exactly happy with it, but he knows I'm old enough to make my own decisions."

Nicholas encircled her trembling hands within his own. "And how do you feel about it, Rosalynn?"

"I'm not quite sure yet." Rosalynn admitted. *But I have decided that you have the potential to break my heart.* The thought was terrifying.

Nicholas would allow her to get by with that statement; until Sunday evening. Then he had a few things that he wanted to declare. "It would be nice if we both could spare more than a few minutes but since we both are on a mission, I must complete mine. Enrique would like to know when we could start our workout sessions."

Rosalynn doubted that Nicholas knew what he was doing to her as he held her hands in his dragging his thumb across each finger. She withdrew her hands. "After the holidays," She stood up then allowing her self the space to cool off. She opened her business folio and presented him with a schedule.

Nicholas read over the graph:

Trainer	Monday	Tuesday	Wednesday	Thursday	Friday
Rosalynn	Giovanni	Enrique	Enrique	Enrique	Giovanni
Carlton	Enrique	Nic /Gio	Nic /Gio	Nic /Gio	Enrique

A frown the size of Texas appeared on his face. He looked up at Rosalynn. "Did you take a look at this?"

Rosalynn nodded. "I did."

"I don't have any training days with you." Nicholas was more than a little perturbed. Giovanni had warned him that was how it would be.

Rosalynn grinned. "I'm not complaining Nicholas. I think the schedule works to our advantage."

Nicholas looked at the schedule again. "Explain."

"Carlton has no excuse as to why I can't have dinner with you. Technically, you're not *my* client." Rosalynn saw the light of understanding turn on in Nicholas's mind.

Nicholas grinned from ear to ear. "Good ole Carlton painted himself into a corner, didn't he?"

"Yep," Rosalynn agreed.

"I'm sure you were more than pleased to point it out to him." Nicholas chuckled.

"More than pleased; it was an effective silencer." Rosalynn gathered up her belongings. "Will you walk me out?"

"I'm offended that you would ask such a thing." Nicholas feigned hurt.

Rosalynn rolled her eyes playfully. "I can tell how wounded you are."

Nicholas decided to surprise her. "I must defend my honor and go a step above."

Rosalynn locked her door unprepared for Nicholas's next move. No sooner than she'd turned than she found herself swooped into the arms of Nicholas Cartellini. She buried her face in his chest taking in the scent of him.

Why did I go and do that? "Nicholas! Nick! Put me down!" She half whispered.

"What if the neighbors see you?" *I am so embarrassed. But I am enjoying every moment.*

Nicholas was enjoying himself as well. He took his time walking to her car. "The neighbors will think I am a wonderful man."

"Nic, do I need to remind you that I am not ninety-eight pounds?" Rosalynn thought that would do the trick.

Nicholas finally reached her car door setting her delicately on her two feet his hands resting lightly on her waist. "No, you don't need to remind me of what a stupid oaf I've been." Nicholas searched her eyes seeing her insecurity there. The insecurity he'd foolishly had a hand in developing. Now it was his responsibility to build up what he'd torn down. "But I need to remind you that you're wonderfully made. Every dip, every curve, every valley was honed and carved out to be appreciated. I just hope the Lord allows me to be the one who will appreciate you for a lifetime." He hadn't meant to spill his guts right then but so be it. He would do so all over again.

Rosalynn could not believe what she was hearing. "Nick, I-"

Beep! Beep!

They both turned to see blaring headlights blinding them.

Carlton. Rosalynn stepped back from Nicholas. "I have to go."

Nicholas eyed her suspiciously. She was pulling away from him. "Somehow, I don't think that was what you were about to say," He challenged her.

"We'll talk on Sunday." Rosalynn ignored his comment as her brother decided to let the whole world know he was waiting on his little sister.

Nicholas folded his arms. "We'll pick up where we left off." He corrected her.

Rosalynn waved bye and slipped into her brother's passenger seat. Nicholas stood there for a few minutes. *So that's how it feels to lay your heart on the line and get no response back.* He looked toward Enrique's living room in time to see a curtain pulled quickly back. *I've got to deal with nosy people.* He headed home to stew in his own mental juices.

8

Giovanni was extremely thankful to see Nicholas bounding across the lawn. The sooner he could get away from Fabritza Ciccone, the better. She and her brother Fabian had shown back up only a few minutes earlier, but she was already getting under his skin.

"Are you going out with the young lady at the hospital?" Fabritza had made no secret of her pursuit of Giovanni. They'd met up last year when Enrique had taken his visit to London. She'd all but told him that she would take him any way she could get him. It was a good thing that Giovanni was a holy man of God. "Miss Ciccone, my personal life is none of your concern."

He was determined to keep things between them professional no matter how personal she wanted to get.

"I was just asking. You don't have to get so uptight. One night with me would relieve all that pent up anxiety you have." Fabritza casually informed him.

Giovanni had been glad he wasn't eating or drinking at the time she had spoken those words: For surely he would have choked to death. He had decided to get as far away from her as possible at that point. He was ever thankful that Enrique had thought it more appropriate to foot the bill for their hotel stay than to have them under roof. *God you know how much a man can bear.*

It wasn't that Fabritza wasn't an attractive woman. Her long wavy raven tresses fell down her back when unleashed. She had a beauty that was native to her homeland and she knew it. Her olive skin absorbed the rays of the sun easily. Her almond shaped eyes nearly midnight in color sat under arched brows. Her aquiline nose directed the admirer to full lips that always seemed on the precipice of a smile. Fabritza could have very well chosen to go into modeling; her longs legs and elegant figure would have brought along with it a high price tag. Why she had chosen a line of work as dangerous as the one he was in was beyond him.

But Fabritza lacked something that mattered more than anything to Giovanni. And that was virtue. Call him old fashioned but there was something in him that was stirred by a woman simply being a woman, one who valued family life and commitments. Naomi came to mind even as he thought about it.

He couldn't wait to see her tonight. *Every night for the rest of my life, if I have anything to do with it,* he thought. He took his mind off the coming evening in order to tease his twin who was more than smitten with the next-door neighbor.

He opened the door as Nicholas was coming up the walkway.

"I trust you had a good evening." Giovanni snickered.

Nicholas pushed him out of the way. "Knock it off. I know you were spying on me."

"I was just trying to escape another Fabritza attack." Giovanni tried to downplay his nosiness.

"Where are they?" Nicholas headed for the kitchen.

"In the music room with Enrique; He's showing off his collection of guitars." Giovanni followed him into the kitchen.

Nicholas took a swig of orange juice straight from the carton. It was something that grated on Giovanni's nerves. "So what did Fabritza do this time?" Nicholas remembered her last calling card had been lace underwear and an open-ended ticket to Venice.

"She offered to relieve me of my tension." Giovanni was too embarrassed to even repeat her words.

"Have you told Enrique about her?" Nicholas pressed him.

"I don't want him to worry about it. He's already got enough to think about. I figure we can handle Fabritza." Giovanni reasoned. "Besides she's one of the best agents Italy has to offer."

"What do you mean we can handle? I'd just as soon as throw her off this case for sexual harassment. If she's thinking with her bottom half she's really no good to us." Nicholas's assessment of her was cold and to the point.

Giovanni saw her through the eyes of compassion. "Fabritza doesn't know Christ, Nick. We have the opportunity while she's here for the next few weeks to be the only Christ she may see. It would be easy to toss her aside but I don't think God would be pleased with that."

"I know you want to remain optimistic about her Gio, but if you take a good look at the situation, Fabritza isn't exactly interested in getting into the Word, but into your pants. You have to learn to pick your battles and this is one you don't have to fight. The Word of God says to flee youthful lusts and Fabritza fulfills both categories. She's youthful and she's full of lust. *You* do the math." Nicholas added pointedly.

Giovanni glared at his twin knowing he was right. "I'd just hate to lose a good agent over something so trivial."

Nicholas placed both hands on the counter. "And I'd hate to pick up the pieces of my twin because he thought he could save the world one harlot at a time. I'm giving Fabritza until after the holidays to change her ways. If her behavior continues, I'm going to recommend to her superior that she be relieved of her duties. Her brother can stay on provided he doesn't blow up."

Giovanni gave in. "Alright. You promise not to act until after the Single's trip?"

"Provided she doesn't try anything *on* the trip, you have my word."

The twins shook hands.

Mariella was relaxing on the couch when Naomi came home. She hopped up eager to share the events of her day.

"Guess what?" Mariella bounced up and down. Her ponytail she'd put in place after getting comfortable bobbed up and down with her.

"What?" Naomi could see that Mariella was overjoyed. For Mariella it could be for any number of reasons. Naomi hoped it wasn't because she had found a boyfriend.

"I got a job!" Mariella grabbed Naomi's hands and drug her into the bouncing ceremony.

"Great!" They bounced together.

"I start as soon as possible. It's temporary, but it's a start and it will help me develop my portfolio." Mariella was nearly out of breath bouncing repeatedly.

"Where will you be working?" Naomi slowed down to catch her breath.

"It's actually not too far from here. It all happened rather strangely how I got the job." Mariella flopped onto the couch. Naomi joined her.

"Go on." Naomi was trying to give Mariella her full attention though her thoughts were drifting to the dinner she needed to get ready for.

"I actually went to interview for a position as a secretary, but it turned out the guy had already hired one." Mariella continued. "He took a look at my design portfolio and thought it had merit so he decided to hire me to do interior design for his new home. I'm to meet him in the morning to take a look at his home and go over my contract with him."

Naomi stared at her mouth wide open. "Mariella, you can't be that naïve, can you?"

Mariella sat up then. "What are you trying to say? That I wasn't hired because of my talent?"

Naomi put her hands up. "I'm not trying to pick a fight but if he's already hired someone it just seems a little too coincidental that he just happens to need an interior designer all of a sudden."

Mariella whipped out Noelle's card. "Here. If you want to validate whether I imagined my job offer today, call him yourself." She stood up, stomping off into the kitchen to fix a snack. "Sheesh, does no one believe in me around here?" she muttered to herself.

Naomi stared down at the card. "Noelle Marks." She said aloud. "I know this guy." She looked to Mariella who was sulking over a bowl of cereal at the kitchen counter.

"Good. Are you happy now?" Mariella took a very large spoon and dug in to her cereal, smacking loud enough for the neighbors to hear.

"Yes. As a matter of fact I am. Noelle is my pastor's son."

At those words, the cereal that Mariella was eating left her mouth like ammunition spraying the counter. She coughed rapidly.

Naomi rushed over to her to see if she was okay but was stopped by Mariella's arm outstretched.

She coughed again. "I'm okay; must have gone down the wrong pipe."

"The wrong pipe indeed," the Holy Spirit spoke.
Mariella ignored that incessant voice that seemed to accost her at the wrong times- Like now.

"Are you sure you're okay?" Naomi had more than a slight suspicion that Mariella's choking was directly linked to her statement although she wasn't exactly sure just why yet.

"Umm hmm," Mariella nodded quickly and hastened to clean up the mess before her.

"Any way as I was saying, he's Pastor Marks's son. Had you gone to New Life with us a while back, you would have met him then," Naomi did recall Noelle giving testimony of finding a home he could call his own. "He's also an associate pastor of our congregation and a prophet of the Lord."

It's a good thing I didn't go to that service that day. The word prophet didn't bode too well with Mariella. "Are you talking about prophet as in the Bible?"

"What other kind is there, Mariella? The prophets of our day are certainly a tad more merciful than the Old Testament prophets but they also serve different functions today. They are still able to hear from God and share what is on his heart for the people of God." Naomi assured her.

The words "hear from God" rang in Mariella's mind. *Sooner or later God was going to whisper in Noelle Marks's ear.* Mariella hoped it was later-- years later. Hopefully she'd be back in Costa Rica firmly ensconced in her own design firm. "I was just wondering." She decided it was best to change the subject. "You want to order out tonight and watch some old movies with me to celebrate?"

Mariella rarely let Naomi into her world and it saddened Naomi that she was going to have to turn down her invitation. "I actually already have plans for dinner tonight."

Mariella shrugged it off. "Okay. I'll call Aurielle then. We'll hook up and do something."

Naomi chewed her bottom lip. "Actually, Aurielle is having dinner with one of her neighbors tonight." Somehow she didn't think it would be wise to let Mariella know that Dr. Thomas was the self same neighbor. But she had an idea. "I'm being picked up so you can borrow my car if you'd like to go see Enrique." Naomi hoped the last word was pointed enough. She did not want to be responsible for aiding her in carousing about town.

Mariella clapped her hands together. "That would be great! I can rub it in his face that I found a job without his help." *And I can share my good news with Jamar. Maybe Seth will be there as well.* She had heard he was back in town from his mission trip.

Before that time, Mariella had been cut to the quick by his bedside vigil and devotion to the comatose Aliya Peyton. *I was front and center alive and awake and yet he paid me no attention.* Enrique had further driven a stake into her heart with his words: *Mariella, its called love. Your perception of relationships keeps blinding you of that emotion.* It had been hard to face the cheery Aliya since then. It was hard to dislike her until Mariella realized that Aliya had known about her feelings for Seth. Then she began to seethe with anger. She wouldn't fool herself any longer. It would be childish to chase after Seth when he was so obviously devoted to another. But she could not explain why she still felt drawn to him.

"He will help you to understand the man who will be your husband."

Mariella was leaning back with her stool at the counter when God spoke. She lost her footing and came crashing down on padded carpet. "Ouch! Oh, my back," she groaned.

Naomi was next to her in an instant. "Mariella don't move."

"I can't move even if I wanted to." Mariella winced at the pain in her backside.

"How many fingers am I holding up?" Naomi held up three fingers. "Too many," Mariella groaned.

"Where are you hurting?" Naomi prompted her.

"The back of my head, my back, and especially my behind," Mariella breathed in and out heavily. "I can wiggle my toes, so I'm not paralyzed. I'll be fine. Let me just rest here a moment." *God, can we be friends? We gotta stop meeting like this.*

"I thought you'd never ask."

All of a sudden, Mariella felt a slow heat rise within her. It felt like a heating pad running up and down her spine. It moved from her spine and circled around her heart, settling there for a moment. Then the sensation moved up her neck to the back of her head massaging the sore area it moved to her forehead and settled there for a moment returning to her heart. *That sure feels nice.*

"Tonight, Mariella, I give to you a new mind, a new heart, and a new spirit. You can sit up now."

Mariella sat up and amazingly she didn't feel dizzy at all. She reached behind her touching her back. *No pain.* Her head wasn't throbbing either. "Did you give me a heating pad?"

Naomi had righted the stool she'd been sitting on. Naomi looked at her strangely. "No. I've been right here the whole time. You aren't delirious are you?"

"Then who touched me? Something just happened to me. I felt this warmth, this heat travel through my entire body." Mariella marveled. "I'm not in any pain."

Naomi knelt down next to her roommate. "My only explanation for you is that God touched you, Mariella." *And it's about time you felt His presence.*

The thought was entirely foreign to her. "But he's invisible. How can that be?"

"The air is invisible as well. But we feel it and we know it exists. The same with God, just on a greater level," Naomi explained.

Mariella just basked in that thought for a moment. "There was something very comforting about His warmth."

Naomi grabbed her Bible out of her purse and turned to the fourteenth chapter of John. "Here. Read this."

Mariella read the chapter out loud. Then she closed the Bible. "So, that feeling I felt was God's comfort?" she flipped to the passage again. "His Holy Spirit?" she questioned.

"You got it." Naomi could see a change even in Mariella's countenance.

"How do I get God to touch me again?" Mariella questioned her honestly.

"Mariella, God not only wants to touch you, but he desires to live inside of you. All you have to do is ask him to live in you." Naomi instructed her.

"Like asking Jesus to come into your heart," Mariella was putting things together.

"Yes. Many believers ask Jesus to come into their heart but they stop there. He not only wants us to have salvation but he wants us to have power to share our salvation with others. The Spirit of God does make you feel good in God's presence but it also warns us, helps us, teaches us about what Jesus wants for us right now and convicts us when we do wrong. Once you ask Jesus for his Spirit, he will give it to you. The only way his Spirit will not live in you is if you intend to do wrong. He will lead you and guide you into all truth but if you repeatedly reject truth, you are in essence telling him to move out. Do you understand?" Naomi could sense that this was an important moment. *Dinner is going to have to wait.*

"I understand. I want the Holy Spirit to help me." Mariella confessed. "Sometimes I think I hear God or know what he wants. There are other times I'm not so sure."

"I'll admit that sometimes I miss what God wants, Mariella. But because my heart is yielded to him, I endeavor not to miss him at all. None of us has hit the benchmark called perfection." Naomi assured her. "But we strive for it."

"Can we pray right now that God will let his Spirit live in me?" Mariella was ready.

"Of course, God's ears are always open." Naomi grabbed her hands and sat Indian style.

How right you are. Mariella bowed her head for prayer.

9

Ginevieve Dubois was still humming inwardly as she closed up her office for the evening. She had nothing planned for the evening except a journey to the local bookstore chain to catch up on her hobby of reading. Once she made it home she would cuddle up with her best friend, her poodle Evian.

Tatyanna had taken off early to help her sister get settled into her apartment while Augusta had left early for undisclosed reasons. Ginny was surprised to find Jamar still on post.

"You know we're not paying you overtime young man." Ginny chided him for staying so late.

Jamar looked up from the fashion journal he was reading and cocked a brow in her direction. "Surely you don't think I'd leave a delicate and fragile Southern belle such as yourself alone in these here parts of town, do you?"

Ginny laughed at his accent. "Thank you for the dutiful kindness you've shown Mr. Davis. I am Southern, but I am neither delicate nor fragile, and I sure don't ring any bells. Don't let the exterior fool you."

Jamar loved to carry on saucy dialect with his co-worker. He also knew she was more delicate than she let on but being the assistant editor at Alpha, Inc. called for gumption. And she exhibited plenty of it when she had to stand toe to toe with Augusta and Tatyanna in the decision making process. He admired her soft-spoken words grounded in the expertise she carried in her field. "I'm not the slightest bit fooled." He came around the counter, nearly towering over her. He grabbed her overloaded brief bag. "Where are we headed?"

"My car is right up the street there." Ginny waited as Jamar locked the door for her. Then she remembered she still hadn't told him about her run in with Mr. Bolivar. She waited until they had reached her car before she told him.

"All set?" Jamar opened her car door for her.

"One more thing; Mr. Bolivar turned down the Single's retreat trip. I believe if you'll see Aliya before she leaves this evening, you can still get your check back. The other option is to find someone else who wants to go." Ginny suggested.

Jamar looked puzzled by her statement. "How could he *not* want to go? It's a paid vacation," He would have a talk with his newfound friend.

Ginny shook her head. "I can't answer that. My piece of advice is don't spend your money unless you know the person is committed to going. I wouldn't suggest you try to convince him. He was rather rude about it. If you ask me, his paradise is his flower shop. There's no room for anything else."

Jamar winced. "Ouch. Do I detect *more* than a hint of cynicism?"

"I really...It's nothing. Don't even think twice about it." Ginny smiled widely.

But Jamar had made an art of reading people and beneath that wide smile that didn't quite reach her eyes Jamar could see that Ginevieve's admiration for the florist had been effectively snuffed out. At first he'd thought she had an overwhelming interest in his stunning bouquets. But the more he'd studied her gestures he'd soon realized that Ginevieve was not wishing for flowers. She had her sights set on the florist himself.

The greatest concealer of earnest affection is apathy. It takes the utmost of emotion to pretend you have no emotion in world, especially that of affection towards another.

Marco Bolivar's poetry rose to the surface. A smile formed on Jamar's lips. *Oh, Marco. You've got it bad. And your poetry is giving you away.* "You have a good evening, Miss Dubois."

Ginny pulled out from the parking lot wondering why Jamar was sprinting back to the shop.

It was close to seven and Aurielle was flipping through her wardrobe like a madwoman. *No. That won't do.* She walked to the end of her closet. *Too flashy, too sassy, too trashy; How did I miss that dress?* She tossed it into the waste basket. *Too corporate, too churchy, too short, too long, needs dry cleaning. Too bright; even for my eyes. Too preppy, too political, too motherly; I don't want him thinking Brady Bunch. Aha.*

Aurielle pulled out a simple silk olive dress that stopped mid calf. The bodice of the dress hugged her curves gently while the dress flowed out at the waist. Aurielle would use a scarf at the waist instead of the belt that accompanied it to soften the look more. She would wear her hair down in relaxed waves so there would be no need of earrings and she decided on a necklace with clusters of jade encircling the front. Her olive clogs with wooden heels would give her a dress casual feel. *Perfect. Now if I can just calm my nerves and pretend as though it didn't take me an hour to put together an outfit then I'll be okay.*

Aurielle hadn't felt this nervous since her first date. *He's just my next-door neighbor. A lot of neighbors eat dinner together.*

Her phone ringing startled Aurielle. She picked it up quickly. "Hello?"

"How far along are you in getting dressed?" Naomi whispered.

"Not very far; you," she asked.

"I've just picked something out. Listen, I wanted to give you some good news."

"What's up and why are you whispering?"

"Mariella received the Holy Spirit into her life tonight." Naomi continued. "I called Enrique to come over and facilitate the on going change. She's very tender at this moment and I didn't want to leave her alone."

Aurielle sat on the edge of her bed. "What happened?"

"It was all rather a strange series of events but it led to me showing her in the scriptures that God wants to live in us not just make Jesus our Savior. We prayed and she invited the Spirit of God to live in her. The next thing I knew, we were both overtaken with the presence of God. Mariella just began to cry and like most of us who encounter the power of the Holy Spirit, she began to confess her heart to God. That was nearly an hour ago. She's still confessing."

Aurielle rejoiced on behalf of Mariella. "It's so refreshing when God gives you a pure heart. I'm excited for her." She couldn't wait to meet the new and improved Mariella. She was going to be a force to be reckoned with.

"Enrique and Nicholas are going to ride out here with Giovanni. They'll stay until we return." Naomi mentioned.

"Let's make plans to celebrate tomorrow with her." Aurielle suggested.

"What about after the Single's trip meeting?" Naomi offered.

"Sounds good; See you at eight." Aurielle danced to the shower. *What a miracle working God I serve!*

When Marco Bolivar heard his overhead bells chime for the second time this evening he knew exactly who it was. Jamar Davis had made a habit of stopping by his flower shop the evenings that he worked to show himself friendly and in turn he'd gained a friend.

"A distinguished poet once said and I quote 'the greatest concealer of earnest affection is apathy. It takes the utmost of emotion to pretend you have no emotion in world, especially that of affection towards another' unquote. Would you happen to know where I could find the poet who penned those soul stirring words?" Jamar looked questioningly at Marco who'd come from the back and stepped to the counter.

Marco applauded his friend's recount of a piece he'd shared from a more romantic period of his writings. "Well recited. How's your evening been?"

Jamar leaned against the counter nonchalantly. "It was going well until I spoke to a lady friend of mine who'd recently had her heart broken." Jamar was reeling him in for Marco was always looking for material for his poetry writing.

"What happened?"

Jamar turned from the counter then and proceeded to paint a picture. "I suppose her infatuation started out simple enough. As you well know, most people don't intend to fall in love. As you've also written, most times love is like that manhole cover that's lifted when you least expect it and in you tumble. It doesn't matter who uncovered it, the only thing you know is you're stuck in it, helpless to do anything about it, and hoping those around you won't think you a fool for falling in there in the first place. Love covers but sometimes you still feel exposed because you know that's the only thing you're covered with."

"Go on." Marco's attention was focused.

"Anyway, this friend of mine must have walked past this manhole called love a thousand times. She stayed on the side of infatuation for a while building up her noble ideals about the one she was interested in. She convinced herself that the man was as noble as the task he carried out from day to day. I say she got confused. She thought the nobility of the task equaled the nobility of the man. One day and I'm quite sure she didn't know when, she fell in love. To her dismay it was unrequited and as we both know there is nothing more painful than falling in love alone. Today, the rose colored glasses were discarded. She saw the noble deed but no noble man behind the deed. The saddened expression I saw will stay with me for a very long time because I saw hope blossom in a young woman's eyes and I saw it extinguished by careless words." Jamar ended his speech, his dropping his head dejectedly.

"Well just tell me her name. I'm sure a bouquet of flowers would cheer her up." Marco got out a pad. He'd make this a benevolent order for tomorrow.

"The lady's name is Ginevieve Dubois and you, sir, are the insensitive cad. Even if you gave her a million roses she would no doubt hurl them all back at you. They would mean nothing to her." Jamar looked him squarely in the eye.

Marco's head was pounding. *Ginevieve Dubois? He'd crushed sweet little Ginny's heart?* "What do I have to do with it?"

"She said and I quote 'I wouldn't suggest that you try to win him over about the retreat. He was quite rude about it. His paradise is his flower shop. There's no room for anything else.' unquote," Jamar saw Marco flinch at those last words.

This is the same Ginevieve who smiled sweetly and returned my ornery attitude with a docile reply and walked out of my shop earlier? Marco could see where this conversation was going. "I was merely teasing her. And if she has a complaint about me, she should tell me in person. Besides she shouldn't take words so seriously."

Jamar wasn't buying his act one bit. "This is coming from a man who makes his livelihood off words? Marco, come on. She challenged the very essence of who you are. She thinks the only thing you can love is inanimate objects."

Marco's temper was rising at the thought. "Let her think what she wants. I don't need to prove anything to her."

"Once again, your poetry is telling on you. Your utmost sign of affection is apathy. Just how long have you had this affection for Miss Dubois?" Jamar came closer to the counter then.

"I would hardly call it affection." Marco defended himself. "She's nice to look at."

"Any man with two eyes could see that, Marco. But no, I believe it is something more. When she told me that you had been rude to her I thought to myself we must not be thinking of the same man." Jamar chided him.

"I hardly consider myself to have been rude. I just don't like being put on the spot. I'm not in a position to take a vacation right now, especially when I'll be gone shortly after the holidays." Marco explained.

"Why didn't you just say that? Why would you be rude to Ginevieve and allow her to think ill of you? Is it because you would rather not give her a reason to be interested in you?" Jamar grinned knowingly.

Marco sputtered. "This is my shop and I will not be counseled about how I choose to live my life!"

Jamar held up his hands in mock surrender. "Fine, suit yourself. Just know that it will take more than a bouquet to get back into the good graces of Ginevieve Dubois. But of course you're not interested in what she thinks. It's your life after all."

Marco was sore tempted to throw something at Jamar for his nosy inspection into his psyche. *I'm not at all concerned about what the prissy Miss Dubois thinks!* "Good night, Jamar."

"There's a ticket still waiting for you. If you change your mind about going you'll need to come to the meeting tomorrow at five-thirty." Jamar knew that as much as Marco argued and resisted he would find himself at that meeting. He was too much of a romantic not to come. That was exactly what Jamar was counting on.

Giovanni rang the doorbell to Naomi's home hesitantly. *Lord help me not to be a bumbling idiot tonight.* He hadn't bothered to ask what the attire was for the dinner tonight but he decided to wear something casual and less formidable. His rust colored shirt accented his tanned physique. His khaki slacks made for a nice combination. Nicholas breathed deeply inhaling the scent of azaleas neatly arranged on either side of Naomi's porch. He tried to keep still but he couldn't help it. He'd been excited since yesterday about this evening and since then his excitement had only been mounting.

As the door swung open he had to make a concerted effort to keep his mouth from gaping in disbelief at the lovely view before him.

Naomi wore a halter dress of chiffon that hung gracefully upon her slender frame. Multi-tiered ruffles started at the waist and ended at the edge of the dress, which flared out stopping just below her knees. The coral color lit up her olive complexion causing it to glow. She wore her raven hair down about her shoulders and back accented by a flower near her temple. She smiled nervously.

"If you keep looking at me like that, I'm going to put on a pair of jeans and a sweat shirt." Naomi's saucy reply pulled Giovanni out of his mental wonderland.

"No matter what you wear, you'd still be appealing to me." Giovanni leaned close to whisper in her ear.

"Alright, break it up you two," Enrique stepped onto the porch then. "Naomi, you look lovely. Don't keep my body guard out all night and I'll think about loaning him out again in the near future," He chuckled.

"What a kind offer." Naomi punched him in his good shoulder.
Nicholas watched the three of them with mirth in his eyes.

Naomi took notice. "I hear life has been treating you pretty good these days Nicholas." Naomi smiled with pleasure when she saw his bashful look.

"Don't start, Naomi. I've had enough ribbing already." Nicholas warned her.

"Fair enough; I'll just have to wait until Saturday to roast Rosalynn." Naomi laughed when she saw Nicholas's eyes widen at the statement. "Don't worry. We'll let her keep a few secrets."

Enrique rubbed his chin. "Is that what you ladies do with your free time? Do you compare notes for more creative ways to drive us out of our minds?" he kidded.

"Actually, we haven't considered that, but I'll make sure to bring it up for discussion on Saturday night." Naomi chuckled.

"And we'll be somewhere nearby eavesdropping." Giovanni assured her.
Naomi knew they could go on like this all night. "Come, let's get going. We don't want to keep the others waiting." She gave Enrique a hug. "Take care of your cousin and help yourself to whatever's in the fridge. She's in her room now. When she's ready, I'm sure she'll talk with you."

Enrique had seen and experienced more than his own share of the Spirit's encounter. "I won't hold my breath," He smiled slightly. "I'm sure God's got everything under control."

Naomi allowed Giovanni to lead her down her steps to the SUV all the while thanking God for removing her nervousness. *Lord, please be glorified in all that happens tonight.*

10

Angelynn sat nestled in her recliner with Josiah as she watched her husband lift Jaia into the air and gently bring her back down to his chest.

"She seems to be enjoying that quite a bit," Angelynn grinned widely at her daughter's high-pitched squeal. "You think she may take on a career in the friendly skies?"

Josiah shook his head. "I think it may be a little too early to tell what either of them will be," he kidded.

Just as he took a seat in his own recliner, Jarah waltzed into the entertainment room with dessert.

"I have homemade chocolate chip cookies fresh out of the oven." She set the platter down on the coffee table.

Josiah licked his lips in anticipation. "You know Mom, if you keep baking these treats for us, we're going to have to hold you hostage here with us for a little while longer," Josiah reasoned.

Angelynn looked longingly at the cookies but declined the offer. "If I am to ever have hope of getting back into a size four, I have to lay off the dessert."

Jarah was a bit disappointed but she didn't let it show. "I understand, dear. As long as you don't become a fanatic about losing weight, I'm okay with you turning down my desserts every *once* in a while," she emphasized.

Josiah looked lovingly at his wife then. "Sweetheart, you look great no matter what size you are." Josiah was secretly enjoying the fact that she'd put on a few pounds. Pregnancy had filled her out in all the right places. No, Josiah wasn't in any hurry to see her size eight-figure return to a size four.

Angelynn blew her husband a kiss. "I know I can count on you as my number one fan to boost my ego."

"Always," Josiah reached over for a cookie.

"So, how are the plans going for the Single's Trip?" Jarah enquired.

"All participants including chaperones are going to be meeting tomorrow. We'll get a chance to meet those who will be participating from other churches, get our room assignments and hopefully our itinerary. I believe the chaperones will have a meeting after the singles are dismissed."

"I know you both must be excited. This will be like a second honeymoon for you." Jarah added.

"I'm looking forward to it," Angelynn agreed. "Though I wish you would come with us."

"The advertisement said Single's Retreat *not* Senior's retreat, dear. Besides, if Jaia and Josiah were on the island with you two, you'd spend all your free time checking up on them." Jarah reasoned.

"She's right, you know." Josiah stood then with the sleeping Jaia. "Jarah's been a great nanny. She'll do fine while we're away."

Angelynn kissed the top of her son's head. "I know. It's just that four days is an awfully long time away from my Sugar and Spice."

They'd been over this before but never in front of Jarah. Josiah could see that Angelynn was not budging on the subject. *It's a good thing I always have a plan B.* He looked to Jarah then. "Jarah, I know you hadn't planned on going, but for the sake of Angelynn, would you consider going on the trip as our nanny? You wouldn't have to participate in the activities. Angelynn and I could check in on the twins in the morning and in the evening when the festivities are over." Josiah looked pointedly at his wife. "Twice a day," he winked.

Angelynn nodded. "I can live with that." She looked to her mother. "What do you say, Mom?"

Jarah knew what she wanted to say, but she also knew it wasn't time to discuss with Angelynn the dangers of being a mother who couldn't let go. She didn't want to see Angelynn make the same mistakes. Even at this early stage she could see a pattern developing. They would have to talk soon. "As long as you keep the visits to twice a day, I don't foresee a problem."

Angelynn beamed triumphantly. "Then it's settled. I'll call Aliya and tell her to add you to the list."

Shemiah grasped Savannah's hand lightly as they ascended the steps to her mother's home. As she rang the doorbell he squeezed her hand for support.

"Are you going to be okay tonight?" Shemiah searched Savannah's eyes for some sign of worry.

"I was just about to ask you the same thing." Savannah gave her beau a smile that didn't quite reach her eyes.

Shemiah pulled her toward him in an embrace. "I've already asked the Lord to keep my temper under wraps."

Savannah exhaled and enjoyed the feel of Shemiah's arms around her. "God is able to keep what we commit to him. I asked him to hold my tongue and to keep me from giving Lysander a knuckle sandwich."

Shemiah pulled back from Savannah surprised. "You would give Lysander a knuckle sandwich?"

Savannah nodded. "I wasn't *always* a law abiding believer. I've had my share of fights."

"I'm glad to find out this bit of information before the wedding." Shemiah joked.

Savannah punched him playfully.

"See, spousal abuse already. What will your family think?" Shemiah laughed.

"The apple doesn't fall far from the tree," Marilyn greeted them from the doorway.

Shemiah and Savannah both looked embarrassed at being caught in horseplay.

"Good evening, Ms. Robinson." Shemiah stepped aside as Savannah smothered her mother in kisses.

"Dinner is already on the table and you two are the last to arrive so let's make haste to the dinning room," Marilyn ushered them in.

"Lead the way." Shemiah heartily declared.

Aliya looked over her guest list for the trip once again. She'd wanted to strangle Jamar for his last minute addition. "If I get one more addition to this list, I'm going to scream."

"You may as well start screaming then because you have two more. Oh, and dinner's ready." Augusta poked her head into Aliya's bedroom.

"Urrgh!" Aliya threw the papers in the air not caring where they landed.

Augusta shook her head. "You know, that was the most intelligent thing you've done all day." She grinned.

Aliya rolled her eyes. "Like you would handle it so much differently," she shot back.

"Actually, I would. I would only count those who show up at tomorrow night's meeting. It's mandatory right? So, even if they have paid, if they don't receive their itinerary and registration, they still won't be able to attend. So why are you beating yourself up tonight?" Augusta leaned against the door.

"I'm trying to set the room assignments in order. I can't do that if people can't make up their minds or if the count keeps changing. Remind me not to volunteer to do this next year or any other year." Aliya hopped up from her bed.

"You can give out room assignments when we get there, sweetie. You won't have a good idea of what you're working with until Friday evening so relax." Augusta walked out to the living room, Aliya on her trail.

"All right, where is my sister and what did you do with her?" Aliya looked quizzically at her twin.

"I'm right here. Look, even I know when to stop stressing, Aliya. What's really bothering you?" Augusta lit the candles on their dinner table.

Aliya fidgeted with her silverware on the table. "Nothing in particular," she muttered.

Augusta helped herself to the steaming white bean chili she'd cooked. "Hmmm...nothing in particular; Then it must be *someone* in particular."

Aliya ignored the inquiry and fixed her own bowl of chili.

"We can play twenty questions or you can come right out and tell me what's bugging you, but I promise you it will be impossible to sleep tonight if you don't tell me." Augusta threatened her.

Aliya's spoon clanged against the side of her bowl. "Oh, alright; Jamar issued me an invitation to Seth's welcome back dinner tomorrow night."

Augusta's spoon stopped midair. *What in the world is that boy up to now?* She was almost sure there was no such dinner planned. She would have heard of it by now. "What did you tell him?"

"I accepted although I'm not sure why. I can't imagine he'd want to see me anytime soon." Aliya reasoned.

"I know you two weren't exactly on speaking terms but maybe he wants to be. Think of it as a good thing. He obviously cares for you." Augusta added.

"That was only pastoral concern. I'm sure if any of his members were seriously injured he would have responded the same way." Aliya spoke as though she was trying to convince herself as well as her twin.

"So, do you doubt what God has told you? Do you no longer think that Seth is the man God intends for you?" Augusta challenged her.

Aliya glared at her sister. "I don't doubt what God has told me but I believe he will tell Seth as well. Even if he has told Seth, human beings have a will of their own."

"Do you honestly think that if God told Seth you were the woman for him that he would run in the opposite direction?" Augusta shook her head.

"As long as Seth Davis thinks that I am incapable of being a wife to him, what does it matter what I think?" Aliya finished her chili hurriedly.

Augusta had made up her mind on the matter of the welcome home dinner. *I'm not going to tell her. Maybe this is Seth's way of ending the stale mate between them. Lord, show him what to do to win my sister's heart. She's not going to surrender without a fight.*

"How did your interviews go this afternoon?" Pastor Marks sat down at the picnic table with his son.

Noelle stretched a bit gearing up for his t-bone steak. "Everything went extremely well. The young lady I hired is perfect for the position. Her name is Tehinnah Adams. She's a recent law school graduate. She's twenty-five and easy on the eyes."

"Did you get her measurements while you were at it?" John remarked sarcastically.

"Dad," Noelle glared at his father. "It wasn't like that. I'm a man of detail that's all. Speaking of which, the strangest thing happened to me today."

Pastor Marks took a sip of lemonade. "Do tell."

"You remember the Hispanic beauty that blew me off today in front of the café?" Noelle was eager to tell his news.

"I do recall the incident."

"Well, she was one of the interviewees today. It turns out that she's got some interior design experience so I hired her to work on my home." Noelle didn't pause for breath.

Noelle's brow rose. "Let me get this straight: The same girl who didn't have two words to speak to you is now your new interior designer? Is that a wise idea?"

"She apologized. She was in a hurry to make it to my interview. How could I not forgive her?" Noelle threw up his hands.

"Does this girl have a name? I have a strange feeling I'm going to be seeing her at my dinner table sometime soon."

"Mariella Estrada."

"The name sounds familiar."

"Her cousin runs EAE Design Group."

Pastor Marks nodded then. "Ah, the gentleman that Augusta is very close friends with? He's a strong Christian. Is she a believer?"

"Yes. She's said so." Noelle sliced his steak.

"Well I'm glad you've found the help that you need. That last interior designer was a disgrace to the field." Pastor Marks grinned.

"I'm only expecting good things this time around." Noelle savored his father's cooking. *In more ways than one,* he smiled to himself.

"You did what?" Seth raked his hands through his hair, clearly frustrated.

Jamar stood and backed away from the table. "Seth, man, calm down. It's only a dinner date."

"One for which I am ill prepared!" Seth yelled.

Jamar had just finished explaining how he'd convinced Aliya to come over for dinner by inviting her to a welcome home dinner for Seth. He'd failed to tell her she was the only guest.

"Don't worry about the details. I've got this all under control." Jamar tried to placate his angry brother.

"Why do you love to interfere in my life? I'm not ready to see her yet." Seth stomped off through the sliding glass doors onto the deck. Jamar followed him.

"What are you so afraid of?" Jamar stepped onto the deck directly behind his brother.

That I will make a complete fool of myself, that nothing I say will come out right. That we'll end up in another argument and never get down to what we really need to say to each other, Seth ignored his brother's question walking past him. "Either you call her and tell her the dinner has been cancelled or I call her and tell her the truth but I will not be backed into a corner on this."

"Then you can call her. At least you two will talk and my goal will still be accomplished." Jamar stood his ground.

Seth glared at his brother for a full five minutes before responding. "If this winds up being a disaster you will only have yourself to blame."

Jamar clapped his hands together. "Then it's settled. All you need do is bring an open heart and a willing mind for dinner and conversation at seven. Agreed?"

"You better be glad I'm a holy man." Seth shut the sliding glass doors behind him leaving his brother on the patio.

11

"Your home is absolutely gorgeous, Trey. Did you manage this all on your own?" Naomi did not hide her obvious pleasure at Dr. Jones elegantly decorated home.

Giovanni had to agree with her. "Nice pad you've got here."

"I'm glad you approve," Trey motioned them to his living room.

Naomi was further impressed with his ivory décor and marble floors that reflected the fluorescent spotlights overhead. "I'm afraid to sit down."

"Go right ahead." Trey insisted. "I believe that living rooms are meant to be lived in and enjoyed." Just then the doorbell rang. "I believe that's the last guest." He hurried off to the door.

Naomi sat with her hands folded smiling faintly at Giovanni. "Thank you for coming. I really appreciate this."

"I'm actually enjoying myself. You look absolutely stunning, Naomi." Giovanni sat across from her on the sofa.

Naomi blushed at the comment. "You don't look so bad yourself." She kidded. *The man is a total babe.*

"Why don't you wear your hair down more often?" Giovanni thought aloud. "The look really becomes you."

"Well, it's more manageable for me in a bun especially when I'm working with patients." Naomi reasoned.

"What areas do you work in mainly?" Giovanni leaned forward, anxious to hear more about her profession.

"I mainly help with deliveries but lately we've been short on staff so if I'm needed down in emergency then I take up the slack there." Naomi informed him.

"Dr. Jones works in ER?" Giovanni enquired.

"Yes. He's one of the best. It's tough though. He's always on call." Naomi fidgeted with her fingers. *Like you.*

Giovanni knew the words she wanted to say so he finished her sentence. "He's always on call like me, huh?"

Naomi looked up. "Well, not exactly like you. He can take vacations." She grinned sheepishly.

Giovanni's reply was cut off by Dr. Jones announcement of dinner. "What's on the menu tonight, Doctor?" Giovanni stood rubbing his hands together like a hungry man.

"For starters we have fresh Caesar salad. Then we have our main course of lemon herb cubed steaks served with asparagus in garlic crème sauce and brown rice pilaf with a side of French onion soup. For dessert tonight we have raspberry mocha cheesecake and your choice of coffee or tea. Will that suffice?" Dr. Jones recited his menu like a five-star chef.

"Are you kidding?" Naomi laughed. "I think what you've prepared is more than enough."

Dr. Jones ushered them into his dining room where his table was set for four. He took the pleasure of seating Aurielle first.

Giovanni seated Naomi and took a seat next to her.

"I'll be right back." Dr. Jones trotted to his kitchen.

"I'll join you." Giovanni hopped up to follow Dr. Jones.

Aurielle was thankful for the reprieve as she stared across the table at Naomi. "You look terrific. That color really suits you."

"Thanks. You look runway ready. I'm surprised Dr. Jones can still form coherent sentences," Naomi giggled.

"Well, I noticed it was hard for him to speak at first." Aurielle chuckled.

She had been a little awestruck herself. He'd chosen an olive dress shirt and charcoal gray slacks for the evening. They complimented each other nicely.

"And how are you doing so far?" Naomi grinned widely at her friend.

"I'm a bit terrified but I'll manage," Aurielle admitted.

"You have nothing to be afraid of. Trey is a perfect gentleman." Naomi reassured her.

"And what about Giovanni," Aurielle teased.

"We're not here to talk about Giovanni." Naomi warned her in a teasing manner.

"Here we are, ladies." Dr. Jones and Giovanni came bearing steaming platters setting them down on the table.

Naomi had to stifle a giggle at Giovanni's getup. He was wrapped in an old apron that read will cook for free. Trey ran back to the kitchen and was back in a flash carrying a huge salad bowl.

"I believe we have everything we need to get started." Dr. Jones whipped off his own apron then. "Mr. Cartellini, will you do us the honor of leading us in blessing the meal?"

"I'd love to."

They all bowed their heads in thanksgiving for what they were about to receive.

Savannah had been more than relieved to find out that Lysander Townsend had been called away on urgent business with his firm and had to hurry back to South Carolina. It had seemed as if a weight had been lifted from her. *Lord, I thank you. I don't know how I would have made it through dinner with Lysander at the table.*

"I will place no more on you than you can bear. Always believe that."

Savannah smiled inwardly at the voice of the Lord. Every one around her talked animatedly. Between the multiple wedding plans and her grandmothers' prospect of opening a restaurant the talk seemed non-stop.

"Oh, Savannah, sweetie, I brought down those photos you wanted for the slideshow at the wedding." Indina handed her an envelope.

Shemiah almost intercepted it but he was too late. "Mother, tell me you didn't."

Savannah pulled out the first baby picture of Shemiah and immediately burst into laughter. "Oh yes, she did. It's payback time, sweetheart."

Shemiah shook his head. "Here we go."

"This one is adorable." Savannah grinned at the picture of Shemiah wearing a diaper along with a cane and a top hat. "I see you were planning to be a groom from the very beginning."

"Just remember that I get to pick out your childhood shots." Shemiah warned her.

"As long as they are not birthday suit shots, you can pick out whatever you want." Savannah noted.

"Are you two always this fussy?" Marilyn wondered aloud.

"You should put a remote in their hands." Andre laughed. "They entertain me more than the shows they want to watch."

"We aren't fussy. We're just very expressive people." Savannah defended herself.

"Sure." Everyone at the table stated at the same time.

"I see I'm outnumbered tonight so I'm going to finish my macaroni and cheese." Savannah loaded her fork.

"Well said." Shemiah chuckled. He enjoyed the easy banter between them. He looked forward to the other expressions that married life would bring. Just *one more month, Lord! Thank you for giving me the patience to wait. I didn't think I had it in me, but you have certainly proven me wrong.*

"So, how do you like it?" Tatyanna helped her sister put away her things.

"I think it's great. It's certainly you. Your style and everything," Tehinnah stood in the center of Tatyanna's condo.

"I hear the "but" in your voice. Come on. Spit it out." Tatyanna sat on a stool at her kitchen counter.

"But I'm definitely going to need my own place after a while. I appreciate your letting me stay for a few months. I can get my own place once I pass the bar and my salary changes from secretary to attorney." Tehinnah sat down on the futon.

"That's fine. I understand your need for independence so I'll enjoy you while you're under my roof." Tatyanna came and plopped down on the floor in front of your sister.

"I understand your need to play mom while I'm under your roof, so I'll play along until I get my own place." Tehinnah grinned.

"If Mom were still alive, I think she'd be extremely proud of you. You've accomplished so much." Tatyanna didn't think of her mother's death too often. It still pained her.

"I feel like I'm at the beginning again." Tehinnah reflected. In many ways she was. She was in a new city starting a new job and living in new surroundings encountering new people. One of whom she was particularly interested in.

"That's how I felt when I came here but I've made friends, met God and things are great." Tatyanna knew she sounded ultra optimistic but she couldn't help it. God had turned her cynicism into joy.

"I hope I can share in that testimony in the near future." Tehinnah spoke with a tinge of humor. "So, what's for dinner?" Tehinnah wasn't too interested in hearing yet another sermon on God right now. He hadn't been able to stop her mother from ending her life so she and God had nothing to say to each other. She had decided it was best not to burden anyone with her animosity towards Him at the moment.

"Actually, we're going just a building over to have dinner with a very special man in my life." Tatyanna informed her little sister.

"You have a boyfriend?" Tehinnah punched her sister playfully. "Why have you never mentioned him in our conversations?"

"Ouch." Tatyanna rubbed the sore spot. "It wasn't that serious then. He's not my boyfriend anyway. We're courting."

"Isn't it the same?" Tehinnah looked miffed.

"No. Courting is a bit more serious than dating. We're not seeing other people and we expect the next step of our relationship to be engagement then marriage." Tatyanna explained.

"I could be meeting my future brother-in-law and you just now decide to tell me? I'm hurt." Tehinnah feigned injury.

"You are such a drama queen." Tatyanna laughed. "Come on. He's expecting us any time now."

Tehinnah grabbed her purse and headed to the door with her sister. "I must warn you that since I am the only present representative of the Adams family, I'm going to have to interrogate him to see if he meets the Adams' family code."

"Go ahead. I think Kevin will welcome every question. Just remember he's not on the witness stand."

Ginevieve Dubois was floating through the bookstore humming a hymn, her arms full of books when she ran headfirst into what she thought at first was a bookshelf. That would have been embarrassing enough, except bookshelves don't talk.

This particularly solid individual said, "Oomph!" It was sound of books colliding with a midsection. That would have been embarrassing enough as well. Except the gentleman now under a pile of books due to a bookworm who refused to get a cart like everyone else in the store was Marco Bolivar.

Ginny put her hands to her mouth in shock. "I'm *so* sorry!" she managed to croak out bending down to pick up the stack of books that covered him.

Marco was about to answer when he happened to look up. *Ginevieve Dubois, the woman who is supposedly upset with me; I wonder if she didn't plan this accident as an attempt to maim me.* "I suppose we are now even." He muttered under his breath. Marco sat upright and helped her with the books. "Did you need some assistance carrying these to the counter?"

"Thanks, but I'll get a cart." Ginny's cheeks looked like cherries as she rushed to pull up an empty cart.

Marco grinned thinking it was cutest thing he'd seen on a woman in a long time. "You don't have to be embarrassed. I'm sure you're not the first person this has happened to."

Ginny turned around to see a silly grin on Marco's face. *Is he actually trying to have a conversation?* She nodded grabbing her pile of books and dumping them into her basket. "I'm going now. Have a good night." She turned and walked off hurriedly.

Marco stared after her clueless. *Was it something I said?*

Mariella was surprised to find Enrique and Nicholas sitting on her couch. Nicholas was fast asleep. Enrique sat reading a Christian magazine. He looked up then.

"Hello." Enrique said softly.

"Hi." Mariella spoke just above a whisper. She looked around. "Where's Naomi?"

"She had an engagement she had to keep. She asked me to come by and keep an eye on you." Enrique put down the magazine and patted the couch where he was seated. "Come on over."

Mariella joined him on the couch. "I'm kinda glad you're here, actually. I believe I have some apologizing to do."

Enrique sat up then. "Apologizing?"

"Yes." Mariella looked down then. "Since I've come to the States, I've been nothing but trouble for you: Refusing to listen, doing my own thing, flirting with every guy I meet. I know Papi would have a fit if he knew what I was doing over here. I fully expected him to be here by now

83

dragging me back to Costa Rica. I know the only reason he hasn't shown up is because you haven't called him. For that, I thank you. I'm sorry for being a disrespectful brat. Can you forgive me?"

Enrique took Mariella's chin in his hand and lifted it so her eyes could meet his own. "Of course I forgive you. How could I not? As long as you honor God and hear him, you'll do fine. Just remember that. I'm not here to be your babysitter, Mariella. I'm just here to help you. I can't choose right or wrong for you, but I can tell you what is right and the Word of God will show you as you read and pray and study it."

Mariella was amazed to find no hint of condescension in her cousin's eyes. "Thank you for being so understanding. I want you to know I found a job today within my field."

Enrique's eyes lit up then. "What company?"

"It's a private job. I'm going to be doing the interior design for a home."

"Who's your client?" Enrique didn't like the sound of 'private job'.

"His name is Noelle Marks. His father is a Pastor here in town." Mariella could see the wheels churning in her cousin's head.

"Ah. Pastor John Marks is a good man. I'm not sure I've ever met his son."

"The job should take a few months tops." Mariella insisted. "It won't interfere with school."

"How are you going to get back and forth?" Enrique wondered.

"Right now, Naomi and Mr. Marks will give me a ride." Mariella assured him.

"Tell you what. If you get your license here, I'll provide the transportation. But you must promise to use it responsibly," Enrique laid down the law.

"Not a problem." Mariella thought as she gave her cousin a hug. "Thanks, Enrique."

"You can let go now. You're choking me." Enrique managed to get out.

"Choking," Nicholas hopped up fully awake in combat stance.

Mariella jumped back. "Whoa. I was just thanking him. You can turn off the attack mode."

Nicholas grinned. "You thought I was asleep?"

12

Carlton stared across the table at his little sister, who seemed more than a little distracted ever since they began dinner. Though Carlton never voiced his true opinion, he often worried about her growing interest in Nicholas Cartellini. *I know I can't control her life, but I really don't want her to hurt,* he battled inwardly.

"What's on your mind? You've been pretty quiet tonight." Carlton helped himself to another portion of baked chicken.

Nothing that I can share with you, thought Rosalynn. She knew Carlton would probably have a fit if he knew she was contemplating a serious relationship with Nicholas.

"Nothing much; I was just thinking about the Single's Getaway and how much fun it's going to be."

"You can't possibly be serious. The *only* reason I'm going is to watch out for you." Carlton downed a glass of homemade lemonade.

Rosalynn laughed outright. "You're kidding, right? I'm a fitness instructor who knows martial arts, Carlton. I'm not your five-year-old sister with pigtails, a low self-esteem and an extra hundred pounds. You've got to change your perception of me. *I* certainly have."

Carlton inhaled sharply at the comment. "I'm just looking out for you Rosalynn. As your brother, it is my duty to do so whether you appreciate it or not." He stood up throwing his napkin down on the table.

Rosalynn regretted hurting his feelings but she couldn't keep pretending that his overprotection didn't bother her. She stood as well. "Look, Carl, I'm not trying to hurt your feelings. You've been there for me all of my life and I appreciate the fact that I can always count on you."

Carlton turned to face his sister then crossing his arms defensively. "But somehow that just isn't good enough anymore, *right?*"

Rosalynn remained silent knowing he had more to say.

"All of a sudden some guy starts paying you some attention and you totally forget about those who are there for you no matter what." Carlton glared at her.

It was Rosalynn's turn to get indignant. "If you're trying to make me feel guilty about my friendship with Nicholas, I'm afraid I have no remorse about it. Nicholas is not here to *replace* you, Carlton. He's not in competition with you."

Carlton waved her words away. "Of course not; He's already completely won you over and when the relationship turns sour, who's going to be there to pick up the pieces?"

Rosalynn couldn't believe Carlton was speaking so negatively. "Why are you already condemning our relationship before it even begins? Don't you want me to be happy?"

"Of course I want you to be happy. But you need to evaluate what that means. Are you considering dating Nicholas because you truly like him or are you considering the boost to your ego at being linked to a great looking guy who cared absolutely nothing about you only months ago?" Carlton stomped off.

Rosalynn felt as though she'd been dealt a blow to the stomach. She sank down in her chair. *Is that what I'm doing? Am I simply using Nicholas' attention to boost my self-esteem? Is Nicholas willing to date me simply because he feels pity for me?* The very thought was enough for Rosalynn to call off the whole dinner engagement. *Carl's right. Nicholas couldn't possibly be serious about me.*

The seeds of doubt had been deeply imbedded and only God could uproot them.

Aurielle, Naomi, Giovanni, and Trey sat in his living room after dinner enjoying each other's company. They'd talked about everything from movies to cars to music and somehow or another the subject of the perfect date had come up. Giovanni was the first to share.

"My idea of the perfect date would be a flight to Venice where dinner would be waiting on a boat along with a two hired violinists playing softly in the background. I would cruise the waterways until midnight talking and sharing my innermost thoughts." He looked directly at Naomi. "The waterways of Venice are beautiful in the moonlight."

Naomi smirked. "I can imagine. Surely you've enjoyed them *plenty* of times judging by your description."

Giovanni flinched at the statement. "Actually, as many times as I've been to Italy, I haven't found anyone special enough to cherish them with." *So she still thinks I'm a philandering playboy.*

Now I feel like a real idiot. "Oh." Naomi flushed. *I've ruined a perfectly good evening with my big mouth.*
Aurielle and Trey could sense the tension.

"So, Aurielle, tell me your idea of a perfect date." Trey was hoping to clear the air by taking the focus off his other guests.

Aurielle thought about it for a moment. "The perfect date to me is simply being with the right person, for the right reasons, at the right time, with God's approval." *I've been on more dates than I'd care to admit.* But none had impressed her as much as tonight had. Dr. Trey Jones had been the perfect gentleman, serving her as if she were a queen. Aurielle knew that his attitude wasn't rehearsed, but genuine. It was one of the things that she liked most about him.

"I'd have to agree with you there." Trey Jones couldn't have put it better himself. "Although I'd favor something outdoors in particular; I spend too much time indoors."

Aurielle turned to Naomi hoping to take the scowl off of her friend's face. "What about you Naomi? What's your idea of a perfect date?"

Naomi looked at Giovanni apologetically. "One where I don't ruin it with my big mouth," She smiled sheepishly.

They all broke out into laughter.

Great comeback, thought Giovanni who smiled at Naomi accepting her offhand apology. Her transparency was endearing. "I'm sure we've all stuck our foot in our mouths a time or two."

Aurielle looked at her watch. It was getting late. "Well, I don't know what your schedule looks like for tomorrow, but I know I have an early day planned." She stood then stretching.

Naomi looked uneasy. The evening had started well enough but she knew the ride home with Giovanni was bound to be filled with tension. *Why do I always have to make jibes about his romantic life? I don't know anything about him, but yet I keep painting the picture of a playboy.*

"If you view him as unfaithful you will never consider making a commitment,"

Naomi was not prepared for the reality of what she was doing. *Lord, are You saying I'm afraid of commitment?*

"When it comes to the opposite sex you are."

"Naomi, Are you ready to leave?" Giovanni's question intruded on her introspection.

Naomi grabbed her handbag. "Yeah, Sure,"

Aurielle and Dr. Jones were already walking to the door.

"Do you mind if I walk you next door?" Dr. Jones looked hopeful.

"That would be fine." Aurielle gave Naomi a hug on their way out. "Call me when you get in. I'd like to know how things are with Mariella." *And with you,* she wondered.

Naomi gave her a half-smile. "Will do," She really wanted to throw herself at Aurielle's feet and beg for a ride home. But to do so would only confirm what the Lord had spoken to her heart earlier.

Though, both couples walked in opposite directions, their hearts were all focused on the same thing: *where do we go from here?*

Tatyanna Adams had hoped her sister and Kevin would hit it off. What she was not expecting was the instant camaraderie they shared. Tehinnah had been a continual chatterbox not pausing for air since Kevin had met them at the front door. If Tatyanna didn't know any better she'd think her sister was interviewing for a date.

Tatyanna had been working hard on controlling her emotions and seeing things for what they really were before jumping too conclusions.

She'd made that particular mistake too many times. *Lord, help me not to jump to conclusions. Help me to be patient and understanding. If Tehinnah does have an interest in Kevin, then help me to deal with it in a godly manner and keep our relationship in tact.*

"How many offices do you have?" Tehinnah leaned in close to Kevin her eyes fastened on him.

"I'm getting ready to close my office in Jacksonville. I'll be expanding my Savannah base. My partners are moving to town." Kevin answered nonchalantly as he sipped ice tea. *I can't believe how much they look alike.* Except for coloring and height, the sisters could be twins. Whereas Tatyanna was polished ebony Tehinnah was caramel.

"Any siblings," she quizzed.

"I have four sisters. Two older, two younger; I'm the middle child." Kevin grimaced. "But not all stereotypes are true."

"I would love to have more siblings. It's just me and Tatyanna. What are their names?"

"Summer who is finishing her last year of college in Atlanta, Spring who is just starting college in Jacksonville, Wintera who is an architect like myself, and Autumn who is an attorney in Los Angeles. Speaking of which, Tatyanna tells me you just graduated from law school. Congratulations are definitely in order." Kevin turned the subject away from his sisters. He'd been teased mercilessly through the years about living with all four seasons under one roof.

Tehinnah beamed under his praise. "It was hard. I dealt with some pretty cutthroat professors my last year but I graduated with honors. I just need to take the bar, and I'll be all set."

"Tehinnah is very bright. Always has been." Tatyanna added.

"Mom always said you were the beauty and I was the brains of the family." Tehinnah's comment held a tinge of sarcasm.

"I think God gave you both your fair share." Kevin glanced lovingly at Tatyanna. "When I first met your sister, I'll admit she took my breath away, but it takes more than beauty to run a company."

Here we go again; the sacred sayings of mom. Tatyanna thought those days were over. "Tehinnah, you've been queen of every beauty pageant you've entered. You don't win just because you have brains."

Tehinnah conceded then. "That *is* true, although intelligence does figure into the big picture."

"Maybe you should get involved with the church youth groups here in town. I'm sure they'd welcome someone with your experience in poise and etiquette." Kevin suggested.

Tehinnah looked at him as if he'd grown three heads. "I don't *do* youth anything. Neither teenagers nor babies are my cup of tea."

"You'd be surprised at what you could enjoy if you gave it a try Tehinnah." Tatyanna encouraged.

"Tatyanna didn't know how much she could enjoy my company until we started hanging out." He teased. "Now we're inseparable." He winked.

The comment seemed to bring up something Tehinnah had wanted to ask for most of the day. "Speaking of company, who's the secretary that works for you, Tatyanna?"

Tatyanna's brow rose at the question. "You haven't been in the city a full day and you're already out scouting?"

Kevin grinned at the sisters knowing full well whom she was referring to.

"Are you going to tell me who he is or not?" Tehinnah folded her arms waiting for an answer.

"His name is Jamar Davis. He's graphic design student here in town and he transferred from New York. He's a really sweet guy."

"He's still in school?" Tehinnah sounded disappointed. *Then he's not as old as I thought.* Tatyanna didn't do younger men. *Too immature,* she reasoned internally.

"He's got one more year I believe. After that, I hope he plans to join our design team." Tatyanna had seen Jamar's portfolio. He definitely had potential.

"Is he a believer?" Tehinnah had already made up her mind about the relationship part but maybe they could be friends.

"Jamar is a strong Christian and firm in his beliefs. He helps assist his older brother who pastors the church right across from our office." Tatyanna went on to describe the services there. "Fresh Fire a pretty young membership with collegiate students mainly making up the population. He's active with the youth ministry there and he serves as the interim pastor while his brother is away on missions."

"Oh." That said it all as far as Tehinnah was concerned. The word youth turned her thoughts completely in the other direction. The word pastor sent her running.

Kevin sat in awe of the pair. "Is this how you decide whether or not someone is suitable for you?" Having lived with four sisters he understood exactly how the female psyche worked. His sisters had made target practice of him and he had cringed as they made mince meat out of their significant others.

Tatyanna and Tehinnah looked at him.

"I wasn't exactly looking for you, Mr. Thomas." Tatyanna pointed out.

"Point taken, but you are a rare find among women." Kevin noted.

"I'm not deciding his suitability." Tehinnah denied. "I was merely enquiring as to what kind of person he was." She spoke innocently.

"If Jamar was here, I don't think he'd see your conversation in the same light." Kevin assured Tehinnah. "If you're so curious, why don't you ask him? He's a real friendly guy and he always welcomes conversation. I think he'd be quite interested to know that a man's age and profession define who he is." *And any unattached male would be crazy not to welcome your attentions.*

"I don't see anything wrong with finding out if you share the something in common with someone who strikes you as interesting," Tehinnah defended her inquiries. "I think in time I'll take you up on your advice." Tehinnah replied saucily.

"Just be ready to answer some questions of your own." Kevin warned her. He chuckled to himself as he thought about Jamar Davis. He seemed to have everyone's love life mapped out except his own. *Well Jamar, it appears that your single days are numbered.*

Ginevieve let herself in to her cozy apartment loaded down with books and groceries. Though petite in nature she possessed an abundance of physical strength that came from her athletic pastimes as a marathon runner and membership in the local mountain bike club. Her Saturdays were spent running or biking, settling down to hot chocolate along with a good book, reflecting on her day and finally curling up to her beloved cat and dozing off.

Though Ginevieve's life wasn't action packed it certainly wasn't humdrum either.

As she put away her groceries, Ginevieve let her mind rewind to her encounter with Marco Bolivar at the bookstore. She'd felt like a total idiot smashing into him. Her words simply amplified her embarrassment. *Thank God he didn't find me in the Christian Romance section. I would have never been able to look him in the eye again.* Not that Ginevieve thought there was anything wrong with romantic fiction for Christians. Quite frankly, she was addicted to it. But to be caught *reading* it, now that was another story. To Ginevieve, reading Christian romance novels automatically implied that there was a lack of romance going on in reality. The last thing she wanted Mr. Bolivar to think was that she was a hopeless romantic, carrying notions of grandeur and chivalry around in her head. *Even if I am,* she giggled to herself.

Ginevieve picked up Evian and rubbed the back of his neck. "Right now, Evian, you are all the Prince Charming I can stand."

The ringing of the phone startled Evian causing him to jump right out of her hand. Ginevieve wondered over her cat's strange reaction to her telephone ringer as she grabbed the receiver.

"Hello?"

"Ms. Dubois?" Marco Bolivar sounded terse on the other end.

I must be imagining things. "Mr. Bolivar? How'd you get this number?"

"You must not check your messages." Marco paced back and forth on his cell phone.

We've got to do something about his attitude. "I just stepped inside a few minutes ago."

"Well, this is my third time trying to reach you. I have your credit card to return to you." Marco adjusted his tone slightly. "You must have dropped it when we collided in the store; Anyway, they were calling you to come to the front desk. After they took down all my information, I offered to deliver it to you myself. "

Ginevieve noted the change. "That was very thoughtful of you."

Marco chuckled at her comment. "Considering what a heartless, insensitive, unfeeling oaf I am?"

Ginevieve's sharp intake of breath was all Marco needed to continue.

"Since you feel I owe you an explanation for not accepting Jamar's generosity, it is because I will be on vacation in another week and I wanted to give some time to planning my absence from the shop," Marco's whispered reprimand sliced through Ginevieve like a knife through cheesecake.

Ginevieve stood speechless clutching the phone barely breathing. *How had he known?*

She was thankful several miles separated them. Her flaming red cheeks would have been indelibly etched into his memory had he been standing before her. "I apologize for making you feel that way. You can leave the card at the front desk tomorrow." She added quickly. *How does one escape from verbal quicksand?*

"No need for that. I'm right outside. I was just calling to make sure you were home. I'm on my way up." Marco closed his cell phone and made his way up the stairs of Ginevieve's complex.

"No!" Ginevieve was too late. He'd already hung up and she could hear him bounding the up the stairs one heroic step at a time. *Lord, help!*

She ran to the restroom hoping to cool her flushed cheeks with water.

13

As he stood barefoot on his patio, Seth Davis admired the frolicking couple walking hand and hand away from the shore. From a distance their life seemed so carefree. *Why can't it be the same for me? Why do I always seem to wind up in a heap of twisted and confused emotions?* Seth had led a pretty uncomplicated and structured lifestyle that is until he had met Aliya Peyton.

From the beginning they had clashed. They differed in opinion, in taste, in attitude. The only thing they had in common was that they loved God. Seth still didn't understand all the reasons why the Lord had said she was the one. At first, he'd wanted answers. Now he was ready to relinquish his feelings on the matter and let God have his way. *But is now the time, Lord?*

Seth reflected back on the time actually spent getting to know Aliya and he found himself lacking. *Jamar has placed me in a precarious situation. I haven't seen Aliya in a while. I have no idea how she even feels about me. How am I supposed to convince her that a relationship between us is Your will?* Seth thought within.

"I don't recall giving you that responsibility."
Should I just call off the dinner and admit that it was my brother's idea? I'm sure she'll be overjoyed.

"Truth is better than compromise."
Seth took in the words of wisdom. He would have to call off the Dinner Date; He stepped back inside to find Jamar. He was at his desk working in his sketch book-- the picture of artistic sensitivity.

"I'm calling off the dinner."
Jamar looked up perplexed. "Why?"

"I'm not ready to have dinner with Aliya. I don't want to force a relationship between us that's not there," Seth stood his ground.

Jamar gave him an unbelieving glare. "So are you saying that you feel absolutely nothing for her?"

"Of course not; Aliya is a beautiful young woman whom I have come to care for very much. Because of that, I can't let you or anyone else influence how I express that." Seth hoped Jamar was getting the point.

"Well I'd say you're a terrible mime because I can't see how you've expressed anything except that she's the last person you'd think of becoming involved with," Jamar snapped.

"I'm sorry if I'm not enough of a *romantic* for you Jamar, but before I just lay my heart on the line I look at the big picture and part of that has to do with mutual feelings," Seth answered stiffly.

"How can you be so spiritual and yet be so *blind*?" Jamar slapped his hand against his forehead. "You're shouldn't be waiting on Aliya to declare her feelings. She's waiting on you to tell her that she may not be what you bargained for but she's a whole lot more than a cookie-cut preacher's wife. You should be man enough to face how you feel whether she rejects you or not. But that's the real problem, isn't it?" Jamar stood toe to toe with his brother his eyes riveted upon his.

"It's not a problem. It's a reality. I don't know how she feels about me. I've been horrible in more ways than one. I haven't tried to understand her point of view. I don't *know* what makes Aliya tick. I feel compassion for her and I want to get to know her better but there's a barrier between us. Maybe it's a barrier of my own making but nevertheless its there. I don't think that can be broken down in one evening," Seth humbly admitted.

"But you've got to start *somewhere*, Seth. Don't hide behind your title and your sermons. If you dish it out, you've got to live it out. Your sermons won't have the impact they need if there's no reality behind your message," Jamar admonished him. "I've watched Aliya over the past few months. Her ordeal has strengthened her in so many ways. I dare venture to say that she's not the same person. Playful and carefree and outlandish though she may be, she's also developed a serious side."

Seth absorbed Jamar's heartfelt words. "I don't doubt that Aliya has changed. I'm simply saying that if there's going to be anything between us, it's got to start with a friendship. The last time we spoke she basically told me not to contact her. Don't expect me to feel gung-ho about round two."

Jamar laughed at Seth's grimace. "Obviously she's not holding grudges or she wouldn't have accepted the dinner invitation in the first place. Which of course I think you should still go through with."

Seth grinned. "Oh, I intend to but it will be on *my* terms."
Jamar could sense he was going to be in trouble. "You're going to tell her the party was for one?"

"Yep," Seth chuckled. "I'm sure she'll go easy on you after I explain it was one of your misguided attempts at matchmaking."

"Sure you will." Jamar scowled. "Just make sure I'm on lunch break."

The tension between them had eased and Jamar was thankful for it.

"Let's pray that I make her an offer she can't refuse." Seth was already formulating a plan.

Aliya and Augusta sat poolside their feet treading water at their complex. Most of the residents were long gone. Only a few people came down at night to enjoy the cool waters. Tonight the Peyton twins found themselves alone.

"I wonder when he'll call." Aliya thought out loud as she was prone to do.

"Who," Augusta sent her a puzzled look.

"Enrique. I'm anxious to hear how things went in Venice." Aliya was grateful for the capture of the man who had been responsible for her kidnapping. "I left a message for him about the meeting on Friday." She looked up to gauge her sister's reaction.

"That's cool." Augusta looked away from her sister then.

"So you're okay with that?" Aliya prodded her.

Augusta still had not looked at her sister. "I'm okay with that." She breathed a sigh of weariness. "I saw a doctor today."

Aliya didn't need her to go on. She knew exactly what Augusta meant. "And,"

"I'm able to have children although I'm going to have to have minor surgery after the trip." Augusta confided in her twin.

Aliya looked worried. "What's wrong?"

"I have fibroid tumors. My doctor suggested you get examined as well." Augusta had intended to wait until after the trip to tell her but decided against it.

Aliya hugged her sister. "Everything's going to be okay, Auggie. I'm glad you got the answer you needed."

"I know I should have depended totally on the Lord. I've asked him to forgive my pigheaded behavior." Augusta leaned her head on Aliya's shoulder.

"So what now," Aliya asked hopeful that Augusta would take an initiative to make contact with Enrique.

"Now, I wait on the Lord to direct our paths." Augusta felt sure of her feelings for Enrique. Her heart beat faster at the thought of seeing him again.

"What about his invitation?" Aliya thought about the exquisite gift from earlier.

Augusta pulled out the necklace.

"You are a sly girl." Aliya giggled.

"It was an offer I couldn't refuse even though I'm quite terrified." Augusta grinned from ear to ear.

"Perfect love casts out all fear." Aliya assured her sister while she

encouraged herself. *If only I could believe that with all my heart.*

Shemiah sat on front steps of Andre Charles' home his arms wrapped snuggly around Savannah as the warm summer winds blew past them carrying the aroma of flowers and freshly cut grass. It was evenings like this one that Shemiah most appreciated. He enjoyed the feeling of protection he felt when holding Savannah close.

"Did you think you'd make it this far?" Savannah's soft voice came from out of nowhere breaking the silence.

Shemiah chuckled softly. "You mean without throwing you over my shoulder and eloping? No, honestly, I didn't."

Savannah turned her head in order to get a full view of her fiancé. "I have to say I'm very proud of you." She grinned from ear to ear. "You've made it hard for me to resist you at times but overall you've been on your best behavior."

Shemiah's brow rose. "I wouldn't talk if I were you. Every time I see you I'm reminded of cotton candy, my favorite childhood treat by the way. This past year has been a bit torturous. It's been like putting dessert in front of a child and commanding him not to touch it." He laughed imagining the picture.

"But there's pleasure to be had in the anticipation and increased joy in the waiting." Savannah encouraged him.

Shemiah touched her cheek tenderly. "I'm glad the wait is almost over. I'm looking forward to our life together."

"Me too," Savannah sighed inwardly. Her feelings for Shemiah had only grown stronger. "There's no one I'd rather share the rest of my life with."

Shemiah rested his forehead against hers. "I love you, Savannah. I love your wit, your charm, the way you lovingly correct. I love your passion for the word of God." He smiled thinking of their debates. Savannah had stirred within him a desire to know God better and to not be satisfied knowing the basics. She'd challenged his thinking in more ways than she would ever know.

Savannah pulled away from him then sensing the desire within her for him rising past what was allowable at the moment. "I love you too, Shemiah. I've never met someone who inspired me to fulfill my dreams and long to be the kind of helpmeet God intended." Savannah knew enough about herself to know she didn't have it all together but she trusted God. "I love the way you handle conflict, the way you stay calm in the midst of crisis. You've been a faithful friend to me understanding where I am but always pushing me toward my purpose." She'd kept all of his words of encouragement sent during her day. "I'm amazed at what God is doing. To think that God foreknew all along the events and the circumstances that would bring us together puts me in awe sometimes."

Shemiah took her hand in his lacing their fingers together. "I'm glad we made the right choices." he brought her hand up to his mouth and placed a gentle kiss there. "The right choice at this moment would be for me to depart before my hormones get the best of me." He grinned sheepishly.

"Well said." Savannah giggled allowing Shemiah to help her up. "It's getting late anyway and tomorrow is going to be a long day with the meeting for the trip and rehearsal."

"What do you have planned afterwards?" Normally they spent Friday evenings together but he didn't want to press the issue.

"How about hanging out with Seth and Enrique? I'm sure they have a lot to share since they've been gone. Maybe we can all hang out for a little bit after rehearsal?" Savannah didn't want to try to cram in the time between the meeting and rehearsal.

"That sounds fine with me. I was going to stop by Seth's on my way home." Shemiah assured her. He'd been checking up on Jamar during his absence since they both lived on the beach. It had become habit. "I'll see what his plans are for tomorrow."

Savannah reached up and planted a kiss on Shemiah's cheek. "Good night then and sweet dreams."

It doesn't get any sweeter than cotton candy he smiled within. "Good night, Vannah." His lips brushed her feathery soft cheek. *May my dreams soon become reality,* she felt her spirit smile.

Columbia stood in the doorway of the twins' bedroom watching Nadia stretch at the computer. She had sent Rodia to put Dee to sleep so she would have a few moments alone with her headstrong daughter. She had decided to table their earlier conversation until after dinner but she could hold off no longer.

"Nadia, we need to talk."

Nadia swirled around in her computer chair an anxious look crossed her features. "I know what you're going to say and you're right. I should have told you what was going on at school but I didn't think it was serious enough to mention."

Columbia came into the room then and sat on her daughter's bed. "I think that was for me to decide. What if this girl had attacked you? At this rate we would have no reason, no motive, and no suspects. I know you treasure your privacy and most of the time I try to respect that, but how can I be confident that you will tell me when things have gone over your head?"

Nadia rubbed the back of her neck wearily. "Most of the time I just ignore her, Mom. Besides you can't always be there for me. Next year I'll be graduating. You can't hold my hand forever and going into the principal's office and making a scene isn't going to make me feel like a young adult."

Columbia could understand her point of view but something needed to be done. "Well, what do you suggest? I'm not going to sit idly by while some girl takes out her attitude problem on my child."

"I'll talk to the principal myself tomorrow. I'll let him know I feel like I'm being harassed and tell him I have a pretty good idea of who's behind it. He's really good about keeping an eye out for trouble when he knows what's going on." Nadia hoped her speech would be enough to ease her mother's mind.

"Alright; But, if any more incidents rise up, I'm going to call a parent conference myself." Columbia rose and stood then.

"Thanks, Mom." Nadia breathed a sigh of relief. *Lord, let her not have to make an appearance.*

"Don't stay up too late." Columbia chided her softly.

"Okay." *Only late enough to beat up my twin,* the mischievous thought formed.

Columbia closed the door back softly behind her. *Lord, protect my daughters from every evil plot of the enemy.*

God was already working on her behalf.

14

Ginevieve rang her hands as she heard her doorbell ring for the third time.

"Moo Moos are common these days. It's perfectly okay."
She heard the muffled voice of Marco Bolivar on the other side of her door.

"Just a minute," Ginny ran around in circles. *Act natural. Be calm. Focus. Just take the card and close the door as quickly as possible.* Ginny was mortified that she was in such a state of distress. *He's just a guy. What am I getting so worked up about? I've dated guys ten times hotter.* But none of them had stirred up attraction and apprehension in the same breath.

"If you don't open up in ten seconds, I'm going to start singing at the top of my lungs. I'm sure your neighbors will enjoy the serenade."

There was silence on Ginny's side of the door. *He wouldn't dare.*
"Ten!" Marco started his countdown.

Maybe he would. Ginevieve vacillated between utter embarrassment and public utter embarrassment. She flung open her door.

"Five!" Marco smiled when he saw her flustered appearance. *Good. She should be ashamed of herself.* "I see all it took was a little motivation for you open up."

More like manipulation. Ginevieve's eyes were downcast as she held out her hand for her card.

"I wasn't prepared for guests." She answered stiffly. "Thank you for returning my credit card." She hoped her comment was blunt enough to make him understand she wasn't inviting him in.

Marco placed the card in her hand, his own lingering there. "Not a problem." *I'm not leaving until she looks me in the eye.* "Even an oaf like me can have a streak of kindness in him."

The instant Ginevieve looked him in the eyes she knew it was a mistake. *I could get lost in those eyes.* She drew her hand out of his own looking away embarrassed at her reaction to such an intolerable man. She'd had time to think about where he might have heard such personal declarations and the trail led to one meddling secretary- Jamar Davis. "Whatever I said about you was said at the spur of the moment, Mr. Bolivar. I apologize if I offended you, but those were my thoughts at the time." *And you seem bent on never letting me live them down.*

"I appreciate your apology, but I think you owe me more than that." Marco surprised himself with his bold statement.

Ginevieve laughed in disbelief. "Excuse me? I think you've gone *too* far."

Marco held out his hand as she proceeded to close the door. "Wait. Listen, I know we haven't gotten off to a friendly start, but I think that if you're going to accuse someone of a heinous crime, you should allow them chance for redemption."

Ginny had to force herself to close her mouth. She knew she looked like a gaping idiot. "I- I - you don't owe me anything."

"But you owe me the opportunity to prove to you that I'm not the louse you believe me to be," Marco crossed his arms his gaze unrelenting.

Ginny couldn't believe what she was hearing. "What are you suggesting?" her expression was one of puzzlement at this turn of events.

"I'm suggesting that you allow me to take you out three times: If you still hold the same sentiments about me then I will consider myself rightly judged. If you don't then hopefully I will have gained a friend and not an enemy." Marco ended his brilliantly crafted bargain. *Thank God for the art of impromptu.*

I'm really in over my head. Ginevieve wished she could find a hole and crawl into it. Any man that was willing to prove he was a gentleman just for the sake of friendship just didn't match the picture she'd painted of him. *Good going, Ginevieve. In a moment of anger you insult the very man you desire to know only to have it all blow up in your face.* How could she even confess that it was her own disappointment in wanting a relationship with him that made her blow up in the first place? *Better three dates and the chance to get to know him than no date at all...but what if I find myself wanting more? What then?*

"What do you say? We can start tomorrow and end Sunday afternoon. I know you'll be getting ready to leave next week. I'll be gone on business the following week. That will give you two weeks to hash out your thoughts." *Hopefully three days will make a lasting impression upon you.* As crazy as the thought seemed Marco was hoping more than friendship would blossom. He would take what he could get for now.

"Fine," She cleared her throat. "Three outings," She refused to call them dates because Marco wasn't interested in her. He was interested in proving a point. *Mental note number one: This man has to have a purpose behind everything he does.*

"Three dates." Marco corrected her seeing through her attempt to trivialize his intentions. *Note number one: This woman is not easily convinced.*

"I take *children* on outings, Miss Dubois." He said pointedly smiling to soften the hardness of his words.

Yep. I am definitely in over my head.

"Does seven sound fine for tomorrow night?" Marco wanted to secure a time. Her expressions even now told him she would try to weasel out of the date.

Ginny swallowed. "Make it eight. I've got that meeting for the trip tomorrow."

Marco wanted to reach out to touch her cheek but decided against it. *Too close too soon.* He stepped out of her doorway then. "The dates are my treats so just enjoy. If you could wear something semi-formal tomorrow, that would be great." Marco's mind was already spinning with ideas of how he could make the next three days memorable.

Ginny nodded. Her mind reeling at the ramifications of what she was setting in motion.

"Would you like me to pick you up from here?" Marco waited for her reply.

"That would be fine." *This is the last thing I want buzzing around the office.* Ginny held in her emotions in check not wanting Marco to see how affected she was by his proposal. She thought about telling him that she'd like for things to remain under wraps but hesitated. *He's seems to be a pretty discreet guy.*

Marco grinned widely. *Bingo. If she thinks I'm going to keep this three-day relationship under wraps she's got another thing coming.* With the fanfare Marco was planning to make it hard for her to let go. The longer he spent in Ginevieve Dubois' presence, the more he wanted to get to know her. "I must be going now. I'll see you at eight." He bowed out and trotted down the hall and skipped down the stairs humming an unfamiliar tune.

Ginny closed her door leaning against it. *Lord, what in the world have I gotten myself into?*

Naomi sat in silence as Giovanni drove. The tension between them could be sliced with a knife. He'd been cordial enough near the end of their visit but Naomi sensed the barrier that had been placed between them.

It's my fault entirely. Every time he advances I withdraw. Naomi was forced to face her own shortcomings. God had hit it right on the nail. Her greatest fear was commitment and anytime something pressed that button she acted out in self-defense.

Naomi chanced a glance over at Giovanni. He stared unflinchingly ahead his emotions masked. Strange now that she thought about it, Giovanni had never masked his emotions around her. *This is my doing and its time for me to try to undo what I've done.* "Giovanni," Naomi didn't have much time as they rounded the corner to her neighborhood.

Giovanni had been mulling over tonight's events himself when he heard Naomi call his name. "Yes?"

"I'm sorry about this evening. I acted totally out of character." Naomi confessed.

"You mean your tongue *isn't* always laced with sarcasm?" Giovanni countered.

"You're not going to let it go easily are you?" Naomi took a deep breath. She knew Giovanni was going to let her have it and rightfully so.

Giovanni's jaw worked as he pondered over how he should respond. "Let's just put it this way: for a man who prides himself on never getting knocked down, you have a strong knack for verbally drop kicking me quite frequently." He pulled into her driveway.

"I know what I said was inappropriate," she began.

"No. That's where you're wrong. What you said was *presumptuous*, Naomi. You presume to know me. You presume to know what I like, how I feel, and what kind of person I am," *What kind of husband I might be.* Giovanni forced himself to swallow his last thought. It was obvious the very notion of a marriage between them was preposterous. Giovanni felt sure that Naomi needed to settle some things within before he could talk about marriage. *I'm not going to play the role of seasonal punching bag.* Giovanni's assessment of her hit Naomi hard.

"You're right, Giovanni and there is no justification for what I said; Can you forgive me?" Naomi gave him such a look of tenderness that Giovanni was hard pressed not to kiss her.

Is this only a performance until the next attack? Her feminine wiles were alive and kicking.

"Forgiveness is unquestionable." He cleared his throat. Naomi looked relieved then. "I appreciate that." She looked toward her House; the lights were still on. "Would you like to come in for coffee?" Giovanni hopped out of the SUV, his nerves jangling, and helped Naomi out of the passenger side.

"That's okay. I've taken up enough of your time for the evening." Naomi nodded in understanding. *He's had about as much of me for one night as he can take,* She pasted on a bright smile. "Alright then," Giovanni walked alongside her conscious of his surroundings. The closer they moved to the front door they could hear the sound of laughter.

They looked at each other questioningly as Naomi let herself in.

"What is going on in here?" Naomi opened her door to find her living room in shambles.

Mariella noted her roommates look of surprise and aggravation. "Enrique was teaching me how to play blind man's bluff."

Naomi shook her head at the overturned Enrique. He'd apparently gone barreling into the couch and flipped upside down. Her lips turned upward in a smile.

"I know a few people who would pay a lot to have a snapshot of this moment." Naomi threatened.

Enrique sprung into action righting himself and tearing off the blindfold. "That's exactly why I pay good money for Nic and Giovanni to break all cameras." He chuckled.

"So this is how you two entertain my roommate?" She looked to Nicholas.

Nicolas raised his hands in surrender. "Don't look at me. It was all The Boss's idea,"

"Where's Giovanni?" Mariella had been given the abridged version of Naomi's whereabouts.

"He's outside waiting for you." Naomi looked to Enrique. *Something's very wrong.* Enrique had known Naomi long enough to know when things were not right. And now was not the time to discuss it. He gave Mariella a hug. "Playtime's over. Even you have to get up and go to work in the morning," Nicholas had already headed for the door. He mouthed the words 'we'll talk' to Naomi. She nodded in agreement.

"I know," whined Mariella "but I sure am looking forward to payday already."

Enrique gave Naomi a hug on the way out. "I've got an open ear." Naomi smiled wryly. "You're bound to get an earful tonight," She couldn't imagine Giovanni not venting.

"We'll see about that. You go easy on yourself. Giovanni is no walk in the park himself." Enrique consoled her.

Naomi let him out and stood at the door for a few moments watching his vehicle pull out of the driveway.

Mariella came to stand behind her. "So... wanna tell me about your hot date?"

"I had a wonderful time tonight." Aurielle hadn't realized how long they had stood on her porch enjoying small talk and the cool evening breeze.

"I'm glad you did," Dr. Jones eyes met hers. "And I hope it won't be the last time."

Aurielle smiled then. "I believe I'm open to a future invitation."

"Good. How about Sunday," Trey hoped he didn't sound too eager for her company.

"I usually eat out with a few of my lady friends that I don't see very much of during the week," Aurielle admitted reluctantly. *I don't want to sound too eager to have dinner with him again.*

"I love to cook and I have plenty of room. I'd like to meet your friends." He encouraged her. *I'd brave an overload of estrogen just to have you in my presence.*

Aurielle was taken aback at the offer. "Really; you'd do that?"

"It's not difficult at all. I just multiply my ingredients." Trey couldn't understand what the big deal was.

Aurielle was so used to making all the adjustments to please whomever her boyfriend happened to be at the time. This was something new to her. "Okay. I'll let you know something by tomorrow evening." Aurielle assured him.

Trey took her hand in his and brought it to his lips placing a feather-light kiss there. "Thank you for a memorable evening."

"The pleasure was mine." Aurielle felt butterflies dancing in her stomach.

Dr. Jones thanked God for bringing Aurielle into his life. He prayed that when the time came he would have the courage to tell her everything.

Naomi pulled her front door closed. "There's nothing to tell really."

Mariella crossed her arms refusing to let Naomi pass. "Not this time. If you can interfere in my love life then I should be allowed equal rights."

Naomi rolled her eyes heavenward. "We went out to eat, I put my foot in mouth and there you have it. Satisfied?"

Mariella backed off then. "Don't feel bad. It happens to the best of us. I've let a bad attitude ruin a good thing more times than I'd care to count."

Naomi flopped down on her couch dejectedly. "I guess I'm the poster girl for bitter diatribes then."

Mariella sat next to her and gave her a sideways hug. "It can't be that bad; Just give him some time to cool off."

"How does a raging inferno cool off?" Naomi wondered aloud.

Mariella looked at her. "What exactly did you say?"

"It doesn't bear repeating. Let's just say I assumed he was a man of many conquests." Naomi winced.

"You hit him below the belt, huh?" Mariella understood then.

"I know that there is a certain accepted lifestyle that comes along with the job, but Giovanni has never struck me as that kind of guy. You sure you haven't been watching too many movies?"

Naomi swatted her with a pillow.

"Ouch! Come on, Naomi. Think back. What has Giovanni ever done or said to give you that impression of him?" Mariella quizzed her.

Naomi didn't have to think hard. "Absolutely nothing; Look, I've apologized, I've asked for forgiveness and he's given it. But I can't expect anything else after the way I've treated him and I won't."

"So are you saying it's better to expect nothing than to hope that God will work things out between you two?" Mariella badgered her.

"I'm saying I can hope until I turn blue in the face but I know I have wounded Giovanni one too many times." Naomi admitted.

Mariella was puzzled. "I don't understand. If you truly like him then why do you keep goading him on?"

"Because I'm more comfortable with him resenting me than I am with him loving me," Naomi's confession broke her. "I screw things up before they have a chance to screw me up." She hung her head in misery.

A scripture came to mind that Mariella felt worth mentioning. "Perfect love casts out all fear. Love doesn't screw us up, Naomi. It makes us whole and complete."

Naomi had heard the scripture before but now it seemed to come alive. *Perfect love won't allow me to harbor fear* she realized. And she had been harboring plenty; the fear of lifelong commitment, the fear that death would end her lifelong commitment; the fear that the man she would grow to love would ultimately leave her for someone else. She had been trying to find fault with Giovanni so there would be no need to commit. *Lord, forgive me.*

"Can we pray?" Naomi looked askance.

"I think that's the wisest thing you've said all night." Mariella grabbed her roommate's hands and they went before the Lord in prayer.

15

Enrique had prodded and prodded but he had yet to pull one iota of information about tonight's dinner from Giovanni. No amount of wheedling from Nicholas was able to stir him up either. Instead he simply gave them a brooding glare that said: no trespassing. Enrique decided to try a neutral route in hopes of easing into what he wanted to discuss. Nicholas left them alone to go check the answering machine.

"How was the food?" Enrique went to the kitchen and pulled out a few glasses. He helped himself to some lemonade and poured a glass for Giovanni.

"Excellent. Paradise to the taste buds." Giovanni accepted the glass from Enrique who sat opposite him.

"What was on the menu?" Enrique enjoyed good cuisine. "Lemon herb cubed steaks, asparagus in garlic sauce, brown rice pilaf, French onion soup, raspberry mocha cake, and Caesar salad." Giovanni spouted off like a true aficionado.

"I'm going to string Naomi up by her toes for not inviting me." Enrique chuckled.

"Maybe she should have. She seems to enjoy your company more than mine." Giovanni didn't even blink.

Enrique's laugh disappeared immediately. "That wasn't in the least bit funny."

"I didn't intend for it to be." Giovanni voice was just above a whisper.

"What exactly are you insinuating?" Enrique tensed. Giovanni was spoiling for a fight tonight. He was angry and he was ready to release it.

Giovanni looked away then. "Just forget I said that."

"I can't forget it." Enrique stood. "First you come in all silent tonight and now you accuse me of having some secret thing going on with Naomi? Why would I encourage you in a relationship with her?" Enrique was near yelling.

"What's going on out here?" Nicholas broke into the midst of them.

"Nothing; just go back to the den." Giovanni waved him off. "Your brother here thinks that Naomi and I are seeing each other behind his back." Enrique's eyes flashed angrily toward Nicholas.

"You two aren't the only ones with relationship issues." Nicholas placed his hands on his hips. "I just got a message from Rosalynn. We were supposed to have dinner Sunday evening. Now it's a no-go. No reason, nothing. I have a good idea who's behind that call.

"My first inclination was to go and smash his head in, but I prayed and I'm feeling charitable now. A body slam will suffice."

Enrique looked toward heaven. "Has everyone lost it tonight?" He shook his head at Nicholas. "Nic, you can't go around body slamming people. God won't be pleased with that either." He turned to Giovanni. "Giovanni, Augusta Ming Peyton has been the only woman I've pursued. You've been with me nearly every waking hour of the day. Don't let your emotions cloud your judgment."

Giovanni stood face to face with Enrique. "Why does she insist on insulting me every time I try to get close to her? She never insults you."

"I don't have the answer to that but from what I understand about Naomi, you definitely mean *something* to her. She usually ignores people that she detests."

"So she drives me away because she cares for me? That's the most ridiculous thing I've ever heard." Giovanni looked at him as if he'd grown wings.

"I didn't profess to be a woman. I'm just telling you what I know about Naomi." Enrique hunched his shoulders.

Nic and Giovanni both folded their arms defensively and surprisingly asked the same question at the same time. "Since when did you become the relationship guru?"

Enrique laughed outright. "*God* is the relationship guru. I just happened to start tuning in to what he had to say. Giovanni, you're upset right now but you'll get over whatever Naomi said, and hopefully soon. You love her. There's no denying it so stop wasting time and help her deal with whatever issues are holding her back from a relationship with you. Nicholas, you care for Rosalynn but you're still testing your feelings because you want to be genuine and real. Rosalynn is feeling a little unsure about where you two are headed. I'm sure if Carlton is involved, he's probably warned her to bow out gracefully before she gets her feelings hurt. He's doing what any brother would and that is simply to look out for his sister's best interests—even if he is misguided. Just talk to him and let him know how you feel. Just make sure I'm present so you don't do anything rash." He joked.

Giovanni was a little amazed. "And your relationship with Augusta," he wondered aloud.

"That I am still working on." He grinned. "It's so much easier to analyze a relationship you're not in."

Nicholas glared at him. "How convenient," Nicholas gave his twin the go ahead.

"Let's get him." Giovanni agreed.

Before Enrique knew anything, his two bodyguards were giving him a nookie.

When Seth's doorbell rang half past ten he thought surely someone must have the wrong beach house. Jamar was in the shower and he was loath to leave his Sunday sermon notes vacillating on the computer. *Probably looking for a party,* he thought.

He hurried to the front door and was welcomed with a surprise. "Shemiah, How *are* you?" Seth ushered him in the front door.

"I'm fine. Just making my rounds as usual," Shemiah sat down on the comfortable couch.

Seth joined him. "That's right. Hey, thanks for watching over my little brother. I really appreciate it." Seth remembered Jamar writing him about Shemiah's visits to check up on him. "How are things going?"

"Pretty good actually; we are a little more than a month away from the big day and I'm really excited. We've had some trying moments in the process but God continually works things out for our good." Shemiah looked around at the sparse furnishings.

"That's good to hear." Seth thought he might as well take advantage of the moment while Jamar was out of earshot. "Have you seen Aliya?"

Shemiah grinned knowingly. "Of course; she's been working really hard to get back on track with helping us prepare for the wedding along with designing Savannah's Mom's dress."

"Does she mention me at all?" Seth wondered aloud.

"I haven't heard her mention you although when your name comes up she stops whatever's she's doing to listen in. I know some of her clients talked about your mission trip." Shemiah could tell Seth was eager for some sign. "So... what are you waiting on?"

"Excuse me?" Seth thought he misunderstood Shemiah.

"I said what are you waiting on? Aliya is not going to come knocking on your door. Maybe she would have done that in the past, but she's not the same person." Shemiah was sure of that. No one could have gone through her ordeal and not have been changed.

"Everyone keeps saying that--"

"Then maybe you should believe it. Or at least see for yourself." Shemiah encouraged him.

"Sometimes ministering half way across the world is easier than ministering right next door." Seth confessed.

"Charity begins at home," Shemiah reminded him.

Seth nodded in agreement. "You certainly have a way with the Word."

"My opinion can sometimes get me in trouble but the Word is always right." Shemiah grinned. "What does your schedule look like tomorrow?"

"I'll be handling some client business in the morning and checking on a certain young lady afterwards. By mid-afternoon, I hope to be putting the finishing touches on my sermon for Sunday." Seth figured he would visit Aliya before the meeting to let her know he was interested in seeing her aside from ministry purposes.

"It sounds like you've got your work cut out for you." Shemiah would have to take a rain check on them hanging out.

"Right now, I'm trying to tie up loose ends with my clients and answer any questions before I head out of town. I want to enjoy the retreat and not be bombarded with calls. I'm pretty much telling my clients not to buy or sell without my counsel." Seth knew that some of his clients were antsy about his absence especially since he had just arrived back in the States.

Shemiah looked at his watch. "I don't intend to hold you up. I was just on my way home and I thought I'd check up on you."

Seth walked Shemiah to the door stopping him just before he opened the door. "Pray for Jamar. I have a feeling that God is going to give him a dose of his own meddling." Seth shared what he'd learned briefly with Shemiah who managed to hide his own mirth.

"I think he just has your best interests at heart but I will pray. There's nothing like a comeuppance from God him self." Shemiah headed down the steps.

Seth closed the door thankful for the words of encouragement from Shemiah. *Lord, thank you for sending a brother when I needed one.*

"You're welcome."

Nadia waited behind her door until her twin walked inside the bedroom fully. She reached for her from behind covering her mouth with her hand. With brute force she swept her feet from under her and she thudded to the floor.

"If you ever interfere in my personal life again, you will be sorry." Rodia flipped her sister until she was underneath her. "I am my sister's keeper."

The two rolled until they were in the center of the floor.

"What I do is my business." Nadia ground out.

Rodia managed to grab a pillow and whacked Nadia with it. "Not when I have to suffer with you too."

Nadia grabbed a pillow as well and the twins whacked away at each other until they were exhausted. This was a common ritual between them when they didn't see eye to eye; which was often.

"Good night." Nadia yawned.

"Good night." Rodia groaned.

Click went the light.

"So what did you think?" Tatyanna asked her sister as they walked back to her apartment.

"He's talented, successful, gorgeous, intelligent, gorgeous, witty, gorgeous..." Tehinnah kidded with her big sister.

"Gorgeous is not a quality." Tatyanna punched her sister playfully.

"You two would make an awesome team together." Tehinnah tapped her sister back.

"You think so?" Tatyanna prayed that Kevin would be the one. They hadn't been courting long but she couldn't think of anyone else that she would want to spend the rest of her life with. *Lord, let it be your will.* They walked in silence for a few minutes before Tatyanna decided to tease her about Jamar. "Any final conclusion yet about our secretary,"

Tehinnah's brow rose at the question. "Is he seeing anyone?"

"No, although it's not due to a lack of offers; I have to run some of our clients out of the building once we're done meeting." Tatyanna admitted.

"He is definitely eye candy. It's a wonder he doesn't model." Tehinnah thought out loud.

"Tehinnah; eye candy; they don't use those terms in law school." Tatyanna chided her. "Considering the man that he is I don't think Jamar would appreciate being called eye candy."

"How about visually appealing in an appetizing way?" Tehinnah had only seen him briefly and never really met him. He had been on his way out the door to deliver an order and while his arresting masculine beauty had stopped her in her tracks he hadn't even given her a second glance.

"Much better," Tatyanna commended her.

"It's just another way of saying scrumptious." Tehinnah giggled.

"If this is how you're going to carry on, there's no way I'm bringing you back by the office." Tatyanna warned her as she fished for the key to her apartment.

"I'm just pulling your leg, Taty." Tehinnah called her by her pet name. "We both know he's too young."

Tatyanna let them both into the apartment turning on her living room lamp as she set her purse on the lamp stand. You're twenty-five, Tehinnah. You act like you're ancient. He's only a few years younger than you."

"Case in point- But, he's still in college, he works part-time, he has no car, he probably still lives at home with mom--"

"He and his brother live together-"

"Same difference; It's a recipe for disaster." Tehinnah defended her case.

"I'm not saying you should get involved, but I didn't hear you mention anything that had lasting eternal or internal value. He's intelligent, humorous beyond measure, determined, dedicated to God, an excellent cook, and he has a servant's heart. On top of that he *is* gorgeous." Tatyanna stuck up for her secretary. "He won't always be answering phones but even if he was, Jamar Davis is a wonderful person."

"That's all fine and dandy but he's just not what I'm envisioning for my life. End of story." Tehinnah made her way to the guest room.

Oh dear sister, God has a way of making you see clearly.

16

Noelle Marks rested against the columns that supported his grand porch. *Any day now, Miss Estrada;* He tapped his foot upon the ornately bricked porch. He had been waiting for the last fifteen minutes. *I hope she hasn't changed her mind.* Just as he was about to give up waiting, a cream-colored sedan strode up his tree lined driveway. *Thank God.* The sedan rolled around his circular driveway to stop directly in front of his home. He descended the steps to meet her.

Mariella hopped from the vehicle with enthusiasm. She flipped her dark tresses off her shoulder. "Good morning Mr. Marks. I'm sorry I kept you waiting."

Noelle stood there staring at her like a starry-eyed teenager. "Not a problem." He willed himself to speak normally. Mariella looked like a tropical dream this morning. He brushed aside the thought.

Naomi waved to him. "Good morning, Mr. Marks."

Noelle peered into the car recognizing the driver. "Good morning. You're Miss Watts, right?" He remembered her face from Sunday services. She had been making frequent trips to the altar lately.

Naomi gave him a pleasant smile. "That's right. This is a very nice place you have here. I'm sure my roommate will help you enhance the beauty that's already evident."

Noelle's brow rose. *"You* two are roommates?" he wondered why Mariella wasn't living with her affluent cousin.

"More like a hired spy." Mariella joked. "She and my cousin are close friends."

Naomi narrowed her eyes at Mariella. "I am *not* a spy. You've been free to come and go as you choose."

"I think that's pretty noble of your cousin to make sure you're being looked after." Noelle added. "I look forward to meeting Mr. Estrada."

Mariella looked mortified at the thought. "That really won't be necessary." *He doesn't even know yet and he's already eager to meet my family.* "Enrique's really busy."

"I'm sure he'd be *more* than happy to arrange a meeting." Naomi gave Mariella a pointed glare. *What was her problem?*

"I don't want you to be late for work, Naomi, and I know Mr. Marks has other business to attend to so we're going to run along and get started." Mariella started up the steps.

Naomi smiled brightly. "I'll see you tonight, then." She waved to Noelle. *I may not be a rocket scientist, but I'm not blind.* The attorney and minister had been looking at her roommate with more than professional interest; Either Mariella was totally unaware or she refused to acknowledge it. *She could definitely do a lot worse.* In either case, Naomi was not about to encourage Mariella in any type of relationship.

Mariella waved profusely at the retreating car. She turned to Noelle giving him a radiant smile. "So, where shall we begin?"

Nadia sat outside the principal's office awaiting his arrival. *Lord, please give me what to say. Help him to see my point of view. I don't want my Mom to have to straighten things out for me.*

"Miss Newcomb? What are you doing here this early?"
Nadia looked up into the kind eyes of her Assistant Principal. Ms. Cinnamon Sugarbaker or as the students called her Cindy was everyone's favorite administrator hands down. Nadia relaxed. "I needed to talk with the Principal."

Ms. Sugarbaker's brow furrowed. "I'm afraid he's out of town on the senior trip. Is it something I can help you with?"

Nadia didn't want to allow more time to pass without dealing with the issues at hand. "I've been having a problem with some girls here. It's been going on for a while and I didn't think anything of it. But I feel that things are getting out of hand."

"Come into my office and let's talk about it."
Just as Nadia was standing, a wiry gray-haired janitor came into the office.

"What can I help you with Mr. Greeley?" Ms. Sugarbaker enquired.
Mr. Greeley looked back and forth between Nadia and the Assistant Principal. He held up two empty spray cans. "There's been some vandalism in the girl's locker room. I saw two girls dump these cans yesterday in the girl's restroom."

Nadia's eyes grew wide. "That's what I wanted to talk to you about." she faced Ms. Sugarbaker. "It was my locker that was spray painted."

Ms. Sugarbaker's countenance was fierce. "When did this happen?"

"I don't know. It was after school when I saw it. That's why I came so early this morning. I think I know who did it." Nadia wrung her hands. *This isn't going as I planned.*

Ms. Sugarbaker looked to Mr. Greeley. "Do you think you can identify the young ladies that dumped the cans?"

"I think so, ma'am." Mr. Greeley nodded.
"Then I'll call a morning assembly for girls only." Ms. Sugarbaker looked sympathetically at Nadia. "This kind of thing will *not* be tolerated. Don't worry Nadia. We *will* get to the bottom of this."

"You mean I'm not in trouble?" Nadia sputtered.

Ms. Sugarbaker gave her a curious glance. "It's not your fault that someone decided to handle their personal differences by destroying school property. This is my territory."

Nadia felt all of the tension drain out of her. *Thank God.*

"If you'll excuse me, I've got to finish my rounds." Mr. Greeley nodded to them both and stepped out into the hallway.

"You can go on ahead to class Nadia. I'll include the assembly in this morning's announcements. Your name will not be mentioned unless necessary." Ms. Sugarbaker assured her.

"Thanks for helping me." Nadia held herself in check, her voice not revealing how she felt.

"That's what I'm here for." Ms. Sugarbaker walked Nadia to the door. She waited until Nadia had trotted down the hallway, before pivoted on her heel in the opposite direction heading toward the media center. *I hope I can nip this in the bud before it escalates.*

Aliya Peyton yawned widely as she opened the door to her shop. She had changed her shop hours from ten to five to open two hours earlier, her body had been feeling the change. Business had become quite lucrative making it necessary for her to put in more time.

Just another day that the Lord has kept me she hummed to herself. She turned on all the lights in her boutique, turned on her sewing machine, started the coffeemaker and headed back to the front door to open her blinds.

"Aiee," Aliya clutched her chest. She whipped open the door.

"I'm sorry. Did I frighten you?" Seth stood anxiously holding a bouquet of lilies.

Aliya glared at him. "Ya' *think*?" She was too busy going off to notice the flowers in his hand.

Seth forced himself to not respond back. "I can come back if this is a bad time." he said gently.

Aliya eyes swept toward the bouquet. "Are those for me?" *I'm ranting and raving and here the man is trying to bring me flowers. How stupid can a girl get?*

Seth held them out as an offering. "That depends on if you like them and if you don't intend to bash me over the head with them once I hand them over."

Aliya giggled. "They are one of my favorite." She took the flowers from him, her hands brushing his. She looked into his eyes then. *Warm and friendly,* She remembered them as cold and aloof at times. *Something has definitely changed him.* "Thank you."

Seth followed Aliya into the boutique tucking his hands into his pockets. *Her beauty hasn't diminished at all.* It was her eyes that troubled Seth. *Sad and somewhat distant;* He remembered them filled with humor and a hint of mischief. She definitely wasn't the same woman he knew a few months ago. *What happened to you Aliya?* He knew in time he would ask her.

Aliya placed her flowers on the counter and turned to face him. "So, what brings you by?"

Seth came to stand in front of her at the counter. "I wanted to see you."

Aliya swallowed hard. "It's good to know there are a few ministers that still believe in making house calls."

Seth grinned from ear to ear. "I assure you this has nothing to do with the ministry."

Aliya's cheeks flamed. "Oh."

"Blushing becomes you. You were never one to blush before. I find it refreshing." Seth chuckled.

Aliya opened her mouth in shock and then closed it. "And you, Seth Davis, never spoke your mind so openly. I find it unnerving."

Seth stepped closer. "So I make you nervous?"

Aliya backed up. *You make me terrified.* "Yes."

"Why?" Seth pressed her.

"Because," Aliya was not about to tell him how she really felt. *No way.*

Seth reached out to tuck a wayward strand of her hair behind her ear. "I'm sure as we get to know each other you'll feel more comfortable around me." he whispered softly.

Aliya thought she was going to swoon any moment now. "I already know you."

Seth stepped back then leaning against the counter. "No, you don't."

He turned toward her. "You know the minister but I want you to meet the man."

Aliya blinked twice. *Is he giving me a come hither look?* This whole conversation was totally throwing her for a loop. As long as Seth Davis was in his stark dark suit hibernating in the stucco and brick building across the street and safely tucked away ensconced in a Bible he was safe. *But not anymore,* Aliya could hear her heart beat thudding steadily in her ears. She took a casual perusal of him. Seth had gone for a casual ensemble this morning. Chocolate turtleneck and slacks with loafers gave him a monochromatic feel that gave his skin a warm glow. Gone was the clean cut look and in its place was a neatly manicured mustache that connected with his goatee. Aliya bit down on her lip to hold in her inner thoughts.

There should be limit to how sexy a minister could be. Especially before eight on a Monday morning holding a bouquet of lilies and smelling like a slice of heavenly pie!

"Aliya," Seth felt as if she were looking straight through him. *I wonder what she sees.*

Aliya popped out of her mental wanderings blushing at the turn her thoughts had taken. "Yes?"

"You know your father and I have talked." Seth waited for some sign of disinterest, continuing when he saw none. "I told him I was interested in you."

Aliya had been putting the conversation with her father aside. He'd been hounding her about Seth since she had regained consciousness. She hadn't wanted to hear it. "Are you?" Aliya folded her hands defensively. As strongly as she felt about Seth, she was not inclined to lay her heart on the line only to have it crushed.

"Interested is an understatement. I know what I want, Aliya." He closed the gap between them.

Aliya clutched the edge of the counter. "What do you want?"

Seth placed his hand over her shaking one and pulled it toward his heart. "Do you feel that?"

Aliya could feel his heart beating erratically beneath her fingers. She nodded.

"I'm just as nervous as you are. I tend to hide it better." he admitted.

Aliya laughed nervously but the laughter faded as she gazed into his eyes.

"Aliya, I want hope and a future and I know that I can have that with you." he said simply and confidently.

"How can you be so sure that there's a future with me?" Aliya suddenly felt dizzy. The wall paper behind him seemed to be tilting.

"God promised me a future with you." Seth declared.

It was the last thing Aliya heard before everything went black.

Ms. Sugarbaker stood on the court of the school gym microphone in hand. Though none of the male students had been invited to the assembly, they would be sure to get an earful.

"Good morning, ladies."

Murmurs of hello and good morning sounded back in tangled, immature female voices.

"As you might have guessed, what I want to discuss with you is of utmost importance due to the fact that you are missing your first period class." she waited for the rest of the voices to die down before she went on. "Sometime yesterday horrible crimes was committed right here at this school by some of your female peers."

Hushed voices and whispers rose as the young girls turned to each other some looking around trying to figure out who might be the culprit. Ms. Sugarbaker continued.

"I say horrible crimes because one was vandalism of school property," she held up the two spray cans used, her hands encased in gloves, "and the other defamation of character." She walked back and forth staring each and every student in the eye. Then she began to climb the gym stands and stood in the midst of them. "I want you to know that this kind of behavior will not be tolerated from any student at this school. We have an eyewitness to the crime and they are willing to identify those who did the spraying. If you'd like to come forward and admit to this, your punishment will be lessened. You have until lunch to make your way to my office. If no one comes forth and you are identified by our witness, you will pay every penalty involved. We will bring in the police to deal with the graffiti. Should you have to be identified the school penalty will be no pep rallies for the rest of the year. I find it hypocritical to proclaim we have school spirit if you are tearing each other down with your words."

Uproar arose at the declaration.

"Settle down!" Ms. Sugarbaker's word quieted the students. "I don't want any martyrs coming to my office. I want the young ladies responsible. You are dismissed." She turned the students over into the hands of their teachers awaiting them.

17

Mariella tried to keep up with the long legged Noelle as he walked her through a brusque tour of his home. *This is impossible!* She followed behind him jotting down his thoughts and ideas. *Such eclectic taste; How am I going to tie it all together?* Mariella chewed the bottom of her lip.

"Mariella,"

Mariella snapped out of her mental anguish. "Yes?"

Noelle gazed down at her apologetically. "Here I've been running my mouth this whole time and I haven't let you get a word in. You're the designer here. I know I have my own tastes but I want you to be able to pull this off. The last thing I want is my peers laughing at me for mixing and matching the wrong styles or furniture. I'm just throwing out my ideas but if they sound far fetched please let me know."

Mariella stared at him curiously. "How did you do that?"

"Do what?" Noelle was puzzled then.

"I was thinking that exact same thing." Mariella wondered.

Noelle smiled then looking away. "I didn't do anything." But he knew better. For a moment he'd been allowed to see into her heart. After all the years he'd tried to resist that particular gifting from God lately it seemed to intensify. It had become a natural part of who he was so much so that he found himself ministering to the hearts of men and women just about everywhere he went. It was no different now. "God knows the hearts of men and women and when we are connected, he reveals some things to us so that we can help each other out."

Mariella pondered that thought for a moment. "Are you saying that God allows us to know the heart of another person?" she swallowed. *I hope he doesn't plan to show mine any time soon.*

"The Spirit of God helps us to discern the people that we come in contact with for several reasons. For one as Christians we should know our brother. As people who live in this world, we should be aware of those who don't have our best interests at heart and steer clear of them. We should be aware of the needs of others especially our brothers and sisters in Christ and be ready to offer encouragement when it's needed."

Mariella knew she would have to read up on this discernment thing Noelle went on about. "Well, I was certainly perplexed for a moment. You were talking about an Afro-Caribbean mixed with a little Renaissance for your living room and I thought how in the world am I going to pull that off?" Mariella shook her head. "But I am beginning to get a vision for it."

Noelle grinned clapping his hands together. "Good." He looked at his watch. "I've got to get going. I hope I left you with enough ideas to ponder over." He reached into his inner coat and handed her a few twenties. "Lunch is on me as long as you are in my employ. Feel free to order in. Your contract is on the kitchen counter. If I have time, I may stop in for lunch with you and take a look at some of your sketches. Make yourself at home and help yourself to anything in the fridge."

Mariella nodded profusely to every instruction. "Thank you, Mr. Marks." She folded the bills and set them on the counter. "I brought lunch and I'm sure I'll be fine with what I have."

Noelle wisely disregarded her comment. "Well, call me at the office if you need anything. I'm going to get the new secretary settled in and then it's off to visit my new clients." Just as he grabbed his brief bag, a mental image flashed in his mind. The scene was of Mariella with a child hugging one hip and him hugging the other. He shook off the thought almost staggering. *Satan, you are a liar. I will bring every thought under captivity to the obedience of Christ. And that most certainly wasn't God.*

Mariella reached out to steady Noelle from falling backward with his bag. "You definitely may want to go with a textured tile for your new flooring."

Noelle appreciated the fact that she didn't play up his embarrassment further. "Maybe so," He headed toward the door walking regally yet carefully.
"I'll see you later."

Mariella had followed him to the door ensuring his safe descent. She closed the door as he drove off and leaned against it. *Time to get down to business,* she exhaled a breath of relief.

"Don't move, Aliya."
Aliya struggled to open her eyes at her sister's command. Finally they flittered open. "Why are you standing over me?' she murmured. Then she remembered. One moment she'd been talking with Seth and the next... well she wasn't sure what had happened. "Where's Seth?"

"I'm right here Aliya." He took her hand in his.
Aliya turned her head to the right. Seth looked down at her in tender concern. It was then that Aliya realized that Seth was supporting her weight. She attempted to sit up. "Nobody panic. I'm fine."

Augusta crossed her arms. "We'll let the doctor make that decision. Seth called me as soon as you went out."

Aliya was not fond of hospitals at all. "I just got a little excited that's all. There's no need to call anyone."

"I'm afraid you're too late to protest." Seth spoke gently as the door to her boutique opened ushering in the EMT.

Aliya glared at her sister. "I can't believe you called in the Calgary. People faint all the time."

"Then it will be no problem for you to allow these men to do their job." Augusta was not budging. She could be even more stubborn than her sister. "If you don't cooperate, I'm going to call off your meeting myself."

"Fine," Aliya snapped, holding out her arm so the EMT could check her blood pressure.

Seth marveled at the twins' interchange chuckling to himself. *Lord, I've definitely got my hands full.*

Ms. Sugarbaker was engrossed in paperwork when she heard her office door open. She looked up to see three junior varsity cheerleaders standing before her. Closing the folder in front of her she stood motioning them to have a seat. She came around to the front side of her desk and leaned against it.

"I believe you have something you would like to share otherwise you would not be here." Cinnamon Sugarbaker wasted no time with small talk.

The girls looked to one another. Finally the tallest of the trio spoke. "We were responsible for the graffiti." She hung her head in obvious shame.

Ms. Sugarbaker knew better than that. "Who promised you a spot on the varsity team for your reckless behavior?" High school was still high school and the rules had not changed.

The shortest of the trio spoke then. "Serena Quintana. She promised us that she would make things easier for us to get accepted since she had the final say."

"I see." Ms. Sugarbaker had a mind to contact the principal right then. While these girls faced serious consequences for their actions, little Serena Quintana was off having the time of her life on the senior trip. She would deal with her when the time came. "Thank you for coming forward and not making this a long drawn out process. Because you have done so, I will not press charges. There are not many more days left of school however, so until the end of school you will help our janitor Mr. Greeley with cleanup around the building and you three will split the cost for the replacement of the spray painted lockers. You are not allowed to attend prom nor the end of the year party. Considering the punishment awaiting Miss Quintana, your three have gotten off lightly."

The freshman that had not spoken was in tears. She looked up at Ms. Sugarbaker. "I am so sorry."

"I think there's someone that you all should apologize to. As far as I know, Nadia Newcomb has done nothing to deserve your obvious dislike." Ms. Sugarbaker had gone to take a look at the locker herself after the morning assembly. She had been disgusted by the insults.

The taller of the freshmen spoke up. "We don't dislike her. We just wanted to impress Serena."

"Was it worth it?" Ms. Sugarbaker asked the age-old question.

"No," the resounding answer was simultaneous from all three girls.

"Make that the first thing you ask yourself in the future. It will help you to make better decisions." Ms. Sugarbaker dismissed them from her office. She sat down and sent up a prayer. *Lord, help these students to turn to you. Help them not to give in to the pressures to be popular for popularity sake. Help them to develop a mind of their own and to think before they act.*

Ms. Sugarbaker picked up the phone. It was time for the unpleasant task of notifying parents.

Noelle was surprised to find Ms. Adams waiting outside his office. She was a full thirty minutes early.

"Good morning." Noelle greeted her.

"Good morning." Tehinnah Adams took note of her impeccably dress boss. *He has very good taste.*

He ushered her into the lobby area. "I didn't get a chance to show you around yesterday." He pointed to the curved Formica counter. This is where you will be setting up shop."

Tehinnah took a look at the space. It was big enough to suit her needs for now. "I assume all your case files are in your office."

"Yes. All my cases are logged by case number and year that I began working on them." Noelle clarified for her. "You are the only one who will have access to those files. As a fellow attorney I know you understand the importance of confidentiality." He handed her a key to his files.

"Yes, I do." Tehinnah listened intently to his instructions.

"I usually work using a weekly itinerary." He handed her a print out. "This is my itinerary for the week. I expect you to prepare these for me by Thursday for the upcoming week. I don't like to schedule client meetings to close together so I allow for an hour between just in case they run over." Noelle noticed she was good at short hand. "There will be times when I'll need your assistance at the meeting so you won't be in the office at all times."

Tehinnah smiled then. "That's good to know."

"Also you're more than welcome to use any of my reference books to help you study for the bar." Noelle noticed Tehinnah's eyes lit up at the thought. "I believe that as time progresses I'll need to make room for you."

"I'm glad you're considering the possibility of growth." Tehinnah bubbled inside with excitement.

"Everything God does, He does with the expectation of multiplying." Noelle spoke matter of fact.

Tehinnah's grin grew. "So you're a believer?"

"Do I believe In Jesus Christ? Whole heartedly," Noelle wanted to make that clear.

"So am I." Tehinnah was actually relieved. It was one of the things that had bothered her with other firms that she had interviewed with. Their disdain for the spiritual had sent her packing. Many of them had offered her packages her classmates would have taken in a heartbeat but Tehinnah had turned them down.

"That's good to know, Ms. Adams. I let my clients know my stance as well and I am not ashamed to say I am a child of God." Which brought on another question; "Where do you attend services?"

"I just arrived in town yesterday, actually. I'm staying with my sister for a while. I haven't thought about a place of worship just yet. I know my sister attends a church here in town." Tehinnah had forgotten the name of the church.

"Well, my father pastors New Life Ministries here in town where I assist him. You're more than welcome to come visit us anytime." Noelle offered.

"Thank you. I will definitely take you up on the offer." Tehinnah was beginning to admire her boss more and more.

Noelle took out a note pad for her. "If there are any office supplies you think you'll be in need of, let me know. There will be a mini-fridge arriving today as well as a laptop for your use. I will take care of your lunch every day and any dinners where you have to accompany me." He reached into his brief bag and pulled out her contract.

Tehinnah took the folder from him and opened it. Her eyes widened. "This is more than a receptionist salary."

"That's because you're more than a receptionist. If you look at the top of your contract, I'm hiring you to be my legal assistant. You didn't think I'd let that mind of yours go to waste did you?" Noelle chuckled.

Tehinnah was speechless for a moment. Then she gazed at Noelle with appreciation. "Thank you, Mr. Marks." *All the more reason to get cracking on my studies,* she mused.

"Don't thank me. I'm honored to have you as a part of my team." He snapped his fingers. "Which reminds me; the company car I ordered should be here by ten. I have an interior designer that may need your assistance from time to time until she gets her own transportation. That may require you escorting her to different stores. Would you have a problem with that?"

"Not at all," Tehinnah assured him.

Noelle looked down at his watch. He wrote down Mariella's name and information and handed it to her. He handed her one of his business cards along with a credit card. "I won't be back until after lunch so feel free to purchase your supplies and order lunch. You can use my business card as a reference for ordering your own at Alpha, Inc. When I come back we can talk over some procedures I have for taking on new clients."

121

Tehinnah managed to keep her mouth from gaping wide open. "Alright, Sounds like a plan."

Noelle grabbed his brief bag and paused for a moment. "I know I just foisted a lot of responsibility on you so please don't feel like you have to accomplish everything today. Take your time. Look around. Get acquainted with the office. I should be back around two. We'll talk some more then."

Tehinnah nodded profusely. "Okay."

Noelle was gone in a flash.

Tehinnah stared at the closed door in amazement. Noelle Marks was a man on the go. *Does that man even have a social life?*

Ginevieve was walking up the hallway toward Tatyanna's office when she saw Jamar walking through the front door. She strode directly towards him.

"Good morning, Ginny."

"Don't you good morning, me!" she hissed. She had a mind to douse him with her coffee.

Jamar gave her a puzzled look. "What's got you up on the wrong side of the bed?"

Ginny glared at him. "Someone paid me a little visit last evening." Jamar set his portfolio behind the counter and turned on his laptop. "Who,"

"Mr. Bolivar." Ginny spat out.

Jamar stilled then turned to face her. "Really?" he looked surprised.

Ginny couldn't believe he was playing the innocent. "What did you say to him?"

"Nothing that you didn't express yourself; that he was rude and unfeeling," Jamar abbreviated his version.

"Jamar, I was just talking off the top of my head. I didn't think you would go broadcasting the information." Ginny threw up her hands.

"Marco is my friend. I thought he should know he was making a terrible impression on a beautiful lady." Jamar's sincere compliment almost silenced Ginevieve-- Almost.

"Don't try to flatter me, Jamar. Your meddling has created a huge mess. You have him thinking that he's got to prove himself by taking me out." Ginny's frustration was evident. "The whole thing is ridiculous."

Jamar leaned over the reception counter giving her a raised eyebrow. "Is it?"

His question stopped Ginevieve short of her retort.

Jamar walked around to the other side of the reception desk. "Are you saying that you are not looking forward to spending time with Mr. Bolivar?" he had her cornered now.

"I plead the fifth." Ginny glared at him. "Look, you are missing the point Jamar. Mr. Bolivar never should have been put in this position in the first place."

"What do you propose be done?" Jamar had to keep himself from laughing out loud. It was obvious Marco was taken with Miss Dubois. *More than he cared to admit.*

"I think you should talk him out of taking me out." Ginevieve was serious.

"I didn't talk him into taking you out. Mr. Bolivar has a mind of his own." Jamar reasoned.

"But you were influential in his decision. You can make him see that this is not necessary." Ginny pleaded.

Jamar shook his head. "Marco Bolivar considers himself to be a man of honor. You challenged that honor and he is bound as a gentleman to defend it. There is no way that I am going to be able to talk him out of it."

"Talk who out of what?"

Ginny and Jamar turned to see Tatyanna coming out of her office.

"Nothing of importance," Ginny waved off the question. "Where's Augusta?"

"She went with Aliya to the hospital. Apparently she fainted and she wants to make sure everything's okay." Tatyanna informed them.

Jamar looked worried. "I'd better call my brother."

"Seth was there when it happened." Tatyanna noticed Jamar stilled at her words.

"*Seth* was there?" Jamar was hoping he heard her correctly.

Tatyanna nodded. "Augusta got the call from Seth and she rushed right over."

"Well, I'll be." Jamar stood with a look of amazement pasted o his face.

"You'll be staying out of that one." Tatyanna grinned. "I think Seth can take it from here."

Ginny eyed Jamar suspiciously. "So you have a habit of sticking your nose where it doesn't belong, huh?"

Jamar grinned sheepishly. "It's been known to happen on occasion."

"Delivery,"

No one noticed when the florist had come in but he wasn't a familiar face.

"These are for... a Miss Dubois?"

Tatyanna was surprised at that. "Is there something you care to share with us Ginny?"

Ginny stood speechless looking at the huge bouquet of multicolored roses and baby's breath. It looked like a floral rainbow. It reminded her of God's promises. *How could he know that I love rainbows?* No one knew that but God.

Jamar took the huge vase from the florist and handed her the card. Ginny opened the card hesitantly and read it silently.

Ginevieve,

May you blush 100 times over! It becomes your delicate beauty.

Your Promise Keeper,

Mr. B

"What does it say?" Tatyanna was curious.

"It doesn't have a name." Ginny quickly concealed the card. *He is not my promise keeper.* She resented those words. They spoke of an intimacy in relationship that she knew was non-existent.

"Name or no name, One hundred long stemmed roses speaks volumes to me." Tatyanna chuckled picking up the tag. "Marti's florist; I wonder what Mr. Bolivar will think about this."

Ginny was thankful Tatyanna walked back into her office missing the fact that her entire face was lit up like a light bulb at the mention of that name.

It didn't escape Jamar's notice. "As you can see we are past the talking stage."

Ginny stomped her foot. "This is your entire fault Jamar." She would have to put an end to these extravagant displays. *This is not a courtship and I will not give in to the illusion of one.* "If you will please, deliver those to Mr. Bolivar and ask him to have them delivered to someone deserving of them."

Jamar felt that one down in his gut. "Ginny, I don't think Marco would appreciate that. The more you resist the more extravagant he's going to get. Take my word for it."

Ginny sighed. "Fine, leave them in the lobby as a centerpiece." She walked back to her office.

Jamar stood holding the vase staring after their editor. *Has no one ever lavished her with gifts?* He couldn't imagine that no one had ever noticed her timeless beauty within and without. *Mr. Bolivar, I hope you know what you're doing.*

18

It's amazing how time flies Rosalynn thought to herself as she waved goodbye to her ten o'clock appointment. She looked down at her watch. *It's almost lunchtime.* Rosalynn had settled into the routine of seeing clients during lunch rather than eating. She found it to be a good way to stave off her hunger by putting the needs of her client first. This afternoon she wasn't looking forward to her next appointment. *Giovanni Cartellini.*

She hadn't heard a word from Nicholas since calling him to cancel their dinner date. Now it was time to face the music. *There's nothing like a family member interfering in your personal affairs.* She would not even kid herself that Giovanni would bring up the issue during their session today. She only searched her mind for a probable excuse. *It's for the best. Nah, He'll automatically refute that. How about...we come from different backgrounds? Nah, He'll find a way around that too.*

There was no further time to wonder as she caught sight of the twin bounding across the lawn toward her.

Help me Lord to find the right words to say. Rosalynn put on her best smile and strode to meet him halfway.

Naomi was caught up in thought as she sat watching the latest news developments in Savannah when she felt a light tap on her shoulder.

"Is this seat taken?" Dr. Trey Jones flashed his perfectly lined pearly whites.

Naomi couldn't help but smile back. "Not at all, help yourself."
Trey sat down, sub in hand and proceeded to unwrap his lunch. "How's your shift going?"

"Okay. I'm thankful for the reprieve though. It seems as though all my patients have been especially irritable." Naomi confided.

"By the time I get to my patients they're usually out for the count." He chuckled.

"Be thankful. I've heard several choice phrases today that don't bear repeating." She sighed drumming her hands on the table.

Dr. Jones chewed thoughtfully, washing his sub down with a long drink of lemonade. "So...did everything turn out alright?"

Naomi didn't even have to second-guess what he was referring to. "They went fine of you count the fact that he probably never wants to see me again." She pushed her hair behind her ears. "I can't believe I insulted him like that."

125

Dr. Jones didn't try to pacify her. He knew his co-worker had a pretty spicy tongue. "Did you apologize?"

"Of course I did, but..." Naomi looked away then not wanting Trey to see the tears that threatened to seep out.

"But...? I can't see Giovanni holding a grudge about something so minute in the scheme of things." Dr. Jones reasoned.

Naomi looked forlorn then. "This isn't the first time I've insulted his character. I'm afraid it's deeper than that."

Dr. Jones wasn't born yesterday but he decided to keep that revelation to himself. "Look, we all have said things that we didn't mean. It may not be the last time either. But judging from the way he was looking at you last night, I doubt things are over between you two."

Naomi felt a small flutter in her stomach. "What are you saying, Trey?"

Dr. Jones folded his hands together and leaned in taking advantage of the fact that he had her full attention. "The man is obviously in love with you Naomi. Give him some time to cool off. In the meantime pray about what's really keeping you from holding back. Get some counseling. I've had problems in the past with the way that I talked to others. I'd be more than willing to let you take a look at some of my resources I've collected over time."

Naomi's heart warmed at his thoughtfulness but she wouldn't allow herself to hope for more. "Thank you. I'd really like to look into it. I'm definitely going to be praying for a change. I don't want to go around hurting the people I... care for." *I don't dare admit to the other.*

But Dr. Jones caught her slip capitalizing on it. "Don't you mean love?"

"Umm...Well..."

"Go ahead. Admit it. It's quite liberating actually." Dr. Jones encouraged her. "Okay. Let me help you." He breathed in deeply then exhaled. "I love Aurielle Foqua."

Naomi gaped at the handsome doctor.

"Close your mouth." Dr. Jones chuckled.

"You do?" Naomi was happy and surprised at the same time.

"Yes. As a matter of fact I believe I fell in love with her when I first saw her. Back then it was her need that I saw but I've discovered it's more than that. She's a wonderful woman." The pride that he felt for her was evident.

"Wow." Naomi couldn't believe it. "Have you told her?"

"Not yet but I plan to." He shook his finger playfully. "And don't go holding this evidence against me. I was confessing so that you could feel more comfortable."

Naomi certainly felt that laughing at his antics. "Okay." She took a deep breath and let it out. "I... I...love... Giovanni Cartellini." The words felt right rolling off her tongue so she said them again.

"You did it." Dr. Jones applauded her softly.

Naomi's hand came to her mouth in shock. "You're right. I said it." She whispered looking around for fear that Giovanni was somewhere nearby.

"Liberating isn't it?" Dr. Jones gave her a tender smile. He prayed that Giovanni would recognize what a gift Naomi was.

"Quite." Naomi didn't know what to make of herself really. This was the first time she'd admitted to anyone even herself how deep her feelings ran.

Dr. Jones spotted the clock and stood to gather up his debris. "Well, young lady, it's about time for me to get rolling. I'll see you tonight at the meeting?"

"What meeting?" Naomi stood as well.

"The Singles' Retreat; you *are* going aren't you?" Dr. Jones queried.

Naomi slapped her forehead. "That's right. I totally forgot."

"Why don't you stop by my place afterward and pick up those resources?" Dr. Jones offered.

"Great idea," Naomi gave him a brief hug. "Thanks for everything."

"No problem." He saluted her.

"You should have been a therapist, you know that?" Naomi chuckled.

"That was my second choice in college actually." Dr. Jones admitted placing a finger to his lips. "But don't tell anybody. It's not supposed to get out that I'm a mushy teddy-bear deep down inside."

Naomi laughed out loud. "I can't wait to tell Aurielle."

Dr. Jones looked dismayed. "You wouldn't."

"You're right; although the look on your face just now was priceless." Naomi waved him off still giggling under her breath. *Dr. Jones you are one of a kind.*

Savannah had been ensconced in the plans for her school's end of the year party and talent show that she hadn't noticed how long her secretary had been standing in the doorway. She motioned for her to enter.

The secretary had a look of worry etched upon her face as she handed Savannah a manila envelope. "The gentleman didn't leave his name. Only this package for you,"

Savannah suddenly felt a strange niggling suspicion about the package. She took the envelope warily. "Is he still here?"

"No. He left as soon as he dropped this off on my desk. He said he was just passing through."

"Thank you." She dismissed her secretary waiting for her to close her office door before she ripped into the package. She was pretty sure she knew the culprit. She gasped covering her mouth as she beheld the contents. Her hands shook as she read the note that accompanied them.

I think these would look great on your wedding web site. It's never too late to call off the wedding. Think about it. Does your fiancé really need to be put through this kind of embarrassment? You have until July 8. The choice is yours.

Savannah let the letter fall from her hands to the ground, a sinking feeling overtaking her. *Never in my life would I have thought someone would stoop so low.* She sat speechless for a moment looking at what appeared to be incriminating evidence. Seven pictures of what appeared to be Savannah in the nude in compromising positions. The artist had done a flawless job of airbrushing that even to trained eye it was hard to tell if they were real or computer generated. But the Savannah knew the truth. *Before I can even prove they are false the lies will spread like wildfire. Shemiah will be defending my honor and I'll be fighting to maintain my reputation.* She had no doubt in her mind the culprit who was behind this. *Ultimately it will bring shame to the Body of Christ and to my family.*

Savannah buried her head in her hands. *Lord, You promised me a lifetime with Shemiah but you never said that it was going to be easy attaining it. What am I supposed to do? If I keep this from Shemiah, he may doubt my innocence. If I give up the man I love Lysander will win. Lord, please show me what to do.*

"Let God arise and let His enemies be scattered."

The verse of scripture was like a balm for Savannah. *God, I'll step out of the way and let you be the boss.* She placed the photographs back in the folder along with the letter. She would hold on to the evidence in case it was needed.

She doubted Lysander would have been foolish enough to deliver the photos himself. She regretted having to share this turn of events with Shemiah but she had to be open and honest with him. She hated to be the sole cause of a family rift. She knew the precious time that could be wasted on holding grudges and letting old wounds fester. *Lord, touch Lysander's mind. Bring him back from this path of destruction he's headed on.*

Savannah felt a peace come over her and a renewed determination. No matter what happens in the coming days she was not going to give up on God or her relationship with Shemiah. If the enemy was spoiling for a fight, he had picked the right opponent. "Let God arise and let his enemies be scattered." Savannah spoke to herself. "Greater is he that is in me than he that is in the world. I will overcome evil with good. God, you are too awesome!" she shouted.

"I'm More Than enough; what else did you expect?"

Savannah couldn't help praise the Lord.

"One more rep and you'll be done." *Thank God.* Rosalynn had been walking on egg shells for the last half hour since their workout had begun. *Fifteen more minutes. I can survive fifteen more minutes.* Rosalynn had been surprised at how cordial Giovanni had been. They'd talked about the weather, the latest trend in fitness, and the best protein bars. Nothing remotely related to his twin in any way. This was what worried her. *Maybe Nicholas has already moved on. Maybe our relationship was so trivial he didn't even bother to mention it to his brother.* The thought saddened Rosalynn.

It was enough for Giovanni to take notice. "So... what's eating you this morning?"

Rosalynn shook her head clearing her forlorn thoughts. "I'm sorry?"

"For a moment you looked as though you lost your best friend." Giovanni had spent the last half hour coaxing her into a state comfortable enough for confession. "Wanna talk about it?"

Rosalynn knew he was baiting her with an open invitation to share her heart but Giovanni seemed too close to the situation to confide in. "I'm fine. It's just been a long morning."

"I see." Giovanni sat up on the weight bench sighing. "Well, at least one of you seems to be doing fine." *Hook, line and sinker,* he smiled.

Rosalynn's eyes widened. "Is Nicholas alright?"

Giovanni's eyes crinkled at the corners as he flashed a wide teasing smile. "I don't think he's going to survive Sunday dinner without you."

Rosalynn huffed. *Blasted! He got me good.* "Giovanni, I am not going to discuss this with you. It's really none of your business."

Giovanni folded his arms in front of him. "It *is* my business when my brother sends objects sailing past my head at the mention of your name. That's where I draw line."

Rosalynn stifled a giggle.

"You think it's funny?"

She shook her head quickly containing her mirth. "I'm sorry."

"Sorry doesn't cut it, young lady. The man is not going to make it until Sunday if he doesn't get rid of the grouchy attitude and I believe you can help with that." Giovanni gave her a coaxing grin.

Rosalynn shook her head. "I can't. Really," *I can't allow myself to be coerced into this.*

Giovanni sighed. "Look, Rosalynn, I don't know why you cancelled the dinner date but I do know this: my brother cares very deeply for you. I've seen him come and go in relationships but...this is different. I'm not asking you to think about this. I'm asking you to pray about it. We both know my brother hasn't made the wisest decisions regarding you, but I think he deserves a chance."

Rosalynn heard her doorbell ring. It was her next appointment. "I hate to run you off, but my next client is at the door." She tried to hide the fact that she was grateful; Giovanni had been slowly wearing her down.

He stood then. "Alright but will you pray about it?" he prodded her.

"Yes. I'll pray about it." She ushered him down the hallway.

Giovanni let himself out as he offered greetings to the next client. Rosalynn pasted on a brilliant smile for her next client. *Lord, help me to think about wiping it completely from my mind.*

19

Seth took a deep breath of salty air as he stood outside Aliya's boutique. He had decided to wait until lunch to check up on her. Their encounter this morning had not exactly turned out the way he had planned. He was thankful that the paramedics had concluded she was okay. He opened the boutique door ready for round two.

"Welcome to Divine Designs. I'll be with you in a moment." Aliya called out chirpily.

Seth followed her voice over to a display of evening gowns. Aliya knelt down in front of a floor-length sequined fuchsia dress. She appeared to be fitting the mannequin with matching pumps, no doubt a creation of her own. Seth took advantage of the moment to study her. She had allowed her hair to grow midway down the length of her back. He noticed she had returned to her natural chestnut color, which gave her golden skin a healthy glow. *Beautiful,* Seth admired the view.

"Fearfully and wonderfully made,"

Seth smiled then. It always amazed him when the Lord intruded upon his thoughts. *I cannot deny the Truth..*

Aliya stood then and whirling around running smack dab into his solid chest.

Seth caught her at the elbow steadying her. "Sorry." he grimaced.

"Seth!" Aliya knew her blush was in full bloom but she tried to maintain a calm demeanor. "I thought you were a customer just looking around." His spicy scent surrounded her.

"Sorry I didn't announce myself when I came in." He would not admit that he *had* been enjoying the view. "We never finished our earlier conversation and I thought maybe you'd like to... over lunch."

Aliya glanced at her wall clock behind her desk. "I can't believe it's almost one. I should have taken a break but I'm already behind on my orders from this morning." frustration laced her voice.

"If it's too much trouble..."

"No, it's fine. I need to take a break, really." Aliya chewed the bottom of her lip. Her mind was still reeling from earlier this morning. She was still trying to get over the fact that God had told Seth they were to be together. Her wayward thoughts had impeded most of her progress this morning.

"Where would you like to go?" Seth queried. He stuffed his hands in his pocket to keep from brushing back her hair that threatened to cascade over her rosy cheeks.

"Hmm... let me see... how about Bistro Savannah?" Aliya offered.

"One of my favorites", Seth admitted. "There's something on the menu for everyone."

"Alright then, let me get my things from my office and we can take off." Aliya hurried down the hallway anxious to collect her thoughts.

As soon as she was out of view Seth allowed himself to relax a bit. He was not sure how to broach the subject of a relationship between them but he knew it needed to be done. *Lord please help me to be sensitive to your voice. Show me how to be open with Aliya. Give us a fresh start today.*

Aliya was searching for her keys when the phone rang. She picked it up reluctantly.

"Hello?"

"How are you feeling?" Augusta's rich voice edged with concern filtered through the telephone.

"I'm fine." Aliya knew her tone sounded clipped and hurried but she couldn't help it. It had annoyed her how Augusta had fussed over her this morning like a mother hen.

"I've ordered take out Chinese. Did you want some?" Augusta ignored her sister's snappy tone.

"I'm on my way out to lunch right now." Aliya didn't let her tone give away any trace of excitement. She had remained tight-lipped all morning about Seth's visit.

"I guess I'll see you at closing. Did you need anything for the meeting tonight?"

"No. I just plan on leaving early today. I have to put together the room accommodations for the trip." Aliya poked her head out of her office catching a glimpse of Seth pacing and humming.

"You take the car. I'll catch a ride to the meeting." Augusta assured her.

Aliya hung up before her sister could probe any further and sped down the hallway toward Seth. "I hope I didn't keep you too long. Augusta was checking up on me." She rolled her eyes heavenward.

Seth had long ago understood the twins' tough love relationship. "She can't help it. I have the same tendency toward overprotection. Jamar reminds me quite frequently." he chuckled.

Aliya was surprised by his warm rich laughter. It seemed to reach way down into his soul. "You should laugh more often," she remarked offhandedly as he ushered her outside.

"I'll keep that in mind." he assured her helping her into his sedan. Aliya sat back and closed her eyes enjoying the camaraderie between them.

Lord, I want what you want for Seth and me. Help me to be open to this relationship in the way that you desire. Help me to guard my tongue and not use my tongue as weapon.

As they pulled away from the curb, Seth spotted Jamar rounding the corner. He waved watching the priceless expression on his brother's face. He knew he was going to have a lot of explaining to do. *Lord, I sincerely pray my brother will receive a taste of his own matchmaking medicine.*

Jamar Davis stood at the front door of Alpha, Inc. with a smile the size of Texas etched into his features as he gazed at the retreating car oblivious to his current surroundings.

"Good afternoon".

Jamar turned to meet the voice that greeted him and collided with the most beautiful pair of eyes he'd ever seen. "Good afternoon." He shook his head at how familiar the woman before him looked. "Have we met before?"

Tehinnah was hard pressed not to stand there for a moment to enjoy the view. Jamar's lightweight periwinkle sweater and slacks hugged all the right muscles. *And I told Tatyanna that wasn't interested.*

"Briefly," She looked downcast.

Jamar looked puzzled. *I'm sure I would have remembered the encounter.* He opened the door for her introducing himself. "Jamar Davis."

Tehinnah gave him a megawatt smile. "Tehinnah Adams."

Jamar knew his mouth was agape but he could not help it. He immediately saw the resemblance as soon as Tatyanna stepped out of her office. Before he could respond, Tatyanna was on the scene making her presence known.

"It's about time you got here. I'm starving." Tatyanna complained looping her arm in her sister's.

Jamar stood there looking dumbfounded.

"I had to wait on some office supplies to come in before I could take a break." Tehinnah filled her in as they headed back outside.

Tatyanna glanced back at Jamar who still stood glued to one spot watching the pair. "Jamar, hold my calls until I get back."

Jamar nodded as the chatting pair stepped out in to the radiant heat once more. *I can't believe this.* In a matter of minutes Tehinnah Adams had managed to jumble his thoughts and muddle his mind.

And that was dangerous.

The last time Jamar had dared to care too much for any woman he had found himself with ringside seats at her funeral. Taking the plunge into emotional attachment had cost too much. He just was not willing to do it again. *No matter how tempting the package.* He regained his focus and turned his attention to his part-time job of pencil pushing and message taking. *No matter how tempting,* he repeated to himself.

Enrique's heart pounded in tune with his steps as he rounded the length of the park in a brisk jog for a final lap. Carlton ran alongside him in silence for which he was grateful. Nicholas kept pace behind them while Fabian and Fabritza Ciccone circled the area conspicuously in his SUV.

As summer had set in, the temperatures had climbed reminding Enrique of his home back in Costa Rica. He missed the smell of ripened fruit and the sound of barefoot children. He brushed the sentimental memories that flooded his mind and focused on the matter at hand. Carlton had been avoiding any reference made to his sister for most of their session but Enrique was a determined man. If he was to live in peace, which was becoming increasingly difficult when fifty percent of his security team was disgruntled, then he needed to straighten things out between the parties involved.

As they came to a standstill, Enrique and Carlton stretched once more. Nicholas hung back affording enough privacy for conversation.

"Carlton," Enrique began carefully forming his words, "I believe that we have a situation that needs to be dealt with." He stood up fully stretching his arms swinging them back and forth.

Carlton had been trying to avoid the conversation since they'd started training this afternoon. Even now he realized he was just putting off the inevitable. He spread his legs and leaned to the right. "As far as I'm concerned, there *is* no situation."

Enrique rolled his eyes heavenward. *Lord, why do your children have to make things difficult?* "Trust me, Mr. Rhodes, there is a situation here. The only reason your head is still resting on your body is because Nicholas is a born-again believer."

Carlton didn't even blink twice at the statement. "His machissimo may flatter my sister but it doesn't impress me at all." He stood then glaring at his new client. "Look, I know Roz, better than she knows herself sometimes. She's excited that someone is finally taking notice of her and when the novelty wears off, so will the relationship."

Enrique's eyes simmered with anger that threatened to be unleashed. "Why do you presume to know what's best for your sister? She's not some star-struck teenager needing to be coddled. She's a grown woman capable of making her own decisions."

Carlton crossed his arms. "I believe she's made her decision already. Nicholas just needs to move on. I'm sure that won't be hard for him."

Enrique understood then. "This is not about Rosalynn's self esteem at all. This is about your need to be in control, Carlton."

Carlton's swift intake was enough for Enrique to know he'd hit the mark.

"Rosalynn has changed Carlton and you have not. You want to hold on to your little sister but she's grown up and moved on. Don't stand in the way of that. You'll live to regret it." Enrique warned him.

Carlton's gaze remained unwavering. "I didn't know you were a licensed therapist." His snide remark rolled off his tongue readily. "Let's make this the last time we mix business with personal." He stormed off in the opposite direction heading toward his car.

Enrique shook his head at the trainer baffled by his callous behavior. Something was seriously wrong within.

"What was that all about?" Nicholas had come to stand behind him.

Enrique turned to face him. "I think it's best if you hold off trying to pursue a relationship with Rosalynn."

"What," Nicholas lashed out.

Great; two irate men in one afternoon; just my cup of tea, "I said to *hold off* not to give up altogether." Enrique brushed a hand through his hair.

"Holding off is temporarily giving up." Nicholas glared at him.

"I'm not here to debate semantics!" Enrique barked out in frustration. "Right now, her brother is emotionally volatile when it comes to his little sister and you two are a combination I would rather not mix." He sighed. "He believes he's protecting his sister."

"What did you say to that nonsense?" Nicholas demanded.

"I told him it had nothing to do with protection but with his need to control her life. I also warned him that he would live to regret it if he continued on in the same manner." Enrique filled him in.

Nicholas threw up his hands in exasperation. "So where does that leave me?"

"It leaves you at step one: waiting." Enrique continued as he watched Nicholas revert to his sulking mode. "Rosalynn has got to break out of the box on her own. She has got to learn how to take a stand with Carlton and keep it." *Lord knows if she can't stand up to Carlton she'll never make it in a relationship with Nicholas.* Enrique knew how intense and demanding his bodyguard could be.

Nicholas didn't want to hear Enrique's advice but he knew his boss was right. Part of the reason he'd been attracted to Rosalynn was due to the confidence she exuded. He was in no way interested in a woman who could not think independently. "I know this won't surprise you but you're right."

Enrique chuckled. "Actually I am surprised. This is the first time you've admitted it. It's a step toward maturity."

Nicholas flagged down Fabritza and Fabian. "Gee, I feel so honored." He kidded.

"Then you're ready for your next level of maturity." Enrique headed toward the SUV.

"Yeah, what's that?"

"Making sure you don't initiate contact with her tonight at the meeting." Enrique was sure steam was emanating from both sides of Nicholas' head.

Nicholas lit up the park with loud protests and groaning. Enrique shook his head. *Lord, you surely know how to bring a man to his knees.*

20

Elder Worth looked across his polished mahogany desk at what had to be one of the happiest couples he'd seen in a long time. Andre Charles and Marilyn Robinson were well into their forties but today they seemed like two giggling teenagers. They were happy and they had every right to be having just completed their pre-nuptial counseling.

"I can't believe it's less than two weeks away." Andre's grin seemed to stretch from California to New York.

Elder Worth chuckled. "Hang in there, Mr. Charles. These few days will breeze right on by."

"Amen to that." Marilyn rested in Andre's assuring hug.

"Is there anything else you need taken care of?" Elder Worth had insisted on covering the cost of the wedding, which was to be held in Second Chance's sanctuary. The Mother's Board was sponsoring the reception at Andre's home.

"You have been so gracious in helping us to prepare." Marilyn smiled warmly. She had been surprised at how enthusiastically everyone had been. The Mothers were throwing her a bridal shower the evening before the wedding at Elder Worth's home. Marilyn had been touched to the core by the love and support she felt.

"Vivian would have my hide if she found out you were lacking in any area." Elder Worth was the head of his church and his home; Vivian was the neck that turned it.

"Tell her she can rest assured that everything has been taken care of."

Marilyn had been honored when Vivian had accepted the appointment as her Matron of Honor. Savannah was to be her bridesmaid. She could picture them now in the lovely royal purple gowns Aliya had recently completed.

Elder Worth placed his hands upon the two of them and proceeded to pray. "Father, I ask a blessing upon this couple as they finalize on earth what you have ordained in heaven. Lord, look on their hearts. Give them peace in the days to follow. Bind every work and plan of the enemy. Let them be blessed immeasurably. Let them find favor with the vendors that will share in this holy occasion. Let their testimony be a witness to the world that you are the God of a Second Chance and that you can produce a love that is worthy to be ignited within never to go out. With the agreement of Jesus we say, Amen."

Marilyn and Andre had not expected to leave the office in tears. Nevertheless, they were tears of joy. And God was pleased to collect them.

Augusta was scraping the bottom of her fried rice container with the futile hope that somewhere more food would appear when Savannah popped her head into the office.

"Heard you were on break; got a moment?" Savannah closed the door behind her as Augusta gave a nod of approval. She moved around to Augusta's side of her desk and sat on the corner.

Augusta tossed her carton into her bin nearby like a skilled basketball player. "It's good to see you." Augusta took notice of the expression on her friend's face. A Furrowed brow was not a good sign. "What's on your mind?" She knew it could not be a good thing. *I hope she's not having second thoughts.*

"Not what, but who," Savannah sighed. She pulled out the manila folder from her brief bag and extracted the note. She handed it to Augusta.

Augusta read the note silently feeling the undercurrent of threat that went along with it. She handed it back to her. "What does he have on you?"

"Nothing; It's all computer-generated images of me in the nude." She stood then pacing.

"Have you told Shemiah about this?" Augusta knew Savannah. This was the kind of thing that turned her inside out.

"I haven't exactly figured out how to broach the subject. Especially when the culprit is so close to home," Savannah went on to describe her initial encounter with Lysander and his recent behavior.

Augusta chewed her bottom lip then stopped realizing her twin's bad habits were wearing off on her. "Just tell him, Van. Shemiah is a pretty understanding man. He'll know how to deal with this. He will defend you. You don't have to feel like you've got to face this creep alone."

"The Lord has given me a plan of action that I intend to follow through with." Savannah confided.

"I don't know if you've thought about this but you need to make sure your website is secure. If it isn't then I would suggest you disband your information. At least that will slow him down." Augusta's mind was thinking strategy.

"I'll take that into consideration." Savannah drummed her fingers on the edge of Augusta's desk. Her eyes caught a glimpse of a chain around Augusta's neck. "You don't usually do jewelry. What's that?" Savannah motioned to her neck.

Augusta hadn't realized when her chain had slipped out but she tucked it away quickly. "It's from Enrique."

Savannah gave her a knowing grin. "Finally going soft on us, are you?"

Augusta glared. "Can it, Van. Besides, no one is supposed to know I'm wearing it." She emphasized.

Savannah chuckled. "Well it's about time. Have you seen him yet?"

"No, not yet but I imagine he'll be at the meeting tonight." Augusta secretly anticipated seeing him though she carefully hid it.

Savannah eyed her suspiciously. "Don't think you're going to manage to escape without a word this time."

Augusta's throaty laugh pierced the air. "Who said anything about escaping?"

"I know you, Auggie." Savannah shook her finger like she was scolding a naughty child. "You have a knack for skipping out under pressure."

"Hey, I learned it from the best." Augusta replied saucily.
Savannah shrugged her shoulders. "Well it's time to unlearn it. Besides Enrique will be hot on your trail," She warned her.

Augusta knew that from experience. She would never forget the time he dropped everything and flew to Kingston just to talk with her. He truly was a man in a class of his own. "Don't I know it," she released a satisfied grin.

Savannah stood then stretching. "As much as I would love to hang out here, I've got to get back to work. My teachers are turning in their grades today and I want to make sure there are no surprises waiting for me or the parents."

Augusta stood hugging her longtime friend. "It was good to see you. I know you and Shemiah usually have lunch today. Where is he by the way?"

He had a meeting in Atlanta this morning, but he'll be back in time for the meeting this evening. Are you coming to rehearsal tonight?" Savannah looked forward to winding down with the praise and worship team. Their Friday rehearsals were a boost for her spiritually.

"I may be a few minutes late, but I'll be there." Augusta had taken up playing her guitar once again in addition to her church rehearsals she rehearsed with Second Chance Ministries. Though she attended New Life, it gave her opportunity to fellowship with other musicians outside her local body.

"Great." Savannah conveniently forgot to mention that it was a strong possibility that Enrique would be there.

Augusta walked her out to the main lobby. "Let me know how everything goes."

Savannah nodded and headed out stopping the reception desk to say hello to Jamar.

"How's that brother of yours?"
Jamar saved the spreadsheet he was working on. "He's doing fine. He just got back yesterday from his mission trip."

Savannah had sent up many prayers that Seth's work would be completed and that he would have a safe return. She was relieved to hear the good news. "Is he in the office?"

"No, he's out to lunch with Aliya." Jamar's lopsided grin expressed her very thoughts.

Savannah opened her mouth then closed it. "Wow. That was quick."

"Tell me about it." Jamar grinned. "And here I thought my brother had no skills."

Augusta was walking down the hall and overheard the conversation stopping in her tracks. "Did I just hear you say that my sister and Seth went to lunch?"

Jamar nodded.

"And she didn't tell me?" Augusta's hands were clenched to her sides.

"I thought you spoke to her." Jamar was sure he had put her through earlier.

"The little sneak," Augusta thought aloud.

Savannah giggled. "I see she pulled a fast one on you."

Augusta glared at them both, which sent Jamar into another round of laughter.

"I can't believe her! And here I was thinking she was hanging on to dear life this morning." Augusta shared with Savannah about Aliya's fainting spell.

"I'm sure Seth is taking very good care of her." Jamar tried to put in a good word for his big brother.

"Can it, Jamar." Augusta didn't want to hear any excuses. She would handle her sister later.

Jamar stifled a laugh saluting his boss. "Yes ma'am."

Augusta marched back to her office in a huff clearly frustrated with her twin.

Savannah shook her head. "Why do those two always seem to light each other's fire?" She jumped as she heard the sharp slam of Augusta's door.

"I don't know, but I don't want to be around when the fireworks go off." Jamar resigned himself to finish the spreadsheet he'd started.

Savannah took the cue from Jamar and headed out. She did not want to be caught in the crossfire. *Lord, help the twins to bridle their tongues.*

Ginevieve Dubois had decided to order a takeout sub from the neighboring building. She'd managed to pass Bolivar's florist without being noticed. Now as she headed back she knew it would be near impossible to pull it off the second time.

Standing on the sidewalk arranging a display in front of his shop was Marco himself. He was chatting amicably with a female customer.

Ginevieve stood there for a moment taking him in. Marco's hair had grown unruly lately and was past his shirt collar. He wore sneakers and carpenter jeans with a plaid shirt unbuttoned at the throat that was as unruly as his dark tresses. He smiled at something the female customer said and with it his eyes crinkled at the corners.

She's definitely not interested in the flowers, Ginevieve deduced. **"Neither are you."**

Ginevieve gasped in surprise her translucent skin not hiding her rosy glow that was increasing by the moment. *Oops! Caught again,* She turned in the opposite direction and headed back around the corner stopping to compose her thoughts. *This is ridiculous! You're going to be on a date with him this evening. If you can't even walk past him without being affected how do you expect to pull off a date?* She took a deep breath, squared her shoulders and rounded the corner again.

Marco was still chatting when Ginevieve walked past him completely ignoring his presence. He excused himself for a moment and trotted to catch up with her pulling open the door to Alpha, Inc.

"A good afternoon, Marco would have been fine." Marco tried to keep his tone light.

Ginevieve looked at him. "I didn't want to interrupt you. You seemed to be engrossed in conversation." *I hope I don't sound jealous because I most certainly am not!*

"Not so engrossed that I would forget my manners." Marco's tone gave emphasis on the word manners. "I wouldn't want to be accused of ungentlemanly behavior."

Ginevieve shrugged as if his presence had no effect on her. "Thank you for holding the door for me, Mr. Bolivar. Have a good afternoon." Ginevieve kept walking, leaving Marco's mouth wide open.

Jamar had heard part of the interchange but decided it would be wise for him not to rub it in.

Marco folded his arms and glared at Jamar? "Well? Aren't you going to say something?"

Jamar glanced up from reading the latest design magazine delivered to their door. "And allow you to take out that temper on me? Nah,"

Marco's eye happened to light upon the waiting area where he saw his bouquet. He staggered backwards like a drunken man his hand going to his heart. "These...what are these doing here?"

Jamar closed his eyes opening one to peek out. "Do you really want to know?"

Marco went to stand in front of the bouquet, which still maintained its morning glory. "I send her flowers and this is how she shows her appreciation; by making them the centerpiece for the *office?*" Marco managed to whisper irately for the sake of maintaining the working environment.

Jamar stepped down from his post to join Marco in mourning. "You have to admit they are a bit overboard."

"Overboard; really," Marco's hand went to his chin rubbing it thoughtfully. "Where I come from, this is a meager gesture of affection."

Jamar chuckled. "Well, for the most part, here in America, you don't send this many roses unless the woman is wearing your ring."

The light seemed to turn on in Marco's head. "Aha! So she thinks I was being how you say...patronage?"

Jamar stifled a laugh. "I think you mean patronizing."

"Yes! That's the word I was looking for." He laughed at his own inadequacy with the English language. He headed toward the door and turned to view his flowers once more. "I wish those beauties could have been appreciated more."

Jamar knew how Marco felt about flowers. In retrospect he wished Ginevieve had handled the situation more delicately. "They'll definitely be admired by our customers."

Marco held his tongue on the matter knowing it was futile. *So she thinks I'm just playing games.* He knew there was one way to put an end to her guesswork. He would have to put in some overtime at the shop but maybe he could pull it off. Seeing his flowers gracing the lobby instead of her office had done something to Marco. Something for which he had no words for yet. He saw her gesture symbolically. Ginevieve Dubois was used to relegating people to a certain compartment in her life. *I will not be boxed in and relegated to some unimportant corner of her life.* "I'm glad someone will look on them in appreciation. Have a good afternoon."

Jamar knew by the look on Marco's face that trouble was definitely brewing for Ginevieve Dubois. *This isn't business anymore. It's personal.*

141

21

Aliya wrapped her pasta once more around her fork and carefully brought it to her lips all the while cognizant of Seth Davis. They had eaten in relative silence for the most part simply enjoying each other's company. It was Seth that spoke first breaking the silence.

"How has business been for you?" Seth took a sip of his beverage waiting for her response.

"Things are going pretty well. I have my sister to thank for that. She divided her time between running the shop and managing Alpha, Inc." Aliya had been surprised to find things running smoothly. Augusta had hired temporary help and had managed to keep her boutique afloat. "I don't know what I would have done without her."

Seth's mouth curved at the corners. "You would certainly be short of a sparring partner."

Aliya chuckled. "So you noticed that our extracurricular activities include arguing."

"You enjoy arguing?" Seth took another sip.

"I find it intellectually stimulating. Like take today for instance, I knew my sister was a little distraught so I managed to take her mind off the situation by arguing. It's a great diversionary tactic. You should try it some time." Aliya giggled watching the myriad expressions light across Seth's face.

"You are a very surprising young woman." Seth folded his hands together on the table.

Aliya noticed his tone took on a more intimate note. "And you are a very nice man."

Seth grinned. "Is that all?"

Aliya laughed out loud. "I don't want my compliments to go to your head."

Seth pointed to himself in mock surprise. "Me? Never; my little brother keeps me very grounded."

Aliya gave him an unbelieving glare. "Really,"

Seth folded his arms. "Yes. Besides, I am well aware of how privileged I am to be sharing this moment with you right now."

Aliya felt herself blush right down to her toes. "Flattery will get you nowhere, Mr. Davis."

Seth reached across the table taking her hand in his. "There's no need for embellishment. I would be lying if I didn't admit to myself how special and rare you are. I'm just hoping in time you'll give me the opportunity to fully appreciate you."

Aliya's heart seemed to skip at those words. For once the queen of talk was completely at a loss for words.

Seth let her off the hook. "I think today is the start of something beautiful. I've enjoyed this time of fellowship with you."

Aliya released a pent up sigh realizing he wasn't proposing. "I have too." She stood allowing Seth to grab her things and escort her outside.

"If you're up to it, I'd like to see you tonight." Seth requested.

"Isn't your welcome back dinner tonight?" Aliya reminded him.

Seth took a moment to explain that there was no dinner and as he watched her eyes light up with understanding he knew his brother was in trouble. "Try not to be too hard on him."

Aliya shook her head. *Wait until I get a hold of him.* "I promise to send him home in one piece." *After I put him back together,* she smiled.

Seth chuckled at Aliya's expression. "You can be quite fierce, you know that?"

Aliya punched Seth playfully. "Your brother deserves a taste of his own medicine."

"I agree with you there and in due time he's going to reap what he's sown." Seth opened his car door for her.

Little did they know, Jamar's harvest was just around the bend.

Noelle opened his front door to the sounds of Christian jazz music floating through his home. *What the...?*

"You did tell her to make herself comfortable."

Noelle conceded that point to the Holy Spirit and made his way down the hall until he came upon his unfurnished living room. He had to pause in the doorway not wanting to interrupt what he saw.

Lying prostrate on the floor with her nose in a material manual and humming Great Is Thy Faithfulness was Mariella Estrada looking totally at home and in her element. *In my home!*

I feel like this is the story of Raven Locks and One Disturbed Bear, Noelle thought. The picture before him made him feel a bit uneasy. He walked back down the hallway to the front door and opened it, closing it loudly this time. He made an extreme amount of noise so as to alert her to his presence.

When he found her the second time, she as sitting up with her feet folded under her. Noelle acted none the wiser.

"Afternoon, Mr. Marks." Mariella looked up at him with wide eyes parting her lips in a gentle smile.

"Good afternoon." Noelle stood in the doorway. "How are things coming along?" He managed to pull himself out of the doorway moving into the bare room.

Mariella rose to stand and Noelle offered her his hand. She dusted herself off. "They are coming along just fine. I'd like to start with this room here. I think I could pull off your Afro-Caribbean theme here." She showed him the sketches she'd been working on.

Noelle was quite impressed. The color scheme was olive and gold, two colors he favored quite a bit. He noticed she had gone for the essence of Africa and left out the idolatrous artifacts, which seemed to be so popular in modern décor. "This looks wonderful. When can we get started?"

Mariella was flabbergasted. "You have no objections?" She looked at the sketch he'd picked out. *I didn't intend to include that one.* It had a feminine flair to it and it was the last one she expected him to choose. She'd gotten off on a tangent imagining how she would want her living room to look.

"Not at all," Noelle looked puzzled.

Mariella didn't feel right withholding the truth so she confessed. "That sketch actually wasn't meant for your living room. I was just playing around with some ideas."

Noelle didn't see what the point was. "Well, I think it's the best one and I'd like to go with that design scheme. Olive and gold are two of my favorite colors."

Mariella could not believe what she was hearing. *First he selects my personal design. Now he tells me we share the same favorite colors?* "Very well; I can order the furniture tomorrow. I'll need to run into town to select the paint and border. We'll need to pick a separate time to search for antique pieces." *I will not let my imagination run wild.*

"I'll see what's on my schedule for next week. We can plan for a day out and about. You just put together some shops that you'd like us to visit." Noelle looked at his watch. "I'm due back at the office, but I should be back here by four to give you a lift home."

"Alright, thank you." Mariella managed to wave calmly as he left the room and breathed a sigh of relief when she heard him pull out of the driveway. Mariella cleared her head and got back to work putting all thoughts of Noelle Marks aside.

Tatyanna sped back to work realizing she had gone way past her break time. It was no secret that her sister could keep her talking a mile a minute.

Today was no exception especially since the topic of discussion centered on her handsome secretary that her sister was obviously not interested in. Tatyanna was hard pressed not to laugh at her. Tehinnah had prefaced every question with 'not that I'm interested or anything but'. She had not seen her sister this animated about anyone.

"Do you realize that outside of your new position you've spent the rest of your time talking about Jamar Davis?" Tatyanna put the question to her sister.

Tehinnah denied the accusation vehemently. "Just because I asked a few questions; Hardly,"

Tatyanna let it go seeing her sister was in denial. "Suit yourself." *I'd just as soon as set up a date with him and get it over with but if she's going to play dumb so be it.*

Tehinnah allowed herself a moment of relaxation reclining her seat. "I think I'm really going to enjoy my job. Mr. Marks seems like a decent guy."

"Not to mention good-looking, spirit-filled and intelligent." Tatyanna threw in giving her sister a knowing look.

Tehinnah giggled. "It would be hard to overlook those qualities."

"So you aren't blind. I was beginning to think you were." Tatyanna joked.

"In the scheme of things what really matters is where a man's heart is." Tehinnah had had enough experience in relationships to know plenty of men who did the 'church thing' but whose hearts were not turned toward God.

"I agree with you there. Kevin and I went through a period of getting to know God for ourselves and making sure that Christ was whom we looked to for fulfillment and completion. Our relationship with God is the only thing that can wholly fulfill us. People are fallible and they will disappoint us but God will never let us down." Tatyanna kept this truth in mind daily. It helped to keep her expectations of others real.

"So you think Kevin's the one?" Tehinnah asked curious to know.

"We wouldn't be courting if I couldn't picture a future with him. Right now, we are getting to know each other and drawing near to God. That's enough for me right now." Tatyanna elaborated.

Tehinnah's eyes shone with admiration for her sister. "I'm so proud of you, Taty. That you've given your life to the Lord and you're pursuing a God-honoring relationship is nothing short of amazing."

Tatyanna grinned. "I know. I just wish I had made better choices before now. I think about all the time I've wasted thinking that people and things could fill the void in my life."

Tehinnah thought back. "I can remember how heart broken you were when Shemiah broke off your engagement." Tatyanna had written her sister to let her know she'd run into him. "How is he doing?"

"He's getting married to a lovely young lady on August eighth. Savannah is such a jewel. I can't wait to introduce you to her." Tatyanna was thankful that she was able to move past her own regrets. Getting to know Savannah had been worth it.

"Will she be at the meeting this evening?" Tehinnah threw in a subtle reminder. Tatyanna had a tendency to plan several things at once.

"Yes she'll be there. Most of the people I've written you about will be there so you'll get a chance to put a name with a face." They pulled up in front of Alpha, Inc.

"I'll meet you back here at a quarter till four and follow you to the meeting." Tehinnah gave her sister a quick hug.

"Sounds like a plan." Tatyanna waved her sister off and headed back to work wondering how her sister was going to react to seeing Jamar Davis this evening.

Rosalynn stood at her kitchen counter tossing a fresh salad when she heard the screech of tires in her front yard. *What in the world...* She looked out the window to see her very own well-mannered, organized, no hair out of place brother parking like a mad-man and jumping out of his car. He slammed the door and approached the house looking battle ready. Rosalynn went back to tossing her salad as if she had not witnessed the entire scene. *Here we go in five...four...three...two...*

Carlton made his entrance slamming the door as he strode through the living room. It wasn't long before he found Rosalynn in the kitchen setting out her salad bowl on the counter.

"Is there something going on between you and Nicholas Cartellini that you're not telling me?" Carlton barked out.

Rosalynn glared at him. "What is your problem now?"

Carlton exploded. "Just answer the question!"

"I don't have to!" Rosalynn snapped back.

"As long as you're under this roof you do!" Carlton yelled.

Rosalynn's eyes widened in disbelief. "Do you really believe that?"

"Did I stutter?" Carlton's words could have frozen New Mexico.

Rosalynn set the fork down that she'd been using and walked past him to her bedroom. Carlton followed her down the hall stopping when she slammed the door. When he reached her door he opened it slowly.

"You're making a mistake." Carlton folded his arms defensively.

Rosalynn threw her clothes on the bed. "No, Carlton. *You* made the mistake of thinking I was a child and not an adult."

"Come on Roz. Where are you going to go?" Carlton reasoned with her.

"It's no longer your concern." Rosalynn zipped up her duffel bag. As she moved past him, he gripped her arm.

"Don't do this Roz. We're family. You know I'm the only one who cares about you." Carlton tried to coax her.

Giovanni's words came to her mind. *My brother cares very deeply for you.*

"I care for you."

Rosalynn was surprised to find that God was right there with her. *Whether Nicholas cares or not God cares.* For Rosalynn that was enough. She looked up into her brother's hard unfeeling gaze. "Not anymore, Carlton. Not any more." She pulled out of his grip and walked down the hall moving faster as she heard him walking behind her.

Rosalynn felt a tangible and very real fear. *Lord, something is not right with my brother. Help him to let go and let you have control.* She kept walking in the opposite direction of her home pulling out her cell phone. She called the first person she could think of.

22

Aliya sat in the fellowship hall of Second Chance, lines of frustration etched in her near perfect features. Due to emergencies, car problems, family issues and such like, she had been forced to move her meeting to five-thirty. *Everyone has known for a month now that we would be having this meeting. You would think they all planned ahead of time to have every human delay known to man to occur on this very day!*

"Be patient, my love."

Aliya closed her eyes and breathed in and out hoping it would abate her rising temperature. *Ten more minutes, ten more minutes.*

"Mind if I join you?"

Aliya opened one eye to find Seth staring down at her with an infectious grin on his face. "Sure. Maybe it will actually work for you."

"Meditating on the Lord doesn't work for you?" Seth questioned her mischievously.

"You know good and well I wasn't meditating on the Lord." Aliya glared at him.

"What so ever things are pure, lovely, virtuous..." Seth started in.

"I know, I know. Think on these things. But they don't allow me to hold on to my temper." Aliya chuckled seeing the foolishness of her own ways.

"Temper, you; you've got to be kidding. I've never met a more jovial woman in my life." Seth said it in a joking manner but he was very sincere.

"Are you serious?" Aliya leaned in enjoying their conversation.

"Yes. In fact, I thought you were so jovial that you couldn't take anything or anyone seriously." Seth admitted.

Aliya was game. "Would you like to know what I thought of you?"

Seth held out his hands in protest. "That's okay. You've told me more times than I'd like to count. You were never shy about it."

Aliya laughed out loud. "That's not what I really thought about you. That's what I said to inspire any type of emotion from you." She had not noticed that others had started to file in. She was going to have to call her meeting to order.

"So what *did* you think about me, Miss Peyton?" Seth leaned over to whisper to her.

"I'm afraid I can't answer that question right now. I have to call this meeting to order." She said sweetly as she waved at Enrique and his security entourage.

Seth conceded the point. "This conversation is far from over." He promised walking away from her to take his seat.

Aliya cleared her throat and called her meeting to order.

"Please bear with me as I take roll this evening. We have quite a few people that will be going on this trip. I will recheck the role at the end of the evening for those that miss this first roll call." Aliya looked down at her pad and began taking roll. "Please say present or here when you hear your name."

The roll took several minutes and it surprised Aliya that everyone was present. "If my count is correct, we have exactly sixteen men and sixteen women on this trip. You will be placed four to a room with 8 rooms. The bungalows can occupy six people comfortably so we allotted for some extra space."

Aliya flipped her note pad and launched into the second portion of her speech. "Please listen to your room assignment: For the ladies room one will occupy myself, my cousin Mei-Ling Wong, Tatyanna Adams, and Ginevieve Dubois. Room two occupants are Vivian Worth, Savannah, Augusta, and Rosalynn. Room three guests are Jarah, Angelynn and the twins, Mariella, and Fabritza Ciccone. Columbia, Aurielle, Tehinnah, and Naomi will occupy room four."

Aliya heard several murmurings so she decided to quell all talk. "We are asking everyone to abide by the room assignments. We took into account those of you who needed certain occupants for security reasons. The object of this trip is to learn more about each other, not necessarily to camp out with your best friend. So expand your horizons. Now for the men: room one will occupy Enrique, Giovanni, Nicholas, and Fabian. Pastor Marks, Kevin, Noelle, and Carlton will occupy room two. Room three guests are Elder Worth, Dr. Gregory Thomas, Jamar, and Marco. And finally, Seth, Dr. Trey Jones, Josiah, and Shemiah will occupy room four. And no, none of these bungalows are adjacent or across from each other."

Aliya's statement produced a round of laughter.

"I know many of you have had a long day so I will get on with the rest of my presentation. At this time, Augusta is going to come before you to let you in on a little surprise." Aliya took her seat for a moment as her twin came to address the crew.

"Thank God it's Friday." Augusta gave an exaggerated sigh.

"*Amen.*" The resounding voice of several called out.

"Well, I think we saved the best surprise for last because we weren't sure who we would choose and why. The surprise is that 5 of you will receive a full refund once we arrive in Kingston. My father decided to sponsor five of the participants. Aliya and I couldn't decide who should receive the discount so we decided to pull names tonight excluding our own." Augusta picked up a bowl with names and swirled it around. She pulled out five slips of paper. "The following people will receive refunds for this trip: Rosalynn Rhodes, Gregory Thomas, Ginevieve Dubois, Columbia Newcomb and Jamar Davis. Congratulations! Back to you, Liya," Augusta winked at her sister giving her the floor as the applause rang out.

"Well we are down to three things left on my agenda. I would like to introduce to you those who will be Group Leaders during this time. These are the people that are authorized to advise you on life changing life-altering decisions that may come up while you are on this trip. I strongly advise you to seek out the wisdom in these men and women rather than relying strictly on your experience or the advice of your peers. We can be a bit biased at times."

"I introduce to you tonight, Senior Pastor of Second Chance Ministries and Second Wind Ministries, Elder Josiah Worth. He and his wife Vivian Worth will serve as senior Group Leaders. Pastor Seth Davis and Pastor John Marks will serve as executive Group Leaders. Josiah Worth and his wife Angelynn will serve as Group Leaders to the Engaged and Courting. These are your group leaders. At this time, I yield the floor for Elder Worth to give us some general guidelines." Aliya took her seat once more to search for her itinerary for the trip.

Elder Worth held up his to stop the thunderous applause and catcalls as he came to address them. "Thank you for the warm welcome. First of all, I must say that I am excited about this trip. I think it high time that someone unified the body of Christ for fellowship. Secondly, I think it would be robbery if we didn't give a round of applause for the young ladies that made this trip possible." Elder Worth faced the Peyton twins and gave them a round of applause. Augusta hid her face. He faced the eager singles and continued on. "Despite all they have been through personally, they have continued to plan this trip and that says a lot about them as faithful women of God. I am proud to know them and I know that Pastor Marks is glad to have them serving in his ministry."

"You're right about that preacher," Pastor Marks grinned from ear to ear, beaming like a proud parent.

"Now, as for guidelines," Elder Worth began. "I'd like to break them up into four categories; singles, courting, engaged, and married. Because there is a mixture of each, I am asking that married couples keep the PDA to a minimum outside the bedroom. I am asking that engaged couples refrain from PDA during the group activities and those who are courting should refrain from PDA during this trip. Well, you may say, why is he asking us to go to such lengths?"

"One major reason is that this trip is not just for fellowship or matchmaking but a time and opportunity to seek God and grow closer to him. Even Moses had to refrain from procreation before he went up to see the Lord. If you will honor this request I believe that you will come away with a richer experience."

"This is not just a time to come and go as you please although I know the Peytons have allotted some free time. There is a curfew. Group leaders will be patrolling and answering questions so you may see us out tending to a need. For the couples that are engaged, curfew is midnight. Courting couples curfew is eleven-thirty. All other singles curfew is ten-thirty. Curfew simply means that you are in your room for the night. What

150

you and your roommates decide to do in the room is up to you. I will warn you that our schedules are pretty loaded so you may want to get all the sleep you can. Are there any questions?"

Carlton raised his hand.

"Yes, sir," Elder Worth pointed to his member.

"I noticed that you didn't mention dating. Where does that fall?" He eyed his sister who turned her head refusing to look at him.

"Well, if the relationship is not serious to make you consider that person as a lifelong mate, then you aren't courting. So I would consider you a single. Does that answer your question?" Elder Worth noticed the distance between Carlton and his sister.

"Yes, thank you." Carlton's eyes periodically fell upon his sister.

"While I'm up here, I'd like to address one more thing. If you are having a personal problem with someone or even if you feel uncomfortable with your placement, please talk to us. We don't want anyone bringing unnecessary baggage on this trip. We have less than a week before we depart so let's deal with any issues now so that we can enjoy one another without reserve."

Aliya took the floor once more. "And on that note, pack light please. We have been blessed with a sponsor for our transportation and that is none other than EAE Design Group. Their CEO who is a member of Second Chance Ministries will be accompanying us and is here with us tonight. Enrique, will you stand?" She joined in as others applauded him.

Enrique waved and blew her a kiss.

"Thank you Enrique for helping us to defray the cost of airfare. Finally, we are winding down. As you know, we are departing July third at four in the morning and we will return July sixth at ten in the evening. That gives us four full days of fun and adventure in Montego Bay. You will receive a full itinerary by email three days before we depart, but I did want to let you know some of the activities we have planned. We will be jet skiing, hiking, and scuba diving."

"For those of you who are less adventurous the hotel always has activities planned onsite. We are going to go into town to shop so bring some spending money. My father has created man made waterfall to enhance the landscape. We will meet there every morning for prayer and the Bible Study at nine. Everyone is expected to be there."

"Now for the things that we forget to think about," Augusta passed out a list of needed items for people to bring as Aliya went over the list. "Please make sure you have any needed medications for this trip. Please make sure you have your passport, driver's license and at least one other form of identification." Aliya continued down her list of important items until she was done. "We don't intend for anything to go wrong, but if something does go wrong, we want to be prepared. Thank you all for your time."

Elder Worth stood and offered a prayer of blessing adjourning the meeting. "Refreshments, veggies, and fruit are to your rear. Please help yourself." He shook hands with Aliya. "That was very informative. I appreciate all the time and effort you have put into planning this trip. I pray that every aspect turns out to be a success."

"I'm counting on it." Aliya smiled back. "If not, my father may never be this generous again." She chuckled.

"I'm sorry to interrupt but I need to borrow my sister for a moment." Augusta cut in politely.

"Go right ahead." Elder Worth walked over to say hello to Pastor Marks.

Augusta pulled Aliya to the side. "I wanted to let you know that I'm staying for the rehearsal. It's at eight so it's just thirty minutes away. You can take the car and I'll get a ride home."

Aliya gave her a sappy grin. "I'm sure you will." She had a feeling Enrique was staying for the rehearsal as well.

Augusta made a funny face. "You have no right to rub in anything, Missy. Especially after your luncheon rendezvous with Seth today," she smiled knowingly.

Aliya gasped. "Who told you?"

"Jamar happened to see you two pulling off. Caught in the very act," Augusta looked smug.

"I'm going to give him a piece of my mind later." Aliya thought about her conversation with Seth.

"I hope it's the mind that's in Christ Jesus." Augusta chided her.
"Do you know he tried to set me up with Seth?" Aliya looked to her sister to be surprised.

Augusta was silent.
"You *knew* didn't you?" Aliya accused.

Augusta burst out in laughter.
"And you didn't tell me? Oh, that is so not right." Aliya complained.

"Look at the pot calling the kettle black! I invited you over for lunch and you didn't even have the decency to tell me you were leaving with Seth." Augusta argued.

Aliya was in a catch twenty-two situation. "Okay. I guess we both were in the wrong."

"It's a good thing I approve of Seth or you'd be in hot water." Augusta wrapped her arm around her sister's shoulder.

"Jamar is *still* in hot water." Aliya pouted.
"I'm sure his brother will think of someway to get him out." Augusta chuckled.

Aliya smiled dreamily. "He doesn't have to think. All he has to do is look at me in that special way and I'll probably give in."

"I see you're *still* a hopeless romantic." Augusta grinned as they walked over to the refreshments.

"I see you're still a *Wanna*-be cynic." Aliya giggled. *What a pair we make.*

23

Though the organizational meeting was dismissed, no one departed. Instead they took the opportunity to enjoy the refreshments and fellowship.

While some took small bites and chatted comfortably, others milled about from friend, introducing one another. The circles of conversation were varied and many. Though several wore a look of assurance and confidence inwardly their minds were brewing. The old adage was certainly true at the moment: looks could be deceiving.

Ginevieve was refilling her cup from the ornate punch bowl when she felt his presence behind her. *Maybe if I ignore him he will leave me to my own devices.*

"Here, let me get that for you." Marco took the ladle out of her hand, pouring the fruity drink into her empty cup.

Well, there goes the ignoring part. "Thank you," she said demurely. "I thought you weren't going." Ginevieve's tone held a trace of accusation.

"I wasn't planning to but I was able to rearrange my schedule." Marco held himself to a cup of his own.

"Oh." That one word held so many questions all of which Ginevieve refused to ask. *What is he up to? Is he trying to intimidate me? What is he trying to prove?*

Marco smiled at her and took a sip of his punch. *She is absolutely baffled that I m going on this trip.* He hadn't taken this much pleasure in the company of a woman in a while. "Would you like to push our date up to nine?"

Ginevieve blinked twice. "What?" "Our date; you know, tonight? I can postpone for an hour, unless you'd rather not waste time. You look fine in what you have on." Marco knew his words didn't do her justice but he had to maintain a level head under the circumstances. He didn't want to scare her off.

Ginevieve thought what she had on was suitable. It was functional and one of her most unattractive suits. The only saving grace of her gray ensemble was the fact that it brought out her auburn hair. Contrasted against her milky complexion, it left her looking ghostly. *No man in his right mind could possibly find this attractive.* She gave herself the once over. "I'm fine with this. Give me about ten minutes to freshen up in the restroom and I can meet you outside." No one was yet privy to their planned outings and Ginevieve wanted to keep it that way.

"That's fine. I'll meet you outside then." Marco headed toward the exit silently pleased that Ginevieve hadn't created a female stir concerning her appearance. He'd heard more than his share of unsavory words from women who were offended by his suggestion. It was good to know Ginevieve wasn't overly concerned.

Ginevieve hurried off to the restroom eager to be free of Marco. She had no idea what he'd planned for the evening but if one hundred roses were an indication of his tastes she couldn't help but think how much more extravagant he was bound to get. *I know this is just his way to prove that he's capable of being considerate Lord so help me to keep my perspective.*

"Are you alright?" Tatyanna sat with Rosalynn her eyes moving to and fro about the room.

"I'm okay. I just wish he would stop looking at me." Rosalynn rolled her eyes. "I'm glad you were able to come when you did." She did not mention to Tatyanna how afraid she had been. She'd never seen Carlton strike anyone but this afternoon had shown her that he was capable of doing so. She shuddered as she recalled how angry he had been.

"No problem. You can stay with me until you decide what you want to do. I'll go with you to collect the rest of your things when you're ready." Tatyanna wanted to take the pressure off of her friend.

"Thanks. I'm going to reschedule my morning appointments and go apartment hunting. The sooner he sees I'm independent, the sooner he'll get the picture." Rosalynn confided.

Tatyanna had been trying to rush to get her settled in her apartment so they could head to the meeting. She'd been holding back one question until now. "So, is there anything going on between you and Nicholas Cartellini?"

"We've talked a few times and he's asked me out to dinner." Rosalynn admitted feeling guilty about not sharing the information sooner.

"I hear a 'but' coming," Tatyanna shook her head.

"But... I accepted and then I cancelled." Rosalynn threw up her hands. "I don't know Tatyanna. I feel all confused about the whole thing. I mean, at first I liked him, then I didn't like him because he didn't like me, then I ignored him because I absolutely detest a judgmental attitude, then he asked me to forgive him and I did and then I got to know him a little and I liked what I saw and then Carlton started in on me with his theories of why I'm giving in to this relationship and I'm just...confused right now."

Tatyanna nodded in understanding. "I think the path is pretty clear, Roz. Take it to the Lord in prayer. Don't force something to happen. If something does happen, don't hinder it. Wait on God."

Rosalynn smiled. "Thank you for listening."

Tatyanna almost hesitated but then she went on. "And one more thing I've learned; you're either going to make room for the insecurities of the relationship or the relationship. They won't coexist together."

Rosalynn accepted her friend's words of wisdom. "I can always count on you to tell me the truth." Rosalynn had come to face a lot of truths in the past few hours but one profound truth stuck out. *There is a friend that sticks closer than a brother.*

Look at her! She has the nerve to look so calm and poised as if nothing has happened.

Carlton looked over at his sister as he explained to Elder Worth about their falling out. "I think it was a huge mistake for her to leave like she did."

Elder Worth had listened patiently to Carlton Rhodes as he painted his sister as the villain in their estranged relationship. He was sure that most of the blame lay at Carlton's feet but his member was not inclined to hear the truth right now. "Would you like for me to schedule you two for a conference on Monday?"

"That would be great. Maybe you can talk some sense into her. She's been acting really unstable these past few weeks and now that she's moved out I'm concerned. I don't want her to be taken advantage of."

You also don't want to relinquish control. It was a silent thought that formed in Elder Worth's mind. He would definitely have to nip this in the bud. Elder Worth had watched Rosalynn's spiritual progression and he had not witnessed any unstable behavior. She was faithful in her attendance and serving. Nevertheless, he knew Carlton's mind would not be at ease until he had confronted the situation. "I'll give you your appointment time on Sunday."

"Thank you." Carlton shook hands with the pastor and departed his thoughts on nothing but Rosalynn. *You're not going to get away so easily Roz.* Carlton missed Nicholas's menacing glare as he departed.

Jamar Davis had been doing pretty well this evening. That is until his eyes rested on the doorway to find Tatyanna and her lovely sister making their way in late and scooting past him to find a seat. From that point on the meeting had sounded like gibberish to him. He couldn't believe she was going on the trip. *Tehinnah;* Her name had permeated his thoughts on and off since early this afternoon. He was slightly relieved that she hadn't come back to the office after lunch but seeing her here was unnerving to him.

"She bears a striking resemblance to her sister doesn't she?" Seth came to stand next to his brother.

Great, Now I'm caught in the act of staring. Jamar cleared his throat. "Who are you referring to?"

Seth chuckled. "Don't even try it. The young lady you can't seem to take your eyes off. Tehinnah Adams."

Jamar looked at Seth annoyance written on his face. "Contrary to your popular belief I am not interested in Ms. Adams." *She's way out of my league anyway.*

Seth decided not to pry. Clearly his brother was in denial. "I just came over to tell you that I'll be in a little later than usual. Aliya and I are going to hang out for a bit on Riverstreet. I should be home by ten."

Jamar laughed out loud. "I'm glad to see that you're getting out past your bedtime."

Seth punched him playfully. "I look forward to the day when you understand what a bed time is. All those late nights are going to catch up with you sooner or later," he promised.

"I've got to finish a project so I won't be home until late either." Jamar admitted.

The brothers went their separate ways as Seth went in search of Aliya.

"How are things going over at Worth It?" Shemiah leaned against the refreshment table talking to his long time friend.

"Things are going really well. Our clients are happy and I can't complain. I was out of the loop for a while but it feels good to get back to work." Josiah spoke of his sabbatical. He had taken the time off to devote some quality time to his wife and his newborn twins. "Angelynn has been working from home, but she's planning to go back full time at the start of the New Year."

Shemiah looked over to Angelynn who was chatting away with her mother and holding on to the twins for dear life. "It's amazing how big they've grown."

"I know." Josiah gazed lovingly at his wife. "I want to savor the moments that I have right now."

Shemiah laughed. "Well, I won't hold you back. Once Savannah and I are married, you may not hear from us for quite a while."

"And how are you managing to hold up? You're just a little over a month away." Josiah teased.

"Lots and lots of prayer," Shemiah confessed. "There are times when the urge to take her into my arms is so intense that I ache with the feeling. But God is a keeper and he's helping me to keep *my* word."

"That's good to hear. Besides, my father would tar and feather you." Josiah kidded.

"I take it you've learned through experience?" Shemiah grinned knowingly.

Josiah nodded. "It took me a while before I got over the trauma of my father catching Angelynn and I in a heated embrace. After that, I thought it best that we wait until we said I do."

Shemiah tried to hold back his laugh. "You; The kid who never did *any* wrong," he questioned.

"The one and the same," Josiah could still remember the look of disbelief on his father's face the night he had entered his study to find his son and finance carried away by their flesh. "I think it was the only time my father told me that he was disappointed in me."

Shemiah pondered over those words. *Lord, I don't want to do anything to disappoint you.* As Josiah was called away by Angelynn, Shemiah said a silent prayer for the happy couple.

Columbia tried not to sound as excited as she felt as John Marks greeted her. She could not help but admit that seeing him tonight had been a pleasant surprise.

"How have you been?" John had been slowly making his way past his own parishioners to talk with Columbia. He had not seen her since Saturday but it had felt like ages.

"I've been doing fine; and yourself?" Columbia looked around self-consciously.

"I've been doing well. How are the girls?" Pastor Marks had run into the twins in the grocery store earlier in the week. It had encouraged him that Nadia seemed to be friendlier with him than previously.

"Rodia is her usual pleasant self, Dee is her usual hyperactive self and Nadia has been in a better mood as of late. She was being harassed by upperclassmen but I believe they are putting a stop to it today." Columbia gave him the brief version of what she had managed to pull out of her daughter. "Prom is tonight so they are scrambling to make themselves ready now."

Pastor Marks looked surprised. "Rodia and Nadia are going?"
"Yes. Brett Hamilton is taking her and Xavier Roberts is escorting Rodia."

Pastor Marks was even more surprised. "So you finally caved in?"
Columbia shook her head. "They are not allowed to date. It's a one time deal. The seniors should have arrived back in town this afternoon from their trip so if you see Brett in between make sure you give him a pep talk."

Pastor Marks looked puzzled. "I thought the prom was a week away."
"I did too but apparently the girls got their dates mixed up so they have really been in a panic getting their selves together."

"I'll give Brett a call since I know I won't make it home in time to see him." Pastor Marks promised.

157

"Thank you." Columbia beamed. "I know you're not obligated to but I appreciate it."

"No problem." John waved off her praise. "I'm glad things are going well for you. May be during this trip we'll get a chance to hang out a little." The promise of a date still hung in the air between them.

Columbia agreed. "I look forward to it."
Her words warmed his heart.

Columbia's cell phone went off interrupting her idyllic moment. "It's the girls. I've got to get going."

"Enjoy your evening." Pastor Marks was on cloud nine as he went for round two at the refreshment table.

Mariella smiled politely as Noelle went on and on about how exciting the trip was going to be but inside she was terrified.

"I had no idea other churches were invited. Did you?"
"No." Mariella managed to squelch out. *I'm going to kill Enrique.*

"I think this is great. This will give me a chance to make new friendships. I have not been able to do that since I've been in town." Noelle admitted sheepishly.

"I'm sure you'll have no problem." Mariella was looking for a way to exit the conversation when her cousin strolled over.

"Noelle Marks? I don't believe we've met officially." Enrique shook hands with the attorney. "I'm Enrique Estrada, Mariella's cousin."

Noelle flashed his pearly whites. "I've heard a lot about you."
Enrique gave his cousin a teasing wink. "I hope only good things."

Noelle laughed at the comment. "You're certainly going to boost the economy once your Headquarters are in place."

Enrique was impressed to see Noelle had done a little research on him. "I hope so. There's been so much press about the personal things going on in my life. I hope it doesn't overshadow the good I'm trying to accomplish."

"Whatever the enemy has meant for you bad, God will always turn it around for the good." Noelle encouraged him.

Enrique nodded in approval of Mariella's boss. "Thanks for the encouragement." He turned to Mariella then. "Are you going to be okay getting home? I've got to stay for rehearsal tonight."

Before Mariella could offer a solution Noelle cut her off.
"I can give her a lift home." Noelle looked askance at Mariella.

"I don't want you to go out of your way." Mariella reasoned.
"It's fine. I'm going to grab a bite to eat and then head back to the office to put in a late shift." Noelle explained.

Mariella glanced over at Naomi who seemed to be engrossed in conversation. *No rescue there.* "Alright,"

Noelle and Enrique shook hands once more before they departed. "Good meeting you." Enrique couldn't put his finger on it, but there was something different about Noelle. It made him feel like he had known him forever. "The men here are meeting down at the beach tomorrow for a day of fellowship. You're more than welcome to join us." Enrique handed him his business card. "Call me and I can give you directions."

"Thank you. Maybe I and stop in for a few hours." Noelle offered. As he followed Mariella outside, his step seemed lighter. *There's nothing like being in the company of the saints.*

24

"Attention, everyone," Josiah called out in the midst of the noisy fellowship. "I hate to give you the boot but we'll be closing down in ten minutes. If you are staying for rehearsals they will begin at eight ten."

Naomi had been talking with Dr. Jones when Giovanni Cartellini came to stand beside her. The two of them shook hands making small talk until Aurielle spotted Trey.

"Excuse me guys. I'll be right back."

Naomi could have strangled her co-worker for leaving her to fend for herself.

"How are you?" Giovanni offered.

"Fine," Naomi stood aloof people watching and sipping her fruit punch.

"It's good seeing you again." *Here I go again.* Giovanni wanted to kick himself. *Boy, you are just a relationship martyr aren't you?*

Naomi gave him an incredulous look. "You're joking right?"

Giovanni looked puzzled. "Why would I be joking?"

Naomi put her hand on hip. "After last night; I thought I'd be the last woman you'd want to see."

Giovanni folded his arms defensively. "Was that the desired effect you were hoping for?" his lips tilted into a half smile.

Naomi shook her head. "Not at all,"

"Then I guess its water under the bridge." Giovanni watched as Naomi's face lit up in surprise.

Naomi received the forgiveness willingly. "I appreciate you forgiving me so easily. I'm still working on that area myself."

"Forgiving others is the easy part. Forgiving yourself is another can of worms." Giovanni grinned. "Besides, you still owe me a date."

Naomi agreed. "I haven't forgotten."

"Good." Giovanni took her hand, glad Naomi was a woman of her word. "I intend to make good use of Montego Bay."

Naomi knew it was time to head out before Giovanni ran away with her heart. "Well, it's past time for me to go. Aurielle and I are going to grab a real meal."

Giovanni released her hand slowly treasuring its softness. "Is it okay if I call you later?"

Naomi relented. "I'm usually in bed by eleven. Aurielle and I will be at the house."

"I'll call you." Giovanni could have sworn his heart had started singing. For once Naomi Watts was not putting up a fight. *This is a miracle. I must document this occurrence.* Giovanni was hard pressed not to hop up and down as Naomi trotted off to catch up with Aurielle.

"I don't think this is such a bright idea for me to go on this trip, Kev." Dr. Gregory Thomas helped his son clean up the fellowship hall.

"Oh, come on, Dad. When's the last time you took a vacation?" Kevin argued.

Gregory was silent.

"Exactly; your last vacation was with Mom. You deserve this time of relaxation." Kevin reasoned.

Gregory discarded the used plates that lay unattended. "Relaxation; You call jet skiing and scuba diving relaxing? Hardly; look, you guys are young and unattached; I've been where you all are headed. I've been in love, married, and you are the product. If you're blessed, you'll find someone who you will experience a great love for. To fall in love once is wondrous in itself, but twice? I won't press my luck."

Kevin knew his father was still smarting over his rejection by Marilyn Robinson. He was hoping the trip would take his mind off things.

"No one is saying that you have to meet someone on this trip. I just want you to enjoy yourself."

Gregory sighed. "Well, I guess it doesn't matter anyway. You signed me up so I'm going."

"Who knows what God has planned for you?" Kevin strolled off to the other side of the fellowship hall.

Gregory looked after his son. *That's exactly what I'm afraid of.*

Fabian and Fabritza Ciccone stood apart from the crowd that was slowly filtering out. They had been responsible for checking the grounds before the people had arrived this evening. Finding nothing suspicious, they had given Enrique, who stood before them now, the go ahead to show up.

"I'm going to stay behind for rehearsal. I need you two to check the house and stay put unless I need you." Enrique addressed Fabian.

"And once you arrive back at the house?" Fabian queried.

"We talk about what kind of security we need for the trip next week. We need your connections in Jamaica. I can't have people getting hurt on my account." Enrique knew he was fair game in international waters which was why he had been limiting his travels as of late.

"Francheska will be meeting us in Montego Bay. We've already arranged for her to be on site at the resort. She'll be there the first of July securing the grounds and running background checks on the current staff." Fabian reported.

Enrique was glad to see that he was thinking ahead. "I should reach home before midnight."

"We'll talk then." Fabian and Fabritza escorted Enrique to the music room.

"It's so good to finally meet the little sister Tatyanna has been bragging about." Savannah hugged Tehinnah and stepped back to look at her. "Look at you. We've got to fatten you up a bit." Savannah marveled that Tehinnah was all legs.

"My last semester of school, I was constantly on the run. I wasn't eating right." Tehinnah admitted.

"Well, there are plenty of us around that will make sure you eat right." Savannah kidded. "If my grandmothers saw you they'd cook a seven course meal."

Tehinnah laughed rubbing her stomach. "Right about now I'm ready for a seven course meal."

"I second that." Tatyanna came to join them. "Tehinnah, Rosalynn is going to stay for rehearsal while we go eat dinner. We're going to come back and pick her up."

While Tehinnah left to grab her things, Savannah took a moment to ask about Rosalynn. "I got her message too late this afternoon. Is she doing okay?"

"She's planning on finding another place. Apparently Carlton doesn't understand what his boundaries are as her brother." Tatyanna had a few choice words for him.

"We've got plenty of room at my father's house. Josiah has a beach house that she can rent out if she's looking for something immediate." Savannah suggested.

"I'll bring it up tonight." Tatyanna felt sorry that she even had to discuss something like this.

"Did she say what the problem was?" Savannah saw Shemiah motioning for her realizing her time was up.

"Her brother is dead set against her dating a particular bodyguard." Tatyanna smiled.

Savannah's mouth came open. "Nicholas?"
Tatyanna nodded.

Savannah was still stunned. "Well, I'll be. Wonders never cease around here these days."

"I know. The same 'I wouldn't date him if he were the last man on earth' Nicholas." The two of them laughed.

"God has a way of changing our hearts to conform us to his will." Savannah reminded her.

"I know. It wasn't so long ago that I thought Kevin and I were totally wrong for each other." Tatyanna sighed.

Savannah pushed her playfully. "Stop daydreaming."
Tatyanna giggled spotting Kevin coming toward her. "You're right. The reality is so much better."

Savannah shook her head as Tatyanna ran to meet Kevin halfway. *Lord, help her to remember those words when testing time comes.* Because Savannah knew they would surely come.

"Alright ladies and gentlemen, let's take our places." Shemiah began as he closed out prayer. "I'd like to say welcome back to Enrique."

Enrique threw up his hand in embarrassment as the hoots and hollers went forth. "Glad to be back."

Shemiah looked to Augusta. "As always we are proud to welcome Augusta Peyton. I'll make a worship leader out of her yet." he winked.

"As you all know we've been trying something different within the music department. As you've seen in the services, God has been releasing prophetic songs. Savannah is going to share the song the Lord gave her based on Psalm 91. Musicians you are going to follow her and we are going to worship the Lord. If I hear something then we'll stay there and develop the notes. Choir, I'm listening for your background if there is any. Does everyone understand?" He continued as heads nodded in agreement. "We are recording these sessions and submitting them to Elder Worth for further consideration." He handed the microphone over to Savannah whose sultry, jazzy soprano voice filled the room.

"Hallelujah, Hallelujah. Come on and lift your hands to the Lord. Put yourself in a place of surrender. Psalm 91 is a place of surrender. It is a place of protection. Allow the Lord to minister to your heart as you listen:

> He that dwells in the secret place of the Most High God,
> Shall abide under the shadow of the Almighty,
> He that dwells in the secret place of the Most High God,
> Shall abide under the shadow of the Almighty,
> I will say of the Lord... he's my refuge and my fortress,
> My God in Him will I trust.
> I will say of the Lord...he's my refuge and my fortress,
> My God in Him will I trust.
> When the enemy camped about me,
> He tried to surround me,
> My God in Him will I trust.
> Choir,"

The choir sang the last stanza and Savannah continued on.

> "Though the terror flies by night,
> And the arrow flies by day,
> My God in Him will I trust."

The choir continued to sing, "My God in Him will I trust."

Savannah sang sermonically as the choir sang softly. "I'll abide under the shadow of the Almighty. Face to face in the glory of the Almighty."

The song took them up to a place of worship and no one was willing to come down.

Ginevieve had imagined Marco was planning something lavish, but she was not expecting this. *I can't believe it.* For the second time today, Marco had managed to delve into her secret desires. *Only my mother knows how much I love horse and carriage rides.* Standing before her was a horse with one of the most beautiful coats. But that wasn't all. Seated in the carriage was a violinist. Ginevieve couldn't take it. *Did he do a background check on me or something?* She had played the violin and cello up until college. She still had her instruments tucked away in her apartment.

   "I know what pleases you."
Ginevieve wasn't expecting God's answer but she was glad it came.

   Marco took her hand and helped up onto the step.
"Thank you." she answered politely.

   Marco loaded himself in and the carriage was off. "It was my pleasure."
Ginevieve couldn't help but grin on his choice of words. "So...where are we headed?"

   "Not too far from here." Marco sat back and relaxed against the seat closing his eyes. "This is a perfect evening."

   Ginevieve had to admit that she was enjoying the ride. The violinist played softly. "It is." *I suppose I can be nice since the moment permits.* "Thank you for the flowers."

   Marco opened one eye looking at her. "Jamar tells me they were overdone."

   Ginevieve flushed. "Just a bit."
Marco sat up completely then. "I think your standards are too low, Ginevieve. You are worth much more."

   Ginevieve swallowed hard. *If he's brushing up on his skills he's doing a mighty fine job.* "That's really sweet of you to say, Marco."

   "I've never had a problem with telling the truth." He grinned.
Ginevieve realized they had stopped in front of a park. Located on the expansive green was a table dressed and set for two with candles and a server.

   "This is wonderful, Marco." Ginevieve allowed him to assist her in getting down. This time the driver forget to place the step down so Marco encircled her waist with his hands and gently lifted her and set her on the ground. *I think I'm floating,* Ginevieve thought to herself.

   "I was hoping you'd like it." Marco led her to the table and seated her first.

   Ginevieve smelled a familiar aroma from the covered dishes. "Is that..."
"Lemon Herb Chicken? Yes, it is." Marco stated proudly.

   Ginevieve squealed in delight as their server lifted her cover. On her plate sat steamed vegetables and rice pilaf along with the chicken. *I have received a slice of heaven tonight.* "This smells delicious."

Marco blessed the food and they dug in. "This is one of the only things I can cook well." he admitted.

Ginevieve's fork stooped mid-air. "*You* cooked?"

Marco shrugged. "Most single men do these days." he continued eating.

Ginevieve wasn't prone to being emotional but Marco seemed to be pulling on every heart string possible. "That wasn't what I meant. It's just that it was a very nice gesture." In fact, everything about tonight had been nice.

Marco allowed himself a glance at Ginevieve to see her stricken expression. He was actually enjoying her company. He was sorry to see that the feeling wasn't mutual. "I guess if I were someone else you could actually relax and enjoy this moment."

Ginevieve had been lost in thought but Marco's words brought her back to the present. "Is that a question or a statement?"

"Both." Marco ventured.

Ginevieve thought about her answer. "Well if you *were* someone else, I doubt I would be having this moment so, no, I don't wish you were someone else."

Marco's eyes lit up. "So you are enjoying yourself?"

Ginevieve smiled shyly. "Would I be committing a crime of I said yes?"

"The most heinous of crimes," Marco's eyes brimmed with laughter.

Ginevieve held out her arms. "Well, I guess you better cuff me and bring me downtown now."

Marco let out a bellow of laughter that echoed in the evening atmosphere.

Ginevieve couldn't help but join him all the while thinking this moment was too good to be true. *Marco Angelo Arion Bolivar has a mighty fine sense of humor.*

"So do I."

Ginevieve's eyes brimmed with tears of joy as her heart responded to the Lord. *Yes, Lord, you most certainly do. I'm beginning to wonder why I never noticed.*

25

How could I let him talk me into this, Mariella berated herself thoroughly; *it's just going to complicate things in the end.* She had intended to get dropped off home. Instead she had been coaxed into joining Noelle for dinner before he dropped her off. *I should have known I'd be no match against his legal mind.* He had argued his way into her agreement.

"Are you comfortable?" Noelle noticed Mariella had been fidgeting for the past ten minutes.

Mariella nodded giving him a stiff smile. "Yes, thank you."
Noelle was relieved to see the waitress approaching with their orders. "We'll consider this a company dinner so don't worry about the tab."

Mariella nodded in understanding taking a sip of her lemonade. *Maybe if I keep my lips occupied with food I'll get by with nodding my head.*

As Mariella sat across from him, Noelle couldn't help thinking about how lovely she was. *And extremely quiet,* "That's a very nice color on you."

Mariella hid her surprise well. "Thank you."
Noelle applauded her. "Two words; At least I'm making progress here."

Mariella's old attitude flared up. "Are you making fun of me?"
Noelle nodded. "Attorney-designer privileges; haven't you read your contract yet?" he teased.

Mariella relaxed a bit realizing he wasn't serious. "As a matter of fact I have. Thank you for being so generous." Noelle had given her a competitive salary.

Noelle didn't know why he felt drawn to Mariella to help her in any way that he could. It was obvious that she had connections and didn't need his money but he was a man of conviction. He had felt inspired to be a blessing and so he was. "Everything I have belongs to God so he is the one who deserves praise. I'm just the steward."

Mariella had never heard it put like that. "Is that what you really believe?"

"It's what the Bible plainly tells us. We get in trouble when we start believing that what we have is ours. We are blessed *to be* a blessing." Noelle explained.

Mariella took a mental note to look the word up. She knew Naomi would be able to help her find scriptures on stewards. "How long have you known Christ as your Personal Savior?"

"I gave my life to God when I was twelve. I haven't looked back since." Noelle spoke between bites. "And you?"

"I've grown up knowing about God, but he was the God of the Bible. He's never been real to me until recently." Mariella was surprised by how comfortable she felt sharing with him.

"How recent," Noelle sensed for some reason this was important.

"Yesterday," Mariella said with assurance.

"Sweetheart, you sounded like a heavenly choir tonight," Shemiah whispered into Vannah's ear.

"Flattery will get you everywhere, Mr. Newman," Savannah teased.

"I can't help but speak the truth. Soon I'll be able to wake up to beautiful music every morning," he declared in awe.

Savannah sighed in resignation. "Well, what I am about to share will definitely not be music to your ears," she assured him.

Shemiah pulled her into an alcove outside of the music room. "Go ahead; I'm all ears," he folded his arms across his chest.

Savannah blew out a calming breath. "It appears that your cousin has not given up on harassing me. A package was hand delivered to my office today with photographs of me that were doctored so that I appear nude in them. The note that was delivered expressed that the pictures would hit the internet if I persisted in marrying you." She finished.

Shemiah could feel his blood rising in his veins. "I have just about had it with Lysander. Let me handle this once and for all. Don't make any moves," he consoled her.

"I just want this nightmare to be over. I knew that our relationship would encounter some difficulties, some opposition along the way but this? This is beyond comprehension." Savannah reasoned.

Shemiah tenderly gathered her close to his heart. "We'll work through this with the Lord's help. God has joined us together and no man can put us asunder. Believe that." He encouraged her.

They turned their thoughts and attentions heavenward and bombarded the heavens with prayer.

"I don't understand why I'm here. I have to get ready for prom," Serena Quintana whined to Brett Hamilton as she slouched on the loveseat in the assistant principle's office.

"I have a pretty good idea of why you're being detained," he confessed.

Serena sat upright then. "Do tell," she goaded him.

Before Brett could respond, the door to the office swung open, and with it several officers who were backed by Ms. Cinnamon Sugarbaker.

"I don't intend to make this a long, drawn out process so let's get straight to the point." she stated to Serena.

Serena flipped her hair back arrogantly. "I'm glad because I don't have all night," she rolled her eyes at Brett. She had no love for him now that he'd turned down her sexual advances twice during the senior trip. *He's such a wuss.*

"Ms. Quintana, after several inquiries into a recent defaming of school property, you have been found to be responsible for the destruction," Ms. Sugarbaker announced coolly.

"What are you talking about? I didn't do anything," Serena snapped.

"Wrong. You supervised underclassmen in the destruction of school property. You were identified by a school employee who saw you, you were handed over by those same underclassmen who received a lighter punishment than the one you will receive, plus, you were caught on camera supervising, handing over the cans, and sanitary items. You didn't do anything; you masterminded everything."

Gone was Serena's sassy attitude. In its place was indifference. "Look, just tell me what I have to do so I can go," she complained.

"I'm afraid it's not that simple," an officer spoke then. "What you did is considered a federal offence. Now, Ms. Sugarbaker has agreed to not press charges, but there are some consequences you will face."

Serena's eyes widened. "It was just a locker," she looked to Brett. "It was a hate crime," Ms. Sugarbaker informed her. "One of which I will not tolerate on my campus. That being said, all of your senior privileges have been suspended, including leaving campus for lunch. You are banned from prom, you are released from the cheerleading squad, your cheerleading scholarship has been revoked, you may attend graduation, but you will not march, and you will give three hours of community service time everyday after school until the end of the school year to the Environmental Club to help beautify the campus. This is in exchange for not pressing charges against you, for then you would have a criminal record," Ms. Sugarbaker outlined for her.

Serena was in tears and outraged. "How dare you? I'd rather die than live like this! You'll be hearing from my lawyers!" she stood up then.

"We have more than enough evidence to arrest you. Please don't force our hand in the matter," the officer warned her.

Brett stepped in as well. "Serena, Ms. Sugarbaker is giving you the sweet end of the deal. You get to keep your freedom, finish all your classes, attend graduation, and still get into college. She's not even suspending you," he reminded her.

Serena fumed inwardly but managed to pull herself together. *That low class worthless trash Nadia is not going to get away with this.* "Fine, I accept your deal." She stared cross-eyed at the administrator.

"I'm glad we could see eye to eye," Ms. Sugarbaker smiled sweetly. "Now, let's clean out your locker on senior row and get your letters turned in," she directed her.

"How do I look?" Nadia swirled in front of her mother dancing from one side of the living room to the other. She wore a floor-length satin and chiffon gown that floated in black and silver waves around her.

Columbia was truly speechless. She had done her daughters' hair right after school today and Nadia's upsweep was perfect for her off the shoulder dress. "You look radiant! You look so fly! I'm going to have to send you with a bodyguard," she laughed.

"That would be me," Rodia stepped into the living room slowly. She was still learning how to walk in stilettos. She wore a gold, form fitting, beaded, floor length gown that hugged her burgeoning curves. Her simple chignon said "classic elegance" and gave Rodia a more sophisticated and mature look far beyond her years.

Columbia clasped her hand to her heart. "Hold me, Lord, where have my babies disappeared to?" she shook her head in part amazement, part sadness.

Rodia rolled her eyes heavenward. "Mom, promise me you will not look like someone shot your best friend when Brett comes to pick us up," she pleaded.

"Yeah, Mom, We can't have you getting' all sentimental and stuff, It's just prom," Nadia reminded her.

Columbia looked reminiscent. "I know sweetie punkins. It's just that you both look so beautiful and young, so mature and so full of promise. I don't want to hurt anyone's children, but if something happened to you both, I... I just ..." she broke off.

The twins wrapped their arms around Columbia. For all her whining, complaining, and nagging, they knew their mother loved them and just wanted what was in their best interests. "It's gonna' be okay, Mom. We promise we won't do anything crazy." Nadia assured her.

"I've been so nervous about everything, but one thing I never doubt is that you love us," Rodia kissed her mother's cheek.

"You love me too," Delia added.

They all looked down and laughed. Delia had found her way out to the living room though she was supposed to be in bed. Columbia picked her up. "Yes, I do, which is why I'm taking you back to bed so you can get your beauty sleep. Tell your sisters goodnight," Columbia kissed her forehead as the sleepy princess of the family waved goodnight.

"Hurry back so we can pray before Brett gets here," Rodia urged.

Columbia thanked God that her daughters were so aware of His sovereignty in their lives. "I wouldn't miss it for the world," she assured them.

Brett was pulling up to his house when he felt his pocket vibrating. He quickly pulled out his cell phone. "Brett, speaking," he answered tersely, making quick work of unlocking his house and running upstairs to change.

"Hello, Brett. Did I catch you at a bad time?" Pastor Marks enquired.

"I'm in a time crunch trying to get ready for prom. We just returned about an hour ago from the senior trip," he stated while garments went flying every which way.

"I hope all went well. I just wanted to call and wish you a safe evening tonight. I understand you are taking Columbia's daughters to the prom?"

"Yes, and I intend to take every precaution to keep them safe, sir," Brett assured Pastor Marks.

"Glad to hear it. Let's lift up your evening to the Lord, then."
Brett bowed his head in obedience as he lifted up his own prayer. *Lord, redeem the time!*

"That's fantastic, Mariella!" Noelle surprised even his own self at how enthusiastic he came across.

"Thanks, I guess," she shrugged.

"I'd love for you to visit us at New Life Ministries this Sunday. My father is the Senior Pastor and I serve him." Noelle gave her a copy of their ministry brochure.

Mariella looked over the material. "My roommate attends your church. I'll consider it," she promised.

"Good, well, let's get you home," he announced.

"Okay," Mariella happily stood up, thankful that she would not have to endure another second of pent up breaths around him. Noelle Marks was one very appealing man.

It didn't escape Noelle's attention that Mariella seemed to want to be rid of him. *It's best this way. No good could come of my attraction to her.*

He that findeth a wife findeth a good thing and obtains favor from the Lord.

Exactly, thought Noelle. *I didn't find her. She's more like an atomic bomb dropped on my well-laid plans. No way am I calling this a good thing.*

170

"Brett, darling, you look so handsome," Anastasia Hamilton fussed over her only son, straightening his bowtie for the fourth time, smoothing his brow, brushing off his jacket, checking him with the precision of a military sergeant.

"Dear, please cease your grooming of the boy so I can take his picture," Bryant Hamilton groaned under the weight of his digital camera, clearly all out of patience with his wife.

Anastasia moved out of the way while her husband dived into his obsession: photography. "So, tell me more about your date," she asked her son. It had not escaped her notice that Brett had not invited his date to dinner, nor had she seen any pictures of the mysterious girl. Clearly, it was someone she would not approve of. Brett had never been so secretive.

"She's just a friend from school. We're not serious or anything," he assured his mother. *Not because I didn't try.*

"That's good to know. Who are her parents: the Cliffords'; the Quintanas'?" Her eye pinpointed the moment her son winced at the names.

"Neither," he replied stoically. "Her name is Nadia Newcomb, her mother is--"

"Columbia Newcomb," his mother cut him off. "I know her kind very well," she snorted. "Poor, opportunistic, always trying to rise above their station in life," she surmised.

Brett's back was to his mother so she could not see the look of outrage that flashed across his visage that he quickly put in check.

"Anastasia," Bryant warned. "Many people said as much about you when we married," he reminded her.

"That's because I am, and I recognize my kind very well. I had education and good looks to recommend me, while she has what-- A beauty shop, three children, all by different fathers? Please!" Anastasia laughed scornfully.

Brett was cut to the quick by his mother's disdain for Columbia. He had no words. He looked to his father who was clearly at a loss for words himself. "I'm leaving. I have to pick up Xavier in the limo. I'll be home by curfew," he strode out the door, not looking back.

His father caught up with him outside. "I'm sorry, Brett. You know how your mother can be," he cautioned him.

"That was not my mother in there," Brett stated coldly. "Lately, she's been getting snobbier as the days go by. She didn't used to act that way; thumbing her nose at other people because they have less than her? I don't invite my friends over, dad, because I'm afraid I won't have any left after she picks them apart," he growled.

"I don't know what's gotten into your mother lately, but we'll figure it out. Things will get back to normal," Bryant promised.

Brett realized then that his family had moved so far away from normal, he wasn't sure they could ever get it back.

"It feels great to have you back with us, Enrique," Savannah embraced her old friend.

"Yeah, man," Shemiah shook hands with him. "I don't know how you find the time, but your licks tonight on that bass were incredible," he acknowledged.

They sat down at the local café to order beverages.

"It's one of the only things that kept me sane during the trial in Venice, he admitted.

"We're glad to see you back here safe and sound," Savannah assured him.

"So am I. I thought about all that I was missing back here in the States," he agreed.

"More like who you were missing here in the States,' Shemiah teased.

Enrique grinned sheepishly. "Hey, what can I say? I've got it bad, and at this point I don't care who knows it," he confessed.

"Not even if she's walking in right now," Savannah baited him as she spotted Augusta making her way to their table.

"Not even then," Enrique went on. "I've come to realize that next to God, Augusta is the most important part of my life."

"Ah, how sweet; don't you think so, Augusta?" Savannah questioned her friend as she watched Enrique turn a few shades of pink.

Shemiah had stepped away from the table briefly to take care of some urgent business; setting Lysander Townsend straight.

"Lysander Townsend, here," the voice spoke clearly.
"This is your cousin, Shemiah."

"What's up?"

"I think you know this isn't about small talk so let's get to the point: if anything derogatory shows up about my fiancée in any form of publication or media, there will be some reckoning. You will be disowned from the family financially and socially. Every membership you enjoy will be terminated. All ties and communications with this family will end. Do you understand me?" Shemiah's tone brooked no argument.

"I was only trying to get her to call it off. She's not the one for you, Shemiah. Let me prove it to you," Lysander challenged him.

"Stay away from my fiancée. This is the only time I will *say* this to you," Shemiah warned him.

"I can't make that promise, but I will say this: may the right man win."

The line went dead and at that moment, Shemiah knew that war had been declared.

26

"Savannah, fancy meeting you here," Augusta greeted her with gusto. "This isn't your usual hangout spot," she noted.

"So true," Savannah admitted mischievously. "Although, I happen to know a certain set of twins loves this joint," she smiled.

"So, this was a happy coincidence, then?" Enrique questioned. He usually had a problem with being done in by women, but not this time. He would be willingly duped any day for a chance to be with the woman he loved.

Augusta hadn't planned on this moment but she was learning to go with the flow and roll with the punches. "Hi, Enrique," she waved shyly as she seated herself. *You would think by now that I would be over his magnetic good looks and natural charm, but clearly I am not,* she mused.

"Hello, yourself; it's really good to see you Augusta." Enrique let his eyes do most of the talking, sweeping over her in a gesture of tender possessiveness.

"Well, it seems as if Shemiah is ready to take off. I'll see you two later," Savannah swept up her things, hurrying off before either party could protest.

They both waved Shemiah goodbye turning to each other with a knowing smile. They had been bamboozled by the best. The funny thing was neither one of them minded much.

"So, how's business been for you?" Seth asked as he and Aliya walked at a leisure pace down Riverstreet.

"Things are going well. Business has picked up quite a bit and I'm grateful for the support I've found in the artistic community here. They've been great especially during my recovery," she noted.

Aliya enjoyed the pleasant silence between them as they walked. She was thankful for it, and for Seth not trying to fill every moment they were together with empty conversation.

"How was your mission trip?" Aliya looked to Seth then. They had found an empty bench near the dock upon which they took a seat.

"It was awesome. It was tremendous. There were so many needs there that I wish we had more manpower. We just couldn't do it all," Seth shared, regret evident in his voice.

"There's always next time, right? I mean, you seem committed to what you do and it is your life's work, correct?" Aliya reasoned.

Seth stared blankly at Aliya. *She was totally correct.* He laughed at himself. "I guess when you put it that way, I sound a little uptight," he chided himself.

"No, I mean, I didn't mean to make you feel as if you don't have a valid point; I'm just saying that I believe the Lord will allow you to complete what you need to in Ecuador. He didn't just bring you there for one-time relationships, but to foster relationships there."

Seth looked in surprise at Aliya. "Okay, who are you, and what did you do with the carefree woman I left behind?" Seth joked.

"That carefree woman grew up," Aliya informed him. "She put away childish things so she could embrace her future."

Seth turned to Aliya then, taking her hand in his. "A future that I want very much to be apart of," he studied her expression, seeing no fear there. He was relieved.

"I want that too," Aliya assured him. "But I want to take things slow, allow our friendship to progress. I feel like I've spent so much time fighting my feelings for you, that I've missed getting to know you," she admitted.

"So, you have feelings for me, do you?" Seth wiggled his eyebrows, causing Aliya to burst out in laughter. "That's such a wonderful sound. You should do it more often," he encouraged her.

Aliya regained her composure. "Lately, there hasn't been much to laugh about, so thank you," she wiped her eyes. "I do have feelings for you, Seth. I just don't want to rush into anything."

"I don't think we're rushing, Aliya. I believe we're making up for lost time," he clasped her hands. "When I got news, that you were kidnapped, nothing, and I mean *nothing* in the world mattered to me at that moment. If you weren't in my life, it would have amounted to great preaching, but not great living." Seth laid his heart on the line. "I know now how selfish, how insensitive I've been. I've been a fool for too long. Aliya, you're the woman I love, the woman I care about. When I was in Ecuador, thinking of home, my thoughts always returned to you, to seeing your face again. I've had plenty of time to think about what I want, and I know this now, more than ever, that you are what I want. I want you forever, and I'm willing to wait until you are ready to share forever with me." Seth raised her hands to his lips and pressed a soft kiss upon each one.

Though she managed not to swoon, Aliya was blown away. "I don't know what to say," she managed to choke out. "I never expected this so soon," she stammered.

Seth smiled reassuringly. "You don't have to say a word. I just wanted you to know how I feel about you so that there is no doubt in your mind concerning my intentions toward you," he released her hands then.

Aliya basked in Seth's admiration, touched by his sincerity. "You've made your intentions quite clear," Aliya acknowledged. "So, the question is, where do we go from here?"

Seth knew the only one who could give them true guidance was the Lord. "We take it our desires to the Father." He stated matter-of-factly.

Enrique motioned for Augusta to move closer inside of the booth they occupied. "I hope you have a few minutes to catch up," he wondered aloud.

"How can I refuse a man who sends me diamonds by hand delivery?" Augusta kidded.

Enrique bowed his head. "You thought it was over the top didn't you," he assessed.

Augusta smiled then. "Just a bit," she agreed. "But it's the thought that counts. It's a beautiful set," she declared.

"Not more beautiful than the woman who wears it," Enrique countered.

Augusta's dry throaty laugh filled the café. "My head won't fit through the door if you continue to flatter me, Enrique."

Enrique placed his hand to his heart. "You wound me, my fair lady. I mean it every time I say it. I never get tired of telling you how gorgeous, sweet, beautiful, talented, feisty, intriguing, intelligent, sexy, did I mention beautiful, you are," Enrique's eyes were twinkling with mischief as he watched Augusta turn all kinds of pink, her eyes rounding when she realized how much attention Enrique was drawing to them by his flowery, yet public declarations.

"Stop it, you show off, you're embarrassing me," Augusta laughed aloud.

"Well, since I'm embarrassing you, I may as well do it big," Enrique reasoned as he dropped to one knee and began to serenade her.

"You are my queen,
You are my dream,
I want to give my love to you.
I won't hesitate,
Please make no mistake,
All of my heart,
I give to you,
One day I'll say,
I do,
Forever I'll say
I love you."

Augusta was in tears as his tender words cut back the thorny places her heart had begun to develop in his absence. She stilled at the gentle touch of his fingers wiping away her tears. Augusta didn't know who moved first, but they were in each other's arms, holding on for dear life, the applause of customers thundering in her ears, like the sound of fresh rain on a steamy afternoon. *Lord, help me to never forget this moment,* she reflected. "I love you too, Enrique," Augusta whispered in his ear.

Calm settled over Enrique as Augusta's affirmation of love settled deep into the core of his being. This moment felt good and right and most importantly ordained of God. He drew back, his mind fixed. "Have lunch with me tomorrow?" he asked.

Augusta nodded. "It would be my pleasure," she looked into his eyes, losing herself in their depths.

Enrique stood then, extending his hand. "Until tomorrow," his devastating smile radiated with untold secrets.

"This is so amazing!" Rodia shouted over the music to Xavier.

"What," Xavier put a finger in his ear to block some of the noise out so he could hear his date.

"Never mind," Rodia shouted again as she swayed from side to side. The disc jockey was a Christian who only played gospel music, and at the moment he was playing one of her favorite artists.

Xavier moved alongside her, twisting, turning, and sliding, creating his own movements to the beat of the music while on the other side of the dance floor Nadia and Brett stood, Brett enfolding Nadia in his arms, enjoying the view.

"I think they hit it off pretty well, don't you?" Brett leaned into her ear to share his thoughts.

Nadia nodded because at the moment it was all she could do. *I can't believe I'm here in Brett's arms!* She shifted her attention around the room at the curious glances that came her way. *I know what they're thinking, but it's only for one night.* Nadia didn't feel saddened by the fact that her mother insisted on them not dating. She was finally beginning to understand the magnitude of what she would be getting herself into if she and Brett got serious right now. *To everything there is a season and a purpose under heaven.* There was no way she would continue to dwell on what could be; she would enjoy the here and now.

A sharp tap came on Brett's shoulders. He turned around annoyed to face one of his teammates. "Hey, man, what's up?"

"Man, this party's 'bout done. We ready to get crunk; a few of us rented a beach house for tonight to get the party started, if you know what I mean," he leered at Nadia. "You ready to ditch this scene?"

Brett shook his head, knowing what the party would lead to. "Nah, man, that's not my thing. We've got other plans," he added.

"I see; you trying to put that on lock already?" the team member smiled seductively at Nadia who had stepped behind Brett.

Before he knew anything, Brett had lifted him by the collar of his tux. "Look, man, it's not like that; and if I hear anything that says otherwise on Monday, you'll be handing over your letters and your teeth;

Got it?" Brett's menacing glare silenced his teammate. He let him fall to the ground.

"I was only looking out for you bro," the teammate dusted himself off.

"Thanks, but no thanks," Brett turned to Nadia. "Let's find Rodia and Xavier and get out of here," Brett suggested clenching his fists and taking a deep breath to calm down. The last thing he wanted was to end his perfect date by putting a fist in the mouth of his teammates. If there was one who was bold enough to approach him with such nonsense, there were others. He looked regretfully at Nadia then. "I'm sorry you were subjected to that meathead," he said gruffly.

Nadia grabbed his hand and pulled him along through the crowed dance floor. "It's okay; after all we knew we would be the talk of the town. Don't sweat it." She urged him with a smile.

"Have I told you how wise and beautiful you are?" Brett smiled as he allowed himself to be led along by the fair Nadia who had definitely caught the attention of more than a few of his friends.

Nadia grinned back. "Tell me more," she replied saucily as they spotted Xavier and Rodia hurrying to meet them.

Shemiah was settling in for the night after a satisfying evening with Savannah when his phone rang. He picked up apprehensively due to the lateness of the hour.

"Shemiah, speaking." He settled onto his couch.

"Hey, Shemiah, I know it's late, but I wanted to run something by you and see if you could help out," Tatyanna's business tone rolled over him.

Shemiah sat upright then. "Sure, go ahead."

"Well, to make a long story short, Rosalynn has been having some family issues and has decided to move out. She's looking for her own place and I wondered if you could rent out your beach house to her?" she proposed.

Shemiah thought on it for a moment. "I'm soon to be married and I'm sure Savannah and I will utilize the house in the future, but if she'd like to stay there for a few months temporarily without cost, she's welcome to. Would staying there until December help out?" he questioned.

"I think that would work for her on several levels. I'll run the idea by her and see what she thinks. I hadn't been thinking far enough ahead when I suggested it to her," Tatyanna chastised herself. *Of course as a newlywed, he'd want to take advantage of the spot,* she smiled inwardly.

"No problem. Give her a few days and let me know before we return from Montego Bay. I'll have my people come in to freshen everything up for her." He assured.

"Thanks, Shemiah, for being so generous; it's one of your best qualities," Tatyanna noted.

"Not a problem. Goodnight, Tatyanna." Shemiah hung up the phone ready to rest up so he could be in top shape for whatever tomorrow held.

Naomi had settled into a surprisingly pleasant phone conversation with Giovanni Cartellini. He'd shared with her about his early childhood experiences, things that had shaped him to become the man he was, things that had shaped his life long interest in personal security. She also understood his fear of committing to a permanent relationship that could be so quickly wiped out through a senseless act of violence.

She listened intently, thinking of how easy it would be to deny their feelings for each other, but suddenly she no longer wanted to. She wanted to be the person in his life that he could find happiness with, experience constancy and faithfulness with, to understand that though death was final, love was eternal, and could live on beyond death. Our mortality should be what made love a necessary ingredient in our daily lives. *I think I finally understand what the Lord has been trying to tell me. Perfect love casts out all fear; the fear of the unknown, the fear of 'what if'. I've been creating all these scenarios in my mind because of fear, but what have I created in my mind based on faith?* Naomi realized that she hadn't been letting the peace of God rule her thoughts but the fear of the enemy. She closed her eyes and allowed herself to really dream of a life with Giovanni, a life that she had been putting on the backburner, because of her fears. *I choose to embrace what you have to offer, Lord, by faith.* Gone was the uncertainty. Gone was the uneasiness. Gone was the ominous feeling that had stalked her every time she thought of Giovanni carrying out his duties. Naomi looked down at her night robe, surprised to see it awash with tears.

"Naomi? Are you still there?" Giovanni had been going on about what a privilege it was to serve Enrique when he heard a soft sniffle.

"Yes, I'm here," she sniffed. "My thoughts just drifted for a moment," she assured him.

"I must be boring you with all this talk," he surmised.

"No, not at all; it's just that you got me to really thinking about your profession and all of the danger seen, and unseen that you face. How do you handle it?" Naomi asked, wanting to hear it from his perspective.

"He that keeps Israel neither slumbers nor sleeps; I know that if God can keep a nation whose enemies surround her and are a constant threat, then my safety is but a light thing with the Lord," his confidence and faith in God rang out.

"With your faith in God, and my faith in His love for you, I believe we can make it through anything," Naomi declared.

"I had the time of my life," Nadia giggled as Brett held her hand in the limo. They were outside her home a full twenty minutes before curfew. Brett and Xavier had been more than perfect gentlemen. They had taken Rodia and Nadia for a carriage ride around Oglethorpe Park. Brett had arranged for a photography session at the park, followed by late night sundaes at a quaint ice-cream shop. It was the perfect end to a beautiful night.

"So have I," Brett murmured as he effectively silenced her giggles with a kiss on the cheek.

Nadia felt the light brush of his lips against her cheek like a permanent imprint. She swallowed. "I've never been kissed before," she watched his face in the shadows, hoping that he wouldn't make fun of her.

"Neither have I," Brett smiled sheepishly. "You don't believe everything you hear, do you, Nadia?" he challenged her.

"Of course not, but you've been on plenty of dates," she reminded him.

"True," he conceded. "But I've never been more inspired to have that first kiss than I am right now," he chuckled.

"Well, you'll just have to live with the inspiration, then. I've decided my first kiss belongs to my husband," she informed him.

"I totally respect that," Brett grinned, "But I don't know if I can wait that long. I plan to wait until I'm engaged to be married," he shared.

Nadia almost burst with the knowledge. Brett Hamilton, All-American, Scholar Athlete, and resident hottie, was saving himself for the right woman. *Now that's what I call a real man*, Nadia mused to herself, proud to be escorted home by a young man with such class and caliber.

Xavier loosened his tuxedo tie so he could finally take a real breath. "I don't know why these monkey suits are required," he said jokingly to Rodia who sat next to him on the porch swing.

"You looked really handsome tonight, Xavier," Rodia stared up at him, adoration written across her features.

"Call, me Xay," he grinned. "I suppose that's why guys put these on," he chuckled. "So, they can bask in some male appreciation."

Rodia looked away then. *Great, now I've really done it.* "I mean, you look nice," she commented coolly.

Xavier touched her cheek then. "I think you're hot, too, Rodia."
Rodia turned swiftly to face him. "You really shouldn't say things like that," she shot him a look etched with hurt. "Especially, when it's not true," she noted.

Xavier stood; insulted that she would think he was playing her. "Have you looked in the mirror, lately? Rodia, you're gorgeous, and if no one's ever told you, then I'm sorry, but I won't apologize for being the first," Xavier assured her.

Rodia stood up then. "I'm sorry, I just... you can have any girl you want ; you don't need to make me feel good about myself, and I don't lack confidence, its just that you're you, and I'm me. Guys like you don't normally pick girls like me," Rodia reasoned.

Xavier was getting hot under the collar the more she went on. "Guys like you? What's that supposed to mean?" he glared at her. "You know what, never mind; I don't want to know," he turned away only to see Nadia and Brett headed up the walkway.

Rodia didn't know what just happened but she felt sure she'd just insulted him and the conversation was far from over. The overhead light came on just then and the front door opened to reveal their mother.

"Evening, Ms. Newcomb," Xavier spoke politely, all trace of hurt gone from his voice.

"Good evening," Columbia voice held a trace of tiredness as she waited for Nadia and Brett to make it up the steps. "Thank you both for bringing my babi—I mean daughters home safely." She winked at Nadia.

"Not a problem," Brett assured her. "Thank you for the privilege of allowing us to be their first dates," he grinned, his smile lighting up the night.

"Thanks, Ms. Newcomb. I definitely had a night I am not soon to forget," Xavier looked Rodia squarely in the eye.

The gentlemen quickly said their goodbyes, bounded down the steps and back to the limousine for they too had curfews.

Columbia opened the door wide to let her little ladies in. "We'll have breakfast in the morning so I can hear all about your first dates," she told them.

Rodia and Nadia nodded in agreement, thankful for the reprieve from interrogation and hurried to their rooms to get ready for bed. Columbia decided she could wait until tomorrow to find out if her two angels had learned any lessons about the perils of dating.

27

Tatyanna opened her door to a tired Rosalynn who stood in her doorway like a wilted flower, watered too many times. "Come in," she urged. "Let me help you with some of those bags."

Rosalynn accepted the help gratefully. She had sped away from the meeting tonight to collect more of her things from Carlton's house before he arrived back home. She didn't want to face him and it was more than that; she didn't feel safe around him anymore. Something had changed about him during their last argument. "Thanks, Taty. I'm just feeling a little drained that's all." Rosalynn had to contact her client list and let them know she was no longer working in conjunction with her brother. Most of them had still wanted to continue to utilize her services for which she was grateful. She would have to come up with a name for her new business and incorporate next week. It was a lot to do but do it she must. She had grabbed something to eat alone and worked on her business plan before realizing how late it was. She had headed to Tatyanna's home then.

"I spoke with Shemiah tonight and he let me know that his beach house would be available rent free until December if you're interested," Tatyanna informed her.

Rosalynn was taken aback by his generosity. "That would be perfect for now. It would give me an opportunity to save up more funds so that I could purchase a home of my own. I could utilize the beach itself for group workouts until it got really cold. I definitely accept his offer. I'll let him know on Sunday and how important it is that Carlton doesn't know where I'm staying," she thought aloud.

Tatyanna sat across from Roz on the sofa. "Do you want to talk about it?"

Roz sighed in remorse. "There's really nothing to talk about. Carlton thinks he owns me, can tell me what to do, who to see, where to go, how long to stay out; it's been going on too long, and I'm sick and tired of it. He has no social life of his own and is not interested in having one. He detests Nicholas, granted he and I have not always been on good terms, but Nicholas has admitted his mistakes, I've forgiven him, and Carlton should just let it go, but he won't." Roz threw up her hands.

"Well, I don't have an overprotective brother, but I can tell you as an older sibling that when someone messes with Tehinnah, it gets me fired up and sometimes when she's over it, I'm still gung-ho about getting back at them. Let's just pray that Carlton will see the error of his ways. If something serious comes of this relationship between you and Nick, it will be difficult to enjoy it with a thorn in your side. He's your only living relative, right?" Tatyanna enquired.

Roz nodded. "It makes this situation really hard for me. I don't want to choose between them," she groaned. "Nick wants nothing to do with me at this point, and I don't blame him. I'm not going to pursue a relationship with anyone until this drama is behind me."

"Let's take this problem to the Lord so that he can work it out. Maybe you won't have to." Tatyanna encouraged her as they bowed their heads and allowed God free course to move on Rosalynn's behalf.

"Here's the plan, Mr. Estrada," Fabian Ciccone handed over a detailed document of safety issues, strategies, and personnel coverage for the trip to Montego Bay. "Our contacts in Jamaica informed us that the resort you will be staying in has the finest security on the island. Your security will be airtight, sir. Fabritza will be monitoring Mariella. When we connect with Francheska, she will monitor Augusta and Aliya discreetly. We will remain with you at all times and at a courteous distance when you are with Diamond Rose," Fabian noted. They had decided to give Augusta, Aliya, and Mariella code names once they reached the island: Augusta was Diamond Rose, Aliya, Pearl Lily, and Mariella, Wild Flower.

Each man looked over the plan, finding nothing at fault with it. Enrique had given Nicholas and Giovanni permission to make sure their interests were protected as well. He did not want any distractions to any man's safety while they were off domestic soil. He had forgone taking the company jets and hired private ones so that they would not be a sure target in international waters.

"The plan looks good," he looked down at his watch: it was well past midnight. "Well, let's get some rest so we can enjoy tomorrow's festivities. Fabian, Fabritza, we'll see you in the morning." Nicholas escorted them to the door, not missing the fact that Giovanni had followed Enrique down the hall. *Miss Fabritza, if you make one more misstep, you are off this assignment,* Nicholas declared to himself.

While Columbia had retired to her room and found herself quickly asleep once more, the night was far from over for her daughters. Rodia and Nadia lay on their bedroom floor amongst blankets and pillows whispering and giggling and spilling secrets.

"You spent an awfully long time in that limo alone with Brett," Rodia whispered accusingly.

Nadia rolled her eyes. "Please Little Miss Porch Swing," she giggled. "I was trying to give you some time alone with Xavier," she countered.

"Did Brett kiss you?"

"Do you think I would tell?"

"Answer the question."

"On the cheek; are you satisfied?"

Rodia rolled over and covered her head with her pillow. "No."

"What's the matter?"

"Xavier didn't kiss me; he didn't even try."

"He seemed upset when we walked up; what did you do, Rodi?"

Rodia rolled over again stuffing the pillow under her chin and looked her twin in the eye. "I think it was something I said," she whispered.

Nadia knew when she used that phrase it was usually a doozie. Rodia was normally a very genial girl, but every once in a while, her words could slice you in two. "Spill it. What did you say?"

"Well, he tried to flatter me, and I basically told him I didn't need it. He can have any girl he wants and I'm out of his league," she finished.

Nadia winced. "Rodi, tell me you didn't say that to Xavier," she closed her eyes imagining his stunned expression.

"But, it's true: he *can* have any girl he wants. I really like him, but I'm not getting mixed up in that contest. Do you know girls have money on who's going to be his next girlfriend?"

"Are you kidding?" this was news to Nadia.

"Where have you been?" Rodia looked at her sister, flabbergasted that she was clueless on this piece of news. "I wish I was but I'm not," she sighed. "I figured him asking me out was just a way to throw people off, you know?" she reasoned.

"Obviously, you were wrong." Nadia smirked.

"What do you mean?" Rodia sat up in apprehension.

"When you were in the shower, Brett sent me a text," she grinned knowingly. "Apparently whatever you said ticked Xavier off so much that he wrote a blog about you and posted it on his web page. Way to go, sis."

Rodi smacked her hand against her forehead. "I'm gonna faint."

"Get this: the title of the blog is, *My Best Date Ever*." Nadia sighed romantically. "It's already gotten a hundred comments. You, little sis, are an overnight sensation." Nadia spoke proudly.

"Did he put my name?" Rodi jumped up and powered up their computer, careful to mute the sound.

"No, but he did mention that it was his prom date. Everybody knows that it's you, Rodi. You can't hide," Nadia giggled.

As she signed on to her own page and went in search of his, she thought aloud. "I'm going to wring his neck," she whispered.

Nadia looked over her shoulder as the blog appeared. They read it in silence.

My Best Night Ever - Cra Xay

Tonight was incredible! I danced, I shouted, I ate a lot, and I hung out with some real cool peeps. I got a chance hang with someone new, someone that helped me to see some things in a different light. It takes a lot for a girl to throw me for a loop, but this girl did. My prom date scored a three-pointer and dunked on my perceptions. Here I thought all this time that I was an equal opportunity guy: you know, give a girl an opportunity to get to know me before she jumped to any conclusions. But, I was wrong, so now I feel I gotta set the record straight. Let me tell you what kind of guy I am: I'm the kind of guy that likes to read, that likes to go for long walks in the park. I'm the kind of guy that prefers conversation over adoration because I can get applause on the court. I'm the kind of guy that judges a girl not on her bra size, but on her brain power. I'm the kind of guy that wants my first kiss to go to my wife, not my girlfriend. I'm the kind of guy who just wants to enjoy life and not rush into things that I might regret later. Just want to set the record straight. If I'm uncool for doing so, that's fine; I'll still be CraXay regardless. This was my best date ever because I know who I am and what I want out of every date I'll go on from here on out. Peace.

Rodia truly felt miserable after reading his blog. *Wow, what a verbal slap in the face.* "I'm never going to be able to show my face again," she clicked out of the blog.

Nadia shook her head. "See, that's where we differ in opinion. Xavier was upset, but he was also convicted. Maybe he didn't realize the picture he was painting about himself; hotshot jock who only dates the popular girls. You just made all guys everywhere step up their game when it comes to dating. He thought he was giving you an opportunity; what he got was an opportunity to get *checked.* I'd say your evaluation was on point."

"Well, I don't think that's how the rest of the student body will see it. Out of the pot and into the flames," Rodia joked.

"Don't sweat it. Just play it cool and things will blow over. Besides, Mom has banned us from dating anyway. It's not like it matters right now," she reminded her.

Rodia climbed atop her bed feeling more miserable by the minute. "I'll just pretend that I didn't insult my long time crush," she yawned sleepily.

Nadia yawned in agreement. "I won't mention it if you don't."
The girls turned in for the night, unaware that by tomorrow their lives would be turned upside down.

"Thank you for an enjoyable outing," Ginevieve spoke in soft tones, mindful of the lateness of the hour and her neighbors. It was nearing one in the morning. They had lost track of time out in the park.

"My pleasure; I would like to meet tomorrow during the day. Would that be alright with you?" Marco was working hard to restrain the urge to gather her in his arms.

"That would be fine," Ginevieve nodded.

"Dress comfortably," he added.

"Okay." Ginevieve waved goodnight and watched as he made his way back to his vehicle. It was a vintage Mercedes in mint condition. *I wonder what he has up his sleeve for our next outing.* He had certainly surprised her tonight with his thoughtfulness and manners. Still, Ginny refused to read more into it than a man who had an ego to assuage and a reputation to restore. *At the end of these three days, we'll go our separate ways; He'll return to his cordial self, and I will continue to admire him from afar.* The only problem was, Ginevieve was beginning to like what she learned about him up close and personal.

"Were you able to procure it?" Enrique closed the door behind Giovanni.

"Yes, and without a problem, I might add," he chuckled.

Enrique had sent Giovanni on a mission unbeknownst to anyone but himself. He hadn't wanted word to get out about his next move, especially with the press still pounding the pavement.

Giovanni handed him the velvet box. Enrique opened it reverently. The ring, shaped like a bud, held a round center stone, with pave set diamonds surrounding it. It was a new creation by his favorite New York jeweler and it was a perfect compliment to his Diamond Rose. His hand shook with the enormity of it all. He anticipated the moment he would slip it across her finger. "Make the necessary preparations for lunch tomorrow. I want everything to be perfect. Tell them I am willing to buy out their restaurant for the afternoon. I want lilies and roses. Spare no expense, just make it happen." He instructed.

"Aye, Aye, captain," Giovanni grinned. He was experiencing his own cloud nine and didn't begrudge Enrique his moment of happiness.

Enrique closed the door and went to the Lord in prayer.

28

Saturday morning dawned bright and sunny for the residents of Savannah. The men's barbecue was scheduled to take place later in the evening at Seth Davis' home and he'd spent the better part of the evening after meeting with Aliya setting things up. This morning he just wanted to enjoy the feel of sand beneath his feet and brisk air whipping at his cheeks as he ran parallel to the beach with Jamar. They slowed to a stop as their beach house was spotted in the distance. It wasn't often he could catch up with Jamar in the morning. He was usually working at his studio he'd set up recently in the warehouse district. Seth had been impressed with his brother's diligence and attention to detail with his work. He'd encouraged him to keep at it and accomplish his educational goals. He knew how easy it was to get sidetracked. Jamar was in his last year of schooling so he needed to maintain his focus.

"Gasping for breath, big bro?" Jamar teased.

"Nah," Seth grinned. "Just thinking," he straightened up reaching as far as he could skyward.

"About what," Jamar ran in place. He wasn't quite ready to slow down.

Seth bent backwards then straightened up. "Aliya; she's different," he considered that thought for a moment. "Or, maybe I just came to my senses; either way, she's pretty incredible." He deduced.

Jamar laughed out loud. "I think it's definitely the latter. Aliya has always been incredible; I think it took you leaving the country to realize that. I'm just glad you're here in one piece," Jamar chuckled.

"I really enjoyed being with her last night," he said with some surprise. "She's very discerning and she knows how to put things into perspective so simply that when she's done speaking, you wonder why you didn't figure it out yourself," Seth spoke with admiration.

"That about describes Aliya to a tee," Jamar agreed.

"She's sweet, playful, yet, I know what happened to her has changed her in some way," he explained.

"I think it's changed us all," Jamar reasoned. "I've learned to appreciate life a little more and not take for granted the people God places in my life," he smacked Seth on the back. "Including an overbearing brother like you," he added.

"Hey, I try to do my best in that department," the brothers walked back to their beach house arms slung about each other in a gesture of comradeship.

God smiled upon their bond of brotherhood and friendship knowing how much stronger it would become.

Aurielle Foqua was used to doing everything herself. She was a techie after all; a computer guru, a regular fix it up, do-it-yourself kind of girl. So, after trying for two hours to install her new sprinkler system, she was still having difficulty, she finally surrendered her superior knowledge over to the God of all wisdom. *Lord, can you help me out here? This is supposed to be a simple task. Am I missing something, here? Please help me to get this done.*

"Having trouble?" Dr. Trey Jones asked. He stood on the sidewalk watching with interest as his neighbor tried to assemble what looked to be her sprinkler system.

Aurielle's head swung up quickly as she stood up brushing herself off. "Actually, it embarrasses me to admit it, but I am," she straightened.

Trey stepped forward onto her lawn and made his way to through her tools strewn about her walkway. "This looks similar to one I installed recently." He adjusted the main line, checked the nozzle, checked the water pressure, and then returned to the front of the house. "Alright, see if it will work." He suggested.

Aurielle turned on the hose. Unbeknownst to Trey, he was standing near one of the sprinklers. "Ah!" Trey jumped out of the way, but it was too late. His entire backside was soaking wet.

Aurielle giggled. "I'd say it's definitely working now," she covered her mouth to hold back the laughter.

Trey sent her a playful glare. "You owe me big time," he warned her.

"How about lunch?" she offered. "You deserve it for coming to the rescue," she complimented him.

Trey looked at his watch. "I've got to check on the status of a patient this morning, but I'm certainly going to hold you to lunch," he promised.

"I'll see you then," Aurielle agreed as she made her way inside her home. She couldn't wait to share lunch with the eligible Dr. Jones.

Mariella was thankful for the peace and tranquility that greeted her at Noelle Marks' residence. Most of his neighbors were out carrying on their routines so she had an opportunity to put some finishing touches on the rooms she'd been working on. She got down to business quickly getting all of the drilling out of the way. An hour later, she was detailing a painted border when she overheard voices. *Funny, I didn't hear them come in,* she wondered.

She moved down the hallway from the guest bedroom she'd been working in when she overheard Noelle speaking. Apparently he'd come to check out the work as well; and he was not alone.

"Well, dad, what to you think?" Noelle remarked.

John Marks perused the room, walking around and observing each aspect, bookshelves, escritoire, plush sofas, animal prints, and antiques scattered tastefully about the room. "I think she's done a wonderful job." He turned to his son then. "If I didn't know any better, I'd think she was applying for the position of wife, not interior decorator," he chuckled.

Noelle had been sipping some orange juice; he nearly choked on the words coming out of his father's mouth. "Dad, please don't go there," he cautioned. "She's inexperienced, barely out of the school room, and too beautiful for her own good," he concluded. "I don't need those kinds of complications right now," he added.

"But, son,--"

Noelle held up his hands to stay his father's further input. "Dad, please, let it go," he urged. "I need someone who is cultured, who is at least established in her chosen career path," he reasoned. "Not someone who is still trying to find their way. Mariella is a talented young girl; she's not ready for a relationship."

"Have you asked her?" Pastor Marks crossed his arms.

"Are you kidding? No, I haven't asked her," he shot back. "Besides, she is under my employ; it would be unethical for me to date her and pay her as well," he surmised.

"Is that why you chose to hire her instead of asking her out?" Pastor Marks challenged him. "I may be old, but I'm not dead, son."

Noelle rolled his eyes heavenward. "Lord, what did I do to deserve this?" He glared at his father. "I've moved back to town. I'm establishing my practice here. Why isn't that enough for you?"

"Son, I just want you to be happy," Pastor Marks implored. "I don't want you to wake up one day with regrets. Having a career is fine, but you know that God has called you to more," he reminded him.

Mariella had heard more than enough. She inched away from the living area and made her way back to the guest room. She gathered up her things and exited the house through the garage, thankful that Noelle's floor plan allowed for a speedy escape. *I will not cry, I will not cry.* It was her mantra as she called for Enrique to pick her up. He will know what to do. She couldn't face Noelle after hearing what he thought of her. *She's inexperienced; barely out of the schoolroom; too beautiful for her own good.* The words kept replaying in her mind. It was the first time Mariella could remember that her beauty did not work in her favor. Instead, it was a liability. She would finish the project quickly and be done with Noelle Marks. It was in their best interests. *Better to know how he feels now than to be disappointed later,* she thought as Enrique's car pulled up to the curb.

"Mom, thank you so much for taking us out to breakfast," Rodia said between bites. "You didn't have to," went on. "Your cooking is the best hands down," she admitted.

Columbia savored the syrup flavored bacon that tasted like heaven. She shook her head. "Every now and then your mom needs a break too," she confessed.

"We know, but you're still the best cook this side of heaven," Nadia agreed with her sister as she took another bite of her omelet.

The noise in the restaurant was nearly deafening, a local little league team entering in to be served before a morning game. Columbia leaned in to make sure her daughters could hear her. "Alright, who wants to go first?" she looked to each twin noting Rodia's look of terror etched on her face.

"I'll go," Nadia quickly volunteered. "Last, night was so fun; after the dance, Brett and Xavier took us for a carriage ride through downtown. I really enjoyed myself," Nadia grinned. "Brett is such a gentleman," she sighed dreamily.

Columbia looked to Rodia. "Well, Rodi, what about you?"

"It was okay. Xavier was cool and all, but last night made me realize I'm not ready to date," she concluded by sipping her orange juice.

"Speaking of which," Columbia dropped the bomb. "I've been rethinking my position on letting you young ladies date."

Rodia's orange juice came spewing out of her mouth. "What did you just say?"

"Mom, please don't play around like that," Nadia huffed. "I really don't want to get my hopes up," she warned.

"I'm serious." Columbia assured them. "I've been thinking about how mature you two have become and I thought to myself that if I've done my job as a parent, then you ladies should know how to conduct yourselves. I have to trust that the standards I've instilled in you will help you to make the right decisions and that you will trust me enough to be open with me when you feel you are in over your head; that being said, I am allowing you to date." Columbia looked to both her slack-mouthed daughters. "This is a Kodak moment: my punkin noodles are speechless," she chuckled.

Nadia swallowed hard. "It's not everyday that a girl gets her emancipation proclamation for dating," she joked.

Rodia was completely mute on the subject. She was still recovering from shock.

"Well, there are some guidelines," Columbia stated emphatically. "You must commit to the same guy, no one over eighteen for one year. If you chose to end the relationship, you will refrain from entering another relationship until you finish your first year of college. Your grade average must not drop. The
only reasons you will have for a valid break up will be if the person you choose to date is verbally, physically, or sexually abusive, or causes you to be at odds with your goals for life. There will be no sexual contact, no mouth to mouth contact, and you dates will occur on Friday or Saturday only. There will be no gentlemen over unless they are invited for dinner. Your curfew will be eleven o'clock. Are there any questions?" Columbia asked as she slid each of her daughters a copy of her guidelines to sign. She'd prayed about it and God had helped her to create realistic and clear expectations for her daughters. She also had copies posted on their doors

and the refrigerator. "You are free to choose; choose wisely. Your first official date will be dinner at our house," Columbia collected the signed copies.

"This is just a formality for me," Rodia noted. "I don't have any prospects," she sighed sullenly.

Nadia was beyond giddy. "I can't wait to tell Brett! He'll be so happy for me," she added, glancing sideways at her sister who looked the picture of a tornado approaching at breakneck speed.

"You have prospects," Columbia corrected. "You just need to apologize for misjudging Xavier," Columbia brought her coffee to her lips and let her daughter digest that statement.

Rodia stared flabbergasted that her mother's words. "How much did you hear last night?"

"Enough to know when my daughter needed rescuing before she puts both high heels in her mouth," Columbia chuckled.

Rodia groaned, placing her head between her head. "How humiliating," she shook her head in regret.

"You don't know the half, Mom," Nadia added. "Xavier wrote a blog about it. Rodia really got him thinking, though. I think he needed to be taken down a notch or two," Nadia reasoned.

Columbia sighed then. "I think that you two should talk on Monday and clear the air. Xavier made some valid points, Rodia. What if he judged you solely based on appearances? He obviously did not, or he never would have asked you out. Sometimes we as women underestimate our worth. You *are* a beautiful, bright, sweet girl: I think you should give Xavier some credit for being mature enough to recognize it," Columbia advised. "Lord, knows when I was your age, guys just weren't that smart; they usually went for the physical regardless if the girl had clouds between her ears," Columbia assured her.

Rodia laughed then at the picture that presented. "I know now that I was wrong about him, but I can be real with you and tell you that it will be a hot day in heaven before I get up the nerve to approach him," Rodia confessed.

Columbia sympathized with her daughter. It was hard to admit you were wrong, but the sooner you did, the better you felt. "It's your choice, but I think that you should make amends quickly. I don't want a repeat of your sister's situation at school, because I will come out there," Columbia warned her.

"On second thought," Rodia straightened at the thought of Columbia paying a visit. "Making amends sounds like a great idea."

As Enrique drove his cousin back to her apartment, he was hard pressed not to pry. Clearly Mariella was upset about something; she had red-rimmed eyes when he picked her up and she had remained tight-lipped the entire drive. *Lord, how can I minister to her?*

Let her know that I love her. Let her know I have a plan for her. Let her know that to everything there is a season and a time to every purpose under heaven.

Enrique dove in. "Mariella," he glanced at her sullen expression.

"Yes?" Mariella hadn't intended on talking. At the moment she was still brooding over Noelle's conversation. *That's what I get for eavesdropping.*

"God loves you tremendously," he shared. "He's working out a plan for you; know that everything has a season, and there's a time for every purpose under heaven," he encouraged her.

Mariella glared at him. "Enrique, I'm really not in the mood," she warned him.

"Sorry," he shrugged. "God just wanted you to know. I'm just the messenger," he added.

Mariella looked away then. "It's His entire fault," she muttered.

"Pardon me?" Enrique leaned over to hear her.

"Never mind," she muttered.

"Mariella, not to pry or anything, but if you ever need to talk about it, I'm here for you; we don't always understand God's ways or God's thoughts, but sometimes it helps to share with others. It can be a great comfort to find that someone else has gone through the same situation." He confided.

"I'll try to remember that," Mariella gave him a slight smile as she got out his car and headed for her house. After all, it wasn't her cousin's fault that she was feeling so unsure.

"Take care, and have fun tonight at the sleepover," he added.

As Enrique pulled away from the curb, he lifted his cousin up once more to the Lord. *Father, when her heart is overwhelmed, lead her to your Son, the Rock who is higher than all of the mountains we face.*

191

29

"You look so beautiful," Savannah gushed as Marilyn walked out of the dressing room in her wedding gown. It was her final fitting and she was getting quite antsy. "I'm going to cry," Savannah waved back the tears as a flood of emotions crashed over her. *It's really happening; my parents are finally getting married!*

"You better not cry right now," Marilyn laughed, holding back her own tears at how beautiful her Divine Design original creation looked. Aliya had decided to name her creation *At Last,* giving hint to the timeless beauty and extravagant beadwork of the garment. "Aliya will blame you if I cry a river all over this dress," Marilyn cautioned her.

"That's right," Augusta noted as she helped Savannah fasten the clasps in the back of her gown.

Vivian Worth stepped out of her dressing room looking fabulously fit for her age in her royal purple floor length beaded gown. She stopped dead in her tracks when she saw Marilyn. "Elder Worth is going to have to pick Andre up off the floor when he sees you," she teased.

"Oh, please, Andre's seen me a thousand times," Marilyn reasoned. "He'll be glad to have the formality over and done with," she assured them.

"But it's so much more than a formality," Savannah interjected. "I've been waiting all my life for this moment, and you're not going to downplay it," she added.

"I'm not trying to downplay the importance of the event," she chuckled. "I'm simply letting you know that if your father had his way, we would have eloped," she turned around in front of the mirror, examining her train.

"And Daddy knows I would have had his hide," Savannah assured her mother as the other ladies laughed in agreement. Everyone knew how adamant Savannah had been about her parents getting back together, especially when she realized they had never stopped loving each other.

"Well, everything has been finalized so I know that Andre can wait just one more week," Vivian reflected.

"You're going to make one beautiful bride, mom," Savannah sighed, admiring her mother's svelte form.

"I second that," Augusta smiled. "One can only hope that one day I'll look half as good at your age," she noted.

"Your day will come," Marilyn encouraged them all. "Just take it one day at a time and get to know your intended," she advised them.

"Just don't let true love pass you by and take every opportunity; enjoy the one that God has gifted you with," Vivian volunteered.

Each lady grew silent, content with thoughts of the very special man that God had placed in their life.

Columbia, Nadia, Rodia, and Delia were on their way out of the breakfast café when they spotted Brett and Xavier. Nadia couldn't believe her eyes. *What kind of coincidence is this?* She thought as they made their way towards them. She noted Xavier's look of apprehension, a direct contrast to Brett who looked overjoyed to see them. She looked to her twin who had stopped dead in her tracks and was actually backing away. *She's got it bad,* she mused as she walked ahead to meet Brett and Xavier halfway, her mother giving a nod of approval as she picked up a complaining Delia in her arms.

"Fancy seeing you out and about this morning," Brett teased.

"Yeah," Nadia replied, clearing her voice. "What are you two up to?"

"Well, we always come here for breakfast on the weekends. It's kind of our hang out spot," Brett grinned sheepishly.

"Oh, I didn't know," Nadia blushed. "My mom wanted to do something special for us. We almost always eat breakfast at home," she informed him.

Brett kicked at a few pebbles, hesitant to pry further, but he figured he would ask her anyway. "So, what are your plans for the rest of the day?" he enquired, trying to appear as nonchalant as possible.

"Well, usually we help my mom out at her shop unless we have practice or we hang out at the mall," Nadia shifted from one foot to the other trying to appear uninvolved. *What is he getting at?*

"Well, Xay and I are planning to hang out at Oglethorpe Park for a little bit after we have breakfast," he shared.

"That's cool," Nadia said, looking to Xavier. "You plan on hanging out there for a while?"

Xavier nodded, but his eyes were directed to her twin who was clearly ignoring him. *So much for small talk,* Nadia pondered to herself.

"Hello Brett, Xavier," Columbia greeted the boys. She had decided to see if she could help overcome this apparently awkward moment that was developing.

Both boys nodded and stumbled over their words paying respect to her. They were really endearingly cute and seemed very conscious of not putting forth a wrong step.

"I overheard you saying that you planned to go to the park today," she looked to each gentleman then to Nadia. "Nadia, why don't you and Rodia meet them at the park later?"

Rodia stared at her mother as if she had grown two heads. "Mom, don't you need my help at the shop today? You told me you've got three clients to do today," she reminded her. "I can help you and Nadia can go hang out," she concluded.

Columbia saw right through her daughter's brilliant plan. "Actually, one of them cancelled this morning so I won't need the help today," she confided. "Besides, I know you young people have some catching up to do," she reminded her.

A light bulb went on in Nadia's mind. *She's giving me the go ahead to establish my relationship with Brett.* The only thing was it would prove to be very awkward with Xavier and Rodia at odds with one another. She looked to her twin, reading her mind. "I don't want to intrude on Brett's time with Xay," she spoke up, trying to clear the way for Rodia to make her escape to her mother's shop. She could always take Delia to the mall if she got bored hanging around the shop today.

"It's not a problem," Xavier spoke, surprising everyone. "Brett and I always hang out," he added. "We were going to play Frisbee. We could play opposite each other; girls against guys," he offered.

"I better warn you that though she may look innocent, Rodia throws a mean Frisbee," Columbia gave the boys a look of mock sternness, causing them all to laugh.

"Then it's on," Brett concluded, happy that his friend had decided to humor him and play nice. He knew he was still upset about how Rodia had misjudged him. They were in mid-conversation about it when he had spotted them coming out of the café.

As they exchanged numbers and agreed to a meeting place at the park, Brett truly felt giddy and lighthearted. *I've got to get myself together or Nadia will have me eating out the palm of her hand.*

As the boys stepped into the café, Columbia looked to her mini-mes, reading the expression on their faces. "Well? Are you ladies ready to resolve some issues this afternoon?"

Rodia rolled her eyes heavenward. "Not exactly, but I guess I don't have a choice, do I," she glared pointedly at her mother.

"Don't take that tone with me, young lady," Columbia warned her. "Not five minutes ago you agreed to straighten out your issue with Xavier. I think this afternoon is as good a time as any," she assessed.

Rodia threw her hands in the air. "Fine; if I make matters worse, don't blame it on me," she warned stomping to the car.

Nadia shook her head in sympathy as she walked alongside her mother back to their car. "Mom, I totally feel her," she confided. "It was so hard to apologize to Brett, but I'm glad that I did," she confessed.

Columbia nodded. "I know it's the last thing your sister wants to do, but it will be good for her. Even if she and Xavier don't begin dating, she will have repaired a relationship. She needs to know how to reconcile with others and do it quickly. If she doesn't, the situation will only fester."

"I hear you," Nadia sighed. "I just hope that they can resolve it today and not let it affect our last week of school," she added. "It's Spirit Week and the last thing Rodi needs to feel is stressed out," she mentioned.

As they made their way to the salon in silence, Nadia made up her mind to reassure Rodia the first chance she got. *Lord, we are too blessed to be stressed!*

Charcoal; check, ribs; check, lighter fluid; check, and marshmallows; check, Jamar ran through his mental list. He had volunteered to pick up the necessary items for tonight's bonfire and barbecue. *Just call me Mr. Domesticated;* he humored himself with the notion.

"Jamar, right?"

Jamar turned in line to find himself eye to eye (a rarity) with the strikingly beautiful Tehinnah Adams. *God, why the torture?* He cleared his throat hoping he didn't sound like a total girl. "Uh, yeah," he replied. *Uh, yeah; is that all you got?* He berated himself. It seemed that whenever this leggy beauty showed up he seemed to lose his wits altogether.

"How are you?" Tehinnah tried again, not wanting to think that she was getting the brush off.

"Fine," Jamar stated his back to her as he literally threw his items onto the conveyor belt. *Lord, get me out of here before I say something or do something really stupid. Like tell her how beautiful she is and how she takes my breath away and I find myself at a loss for words, something that doesn't happen to me-ever.*

Tehinnah stared at him, miffed by his obvious disinterest. "It looks like you're getting ready for a good time," she noted.

Jamar turned to face her again, his eyes shifting between Tehinnah and the cashier. "The men are having a barbecue tonight. It's kind of our quarterly get together so to speak," he sounded as calm as possible, resisting the urge to admire her from head to toe. It was hard to tamper down the artist in him. He could imagine her in repose as he sketched. She would make a fabulous study.

Tehinnah could see his mind was otherwise occupied and wasn't really focused on the conversation. "Well, I hope you have a good time tonight," she wished him well as he paid quickly and hurried out of the grocery store as if his car was on fire. "Bye," she waved, speaking more to herself than Jamar for he was already out the door, walking at breakneck speed. *Clearly, he's not that into you, girl,* she acknowledged to herself as she paid the cashier and made a fashionable exit, all male eyes trained on her in open appreciation.

"Hey, baby," Kevin greeted the love of his life and seated her before they sat down for brunch.

Tatyanna leaned into his kiss on the cheek, thankful that Kevin could get away from his office for lunch today. She enjoyed their quality time together sharing in the Word, but she also understood he had many projects with deadlines that were closing in on him. "Hey, yourself," Tatyanna beamed. "How are you today?"

"I'm feeling fine, I'm having lunch with the most beautiful woman in the world, my projects are ahead of schedule; I'm in love with God and He loves me back; what more could a man ask for?" he wondered aloud.

"That's good to hear," Tatyanna breathed a calming breath. "I know you're excited about Enrique's project being near completion. Tell me about it," she encouraged.

"Well, everything is pretty much completed structurally. We've got one more walk through this week and then come the interior designers. Everything should be ready for grand opening by the end of July," he summarized.

"That's wonderful. I know he must be bursting with anticipation," Tatyanna surmised. "So, where were we," she opened her pocket sized Bible to the thirty-seventh chapter of Genesis.

"I believe we were right at the part where Joseph is telling his brothers and father about his second dream," Kevin flipped to the marked page in his own Bible.

"Do you think that was a wise decision? Clearly, his brothers were not fond of him," Tatyanna reminded Kevin.

Kevin folded his hands together pondering the question. "Well, I believe Joseph had the best of intentions when he told them. After all, he didn't give the interpretation of the dream; his father did. I think Jacob recognized what his son was saying and openly rebuked him, hoping it would satisfy the other brothers' dislike of Joseph."

"I never saw it in that light," Tatyanna reread the passage. "It was almost as if he were telling Joseph he was right in believing that one day he would rule over his brothers while at the same time gently rebuking him," she concluded.

"Perhaps there is something to be learned from the wisdom of Jacob. Sometimes fathers have to be careful not to give too much encouragement in the face of open dislike. Some say that Jacob favored Joseph with the coat but I don't think so," Kevin shared.

"I agree. If you go back a few chapters, Reuben, Jacob's firstborn had already lost the right to the inheritance by dishonoring his father with the maid of Rachel. Joseph was the oldest child of Rachel, so, technically, he was next in line to inherit. Jacob was making it clear who would inherit next," Tatyanna deduced.

"When you think about it which makes it even more incredible that Reuben would try to save him from the pit when he had the most to gain by allowing Joseph to be killed," Kevin thought aloud.

Tatyanna tapped him playfully. "Now, Kevin, don't get ahead of me; we're studying together," she reminded him as they put away their Bibles to attend to order their food.

"Aliya, I forgot to tell you," Augusta hurried to put away bolts of fabric for her sister. "Enrique called me about having lunch this afternoon; I accepted so I hope that you've got some lunch plans," she looked pointedly at her sister. "I know how you forget to eat."

Aliya shooed Augusta out the door. "I promise to eat if you promise to stop nagging," she grabbed her sister's bags as she helped her to the door. "I'm going to the beach house to help Angelynn decorate for tonight after I clean up here," she assured her.

"I know you; try to catch a nap, okay?" Augusta hugged her sister. Every now and then, Aliya suffered from bouts of tiredness.

"Alright, and make sure you change," Aliya perused her sister's rumpled attire. "The Billionaire's Sweetie shouldn't look anything less than perfect," she teased, knowing how much Augusta hated that title bestowed upon her by the press.

"Watch it, Pastor's Hottie," Augusta laughed, barely making it out the door before Aliya could respond.

Aliya shook her head at her sister who had somewhere along the way gained a very keen sense of humor. *It's about time, Auggie.*

Nicholas Cartellini had an hour to himself and strangely, he didn't know what to do with the time. Enrique had informed him of operation Lunch Proposal and he had been overjoyed for his boss. At the same time, he had felt a little bit hollow as he was reminded of his current relationship status. He had been following Enrique's advice and had not made any effort to contact Rosalynn, but it was driving him up the wall. He had gotten used to seeing her next door, seeing her in services, seeing her in passing as their mutual friends connected. Seeing her last night at the meeting had been like receiving a roundhouse kick to the head. An hour was too long to let his mind lie idle. He pulled out his mat and was readying himself for a session of stomach crunches when he heard the doorbell ring. He was on his feet in an instant, all senses alert and ready when he swung open the door and was greeted by an unbelievable sight: Rosalynn Rhodes standing on his doorstep with a sweet smile and a peace offering.

"I know this isn't dinner but, would you care to have lunch with me?" Rosalynn braved the apprehensive look Nicholas gave her. Clearly he wasn't overjoyed at the sight of her standing before them. He had every right to be upset since she was the one who had reneged on their dinner date. But, it was time to clear the air. She didn't want to fly to Montego Bay with unresolved issues hanging between them.

Nicholas didn't know what to say, but he certainly wasn't going to look this gift horse in the mouth. "Here?"

Rosalynn looked around, taking notice that everyone was out for the day. "Here is fine," she agreed.

Nicholas stepped aside allowing the sweet fragrance of lavender to tantalize his senses as Rosalynn stepped over the threshold. He clapped his hands together in readiness. "So, what's for lunch?"

Rosalynn began unpacking her savory treats with a grin. "I've got an Italian sausage Panini and a chicken and broccoli Panini," she put them on the plates Nicholas had set out.

"That sounds delicious," he thought aloud. "We've got some apple juice, ginger ale, and root beer; what would you prefer?" he swung away from the fridge then to fill their glasses with ice.

"I'd love some ginger ale," Rosalynn requested as she seated herself at the counter.

Nicholas took a moment to really look at Rosalynn and appreciate her for who she was: a warm, kind, young woman who knew what she wanted out of life; a woman who could touch your heart with her sweet spirit, yet who could also deliver a swift kick in the rear when you needed it. *That's my Roz,* he thought to himself, pausing mid-thought. *My Rosalynn,* Nicholas realized then that he was in too deep and he didn't want to be rescued from the sweet company of Rosalynn Rhodes.

Tehinnah was trying to crunch in some hours of study before she attended the Women's fellowship but the incessant knocking on her sister's apartment door pulled her right out of her studies. She had tried to ignore it for as long as she could, but there was no help for it.

"Coming, Jeez!" Tehinnah swung open the door to see a boatload of luggage stacked in front of the doorway. The culprit was gone. There was a note attached to one of the larger bags. It read: Good riddance, Your Ex-brother Carlton. *Of all the rotten, dirty things to do.*

"What's this?" Tatyanna had just made her way off the elevator, still caught up in the euphoria of a beautiful lunch date.

Tehinnah shook her head in disgust. "Apparently Carlton couldn't wait to be rid of his sister," she pointed to the luggage stacked haphazardly in front of the doorway.

"Here, let's get these things moved inside," Tatyanna grabbed some of the smaller bags.

Tehinnah joined her, tag-teaming the heap as they went, until all of Rosalynn's things were safely inside.

"What a jerk," Tatyanna had worked up a bad attitude by the time they had finished. "I would have never believed he could be so cruel if I hadn't witnessed it for myself."

"I'm just glad that your friend wasn't here; no doubt there would have been trouble," Tehinnah noted. "I tell you, I haven't been here long, but I've just about had it with the men in Savannah; it seems as though the sane ones are taken," Tehinnah walked back to her room then to resume her studies.

Tatyanna couldn't help wonder if this was the end or if Carlton's blatant disrespect was just the beginning.

"This is beautiful! How did you find this place?" Ginny asked as she and Marco pulled up to the Bonita Horse Ranch.

Marco shut off the engine quickly and hopped out to open Ginevieve's door before she could exit. "I endeared myself to the owner by providing beautiful bouquets for all of his special occasions. He told me that I had an open door anytime I wanted to ride," he shared. "He's actually away on business this month, so I won't be able to make introductions this time," he smiled.

Ginny didn't like the way Marco had insinuated that there would be another time. "How unfortunate; maybe you could introduce him the next time he comes by your shop," she offered.

"That's an idea," Marco agreed, not wanting to argue at the moment. He knew he had faith that Ginny would return. "Come on, let's have some fun."

They made their way to the stalls where the horses were located. They appeared well taken care of from what Marco could see. His family owned their own operation in Spain, but he tried not to look too educated. He didn't plan on having to answer too many questions concerning his past. He groomed the two horses his friend had suggested for their outing, Cinnamon and Spice, and led them out of their stalls toward Ginevieve.

"They're beautiful," she spoke quietly and reverently in appreciation for their majestic stature. "And well taken care of," she added.

Marco led the horses over to an excited Ginevieve. "This here is Cinnamon," he rubbed the back of the pinto. "She's a Galiceno, imported from Spain. She'll do you well, today," he continued. "She's got a bit of a running gait but she's a family horse and excellent when it comes to trail riding," he grinned. Cinnamon was also suited to children and small adults but somehow Marco knew that would offend Ginny's sensibilities so he didn't mention it. "I'll be riding Spice, who's a Florida Cracker. He too has his origins with the Spanish and will make a great partner on the trail we're about to embark upon."

"Let's get this show on the road," Ginevieve was excited and enthused. She hadn't been horse back riding in years. It was something she missed. *If I'm not careful, this man is going to maneuver his way into my heart without my even realizing it,* she mused. She had to give it to him: Marco really had been conducting himself as a gentleman. Still, she wasn't about to let her guard down one bit.

"We'll have lunch once we return. The trail is about four miles long. It'll take us about an hour. There's a manmade pond near the middle. We'll stop there and eat," he informed her.

Ginevieve nodded her head in agreement. As she readied herself for the saddle, she felt sure hands lift her up onto the horse with one swift, yet graceful motion.

"There you are," Marco chuckled at the look of disbelief on Ginny's face. "You're not as heavy as I thought," he joked.

Ginevieve made a face at him. "Whatever," she muttered as he laughed without reservation.

Marco swung up into his saddle like a professional circuit rider. "Off we go into the wild, blue, yonder," he sang merrily as he led them up onto the trail.

Wild, blue, yonder, indeed, Ginny thought to herself while trying not to imagine herself riding off into the sunset with the most perfect guy she had ever met.

30

Xavier lunged for the Frisbee that went sailing over Nadia's head, making a perfect midair catch.

"No fair," Brett called. "You've got height advantage over us," he hollered.

"Hey, I didn't call teams," Xay reminded him. "You and Rodia thought you could take us down," he added. "We just had to let you know who was in charge," he boasted, high-fiving Nadia.

Nadia laughed at Brett's expression of defeat. It had been a great idea to split up and help to smooth over the issue between her sister and Xavier and have some fun at the same time. "Maybe next time," she giggled, then caught her breath as Brett and Rodia ran towards them getting ready to charge.

Nadia turned and ran, pumping her legs as fast as she could, but she was not match for Brett who was quickly gaining on her. Rodia on the other hand stopped short of Xavier, breathing hard, and holding out her signal for time out. "It wasn't," she panted, "my idea," she continued, "to charge you," she finished, clearly still trying to catch her breath.

Xavier sighed then. "Of course it wasn't; Brett has a habit of drawing people into his harebrained plans; besides, we both know you probably want to kick me in the shin if anything," he reasoned.

Rodia glared at him then. She was just beginning to enjoy this afternoon; now she was reminded of why she hadn't wanted to come along in the first place. She turned away then.

"Wait," Xay trotted around her blocking her escape. "Look, I was a jerk for writing that blog," he admitted. "But I was upset," he paused, and then just went for it. "Because I wanted you to like me, and trust me, and think about me the way that I've always thought about you," he confessed.

Rodia leaned back then. "You thought about me?"

"Yeah, I've thought about you," he nodded, swallowing hard, realizing how difficult it was to just slap your heart on your sleeve. "I thought to myself, that if I ever get the opportunity to ask Rodia Newcomb out, I'm going to go for it; I'm not going to hesitate because she is...wow, she is...kind, beautiful, courageous, funny, and way smarter than I am, and I'd be a fool not to let her know I'm available," he grinned.

Rodia looked at Xavier as if he had grown two heads. "Okay, that was overwhelming," she took a breath then, noticing Nadia and Brett had taken a seat on the other side of the park. "I'm...I don't know what to say, Xay," she looked down at her shoes.

"Say you'll give me a chance," Xay grabbed her hand, causing Rodia to look at their hands joined together, his hard in some places, but gentle; hers, sweaty from the nervous energy coursing through her. "I'd like to be your friend, Rodia, if nothing else," he continued. "But I'm hoping for something more." He admitted.

"Hallelujah to God; they aren't tearing each other's eyes out," Nadia gazed at her twin and Xavier.

"Your mother is a very smart woman," Brett chuckled. "I'm glad she allowed you to hang out today."

"Well, it wasn't really a big deal since I'm dating now," Nadia stated nonchalantly.

Brett shook his head as if clearing his ears. "Come again, I didn't quite hear you," he turned himself so that he was looking directly at her.

"I said it's not a big deal, now that I'm allowed to date," she grinned.

"Dating who?" Brett inquired. "Why didn't you tell me you were available?"

"Because it just occurred oh, a few hours ago," Nadia admitted.

"You're serious?" Brett looked hopeful. "You mean you're no--"

"No, I'm not seeing anyone..." Nadia grinned. "Yet," she added saucily.

"Are you throwing hints?" Brett leaned in close. "Because I'll make myself real clear: whenever you're ready, I'd like to pickup where we left off last night."

Nadia felt herself melt inwardly. "I'd like that too," Nadia let out a breath of relief.

Brett took her hands in his. "I don't want you to feel rushed; after all this would be your first relationship. But I want you to know there's no one I'd rather be with than you. If you need time to think about us, take it," He encouraged her.

"Alright, I'll do that," Nadia decided. She had much to contemplate. "My mom laid down some pretty intense rules so I want to make sure you can honor what she is asking of us," she added.

"I'm not fond of rules but I'm willing to do what it takes to make our relationship work," he confided.

"Well, I think the first thing we should do is pray about it. Dating is a serious thing and I want to make sure that I'm doing the right thing," Nadia confessed.

"I agree. There's no better time than the present," Brett said as they bowed their heads and went before the Lord in prayer.

"It's so beautiful here," Ginevieve took a moment to stare out at the pristine scenery before her. The landscape looked like it came straight from a postcard. "I could stay here all day," she murmured.

"Lunch is ready," Marco whispered. He had come up behind her, close enough to touch the tendrils of hair that curled at her nape.

Ginevieve swung around nearly missing the edge of the lawn. "Oh, you startled me," she laughed lightly as he grasped her elbow and assisted her onto more solid ground.

"Not intended," he assured her.

They took their seat then on a blanket Marco had managed to bundle along with the rest of their things. They ate in pleasant silence, enjoying the sights and sounds around them. Ginevieve figured this was as good a time as any to pry into the personal life of Marco Angelo Arion Bolivar.

"So, what brought you to Savannah?" Ginny asked between bites.

"I came for school," Marco answered. *I know where this conversation is headed and I do not intend to let it get that far.*

"Really," Ginny didn't expect that answer. "What did you major in?"

"Broadcast Journalism," he replied.

"Wow, I never would have guessed," Ginny wondered aloud. "But I'm not surprised."

Marco lay sideways on the blanket dipping his strawberries into whip cream. "What's that supposed to mean?" he raised a brow, taking a bite out of the strawberry.

"With your looks, you would do quite well in broadcasting," Ginny surmised.

Marco gave her a curious look then. "So you think its all about beauty and no brains?"

"Of course not," Ginny assured him. "I'm merely stating the obvious. Those who look well do well," she noted clearing her plate into a small bag they had brought along for trash.

Marco fought to maintain his composure. "I find that to be entirely false. There's a lot more that goes into journalism than looking good. You have to be good at your craft in any profession," he informed her in a crisp tone. "God happened to have other plans for me," he added. *Plans you couldn't begin to imagine and would probably laugh me to scorn if you found out.*

"Did you ever report or work as an anchor?" Ginny enquired.

"No, chyron was my responsibility. I typed the titles for the teleprompter," he clarified. "I'm a behind-the-scenes kind of guy." Marco confessed.

"I'd like to see some of the things you've written," she took the rest of their belongings and placed them in the basket they had brought along.

"I don't really share what I've written with people," Marco gave her a morose look then.

Ginny returned his look with one of her own. "I'm not just anyone," she replied saucily. "You can include some of your writing in our last date," she suggested.

"I'll consider it," Marco helped her to her feet then. He had no intention of letting Ginevieve in on what he had planned. He lifted her once more into the saddle making sure she was settled before he handed her the reigns.

Ginevieve reached for the reigns, her fingers brushing his, sending a spark down her spine. She tried to pull away but he held her fast. She looked into his eyes, seeing more than friendly banter.

"I really enjoyed being with you today," Marco wanted to say more but he knew it would make her feel uncomfortable.

"I had a really great time," Ginny tried to hide the quavering in her voice. "I'm glad you invited me." She was also a little saddened by the fact that their outings would soon come to an end.

"There's no other woman that I could picture sharing this moment with," his words were so direct, his look so piercing that Ginevieve nearly took a tumble over the side of her horse. "Whoa, there; steady, now," he chuckled.

Ginny laughed in embarrassment. "I'm good," she asserted. "I just need to get my bearings again."

Marco left her side then to swing up into his own saddle. "Alright, little lady; Just follow me and take it slow," he reminded her.

Ginevieve thanked God that she had some time to stew in her own mental juices and digest just what it was that Marco had just hinted at. Those were not the words of a friend, but something much deeper. *Lord, I'm sinking here! I need you to rescue me.*

Just remember. Love is a choice.

Ginevieve understood what the Lord was saying but she felt as if she had no choice in the matter. To deny what she felt for Marco was like denying she needed air to breathe. No matter how she felt, she had no intentions of acting on it. Love for her had never led to anything good.

Nadia and Rodia waved Brett and Xavier goodbye as calmly as they possibly could. They made their way inside their home politely and then they did what many normal teenage girls would do: they screamed.

"Oh, my God; Brettaskedmeoutandicantbelieveit," Nadia jumped up and down in sheer random madness.

Rodia was no better, giddy with her own excitement. "Xayandiarethinkingaboutdating!" she said breathlessly.

"What in the world is going on out here?" Columbia came waltzing down the hallway. "I just put your sister down for a nap," she complained.

"Sorry," the girls brought their voices down to a whisper.

"So, I take it you ladies have some exciting news to share?" Columbia leaned against her counter.

"We're still in the decision-making stage, but we've definitely made some progress," Nadia shared.

"They both asked us out but we're weighing our options," Rodia's sophisticated tone caused Columbia to raise a brow. "We don't want to seem too eager," she reasoned.

"Whatever you two decide, I'm here for you," Columbia enfolded them in her arms. Letting go was going to be harder than she thought. "Just so you know, no decision-making until after the holidays, okay?"

The girls agreed, content with the fact they could even have this conversation. Thirty days ago if someone had told them their mother would relent on her stance with dating, they would have laughed that person to shame.

Columbia sure is mellowing out in her old age, Nadia smiled inwardly. There was no other place she wanted to be right then than in the sheltering arms of her mother.

Rosalynn couldn't think of a time when she had better food or better company as she helped Nicholas right the kitchen once more. They worked in companionable silence, wiping, sweeping, shifting and working around each other like well oiled gears. They finally seated themselves on a comfy oversized loveseat whose view was to French doors which opened onto a pebbled patio.

"Thank you for bringing me lunch," Nicholas began wanting the break the tension of the issues that loomed suddenly before them.

Roz smiled genuinely. "Not a problem. I just wanted to come by and set some things straight between us," she went on. "I apologize for the way I've been acting; I've just been a little confused about how I feel, what's really happening between us," she admitted.

Nicholas let out a frustrated breath. "I thought I was making myself pretty clear, Roz. I think the only thing that's clouding the issue is that meddling brother of yours," he noted.

Roz acknowledged the truth regretfully. "I know; that's why until I sort out these issues with Carlton, I won't pursue anything with you at this point," she declared.

Nicholas bit back a sharp retort. *This is just enough to tempt a man to curse.* He swallowed his pride. "If that's what you want, I'll respect your wishes," he stated with a calmness he didn't feel. "I just don't think that putting your life on hold is going to help. Carlton gets exactly what he wants—you putting your life on hold," he reasoned.

Rosalynn could tell her decision was not on his favorites list but she had to make it nonetheless. "Nicholas, its not my intention to make you feel like you're being left high and dry but I don't want to bring baggage into any relationship, and right now, Carlton is baggage," she sighed. "Can we have dinner after the Montego Bay trip? I feel that I will hopefully have some closure by then. We're meeting Elder Worth on Monday." She informed him.

"Maybe Elder Worth can talk some sense into him," Nicholas thought aloud.

"Whatever happens, one thing I am sure of; Carlton has no say in this relationship. I plan to make that perfectly clear," she stated pointedly as she stood gathering her things.

Nicholas felt a tad relieved upon hearing that. He walked her to the door then. "I suppose one week isn't too long to wait," he relented.

Roz turned then, about to return his remark with a snappy comeback when she realized they were nose to nose. She could smell sandalwood and spice emanating from him.

Nicholas lost his train of thought as he stood toe to toe, nose to nose, forehead to forehead with the sweet, loveably spicy Rosalynn Rhodes. He closed his eyes, stepped forward, and sealed their lips together briefly tasting garlic and sesame. He pulled away as quickly as he had stepped forward taking in the look of wonder on Rosalynn's face.

Rosalynn put her hand to her lips which still tingled from the brief but intense contact of Nicholas' lips against hers. Heat suffused her entire body, its intensity in certain unmentionable parts not lost on her. "That wasn't fair," Roz spoke breathlessly narrowing her eyes. "You kissed me on purpose," she accused.

Nicholas laughed out loud. "You look so adorable when you're angry," he declared.

Rosalynn stomped off to her car. "I won't dignify that with a response," she shot back over her shoulder. "You try that again and no measure of security is going to save you," she warned.

Nicholas followed her out to her car hurrying to catch up. "I'm not sorry for kissing you," he confessed. "I've wanted to do that for quite some time," he chuckled.

Roz swirled on him then, clearly offended. "I don't know what you take me for, but you better not try that again!" she huffed.

Nicholas stopped then crossing his arms defensively. "Are you upset that I kissed you or that you *liked* it?" his brow rose at the suggestion.

"Men!" Rosalynn fumed as she opened her car door and glared at him. "This break is definitely in order," she reasoned. "Seeing how you're beginning to lose your mind!"

Nicholas laughed and waved goodbye as an irritated Rosalynn pulled out of his parking lot and sped off.

Yep, Nick chuckled to himself, *she definitely liked it.*

31

As Augusta stepped into the swanky restaurant for lunch, she was glad that she had changed clothes and tidied herself up. Though a small establishment, *Panache* eatery was definitely five-star cuisine. A valet had met her up front and told her all was taken care of. She had been ushered inside the establishment, taken to a private dining room with a full live orchestra and been seated.

The room had the feel of a secret garden at night, its living vines and stone walls the perfect storybook setting. She's been served sparkling pomegranate cider and had a host of desserts lain out before her. When Enrique appeared, she knew something was definitely not quite normal. He wore a tuxedo and carried a dozen calla lilies. Augusta felt her stomach somersault. She took another sip of the cider to calm her nerves.

"What have we here," Augusta sipped calmly. "You must have had some meeting with Kevin today," she smiled up at him. She never got over how dashing he looked. He had trimmed his hair since arriving back in town, making him look less the renegade and more the refined, debonair businessman he was.

Enrique knew he had her at a loss for words and he took pleasure in surprising the no nonsense Augusta Peyton for once. "Kevin and I did meet. Things are looking great and I'm really pleased with his project management skills. As a matter of fact, I offered him a contract with our firm to build all of our future sites here stateside," he confided.

"I know he must be elated," Augusta slid over making room for him in the alcove.

"Enough, business; how are you doing?" Enrique enquired.
Augusta took a moment to answer. How was she really? "I haven't really thought much about how I'm doing to be honest with you," she admitted.

"I know," Enrique took both her hands in his. "You've been so busy taking care of everyone else that you've been neglecting yourself," he declared taking his bouquet of flowers and placing them in the crystal vase prepared for their arrival. "So, I've decided to do something about it," he informed her. With the clap of his hands, the orchestra began a rendition of some of her favorite hymns as a chef brought in their lunch.

"Curried shrimp over steamed rice and broccoli," the waiter placed a platter before them and lifted the lid.

Augusta's mouth watered as the spices teased her. "That smells delicious," she gave Enrique a heart-stopping smile. "Thank you," Augusta tried to remain calm, her senses overloaded from sight, touch, and smell. Both the man and the cuisine were appealing in their own way. "You didn't have to do all this," she looked around them.

Enrique smiled at that thought. "Yes, I did. I'm glad to be here, right now, with you, sharing this moment."

"Well, it's good to have you back," Augusta meant those words more than she could say. "I found myself worrying about you and how you were faring halfway across the world," she told him.

"You mean when you weren't avoiding the press?" he chuckled. "You heard about that?" Augusta shook her head embarrassed at the memory of reporters camped outside her door demanding an interview with the Billionaire's Sweetie.

"How could I not? Nick and Giovanni kept me quite informed." He reminded her. "I didn't try to contact you because I knew they would probably be taping our conversations. I didn't want you exposed to the press more than necessary." Enrique confessed.

Augusta shook her head at the notion. "Well, I'm glad it's over, at least for now."

As they bowed their heads and blessed the food, Enrique prayed that the press would not get wind of his next move. It made Billionaire Sweetie look like a walk in the park.

"To life, love, liberty, and the pursuit of a happy marriage," Shemiah toasted Savannah's parents.

He and Savannah had decided to treat her parents to a day cruise in honor of their eminent nuptials. It was a beautiful day, the weather perfect for taking in the sights.

"Cheers!" Marilyn and Andre shouted joyfully. They were counting down to the big day.

"Now, Mom, you aren't allowed to move in until *after* the wedding day," Savannah teased. Her mother would be moving in with them after the wedding. She was beyond happy: for the first time, if only briefly, they would live as one united family under the same roof.

"There's nothing wrong with having my bags packed and ready to go," Marilyn teased back.

"To hear Gram Parker and Gram Tot tell it, you've got more than your bags packed," Savannah giggled.

"Gram Tot accused your father the other day of trying to walk out with her good China," Marilyn laughed.

"As if I want China," Andre shook his head.
"You know parents act in strange ways when it comes to weddings, no matter how old their children are," Marilyn reminded Savannah.

"I'm so glad I can count on you and Dad to be normal, rational human beings," Savannah grinned from ear to ear.

Both her parents gave her a deadpan serious look.
"Okay, almost rational," Savannah laughed.

Andre and Marilyn looked at each other with a secret knowing in their eyes. "We'll be as rational as we can," they agreed. "Until the good pastor sends you on your way; then we're going to turn that aisle into a dance floor," Andre chuckled.

"And now we shall have the dessert menu," Enrique clapped his hands once more. The waiter came to remove their china and handed Enrique the menu.

Augusta held up her hands in protest. "Enrique, I couldn't eat another thing at this point, really," she rubbed her tummy. "Everything was perfect," she praised the waiter.

Enrique was not taking no for an answer. "Here you are. You may not want anything right now, but maybe you'll find something you'd like to take home. It's a personalized menu, by the way," he handed it to her.

Augusta figured she would humor him. "Oh, alright, let's see it," she took the menu he offered and opened it up to browse. It read:

Augusta Ming Peyton
Proposed Menu

A Man in Love - dipped in strawberries

Desires Eternity - chocolate fudge dripped

Holy Matrimony - sealed with chocolate kisses

Lovely Augusta - a mint sherbet

Will You Say Yes? – hope filled cheesecake

Marry Me – caramel and vanilla merged together

Augusta's eyes were flooded with tears by the time she reached the bottom of the menu. She covered her mouth, floored by the lengths Enrique had gone to for this moment. It was private, it was personal; it was her moment to savor. She hadn't realized she had closed her eyes

209

until she looked up. Enrique had kneeled before her. A red pillow in hand with one jewel encrusted shoe poised perfectly and one in hand.

Enrique had never felt more overwhelmed with the presence of the Lord than he did right then. When he looked into Augusta's eyes, he saw the man he used to be, the man he was at this moment, and the man he wanted to be.

"Augusta, I offer myself to you, all that I am, and all that I hope to be as your husband, your protector, your partner, your co-ruler in this world. I offer this slipper to you as a symbol of the queen you are in my life. I pledge my heart to you, I pledge to treasure you as the queen you are. God has knit my heart to yours and I never want to undo what He has done. You, Augusta, have shown me what true beauty is; endurance, trust, confidence, determination, faithfulness, holiness, submission, and most importantly purity of soul. I've never met a more selfless woman than you. I want to walk with you everyday; I want to share everything this life has to offer us. I want you now; I want you forever, Augusta. Will you make me eternally blessed? Will you marry me?" Enrique pleaded his heart in hand.

"I will marry you with pleasure," Augusta laughed wiping tears that flowed faster than she could contain.

Enrique removed her heels and replaced them with the jewel encrusted glass slippers. "Your sister designed these for a mystery client a few months back," he confessed. "The jewels are not imitation."

Augusta stared down at the exquisite shoes. "They're beautiful," she choked out, overwhelmed with the enormity of it all.

Enrique held out his hand to stop her from rising. "I'm not quite done; do you think I would let you go home empty-handed?" he clapped once more and Giovanni appeared with a box shaped like a budding rose. He delivered it to Enrique with military precision, saluted his boss, and then disappeared from sight.

"A rose for My Rose," Enrique handed the box to Augusta. "Open it," he encouraged.

Augusta was literally shaking as she unfolded the petals of the box. Inside laid a velvet box. She gently took it out and flipped open the lid. The ring was indescribably exquisite. It was a diamond crafted to look like a rose. "I'm undone," she whispered.

Enrique lifted the ring out and set the velvet box inside of the gift box. He took her hand in his, sliding the ring onto her ring finger. "With this ring, I pledge my heart, my love, my faithfulness. I am yours," he declared bringing her hand to his lips to place a kiss there.

Augusta had always prided herself on being the strong sister but she felt her knees go slack at his touch and knew at that moment she was a goner.

"I'm really glad you ladies decided to come early and help out," Angelynn called from the kitchen where she was preparing appetizers for the women's fellowship later that evening.

"Not a problem," Aliya called out from the family room where she was dusting knickknacks.

"I love to decorate," Naomi called from the dining room.

The ladies converged in the family room where Naomi was bringing more decorations. "Alright, let's see what we've got left to do," she thought aloud looking around. "The decorations look great, Naomi," Angelynn praised her close friend. "If Jarah hadn't taken the twins off my hands, I would be in big trouble," she recognized.

"It does look great," Aliya added. When she had arrived not much more needed to be done. The beach house had needed a little airing out but other than that it was an elegantly furnished getaway. "Angelynn, you've got great taste," Aliya complimented her.

"What's tonight's theme?" Naomi questioned.

"It's P.M.S. which stands for Praise My Savior," Angelynn shared. "We're also going to talk about PMS: Protecting My Spirit, Soul, and Sexuality; so many times we leave ourselves vulnerable to the attacks of the enemy. I want to share tonight a little about how you can have the right PMS and do what is necessary to keep yourself in this world," Angelynn summarized.

"Wow, I can't wait," Aliya clapped her hands together in youthful glee.

"You always amaze me how you come up with such practical ways to apply things we know and are familiar with." Naomi shook her head in wonder.

"It's a gift from God; I'm just learning to thank Him for it," Angelynn acknowledged. "Well, let's finish up and then we can have some chill time before the others start arriving."

The ladies had a plan and their Lord was with them overseeing their success and working with them to perform His Word.

Ginevieve waved goodbye to Marco as he drove away, wondering what wonderful surprise he had in store for her. She was desperately trying to hold on to her fears where he was concerned. It was becoming more and more futile by the moment to pretend that what she felt was some infatuation or passing fancy. Marco had effectively silenced all the voices in her mind. He was turning out to be a pretty kind, caring, thoughtful, and selfless individual. Ginevieve knew her past experiences were warring against her present happiness. As she went to prepare for tonight's fellowship she'd been invited to, she prayed the Lord would show her how to direct her thoughts. *Lord, I need you now, more than ever. Rescue me from the mistakes of the past. Help me to live in the now. Amen.*

32

Saturday Evening...

"Welcome Ladies to our quarterly Women's Retreat!" Angelynn announced as ladies began to file into her family room. "I'm Angelynn Worth, your hostess and moderator for the evening," she began. "Tonight's focus is P.M.S. which stands for Praising My Savior and Protecting My Spirit, Soul, and Sexuality. It appears everyone is here so I'll make the introductions sweet and to the point tonight." Angelynn's eyes swept the room as she familiarized herself mentally with faces.

"Okay, I'm going to start to my left: we have Aliya and Augusta Peyton, twin sisters and entrepreneurs, Savannah Charles, soon to be Newman, Tehinnah and Tatyanna Adams, Naomi Watts, Aurielle Foqua, Mariella Estrada, Rosalynn Rhodes, personal trainer extraordinaire, Columbia Newcomb, Jarah, my mother, and Vivian Worth, my loving second mother," She finished. "Last but not least, we have a newcomer, Miss Fabritza Ciccone whom I had the pleasure of meeting recently. She currently works with EAE Design Group and I'm glad she decided to take me up on the invitation to join us. At this time, refreshments are available so catch up, mingle and enjoy one another. We'll return here in an hour for our discussion session. I know the sun is going down but feel free to roam on the beach a bit," Angelynn encouraged feeling pleased with herself as the ladies connected with each other like old friends.

"Over here!" Josiah waved. "I'm open!" he shouted. Clearly his teammates hadn't heard him as one sailed right past him with the ball making a touchdown.

"You know you were out of bounds, dear brother," Seth taunted Jamar as the other men debated if the touchdown was good.

"Give me a break, man; this is sand we're working with here," he chuckled.

"Yeah, yeah," Seth gave him an incredulous look. "Always pleading mercy when it's your team," he observed.

"Alright gents, dinner's served!" Shemiah called from Seth's deck.

All men headed toward the beach house, all thoughts of football gone at the mention of dinner. The menu was impressive: barbecue ribs, chicken, potato salad, macaroni and cheese, fried tilapia, smothered pork chops; their respective mates and partners would have a fit if they saw the menu but it was guy's night out. Seth and Jamar raced back to the house to find a scene typical to the male population: heads kicked back, feet kicked up, and a smorgasbord of food piled high atop each plate. As each man honed in on their plate, they gave the floor over to the newest members of this male frat, Fabian and Noelle.

"I'm Noelle Marks, attorney and son of Pastor Marks. Thanks for having me out here," he took his seat then.

Fabian cleared his throat and stood. "I guess that leaves me," he began. "I bring you greetings from Venice, Italy. I work for Mr. Estrada. Glad to meet you all," he replied stoically.

The men looked to each other, then back to their new guests. Josiah was the first to speak. "I see we're gonna have to loosen you two up," he warned playfully.

The men laughed in agreement. Noelle and Fabian didn't know just how serious they were.

"How are things at the hospital?" Angelynn asked Naomi as they sat on her deck facing the beach. A beautiful sunset was nearing its end as they chatted.

"Hectic," Naomi admitted. "We're short staffed right now so we're making do with what we have and trying not to overtax anyone," she shared.

"Understandable," Angelynn sympathized. "How's Giovanni?"

"Things are okay between us," Naomi smiled. "He's a great guy; we're sorting some things out," she confided.

"I totally agree with your assessment."

The voice came from behind Naomi and caused the hair on her nape to stand at attention.

"Oh, hello Fabritza; we weren't aware you were there," Angelynn waved her over.

Fabritza took a seat between them, crossing her long legs so that her skirt rose a bit higher than was publicly polite. "Yes, as I was saying," she continued, "Gio is a fabulous guy; I mean, he's so sensitive, polite, and thoughtful.

She's describing Gio? Naomi thought to herself.

"He's so very helpful. I just love the way he looks when he's trying to explain something; so intense, it just makes me crazy when his brows cross together when he's concerned...I'm sorry, I shouldn't be going on and on," she eyed Naomi slyly. "He's your friend, so you know how special he is," she assured them.

Naomi was speechless. "I'm sorry; are you two co-workers or something?"

"Yes, we are as a matter of fact. We spend late, long hours together," she smiled in satisfaction. "Trust me, he knows his way around *everything*." she gave Naomi a saucy look.

"I've told Enrique that meeting Giovanni was one of the best things that ever happened to me," she boasted proudly. "It's truly a wonder he hasn't married yet," she confided. "But I plan to remedy that soon enough," she smiled knowingly.

Naomi had heard enough and she could see from the look on Angelynn's face, that she too had received more information than she wanted to know about Fabritza. It appeared Enrique had female security on his payroll. *How cute,* thought Naomi sarcastically; *she's probably imagining little martial arts commando babies.* "Well, I think I hear Savannah calling me," she stood up making her escape. "Excuse me ladies," she hurried into the beach house to find a place to calm her roiling emotions before it became obvious to all that her world had just been flipped upside down.

"Gentlemen, I've come to share with you this evening from the topic of *Real Manhood.*" Elder Worth's voice resonated through the living room. The men had settled themselves on any free surface in Seth's living room: Seth, Enrique, Shemiah, Jamar, Kevin, Giovanni, Nicholas, Trey, Noelle, Pastor Marks, Fabian, Josiah, and Dr. Greg Thomas; each man with his own strengths, fears, disappointments, and pressing issues crowded into one space to hear from a veteran in the faith and in life.

"Real manhood is not what you do," he began. "It's who you are. It's the combination of your choices in light of the Word of God. Manhood is not about being the boss; it is about knowing when to step back and let your wife do the leading. Real manhood is not about having the directions but about letting God direct your path, your family, your career, your emotions, your money, your ministry, your everything," he concluded. "These days, people have gotten the impression that you wear your manhood, or that your manhood is determined by who is walking arm and arm with you. If you don't allow God to shape and define you, you will find yourself walking around with a figment of your imagination. You'll be like the king who thought he had on clothes because no one was honest enough to tell him otherwise. I speak to you tonight and tell you to reclaim your manhood. Reclaim your integrity, your chivalry, your desire to protect at all costs, to cover the ones you love, to stand in the gap and pray for your loved ones, and recover your call to action and responsibility. We want our nation to be healed, yet we will not take responsibility for its sickness," Elder Worth's fervent voice pierced the uncertainty that lay within the hearts of those before him.

"Stop handing over your manhood! Stop backing down from confrontation. God created you for combat, to protect those that have been entrusted to you. Many things you face will seem insurmountable, unfair, and downright depressing. But we are living in a time when so much opportunity is available to us. Take advantage of every opportunity God hands you," he finished. "Let us take our concerns to the Lord."

"And now that I've filled you in on the power of praising your Savior in spite of your circumstances, I bring to the forefront, a woman who is a fount of wisdom. She's going to share with you about protecting your spirit, soul, and sexuality. Vivian," she called as the women applauded.

Vivian stepped forward then, giving her daughter-in-law a kiss on the cheek. "Thank you ladies for such a warm welcome," she chuckled. "Most people call me Mother Worth, but tonight, I just want to be Viv; is that alright?" she looked into the hopeful faces as the women gave their nod of acceptance.

"Well, I want to hit three things really. I want to talk about protecting your spirit from predatory people, protecting your soul from unhealthy emotional ties, and protecting your sexuality from the influences that are pervasive to our culture." She began.

The women murmured their approval, some nodding in agreement of her topics. Vivian continued on.

"It is so important to protect yourself from predatory people. If you find yourself feeling emotionally drained, depressed, unenlightened when you leave a person's presence, they may be a spiritual predator. Ladies, don't become someone's emotional trash can. If you're listening and you don't hear a verse to encourage or don't feel the unction to pray, end the conversation. A good question to ask might be: have you prayed first? Have you spoken to the person? Have you consulted your leader? Spiritual predators look for those they consider uneducated in the faith, young in the faith, or disillusioned with the faith. There is much to be said on all counts, but I'll let your leaders teach further on those subjects. Emotional Ties are natural to the Body of Christ. Jesus prayed that we would become one, and I tell you, we still have a way to go. So, what is an unhealthy emotional tie and how do we protect ourselves? An unhealthy emotional tie is when you attach yourself to someone that is illegal in relationship, illegal in access, or illegal in provision. Let me explain. It would be unhealthy for me to become emotionally attached to Pastor Marks because he is not my husband. It would be spiritually illegal. It would also be illegal in access because there is a part of my emotions that should be reserved for my husband alone. It would also be illegal in provision because there are needs I trust him to provide that should only be provided by my husband and more importantly by God. Finally, I must protect my sexuality from the influences that are pervasive to our culture. We are living in a day and time that as soon as you step outside the confines of your home, whether you want it or not, the world is demanding your attention. The marketplace is the exchange of ideas, culture, belief systems, and the world's clarion call to sexual promiscuity. We cannot escape it. As a matter of fact, Jesus did not pray for us to escape it. He prayed that we would be able to share his truth while still in this world. How do we protect our sexuality? We must put on the whole armor of God. We must gird ourselves with the truth about sex, we must renew our minds with the Word, we must ask God as David did to keep our eyes from beholding worthless things, we must put on the breastplate of righteousness, we must run as fast as we can from sex outside of marriage, we must carry the shield of faith, believing God's plan for sex is better than instant gratification. We must think on the things that are pure, just, lovely, virtuous, and worth reporting. We must allow God to invest his visions in us, to purge the hard drive of our minds. We must take action by not placing ourselves in compromising positions. We must have standards, boundaries, goals for our future that we will hold to and act with honor and not give in. Fear says if I don't have sex now, I may never have sex. Fear says, 'I'll have sex to prove my love.' Fear says, 'I just want to watch just one video to see how it's done so that I won't be completely ignorant of the facts on my wedding night.' Ladies, if it makes you go against the principles clearly laid out in the Word of God, don't do it," Vivian warned. "I hope that I have shared something tonight to get you searching the Word and thinking about your own plan for these three areas of your life. When you protect your spirit, protect your soul, protect your sexuality, you can come to a marriage as a whole person. If you haven't protected yourself in these areas, the wonderful thing about grace is that it is not too late to change," Vivian encouraged them. "Thank you ladies for not thinking me too old or outdated to share with you tonight," Vivian blew them a kiss as she took her seat.

"Come on ladies, let's give Vivian another hand," Angelynn smiled widely. "I tell you, that message was overwhelming and so very powerful. Knowledge is power, isn't that right ladies?" Angelynn noted mentally that some were floored by what Vivian shared. "We're going to go ahead and serve our main entrée and then we're going to head outside for a surprise my husband have planned," Angelynn waved, dismissing the women to mingle further as she went in search of Naomi.

Ginevieve stood mesmerized in the inner courtyard of an antebellum home Marco had rented for the evening. In the center of the enclosed courtyard a candlelit table for two was elegantly laid out. The courtyard was lit up by small decorative lights hidden among the rose bushes that nearly overtook the space. He had chosen not to pick her up this evening but had instructed her to be outside by seven. A chauffer had awaited her outside her home and whisked her away. The historical home was one Ginny had planned to explore when she had the time, but she had never gotten around to it. Savannah was so full of nooks and crannies and hidden treasures that one could spend a lifetime traversing the city and never tire of its delights. As Ginevieve stepped forward she felt a bit self conscious in her bronze beaded one shoulder gown. He had told her formal wear and so here she was, her hair twisted in an artful array of curls. She didn't see Marco yet, but she sensed his presence, just as she did every time he entered their offices bearing flowers. She could be hard at work making revisions to some graphic when a sensation would come over her. Somehow it was always tied to his arrival. It had bothered her at first, but now she was used to it and had learned to live with it.

"Dance with me?"

Ginny turned abruptly at the voice behind her, her comment lost in thought as she took in the very arresting sight of Marco Angelo Arion Bolivar in formal wear. "I...don't hear any music." Ginny managed to choke out. *Help me, Lord! I'm drowning here!*

"Not a problem," Marco assured her as he led her by the hand to the center of the courtyard.

Ginny went along, clearly overwhelmed but not quite knowing what to say or do to reverse her loss of control over the evening. As soon as Marco grasped her hands in his, an orchestra began a waltz. Ginny looked up and was surprised by a full orchestra playing overhead on the balcony above them. "Wow, Marco," she giggled nervously. "Okay, you won; game's over," she relented.

Marco's brow went up as if in question. "I'm not playing any games, Ginevieve. I'm here for the long haul," Marco promised as he ushered her into a sweeping turn.

Ginevieve's heart beat just a little faster at his words. "Isn't the temperature nice out?" she attempted small talk totally ignoring Marco's promise of something deeper between them.

"You're what makes tonight memorable, Ginny. You look absolutely stunning," he complimented her. "Come, let's have a seat." He led her over to their table, pulling out a chair for her to be seated.

"What's on the menu this evening?" Ginny clasped her hands together in delight. It was obvious Marco had gone to a great deal of trouble to make sure all was as it should be.

"Well, I figured a Cajun girl would appreciate some Cajun dishes," he smiled as he uncovered their dishes for the evening.

Ginny clapped her hands to her cheeks in utter surprise. She had been feeling a little homesick lately and the dishes that lay before her brought out so many memories of home. "This is fantastic! Thank you for being so thoughtful!" Ginny felt compelled to hug him, but she didn't know how well that would go over. Before her lay catfish kabobs, on a bed of dirty rice, served with Creole flounder with lemon couscous and Tabasco sauce.

"We have mixed berry tea to cool your palate," Marco assured her as he sat opposite. "Let's bow our heads and give thanks to the Lord," he suggested.

Ginevieve agreed and as she bowed her head, she was praying for more than food. She was praying she would be able to leave this evening in the Lord's hands.

"Are you okay?" Angelynn had managed to find Naomi outside behind the beach house deep in thought.

Naomi turned to her eyes reddened. "I'll be fine. I didn't mean to worry you," she assured Angelynn.

"I just don't want you to go jumping to conclusions. Giovanni doesn't strike me as a person who would play games with your feelings," she warned.

"I know that. Deep in my heart I want to believe that, but, Angelynn, she just reinforced so many things that I've been feeling," Naomi countered.

"Sometimes our feelings can mislead us, Naomi. When you are in a relationship, you have to learn to trust. I learned that the hard way. If I had continued down the path I was going, Josiah and I would not be married right now. Just because a woman has an interest in a man doesn't mean he automatically returns the interest. Giovanni is definitely interested in you. Don't throw away the opportunity for a great relationship without giving it a chance," she counseled.

Naomi nodded in understanding. "I hear you," she acknowledged as Angelynn wrapped her arm around her friend.

"Come on inside," she encouraged. "Your opportunity to set things straight may be just around the corner."

"That was an excellent meal," Ginny clapped. "Compliments to the chef," Ginny noted.

"You're welcome," Marco grinned at the look of disbelief that crossed Ginevieve's face. "And now, for the entertainment," Marco took that moment to rise from the table to retrieve a scroll he'd secured on a branch nearby.

Ginny giggled filled with giddy excitement and cautious anxiety at the same time. *He cooks, he creates the most beautiful floral arrangements, he rides horses, he's gorgeous, polite, and definitely a romantic. What doesn't the man do? This can't be real.*

The Father knows how to give good gifts.

Ginevieve didn't have time to respond to the Voice of the Lord as she watched Marco slowly unravel his scroll and get down on one knee before her. The orchestra had begun to play once more, softly, the strains of violin strings curling around her like a warm blanket on a wintry night. She felt drawn to and pulled into the moment before her. If she wanted to ignore Marco's intentions, she couldn't any longer.

"This piece is entitled Autumn Beauty," Marco made a comical show of his presentation, lightening the mood a bit. "Here we go," he cleared his throat.

"Brilliant hues,
Magnificent shades,
Like leaves that brave the change that comes with time,
Or the sunset that illuminates a certain time,
Before it gives way to the brilliance of the
Moon and the stars-- autumn beauty,
Like the cosmic flash in distant galaxies,
Flying past but not really seeing me,
The flash of amber eyes,
Showing anxiety,
Not knowing what to think of me,
Yes, autumn beauty.
Like golden curls that dance in the play of light,
Or the freckles on skin smoother than ice,
Like the words carved eternally into the bark of a lone tree,
Or the drops of water
That slide down a glass of refreshing tea,
Oh, that I could be that glass to your tea,
To enfold the very essence of you with the essence of me,
Each and every sight, form, touch, smell, taste,
Exemplifies,
Personifies,
The autumn beauty that is you," Marco finished with a bow.

Ginny didn't know whether to clap or run, so moved was she by the images he evoked. She blinked twice. "Was that...?"

Marco chuckled as he took Ginevieve's hand, guiding her out of her seat. "Yes, it was for you," he confirmed.

"I'm impressed," Ginny whispered. She had never been shy but she wasn't used to this much attention.

"I was hoping you would be," Marco admitted. "So impressed that we could continue this friendship and see where it leads us?" he pressed.

Ginny stepped back then, feeling almost as if she'd been doused with ice water. "Marco, this is as far as this relationship goes," she released his hand. "The most I can offer is friendship," Ginny stipulated scrambling for reasons. "I'm focused on my career and anything else would be a distraction," she emphasized.

Marco felt the wound to his heart and lashed back. "I won't spend any further time distracting you," he coolly returned. "Your driver is waiting," he pointed toward the open gate turning away from her then. He would not allow her to see the hurt written across his features.

219

Lord, you know I'm not ready for anything else right now. I don't want to give him any false hopes, but I feel horrible.

Ginny felt suddenly bereft in that moment and she knew as she walked away that she had not only lost the chance for a meaningful relationship, she had lost a friend.

33

Angelynn and Josiah had indeed surprised their guests when both groups, the Men and the Women's fellowships, had wound up on the beach at a bonfire prepared for both groups. Elder Worth and Mother Worth had turned in for the evening, which left Angelynn and Josiah with their hands full. They had decided to adjourn both their meetings with roasting marshmallows and singing praise songs. These times were an opportunity for everyone to fellowship, catch up, and unwind from a busy week.

"I'm so glad to see you," Aliya gave Enrique a crushing hug.

Enrique set her on her feet easily, laughing. This was the Aliya he remembered; wild, crazy, impulsive, and adorable. "You're supposed to be recovering, I hear. It certainly doesn't look like it," he chuckled.

"My friends and family exaggerate too much," Aliya shook her head. "I feel great," she assured him.

"That's good to know," he grinned spotting Seth coming toward them. "I know you have a reason to smile a lot more these days," he teased.

Aliya blushed at the innuendo. "Don't give me a hard time," she threatened jokingly.

"I won't; it's good to see you happy, Aliya. That's what I want most for you," he touched her cheek affectionately.

"If you wanted that, you'd convince my sister to put a ring on her finger," she chided him.

Enrique smiled knowingly. "I'm sure she'll get around to it," he commented off-handedly. He and Augusta had agreed that they would wait until they returned from Montego Bay before they announced the engagement.

"She had better," Aliya tapped him playfully before she joined Seth on the other side of the bonfire.

"What's that all about?" Jamar wonders aloud as he observes Tehinnah's playful manner with Noelle Marks.

"Apparently, he's her boss," Kevin sipped on his drink, having overheard Jamar's musing.

Jamar waved the comment off. "I'm sorry, I shouldn't have said that aloud," he grimaced. "It's none of my business," he apologized.

"I'd beg to differ considering the girl makes it her business to ply her sister with questions about you," Kevin revealed.

Jamar took a step back. "Come again?"

"You heard right. For a girl who seemed pretty interested in you, she sure is playing fast and loose this evening," Kevin noted.

"All the more reason to steer clear," Jamar shook his head in disgust, glancing back once more at Tehinnah before he headed toward his beach house to refill refreshments.

The moment Jamar headed towards the beach house, Tehinnah turned off the charm she was abundantly lavishing on Noelle.

"I'm gonna grab some marshmallows; would you like some?" Noelle offered.

"Nah, I'm cool," Tehinnah waved him on. She was hoping to corner Jamar on his return so she had to act quickly and make the most of her time.

Noelle noticed the scathing glare that Mariella was giving him across the way. He hadn't seen her since Friday, but everything was coming along well at his home so he gave no further thought. He considered most women to be moody creatures of indecision and figured Mariella was no different. "Suit yourself," Noelle called over his shoulder as he went to hang out with the twins at the fire.

"Hey, Mariella," Enrique came up behind his cousin, startling her out of her thoughts.

Mariella turned pasting on a smile as wide as Texas yet as false as cubic zirconium. "Hey, what's up?"

"I don't mean to pry, but you haven't been your usual self since this morning," Enrique had paid close attention to her for the last ten minutes. Something was definitely wrong. "I'm concerned about you," he touched her arm, wanting her to feel his reassuring presence.

Mariella gave him a genuine smile then. "I'm fine, just a little tired that's all," she admitted.

"You want me to talk to Mr. Marks?"

"No!" Mariella nearly panicked. "I mean, it's not necessary," she added. "I'm almost done with his project."

"Alright, I'll trust you to make sure he's not overworking you," Enrique warned her. "But if I don't get my spontaneous, bursting with life Cousin back, I'm making a phone call," he ended ominously.

Mariella knew he meant business. "Deal," she shook hands with trepidation. There was no way she was letting Enrique know what was going on with Noelle. She would have to figure it out on her own.

Naomi, Trey, and Aurielle played Battle of the Marshmallow, a survival of the fittest sugary treat. They laughed hysterically as Aurielle's was the first to take a dive into the fire.

"You are terrible at this! That's your seventh marshmallow that has bitten the dust! Give it up!" laughed Trey.

"You gotta admit, Auri, that's pretty pitiful," Naomi shook her head in pity.

"I will defeat you," Aurielle promised Trey.

"You just might, but it won't be tonight," he grinned.

Nicholas had enjoyed a brief run with Rosalynn and as they parted ways, his eyes caught upon a very unpleasant scene: Fabritza practically draping herself around his brother who was doing his best to feign politeness, all the while presenting a very confusing picture to Naomi who stood frozen, hands clenched at her sides, clearly distressed by what she was witnessing. *My brother has rescued me from my stupidity more times than I care to count; the least I can do is return the favor,* he thought as he made his way to Naomi side. He was determined to nip those thoughts in the bud that were clearly evident upon her face.

"Fabritza, the only reason I am still holding on to my smile is due to the fact that I'm not a man prone to making scenes," Giovanni managed to speak between clenched teeth. "Kindly remove your hand from my shoulder. We are not a couple; we will never be a couple—ever. Am I making myself clear?" he shot her a look that could have melted every glacier known to man.

Fabritza laughed playfully but quickly removed her hand. She had accomplished what she had purposed: Naomi's obvious disgust at Giovanni. The sooner the nurse gave up her hopes of a relationship with Giovanni, the sooner she could convince him they were made for each other. "Crystal clear, Giovanni. Well, it's time for me to get my beauty rest; you're more than welcome to make sure I'm tucked in," she offered.

Giovanni glared at her, realizing working with Fabritza was becoming a part-time job. "No thank you," he replied coolly.

Fabritza shrugged her shoulders as if his wishes meant nothing to her and sauntered away.

Giovanni shook off the feeling of disgust that Fabritza left in her wake. *Lord, deliver me from evil.* She may have been every man's dream, but when it came to what mattered most to Giovanni, she was a beautiful nightmare.

"Going somewhere?" Nicholas had managed to catch up with Naomi before she turned to run away, for that was the expression stamped all over her features.

"Oh, Nick, hey," Naomi unclenched her hands, and slowed her breathing. "Just going to head back to the beach house," she mustered a smile.

"I'll walk you there," he offered.

"No, that's okay," Naomi grabbed her things and began packing them up.

"Naomi," Nicholas stopped her then.

223

"Yes?" Naomi tried to look earnest and carefree though she felt anything but.

"My brother's only got eyes for you," he declared.

Naomi stepped back. "He's got an interesting way of showing it," she replied jokingly.

"Fabritza is a nuisance to all of us," Nicholas confided. "I won't lie to you; she wants Giovanni, but the feelings aren't mutual," he pointed out. "You couldn't help but notice how uncomfortable he was," Nicholas went on.

Naomi held up her hand not wanting to hear more. "No, I couldn't help but notice how familiar she was with him," Naomi shot back. "Giovanni's a big boy; he doesn't need anyone offering explanations for him," Naomi added. "I trust Giovanni; he doesn't make it easy, but I do trust him." Naomi realized she actually meant it.

Nicholas was floored and impressed at the same time. "Good; well, sorry if I overstepped my bounds," he grinned sheepishly.

Naomi smiled, feeling her spirit revive. "Give us women some credit for seeing beyond the surface," she teased.

"Yes, ma'am," Nicholas saluted her as he watched her head up to the Worth's beach house and make it safely inside.

If my brother doesn't propose he's an idiot and a half, Nicholas thought, turning back to join those left around the fire.

"Ladies and Gentlemen, thank you all for coming to the fellowships tonight. We thank you all for taking time out of your busy schedules to break bread, learn, and play together. Let us bow our heads as my wife leads us in a closing prayer," Josiah suggested.

"Heavenly Father, ruler and creator of all life, we thank you for this evening and we pray that you would bless those who will travel home as well as those who will remain here on the beach. Thank you for what you have spoken to us and what we have hidden in our hearts. Let us live out your truth and love until next we meet, amen."

Everyone followed suit with their own amen, the ladies walking back to the beach house, the men staying to clean up and make sure their bonfire was out completely.

Angelynn and Josiah took a moment to wish each other goodnight in that timeless way that keeps marriage alive, love on fire, and hearts united: a kiss.

Marco stood in the same spot Ginevieve had left him in an hour ago, dejected and disappointed at the turn of events. He had been unprepared for her complete rejection of anything beyond friendship between them. He had felt so connected and at home in her presence the past three days. He drew his hands through his hair in frustration. *What had happened? Where did I go wrong?*

You thought that you could change her heart. Love is an internal attribute. It is more than what you do. Ginevieve has to love herself first before she can accept the love of someone else.

Marco reflected on what the Lord had spoken to him He thought back to the conversations he had shared with Ginny and recalled nuances of speech and even her perception when he complimented her. She generally thought he wasn't serious. Now he realized that she didn't think he was serious because she held reservations about her own self-worth. He closed his eyes in understanding. *Lord, please breakthrough to Ginevieve's heart and let the truth of her value in you shine through. Help her to cast all of her cares, fears, and insecurities on you,* he prayed.

As Marco walked away from the place where he had expected a new beginning, he moved forward with new determination to show Ginny not only how much he cared for her but how much God cared as well.

Little did he know Marco had all of heaven backing his plans.

Tehinnah had decided not to remain at the women's sleepover in light of her embarrassing episode on the beach. She had cornered Jamar on his way back down to the beach, attempting to act nonchalant about the encounter when he gave her a direct tongue-lashing. Tehinnah was not soon to forget the set down which was still ringing in her ears as she drove back inland.

"Look, I'm aware that you seem to think I'm interested in you, and I'm not sure who gave you the impression, but I'm not in the market for a relationship. Besides, you seem to make no distinction between men. I suppose one of us is just as good as another, right?"

Tehinnah realized then that her plan to incite his interest had backfired. He'd walk past her rejoining the others for the closing prayer, his eyes never returning to hers even after the parties went their separate ways. To Jamar Davis, she was not just invisible, but disreputable. Tehinnah prided herself of having a good reputation, and to imagine someone thinking anything less was completely intolerable.

Somehow, someway, she would have to restore her credibility. Tehinnah was determined that it would be sooner rather than later.

34

Sunday morning is never dull in the city of Savannah. Cars aligning streets, families walking hand in hand signify the time honored ritual of church attendance. If you drive slowly enough through a neighborhood, songs, music, and reverie can be heard like a flower opening its buds to the sun, so the people of God prepare their hearts and minds to receive the presence of the Lord.

Sunday morning...

"Mariella, we've got a good hour before we have to leave for church, honey," Naomi called out as she walked past her roommate's door.

Mariella poked her head out of her bedroom, sleep still in her eyes. "I meant to tell you last night but I've decided to join Jamar at Fresh Fire this morning," she closed her door then thought better and opened it again. "And before you get the wrong idea, I have no designs on Seth. Clearly he's besotted with Aliya," she noted.

Naomi was taken aback by Mariella's attitude. "I don't mean to pry but is something wrong?" she questioned.

Mariella didn't want to drag anyone into her own personal drama so she kept her conversation surface and light. "I do plan to visit New Life, but I'm just not up to it quite yet," she explained.

Naomi folded her hands across her chest. "Okay; just know that you can talk to me, Mariella."

Mariella reached out then to hug Naomi. "I know," she assured her. "Once we get back from Montego Bay, I'll join you for a visit to New Life," she promised.

Naomi grinned then. "I'm planning to hold you to that," she warned as she headed out the door.

Mariella managed to keep her composure until Naomi was safely out the door then she sagged in relief. How was she going to look Noelle in the eye without feeling angry, disappointed, and let down? His display of affection last night towards Tehinnah, his new secretary, had made Mariella truly nauseous. *Lord, I need your guidance,* Mariella prayed.

Stop leaning on your understanding. Trust me to know what is best for you.

Mariella exhaled a frustrated, pent up breath. *How could a man who is so set against me be good for me?* As she got ready for service, she couldn't stop pondering the thing that troubled her the most.

"Is this seat taken?" Rosalynn enquired to the unfamiliar parishioners that nearly filled the row where she planned to take refuge during service. Her strategy was simple: steer clear of all men until after service. She was thankful that she could find a seat close enough to enjoy praise and worship and far enough away from the distraction of her brother's malevolent glares.

Today, Savannah was taking the lead in praise and worship with a new song of praise. Rosalynn allowed the words to wash over her and fill her with the peace that came from worship. The words pierced her heart as she sang along.

"I just want to love you more,
I just want to love you more,
I just want to love you,
More than yesterday
I just want to serve you more,
I just want to serve you more,
I just want to serve you,
More than yesterday

Make my life an offering
A living sacrifice to the Lord I bring
A living sacrifice to you
My Lord King

I just want to give you more
I just want to give you more
I just want to give you
More than anything,"

Rosalynn allowed the vow to flood her soul and replace the worries that had harbored there since last night. She closed her eyes and shut out the distractions that sought refuge in her mind and set her heart to seek God for that was the place where she found joy and comfort.

Little did she know how many angels were looking in on her display of gratitude and wondering about that tiny word she had uttered from her lips-- redemption.

Nicholas couldn't help noticing how radiant Rosalynn was today. With her braids streaming down, her face directed toward heaven, he was transfixed for a moment on how beautiful she was inside and out. He found himself regretting being closed in between his twin on one side and a very distracting female bodyguard on the other side whose sole intent was to distract him this morning. *Lord, help me to hold my peace,* he prayed.

"I'm so glad you could meet with me this morning," Augusta gushed with pleasure.

"I'm never too busy for you or your sister," Pastor Marks assured her. "I'm glad you gave me a heads up last evening about your engagement and afforded me the opportunity to share a few words of wisdom and instruction with you," he added.

Augusta took out pen and paper and readied herself to receive from her pastor.

"First, I would like to say that your father had spoken to me of Enrique's desire to marry you a while back. Before he left for Jamaica, he asked me to look into the matter, to take measure of the man so to speak. He gave his blessings provided that Enrique could come up to par and be found worthy of you," Pastor Marks informed Augusta, watching the play of emotions across her face; clearly she was not aware of how much meddling her father had attempted. He continued. "I want you to know that I approve of your engagement and that Enrique is a fine gentleman. His reputation of fairness, kindness, and generosity precede him and he is spoken of very highly by his pastor, his spiritual family, as well as the business community. That being said, I will begin your marriage and family counseling sessions after we return from Montego Bay. I do understand your desire to keep this under wraps due to the media attention it may engender," he assured her.

"Thank you for understanding," she breathed a sigh of relief then. "Enrique and I have agreed that I won't wear my ring until we return from Montego Bay," she confided. "How long of an engagement period would you suggest?"

"Every case is different, but I would suggest you really concentrate on learning each other as mates since you know each other as friends," he advised.

"That's sounds fine with me," Augusta wrote rapidly. "I won't begin wedding planning because I want to focus my full attention on getting to know Enrique."

"Unfortunately, most people make the mistake of trying to plan their wedding at the same time they should be learning their life partner," Pastor Marks regret was apparent.

Augusta took in the advice with an open heart. "I trust your guidance Pastor Marks. I'm very thankful for you opening your schedule up at the last minute."

"One last thing: Elder Worth, Enrique's pastor, will be personally guiding you both through the process of engagement. I don't think you could have a better role model in your lives. Once we return from Montego Bay, you will meet with us both," He concluded. "Now, let us pray and ask the Lord's continued blessing as you transition from single hood to marriage."

"Today, I want to share with you from the subject, Fire Works," Elder Worth paused for a moment to allow the topic to implant itself on the hearts of his congregation.

"Fire has many purposes; it can warm, it can sterilize, it can purify, it can enable food to be prepared. But fire out of control can destroy a life," he warned as he allowed the swells of amen to build his enthusiasm. "As we see in our text today, Elijah had issued a challenge. He was challenging the idols of his day, the idol worshippers of his day, and the idol masters of his day to a spiritual showdown. I don't know if you recognize it or not, but we are heading toward a spiritual showdown," he declared. "Elijah said something that we need to recognize today as the prevailing thought that should set the standard of our lives in a culture so infiltrated with cynicism, doubt, and unbelief. He said, 'the God who answers by fire, let him be God!" his authoritative voice pierced the atmosphere. "I want you to know today that God still answers by fire! I want you to know that God still speaks today!" Elder Worth calmed himself then. "The question is not whether God still *speaks*; the question is: are *you* still listening? I invite you today to join me at the altar to receive the God who answers by fire. He wants to endue you with his power. He wants to baptize you with the Holy Ghost and with fire. He wants to take away your uncertainties, he wants to reveal the mysteries in his Word, he wants to help you live a life pleasing to Him right now," he encouraged. "Come to the Lord, come now, and receive the God who answers by Fire. Come accept his son, Jesus Christ into your life so that he may give you the Spirit of God that will help you in every area of your life."

Elder Worth ended his sermon leaving much unspoken. God was drawing the people and doing His work around the altar. He was wise enough to let God have his way.

"Today, before I begin, I'd like you to join me in welcoming all of our first time visitors," Seth applauded all of the new students who had decided to visit this morning before turning his eyes upon his personal guest.

"I'd also like you to give a warm welcome to Ms. Aliya Peyton," Seth identified her with an outstretched hand. "Next to my mother, she is the most important lady in my life," he declared, gazing at Aliya with enough heat in his eyes to start a fire. His congregation didn't help at all with outburst of well-wishing and giggles. Seth cleared his throat. "And now, in all seriousness, let us turn to the Word of God. Today, I want to speak with you about Faith on Fire."

Pastor John Marks was knee deep in the Word of God when he glanced up and was thrown for a loop. It was a good thing he had mastered pressing on even when being caught off guard. "God's power is evident because he uses ordinary people to do extraordinary things. This Firepower we are talking about today can't be produced mechanically, artificially, or scientifically. It is produced in our lives supernaturally. It is the power of God given to us by His Holy Spirit; not just any spirit. This power can't be bought or sold. It is freely given by God and freely received by men. You can't even decide who will receive it. It's not something you can discriminate against. Those whose hearts are yielded to God and received the Spirit of God are candidates for this Firepower!" Pastor Marks proclaimed as he stepped down from the pulpit to walk among the congregation who were up on their feet, engaging in the sermon; as much as they were listening, they were participating as well.

"We must use the Firepower of God if we hope to accomplish anything meaningful and purposeful in this world! We must engage our culture, walking out our faith in confidence! It is then that people will say the kingdom of God has come. With His Firepower you can unlock doors of understanding, bring resources to the poor, and shed understanding on the lives of the lost. When you can help someone in need, you are bringing the kingdom; when you can help someone turn from a destructive lifestyle to one of productivity, you are bringing God's Kingdom near," he stopped in front of Columbia Newcomb and her daughters, his surprise visitors for the day. "I encourage those of you who need God's Firepower to come forward today; come meet the God of the Universe at the altar today. He thinks so much of you, that He is ready to answer you at the same time He controls the universe. He is a personal God and He is here to give you the power you need today," he assured the congregation, personally leading some to the altar who stepped forward.

Columbia was one of the first who walked forward, her daughters joining her. She was led to visit New Life this morning, and with her pastor's approval she had hurried over to Pastor Marks' service. It was exactly what Columbia needed to hear. She had received Christ but she knew that something was missing in her relationship. She needed His Firepower and she was ready to ask for that power today. The moment she and her daughters made it to the altar the Spirit of God swept through New Life like a rushing wind. It was the culmination of everyone's expectation multiplied by their faith. It was what many had waited for but no one was quite prepared for, including Pastor Marks. One thing was certain: New Life would never be the same.

"Since we are surrounded as the Word says by such an enormous crowd of faith fans, let's make sure that we strip off the weights that slow us down. We don't want our fire for God to cool off. How do we do this? We have to fuel our faith with prayer, we have to learn the discipline of endurance, we have to let the Word be our guide, and we have to keep our eyes on Jesus who is the lover of our soul and the greatest champion of faith. He died for the hope of our salvation! He endured the shame of the cross, disregarding the embarrassment so that we could have eternal life and a full, satisfying life right here on earth," he concluded. "When you think of the hostility Jesus endured from sinful people you can be encouraged to not give up, to keep your faith lit for God, to let your faith overcome depression, overcome fear, and every other distraction that life will bring. If you feel like your faith has been snuffed out by the difficulties you face, if you feel like you need to ignite your faith, or if you feel like you need to refuel, I want you to come forth so we can pray with you, whatever your need today." Seth opened his arms in a gesture of welcome as the people came forward, some running, some walking, some young, and some old to receive prayer and find direction for their lives. Seth was always humbled by the response to the Word of God. *Lord, use me today for your glory. All of you and none of me as I agree with your people in prayer today,* he prayed, closing his eyes and stretching forth his hand to pray for the first of many souls reaching out to the Lord.

"That was a wonderful sermon, Elder Worth," Rosalynn shook hands with her pastor.

"Thank God he spoke through me today," Elder Worth clasped her hand in a firm grip. "I couldn't have done it without Him," he informed her.

Rosalynn moved along, not wanting to take up all of the pastor's time, seeing as she would be meeting with him tomorrow.

"Roz, wait."

The clipped tone caused her to freeze in her tracks. *Carlton.* She turned to face him. "What is it?"

Carlton's lips were pressed together in a firm, grim line. "You can't avoid me forever, you know; it's not very Christian of you," he pointed out.

Roz held back the quick retort that sprang to her lips. "I'm not avoiding you. I'm clearing my personal space of destructive people," she informed him. "You and I have nothing to say to each other. You made it very clear where we stand when you deposited my things outside of Tatyanna's door. I stopped being your concern the day I left *your* home, remember?" she spoke in a measured tone watching the look Carlton gave her melt ice as he spun away from her in a huff.

Good. Let him chew on that for a while, Rosalynn decided as she headed to Tybee Beach for an energizing run.

Sunday afternoon...

Tehinnah waved enthusiastically at Noelle as he greeted visitors after service. He gave her a megawatt smile and waved back as he continued in conversation with a young couple. *I don't know why I didn't recognize it before but Noelle Marks is one fine brother,* Tehinnah pondered to herself.

"If I didn't know any better, I would think you were flirting with your boss in church," Tatyanna spoke from behind Tehinnah.

"Then you'd be thinking right," Tehinnah giggled waving her fingers at her boss, the pastor's son.

Tatyanna snatched her sister and drug her off to a more unoccupied area of the church as most of the congregation had begun to filter into the vestibule. "Tehinnah, what is wrong with you? First Jamar; now Noelle," Tatyanna questioned her sister in a near whisper. "Didn't those fancy law professors tell you not to mix business with pleasure?" she chided her.

Tehinnah rolled her eyes. "I'm not twelve, Tatyanna. I can handle a complicated relationship. He's gorgeous, ambitious, employed, single, without kids, and saved; how many men do you presently know that fit that description?" Tehinnah rolled the qualities off her tongue like she was describing a fine wine.

"Look, I'm just trying to warn you," Tatyanna pleaded with her sister. "Don't jump into anything too soon. Give yourself time to settle in to your surroundings. I haven't known Noelle for very long but he doesn't strike me as a man who's ready for commitment. I just don't want you getting involved because you're looking for a temporary fix," Tatyanna reasoned.

Tehinnah dropped her façade for a moment, letting her sister see clearly into her heart. "Oh, trust me, a temporary fix this is not," she assured her. "I've been informed quite specifically that Jamar is not interested; I'm not wasting my time on someone who is clearly unappreciative of what I have to offer," she stood a little straighter, tilting her nose in the air.

"Ah, I see; Jamar gave you the brush off. You think Noelle is the answer? Tehinnah, this is a disaster waiting to happen. If you hope to have any chance with Jamar, dating someone else is not going to convince him that you're interested." Tatyanna advised.

Tehinnah waved away her sister's advice. "I just want to have a little fun, hang out, and spend time with someone who values my company; I don't want to be alone and I don't plan to be," Tehinnah's statement was final, leaving no room for argument.

As she walked over to Noelle who was apparently all too happy to see her, Tatyanna could only throw up her hands to the Lord knowing her sister was choosing to learn her life lessons the hard way.

35

Naomi had truly enjoyed Pastor Marks' sermon today but as she gathered her things her mind returned to other matters from this morning, mainly her roommate. Mariella was clearly avoiding attending services but Naomi knew it was more than that; Mariella was clearly avoiding her boss. Naomi had been dropping Mariella off at very odd hours so she could work on completing Noelle's interior design for his new home. She hadn't thought anything of it at first, but the thought began to nag her that something was amiss. It wasn't until last night when they were before the bonfire that Naomi noticed Mariella's pained glances at her boss. *Had Noelle been inappropriate in some way? Was Mariella afraid to mention it for fear it would cost her job?* Naomi wanted to share with Enrique what she was feeling but she didn't want Mariella to feel as though she were spying on her. *Lord, show me how to broach the subject so that all parties involved are treated with respect.*

"Hello, beautiful."

Naomi was taken completely off guard by the comment. She whirled to find Giovanni Cartellini standing before her, a single rose in hand and a grin so bright it competed with his crisp white dress shirt he wore under a camel blazer and jeans. The man looked arrestingly handsome and relaxed. Nothing was more attractive to Naomi than a man who was comfortable in his own skin. She smiled warmly allowing the anxiety to ebb away as he handed her the long stemmed rose.

"Hello, Giovanni," Naomi blushed. "This is a pleasant surprise," she added. She wanted to keep an open mind and trust that their relationship was real; that Giovanni wasn't playing with her emotions.

Giovanni had been anticipating making his way over to New Life today. As soon as his congregation had sung amen he had high-tailed it out the front door to catch Naomi before her service ended. He had a feeling she had gotten the wrong impression the other night. He was thankful he'd made it in time. "I wanted to ask you a very important question in person," he stepped a little closer.

Naomi's heart beat a little faster at his nearness. "And what might that be?" she teased him, taking a step backward.

Giovanni caught on to her cat and mouse game stepping closer. "Would you do me the honor of having dinner with me tonight?" he voice coming on a whisper smoother than melted molasses on a summer day.

Naomi swallowed once, twice, backing up again. "Tonight?" her brave voice ended in a squeak.

"Tonight; does seven sound like a reasonable hour?" Giovanni made no further attempt to come closer, though her scent, cinnamon and vanilla, enticed him to come closer. It did not help him one bit that the woman he desired smelled like a sugary treat. He reined his senses in.

"Seven sounds fine," she managed to croak out nodded vigorously.

"Alright, then," Giovanni smiled then backing away, not daring to touch her lest he couldn't stop himself. "I'll pick you up at six-thirty," he tamed his excitement, measuring his tone lest she think him some love-crazed idiot. He had Josiah Worth to thank for the use of his beach house this evening. He had wanted their first official dinner to be special and memorable. He would make preparations after their security meeting this afternoon.

"Okay," Naomi nearly sighed then caught herself. *What are you doing acting like a puddle of emotions? Get yourself together!* As she watched Giovanni walk out of the sanctuary, she stood transfixed, gripping the single rose in hand. Tonight would be her first official dinner date with Giovanni. It had been a long time coming but definitely worth the wait. Naomi couldn't wait to see the look on Aurielle's face when she revealed she had other dinner plans.

"Thanks for giving me such a pleasant surprise today," Seth grinned as he held Aliya's hands in his own.

Aliya blushed becomingly. "What a surprising introduction," she teased him.

"I like to make my intentions clear so that there's no misunderstanding between me and the flock," he chuckled.

"I was really encouraged by the Word today," Aliya smiled up at him, love shining in her eyes. "With less than a week before we head out for Montego Bay, I'm definitely going to draw on what you've said today," she added.

"I know that your schedule is going to be busy this week so I will try not to intrude on your time too much," Seth informed her. "But if you have some time for lunch this week, I usually take my break around twelve. I have a few counseling sessions this week and I'll be meeting with a guest pastor who'll be speaking for me over the holiday," he confided.

"I would love to but with Savannah's mother's upcoming nuptials and Savannah's wedding right around the corner, I won't be taking any breaks this week," Aliya told him regretfully.

"Well, I'll just have to be very inventive this week in getting your attention," Seth teased.

Aliya tapped him playfully. "If you gave me any more attention, your congregation will think we're going to elope," she joked.

"You know, come to think of it, that's not a half-bad idea," he rubbed his chin thoughtfully.

"Seth Davis, when did you become so incorrigible," Aliya questioned him, totally shocked that he would say something so out of character.

Seth pulled her close then. "About forty-eight hours and counting," he chuckled.

Sunday Evening...

"Welcome," Dr. Trey Jones ushered Mariella and Aurielle into his home. "You all can make yourselves comfortable in the family room. There are some appetizers there for your benefit," he directed them as he made his way back to the kitchen to complete his dinner preparations.

Aurielle and Mariella didn't hesitate to follow his directives.

"He's got great taste," Mariella noted, her designer's eye taking in every detail. "Simple, classic, and not overpoweringly male," she observed aloud.

Aurielle shook her head. "Girl, get your head out of the clouds and just enjoy yourself," she admonished Mariella. "I'm glad you're here, Mariella," she put her arms around her. Aurielle understood how hard it could be navigating your way as a new believer.

Mariella went to inspect a painting on the wall. "Thanks for inviting me. I didn't have any plans today after service."

Trey entered then. "How was service for everyone?"

Mariella became animated then. "Pastor Seth spoke about Faith on Fire; I learned that I've got to keep my faith fueled by praying more and learning God's Word. I've been reading a few verses everyday, but it never seems like its enough, you know?" she explained sitting down on a recliner near the fireplace.

Trey sat across from her on his recliner. "I know exactly what you mean. Elder Worth spoke to us today about Fire Works; it was a play on words but he told us that God still speaks to us today. He challenged us to listen for the voice of God. He challenged us to really be submitted to following God when we hear Him. I know I haven't always listened when God was speaking to me. It's an area that I have to continue to grow in. His Word is one of the most direct ways He speaks to us, but sadly enough, most believers aren't even reading His Word daily," Trey spoke candidly.

"Pastor Marks talked to us about the Fire Power of God, His Holy Spirit. It is the power of God that helps us to do right, talk right, walk right, live right, and certainly to love right," Aurielle shared. "I didn't know what real love was until I met God," she turned to Trey. "And I had certainly never seen love in the flesh until I met Naomi and Trey," she confessed. "They were both living breathing examples of God's love for me," she shook her head at the memory. "And trust me; I did everything I possibly could to make myself unlovable and difficult."

"No matter how difficult she tried to be, I could only see her in the future," Trey revealed. "I believe that when we open our eyes and gain the correct perspective about people, people with flaws who are made in the image of a flawless God, then we can begin to really love like we are supposed to," Trey concluded as his timer in the kitchen went off.

"Looks like dinner is ready," he stood then ushering them into the dining room. "Let's break bread together, ladies."

Enrique had just concluded his security team session when Nicholas pulled him aside. "What was it you needed, Nick?"

Nicholas was thankful that Fabian, Fabritza, and Giovanni had gone outside to do a perimeter check so that he could voice his concerns. "I wanted to make you aware of the tension that is going on between Giovanni and Fabritza. I fear that it is beginning to weigh on my brother and interfere with his personal relationship with Naomi."

Enrique was taken aback. "I noticed Giovanni wasn't his cheerful self in service today, but I thought that maybe he was feeling a bit under the weather," he confessed.

Nicholas shook his head vehemently. "Last night at the fellowship Fabritza was all but pawing my brother. I have a really bad feeling about Fabritza going to Montego Bay with us. I believe she's only going to stir up trouble."

Enrique blew out a breath of frustration. "We need her presence there at least until Francheska can join the team. Then we can give her walking papers," he decided. "I know that you two have not gotten along in the past, but if you can hold on until we make it to Montego Bay, we can settle things there. I'll explain to her that there are too many conflicts of interest involved to keep her on the team," he concluded.

Nicholas nodded in understanding. "It's your call, boss. I'm just making you aware that things have not improved," he warned.

Enrique trusted Nicholas' judgment. "Let's pray that Giovanni will be able to keep his cool and that Fabritza can do her job until we release her from the responsibility."

Both men bowed their heads and lifted the situation up the Ultimate Problem Solver.

"Here are the keys and the code," Shemiah handed the key cards over to Rosalynn. "It's pretty peaceful out here once the sun sets," he assured her.

"Thank you so much, Shemiah," Rosalynn threw her arms around her long-time friend. "I'm so grateful for your friendship," she held back her tears.

"Hey, no need to cry," Shemiah gave her a sisterly hug. "What's most important is that you and Carlton work things out," he declared. "Take your time, get your bearings; I'm not in a rush, okay?"

"Okay," Rosalynn nodded.

"Here's my number, here's Pastor Davis' number in case of emergency, and you have Elder Worth's number as well, correct?" Shemiah wiped the trace of worry out of his voice.

"Yes; thank you all for your kindness," Rosalynn had received a call from Elder Worth, a check from the Benevolent Ministry at Second Chance, and a call from Pastor Davis letting her know he would check on her from time to time. It was seeing the people of God display so much concern, even leaders from other churches truly work together and show their care for her that had her crying tears of thankfulness. "I know to some people this may seem like a light thing but Carlton is the only family I have; he's been there for me and this has just completely thrown me off guard,' she confessed.

"You're wrong on one account," Shemiah corrected her. "Carlton's not the only family you have. You've got your sisters and brothers at Fresh Fire, New Life, and Second Chance. We're going to do what we can to help you, Roz. We love Carlton and we love you. We all want to see you two work this situation out if you can," Shemiah assured her.

Roz thanked Shemiah again and as he got into his car and set off back into town, she wondered whether she and Carlton would ever have the family relationship she had worked so hard to cultivate restored to them. *Lord, help me to forgive him for shutting me out,* she prayed fervently. *Forgive me for my actions today for I was just as wrong as he was in my attitude,* she pleaded. *Help me to make the right decision on tomorrow,* she ended her prayer as she went inside to unpack and settle into her next phase of life.

"Pastor Marks, I didn't know you could move like that," Nadia teased. "One moment you were in the pulpit, the next moment you were running down the aisle," she observed cheerily, her mother and sisters laughing.

Pastor Marks looked down his nose, past his glasses at Nadia with his most serious look. "If I didn't know any better, I'd think you were calling me old, Nadia," he glared in a joking manner.

"Oh, no she's not," Delia exclaimed. "She calls you DP," she assured him.

Nadia and Rodia looked at each other in surprise and attempted to silence their little sister who obviously understood more than she let on.

"What's that?" Pastor Marks grew more curious by the moment. Delia put on the sweetest smile and spoke up proudly. "Daddy Prospect," she turned to her Mommy then. "What's a prospect, Mommy?"

Columbia was thankful that her complexion masked her blush because she was thoroughly embarrassed. "It means something you consider," she explained as she glared at her daughters.

Pastor Marks grinned wide then completely amused by the trio. "Why, thank you for the compliment, girls," he took a sip of lemonade then turning his attention to Columbia. "I don't mind being a Daddy Prospect at all," he tipped his glass in salute to the slack jawed twins.

Gram Tot and Gram Parker, Savannah's matriarchs were busy clearing away Sunday dinner when they heard a knock at the door.

"I'll get it!" Savannah called out. She ran to the door, expecting to see Shemiah but after peering out the window, she didn't see anyone there. A feeling of uneasiness passed over her. She opened the door carefully. Outside on her porch was a newspaper. Savannah picked up the paper and the front headline caught her attention immediately:

School Director Poses Nude- Parents Demanding Resignation

A note slipped from between the newspaper folds: **Time is winding down. Call off the wedding or the headline will read worse than this one.**

"Of all the rude, despicable, ungodly--"

"Honey, what's wrong?" Shemiah came up the stairs to the porch.

Savannah couldn't even speak she was so angry. She handed the mock newspaper over to her fiancé along with the note. "He doesn't intend to stop, does he?" she threw up her hands. "Someone has got to talk some sense into the man. This is blatant harassment and I *will not* tolerate it, relative or not," she finished.

Shemiah sighed in resignation. "I've tried talking to him man to man, but he seems bent on rebellion. I'm not going to allow Lysander one more thought outside of prayer," he hugged Savannah close and comforted her. "Come on inside' let's inform your family of what we are facing and let's bombard heaven tonight."

Savannah was thankful for a man who trusted God and took him at His word. "Yes, let's bombard heaven tonight."

"Well, what happened?" Lysander paid his messenger as he sat in his vehicle up the road from Savannah's grandmother's home.

"She looked terrified but then some guy showed up talking about bombing heaven and then she got all excited," the man told him scratching his head. "Are you *sure* you want to mess with these folks? They seem like good people," the man questioned.

"I don't pay you to think," Lysander snapped. "I pay you to deliver packages. Got it?" Lysander's tone brooked no argument.

The messenger saw the look of pure fury on his face and guessed it would do no good to tell Lysander that he spotted three men dressed in white guarding the house after the woman and the man went inside. "I think this will be my last delivery. You're on your own," the messenger decided.

Lysander cursed profusely then and sped off.

The messenger shook his head glad to be rid of Lysander and suddenly sure that he had done the right thing.

"Thank you for such a wonderful dinner," Aurielle sipped her coffee out on Trey's deck. Mariella had decided to take an informal tour of Trey's home to allow them some space to talk.

"Not a problem," Trey assured her. "I've enjoyed the company immensely and I hope you can join me again soon," he offered.

"Maybe after we get back from Montego Bay," she considered. "I am so looking forward to a few days in the Caribbean," she sighed.

"This will be my first vacation in three years," he confessed. Aurielle's brows rose at that statement. "No wonder you don't have time for much of a social life," she teased.

Trey stepped closer to her. "If you were apart of my life, I'd make time for you," he assured her.

Aurielle gave him an incredulous look. "You barely make time to sleep, much less time for a relationship," she corrected him.

Trey took her hand in his. "I keep myself busy because to be honest with you, I don't want to come home to an empty house. Life is always better when we have someone to share it with," he looked into her eyes then, sure she had read his meaning clearly.

Mariella came outside then to join them. "Your art collection is very impressive," she told Trey unaware of the moment she had interrupted.

Aurielle stepped back then forcing him to release her hand. "Well, I think that it's about time for me to take Mariella home now," she cleared her throat.

"In other words, this discussion is closed?" Trey chuckled. Aurielle gave him a look of warning.

"Okay, I won't press," Trey walked behind her. *Today.* "Thanks for having me over, Trey. You are a fabulous cook," Mariella complimented him.

"I aim to impress," Trey grinned. "Well, you sure impressed me," Mariella smiled then leaned to whisper not too discreetly. "Aurielle, he's definitely a keeper," she smiled up at her friend while Trey chuckled at her audacity.

Aurielle glared at him. "Good evening, Trey," she waved and ushered Mariella through the front door before she said anything else.

"Good night," Trey waved at the pair, his eyes trained on the lovely Aurielle Foqua, a woman of many protestations, all of which he planned to dismantle in due time.

36

Sunday Evening...

Columbia was pleased that her daughters were enjoying Pastor Marks' company. He had invited them to dinner after service, explaining that his son would be heading back to work and he would rather not eat alone. It was touch and go for a moment when Delia had brought up the issue of John being a new father but Columbia was surprised he had handled the statement so well. She noted his ease around her daughters and couldn't help admire the fact that he seemed able to hold a conversation with all three and was genuinely interested in what they had to say.

"This is my firstest year in real school," Delia told him seriously.

"Yes, I heard," Pastor Marks nodded. "Your first year is one of the hardest. You have to learn how to stay awake, when to potty, and how to eat without making too much of a mess," he continued. "Not to mention all those hallways and doors that look the same," he reasoned with her.

Delia's eyes lit up. "I thought it was just me. You noticed it too?" she asked ready to leap out of her seat.

Columbia knew she was a goner when she saw how comfortable he was with Delia. She was just about to comment when she felt her phone vibrate. She pulled it out, excusing herself from the table. "Hello?" She stopped in her tracks. "She did what?" Columbia was hard-pressed not to yell. "I'll be right over." She hung up and rushed back to the table to grab her things.

"Is everything okay?" Pastor Marks' concern was evident.
Columbia shook her head. She was literally shaking. "My shop was broken into and vandalized," she stated as calmly as possible.

Nadia and Rodia jumped up to steady their mother.
"I'm coming with you," Pastor Marks called for their waitress, leaving a sizable tip.

"Why would someone break into the shop?" Rodia couldn't believe what she was hearing.

"They caught the girl. Her name is Serena Quintana." Columbia rubbed the space between her eyes feeling a headache approaching.

"Oh my God," Nadia murmured. "That's the girl that trashed my locker. She must be insane," Nadia concluded. "She got off pretty light with the principal but this is not school grounds."

Columbia could not believe what the world was coming to. "She did this over a boy? Pray that I don't get my hands on her," she determined as she walked out with Delia on her hip, her daughters on her trail and Pastor Marks not far behind asking for the peace of God to guard Columbia and keep her from doing anything drastic.

Giovanni led Naomi blindfolded up the stairs of Josiah's beach house carefully unlocking the door and guided her inside. He had been anticipating this moment from the time she said yes this afternoon up until now.

She had chosen a scarlet dress that draped her curves gracefully and ended well below her calves along with a cashmere sweater to match and scarlet pumps that added height to her petite frame. Giovanni had second thoughts then about dining alone but then waved off the feeling. He could handle this. Naomi had been quite amicable about the blindfold and now all of his hard work was paying off.

"Take off your shoes," he commanded.

Naomi stepped out of her shoes and onto something very soft. *Flower petals!* "Can I take off the blindfold now?"

"No, Little Miss Impatient," Giovanni chided her. "It will be my honor." He slid the blindfold off.

Naomi opened her eyes slowly expecting to adjust to light but found the room softly lit with candles. She looked down and took a sharp intake. The entire floor was completely covered in rose petals.

"In many cultures it is said that the feet of royalty should never touch the ground," Giovanni noted taking her hand in his and bowing to kiss it. He stood once more. "Tonight, I'd like to invite you to indulge me in treating you like a queen," Giovanni requested.

Naomi was a bit stunned for words so she nodded in acquiescence.

Giovanni walked her through the rose petals and seated her on a chaise lounge. He clapped hands and out came a young lady with a steaming bowl of water. "Your first beauty treatment this evening is a foot massage for those feet that you spend all day on," he noted. "Get comfortable and I shall be back in fifteen minutes with your dinner."

Naomi couldn't believe he was going to all this trouble. She was going to thank him when his finger came down upon her lips silencing her effectively. "Not a word," he warned. It was then she noticed the sound of gospel jazz floating through the air. She closed her eyes as the young woman went to work on her tired feet. *Thank you, Lord!*

Columbia stood in the middle of her shop or more specifically what was left of her shop. The damage done was repairable but the feeling of invasion that Columbia felt seemed to stay with her long after they had straightened up, Pastor Marks working alongside her and the girls to clean up before business day on Monday. Thankfully her insurance covered the property damage but she would have to call some of her clients to reschedule until after the holidays. Serena had done quite a work: she had bashed in several hair dryers, smashed her mirrored wall, and poured most of her hair products down the drain.

"Miss Newcomb, are you planning to press charges?"

Columbia looked around her shop. "No, pressing charges will not solve Serena's problems. If you can see to it that she gets five hundred community service hours, she can work them off right in this shop," Columbia decided.

Nadia and Rodia both looked at their mother in disbelief.

"Is she serious?" Nadia wondered aloud.

"I think she is," Rodia murmured more to herself than anyone else.

"I can't make you any promises but I will give your recommendation to the judge," he offered.

Columbia walked the officer to the door. "Thanks, Officer."

She turned around and looked at her bewildered children and Pastor Marks who stood ready to take on the next project she handed out to him. "Well, I believe that the shop will remain closed this week and I will reopen after the holidays," she decided, releasing a pent up breath.

"I think that's a good idea. I have some brothers at the church who own a remodeling business. I'm sure they would be willing to take on this project with little cost. You can trust them to work while you're away and set your mind at ease a bit," Pastor Marks suggested.

Columbia looked thoughtfully at him. "Thanks for your help tonight. You didn't have to stay," she added.

"I wanted to," Pastor Marks stated emphatically. "I want you to know I'm here for the long haul, Columbia."

Columbia wished she could lean on him in that moment. She had spent years building her business all to have it carelessly destroyed by an angry hormonal teenager. "Are you sure?" she kidded. "It can get a little rocky on this road I'm traveling."

"I've dealt with plenty of rocky roads. This here is smooth sailing," he gave her shoulder a gentle squeeze.

As Nadia watched Pastor Marks gaze compassionately at her mother, she decided right then and there that Pastor Marks might just make a great DP after all.

"That was a fantastic massage," Naomi sat on the floor with her legs folded beside her finishing off one of her favorite meals: barbecue ribs slow roasted and so tender the meat rolled off the bone. "Where did you find her?" she spoke between bites.

"She's contracted to work with agents," he confided. "She owed me a favor and I called it in," he informed her.

"Well, thank you is not an adequate enough statement," Naomi sighed appreciatively.

Giovanni lay sideways on the floor admiring her from his viewpoint. "I was very tempted to massage your feet myself, but a man has to be aware of his weaknesses," Giovanni sipped his sparkling cider eying her over the rim of his glass. "And you, Naomi, are definitely my number one weakness," he confessed. "Here," he leaned forward with his linen napkin. "You've got some sauce still left on your bottom lip," he took the napkin and lightly fanned across her bottom lip.

Naomi sat as still as a lion seeking to go unnoticed.

"You seem to need some further assistance," Giovanni noted taking the napkin down and without any thought traced his tongue across the sticky sauce on her lip tasting sugar, spice, and a trace of strawberry lip gloss. "Great combination," he leaned back taking in her glossed over eyes.

Naomi was speechless. The man had taken her from zero to one thousand in under three seconds.

"Naomi?"

"Run! Run! Flee! Get going now! Move it, Girl! Think later, run now!"

Naomi leaped up from the floor and raced to put her shoes on. "We've got to go," she spoke decisively not realizing she had left Giovanni grabbing the air in front of him.

"Naomi, wait," Giovanni hopped up and met her at the door, tugging on his shoes.

Naomi shook her head fumbling with the lock and then bolting outside and down the steps like the beach house was on fire. *Clearly more than the beach house is on fire. What in the world was I thinking?* Naomi paced outside waiting for Giovanni to make his way down stairs.

"Naomi, look, I'm sorry if I startled you," Giovanni's desperation was evident in his voice.

Naomi swung around. "Startled me? You don't know the half of it," she practically yelled. "Thank you for the lovely dinner and massage," Naomi reigned in her panic. "Now I am ready to go home," she declared crossing her hands over her chest in defense mode.

Giovanni hands clasped on top of his head looked rather remorseful. "I blew it didn't I? It's just that the sauce wouldn't come off and you were looking so beautiful and edible," he wiggled his eyebrows.

Naomi shook her head regretfully. "Giovanni, we cannot have another dinner date alone," she got into the car as he unlocked the doors.

Giovanni sighed. "Understood," he helped her inside the car then ran back up the steps to secure the beach house. He would return later, clean up, and take a very, very cold shower.

As he put on his seat belt, he felt a pang of regret. *Why did I go and kiss her?* Now he couldn't stop thinking about how soft her lips felt beneath his. He looked at her then. "Naomi, I apologize for taking advantage of the moment. Will you forgive me?"

Naomi breathed out a relaxing breath. "Yes," she sighed. "Would you forgive me for wanting you to continue?" she confessed.

"Yes," he managed to croak out. That statement caused Giovanni to put the car in gear to deposit Naomi safely back home; with the quickness.

Mariella was engrossed in her leisure reading when her phone rang. *What now?* It seemed to her that she was always being interrupted at the most interesting part of the story.

"Hello?"

"Mariella, hey, this is Noelle."

Mariella sat upright. "How can I help you?" her tone was cordial but distant.

"I was just checking on the house this evening and I was surprised and pleased," he noted.

"How so," Mariella had all of her defenses up.

"Well, it appears you're practically done. I hadn't thought you'd be this far along; I've hardly seen you working and I've been here every day," he commented casually.

"It's not unusual for our paths not to cross. I usually get a ride out with Naomi," Mariella reminded him. "I should be done this week," she assured him. *Then I will be out of your life for good.*

Noelle paused. "See, that's just the thing," he hesitated.

Mariella looked at the phone in irritation. "What's the problem?"

Noelle had to get to the root of his problem. The part he didn't want to address. The part that had been nagging him all day; he had sensed very strongly that Mariella was avoiding him. He had brushed off the feeling on Saturday night but when he was in prayer at the altar, he had seen a fleeting vision of Mariella crying over a paper with his name on it. She had crumpled up the paper and then trashed it. Noelle hadn't wanted to rely on what his Spirit was saying. He wanted to believe everything was fine between them, but he couldn't seem to get any work at the office done. He had decided to call her and make sure everything was okay. Noelle charged ahead.

"I have this tiny feeling that the reason why you've almost completed a project that should take you at least three months is that you've been working extra hard to complete the job with the hopes of getting rid of me, am I right?" he summarized.

Mariella had no words. Her mouth formed a perfect oval but nothing came out.

"Have I done something to make you upset, Mariella?" Noelle pressed.

Only if you include trampling my self esteem in the dirt, she noted. "I can't talk right now," Mariella stalled. "I've got to go," she hung up quickly before he could say more or coax it out of her.

Noelle listened to the dial tone. *Well, Lord. That went well.* ***How do you expect your future wife to respond when you say she isn't good enough for you?***

Noelle was blown away by that statement. *My Wife; when did I? What?* Then the Lord took Noelle back to the conversation he had with his father. He realized that Mariella must have been there. Noelle fell to his knees. *Oh, God, no! My Wife? God, this is not funny.*

Do you hear me laughing? You have been warned several times but you chose to go your own way. Now you must deal with the consequences of disregarding my voice.

Noelle bowed his head in repentance wondering how in the world he was going to deal with this revelation. *What am I supposed to say to Mariella?*

Rest assured, she knows. She was praying you would never find out.

Those words struck Noelle like a blow to the head. Here he thought he was on top of the world. Now he realized he was in the lowest of gutters with God and with Mariella. He had been so busy denying what he was feeling that he had unwittingly hurt her in the process. *What can I do to make this right?* He wasn't ready to ask what he could do to win Mariella's heart. He knew he wasn't worthy of it.

Ask her forgiveness. Listen to your father. Be healed from your past or you will ruin any chance for your future happiness.

Noelle humbly gathered up his things and headed home to talk with his father. *Lord,* Noelle finally submitted, *I am available to you.*

Mariella had no time to process what had happened between her and Noelle due to the fact that her roommate had come home flustered and animated. She had never seen Naomi so riled up so she listened patiently as her roommate recounted her romantic night out.

"One minute I was eating barbecue and the next minute he was licking my lips!" Naomi was still in shock touching the spot Giovanni had tasted. "I was completely thrown," she shook her head. "This is why my Mamacita told me I could never go on a date alone," she reasoned. "one minute you think you're in control; the next minute you know you've lost your mind," Naomi shared.

"Other than the lip licking, how did things go?" Mariella tried to calm her roommate who was turning more hysterical by the minute.

"You expect me to think beyond that? Well, I guess I can divide the time: before lip licking; after lip licking," she decided.

Mariella rolled her eyes heavenward. "Do I need to call Giovanni and tell him how he has ruined you for any other relationship?"

"He would be too pleased by half," Naomi shook her head ruefully. She decided to turn a corner. "So, are you going to tell me what's going on between you and Noelle or am I gonna have to shake it out of you?"

Mariella's eyes widened in surprise. "Who *are* you people?"

When Pastor Marks entered his darkened living room he was not expecting to find his son lounged in a corner looking tired, dismal, and exhausted. He entered the room sensing that this was definitely a spiritual matter and not a natural one.

"Something wrong?" he posed the question casually. Noelle was prone to bouts of righteous indignation at times and tonight, John was simply not in the mood.

"You were right. About everything," he conceded.

Pastor Marks knew instantly to what he referred. "So, she's The One." He questioned.

Noelle nodded stoically.

"What do you plan to do about it?" He came and took a seat opposite his son.

"I've got to repair some things before I can do anything about it. I believe she overheard us the other day at the house." He sighed regretfully.

John resisted saying 'I told you so'. He knew it would only add to the guilt Noelle was obviously dealing with. "Maybe there is something I can do," he said thoughtfully.

"I don't see what can be done. She's obviously never going to visit our church, she'll be done with my house by the time we head out for Montego Bay," he thought aloud then stopped short, laughing at himself. "I just realized the Lord allowed her to design the interior of *her* home," he smacked his forehead. "I really should have seen this coming."

"I may be able to convince her to redesign our class room spaces at the church. After all, they are in need of help," he added. "It's a legitimate project," he concluded.

Noelle nodded in agreement. "Whatever you can do to keep her in my life, I'd be grateful. Hopefully she won't avoid me entirely in Montego Bay," he spoke with renewed optimism.

"The best thing we can do now is pray for her son, that she will accept your apology and that God will heal her heart, and yours," his father gave him a very pointed look.

Noelle nodded. "And mine," he confessed as he bowed his head in prayer along with his father.

For once God did something he hadn't done in a long time when looking at Noelle Marks. He smiled.

Mariella settled herself in for the evening thinking back to Naomi's last comment.

It's not rocket science, Mariella. The first day I met him I could tell Noelle was clearly taken with you.

Taken or not, he's definitely fighting it, Mariella let that thought settle in her mind on her way to sleep. *No way am I putting myself In harm's way,* she decided as she drifted off to sleep.

37

Monday morning in Savannah was as busy as any other metropolis. The air was punctuated with the sounds of well-wishers, the pitter patter of joggers and dog walkers, the sounds of frustrated commuters who spoke with the blare of their horns. The weekend was over and the relaxed atmosphere that had overtaken the city was nowhere to be seen. All over the city everyone was at work, saint and sinner alike. But there was much unfinished business between those in the community of faith.

Elder Worth crossed his legs several times as he tried not to interrupt the indomitable Carlton Rhodes. He cut a dashing figure in his hand tailored navy blue pinstripe suit. He played the part of concerned brother to a tee. It took everything within him as a Pastor to listen to the bitter diatribes flowing from the mouth of a man he had given more credit to for good sense than he apparently deserved.

"I am extremely disappointed in her, Pastor," Carlton went on warming to his subject. He had decided to come in to see Elder Worth thirty minutes early so that he could attempt to persuade him to his way of thinking. "She's very naïve to think that someone like Nicholas Cartellini could take a genuine interest in her. I knew she had low self-esteem issues but I never thought things would go this far. Maybe I haven't given her enough praise for how far she's come, but she's got a ways to go," he continued. "I never expected her to get this far," he spoke almost as if he were commenting to himself. "She's still got several problem areas to work on, though; cellulite doesn't just disappear overnight. She's got to apply herself to her toning regimen," he added sounding like a man in despair.

Elder Worth was prohibited from replying by Rosalynn herself striding through the door and greeting them both in a decidedly cool manner. Elder Worth stood then motioning for her to be seated across from Carlton. He took in her very feminine dress, stiletto heels, and confident smile and perceived that this was not a woman who lack self esteem but who rather had been repressing her self image to accommodate a tyrant of a brother.

"Please, be seated," Elder Worth waited until Roz was seated before he took his own seat once more. He looked to both siblings and bowed his head to pray for them both. Once he had heard what the Lord was saying, he cleared his throat and proceeded.

"Mr. Rhodes, for the last thirty minutes I have allowed you to pour out your heart, to share your concerns with me, and to give me your opinion on what is going on with your sister. Because you are both members of my congregation that many look up to, I am grateful that you chose to seek spiritual guidance and counsel: many do not. For that, Mr. Rhodes, I commend you. However, in listening to your concerns, I believe that the concern does not lie with Rosalynn, but with you, sir," Elder Worth watched as Carlton reared back, ready to take offence but he held up his hand.

"Hear me out; Carlton, your sister has been faithful to this ministry, she has been committed to helping your business grow here in Savannah. Furthermore, her reputation is above reproach. I have spoken to several congregants and not one of them is aware of a budding relationship between your sister and Mr. Cartellini; which generally indicates that there is none at this time," he looked to Roz who confirmed what he said with a nod of agreement.

"As I have listened to you, you have not one time given your sister a direct compliment. It has been couched in terms of her needing further improvement. You sir, have not done your duty to build her up and I am in wonderment over how she has managed to live so long in an environment   filled with negativity. I believe that Rosalynn is to be admired for having the courage to leave such an environment and carve her own path in physical fitness. She has my full support and backing to go forth in the calling of restoring and educating those around her about the importance of physical health. If she chooses to associate with you, that is completely up to her. I would caution you though about slandering this young lady's name to the members of my congregation. I will not tolerate it. Furthermore, I recommend you come in for counseling concerning your own self-esteem. Apparently it must be in pretty bad shape if you cannot see that your actions and behaviors have been a way to boost your own self-esteem." Elder Worth folded his hands together and waited for the explosion he knew was coming. Carlton did not disappoint. He leapt up from the seat as if he were sitting on a bomb.

"How dare you?" he shouted pointing at Rosalynn. "She is nothing but a plaything to him," he shook his head in disgust. "As far as I'm concerned, she's no longer apart of my business. I'll take my services elsewhere," he turned to leave then looking back at her once more. "It's a good thing you're not my real sister. I would never tolerate her behaving like a whore," he strode off, leaving Rosalynn staring after him with her mouth open.

She hopped up from the chair and headed down the hallway after him. "Carlton! Explain yourself!" she caught up with him, stopping just short of touching him as he whirled around to face her, a look of pure malice etched into his features.

"You heard me. Mom and Dad adopted you," he laughed maniacally then. "Didn't you ever wonder why we were so beautiful and you were so...you?" he chuckled shaking his head at her obvious ignorance. He looked her up and down. "You never did measure up," he smirked.

Rosalynn slapped that self-assured look off of his face before she knew what had happened. "You bastard," she whispered.

"No, my dear, that would be *you*," he corrected before he turned away and walked calmly away as if he had not dropped the most devastating blow to her self-esteem.

Elder Worth stood behind her gently grasping her shoulders. She slumped against him for support, the full impact of Carlton's words crashing down on her, the weight of them nearly taking her under. *I was never a Rhodes.*

"Rosalynn, I know this may be hard to take in , but please remember that out of all the children in this world, you were chosen to be apart of a family. Carlton can never take that away from you," Elder Worth encouraged her. "You were their child, but most importantly, you were God's child. He'll never leave you nor forsake you. You can bank on that," Elder Worth assured her as she turned in her spiritual father's arms and received his hug, warming her soul with the comfort of God's love.

Rosalynn knew what she would do today. She would give herself a new identity. She would carve out a new path. *Rosalynn Rhodes is no more. Rosalynn Godschild I will be. I will never let another man define my destiny.* She would forge a new path beginning with a new name. She would forgive Carlton for his cruelty and trade it in for the confidence that her future was in the hands of God and no man, not even Carlton, could dispute that fact. *Lord, forgive my anger. Help me, Lord.*

Mariella walked through every room in Noelle's palatial home checking and rechecking her handiwork. She had been working her butt off to complete as many rooms as she could. The job she had lovingly put so much work into had now become pure torture. It had become the place where she had realized that she was nothing more than a convenient employee in the scheme of things. She had begun working before dawn this morning and was nearly complete. When Noelle stopped in for his routine inspections, he would find everything neatly labeled. She'd chosen different themes for his guest bedrooms. One was French Romanticism, another was heavily influenced by Moroccan culture, and the last was designed to give the guest a Rustic and Country feel. This was the room she most connected with. She threw herself over the bed haphazardly, exhausted from her efforts. Before she even realized it, she had dozed off, the line between reality and fiction blurring.

"Mariella, sweetheart, open your eyes," the voice spoke with quiet determination.
Mariella opened her eyes, smiling sweetly.
"I love you so much," the voice nuzzled along the side of her neck, kissing the tendrils of hair there. "You are the best thing that's ever happened to me," the voice acknowledged.
Mariella closed her eyes, enjoying the feel of soft lips against hers.
"I'm so glad we're having a child here, Noelle," she sighed.

Mariella bolted upright, her eyes wide open. She looked around.

"Mariella, where are you?" Noelle called from the hallway.

Mariella burned with embarrassment. *Oh, God, what was I thinking?* "Coming!" she hopped up, straightened the comforter she had been napping on and tidied herself pulling furiously at her clothing. She had thought he would be too busy with depositions to come by this morning.

Just as she thought to meet him in the hallway, she looked up and found him standing in the doorway, blocking her exit. She felt like a caged animal in that moment. *I hope he can't read minds.*

"You've come a long way since Saturday," he noted, his hands bracing the doorframe on both sides, preventing a graceful exit, his eyes roaming the room taking in all the additions. There was a four-poster bed, beautifully patterned wallpaper with wildflowers, and antiques on a side table. Most of the furniture looked as though it had been aged and appeared very rustic. *Very impressive,* He tried to appear nonchalant. "Have you been working overtime?" he let his gaze travel around the room once more.

"A little," she admitted, not looking him in the eye, and giving herself time to appear cool, calm, and aloof. She was feeling anything but.

Noelle sensed something was not right. He could feel the tension radiating off her. "Are you okay? You look a little flushed," he noted.

Mariella snapped to attention. "I'm fine. Listen, do you mind if I take the rest of the day off, being that I'm ahead and all?" she gathered her bags glancing his way briefly.

"No, go ahead," he waved her question away. "Do you need a ride into town?"

Before she could answer, she heard the familiar horn of Naomi's car. *How did she know?* Mariella shrugged. "Looks like my ride's here," she hurried past him and down the hallway. "See you Tuesday," she called out, walking as fast as her legs would take her.

Noelle had walked out to the front of his house and stood looking through his bay windows as his employee beat a hasty retreat to Naomi's car. *What just happened here?*

She knows.

Knows what?

She knows what you know. What you have worked so hard to deny.

Noelle knew in a flash of memory exactly what God was referring to. *She can't know!*

She does.

How?

She has the gift.

What's she going to do with what she knows?

Wouldn't you like to know?

God, we've been over this before. She's too...everything!

251

Who's in control of your life? You or I AM?
Noelle knew then what he had to do: *Fire her.*

The rest of the week passed in a blur and haze. Savannah and Shemiah finalized their wedding details along with the details for Marilyn and Andre's rehearsal dinner. Aliya frantically completed all the flight plans and arrival itinerary for Montego Bay while holding Seth at bay with flowery emails and phone calls; Enrique made it his business to see Augusta at the start of everyday, meeting her at her office with her favorites: cinnamon raisin bagels and café au lait with caramel sauce topped with whipped cream. His whispered compliments made it hard for Augusta to concentrate for the first fifteen minutes of work, but kept a constant Mona Lisa smile glued to her face for the rest of the day; Marco and Ginny did their best to avoid each other which proved not to be hard at all- Marco never mentioned Ginevieve when bringing by deliveries and Jamar was told not to notify Ginevieve when he came by. It was a simple arrangement. It was a horrible arrangement according to Jamar who argued that he could not imagine two people more suited to each other than Marco and Ginny, to which he was rewarded with an icy glare from both parties the one time they all collided in the lobby of Alpha, Inc, and he had the audacity to mention it. Jamar himself couldn't stop thinking about Tehinnah; He found himself pausing at Tatyanna's doorway overhearing their conversation by speaker phone, then stomping away furious with himself for caring about a woman who was a bonafide flirt in the worst way.

Josiah spent the week calming his wife's fears about taking along their twins, Jaia and Josiah, while Elder and Mother Worth set about the grueling task of counseling Carlton, a man with very deep wounds of insecurity and inadequacy he hid very well. Elder Worth had been surprised to see him return to his office late on Monday, humble and broken, confessing that he was wrong and that he hadn't intended to hurt Rosalynn. Adopted or not, she was the only person in this world that he had left that held any connection to the family he once knew and loved. Elder Worth knew that Carlton had a long way to go in his process of healing and asked him to refrain from making further contact with his sister until it was deemed a wise time to which he surprisingly agreed. Enrique readied his entourage and made sure from a financial and logistical standpoint that all was ready for lift off Thursday morning. Thus, Tuesday and Wednesday found all the believers making preparations spiritually and naturally for the Singles' Summer Retreat. It was a trip no one wanted to take for granted and certainly none would soon forget.

38

The Night before Take off...

"Mariella, are you okay with going on this trip?" Naomi was packing her bags and checking to make sure she had her passport and recommended documentation.

Mariella nodded her head vigorously. Except for Monday, she had called in sick for work every day this week. She was putting off the inevitable: a meeting with Noelle. He had sent a beautiful bouquet of pink roses encouraging her to get well soon. That had been the last straw. She had resigned this morning by voicemail and email, citing conflicts with her educational preparation. She knew that wasn't the real reason. He had responded back that he had intended to terminate her employment but that he wanted to talk with her before doing so. She had responded that no further explanation was necessary being that she had done the honors. And so began the email war. Back and forth they had battled. He had still wanted to meet with her. She declined. He had wanted to give her one last payment. She had rejected his generous offer. And on it went. The more she resisted, the more he insisted. She had finally stopped replying, realizing that she was dealing with a lawyer who was used to stating and winning his argument. He had not emailed her since Wednesday afternoon. Here it was Wednesday night and still no sign of an email. It was a good sign. Mariella had cited education as her reason for letting go of the interior design job, but the real reason had more to do with the man than the workload. The real reason was every night she dreamed. She had never been a dreamer. If she did dream, she couldn't remember enough to make sense of it. But these dreams were vivid, tangible, and all too real. She remembered every detail. She dreamed of a life with Noelle Marks. The dreams were in such detail, she thought she might be losing it. Mariella didn't know who to tell, who to confide in. Most people would think her crazy or at the least delusional and in need of medical help. How could she explain that she was dreaming about a man who she *knew* was completely against being in a relationship with her? *If I don't tell someone, I'm going to explode.*

Naomi noticed her roommate's complete silence, definitely out of character for Mariella. "Mariella, are you feeling ill again? I know you haven't been sleeping lately," Naomi came and sat next her on the couch. "I've heard you moaning and thrashing around at night. Are you having nightmares?" Naomi's concern was evident. She knew Mariella was battling something. She couldn't help but feel that it had something to do with her former boss.

Mariella broke down then. "I don't know *what* to call them! I just wish they would stop!" she buried her face in her hands.

"Can you tell me about them?" Naomi questioned softly.

"I'd rather not," she shook her head solemnly, raising her head, her eyes red rimmed and pleading.

"Maybe I can help you with their meaning," Naomi offered. She couldn't stand to see Mariella so tortured.

"Oh, I know *exactly* what they mean," she wiped her eyes. "They mean trouble in all capital letters," she sniffed.

Naomi was intrigued then. "Explain, if you can," she sat back relaxing her position on the couch.

Mariella sighed then in resignation. "Every night, I dream I'm happily married with a son, and living in Savannah," she groaned.

Naomi's brow rose in confusion at her obvious agony. "So, what's so horrible about that?"

Mariella stared unflinchingly at Naomi then. "Noelle Marks is the man I'm married to in the dream."

At that very moment, Pastor John Marks and Noelle were already on board the men's jet awaiting the other passengers. He was hoping his son would relax on this trip. It seemed as though Noelle was under intense pressure but was choosing to go it alone. *Lord, whatever it is, please give my son the release he needs.*

"What's eatin' you son?"

Noelle turned to his father then, a haggard look upon his face. "Do you *really* want to know?"

Pastor Marks gave his son a disbelieving glare. "What kind of question is that?"

Noelle allowed his head to fall back against the seat before he released a pent up breath. "Are you ready to be a father-in-law?"

Pastor Marks looked taken aback. "Son, who? How? You just arrived back in the city; and don't tell me it's Aliya," he warned.

"No, it's definitely not Aliya. I could live with that," he reasoned.

A light dawned in Pastor Marks' mind. "It's *her*."

"*See*," complained Noelle. "I don't even have to mention her name. How *do* you do that?" Noelle wondered a little annoyed with his father.

"Well, you could have done worse. I had a feeling about her."

"Well, I don't want any feelings about her," Noelle concluded.

"So, you're gonna fight God on this?" Pastor Marks questioned.

"No; I'm simply going to be slow in acknowledging His will," Noelle reasoned.

"Have it your way," Pastor Marks picked up his worn Bible, the undertone of warning evident in his tone.

Noelle knew that even as he made that statement, it was futile. His days as a single man were numbered. He could certainly do worse than Mariella. He had even tried to broach the subject but she was flat out refusing to meet with him. *She definitely knows.* The Word of the Lord came back to him, then. How he would move forward next, he had no clue. He would have to trust God to bring it all together. And if there were one thing Noelle Marks was *not* good at doing, it was trusting God.

Naomi hugged Mariella tightly.

"Oh, sweetie, what must you be *thinking*?" Naomi still couldn't wrap her mind around the fact that Mariella was having prophetic dreams.

Mariella pushed her away. "You don't understand. He doesn't like me-- At all. I overheard him talking with his father about me. That's why I quit. I can't face him; I just can't bring myself to do it," she stood then walking to stare out at her garden of flowers, a comforting reminder of all she had left back in Costa Rica.

Naomi came to stand behind her. "Mariella, trust me when I say that sometimes what men say is not what they feel. Noelle definitely feels something for you. I've seen the way he looks at you when he thinks no one is looking," Naomi spoke remembering the way he kept his eyes glued to her roommate at the bonfire last week.

Mariella brushed aside tears. "He may feel something, but it's not something he will openly acknowledge. I've seen what happens to women who are drawn into a one-sided relationship. I refuse to settle for less. I want everything a marriage should be: passionate, exciting, sweet, comforting, purposeful, with both people giving one hundred percent to making one another happy."

Naomi tended to agree with her. "If Noelle is not in the place to give his all in a relationship, then pray that God will bring him to that place. But more importantly, how do *you* feel about all this?"

Mariella shrugged. "I don't know *how* to feel. Is he attractive? Yes, annoyingly so. He's brilliant, well-respected, and he certainly knows more about the Bible than I do. I'm not his equal in any way and he certainly wasted no time pointing that out to his father," she reminded Naomi.

"Just be you, Mariella. You deserve true love. Wait on the Lord and let him shape Noelle's heart and yours too," she advised. "Don't rush anything between you two, but don't resist what the Lord may be doing either," she counseled.

Mariella took in a deep breath and released it. She felt so much better now that she had gotten that burden off her chest. She hugged Naomi and gave her a grimace of a smile. "You're the best roomie in the world."

"I know," Naomi joked. "Now let's go have some fun in the sun. After all, this is the perfect opportunity to just be you and let Mr. Marks make up his own mind," she reasoned.

Mariella couldn't help thinking she was right. She would try not to take herself so seriously. Instead she would do some soul searching and relaxing. God was in control and she couldn't think of a better person to release her cares to than Him.

On the Lady's jet

"Alright ladies, everyone is just about here. We're waiting for Mariella and Naomi and then we'll hear the pilot's instructions before take off. Does everyone have what they need? Passports? Medication?" Aliya questioned.

A host of groans, nods, and grumbles resounded.

"I know it's the middle of the morning, but you'll thank me later when you see the blue sky dawning and the amazing ocean view," she chuckled.

Angelynn seconded Aliya. "Montego Bay is gorgeous this time of year. You won't regret going; this is the off season so you'll enjoy some quiet along with some great deals," she assured the sleepy women.

"For those of you who haven't flown in a while I recommend you drink lots of water and get some rest now." Aliya ended as Naomi and Mariella boarded the jet. "We'll be landing at Don Sanger Airport where Enrique's contacts will greet us and escort us through customs. We will do most of our activities on or near the resort grounds." Aliya concluded just in time for them to turn their attention to the pilot's instructions.

On the Men's jet

"First of all, we'd like to thank everyone for being on time, being patient with our security check, and just having an accommodating attitude," Elder Worth began. "At this time, I'll turn it over to Enrique," he ushered him to the center aisle.

Enrique reviewed all the details he had received from Aliya and his contact person upon arrival into Montego Bay. "After we make it through customs, Mr. Aslan Peyton's staff will meet us and transport us to the resort. Does anyone have questions thus far? If not, relax, rest, and look over your itinerary. We've got quite a bit of sightseeing to do in four days," he grinned.

Elder Worth patted Enrique on the back. "Thanks, Brother Estrada. Let's all bow our heads as we invoke the Lord's presence, favor, and protection on this trip."

39

Montego Bay Day 1

This is incredible Rosalynn couldn't help thinking. It had become her catchphrase since everyone had touched down in Montego Bay an hour ago. She had been one of the few who had remained awake for most of the trip, not wanting to miss one moment of her adventure. The heavens had opened up bursting with incredible rays and spectrums of colors over the waters. It was a sight that would live in Rosalynn's mind and memory forever. Truly the heavens had declared God's glory this morning. She couldn't help but feel that this trip would change her in some profound way.

They had been quickly hustled through customs and escorted outside where five minivans awaited them. Rosalynn and the others barely had time to register the minor details of their trip. It seemed they had been caught in a maelstrom of activity with the men collecting their baggage and loading everything up haphazardly before they were on their way moving through the town streets, the winding and twisting roads moving upward into the mountains as they made their way to the resort.

Rosalynn's van consisted of the ladies who would be rooming with her: Vivian Worth, Savannah, and Augusta. Seth and his brother Jamar were also riding along with them. Rosalynn couldn't help but notice how much the two looked alike but seemed to be so different in personality. Jamar had no problem befriending everyone and livening up the journey to the resort.

"We made it!" Jamar yelled aloud to his fellow passengers as their bodies swayed in time with the driver's maneuvering.

Savannah and Augusta couldn't help but laugh at Jamar's enthusiasm. "You sure are psyched," Savannah noted.

"Look at us," Jamar waved his hands. "This is going to be so awesome! Were you up this morning? The view coming in was incredible," Jamar sighed.

"I have to agree with you there," Rosalynn grinned in agreement. "That was the first word that came to mind. The sunrise was breathtaking. God has certainly smiled down on this part of the world," she looked out the window at the intensely green foliage as their ascent steepened.

"I can't wait to see the resort," Augusta joined in the conversation. "My father has poured so much of his time and heart into this venture. I'm so glad that you all decided to come," she added. "I know he'll be happy to see all of you," Augusta's smile rivaled that of the sun shining brightly before them.

Everyone sat back enjoying the landscape and the majestic view. This was definitely shaping up to be a pleasant trip. Augusta prayed that all would go well for everyone in attendance.

"I had no idea we'd be headed to the mountains," Shemiah mentioned casually. "We're going to have an incredible view," he commented offhandedly to those who were riding with him. Everyone seemed to be trying to catch up on their sleep. He had the pleasure of riding with Dr. Thomas, Naomi, Aurielle, Tatyanna, her sister Tehinnah, and Kevin. They had been grouped by the persons they would be traveling with during their outdoor excursions.

"Looks like the ladies are still trying to get their beauty sleep," Trey chuckled.

"I can't say I blame them much," Kevin yawned aloud. "It's not everyday a person leaves at four in the morning to catch a flight," he stretched his arms wide. "But it was worth it," he grinned looking at Tatyanna who had leaned into his shoulder. "This is about as close to seeing her in the morning that I'm going to get before the wedding bells ring," he chuckled.

Trey high-fived Kevin from the back seat. "You sure right about it, bro," he smiled then as he listened to Aurielle's light snore. "I'm glad we've got most of our events planned as group events," he sighed. "I'm not sure I'd be able to stay away from Aurielle," he admitted.

"Yeah," Shemiah chuckled. "This is going to be a lot harder than I imagined," he confessed. "I may have to elope if worse comes to worse," he joked. "We've got four pastors on this trip so we've covered the clergy part."

Kevin and Trey laughed aloud at that. One could never have too much spiritual ammunition.

"Are we there yet?" an irritated Fabritza drummed her fingers on the window, anything to drown out the gurgles of the twins who were beside her. *Of all the vans to place me in, of all the room assignments, they put me with the noisiest!*

"We'll be there in about thirty minutes," Josiah passed the message along to Fabritza. Her irritation with his children was evident. He would have to speak with Aliya about possibly giving her another room assignment. He would personally pay the difference if need be.

At that moment, Jaia decided she wanted to exercise her lung power.

"Oh, sweetie, we'll be there soon," Angelynn cooed to her daughter. She was sandwiched between Jarah and Fabritza. Her mother could sleep through anything, her head resting against the van window. Apparently Fabritza could not. Angelynn was made well aware of this as

Fabritza grunted, sucked her teeth, and surprisingly swore under her breath more than once. *There is no way she is going to make it in a hotel room with us,* Angelynn silently acknowledged. She would talk with Aliya as soon as they hit the pavement.

Mariella rolled her eyes at the comment from the primadonna. She wanted so badly to give Fabritza a set down but realized it wasn't her place to do so. *Lord, help me hold my peace.* "The countryside here is incredible," she commented aloud. "Are we going to get the opportunity to sight see much?"

Josiah looked at their itinerary. "Apparently so; we're going to have a tour guide with us for our excursions so we'll learn a little about the city as well," he assured her, his focus split between being cordial and tuning his ear to his wife and children.

"Well, *I'll* probably spend most of my time at the spa," Fabritza's tone spoke loud and clear: she was not here to fraternize or make friends. Her whole attitude didn't set well with Josiah. He would make sure Enrique was aware of the situation. Right now, it could wait. He was not going to let one woman's self-importance spoil this moment of tropical beauty.

Aliya, Ginny, Columbia, Noelle, and Pastor Marks were wide awake taking in the sights together. The only person asleep on their van was Marco. Their driver was several cars behind, but they didn't mind. He seemed to know where he was headed, so they left the driving and directions to him.

"How long has it been since you've seen your father?" Noelle questioned Aliya.

"About three months, but it seems like forever," Aliya sighed. She was a total Daddy's Girl without shame. Their relationship had been a bit strained since she had received the Holy Spirit's baptism but God had been steadily drawing her father into a closer relationship since Aliya's near kidnapping. Her father had been reaching out in spite of their difference of opinion and for that she was grateful. Aliya was hoping that through this trip, this unifying of believers from different churches, that her father would see the power of one Lord, one faith, and one baptism. Aslan needed to experience the Spirit's power and see it reflected in the lives of those around him.

"I know he'll be happy to see his baby girl," Noelle teased.
"I miss *my* babies already," Columbia sighed. She had left Nadia, Rodia, and Deliah in the care of a trusted neighbor until she returned. Though they were old enough to take care of themselves, she didn't want them without adult supervision of any kind.

"They'll be fine," Pastor Marks patted her shoulder. "They seemed to be more excited about this trip than you were," he eyed her pointedly.

"That's because they were anxious to get me out of their hair," Columbia shook her head ruefully. She had closed shop and reopen after she returned.

"I think they knew you needed this vacation. I only hope that you'll make some time for me in between those spa visits," Pastor Marks looked at her meaningfully.

"I certainly intend to," Columbia smiled sweetly in return.

Though she was awake, Ginny chose not to immerse herself in conversation. Instead, she enjoyed the view and tried to ignore the man seated next to her. She was painfully aware of his scent, his presence, and how badly she owed him an apology. She had ended things between them awkwardly and abruptly. He had bustled himself into the van, not bothering to mumble even a word of greeting to her. It was what she had wanted, but now it seemed so wrong. It seemed to her that Marco had shut himself off not only from her, but from Jamar as well. She didn't know how she could fix this gap that was widening between them. She wanted to be friends but she knew that would only encourage him to think there might be more. The only thing stopping her from opening up to a relationship with Marco was fear itself. So, instead of apologizing, Ginevieve let things stand as they were. She was bound to her fears, her insecurities, and nothing could release her but the Word of God.

"I do believe we are nearing the resort entrance," Enrique spoke up. The men in his van all grunted in acknowledgement.

Greg Thomas, Elder Worth, Fabian, Carlton, Nicholas, and Giovanni would be riding together on their excursions. The tension in the van was so thick, it could be sliced and the day had only begun. Enrique was surprised that Carlton had remained silent during the entire drive. He could only attribute it to the calming presence of Elder Worth. As long as no one mentioned the elephant that was sitting in the van with them, that of Nicholas and Carlton's conflict, they would be fine.

"I'll be thankful when I can stretch out a bit," Greg noted.

"I hear you man," Carlton stretched. "First thing I'm going to do once I unpack is hit the gym," he exhaled.

"Just keep in mind there *is* an itinerary and we are expected to follow it," Elder Worth reminded him.

Carlton nodded in understanding. "I'll make sure I'm where I need to be, Pastor," he loosened his neck by rolling his head from side to side.

Nicholas and Giovanni looked at each other then, their thoughts simultaneous. *We'll check on Rosalynn.*

The men's' full attention was captured by the breathtaking view as they drove up a paved lane facing the front of the resort. The white and coral edifice was surrounded by lush vegetation and colorful flowers in varied shades. Jamaican Dreams Resort. It was a little bit of heaven on earth. Aslan had described it that way, and Enrique could see that he had not exaggerated.

"Daddy!" Aliya wasted no time running to Aslan Peyton and flinging her arms around his neck, his towering body absorbing the impact of her embrace. Augusta shook her head as she helped with the unloading of the various bags, setting them on the ground.

"Is she always like that?" Seth chuckled taking the bags from Augusta's possession and handing them over to the bellhop.

Augusta grinned at him then. "She's a Daddy's Girl to the core. You best be remembering that," she teased.

Seth recalled his last meeting with Aslan Peyton. It had been brutally honest yet he had developed an attachment to the man. He had remained in contact with Aslan unbeknownst to Aliya. He looked forward to talking with him at length about his intentions towards Aliya. "I'm pretty sure your father won't let me forget it," he assured her.

Augusta was just about to respond when she spotted her cousin Mei Ling whom she hadn't seen in ages. She completely forgot everything and ran to greet her.

Seth stood there with a wide grin on his face thinking to himself that when it came to family matters, the twins were more alike than they realized.

"Oh my goodness, Ming-Ming, you look great!" Augusta stepped away from the embrace of her cousin who strongly favored Lucy Liu in appearance. She had even been accosted for an autograph a time or two because of the resemblance.

Mei Ling's musical laughter rang out. "And you, cousin, look like a woman in love, or am I mistaken?" she questioned teasingly.

Augusta blushed then. "You are on the money, honey," she giggled.

Mei Ling looked over her cousin's shoulder then at the tired, motley crew walking towards them with several bellhops in tow. "Well, did you bring the whole city of Savannah with you?"

Augusta laughed then. She could always count on Mei Ling for her wry humor. "No, silly, just some friends of mine; soon to become your friends too," she warned. She knew Mei Ling had a habit of being somewhat of a loner. She was counting on the saints to draw her out of her shell and get her to loosen up. News corresponding in one of the most politically charged countries of the world was no small feat. Mei Ling needed this break away from the upheavals that were taking place in China.

"We'll see," Mei-Ling replied as she went to catch up with Aliya who was headed over to the vans with directions. "And use that nickname like a spare tire," she warned.

Aslan stepped forward then to give Augusta a kiss on the cheek. "Hello, love," her father wrapped her up in his arms for a comforting embrace before releasing her. "I just let Aliya know that since this is the off-season we don't have a full service staff but rest assured that your friends will be well taken care of," he rubbed her hair absently. "Aliya has just been sent to inform your guests that lunch will be served in the main dining area in one hour with a brief overview of the history of the area by a local professor. Afterwards, they can rest up, familiarize themselves with the resort and amenities and then dinner will be held at seven sharp. It is the same time every evening with lunch at one," Aslan make quick work of the necessary details.

"Okay, Papa," Augusta breathed a sigh of relief. They had all made it in one piece. She looked around then. "You've done an awesome job, Papa. I'm so proud of you; I know how much work you put into it," She took his hand in hers, squeezing tightly.

"Well, I'm thankful that it's completed. The grand opening will take place at the end of the month. Your mother and I plan to take a vacation then. She wants to go to Australia of all places," he grimaced. "Between their accent and mine, it's sure to be interesting," he declared.

"Where is mom?" it had taken her a moment to realize Phet was absent.

"She's in Kingston still. She was doing some last minute counseling. She'll be joining us tomorrow," Aslan assured his daughter. "She's looking forward to seeing your friend again. We both are," Aslan threw in a hint. He knew that Enrique had intended to propose. He wondered if he had followed through.

Augusta grinned widely. "I'm sure she'll be pleased with the news we plan to share," she hinted.

Aslan was interrupted by Mei Ling before he could respond. "You have a call on line 3 and line 5, Uncle," Mei Ling spoke apologetically. She hated to intrude on the moment.

"We'll talk soon," Aslan promised.

Augusta released her father's hand then, nodding in understanding. She filed in with the rest of the crew and headed inside the lobby to check in, a slight bounce in her step as she walked into this new season.

40

"Thank the Lord we arrived in one piece!" Vivian exclaimed. She had slept most of the drive into the mountain desperately in need of the rest.

"I know what you mean. All I want to do is take a hot shower and curl up in bed," Rosalynn sighed. "I can't believe we've got to get ready for a lecture in *one* hour," she groaned.

"Look at the bright side; at least it comes with lunch. Then, you're free to roam the grounds for a few hours before dinner." Vivian reminded her.

Augusta entered the room with her duffle bag on her arm. "Liya warned you all how it would be in Mo Bay," she chided them. "This trip is her baby and I'm going to let her take the reigns," she admitted.

"I'm going to shower and change, and then meet my husband downstairs to discuss tonight's Bible Study," Vivian informed them.

"Hey, make it happen," Roz threw herself onto the beautifully made bed. "This feels like heaven," she murmured.

"Too bad you have to share it," Savannah giggled as she plopped down on the other side.

Roz lifted her head up then plopped it down once more. "Where've you been?"

"Trying to console a grown man," Savannah shook her head. "Shemiah didn't realize that all of the men are in an entirely different wing from the ladies," she flung herself backwards landing on Roz.

"No midnight rendezvous on accident then?" Augusta joked. "You've got that right," Roz noted. "This trip has been planned down to a science. If anything wayward is going to happen, you will not be able to say opportunity was presented. The Pastors have covered all bases," Roz stated pointedly. "Including keeping that pesky brother of mine away from me, for which I'm truly thankful for."

"I hope you two will be able to overcome your differences; he's your brother after all," Savannah reminded her.

"Turns out he's not my brother," Roz slapped a hand over her mouth then; she had no intention of revealing that.

Savannah sat up then and Augusta was glaring at her. "What do you mean, he's not your brother?" they asked in unison.

Roz sat up on her side. "I probably shouldn't be talking about this," she thought aloud.

"Too late; you can't just drop a bomb like that on us and then leave it," Savannah huffed.

Rosalynn sighed. "I suppose you're right. Carlton admitted in our meeting on Monday that he wasn't my real brother. He said I was adopted. I did my research; he's not lying," she hung her head then.

"Are you *sure* it's not the other way around?" Augusta was pensive.

Rosalynn flung back her head in laughter. "You sure know how to make a girl feel better," she wiped at a tear.

Savannah tried not to look at Roz in sympathy. She couldn't imagine how it felt finding out her parents were not really her parents after nearly thirty years of life. "Roz, it's going to be okay," Savannah wiped another tear from her friend's eye as she grew angry at the thought of Carlton's casual delivery of such life altering news.

"My heart knows that," she sniffed, "but my head is still catching up. Elder Worth told me that Carlton is really sorry for how he told me and that he's seeking counseling, but I'm just not ready to talk with him. He knew the entire time. I mean, I've always had this feeling like I was disconnected in some way but I could never explain why. Now I know. Oh, and before you hear it from somewhere else, I've changed my name. It's Rosalynn Godschild, now," she sniffed.

Augusta and Savannah were shocked speechless for once in their lives.

"Have you talked to Nicholas about any of this?" Augusta was aware of the budding relationship between the two of them.

Roz gave her an incredulous glance. "Are you serious? We agreed not to talk about anything serious until I could deal with my family issues. Turns out I've got *more* family issues than I imagined," she laughed ironically.

Savannah shook her head then. "Sweetie, you've really boxed yourself into a no-win situation. As long as you live, there will be some sort of family issue," Savannah shared. "Take me, for instance; an absent father, a bitter mother, two meddling grandmothers, and now God has moved in my family in a way He never could if I wasn't willing to put all of the issues in His hands," she counseled. "Shemiah and I still have issues to face when we return to Savannah, but the beauty is that we will face them together. I know Nicholas cares about you enough to stand by you during the difficult times. Don't deny him the opportunity to be there for you," Savannah handed her the tissue box.

Roz took several graciously. "I just don't want to come into a relationship with emotional baggage," she reasoned. "Nicholas doesn't deserve to be saddled with my problems."

"They will only be problems if you refuse to cast your cares to the Lord. God is here and I think we should hand over your cares right now. Don't you agree?" Savannah grabbed one hand as Augusta now seated on Rosalynn's other side grabbed the other.

Roz nodded in agreement and thanked God for two praying roommates. She felt sure she would need their prayers again.

"Well, that's settled," Aliya blew a breath of relief. Josiah and Angelynn had come to her almost at the same time stating their desire to have

Fabritza Ciccone removed from Angelynn's room. *The festivities haven't even begun yet and she's already causing trouble,* Aliya thought. She had spoken with Enrique who had paid for another room already. Fabritza would room with Francheska Cartellini, cousin to Nicholas and Giovanni, and a fellow operative who would arrive by dinnertime. *This should prove to be interesting.* Aliya did not want to see the look on Francheska's face when she realized she would have a roommate.

Enrique paced back and forth on the plush, carpeted floor, thankful they were in another wing of the resort. His English was completely gone and he was speaking fluently in Spanish while Giovanni and Nicholas looked on, periodically looking to each other. Enrique finally cooled down, managing to get a few words in English.

"The nerve, the unmitigated gall of that woman," Enrique spat out.

Giovanni and Nicholas knew exactly who he was talking about.
"How dare she insult my friends like that?"

Gio and Nick wisely kept quiet, choosing to unpack rather than engage Enrique in his personal venting session.

"She's getting an all expense paid trip and this is how she responds to hospitality?"

Gio and Nick tried to make their way to the balcony.
"Hold it right there."

They stopped in their tracks.

Enrique turned to face them, his anger evident on their faces. "Just so you know, she'll be rooming with Francheska once she arrives."

Giovanni's mouth went wide open, his eyes widening like huge saucers. "If Francheska gets wind of her fondness for me, she'll tear her to shreds without a thought to anybody."

Enrique's gaze was unwavering. "What better way to help her keep her flirtatious behavior under wraps?"

Carlton was slapping on aftershave like a madman when Kevin stepped out of the shower. Noelle and his father Pastor Marks had already refreshed themselves and were out on the balcony having some father-son time Kevin noticed from the open windows. Noelle appeared to be in deep thought. Kevin turned his attention to his other roommate then who was drowning himself in aftershave and checking himself out from all angles.

"So what's the deal?" Kevin lounged in one of the many recliners in their massive room. It was probably where he would kick back tonight.

"Were you *blind* earlier today?" Carlton asked.
Kevin gave him a quizzical look then. "What are you talking about?"

"I'm talking about the Asian babe? I thought Lucy Liu was vacationing with us. Turns out she's the Peytons' cousin," Carlton rambled off what he had managed to find out through some carefully placed questions.

"Sorry, man; my heart's been taken a long time ago," he shrugged. "Besides, this retreat is mainly a spiritual one. Elder Worth will be the first to tell you there won't be any holy hookups going on," Kevin warned.

"I just plan to introduce myself, that's all. You don't have to get all spiritual about it," Carlton snapped.

"Hey, I'm just telling you straight, man. She's pretty, but she seems pretty kick butt to me," Kevin observed.

"I love a challenge," Carlton grinned wildly. He had felt like someone had kicked him in the gut when he had locked eyes with the Asian beauty. *Spiritual or not, It's time to get my game on,* he decided.

Pastor Marks was glaring at his son. For the third time today. Noelle had taken it upon his self to assist Tehinnah with her luggage, laughing and joking like honeymooners all the way to her room. He had been saying his goodbyes, his father chaperoning them both when Mariella had opened the door across from Tehinnah's room. She had gasped in surprise, recognized *who* he was talking with and slammed the door. Noelle had stood there like a deer caught in headlights. He had no one to blame for the predicament he was in.

"Do you *realize* the impression you left on Mariella?" John scolded.

"It wasn't intentional! She shouldn't be so *presumptuous!*" Noelle shot back. "There is nothing between Tehinnah and I; she's an *employee* for God's sake," Noelle waved his hand furiously.

"You did nothing to correct her perception of what she saw," John reminded him.

"Let her think what she wants! She's bound to anyway," Noelle turned away from his father then. "She asked me not to contact her. I am honoring her request. She can't get upset with me for enjoying the company of someone else," he leaned against the railing, ignoring the breathtaking view.

"What about what God wants? Have you thought about Him since we landed?" John came to stand next to his son.

"Dad, my hands are tied. Mariella won't even hear me out," he threw up his hands in frustration.

"Have you thought that maybe you are giving her ample reason *not* to hear you out?" John spoke the rebuke softly but it sliced through Noelle's anger.

Noelle looked to his father then. "Are you--?"
"I'm saying, son, that no woman wants to hear anything from a man who appears to have roaming eyes and divided attentions," John stated simply. "Your playboy persona has finally caught up with you."

Noelle stood stock still. "I've never been one to play the field. I've done my share of flirting but it has all been harmless," he defended.

"Until now, son, until now," Pastor Marks left his son to think on that.

Fabian Ciccone decided to check the grounds one more time. He had been about to step into the room allotted to his current boss for this trip when he had heard Enrique going on and on about Fabritza, his trouble making sister. Ever since they had been assigned this post, Fabritza had been wreaking havoc. He stood to lose his promotion with their organization if he could not get his sister's behavior under control. No matter how he had tried to get her to back off, she seemed to have an obsession with capturing the attentions of Giovanni Cartellini. Clearly, he wasn't interested and had already set his cap for Enrique's close friend, Naomi. Fabian couldn't blame him on that score. Naomi was a breath of fresh air: Fabritza on the other hand was a blast of heat, scorching anything that dared to get in her path. Fabian had managed to lead a very quiet and peaceful life in spite of what he did professionally. He kept to himself, didn't get involved emotionally with his clients, and his love life was non-existent. It wasn't that he hadn't had offers of a dalliance here and there: but he was a one man woman. When and if the time ever came, Fabian knew that he would give this profession up in a heartbeat if it came between him and the woman who managed to capture his affections. His parents had been dead set against him going into this line of work, his father expected him to carry on their business of producing sparkling ciders. When his twin Fabritza had decided to follow him into espionage, his father had nearly suffered an apoplectic fit. Fabian's mother who could have persuaded him otherwise had passed away when he was twelve. There was no mother figure to steer him away from the taste of adventure, and so off he had gone, Fabritza following behind him. Even during their training, he had been her protector, though he couldn't protect always. She had made a name for herself at the academy as the no nonsense, kick butt officer, who was just as good, if not better than her male counterparts at ferreting out and then taking down those who posed a threat to national security. She was wild, brazenly beautiful, and no man could tame her. Those who had tried to cast her in the traditional role of wife found themselves frustrated by her obvious wanderlust. Fabian seemed to spend half of his operative missions getting her out of one relationship issue or another. He couldn't afford for her to blow this job. He would lay down the law after dinner. It was going to be business or she was going to have to be reassigned. He was so deep in thought that he didn't see the young woman coming around the corner and plowed straight into her.

I cannot believe him! Mariella fumed to herself as she unzipped her bag and began yanking open dresser drawers, moving in swift rhythm to unload her belongings. *Just another reason to avoid him altogether,* she decided. *He's just not into me, but he doesn't have to flaunt it in front of me!* She huffed. *I just wish I had never met him, never worked for him, never dreamed about him! Thank God I didn't make a fool of myself by telling him I actually felt something for him! This situation is so impossible I could just scream!* Mariella stuffed her bags under the four-poster bed. It was then that she noticed Jarah in a recliner in the far corner of the room rocking the twins to sleep.

"You want to talk about it?" Jarah could tell that Mariella was furious. She had been grunting, shoving, and slamming dressers since she had entered the room.

"I am *done* talking! I am done thinking! I am done praying about it!" she folded her hands and plopped down on the edge of the bed. "Men," she huffed again. "I am so *over* the drama!"

"Indeed," Jarah gave her a knowing smile.

Aurielle and Naomi stood behind Tehinnah who was waving goodbye to her boss and closing the door to their suite. She turned and was startled by how close they were. "You ladies made use of the shower yet? I sure need to refresh myself," she said casually.

Naomi and Aurielle continued to glare at her.
"What?" Tehinnah asked in innocence, and then folded her hands in irritation. "Okay. What did I do now?"

"You seem to be getting quite chummy with your boss," Aurielle noted.

Tehinnah rolled her eyes then and stepped away from the door taking her bags with her. "There's no crime against getting help with my bags, ladies. There nothing going on between Noelle and I. He's a really nice man and a sweet guy. He was just offering some assistance. What's *with* everyone around here?" she shook her head as she unpacked quickly.

"So it's Noelle, now? What happened to Mr. Marks?" Aurielle goaded her.

Tehinnah stilled then. "Look," She stood to face Aurielle. "I don't know what this is about, but as far as I know, he's a free agent. I'm single, and if anything *was* going on, it would really be none of your business," she snapped.

"I wish it were that simple," Naomi stepped forward then. "You see, I think that there is someone else involved," she revealed.

"Who is it?" Tehinnah wanted to know who this phantom woman was. Noelle had never mentioned to her that he was seeing anyone or even remotely interested in another woman. He'd had no women visitors except for a few attorneys and clients. Tehinnah had seen his interaction with them and it was all business.

"I'm not at liberty to say," Naomi confessed. "I only ask that you consider the possibility that you could be hurting someone without even meaning to," she urged.

Tehinnah thought back to the flash of a door opening across the hallway, a girl stepping out and then slamming the door again. *Hmmm. I think that's something to look into.* "Well, I don't plan to become a pawn in anyone's game. I'm going to ask Noelle myself after dinner," she decided.

Naomi grimaced at the thought. "That's your choice," she offered.

Tehinnah was even more determined then to get to the bottom of this. No way was she going to be played. Noelle was a fine figure of a man, but if he was already attached, she wanted nothing to do with getting in the middle. She wanted to remain drama free on this trip. She was already avoiding one man. It wouldn't do to have to avoid two. She enjoyed Noelle's company but if it caused confusion, she would have to curtail their fellowship. At least until they returned to their working environment.

"I'm sorry if I came off brash or rude, Tehinnah, but you don't want people to get the wrong impression of you," she advised. "I speak from experience."

"I'll try to remember that," she answered thoughtfully as both ladies headed out to explore downstairs.

41

"Welcome to Jamaican Dreams Resort and to Montego Bay!" Dr. Zeeland Carr announced as the appetizers for lunch were being set before everyone in the main dining room. "I trust that you have at least settled into your rooms and had time to freshen up," he grinned. "I along with my assistants will be your tour guide of Montego Bay and will be traveling along with you on your various excursions to answer any questions you may have," he assured them as a projection screen descended in front of them. "Let us begin."

As Aliya looked around, she grew frustrated. *Lord, this isn't at all what I intended. I wanted everyone to mingle. I see I'm going to have to do random seating for dinnertime.* Aliya knew that some thought she was being a pain in the butt, but she wanted her friends to break out of their zones of familiarity.

Seated at her table were her twin, Enrique, her cousin Mei Ling, Naomi, and Mariella. At the table directly in front of the tour guide sat Seth, Dr. Greg Thomas, Noelle, Tehinnah, Tatyanna, and Kevin Thomas. Directly behind her sat Enrique's entourage: Fabian, Fabritza, Nick, and Gio, along with Dr. Trey Jones and Aurielle. Seated next to them were Elder Worth, and Vivian Worth along with Marco, Jamar, and Carlton. Seated behind that table was Shemiah, Josiah, Savannah, Angelynn, Jarah, and the babies. And seated to their left were Pastor Marks, Rosalynn, Ginevieve, and Columbia. This afternoon's seating for luncheon had been a free for all, with most seated with their friends and fellow love interests.

This simply will not do. If we are going to get connected, we have to do more than go on a trip together. We have to get to know each other. She would talk with Elder Worth about what they could do to break up the monotony. They would be having Bible study at nine at night and nine in the morning.

"This resort has 288 rooms with three championship golf courses for those who you who are aficionados. There are two luxurious spas located right on the grounds and we open up to a private beach. Most of what you have planned, we will accomplish right here, but let me give you a briefing on Mo Bay if you will," he continued.

Everyone nodded in agreement as waitresses filed in bearing the main course of yellow tail fish seated on a bed of red beans and rice, plantains, callaloo. Everything smelled delicious.

"Jamaica is one of the most successful black democracies in the world today. One of the most traditional ways our country has earned money is through agriculture. Our debt burden has grown but since we have a new prime minister, many are moving back to the island and rekindling the enterprises that died. Indian groups originally settled Jamaica and then the Arawak Indians arrived several thousands of years later. Columbus visited Jamaica in 1492, but Spain did not establish colonies here until 1509," Zeeland grew more passionate as he went on.

"The first slaves arrived in 1513 and it wasn't until 1655 that the British overran Jamaica demanding their imperial slice of the pie. It wasn't until 1739 that the British signed a treaty with Jamaica but it would be another ninety-nine years before slavery here would end. We became a British colony in 1866, but we did not get our independence until 1962. So, there you have it: a brief overview of Jamaica's history," he gleefully cheered.

"Our national dish is ackee and salt fish which you should try before you depart our lush island. About seventy-five percent of our population is Black African, about fifteen percent is Afro-European, and the rest is a mixture of Asian, Indian, and a small population of Jews. Some of the places we'll be visiting are Doctor's Cave Beach which is about a five-mile stretch of pure, white sand, such as you won't see anywhere," he promised. We'll hit the North Coast Marine for some scuba diving. There are some awesome coral reefs you have to see to believe. We'll dine by candlelight at the Sugar Day restaurant and we'll also visit the town of Falmouth. All in all, I believe you've got a great tour planned and I can't wait to head out tomorrow at ten-thirty. Thank you for your time," the professor bowed as he was given a polite applause.

Aslan entered the dining room then and shook hands with the professor before he took his seat. "I want to thank all of you for patronizing my resort and for befriending my daughters and not thinking it robbery to join them on this trip. I've wanted them to come home for some time and I can't think of a better occasion for them to return. I hope you will take advantage of the amenities that are all-inclusive in your package. You are special guests here and if there is anything you have need of, please feel free to let me know. I will be on hand to personally serve and assist you," Aslan finished to the cheers, catcalls, and hoots of everyone in the dining room.

Everyone continued eating lunch partaking of pleasant conversation. They would be free in an hour to explore the grounds and relax before dinnertime. It would be their first chance to really kickback and reflect on their trip thus far. There was anticipation mixed with apprehension as that reality dawned in several of their minds.

"Need some help?" Dr. Greg Thomas spotted Jarah struggling with the door to the outdoor patio area all the while juggling baby bags, and a twin stroller. He reached out to hold the door open for her as she made her way outside.

"Thank you so much," Jarah gave him a winsome smile, a little out of breath. "That was very gracious of you," she adjusted the hood of the stroller to block out the direct rays from hitting the twins as they cooed together.

"Not a problem," Greg returned her smile with one of his own. "I planned to do a little reading out here myself," he shrugged showing off his tome. He had decided he needed to occupy his mind with thoughts other than thinking about Marilyn Robinson and her upcoming nuptials. He wanted to think he was over her but every now and then he thought about what they might have become had Andre Charles not entered into the picture. When he saw them together, their love was apparent. If there was one thing Greg didn't begrudge anyone of, it was a happy ending. He had lost his wife to breast cancer and the time he had spent with her he would cherish for the rest of his life, but he was ready to move on. Marilyn had helped him to move past grieving and to begin to enjoy life once more. It was one thing he was thankful for.

"I know everyone is all excited about exploring the grounds, but I'm just here to help out really," she admitted. "I've no interest in going further than the pool and the Jacuzzi," she chuckled.

Greg couldn't believe his ears. He felt the same way. "My son dragged me along on this trip because he felt I was becoming maudlin. I'm really here just to please him," he confessed, a conspiratorial twinkle in his eye. "Maybe if we put our heads together, we can manage to stay under the radar and kick back a bit," he suggested.

Jarah laughed then. "Most definitely," she agreed taking in the suggestion and really seeing Dr. Gregory Thomas for the first time. She had seen him before because his office was connected to her physician's office, but other than that, she had not thought about the man beyond his lab coat. Greg stood over six feet tall, his presence not foreboding but commanding; he was the rich shade of mahogany, and was perfectly groomed from his salt and pepper low cut, perfectly tapered hair to his clean shaven face, sculpted cheekbones, and chiseled jaw line, to his polo shirt without wrinkle tucked into his camel colored slacks which showcased his flat stomach, and toned upper body. *He can't be a day over fifty,* she thought to herself feeling suddenly very old and dowdy in her peasant skirt and empire waist top. "I plan to keep company with these two lovely jewels," Jarah reached into the stroller, adjusting their blankets.

"I'd be honored if you would allow me the pleasure of your company from time to time," Greg requested. The fact that Jarah was beautiful and unattached did not escape his notice.

Jarah blushed then, and turned away embarrassed that she was blushing. "That would be nice," she offered, while simultaneously trying to ignore how her heart raced at the thought of spending time with Dr. Thomas.

Greg smiled widely then, glad he had gained a friend. "I'll see you around then," he departed, allowing himself some time to think and some time to plan his next excursion with the lovely Jarah.

Jamar and Marco had decided to take a turn through one of the manmade trails on the hotel grounds. Jamar could tell that Marco was agitated and a little overwrought about something. They had gotten about half a mile up the meandering path before Jamar decided to break the silence.

"Spill it." Jamar eyed Marco with a look of annoyance and irritation.

"What? I have nothing to spill."

"Sure you do; you look about ready to explode," Jamar observed.

"It's nothing the good Lord can't handle," Marco shrugged nonchalantly.

"So you're not the slightest bit put out by the fact that Ginny is giving you the cold shoulder?" Jamar prodded.

"I'm giving her the space she wants. End of story," Marco continued up the trail.

Jamar followed behind him, kicking the rocks along the trail. "I don't know," Jamar thought aloud.

Marco halted on the trail, a glare evident upon his face. "You don't know *what?*" he ground out.

"If I were desperately in love with Ginny, which I'm not," he assured quickly, "I wouldn't be making it convenient for her to forget me," he threw down the verbal gauntlet.

Marco rushed toward Jamar, shoving him, and catching Jamar completely off guard. "What do you know about love anyway?" he stared down at his friend who was ungraciously seated on the ground. "Back off, Jamar; just back off," Marco pointed at him and stormed away up the trail leaving Jamar in shock at the explosion of emotions he had just unleashed.

Jamar smiled to himself. *What do I know about love, my friend? Plenty.*

"This is such an incredible place," Aliya twirled about as Ginevieve and Tatyanna walked with her through the botanical maze located to the rear of the hotel. "I'm so proud of my daddy. He's seems to have mellowed out too," she commented thoughtfully.

"I have to agree with you there," Tatyanna ran her fingers over the hedges as they walked along. "Maybe the Lord is doing a work in him," she encouraged.

"If God can change my heart, he can change anyone," Aliya assured her, noticing that Ginevieve had grown really quiet. "Right, Ginny?"

"Huh? Oh, yeah, right," Ginny gave a tight smile then, looking around and appearing as though she were interested. "Your father has a really creative eye," she observed.

Tatyanna and Aliya looked to each other then to Ginny trying to decide which of them would broach the subject.

"So, Ginny, how've things been going?" Aliya began, pulling a rose free from the bush they had just passed, inhaling its fragrant scent.

"Fine," Ginny shrugged, her eyes focused on nothing in particular.

"That's good to hear," Tatyanna eyed Aliya. "Because we were beginning to worry about you," she managed to get out without sounding overdramatic.

Ginny turned around then. "Worry? For what? I mean, I'm fine really, really, fine, its not as if I've blown the best thing that ever happened to me," she broke off, gasping for air, blinking back unshed tears. "I'm going to be fine," she rehearsed to herself. "Perfectly fine; this'll all blow over, and I will have been saved from making a total fool of myself over-"

"Whoa." Aliya stopped her with a held up hand. "Breathe, girl."

Tatyanna had tissue on hand which Ginny took graciously then ungraciously blew into loudly, the tears flowing now.

"I'm such a fool," she sniffed.

"Does this have anything to do with a suddenly moody, highly disgruntled florist?" Aliya guessed. She hadn't seen much of Marco this past week, but when she had, he had been in a hurry and not in the mood for conversation.

Ginny nodded profusely. "I-I ch-challenged him to show me he could be kind, and sweet, and he passed with flying colors," she sniffed.

"I'm not following you," Tatyanna patted her co-worker's shoulder. "What's the problem then?"

Ginevieve shared with them her encounter with Marco, his adamant refusal to come on the trip, her misgivings about him, his plan to prove himself, and her rejection of anything more between them. By the time she was done, all three women were crying, Tatyanna and Aliya at the sweetness of it all and Ginny at her loss of opportunity to gain a friend.

"What are we going to do?" Aliya sniffed.

Tatyanna reared back in surprise. "What do you mean what are we going to do?"

Aliya waved her hand at Ginny. "Look at her! We can't let Ginny continue like this! This is supposed to be a fun trip," Aliya's stomach turned as Ginny's heart wrenching sobs continued. "Look at her and tell me how can we think of having a good time?" she stated pointedly.

Tatyanna folded her arms defensively. "What do you propose we do about it? We can't very well *make* Marco speak to Ginny," she reasoned.

Aliya grinned mischievously. *"Can't we?"*

Fabian was so relieved the luncheon was over. He couldn't wait to complete his current mission; to find out more about the stunning young woman he'd had the pleasure of running into. *Literally,* he grinned to himself. He had been lost in thought when he had plowed into her, spilling the drinks she was carrying. He had quickly helped her clean up, catching only her name before she had hurried off. *Mei Ling.* He could still smell the fragrance of her long ebony locks that had swept along his arm as he had helped her to clean up. *Cucumber melon;* It was one of his favorite scents. He had contented himself at the luncheon with a seat near enough to watch her, but far enough to not draw any unwanted attention. It turned out that by keeping a keen ear tuned in, he had learned that she was cousin to Aliya and Augusta Peyton, a little fact he tucked away for future use. She was also a news correspondent in Beijing, and here on holiday. That last piece was a little disheartening, but it helped him come to a swift decision. Somehow, someway, he had to make her acquaintance. He had four days to impress upon Mei Ling that she was definitely someone he wanted to know better and maybe even forever.

Enrique and Augusta followed Aslan into his massive office and personal library, feeling dwarfed by the sheer height of his bookshelves and the cathedral ceiling. There was a ladder that led to a second level which housed a loft for reading. It was the booklover's dream.

Augusta was really impressed by her father's attention to detail. She felt sure that he was probably pressing her mother to sell their home in Kingston and live on the grounds. She couldn't blame him. As she and Enrique sat before him on a plush, leather settee, she knew that her father's heart was firmly ensconced in Jamaican Dreams.

Augusta twined her fingers with Enrique's and boldly declared, "Papa, Enrique asked me to marry him, and I said yes," she beamed.

Aslan who had seated himself across from them rather than sitting behind their desk didn't even bat an eye at the declaration.

"I expected as much," Aslan teased, his eyes alight with merriment. "It's not everyday that a man sees his daughter radiating joy and contentment," he commented. "So, when are the nuptials to take place? What about an engagement party? All of your friends are here, correct?" Aslan's mind was fast at work.

"Actually," Enrique began cautiously, "we haven't announced it to anyone. Not even Aliya knows. Only two of my bodyguards know for security reasons," he continued. "If word gets out before we return to the States, I'm afraid it could thrust us right back into the spotlight," he reasoned. "It could also create unnecessary security concerns as well," he added.

For a long moment Aslan didn't say a word. He was so quiet, so thoughtful; you could hear the whir of the ceiling fan above them. Finally he spoke with such calm and simplicity that his request threw Enrique and Augusta for a loop.

"Since it is imperative that all measures be taken to protect my daughter and you have received our blessing, I see no reason for you to leave Jamaica as nothing less than newlyweds."

"How are you faring?" Seth asked Aliya as they sat on a wrought iron bench near a golf course.

Aliya and Tatyanna had been consoling Ginny when Seth rounded the corner of the maze, taking them by surprise. Tatyanna and Ginny had walked back towards the resort leaving her alone with Seth. She prayed he was not privy to Ginny's situation. She had distracted him and led him out the maze continuing to walk and talk until they had found themselves seated by the golf course before he had to attend the Group Leader's meeting.

"I'm great," she sighed. "Couldn't be happier; seeing my father, having my cousin here, being escorted by a dashing pastor- it's all too much for me," she giggled.

Seth shook his head at her sense of humor. "Well, I'm glad to hear it," he tucked a strand of her hair behind her ear. "You always amaze me how you can go from one emotion to the other in the blink of an eye," he joked.

Aliya stilled then. "What do you mean?"

"I heard you crying," Seth admitted. "Although what you were crying about, I have not a clue. You would tell me if I did something to hurt you, right?" Seth's concern was evident.

"Of course," she touched his shoulder then in reassurance. "It had nothing to do with you; I was just sympathizing with a friend," she confided.

"Well, I pray that I never give you cause to shed a tear," Seth leaned forward, touching his forehead to hers as he gazed into her eyes.

"Only tears of joy," Aliya whispered. She closed her eyes as she felt the soft pressure of his lips upon her forehead and basked in the sweetness of the moment.

42

"Hey, boss man," Tehinnah stood behind Noelle who had located the fitness center and had decided to work off some of the stress he was feeling.

Noelle set the weights down carefully, taking a deep breath as he did so. "Hey, what's up?" he pulled his towel from his back pocket and wiped the sweat beading on his forehead.

Tehinnah took her time testing out equipment and walking around the spacious center before she made her way to stand before him. "I'm just checking out the place; there's really a lot to do if you are fitness oriented. There's even a juice bar near the indoor pool," her voice lit with excitement.

Noelle grinned then. "Nothing like a good swim after a great workout, and nothing like a good smoothie after a good swim," he admitted.

Tehinnah sat down then. "Thanks for helping me earlier with my things," she picked up a smaller set of weights then. "I hope I didn't cause any problems for you," she hinted.

Noelle swiped the back of his neck, his hand stilling at the statement. "Come again?"

"You know; the girl who looked seriously irate, who slammed the door," Tehinnah reminded him. "Doesn't she work for you?" Tehinnah was sure she had seen her in passing a few times at the office.

"She *used* to work for me," Noelle wasn't planning on divulging any further information. It seemed like Tehinnah was fishing for something.

"Oh." Tehinnah recognized the tone that stated this subject was off limits. She was just about to leave then, when she looked up and saw the very woman in question was standing in the doorway, mouth pursed in disapproval. Her huff of irritation alerted Noelle to her presence.

He stood then but it was too late to say anything for Mariella had already turned on her heels.

"Looks like you made a great impression on her. She doesn't even want to share the same space with you," Tehinnah joked.

Noelle gave her a warning glance. "Don't. You know nothing about Mariella."

"I know enough to realize you're in deep, boss." Tehinnah deduced. "Just know that I will not be a pawn in whatever game you're playing," she shot back.

Noelle reared back in surprise. "Game," he laughed, "This coming from a woman who spends time throwing herself at me to gain the attention of someone else? *Don't* talk to me about games, Tehinnah," Noelle stormed off, his last words leaving Tehinnah stunned and embarrassed.

Touché, Tehinnah admitted to herself.

Pastor John Marks and Columbia were content to seat themselves in the main lobby of the hotel, observing the comings and goings of their friends as well as the other patrons of the hotel. Between his counseling sessions and her preparations to close her shop temporarily, he had managed very little time to talk with her. They weren't particularly moved to explore the grounds just yet but found themselves merely enjoying each others' company. Once they kicked off the outdoor excursions, all attention would be focused on making sure the singles were having fun.

"How are the girls holding up?" Pastor Marks knew Columbia had made a call home right after the luncheon was ended.

"They seem to be doing fine," Columbia found that to be a relief. Her daughters meant the world to her and it had largely been due to them that she had decided to go on the trip. In some ways she felt a bit odd being with so many under-thirty singles but she was definitely enjoying herself thus far. The food, the hospitality, the kindness and genuine desire to please from the bell boy to the maids was par excellence. She was thoroughly impressed. "Dee's tooth came out and she was a bit fussy about it, but other than that things are just fine," she sighed in content. She was seated across from John and the view was more than to her liking. He had dressed down a bit in a crew necked shirt, khaki slacks and loafers. John was a man who was solidly built, and groomed just short of being too pampered.

"Well, I'm glad to hear it. So tell me, what are you hoping to get out of this experience?" John leaned back in his chair then, taking in the very appealing woman who was before him.

Columbia had changed into a sleeveless summer dress that fell graciously at her calves, and molded gently to her motherly curves and showed off her toned arms. He liked the fact that she exuded confidence with the skin she was in. She favored braids and this trip was no different. Her braids were twisted into a bouffant with a chignon completing the style. She looked stunning, and radiant, and if John didn't think she would balk at his proposal, he'd suggest they elope. He had known for a while that he was in love with Columbia Newcomb. How could you not love so fearless, so confident, so faithful a woman? He had seen her handle some very difficult situations with fairness, prudence, and judgment. She wasn't infected with the angry black woman syndrome: she had learned to win playing the cards she had been dealt without excuses but filled with hope. She was raising three children alone and doing a stand up job. John couldn't be more impressed and he was honored that she had let him into her life. It wasn't going to be easy convincing her, but the rewards of seeing Columbia laugh, love, and live would be immensely satisfying.

"I plan to milk this trip for all its worth," Columbia chuckled. "This may be my only time in the near future that I can pamper myself and not feel the slightest twinge of guilt," she confessed.

John gave her a nod of agreement. "Pamper away, love," he encouraged. "Just know that the best of your pampering has not even begun," he promised.

"You can't be serious," Enrique had recovered from his initial shock at Aslan's suggestion.

"Daddy, no one even knows we're *engaged*," Augusta reminded him.

Aslan would not budge on his suggestion. "We have all of the things here on site that you would need; we have an event planner, a wedding planner, both of your pastors, your family, and your close friends. We can announce it as an end of the trip party. You and Enrique can make it a surprise nuptial ceremony. Celebrities do it all the time," Aslan reasoned. "As your bride, Augusta would be able to receive all the protection she truly needs. You all would return to the States happily married and you will have performed the greatest coup against the press. They will be upset, but they will also be clamoring for the exclusive interview. Everyone is happy, and you can put to rest these ridiculous Billionaire Sweetie snippets in the local papers."

Augusta looked to Enrique then, realizing with great surprise, her father was correct. Enrique took her hands in his.

"Whatever you decide, sweetheart, I'm content," Enrique gazed into her eyes; his own filled with love and comfort.

Augusta took a deep breath and released it knowing that her decision had been made. "I agreed to marry you, Enrique. I love you so much, and I'd be more than happy to spend the rest of my life with you. I think it fitting for us to wed in the very country you followed me to." She turned to her father then, grinning. "I will leave this island as Mrs. Enrique Estrada." She was caught off guard as Enrique swept her off her feet in a hug, spinning her around.

Aslan too was caught off guard by the display of emotion and longed to have his own wife near to share the good news.

Fabritza had been scoping out the right moment to approach Giovanni after the luncheon. Her brother, Gio, and Nick all had shifts to check the grounds. It was Giovanni's turn, and Fabritza had been trailing him for a few minutes and staying far enough behind to not be detected. The man had six senses. She was just about to approach him when an arm clamped around her mouth and a strong hand tightened around her midsection, pulling her off the path and into an alcove of trees.

She fought hard against the attacker until she heard his voice.

"It's me," Fabian whispered relaxing his grip. "Didn't want you causing unnecessary alarm," he released his sister.

Fabritza swung around wildly, the air rushing back into her lungs. "What the *heck* did you do that for?" she glared, furious that he had interrupted her lone opportunity to get Gio alone.

"Giovanni can be quite dangerous when he is caught off guard. I wouldn't recommend approaching him. Now or later," he warned.

"If you're trying to warn me off, you'll have to do better than that," Fabritza lifted her chin haughtily.

"Stay away from Giovanni. That's not a suggestion; that's a command," Fabian spoke very softly. "This obsession you have with the man is going to cost you your job on the case," he informed her. "Nicholas has been given directions to report any misconduct from you," he confessed, watching her eyes widen at the revelation. "Trust me on this when I say he will happily terminate your part in this operation. You were hired to be a professional and do your job. That is the extent of your involvement with Mr. Estrada and his personal security team. Do I make myself clear?"

Fabritza swallowed hard and nodded, playing the obedient team player all the while seething with anger at the nerve of Nicholas Cartellini. "Perfectly," she answered sweetly.

"Good. If you choose to go against the wishes of Mr. Estrada, you will be called in for insubordination, given a psych evaluation and you will be suspended, not just from this case but from any other case for twelve months. I hope you are not willing to risk it." Fabian left her then to contemplate how she would seduce the impenetrable Giovanni without getting fired because this thing between them was far from over.

"What in the world possessed me to go along with this in the first place?" Jamar asked himself aloud.

"Perhaps it was your desire to see your good friends get along for once," Mariella giggled as she sidled up alongside him.

Jamar, Ginny, Rosalynn, Mariella, and Marco had decided to take advantage of one of the amenities of the resort not included in their package: horseback riding. Jamar had never been horseback riding but felt inspired after he saw the look of excitement flitter across the faces of two people who seemed determined to avoid each other at all cost. He had no idea how he was sacrificing himself until he had, with much assistance, mounted his horse. He was determined to grin and bear it so that Marco and Ginny could spend some quality time together. He was excited that Roz and Mariella had joined him in his impromptu plan. Aliya and Tatyanna had made all the arrangements for the trip. They would all ride out four miles further into the mountains but would drop back until Marco and Ginny were left leading the pack. They would trail behind them. It had seemed like a perfectly reasonable plan and seemed to be working well with one exception: No one had informed him of how uncomfortable his ride would be. He was definitely going to need that Jacuzzi later.

"Are you enjoying yourself?" Marco tried to keep his tone light as he rode next to Ginny on the mountain trail. It had not been his bright idea to go horseback riding and place himself in the same vicinity as Ginevieve, but he was thankful for it nonetheless. Sometimes Jamar Davis could be a royal pest, but most of the time he got it right. He would have to thank him later for his ingenious move.

Ginny looked at Marco out of the corner of her eye. He looked carefree and wildly romantic, like some character straight from the cover of a historical romance novel. She had determined that since she was among company, she could be civil. "Immensely." She replied.

Marco smiled to himself then. "That's good to know, considering the company," he joked.

"I'm enjoying the scenery," she stated pointedly. "Company not included," her words held a tinge of sharpness.

Marco rolled his eyes then. "Far be it from me to think you were enjoying my company. I assure you, I am not ignorant of where I stand with you," his tone only expressed remorse which surprised Ginny.

"Friendship wasn't enough for you," Ginny reminded him.

"You're right," Marco conceded. "I'm sorry for the way I handled things. I wish we could start over," he confessed.

Ginny gave him a look of surprise. "Do you *really* mean that? I mean, can we truly be friends?"

Marco knew that if he was going to have any chance with Ginny, he would have to begin somewhere. "I believe we can be friends. Friendship is the cornerstone of any good relationship. I won't lie to you and say it will be easy being your friend, but I can tell you my life has been better because of your friendship. You challenge me to be better, you berate me, you criticize me, and you make me see myself from a different angle. You're honest with me, and I appreciate that." Marco opened up to Ginny then. "I realized I can be pretty arrogant and sometimes even pompous when it comes to what I want. I need you to keep me in line," he grinned.

Ginny laughed out loud then. He was being outrageous and laying it on thick, but she admitted to herself that she had missed his company too. "Okay, Marco, you win," she eyed him over her sunglasses. "But don't pitch a fit when I remind you that you asked for this friendship," she warned.

"Fair enough," Marco agreed.

They continued along the path, conversing freely, totally oblivious to the cheers and high fives behind them and the grimace on Jamar's face as he adjusted his seat once more. They had one more mile to go before he dismounted and hauled himself off to the Jacuzzi before dinner.

Aliya had thought to sneak off to the spa while everyone was outside sightseeing so she was surprised to see Mei Ling seated comfortably, her turbaned head thrown back, her eyes covered with cucumbers, her face undergoing a mud treatment, her temples being massaged thoroughly. She took a seat next to her cousin and prepared herself for relaxation. She breathed deeply and allowed the therapist to take her bags and place them in a secure place. She leaned over to her cousin's ear and pursed her lips ready to scare the bejesus out of her.

"Don't even think about it, Liya," Mei Ling warned her.

Aliya stopped just short of uttering a word, her eyes rounded in surprise. "*How* do you *do* that?" she wondered aloud.

Mei Ling smiled then. "You have a dainty tap that you do with your feet when you stop. I could always tell when you were sneaking up behind me," Mei Ling revealed.

Aliya's mouth was wide open in shock. "Really? You mean all this time I've been thinking I'm so stealthy when I'm actually giving myself away?" she shook her head in disbelief.

"Don't beat yourself up about it. Most people have a habit that is so ingrained they don't even realize it. Be glad yours is harmless. What's been going on with you?" Mei Ling was a stickler for changing the subject when you least expected.

"Well, when we last caught up Divine Designs was just getting off the ground. We've been doing well so far, keeping our head above water, what with the economy being what it is," she sighed. "Augusta is doing well, gaining more clients within the region. I'm really proud of her. She's finally realizing that she has the love of a good man," Aliya sighed.

"And what about *you*," Mei Ling asked pointedly. "Are you recognizing that you have the love of a good man as well? I couldn't help but notice at the luncheon that a certain pastor couldn't take his eyes off you," Mei Ling teased. "If the building were on fire, I don't think he would have noticed," she laughed.

Aliya blushed furiously then. "We're just friends," she defended.

"Umm hmm," Mei Ling grinned knowingly. "For now." She promised. "That man is practically running around with wedding bells above his head. He may not have signed the papers yet, but he's definitely sold on you, Aliya." Mei Ling assured her.

Aliya eyed her cousin thoughtfully then. "And when did you become an expert on men in love?"

Mei Ling's eyes darkened with an unnamed emotion. "When I realized that my fiancé was content to remain engaged for the rest of our lives," she exhaled. "Trust me when I tell you, it is not a discovery you want to make."

"I'm sorry Mei; I had no idea," Aliya touched her cousin's arm in comfort.

"It's no biggie," Mei Ling forced a cheeriness that she did not feel. "I'm over it," she decided then. "Besides, there's nothing like running into an incredible looking guy to remind you there are plenty of fish in the sea," she perked up then.

"Who are we talking about?" Aliya was curious to know.

"I didn't catch his name, but judging by the looks of him, he's definitely dangerous. He's got a twin sister, I believe; I think he's Italian."

Aliya's eyes nearly popped out of her head. "Fabian?" Aliya went into a wild fit of giggles. "Wow, I never would have guessed," she giggled again.

"What's so funny?" Mei Ling raised her brow.

"I didn't think your tastes ran to tall, Italian, and dangerous," Aliya shrugged.

"Well, one would have to be dead not to recognize that Fabian is one finely made specimen of mankind. God certainly patted himself on the back," Mei Ling joked. "We ran into each other literally as I was helping Uncle earlier today. I tell you, girl, there are very few things that leave me speechless, but he is one of them," Mei Ling sighed dreamily. "I hope I don't make a fool of myself at dinner," she whispered.

"Let's hope not. I don't know much about him, but he's in the employ of Enrique, who happens to be a very good friend of mine. There's something to be said for a man that you can trust with your life." Aliya noted.

"So he's law enforcement? Ugh," Mei Ling shook her head regretfully.

"Worse; he's government intelligence," Aliya informed her.

Mei Ling's smile was completely gone. In its place was a frown the size of Texas. "That's too bad. I really could have enjoyed making his acquaintance," Bad memories from her recent past flooded her mind. She swiftly pushed them aside.

"Well, I wouldn't count him out just because he's involved with the law," Aliya reasoned. There are far worse things to be involved in." Aliya closed her eyes choosing to drift into the comfortable silence between them.

Mei Ling wished she could agree with her cousin, but experience had taught her differently. She could hear the jeers and mockery as she had been arrested without cause, stripped of her dignity, molested and tortured for the sake of incriminating footage that she had not possessed. It was an experience she would not forget. No one knew why Mei Ling had decided to take leave and come to Montego Bay; and she preferred to keep it that way.

43

"Who ever heard of a non-alcoholic resort?" muttered Fabritza. "I need a stiff drink," she complained as she seated herself at the counter of the lobby café.

"I'm in agreement with you," Carlton plopped down next to her at the counter. He extended his hand. "I'm Carlton. And you are?"

"Fabritza, who is not interested," she clarified to his amusement.

Carlton nodded in understanding. "Just being friendly,"

Fabritza laughed derisively. "That's what they all say," she flipped her long silky strands. They billowed like a curtain over her shoulder.

"What's got you so riled up? Your boss laying down the law?" Carlton joked.

Fabritza seized him with a stare that froze his laugh in place. "Actually, yeah; There is something I want that I've been forbidden to have," she pouted.

"Explain," Carlton's mind was already formulating a plan.

"Well, I have a thing for Giovanni and I just know if his meddling brother weren't involved, he would have given in to me by now," she reasoned. "Anyway, my brother all but told me they're planning to fire me, if Giovanni and I have anything but a working relationship," she finished. "He's completely ignoring me for some backwoods nurse!" Fabritza hissed.

"You mean Na--"

"-Don't even utter her name," Fabritza held up a hand of protest.

"Tell you what; let's make a deal," Carlton ventured, "I'll keep Naomi distracted if you can do me a favor as well."

Fabritza looked steadily at her newfound friend. "What might that be?"

"I've taken a vested interest in a certain lady in the building. The problem is, so has your brother. If you can keep him occupied while he's here, I'll take care of your little problem with Naomi." He assured her.

"How?" Fabritza knew that short of killing the woman, Giovanni wasn't going to take his eyes off her.

"I'll simply make sure Giovanni understands that Naomi's been around the block so to speak. I'll drop a few hints, make him believe we've been carrying on because he's been inattentive. She'll never know what hit her," he grinned in mischief. He had not missed the interchange between Fabian and Mei Ling earlier today. He'd been about to approach her when the clumsy guard had crashed into her. He'd been apologetic; Mei Ling had been flustered and blushing profusely. The only thing that went through Carlton's mind was *I saw her first*. He was becoming more incensed with Enrique and his goons by the day. First they had practically destroyed his relationship with his sister; Now, one of them was after Mei Ling. This time, he would beat them at their own game: he would use Fabritza to accomplish his own purpose. He had found an ally in the camp.

"I hope everyone is doing well," Elder Worth addressed all of the clergy who were present for their first meeting.

Josiah, Pastor at Second Chance, Seth, Pastor of Fresh Fire, and John, Pastor of New Life along with Vivian Worth and Angelynn Worth sat at the conference table, their minds, hearts, and ears ready to solidify the plans for the devotional time here on the island.

"Here's what I want to do: we have five sessions of study, and I have been informed that the last evening is a special surprise which Mr. Peyton will share with us momentarily." He continued on. "I propose that the ladies do a joint session on the last morning, I cover the tonight's session, and Josiah cover tomorrow morning, Pastor Mark's cover tomorrow night's session, and Seth cover our last morning devotion on the our last day here. What do you think?" he smiled brightly.

Everyone began to speak at once, putting forth ideas for the devotion time until Elder Worth held up a hand. "Wait; one at a time please," he chuckled.

After a few minutes of deliberation, they were able to formulate a schedule and topics:

Day 1 Evening - Elder Worth - The Purpose of your Singleness
Day 2 Morning -Josiah Worth - Sanctifying Your Single hood
Day 2 Evening- John Marks - From Wholeness to Oneness
Day 3 Morning - Vivian Worth - Age is nothing but a Number
Day 3 Evening- Seth Davis - Guarding Your Heart
Day 4 Morning- Angelynn Worth - Dealing with Your Issues
Day 4 Evening- Closing Festivities

Aslan entered the room with Enrique and Augusta on his heels just as the Pastors and leaders were finalizing their plans. Elder Worth ushered Mr. Peyton forward to address them.

Aslan cleared his throat , knowing that what he was about to say would not sit well with some, but would be accomplished, even if he had to pull strings to hire a justice of the peace. He had already contacted his friend in the States who was settling all the license requirements for his daughter and her fiancé.

"It is with great pleasure, but also with great seriousness that I come before you all and ask for your strictest confidence and confidentiality with the matters I am about to share," he began. "About one week ago, with the knowledge of their pastors, and my approval, Enrique and Augusta got engaged to be married," he noted the surprise in some faces but went forward. "However, due to safety issues, I propose that since they are here among friends, family, and clergy that they tie the knot here at the culmination of our celebration; and they agreed." Aslan concluded and then watched as bedlam transpired. From looks of disbelief to looks of betrayal, to embraces of happiness, and handshakes marked with uncertainty, Enrique and Augusta received congratulations with mixed feelings.

Elder Worth spoke then. "If it were any other couple, I would definitely not approve of so hasty a ceremony; but I believe that Enrique and Augusta are at a place where they have the facts, they have sorted out their personal issues, and can move forward together. You two will be seeing me as well as Pastor Marks over the next few days for counseling." Elder Worth emphasized. "It would do us great honor to officiate at your wedding," he hugged Augusta then.

"I second that," Pastor Marks added himself to the mix.

"Please be reminded that you are privy to confidential information," Aslan warned. "Not even my other daughter is aware of this wedding," Aslan gazed directly at Pastor Seth Davis, his eyes telling their own story. "Thank you for your time," Mr. Peyton ushered Augusta and Enrique out so the Pastors could continue their planning.

Elder Worth settled himself at the conference table, all eyes on him. "Now, I know some of you have misgivings about ending a singles' getaway with a marriage, but what better ending?"

Josiah raised his hand. "Father, with all due respect, I'm hard pressed to see how this is going to be kept a secret. Do you know how many plans have to be laid in three days? It will take a miracle for everyone to remain clueless," he reasoned. He was excited for Enrique and Augusta but he knew fallout was inevitable. Someone was bound to be upset; whether it was the surprise or the secrecy of it all, or simply not having the suitable attire.

Angelynn raised her hand. "If I may interrupt, gentleman, I think the focus should remain on the single's getaway but in the meantime, Mother Worth and I will make sure that Augusta has the assurance she needs during this process."

Seth had decided to remain silent until now. "My concern," he added, "is that Augusta may gain a husband, but she may very well lose a sister in the process. I don't think it wise to leave her sister out of the loop. This wedding is going to upstage all of the hard work Aliya has put into planning this trip. She's not going to see it as a surprise; she's going to see it as a betrayal of trust by two people she loves dearly."

"You do have a point, but everyone knows Aliya can't hold water when it comes to secrets; what do you suggest we do?" Josiah countered.

"I believe the only person who can convince her of the seriousness of keeping this wedding a secret is Enrique. He will be able to express to her the risks involved if this should get out to the press, but more importantly to the wrong people," Seth declared.

Everyone agreed that this was the most sensible thing to do. Pastor Marks along with Enrique would meet with Aliya before devotions.

They bowed their heads and prayed for the trip's participants, asking God's presence to cover them, His angelic hosts to protect them, and evil to be removed from their midst. It was more than an hour before the leaders departed the conference room, refreshed and ready to carry on the work of the ministry.

Rosalynn waved goodbyes to Ginny, Marco, Jamar, and Mariella as she boarded the elevator. She had truly had a wonderful time with them. Though she knew next to nothing about horses, the guides had assured her that she had done beautifully and even declared she had a natural seat. Roz had blushed when he winked at her and offered to give her a private tour of the grounds before she left. *As if!* She had noticed the forthright manner and boldness which the men here on the island were in abundance of. She was flattered, but she was not fooled. There was only one man she was interested in, she thought to herself.

"Going somewhere?"

Roz nearly shrieked, jumping at the voice behind her, turning in surprise. She had no idea that someone was in the elevator with her. She immediately relaxed when she realized it was only Giovanni. "I should knock you out for that," she glared jokingly.

Giovanni grinned slyly. "Hey, I was here first," he reminded her. "You look like you were thrown from a horse," he chuckled.

Roz leaned back against the elevator wall which seemed to be crawling at a very slow pace. "Almost, but not quite; A few of us went horseback riding. It was my first time," she admitted.

"My brother would have loved to have taken you," Gio pointed out.

"Your brother and I are not really hanging out these days," Roz informed him.

"Is that so?" Giovanni crossed him arms. "Would this have anything to do with that pipsqueak brother of yours?"

Before Roz could answer, the elevator doors opened. "Pity, here's my stop," she rushed out waving to Gio before hurrying down the hall.

Giovanni stuck his head out of the elevator calling out. "This conversation is far from over," he warned before closing the elevator once more. He could not for the life of him understand why people complicated the matter of love. He would have to be enlightened in the near future.

"I can't decide whether to kick your butt or kiss you," Marco shook his head at Jamar as he entered their suite.

"Neither one of those choices is acceptable you know," Jamar chuckled. "In either case, I would be forced to defend myself, and Ginny would never forgive me if I tattooed your pretty face with my knuckle prints," he joked.

"Yeah, yeah," Marco waved. "You Americans are all fists and no finesse. I would not fight you, friend, unless a sword was involved. I am a Master Swordsman, trained by one of the best. You would not stand a chance against me, I am afraid," Marco bowed his head in mock sorrow. He did not even bother to mention he was also trained in mixed martial arts as well. A gentleman didn't reveal all his secrets.

"Hey, I can't argue with you there; but you should thank me for helping your cause. Judging from what I could see, it certainly didn't hurt you." Jamar undressed in a hurry, recognizing the time would soon come upon them for dinner and Bible Study.

"You are right," Marco tugged off his shirt and went rifling through his duffle bag for something a bit more formal for the dinner. "Ginny and I are friends now," he grinned to himself.

Jamar stared at his friend incredulous. "She actually *believed* you? You're good," he laughed.

Marco eyes crossed then in annoyance. "I have every intention of honoring the lady's request. I'm going to be the best male friend she's ever had," he glared.

Jamar laughed all the way to the shower. Boy was Ginny in for a shock when she discovered her new BFF was in fact planning to become her groom.

Francheska Cartellini dropped her bags onto the floor in relief and exhaustion and threw herself across the bed, not bothering to take off her holster and gun. She had been delayed in her arrival to the island due to a shakedown and arrest in Venice of two well-known weapons smugglers. It had brought her immense pleasure and satisfaction to see them brought down. She had single-handedly delivered their whereabouts to her superiors but not without losing something of herself in the process. She had been tracking the case from the inside as usual, playing the unsuspecting girlfriend, but this time, she hadn't been playing. She had been growing close to the weapons dealer during the four months she had been under cover. He had truly been a caring individual, not even pressing her for sex after she had shared her religious convictions. He had been very respecting of that, and it was then that she had found herself wishing things were different, that he wasn't a criminal, and that she wasn't an agent. When everything had played out, it had turned out, that Carlito Brunelli wasn't a weapons dealer at all. He was Dominic Francois, a *French* agent, highly sought after, and apparently thorough, and ruthless in his approach to rooting out organized crime. *I can add heartless to his many qualities,* Francheska thought. Francheska had been so furious at the revelation she could not even think straight. She had not even found out from him, but from her boss. He had allowed himself to be handcuffed and carted off with all the other men, leaving her torn and heartbroken for falling for a criminal and he was *anything but!* Her boss had laughed off the whole thing as if it were some joke saying, 'he couldn't be sure if you were a double agent or not,' and sent her on to the next assignment her cousins were working. *Double agent, my foot! He knew exactly who I was the entire time!* Francheska had fumed all the way from Italy to Montego Bay, calling herself all kinds of fools and thankful that he hadn't taken advantage of her. *But of course not; it was against policy. Agents didn't get involved with agents-- Ever.* Francheska wasn't upset about the policy. She was a godly woman and so that policy had never bothered her. Until now; until she had the audacity to fall in love.

Francheska was so involved in her maudlin thoughts that she didn't notice the other female coming into the room from the shower, her towel wrapped securely around her, humming an Italian tune until she shrieked. Francheska, in breakneck speed, righted herself, rolling to her knees, simultaneously pulling her gun out of her holster and aiming it at her intruder.

"Talk fast."

"I'm Fabritza Ciccone. I'm an agent on the Estrada case. If you're not Francheska Cartellini, I guess I won't live to tell it, will I?" Fabritza was not without protection, her dagger hidden in the folds of her towel. She was a fast and excellent marksman.

Francheska didn't lower her weapon. "Show me your identification. Back up slowly, and throw it to me," She ordered. "Now," her voice like steel moved Fabritza to action.

Fabritza did as she ordered, a bit peeved at the militant Cartellini. Obviously she was upset about something. She tossed it onto the bed in front of Francheska. "Could you lower your weapon? It wouldn't do to have to explain to our boss that you shot me," she reasoned.

Francheska identified her as an agent and lowered her weapon, placing it back in her holster. "You really should be more-" her statement was cut off as a dagger went whizzing past her, slicing her holster strap and making it's way into the headboard behind her.

Fabritza raised an eyebrow in mock innocence. "Careful?"

44

Dinnertime at Jamaican Dreams

Dinner was definitely something that everyone had been looking forward to, especially since they had worked up an appetite for it. Whether it was through walking the trails, working out at the gym, going horse back riding, or planning the activities for the spiritual growth of the singles, everyone seemed ravenous, but on their best behavior. Aslan had stated that dinner was a formal affair. Translation: no jeans, no sneakers allowed. The ladies and gentleman had no trouble complying. As a matter of fact, they had expected such a dress code. What they had not expected was to be seated by drawing. Such as it was, one hoped that one's dinner companions would be just as appealing as the menu for the evening. It appeared that the seating for the morning and evening dinners would become permanent. Some were overjoyed with the prospect; some were incensed, each table being given a festival theme: Island Fantasy, Island Carnival, Island Du Jour, Island Dreams, Island Masquerade, and Island Dance.

Located at Island Fantasy were Shemiah, Savannah, Josiah, Angelynn and the twins, and Columbia who seemed as though she was going to drown in all the domestic bliss happening at her table. She eyed Pastor Marks regretfully. At the Island Carnival table behind them, sat Jamar, Tehinnah, Dr. Greg Thomas, Jarah, Aurielle, and Dr. Trey Jones. One couldn't help noticing how friendly Dr. Thomas had become with Jarah. Located at the Island Du Jour table was Seth, Aliya, Marco, Ginny, Tatyanna, and Kevin. This table was clearly in need of a chaperone, but was not far from them. Next to this table was Island Dance, with Pastor John Marks, Elder Worth, and Vivian Worth, and Aslan Peyton seated majestically with a view to all other tables. Directly in front of them was the Island Masquerade table with Mei Ling, Carlton, Naomi, Mariella, Noelle, and Rosalynn; an appropriate table seeing as nearly everyone seated was wearing a mask of one kind or the other. And seated in front of them, towards the front of the dining area, was the Island Dreams table. Seated were Fabian, Francheska, Nicholas, Giovanni, Enrique, Augusta, and much to everyone at the table's dislike, Fabritza. Looking at the table, it would be more aptly named Island Intrigue.

These dinner guests would have to tolerate each other no matter how pleasant or distasteful, for the next few evenings. It was enough to make the Pastors pray that much harder that church love would prevail and that God himself would place a guard over the lips of his people.

"Good evening, everyone," Aslan stood at his table. "I trust that everyone is finding their way and enjoying their stay here at Jamaican Dreams Resort," he waited until the applause died down before continuing on. "Tonight, my chefs have a treat for you. You will be the very first guests to witness their presentation of dinner, so sit back, enjoy the presentation, enjoy the music, as they give you the Jamaican Dreams Cuisine Royal Culinary Welcome," he sat down as the lights dimmed.

All of a sudden the dining room became a swirl of color and lighting as the Christian reggae music began to pulsate through the atmosphere. Several chefs stepped onto the scene, huge platters in hand lifted high above their heads as they set them on an extravagantly decorated table. They lifted the lids and lit each dish, the timing a precision of their performance resembling that of an orchestral concert. The waiters moved in time as well, their maneuvering taking on the form of ballerinas performing Swan Lake, no one missing a step until every table was served and everyone applauding the genius of the waiters and chefs. Elder Worth delivered the prayer and everyone delved into the delicious entrée set before them.

"This is scrumptious," Francheska groaned, closing her eyes in satisfaction and delight. After eating airplane food, this was a divine treat.

"Glad to see you've still got an appetite, cousin," Nicholas chuckled as he sipped his sparkling cider.

"Don't start, Nicky," Francheska teased, her eyes brimming with mirth at the look on Nick's face.

"Nicky?" Fabian teased. "What did you do to earn *that* nickname?"

Giovanni nearly choked on his sparkling cider, waving a hand in protest. "That's classified information. Family secrets and all that, you understand," Giovanni glared at Francheska. The woman hadn't been there twenty four hours yet and already she was setting Nick on edge.

Nick glared at his cousin. "Alright, Checkers," he warned.
Francheska swallowed audibly at that particular name, surprised he still remembered it. "Say no more," she held up her hand. "I'll be on my best behavior," she grinned.

Enrique and Augusta gave each other a knowing grin. It was only a matter of time before the cousins outed each other. They were curious to know the origin of the nicknames.

"You seem mighty quiet tonight," Enrique noted to Fabian who had devoured his entrée and moved onto dessert at breakneck pace.

Fabian gave his boss a side glance. "It would do well for someone to remain just the tad bit on guard at this table," he spoke rather softly. It was not his intent to insult his colleagues: clearly they were enjoying a reunion of sorts with their cousin, Francheska. He had to admit she was quite on the beautiful side, her coloring that of caramel, her hair a deep reddish brown, her eyes almond shaped and the color of chocolate, not to mention very expressive, and her body curved in all the places a man didn't mind resting his hand; but she was an agent so that was the end of his speculation on the desirability of one Francheska Cartellini. Not to mention, he was quite inspired by another young lady who was having a hard time resisting an occasional smiling glance at him. Mei Ling Wong had swept into the room on the arm of her Uncle looking like Asian royalty, wrapped in a crimson kimono that stopped at her calf, her hair done in an artful do, chopsticks holding it in place. She was a mix of beauty and mystery. It had taken considerable effort to reign in his mind and emotions and focus on the present matter at hand.

Enrique merely grinned at Fabian's comment. "I'd say we're all struggling with diversions tonight, wouldn't you?"

Fabian's head swung around at the thought.

"I've got eyes, man. I can see clearly," Enrique spoke softly. "It appears the lady would rather she was at this table as well," he noted.

Fabian scowled then. "I'm not here for my personal enjoyment," he sipped his drink methodically.

Enrique could remember when he was just as uptight. He still was, but for far more different reasons. "Well, I'm glad you're alert and on guard," he decided to leave the matter for now. It would not do for Fabian to become his opposition. After all, he needed him to keep a tight reign on his loose sister.

Giovanni was listening to Francheska fill in Augusta on what it was she did in Italy when he felt a foot rubbing his calf. At first, he had thought it an accident; until it happened again. He looked up then, narrowing his eyes at Fabritza, who seemed to be deeply enmeshed in the conversation between the two women and totally oblivious. Giovanni, not wanting to cause a scene, continued to eat until it happened again. He stomped as hard as he could.

"Ouch!" Fabritza screeched causing the conversation at her table and those nearby to cease. "That was my toe," She rubbed her toe.

"I'm sorry," Giovanni held up his hands in innocence. "I thought it was a pest that had gotten loose. I wouldn't want you ladies to be traumatized by such a pest making its way onto the table." He looked all seriousness and Enrique was hard pressed not to burst from inhaled laughter.

Fabian gave his sister a chilly look which she shrugged off. "Maybe we should all keep our feet a little closer to ourselves to avoid anymore maiming," Nicholas spoke diplomatically, wiping all humor from his tone.

"I agree," Francheska eyed her roommate with suspicion. She would get the full story from Giovanni later. She needed to know just exactly who she was rooming with.

"You really *do* look quite beautiful," Carlton's enthusiasm for Mei Ling's kimono was well known by the time that desserts had been ushered out to the table.

"Thank you," Mei Ling smiled to be cordial, but she honestly wanted to be somewhere else, more particularly, at another table. She couldn't seem to keep her eyes from gravitating towards Fabian Ciccone. He looked at ease and relaxed in his navy blazer and slacks, his dress shirt opened at the throat to reveal suntanned skin. Fabian had done more than his share of returning her glances with interest. Mei Ling reminded herself of the purpose of her trip. Romantic involvements certainly did not top the list, but still she was intrigued.

"No need to smother the woman in compliments," Rosalynn uttered to herself, careful to keep eating and chewing so that she would not have to participate in polite conversation. The silence was so thick at her table; it could be sliced like a three-tiered wedding cake. She was sandwiched in between Noelle Marks and Mariella Estrada, neither whom seemed interested in conversation, their glares, exhaled breaths, and manhandling of dinner utensils seemed to be speaking volumes between them. Rosalynn didn't know much about them but she knew there were undercurrents between them.

"How are you enjoying things so far?" Noelle enquired to Rosalynn. Since no one was inclined to get the conversation ball rolling and it seemed Carlton, the other gentleman at his table, was clearly besotted with the Asian beauty, he figured he would give it a go.

Rosalynn looked at Noelle, humor lacing her words. "Ah, the gentleman speaks," she murmured her mouth tilting in an almost smile.

Noelle had the manners to look embarrassed. "Pardon me for not asking sooner," he apologized. "I haven't been the most sociable guest here. I've had a lot to think about," he admitted.

Mariella shot him a glare that could have killed a lesser man. Rosalynn ignored her look. "I understand that. Even though Elder Worth said to leave our issues back in the States, that's easier said then done," she confessed taking a sip of her sparkling grape cider.

"Most definitely," Mariella spoke up on the other side of Roz then. "There are many things that are better left unsaid until we return to the States."

"However, there are some things that cannot wait to be said," Noelle glared pointedly at Mariella.

Roz leaned back in her seat then. "Why am I getting the feeling that you two are on a different page than the rest of us?" she joked.

Noelle wiped his mouth throwing down his napkin. "Because we *are*," he ground out.

Mariella waved her hands in frustration. "Okay, Noelle, you want to talk, talk. Just get it off your chest now, okay?"

Naomi tried to intervene then. "Mariella, please, don't bait the man," she chided.

Noelle closed his eyes in resignation. "Mariella, this isn't how I wanted to talk to you. I don't want you to be upset," Noelle sighed.

Mariella picked up her spoon then, digging into her dessert. "Look Noelle, I know I've been avoiding talking to you, but trust me, it's with good reason," Mariella began.

"I know." Noelle stated plainly.

"I just- what do you mean, *you know*?" Mariella halted in her conversation. At this point, even Carlton had ceased his attempted flirting with Mei Ling.

"I think you know what I mean. The Lord told me that you know. That's why you wanted to quit. That's why you've been avoiding me," Noelle rubbed his neck. "To be honest, that's why I fired you. I wanted to explain, but you wouldn't let me. Do you think you're the only one who's affected?" he spoke softly then.

Mariella was completely stunned by his words. It was too much. "I don't know what to think. I've hardly been able to sleep; but I do know that I need this time, Noelle. Please, don't ask me for more right now," Mariella's desperation was in every word she spoke.

Noelle nodded in understanding. "Okay. But if you change your mind, I'm ready to talk when you are. Just don't avoid me," he added.

Mariella gave him a tremulous smile. "I can handle that," she conceded.

Roz cleared her throat then. "This episode of Jamaican Dreams has been brought to you by Noelle and Mariella," she kidded.

Everyone broke into laughter, including her brother. Rosalynn thanked God for her interminable sense of humor and received a wink and lifted glass from Nicholas who had been watching her most of the evening. She blushed thinking that in this moment, her cup of joy was full.

"Wow, I didn't know fireworks were included in the package for the vacation," Jamar joked and received a nudge to the ribs by the saucy Tehinnah.

"Hush, that's my boss you're joking about. I thought I was going to have to rescue him from sticking his foot in his mouth one too many times," Tehinnah grinned. "He's not handling his attraction to Mariella well at all," she noted.

Jamar looked pointedly at her then. "I could say the same thing about you," he pointed out.

Tehinnah looked at him quite comically. "Excuse me?" she was given a knowing glance by the older people at her table.

Jamar shrugged. He decided to lay it on the line. "You're obviously attracted to me but you've decided to write me off because of my age. If you would but open your eyes, you'd see that we were meant to be together," he assessed.

Dr. Greg Jones who had been drinking his Jamaican cola nearly choked, sputtering and coughing. Aurielle had been nice enough to give him a few aggressive pats on the back to get him breathing again. "Man, you've got to be a little less obvious," he chuckled.

Tehinnah rolled her eyes then. "Jamar, you don't know me enough to 'assess' my likes and dislikes. Yes, I find you very attractive; but it takes more than attraction to make a relationship work. And for the record, it's not just your age that I have an issue with," she continued eating as if she had not just given Jamar Davis the set down of his life.

Dr. Greg Thomas pointed a finger towards Jamar. "Son, quit while you're ahead; you've got a lot to learn about women."

Jarah looked at him pitifully. "That really wasn't well done of you, Jamar, is your name? This is not the place or the time to declare your feelings and it is ungentlemanly to declare that all the feelings are entirely one-sided, when *clearly* they are not," Jarah looked at him over her glasses.

Jamar felt truly chastised then. "I think I'll take your advice, Dr. Thomas," he acknowledged. "I apologize, Tehinnah. It was not my intention to embarrass you," he looked to her then, sincerity evident in his eyes.

"I accept," Tehinnah smiled so sweetly at Jamar, it made his knees a little weak.

"Now, you're getting somewhere, son," Dr. Thomas chuckled.

Shemiah, Savannah, Josiah, Angelynn, and Columbia sat back listening to the low din of voices and conversations as gospel jazz floated through the air. They were basking in the atmosphere of good food, good friends, and surprising entertainment. The singles who had chosen to come on this trip were a diverse group of people with diverse issues. Those issues were bound to surface and unfold as some had tonight.

"Do you think it was a good idea to seat everyone so randomly?" Savannah thought out loud.

"Well, considering that Roz hasn't strangled her brother, Fabritza has yet to be thrown off the security team, Tehinnah hasn't smacked Jamar, Marco and Ginny seem to be conversing and not glaring at each other, I'd say we're doing fantastic," Josiah chuckled.

"Keep in mind, we've got three more days," Shemiah pointed out. "I'm praying hard that we make it through unscathed," he ran his hand along the length of Savannah's arm.

"The Lord will have His way whether we agree or not," Columbia added. "I'm just happy to see my Pastor enjoying himself; he deserves it," she looked to Seth who seemed enthralled by something Aliya was telling him.

"I almost thought that Pastor Marks was going to pull his son by his boot straps earlier," Savannah noted.

"My money was on Enrique," Josiah argued. "You can rest assured that he was not going to let Noelle upset his cousin," he assured them.

"What was going on?" Angelynn questioned them.

"Apparently Noelle has developed a tendre for the girl," Columbia recalled John and Noelle arguing about it.

"A tendre?" Shemiah appeared clueless.

"A crush, sweetie," Savannah, ever the educator enlightened her fiancé.

"Does *Enrique* know about this?" Josiah's brow rose at the observation.

"I don't know, but I'm not about to enlighten him at this moment." Shemiah reasoned.

"Well, we will look out for Mariella and make ourselves available to help her if necessary," Savannah decided, the ladies agreeing with her.

Shemiah praised Savannah for always doing what she could to keep the peace among friends and associates. She had a way of setting peoples' minds at ease. It was one of the things he loved and admired about her.

"Has anyone been formally introduced to Francheska Cartellini?" Angelynn wondered.

"Not yet, although I believe she just arrived maybe an hour ago at the most," Shemiah looked to Josiah for confirmation.

"I believe so," Josiah nodded.

"We'll make sure that happens tonight then," Angelynn made a mental note.

"I understand she'll be traveling back to work with Enrique's team," Shemiah revealed. "I think it would be great if you ladies showed her around and made her feel welcome. Enrique already made sure she was added to the nuptial celebrations," Shemiah told them.

Columbia finished her dessert then. She was a little saddened that she wouldn't be spending any time with John during dinner, but she couldn't think of better people to share fellowship with. Shemiah and Josiah had explained that they were best friends and that Savannah and Josiah had been childhood friends. Savannah had returned home to care for her mother and face her own past issues. In the process, God had brought Josiah's two best friends together with lots of prayer and divine intervention. Angelynn had even expressed her jealousy over Josiah's friendship with Savannah. Looking at the happy couples now, you could not tell there had been any kind of discord between them. But that was the point of church love as Josiah had put it. It caused you to forgive and heal, to love and relinquish the pain of the past, to release people and free them from their mistakes and accept that they were still in the process of being shaped by God and for His purposes. Columbia sipped her sparkling cider thoughtfully. *Church love is what I need. I won't settle for anything less than love that makes me whole and complete. Lord, I need Your perfect love that casts out all fear.*

You have it in abundance, Columbia. I will use you to help others receive my perfect love. Don't let anyone try to place you in bondage. Remember, I have set you free.

Columbia let the voice of the Lord settle over her like a silk robe. She was surprised to find her eyes a bit misty and was thankful no one seemed to notice.

45

Every one lingered in the breezeway after dinner before they were led outside to their Bible Study for the evening. It was an opportunity for guests to mingle and befriend newcomers as they waited permission to move into the next setting. Fabian wasted no time in making his way towards Mei Ling for a formal introduction.

"I believe there's a certain Italian making very purposeful strides towards you," Aliya informed her cousin Mei Ling. "Twelve 'o clock," she added.

Mei Ling couldn't help but tense up. Fabian was directly behind her so she couldn't turn around without being obvious. "How do I look?" She asked Aliya.

"Stunning; Breathtaking; Amazing; Refreshing," Fabian stood behind her now, eyes brimming with humor.

Mei Ling closed her eyes in embarrassment, mouthing the letters O-M-G to her cousin. She opened her eyes turning to greet Fabian and found she had to take a step back to look up at him. "We meet again, under better circumstances," she said lightly.

Fabian took her hand and brought it to his lips, his eyes meeting hers. "It was a pleasure running into you," he said, a smile playing at the corners of his lips.

Aliya started fanning herself. "Well, I do believe I'll run along now," she hightailed it down the breezeway leaving Mei Ling to fend for herself all the while giggling. *Mei Ling, oh, Mei Ling, what have you gotten yourself into?*

Mei Ling, flustered by Fabian's approach gently removed her hand.

"So, I understand you and Aliya are cousins?" Fabian asked determined to find out what he could.

"Yes, but I live in Beijing. I'm a journalist," she informed him in her most business-like manner.

"Do you travel frequently?" Fabian pressed on.

"Not really," Mei Ling admitted. "I generally go where my work takes me with the country."

"How would you feel about having a visitor?" Fabian went directly to the punchline.

Mei Ling was surprised but not displeased about his bluntness. "Are you always this direct?"

"In the things that matter," his eyes seemed to spark with determination.

"Is that so? You barely know me," she reminded him.

"In my line of work, I am called to make good judgments, sometimes instantaneous. For me, it can be a matter of life and death. I am still alive because I am very rarely wrong," he smiled gently.

Mei Ling laughed nervously. "Well, in that case, I believe that I can tell you that I can't answer your question just yet."

"Fair enough," Fabian nodded. "But you will answer before we leave this island, correct?"

"Yes, I will give you an answer," Mei Ling decided.

"I am sure we will get an opportunity to further our acquaintance," Fabian tucked a strand of hair behind her ear.

"Is this gentleman bothering you?"

Fabian and Mei Ling turned to find Carlton staring daggers at Fabian.

"I'm sorry. Have we been introduced?" Fabian wondered aloud. He was not accustomed to being interrupted when speaking to a lady.

Mei Ling made the introductions quickly. "Fabian, this is Carlton. Carlton, Fabian Ciccone. We just met here," she clarified to Fabian. She was attempting to be as polite as she could to Carlton who had irritated her to no end with his incessant compliments and fawning. He had almost appeared a little drunk but she knew this was a non-alcoholic resort. Still, she had wondered.

"Mei Ling, I believe that the Bible Study is about to begin. I've saved us some seats near the back," he presumed to place his hand on her back and guide her away but was stopped by Fabian's grip on his shoulder.

"I don't believe you gave the lady an opportunity to accept your offer," Fabian smiled politely, a total contradiction to his steely tone.

Carlton gave Mei Ling his most charming smile. "Would you like to join the Bible Study now?"

Mei Ling had dealt with Carlton's kind before and she knew he needed a direct refusal. "Thank you for your kind offer, but I'll be sitting with my family," she let him know. "I also don't want you to be confused so I will tell you now: I have no plans for furthering our acquaintance beyond what is socially required. I hope you will respect my wishes," Mei Ling informed him.

Carlton's hand was removed by Mei Ling herself and she couldn't help but detect his simmering disapproval of her. He stormed off without another word.

"Thank you for coming to my rescue, but I could have handled it," she assured him.

"You handled me quite well, so I have no doubt of your capabilities," he remarked candidly watching her comical expression. "However, you shouldn't *have* to handle unwanted pests."

Mei Ling gave a shout of laughter as she allowed the outrageous bodyguard to lead her into the conference room for Bible Study.

"So what's the deal with my roommate?" Francheska spoke candidly to Giovanni as they waited outside the conference room.

"I'm sorry you got dealt a bad hand this time around, Chess," Nicholas referred to her by her family nickname. "She was having difficulty with another set of roommates from my understanding." He informed her.

"Well, she seemed a bit high strung. How did she wind up on this case anyway?" Francheska drilled him.

"Well, due to the kidnapping attempt that was tied back to Battaglioni, she and her brother were sent as extra security. Apparently the Italian government is trying to crack down on the international crime syndicates," he shrugged offhandedly. "Oh, and by the way, she has an unwarranted crush on me. I have absolutely no interest in developing any relationship beyond business. Though she is good at what she does, she has been a continual thorn in the flesh," he confessed.

"Well, I'm here to add whatever assistance you need. I'm assigned to Enrique for the next six months. I just wanted a heads up. One thing I do know; she's pretty proficient with a dagger," Francheska eyed her cousin for a reaction.

"She's a weapons expert but daggers are her preferred instrument of punishment," he laughed without humor. "She can be pretty ruthless.

"Well let's hope she will remain on the right side of the law. She strikes me as a bit of a renegade, capable of duplicity, and not above scheming to get what she wants." Francheska finished her drink, tossing it back in a most unladylike manner.

"Sounds like warning words for me," Giovanni muttered to himself, taking the words to heart. He did not want to find himself dealing with an enemy within the camp.

"Thank you all for joining us this evening as we embark upon a little enlightenment for this singles getaway," Elder Worth began as many were getting seated. "This is the conference room we will be utilizing for our evening sessions. Our morning sessions will be held by the outdoor pool near the manmade waterfall. There are pens and notepads located at the rear as well as coffee, tea, and pastries. Please help yourself to refreshments during the study. I will warn you that we may do some moving around and written reflection exercises so you may want to come prepared," Elder Worth noted the rolled eyes of Carlton and the sour expression of Fabritza. "I'll give you a few minutes to collect what you need and then we shall begin."

Savannah had just poured herself a nice cup of steaming coffee when she happened to look up. She nearly sent the carafe crashing to the ground.

There standing in the conference room doorway and looking smugly handsome and sophisticated was none other than Lysander Townsend, rogue extraordinaire. Savannah could not believe her eyes.

"Calm down, sweetheart," Shemiah stood behind her leaning to whisper in her ear. "You don't want to appear overset by his appearance," he urged.

"I can't believe his audacity, his gall," Savannah hissed. "He just can't leave well enough alone," she expelled a frustrated breath.

"I'll see if we can't get this resolved. I don't know how he managed to reserve a room, but he shouldn't be here," Shemiah rubbed the tension from her shoulders. "I'll speak to Aslan about the matter."

Savannah waved the notion away. "It's a free country. Besides, being an attorney and all, he'd probably file a lawsuit for being ejected from the hotel."

"Well, if he harasses you in any way, he *will* be ejected from the hotel, and I won't *need* Aslan's approval for that," he promised.

Savannah smiled up at her Chocolate Latte then. "Honey, that's so sweet of you, wanting to come to my rescue, but I'd feel better if you used proper protocol. Lysander is just weasel enough that I'd rather you not have anything to do with it personally. He'd like nothing better than to delay our happiness," Savannah reminded him.

"You're right, baby," Shemiah gave her a brief hug. "I'll see Aslan right after our Bible Study," he decided.

"Who knows? Maybe tonight's Bible Study will soften his hardened heart," Savannah was hopeful. She had better things to do than to spend her time on the island avoiding Lysander.

"Let's hope so," Shemiah placed his hand lightly on Savannah's back, guiding her toward the front of the room.

"Martin Luther once stated that there is no lovelier, friendly, or charming relationship, communion or company than a good marriage," Elder Worth began, allowing for a little bit of laughter and a whole lot of Amens at his opening remark. "I agree wholeheartedly with Mr. Luther, and I'd add that your marriage relationship will be no greater than your marriage commitment to the Lord. You are apart of what Paul calls one of the great mysteries of the Gospel. You are apart of the Bride of Christ. When you received Christ, you promised yourself to Him. He sent his Spirit to seal that promise, indeed he left you with the sign of His promise to you to return. When he returns, we will participate in the marriage supper. Jesus is waiting for His Father to release Him to return. Until then, you, the Bride, are keeping your garments ready, keeping your soul and spirit pure with the guidance and empowerment of His Spirit. This is no rehearsal for heaven. This is preparation. If you are not committed to the Bridegroom of your soul, you *will* fail in all other commitments. And so tonight, we open up tonight to speak with you about the purpose of your singlehood." Elder Worth began to walk among the guests then.

"In First Corinthians, you will find Paul laying out some foundational principles concerning the unmarried man and woman. Their concern is for the things of God and how they may please him. In today's society, you will very rarely encounter encouragement to immerse yourself in the affairs of God. You are constantly bombarded with advice on how to look better, feel better, speak better, dress better, and it is all surrounded by one word: self," Elder Worth continued, noting the many nods in the affirmative. He turned around then.

"In many cases, the ministry of the body goes lacking because our singles are so involved in bettering themselves, they have left their first work: bettering their souls. If you are to ever become one soul with another person, would it not behoove you to work on your soul? No one graduates from this life. Every day you breathe, you have an opportunity to work on your soul, on your spirit, and become the person that God desires for you to be, whether you marry or remain single," Elder Worth went to his demonstration table and held up two glasses, one with oil, one with water.

"When you marry, the two become one. If my partner has taken the time to purify themselves and I have chosen to remain as I am, as this oil here, what will happen when our sexual union creates oneness? Will we wind up always having to shake things up in order to remain one? Will we find ourselves slowly drifting apart, floating in opposite directions, a wall between us because I chose not to prepare myself for one of the most life-altering decisions I would ever make?" Elder Worth placed the glasses down, noticing he could hear a pin drop.

He then picked up two glasses of water and held them up. "If both parties, male and female, respond to God in singleness, allowing God to keep them pure, allowing God to cleanse them from secret faults, allow themselves to become transparent before God, then the result will be the merging of two souls who meet each other on the equalizing plane of holiness, trust, faith, wholeness, and love." He poured the glasses of water together. "These are the relationships that stand the tests of time. They survive the shaking, the stirring, the pouring out, the filling up; these are the people you remark upon who, when you see them, you see an example of Christ and the church, the partner who finishes the others' sentence, the couples you can't tell where one ends and the other begins. It isn't that nothing comes to challenge or test their union. It is that they understand that marriage is not just about being happy, but about being holy. It's about being a living example of how very much Christ loves His church and how she loves Him right back. The passion, the fervency, the desire to love and to honor, and to cherish is not one-sided. The desire to obey and please and submit is not one-sided. You learn how to become one with someone else, by becoming one with God. If you are serious about getting married, you must be serious about being single."

Lysander listened to the preacher with a cynical heart. *I'm not obeying some woman! He's got these people brainwashed with all this psychobabble he's spouting off. If I get married, she's gon' know who's wearing the pants.* He devoured Savannah with his eyes. *That's what's wrong with my cousin now. He's been suckered. She's got him wrapped around her finger. She wasn't ready for a real man.* He rolled his eyes as the preacher continued, wondering how long he would have to listen. *Christ and the Church. People always got to bring God into the equation. I don't need a crutch. I'm fine without Him.*

Lysander didn't know that God was ready to call his bluff.

"Singlehood is your responsibility. You can't blame your spouse for what you bring to the table. The next few days, I want you to think about these questions: What constitutes a good marriage? What do you stand to gain by getting married? Will anything in your past affect your marriage? Are you satisfied with who you are right now? If you could get married at the end of this week, would you be ready? Have you practiced being intimate with God? Have you sought God as much as you have sought a relationship? Have you practiced responsibility and promise keeping with God? I want you to keep in mind that marriage is not the finish line; it is the starting line to a new you. Once you marry, you will *never* see the single you again. Even those who have divorced and tried to return to the single life never truly return. They have apart of someone else within. This is why sexual sin is lethal to your spirit. Every time you have casual sex, illegal sex, you are joining not just physically, but spiritually with that person. God want us to unite with one person, not spread ourselves and our soul thin through multiple partners. I know that I have given you much to think about, but I challenge you to let your purpose in singlehood be fulfilled. Let God shape your character. Let God guide you into healthy friendships. Test your relationships with real life settings. Those who know you should never be shocked by your responses, unless you've been living a double standard," Elder Worth concluded, garnering a chuckle from the group.

"As we end this bible study, I have a parting gift so to speak. Tonight, each of you will receive a small bottle. Inside is oil and water. I want you to write down five things that would be water, or would flow in a relationship you were apart of. Then I want you to write down what would be your number one oily issue; in other words, what would make you reject joining your soul with someone else? We'll ask a few of you to share in the morning, so be prepared. Please take a bottle on your way out tonight." Elder Worth turned the floor over to his wife, as thunderous applause went forth.

"Well," Vivian began. "I've heard my husband talk about marriage many times, but I don't believe I've ever heard an analogy like that," Vivian clapped her hands together. "I pray that everyone will get some rest this evening and remember your curfews," she gave a serious, but comical look. "Let us bow our heads as I ask Josiah to lead us in a closing prayer."

Josiah cleared his throat and began enthusiastically. "Father, we thank you. Lord of love and life, we give you praise. We thank you for every heart and mind that was open to hear what Your Spirit is saying to this assembly of believers, and even the skeptics we might have among us. God, we ask you to forgive us for not making the best use of our singlehood. We ask that you help those who are engaged to continue the shaping process that they may bring themselves wholly to their marriage. We ask for married couples that our covenant be strengthened while we are here, and let nothing put any couple asunder. We pray that every single person will grow from this experience, that we will all search our hearts, and sanctify ourselves so that you may sanctify us completely. Thank you for keeping us all safe as we depart from this study but never from your presence. In Your Son's life giving name. Amen."

Many left in a reflective mood, eager for the solitude of their rooms. Still others remained behind as curfew wasn't in effect for another fifteen minutes. No one left without a gift.

Aslan apologized profusely to Shemiah. He had been under the impression that Lysander Townsend was with the Singles' Getaway group.

"I will handle the matter immediately. It's really quite simple. The resort is reserved at this time for your group. He's not on the list of guests therefore he can receive a full refund. I know several other resorts here in town that will accommodate him. He will have no legal recourse," Aslan assured Shemiah who visibly relaxed at the thought of Lysander being removed from the resort. *If only we could ban him from the city.*

"Unfortunately, he was given an agenda of your off campus sites so he may show up there, but the relief is that he will not be underfoot during your entire stay," Aslan felt terrible that he had allowed something so important to slip under his radar. "I should have checked with Aliya before admitting him. He seemed so sincere, claiming to have missed his flight, and all," Aslan grew angry just thinking about the tale the man had regaled him with.

"Well, I'm sorry that you have to be privy to a family disagreement. The man is apparently obsessed with my fiancé. I appreciate your being so discreet in dealing with the matter, Mr. Peyton," Shemiah shook hands heartily.

Aslan thanked God he was now converted. Lysander Townsend would be somewhere pushing up daisies if God had not gotten a hold of Aslan's heart. *Lord, help me deal as diplomatically as I can.*

46

Enrique was very glad that Aslan had afforded him the use of his study to speak with Aliya. He had agreed with the ministers that Aliya should not be out of the loop regarding the nuptials that were to take place. He however, felt that her sister should be the one to deliver the news. So, there they sat, just a few moments away from dropping the bomb. He prayed Aliya could handle the fallout.

"You two look like you're about to be put on trial," Aliya joked. "So spill; what's the deal?" she squirmed radiating energy in her usual quirky way.

Augusta squeezed Enrique's hand for courage and spoke. "Enrique and I are getting married," she began watching the surprise and joy rise upon Aliya's face. "At the end of the Getaway," she finished watching Aliya's smile form a confused frown.

"I don't get it." Aliya scratched her head. "Aren't you supposed to get engaged first?"

"We were engaged," she held up her hand knowing what was forthcoming. "It was only last week; we wanted to keep it quiet because we were coming on the trip and had no intentions of marrying here, at least at first," she looked to Enrique. "I didn't want to cause a commotion or draw any media attention," Augusta, ever the reasonable twin assured her.

"And of course, me being who I am would not have been able to keep quiet," Aliya surmised. "That about sums it up doesn't it?" Aliya snapped, annoyed at her twin. "I'd like to think I've grown some in that area, but apparently you think not," she shook her head. "Continue."

Augusta looked hurt. "Liya, much as I love you, we both know you struggle with keeping secrets. This was not just about me, but about Enrique, and you. You were *kidnapped* for God's sake!" Augusta calmed herself down, not wanting to be overheard.

"Aliya, I pray that you won't hold this against your sister. Can you imagine if the press knew I was getting married? It would put everyone that is here at risk. I still have enemies, Aliya. I also did not want to have a media circus parading around and ruining your retreat," he added.

Aliya was frustrated with them both. "Don't act like this was about considering what I wanted," she fumed quietly. "I'm not so petty as to think that your wedding upstaged my plans," her voice was filled with emotion. "I love you both so much and I thought that you would eagerly share something that I feel that I've been a part of since its inception. I guess I assumed too much," she deduced.

Augusta went to her twin, wrapping her arms around her. "Forgive me, Aliya, for underestimating you. I never wanted to cause you pain and you're right; you have been there for me the whole time, pushing me towards happiness, pushing Enrique toward what he had to think was insanity," her heart lifted as she heard Aliya laugh at her interpretation of their courtship. "I was running, he was chasing, and now I'm happily caught," she wiped away her tears as well as Aliya's and reveled in the feel of her sister's hug, her unconditional love tightening round her.

"Don't you ever leave me out again," Aliya shook her finger at her, then grinned sheepishly, "Well, except for, you know, those parts," she giggled. She went over to Enrique, giving him a gigantic hug. "Now, you'll be my only brother. There'll be no escaping me," Aliya warned.

"I would never want to escape such an adorable sister," Enrique kissed her hair. "Or relationship coach, I might add," he chucked her under the chin.

Aliya turned to her sister. "I believe, Auggie, we've got a wedding to plan in short order," she decided.

Enrique excused himself from the chatter and headed to his room, thankful that God had soothed the hurts and poured out his forgiveness among them.

"What do you mean my room has been cancelled? That can't be correct," Lysander looked at the printout before him. He had received a request denied receipt when he had attempted to pay for his room.

"It is very correct, sir."

Lysander turned to find a man far shorter than he was, yet of a stocky build standing before him.

"I'm sure there is some misunderstanding," Lysander began. "I reserved this room." He showed Aslan his confirmation number matching the one on his rejection paper.

"There is no misunderstanding. You sir, reserved the room under pretense. You are not registered with the Singes' Getaway group, the only group on the premises this week; therefore you are not a guest here this week. Your deposit has been returned to your card. I have arranged a complimentary stay for you at a resort about 20 minutes drive from here. My van will drive you there personally. I am sorry for the inconvenience," Aslan added.

"This is *more* than an inconvenience! *This* is an outrage!" Lysander ground out in his most condescending tone. "I have never seen such incompetency," he began but was shut down by Aslan's menacing glare.

"If you look closely at the facts, sir, you will see it was your incompetency in failing to mention you are not a guest of the singles', nor are you even considered a *friend* to the guests. They not only did not expect your company, they do not *invite* your company. They are evidently here apparently to *Getaway* from more than one thing," Aslan's voice was like a whip lash, each word cutting, leaving an indelible mark.

"You can take the hospitality I am affording you, or you can leave the island. Montego Bay doesn't take kindly to stalkers or those who threaten our tourism trade with harassment. I need only speak a word and you, sir, would find yourself being escorted to the first plane departing for the States. Am I making my position clear?" He raised his brow at Lysander who recognized that he clearly did not hold the upper hand. Aslan was not cowed by him at all.

"Thank you for your accommodations," Lysander hurried out the door, his bags being rolled out along with him and loaded into a waiting van.

He was still fuming at his set down as he stared back at the palatial Jamaican Dreams Resort. He mind was full of thoughts of revenge when his driver lost control of the van sending them sliding off the soft shoulder of the road, his van overturning several times, landing sideways and hanging and inch short of a complete plunge off the mountain, Lysander and his driver knocked unconscious left to roaming robbers, ravenous wildlife and the cooling night air of the mountainside.

Lights Out

Though everyone had gone to their rooms, sleep was the farthest thing from their minds. There was much discussion and much contemplation about the day's events as well as the Bible Study that had taken place. Everyone was far from notions of sleep.

In Aliya's room

"I see somebody was holding an umbrella today because it was raining men," Aliya teased Mei Ling.

Mei Ling could feel the heat from her cheeks spreading to her ears. "Please don't start, Liya," she flopped onto the bed, flipping the covers and buried herself in the luxurious sheets. "I was actually only looking for the attention of one man," she fully acknowledged. "Instead, I was nearly forced to defend myself."

"Really?" Tatyanna who was pulling out her sleeping mask looked at Mei Ling surprised.

Ginny rolled her eyes. "You didn't see Carlton trying to maul her?" Ginevieve was becoming familiar with all the new people she had met as a result of the Singles' Getaway and could now put names with faces. "I think he was coming on a little too strong. Didn't someone inform him this isn't a Singles' Hookup?" Ginny made herself comfortable on the pull out bed.

"Apparently not; I thought it was really sweet of Fabian to escort you in to Bible Study. Clearly, you were not uncomfortable," Aliya teased.

"He's a very engaging young man," Mei Ling's voice was uncommitted to the topic.

"Not to mention beyond gorgeous," Ginny teased. "You go girl," she giggled.

"You of all people need not be teasing anybody," Tatyanna playfully pushed Ginny. "You were positively seeing stars today when you rode with Marco."

Ginny folded her hands over her chest defensively. "Marco and I have agreed to be friends. Nothing more, nothing less," she glared at Tatyanna. "We are not romantically involved at all," she assured them.

"Methinks the lady doth protest too much," Aliya smiled knowingly. "I honestly don't know how you've managed to resist him. He's sweet, kindhearted, an excellent poet, hardworking, and not bad to look at," Aliya threw in as a side note.

"And he loves God," Tatyanna added.

Ginny placed a pillow over her head. "Goodnight, ladies," her voice was muffled by the pillow.

Tatyanna and Ginny threw their pillows at her then.

"Oh, so now you want to say goodnight when the spotlight is on *you*? Unfair, Ginny," Mei Ling tried to pry her pillow away.

Ginny refused to let go. She was done talking whether they liked it or not. "Goodnight."

Tatyanna pouted like an unsatisfied child. "We'll let it slide for now. Just remember we've got all day tomorrow," she warned.

Ginny groaned her mood turned sour at the thought that come tomorrow their eyes would be on her every action, trying to interpret them. *Good grief.*

In Vivian's room

Savannah, Augusta, and Rosalynn sat Indian style on the floor in the living area of their suite munching on popcorn. Vivian had turned in for the evening and the room she had taken had its own private door which afforded her some privacy.

"I've got a question for you two," Roz dove into the popcorn, grabbing a handful and popping a few into her mouth.

"Go ahead," Savannah was quite sure that Roz had lots of questions. They all did after tonight's Bible Study.

"Well, I'm sure you all are aware of the fact that Nicholas and I are considering seeing each other, and well, Nicholas is a lot more sure than I am right now especially after what Elder shared tonight about truly becoming single and dealing with your issues and all," her stream of words flowed out without a single pause. "I just want to ask, how did you know?"

"How did we know what?" Augusta asked.

Roz rolled her eyes heavenward. "Come on, guys," she threw up her hands in impatience. "How did you know that Enrique, that Shemiah was 'The One'?

Augusta began first. "Well, for me, God had to knock me over the head several times for me to get it. It wasn't so much about knowing he was 'The One' as much as it was about knowing that God had pulled me from his side, and He was ready for us to know each other. I had to stop fretting about my hang ups; thinking I wasn't enough; thinking I couldn't fulfill my part of the marriage covenant. Understanding that to be right with God and pleasing to Him is to take Him at His Word and accept His plan for your life. If that plan includes marriage, you have to be okay with that and not doubt that GOD knows you, created you and will perfect you," Augusta shared.

Savannah nodded in agreement. "Roz, I'll be real with you; when I returned home, I had my sights set on someone entirely different. I felt totally blindsided by Shemiah. I thought he was stuck up, opinionated, and hardly worth my thoughts. I'd have to be blind to miss the fact that he was gorgeous, but looks aren't everything. When I tried to avoid him, it seemed as though God kept placing him in my path until it was undeniable. We formed a friendship, we got to know one another, he courted me, he saw me in my good moments and in my bad moments, and as we walk through our engagement process, I learn something about him all the time. I realize that we will always be learning about each other, and hopefully growing together and appreciating the changes that God makes in us. I won't say I've 'got it all together' or that I haven't faced any challenges since I've gotten engaged, but I am positive that Shemiah is the man of God he says he is. I am positive that I want to spend the rest of my life with him, loving him, honoring him, leading with him, and growing with him. He's the real deal," Savannah sighed thinking about her Chocolate Latte.

Roz had pulled her knees up to her chin and wrapped her arms around her legs as she listened to her friends, her sisters really, share their experiences. It felt good to know that she felt some of the same sentiments regarding Nicholas. No, she hadn't heard a voice from Heaven telling her he was 'The One', but when she was with him, there wasn't anyone else that she wanted to be with. When she was with him, she wanted to be better than she was. She would use this time to clear her mind of distractions and seek God. She had found herself feeling at peace with the fact that she was not Carlton's blood sister. She shuddered at how trusting she had been this whole time. He had taken advantage of her desire to have a familial tie and he had tried to use that sincere desire to control her life. Though he had expressed some regret, it did not change what he was: a smooth manipulator. Roz would not let him back into her life on an intimate level ever again. He had tried to destroy her with his revelation. He had not counted on God to lifting her out of that pit of depression that had been dug for her to fall into. He had counted her out, thinking that his blow would be the defining, crushing blow that would knock her out. But God had greater plans for Roz. Far beyond what Carlton could perceive. She was regrouping. She was healing. She was reorganizing her life for a mighty comeback. God had caused her to triumph and she was glad.

As the ladies settled in for the night and gave each other hugs, Roz took in the words from her friends, pondering them in her mind until she fell into a deep sleep.

In Jarah's room

Angelynn and Mariella sat side by side on their suite's sofa nursing their coffees and just chatting and catching up. Jarah had put the twins to bed and was already asleep.

"How have things been working from home?" Mariella questioned.

"It's taking a little getting used to. Jarah's been a great help to me. She's gotten her own place, but we still have her suite on hand for when she wants to stay over. I freelance now so most of the work I can email. It feels great to be able to set my own schedule to work," she admitted.

"Jaia and Josiah IV are so beautiful! I can understand how reluctant you must be to let them out of your eyesight," Mariella chuckled. "You must have to fight Josiah for snuggle time," she teased.

Mariella shook her head at the thought. "No, actually, when Josiah comes home, he holds out his arms and says, 'where's my babes?' I just hand them over and drop a quick kiss on his lips. He's entitled to his bonding time. One time I found him kicked back in his recliner, both arms full of baby, his head thrown back, his mouth wide open; it was too precious. I'm so glad he's a hands-on father, throwing himself wholeheartedly into what he does," Angelynn took one last sip before setting her coffee down. "So, what's been going on with you? Naomi told me you resigned from your part-time job. Was it getting to be too much for you?"

Mariella took a deep breath then. "Normally, I wouldn't share this with anyone, but I feel like if anyone could give me some advice, you could," Mariella began, appreciating the fact that Angelynn was ready to listen. She forged ahead. "I resigned from my position because I was too afraid to admit what was happening between Noelle and me," Mariella confessed.

Angelynn had sensed that something was going on between them, especially since dinner this evening. "Go on," she encouraged her.

"I guess I should start from the beginning," she sighed. "I was hanging out at a café downtown when I first spotted him. I of course

311

noticed how good looking he was; I'm not blind. Then, I heard this voice that I now know had to be God. He told me that one day I would make this man a good wife," Mariella paused, letting Angelynn digest that fact. "As you can imagine, I was shocked, so shocked in fact that I ended up spilling my drink all over me. I was on a way to an interview and I had no time to change. He offered to assist me and asked for my name. I was *really* rude to him, partially because I wanted to ignore what I heard. I wound up making it to my interview on time only to find out that he was the person conducting the interview. I couldn't believe my misfortune. Then, he told me the position had been filled but he offered me the job of interior decorator for his new home," Mariella swallowed.

"Wow," Angelynn could only utter.

"I thought I could handle it. I thought I could handle being close, remaining uninvolved, but I could not. Whatever I chose, he was in agreement with it; He always had a compliment about my work. He seemed to be in my brain to the point of freakiness. Then, one day, I came in to work early and I overheard him speaking with his father. I found out exactly how he felt about me and it was not flattering at all. I felt so embarrassed, you know? I had begun to think that maybe, this could work, sometime way in the future, you know what I mean? But when I heard him," Mariella's voice broke.

Angelynn touched her shoulder in understanding. "You don't have to go on," she spoke softly. "I can see this is upsetting you."

Mariella waved away the words. "It's okay. It's just that after I resigned, I began to have this dream, a recurring dream about us. I don't know what to do. I feel so *angry* with him and I don't want to feel anything at all. Tonight he told me that he knew. We haven't even spoken, but I know exactly what he's referring to! Don't you find that ludicrous? I have no intentions of talking with him until we return to the States. I don't want to deal with this. I came here to go to school, get my degree, and return to Costa Rica. This is a complication I didn't expect and I daresay that God is *not* going to let me forget any of it," Mariella sighed resignedly.

"Mariella, I know we don't always understand God's ways but He has our best interests at heart. I think we should take your concerns to the Lord. What do you say?"

Mariella was in total agreement, and as they bowed their heads, she was thankful to have a friend to confide in who would bear her burdens as she went to the Lord in prayer.

47

In Columbia's room unlike others, everyone was wide awake and using the gift of gab without restraint. Columbia, Aurielle, Tehinnah, and Naomi lounged in various states of comfort in the living area.

"So, what do you think makes a good marriage?" Columbia asked her temporary roommates.

"I think it's all about your desire to improve your relationship to God. The closer you get to God, the closer you get to each other in a marriage where both parties are seeking a deeper relationship with God," Naomi shared.

"I'm not too concerned about that question," Tehinnah confessed. "I'm still stuck on his question about the past," she sighed. "I mean, who doesn't have a few skeletons in the closet?" she reasoned.

"Forget skeletons. I have three wonderful children, all out of wedlock. The evidence of my disobedience is ever before me, precious as they are," Columbia looked to each woman surprised to see no sign of censure in their gazes.

"We've all got issues; it's how we deal with those issues that will determine if we will build healthy relationships or not," Naomi added. "My past will most definitely affect how I view my relationship with my husband. Coming from an adoptive family, I can't begin to tell you how much I look forward to one day having children of my own. I made a promise to myself that they would know their father and mother," Naomi's voice rang with passion. "I've always wondered who my natural parents are. It's a curiosity that has remained with me all of my life," she admitted.

"Can you imagine getting *married* at the end of this week?" Tehinnah rolled her eyes heavenward. "I don't even have any prospects for a *date*, much less a husband," she laughed.

Aurielle sighed dreamily. "I can't say I'm in the same boat on that. Dr. Trey Jones is definitely marriage material but we're not seeing each other exclusively. He's much too committed to his career goals right now to even think about a steady relationship, though he insists otherwise," she stretched lazily.

"Are you serious?" Naomi shot her an incredulous glance. "I've seen the way Trey looks at you; that man has wedding bells ringing over his head. If you can't hear them then you must be deaf," Naomi pushed her playfully off the sofa they shared.

"So, most of the guys on this trip are already spoken for, aren't they? I'm just along for the ride," Tehinnah deduced.

"Let me fill you in: Pastor Seth and Aliya are definitely an item, Augusta and Enrique are seeing each other exclusively, Shemiah and Savannah are engaged, Kevin and Tatyanna are engaged, Marco is single but focused on getting Ginny's attention, Jamar is single, Pastor Marks is in love with Columbia," she was interrupted by Columbia dismissing that notion, "Nicholas is single but interested in Roz, Giovanni is determined to win Naomi over, Fabian and Carlton appear to be involved in a battle for Mei Ling's attention, Noelle is fighting his attraction to Mariella, and Dr. Greg Thomas seems to be developing a relationship with Ms. Jarah, which goes to show you, you're never too old for romance," she finished watching the comical reactions of her roommates. "What?"

"How in the *world* do you know all this? I never see you hanging out," Naomi wondered.

"I don't do a lot of talking. I observe, I notice things; I guess you could say I'm sort of a people watcher. Human behavior fascinates me immensely," Aurielle shrugged.

"Well, I guess I was right," Tehinnah decided. "I'm clearly a fifth wheel, but it's cool; I didn't come looking for a mate," she assured them.

"You're not off the hook either," Aurielle eyed her suspiciously. "You've got a thing for Jamar so don't try to play the innocent," she laughed.

"Whatever I have, it's not going anywhere; he's *too* young, too *cocky*, and he had the *nerve* to act as if he wasn't interested in me. It will be a snowy day in Hawaii before I give him the pleasure of *my* company," Tehinnah spoke defiantly.

"So what irritates you more? The fact that he didn't fall at your feet or the fact that he wants you to admit you like him more than a little bit," Naomi teased her.

Tehinnah tossed a throw pillow at her. "What*ever*," she snorted. "Playing hard to get is *my* role not his. Anyway, I can ignore him just as easily as he can ignore me."

Columbia smiled knowingly. "It will be interesting to see how long you can ignore him. He's a pretty outspoken guy. He's seems to enjoy provoking you; I can't imagine you holding your tongue," Columbia chuckled.

"Trust me; I can do anything well if I put my mind to it. Tomorrow, Jamar will find himself *completely* ignored and *thoroughly* frustrated," Tehinnah huffed indignantly.

As the ladies turned in for the night, they couldn't help think but reflect on Elder Worth's assignment for tomorrow morning. They also couldn't wait to see God overthrow Tehinnah's plans.

Midnight Security Check

"All is secure on the east side," Giovanni who was partnered with Francheska spoke into his headset to alert Nicholas.

"All is secure on the west side," Nicholas responded in kind. "Diamond, Lily, and Wildflower, are secure," he motioned to Fabian and Fabritza who gave him the thumbs up. "South and north sides are secure as well," he noted.

"We'll meet you in the lobby then," Giovanni walked inside then and ran into a frantic Aslan. "What's wrong Mr. Peyton?" Giovanni stopped him midstride.

Aslan looked a bit frantic. "I sent my driver to escort Mr. Lysander to his hotel. It's been hours since they left. I'm concerned something may have happened to them," he sounded worried.

Fabian, Fabritza, and Nicholas had joined them as Aslan spoke. "We'll take a look for you," Fabritza and Fabian both offered. "You can send us with another van driver and call the local authorities just in case there's been an accident," Fabritza offered. She was up for some action and wasn't in the least bit tired.

Giovanni and Nicholas gave the go ahead and they were off to ready the van to investigate the situation.

Aslan shook his head regretfully. "He was not a very pleasant fellow, but I hope he is okay and that everything is fine," he headed to the reception desk. "I'm going to notify Shemiah. He may want to go along with them."

Nicholas and Giovanni said a prayer for the safety of everyone involved and made their way to their room to share the news with Enrique.

"No interviews," Marco stated adamantly to his public relations manager. "I don't want to have to repeat myself again on this subject," he growled into the cell phone. It appeared that his publishing company had gotten a hold of some photographs of their new author and was pressing him to place a head shot on the back of his novel as well as participate in a few interviews. "I'm not selling myself. That was not part of the deal. Have I made myself clear?"

Marco listened as the publicist droned on and on about the buzz that was already being put out about this mysterious new author. No one knew if he was male or female and Marco wanted to keep it that way. He walked from one side of the room to the other pacing impatiently. "Look," he finally stated his tone unflinching. "If you can't respect my wishes then the book deal is off. I can write for pleasure and continue to enjoy my privacy." He grinned then at the direction the conversation shifted. They were more than willing to respect his wishes, sending all enquiries to a private post office box which would then be forwarded to his home address. No press, no interruptions, and *certainly* no questions about why a handsome florist had taken up writing romance novels. Marco breathed a sigh of relief. He would fly out to meet the publishers next week and finalize the deal; he would be writing a three-book saga after this first novel was released. This of course would drastically alter how he spent his free time. He would hire another experienced helper so that things would continue to flow smoothly at the shop. After signing off with a cordial goodbye, he turned to find Jamar standing before him, his mouth wide open.

"I don't suppose you can pretend you didn't hear any of that conversation can you?" Marco asked sheepishly.

Shemiah prayed as he rode with Fabian and Fabritza down the winding, curving mountain road, looking periodically over the sides of the mountain into darkness so thick, you could slice it. *Lord, I ask that Lysander be alright. Give him another chance at life, Father.* He had been nearly asleep when Aslan had knocked on his door with the news that his cousin had not made it to his destination after checking the other hotel he had been sent to. Aslan's face had been shadowed with regret and remorse at the circumstances. While Lysander was not the most pleasant guy to deal with, Shemiah certainly didn't want his cousin to come to harm.

"There!" The driver shouted. "It's our company van," he carefully pulled to the shoulder of the road, his headlights shining like a beacon of refuge.

Everyone moved into action, Fabian taking the flashlight with him and moving swiftly but carefully towards the wreckage. The van was lying precariously to one side, its eminent tumble down the mountain unpredictable but inevitable. Lysander was amazed that it seemed to precariously hang in the balance. Fabian and Fabritza probed closer peering into the passenger side window where Lysander's head lay against the dashboard. Checking his pulse, Fabian noted it appeared steady and strong. The driver had taken the brunt of the crash, and it appeared he was already dead. They would try to get Lysander out without jarring the vehicle and sending it careening to the bottom of the mountain.

"He's alive but unconscious!" shouted Fabian. The next thing he knew strong hands were helping him pull Lysander free from the wreckage, the van tipping further but not releasing its hold on the crag in the side of the mountain.

Shemiah wiped the sweat from his eyes as he looked into the still, bloodied, and bruised face of his cousin. He was thankful to God for this miracle. He felt sympathy for the family of the driver but gratefulness that for now, his cousin lived. All thoughts but keeping Lysander alive were wiped out of his mind as he heard the rescue vehicle approaching.

Jamar folded his hands across his chest, his brow raised mockingly. "Do I really have to pretend I didn't hear what I think I heard? I thought we were friends," he scolded him.

Marco pointed an accusing finger at him. "Ah, but you, my friend, have a bad habit of trying to help out where help isn't wanted," he reminded as he sat on the edge of the bed.

Jamar pulled up a chair. "So spill; you give me the full story and I vow not to use it against you. If you leave me with my suppositions then I'll be forced to fill in the details with my own imagination," he grinned mischievously.

Marco shoved a hand through his hair in frustration, muttering something about idiot editors and pushy publicists ruining his vacation. "I'm an author and a florist," he confessed.

Jamar shrugged. "Okay. So you write. What's the big deal? Apparently, you just cashed in, so I know money's not the issue," Jamar deduced.

Marco fell back against the bed in resignation. "I write romance novels," he explained.

Jamar's lips formed a silent o. "Well, those are really popular; you should do quite well," he smirked. "And get lots of attention," he added.

Marco bolted upright. "See? That's what I mean. I don't want the attention for a lot of reasons." He scowled.

"Name them," Jamar was curious to know what had his pants in a knot.

"Well, first of all I don't want to be in the spotlight, second, my family would have a heart attack if they knew, and most of all, I am not prepared for my father to find me." Marco shook his head then. "I left his house at eighteen, and never looked back. I turned my back on running the family business to chase my dreams and he never forgave me for that. If he knew where I was, he would be here with the snap of an eye, demanding I fulfill my responsibilities to the family." Marco's bitterness was evident.

Jamar had always had a very nagging suspicion that there was more to his friend than he revealed. "I believe the phrase is in the blink of an eye," Jamar chuckled then his tone turned serious. "Are you royalty or something?"

"Not quite, though close, due to my family's prominence in the winemaking industry. We produce non-alcoholic wine, but it is the best in our country. I have no intention of bringing my family into the public eye therefore I've taken some measures to ensure that I remain out of the public eye," Marco explained. "I'm not using my name for the novels I write, I have requested no photography, no interviews, and all of my mail is directed to a post office box in another state. No one knows whether I'm male or female," He informed him hoping Jamar would realize the extent to which he wished to keep his profession under wraps.

317

Jamar could only stare at his friend in awe. "I'm impressed; However, I hate to burst your bubble; you've inadvertently set yourself up for serious investigation, Bro. If your novels are anywhere near as good as your poetry, there will be women breaking down your door for a chance to meet you, especially when they find out you're young, single, wealthy, and fully male," Jamar concluded. "And you're decent looking according to Ginny," he joked. "Many reporters would see this as a challenge: who can crack the code of the successful author who chooses to remain anonymous?"

Marco closed his eyes, a headache already forming at the thought of his calm, cozy, idyllic world being invaded by the press. "Let's just pray that my success will fly under the radar of the press. The Lord promised to hide me in His secret place," he reminded himself aloud.

Jamar just laughed at Marco's naivety. "He also promised to make your name great and that your gift would make room for you and bring you before kings," he paraphrased.

Marco threw a pillow at his smug roommate. He couldn't help but think in that moment that his days of quiet were numbered.

Pastor Seth Davis and Dr. Trey Jones kicked back on the balcony in their suite recognizing they weren't the only ones who couldn't sleep. Clearly the ladies were also burning the midnight oil across the courtyard in the opposite wing. With news of Shemiah's cousin's appearance and then disappearance, Josiah was downstairs awaiting his best friend's return. Seth and Trey were nighthawks, each due to their profession: Seth had spent many sleepless nights on his knees in prayer for his members; Trey had spent many sleepless nights on his feet in prayer for his patients' prognosis after an emergency surgery. Each man was comfortable with little sleep and lots of coffee.

"After this trip, I plan to take a *real* vacation," Seth chuckled. Trey looked to him in agreement. "I know what you mean, man. I didn't know self-denial could be so excruciating," he sighed thinking of how he had already been tempted to break curfew. He had spotted more than one secluded setting at the resort by which he could talk with Aurielle without so many listening ears. But he realized this trip was not about them; it was about making sure he was right with the Lord, and in turn making sure he was the right man in her life. He didn't want his heart broken because he had handed it over to the wrong woman.

Seth breathed a sigh of frustration. There was so much he wanted to say to Aliya but he doubted she was ready to hear it. Words like love and forever and marriage were right on the tip of his tongue, yet he held back sensing her reservation with him. She was still feeling her way in their relationship and he didn't want to experience setback because he was moving in haste. If he believed that Aliya would say yes, he would ask her to marry him at the end of the week; but the fact was, she wasn't ready. "I'm doing my best to take things minute by minute, but when I look at Aliya and see our future together, I realize I'm more impatient than I realized," Seth confessed. "I want to love her, honor her, cherish her, and come home to her, share the excitement of her accomplishments with her forever. I didn't realize until this trip how much I want to be a husband to her. I've totally floored myself," Seth's surprise at the intensity of his feelings was clearly written upon his face.

Trey chuckled. "Yeah, Bro, you've got it bad," he agreed.

"I'm considering proposing but I don't want her think it's about anyone but us. I'm not in a race to the altar but I do want to officially declare my intentions," Seth thought aloud. "I don't want her to think I just got 'caught up in the moment' and have her reject my proposal."

"That would suck big time," Trey stood then stretching. "Just pray about it, man. It's a serious decision and you definitely want her to take it seriously," he warned.

Seth nodded solemnly. He and Aliya had butted heads because their approaches to situations at times were polar opposites. Lately, though, they hadn't had any disagreements. It had felt eerily right. "I hear you, dude. Go on get some shut eye. I'll be up a little longer," he sighed.

As Trey reflected on the evening's Bible Study, he couldn't help thinking about his own predicament. Until he dealt with his family back in Trinidad, he wasn't free to make any commitments. According to his family, he was already engaged to be married.

48

Montego Bay Day 2

"Good morning, everyone," Josiah the younger sat casually on a rock near the waterfall whose waters poured over the rocks with relative calm. "It's so good to see each of you ready and eager to begin this morning's study. Before we begin, let us lift up a prayer for Shemiah as I'm sure most of you have noticed his absence this morning as well as that of his fiancé, Savannah. His cousin to his surprise arrived on the island last night and to make a long story short, he was in a car accident on his way to check into a hotel. His driver perished in the accident and Shemiah's cousin is in critical condition. He is in a coma and is suffering from internal injuries. No one knows quite yet the extent of the damage and they are still awaiting tests. Shemiah's parents, along with other family members are being flown in courtesy of Enrique's generosity. I am sure this is weighing heavily on Shemiah's heart, so as we pray, let us lift up Lysander, Shemiah, and their family members," Josiah allowed for the bowing of heads before he continued on. "Father, right now, we lift up our friend Shemiah to you. We lift up his family members, and Lord, we ask that you place your able hands upon Lysander. We ask that you do what no doctor can do without your wisdom. We ask that you heal Lysander from the inside out. Make him whole in mind, body, soul, and spirit. Let the blood that you purchased us with show forth its power in the life of Lysander, Shemiah, and their family. Most importantly, let your will be done. Use this situation to bring out your expected and good end and receive, Father, all the glory, and honor, and credit that can come to you when Your will is done. Comfort those who need your comfort, heal the rifts, and allow forgiveness to manifest in the middle of it all. In Your Son Jesus' name," Josiah ended with a collective amen. "We will continue with today's agenda after our study."

Columbia was right outside the patio area taking a phone call from her daughters. Today was bound to be filled with activity so she wanted to make sure the girls were okay back at home. A flustered Rodia answered.

"You sound out of breath," Columbia chuckled. "I take it Delia is giving you a run for your money?" She was thankful the girls had graduated and celebrated and that their school had chosen to do senior prom and senior trips after making sure the students had fulfilled their obligations. It allowed her daughters who had graduated early to enjoy their summer, help out around the shop, and babysit Delia until they began school in the fall. Though they would still be in town, Rodia and

Nadia had opted to get an apartment on their own. Pastor Davis had helped out with assisting them in getting an apartment that was close enough to home, church, and school, and in a relatively safe neighborhood. Since they were nearing eighteen, the twins were chomping at the bit for independence. Columbia was glad they wouldn't be moving out until September. It gave her a few months to acclimate herself to the idea of her Punkin Noodles off on their own.

"I'm glad your trip is halfway over now. Delia has definitely been a form of birth control since you've been gone," she kidded.

"What has she been up to now?" Columbia could only imagine. She was growing up so fast right before their eyes. Since she had been attending Second Chance Preparatory School for Inner City Youth (S.P.I.C.Y.), Columbia had been amazed by her academic progress.

"Let's see, where should I begin? She let the neighbor's poodle outside; she nearly flooded the bathroom when she left the water running. She ate a pack of laxatives thinking they were chocolate candy," Rodia giggled. "I think she never wants to see chocolate again."

"She does have a bad habit of eating sweets no matter where she sees them. I hope she learned her lesson," Columbia shook her head in resignation. Delia still needed some instruction when it came to basic life skills.

"Oh, yeah, and our neighbor has been cool. She's pretty nice," Rodia admitted. When Rodia first met Ms. Stiegel, she thought she was going to be a nightmare. Turned out she had three grown daughters and knew the ropes. She was kind, but tough in the way she needed to be.

"You know I wouldn't leave you with someone I didn't trust," Columbia playfully scolded Rodia. "Listen, I've got to go to devotional, but tell the girls I love them and miss them and I'll call you all later," she promised.

"I will, when those two slugabeds get up," Rodia assured her. "And Mom, I'm glad you're enjoying yourself," she added.

Columbia's smile deepened at the comment. "Thank you, baby, that means a lot," she choked up at the words.

"And you know what else? None of us would mind if you brought back a father too," Rodia hung up then knowing she had left her mother holding her phone with open-mouthed surprise.

"Who would like to share next?" Josiah sat casually enjoying the responses from last night's challenging sessions. "The next part of that challenge was to name the one oily issue that would cause you to end or not even begin a relationship with someone," Josiah looked to each person, noting the myriad of expressions. Aliya was the first to speak up.

"One oily issue for me would be a person who can't forgive easily," she spoke with passion emanating from every word. "Considering the fact that I screw up on a daily basis, a person in relationship with me would have to be able to forgive and forget and not hold grudges," she finished.

"Well said, Aliya. Anyone else," Josiah offered, giving over the floor to Aurielle who had raised her hand.

"My oily issue is snobbish behavior. Looking down your nose at anyone because of uncontrollable things like race, gender, heritage; those things really turn me off from wanting to be involved with someone. No one can control the circumstances by which they are brought into the world. If they are working and striving to improve their lot in life in an ethical way, they should not be ridiculed, denied basic rights, or treated as less than human," Aurielle calmed herself, realizing she was about to step on her soap box then. She smiled shyly as she received a few amens.

"Thank you all for sharing your heart with us this morning. Today we are going to continue where we left off. We began last night to talk about Sanctifying Your Singlehood. To sanctify means to set something apart for a specific purpose or to a specific person, namely God. So, I ask the question; what are you doing to set your single life apart? How do you carry yourself as a single that makes you different from the next single person? I'll share with you one of the ways I set myself apart as a single person: I refused to engage in casual sex, but not only that, I refused to engage in casual dating. You can only imagine how much teasing I got for being a non-dating virgin football player," Josiah allowed the murmurs and giggles to die down before he continued.

" It was embarrassing at times, it was excruciatingly difficult at times to say no, I felt isolated at times, misunderstood, and very often I was the butt of many sexual jokes—but it was worth it. Looking back on that time, I can't say that it was easy, but I can say I wanted to please God more than I wanted to be the big man on campus. I have kept in touch with most of my college buddies. Some are happily married, some are happily married for the third time; some divorced, some separated, some heartbroken, some are dealing with chronic diseases from unsafe sexual practices, and my friend who is living with HIV can't bring himself to enter into a relationship for fear he will be abandoned once he fesses up. I married shortly after graduation and so my sacrifices will not be yours. Yours may be setting yourself apart in the time you give to God alone. It may be in denying yourself an activity that most of your single friends engage in. It may be a heart issue, like reserving your romantic feelings for the one that you will marry. Whatever it is, I urge you to commit to that today; recommit yourself if necessary. Decide what it is about your singlehood that will be different from the way you have been conducting yourself as a single person. Let's go to the Lord now in prayer. I challenge you as you go about our planned activities to think about how you will sanctify yourself and write it down."

As they bowed their heads in prayer Josiah gave God a silent thank you for using him to speak to the singles today. He hoped his words would fortify them and encourage them to take a stand for God in a way they hadn't thought of before today. He couldn't imagine the effect his words were making on the hearts of those who were yielded to God, and the hearts of those who were not.

Doctor Cave Beach Excursion

"This sand feels incredible beneath my feet," Aliya sighed appreciatively. Things were going well; most of those attending the day trip were enjoying themselves. Some had headed straight for the water, some had decided to take on the locals in a game of beach volleyball, and still some had chosen to take refuge under an umbrella and just stretch out and enjoy the sound of the waves and touch of the sun caressing their bodies. Aliya found herself walking the five mile stretch of white sand which seemed to go on forever. She and Augusta had chosen to take some time out with each other today.

"I know what you mean. I'm inclined to forgo a pedicure altogether. You know what they say: as long as you have sand and salt water, you don't need much of anything else," she inhaled the ocean scent deeply. Not many people were out yet, a stray couple here and there, a mother and child collecting shells. It was the perfect day and she was walking close enough to the water to bask in the cool refreshing waters of the tide coming forward and receding back in a steady rhythm.

"How are you *really*?" Aliya glanced sideways at her twin.

"I might ask you the same thing," Augusta teased. "You and Seth seem to be inseparable these days," she pointed out. "I'm glad to see you open up and give your relationship a chance."

"He's such a sweet guy, and so considerate of me," Aliya shared. "I'm trying to take things slow so that I don't make a mess out of it," she admitted. "He's got a lot on his plate. Did you know he's a stockbroker?"

Augusta shook her head. "No, I had no idea," she shrugged. "Does it matter in the overall scheme of things?"

"Not really; I was just surprised to learn that he was a working professional, not just a pastor. I can't imagine where he gets the energy from," Aliya shared.

"Probably from the same place you get your energy from: God himself. And you're no wilting violet yourself you know. You organized this trip, you run your own clothing store and you have your own clothing and shoe line. I would say that your business know how and his investment know how will one day become a very powerful unit and put a big smile on God's face," Augusta decided.

It seemed as though a light had dawned in Aliya's mind then. "I do believe you may have a point, although I don't wish to become a publicly traded company just yet," she informed her twin.

"Don't think so far ahead right now," Augusta laughed at her twin who had no idea just how much her twin could tell that her thoughts were churning away. It was like a neon sign on a pitch black night. "Just get to know Seth. He's clearly enamored of you," she smiled knowingly.

"I can't say it's been a hardship. Ever since he returned from his mission trip, he's been kinder, softer, more forgiving," Aliya noted.

"Aliya, I don't know if anyone shared this with you or not, but when you were in a coma, Seth was...he was a different man. I think seeing you there, so still, so unlike your usual bubbly, talkative self really *affected* him. He was at your bedside nearly everyday, and it was not the polished, polite, I-have-all-the-answers-Pastor Seth; it was the man. He was broken. I remember coming to your room one morning and he was on his knees, holding your hand, pleading for your life. I didn't enter the room, but I waited until he left. I never told him what I saw, but I knew from that day on that he was the right man for you. Seth really cares about *you*, Aliya. If it were just surface, just performance, he would only have come to see you for appearances. No one was there. It was you, Seth, and God. I know I've been a bit pushy," Aliya gave her a disbelieving stare. "Okay, very pushy about you reaching out to Seth, but that's why. He's the real deal."

Aliya gave her sister a crushing hug, nearly toppling her over. "I appreciate all of your pushiness, Auggie. You just gave me an amazing gift, really," Aliya thought about how much she had questioned Seth's sincerity. There were no longer any doubts. "Thanks sis," she wrapped her arms around her as they walked back towards their pitched umbrella.

"Anytime," Augusta felt a smile reaching all the way inside her soul, pulling out joy and releasing it for everyone who had eyes to see. "As for me, Enrique and I are having a hard time containing our excitement. Two more days and we'll be one," she shook her head, still not believing that the whirlwind decision was coming to a head. "Dad has everything running smoothly. I merely told him I wanted a Fireworks Theme and he went from there."

"Mom will be here this afternoon when we return, right?" Aliya picked up several shells that were perfectly formed.

"Yes, and she's meeting with the caterer concerning the menu and wedding cakes. Everything is set. I ordered his ring online and it should be arriving tomorrow. I'm just floored by how smoothly everything is going," she admitted. "Now, if I could just stop Enrique from looking at me like he wants to devour me, I'll make it." She stated casually.

"What?" Aliya gasped in surprise.

"Good to know you haven't noticed; just wait until it's your turn. You'll see exactly what I'm talking about," she laughed.

As they walked arm in arm up the beach, Aliya couldn't help but anticipate the day when Seth would look at her like that.

Giovanni was enjoying the cool waters of Doctor Cave Beach and was having what he would call a very engaging conversation with his cousin Francheska who was sharing some of the details of her latest criminal showdown when he felt something stroking his unmentionables underwater.

"Christ!" he shouted, diving underwater to find the culprit whether man or beast. He dove back up quickly, hearing the tinkling laughter of the culprit. *Definitely human,* he thought.

Francheska hadn't seen Fabritza enter the water and neither had he. He would have exited immediately. Apparently his senses were off when it came to water. He would have to remember that. He saw his cousin stifling a laugh, giving him an innocent shrug.

"Fabritza, you sure know how to make an entrance," Francheska scolded her.

Fabritza gave an innocent smile as she treaded water along with them. "I'm sorry if I bumped into you, Giovanni," she gave him a coy look.

Giovanni narrowed his eyes, knowing the vixen had been very deliberate in touching him. It was nowhere near innocent and he was tired of her games. "That makes two of us," he spoke solemnly. "It would have been great if you could have remained on this case, but unfortunately, your actions are reprehensible," he treaded away from her then. "Chess, I'll see you back on shore."

Fabritza's look of panic was priceless. Francheska raised her brows at the retreating back of her cousin then turned to face an irate Fabritza.

"Do something!" Fabritza screeched.

"Like what? Obviously you've angered him beyond reconciliation," she glared. "You're wasting your time if you think Giovanni gives one iota if you are thrown off this case," she assured her.

Fabritza's voice was fever pitched as she unloaded her profane language like ammunition on Francheska. "You think you're something? Well, forget all of you! I don't need this assignment!" she furiously sputtered.

Francheska held herself in check. "Are you done now?" when no response was forthcoming, Francheska's steely eyes bored into hers. "I have done nothing to provoke or inspire such anger, rage, and filth from you. If you want to have any chance of remaining in the field of Intelligence, I suggest you patch things up with Giovanni, take a vacation, and return to Italy with a mind to work. Your reputation is at stake here. You can take my advice or you can be vindictive and further add to the notion that you are a hotheaded vixen and incapable of working your assignment without fulfilling your sexual urges," Francheska's every word was like a lash of correction. "That appears to be the consensus floating around the Italian Intelligence headquarters. Having met you myself, I'm almost inclined to agree, except, that you are a woman, and in this line of work, we've got to stick together. I hope you're smart enough to apologize and move on," Francheska added before she moved toward the shore, leaving Fabritza wet, angry, and alone.

"That was some quick thinking you had going there," Marco complimented Ginny for helping their team win the final point in their volleyball game. The locals had been very friendly and good sports, congratulating them heartily, moving on to the next game without a second glance.

"I know a little something about handling the ball when it's in my court," she mentioned as they settled into a casual stroll up the beach.

"I can tell. Did you play in college?" He questioned.

"Just for fun; I played in high school though," Ginevieve revealed.

"Hmmm, I would never have pictured you as the athletic type," he thought aloud, realizing too late he had inserted his foot into his mouth.

Ginny looked askance. "Why not?"

"Well," Marco wasn't sure how he was going to dislodge his foot from said mouth but he knew he had to do it quickly. "you seem very feminine; the way you dress, the way you wear your hair, the way you walk; when I look at you, I imagine tea, crumpets, and long canopy driveways leading to a formidable mansion set on rolling hills as far as the eye can see with an intimidating father waiting on the front step, shotgun in hand as I approach to ask permission to pay addresses to his daughter," he finished, delighted to see mirth simmering underneath Ginny's very serious expression.

"So I appear to be the epitome of ladylike behavior?" Ginny giggled, amazed at how closely Marco had her pegged.

"Yes, and I hope I have not offended you by saying so," Marco added quickly. "There's nothing wrong with a girl playing sports or anything, it's just that until I saw you today, I would never have suspected you were even remotely interested," he confessed.

"Let's just say that I'm full of surprises," Ginny gave him her sweetest smile and sauntered away.

Marco didn't take his eyes off of her for a minute, thinking to himself how much he'd like to know everything there was to know about Ginevieve Dubois.

49

Late afternoon

Doctor Cave Beach proved to be such an enjoyable outing that no one wanted to leave for North Coast Marine. Instead, everyone had chosen to return to Jamaican Dreams Resort to refresh and change for dinner.

Giovanni was one of the first to arrive downstairs, a scowl etched upon his features. It appeared Naomi was not speaking to him and with good reason. If appearances could be counted, it had seemed to her that he had enjoyed frolicking in the water with Fabritza Ciccone. The scantily clad Fabritza had followed him down the beach where he had sought to cool his temper, apologizing profusely. She had claimed that she would no longer approach him in an inappropriate manner, taking his hand and begging him not to report her actions. He had looked up then to see Naomi approaching them. For all intents and purposes, it had appeared to her that he was having a lover's tiff when it was the furthest thing from the truth. He had tried to speak with her on their way back from the beach, but she had completely ignored him, giving him an icy glare of warning. Giovanni sighed regretfully. He was really beginning to resent Fabritza's presence. He was also tired of being accused of being a philandering playboy. *If she doesn't trust me now, she'll never trust me in a relationship.* It made him upset and resentful that he had done nothing to encourage Fabritza's advances, yet he was considered the guilty party. He suspected Naomi had some insecurity in the area of other women and it was high time she dealt with them. He was still mulling these sentiments over in his mind when he saw her walking toward him, her steps coming to a screeching halt when she realized it was him and not his twin she was approaching. She went to turn away.

"So this is how it's going to be between us? Are you going to run away every time I do something that upsets you?" Giovanni ground out. He had thrown down the verbal gauntlet and he was primed for an argument as she swung around and marched toward him.

"*Upset* me? I would have to *care* in order for it to upset me," Naomi shot back.

"So you don't care if incredibly beautiful women grovel at my feet?" he countered.

"As long as it's not me," she straightened, her nose lifted in the air. "You are a grown man and your decisions are yours to make," she reasoned. "You don't owe me an explanation for your behavior."

"I don't owe you an explanation, but I want to give you one," he came closer not missing the tears that threatened to slip from her eyes.

Naomi stepped back, unsettled by his nearness. "That's considerate of you but not necessary."

"Oh, it's *very* necessary to explain to the woman I love that I was being accosted *unwillingly* by an obsessive female who I hope will be on her way back to Italy by the end of the week," he spoke softly, touching her cheek hesitantly.

Naomi's look of surprise was priceless. "You *love* me?"

Giovanni released a megawatt smile upon Naomi. "Is that *all* you heard?"

Naomi's grin was telling. "No, that's not all I *heard*, but that's all that *matters*," she laughed softly as she leaned into his embrace.

Fabritza was humming an Italian tune, thankful that Francheska had already gone down to await the van for dinner at Sugar Day. *Finally, a little peace and quiet!*

She was sure that her dress was going to be a hit. The girls had managed to stop at a clothing shop before they headed back to the resort and she had picked up the cutest wraparound halter dress. She was so caught up in admiring her own image that she didn't hear the rampant knocking at first.

"Who is it?" she shouted.

No one answered oddly enough. Fabritza drew out her dagger as she headed to the door. She swung it open and stood in shock. "What are you doing here?"

Her superior officer, along with another gentleman she did not recognize stood before her.

"I think we both know why I'm here, Fabritza," he walked past her into the room, the gentleman following. He turned to face her. "You have exactly thirty minutes to pack your things. You are officially off this case."

Fabritza moved her lips, but no sound came out. She was too stunned to speak.

"I've had you monitored since you got here. I know about your plans to seduce Giovanni. You are out of line Fabritza. I will not have you endangering this case with your antics. You have been warned more than once. The only recourse I have now is to reassign you. That is, unless you'd like to take a twelve month vacation?" his brow rose.

"N-no!" she managed to stutter. Intelligence was her life. If Fabritza had that much time off, she didn't know what would become of her. "Reassignment is fine," she gritted her teeth. Inside she was seething with disbelief and rage.

"Good. I am glad we are in agreement. You have been reassigned to France; an important biological weapons mission. My man here will see you out and to our plane. You will report to the French

Embassy in 24 hours. Make sure you rest up. That may be the only rest you get until this threat is disarmed."

Fabritza nodded to her superior. She had the utmost respect for him. She was honored that he had come to collect her. But she would not forget this thwarting of her plans. *Another time, Giovanni,* she promised.

Montego Bay Hospital

"The family of Lysander Townsend?" the doctor, chart in hand, peered over his glasses, his eyes searching the waiting area.

Shemiah and his father quickly stood in acknowledgement.
"Yes?" Shemiah held his breath. Lysander had come to for a few minutes last night but had drifted back into unconsciousness. He and Savannah had remained at the hospital all night. Indina and Isaiah Newman along with Zara, Lysander's mother, had arrived a few hours ago. Savannah sat sandwiched between the two ladies, offering them her support.

"I regret to inform you that Lysander has passed away. We'll know shortly, but I believe there was internal bleeding on the brain as well as well as some punctured organs. If you'd like to see him, please, follow me," the doctor turned on his heels.

Savannah held on to Indina and Zara as they poured out their tears. *God, have mercy.* Lysander Townsend had not been her favorite person in the world, but she would not have wished this tragedy upon anyone.

Shemiah and his father gathered Indina and Zara and headed back through the ICU doors where family was allowed.

The reality of what had happened hit Savannah with such brutal, raw, emotional force, that she felt like the wind was knocked out of her. *Oh, God. If we would have never insisted that he leave the resort, Lysander would still be alive today.* Savannah held her head in her hands. *It's all my fault!* Savannah knew what she had to do. Somehow she had to make things right. *It would seem that what Lysander had wanted in life, he would gain in death. There would be no wedding.*

Both doors slammed shut at the same time, causing two women who knew very little about the other to finally square off.

"Hello." Mariella flipped her hair over her shoulder, careful to school her features into a look of nonchalance.

"Hi," Tehinnah gave her a look of disdain. "It's Marvella, right?"

"No, *Mariella,*" Mariella corrected her. "And you're Tehinnah."
"That's me," Tehinnah smirked. "Better known as the other woman," Tehinnah smiled sweetly.

Mariella gasped. *The nerve!* "Well," she huffed.

"That's all you got to say?" Tehinnah shook her head. "Apparently he's not yours then."

Mariella gave her an icy glare. "I don't know what-"

"Girl, please!" Tehinnah rolled her eyes. "I know you think that Noelle and I have something going. But let me make it plain: if Noelle *was* mine, you would know it," Tehinnah stepped closer to Mariella.

Mariella, not intimidated by her posturing, stepped forward as well. "Let me make myself clear: I don't have time for junior high antics so if you want to continue this conversation, you'll have to do it alone."

Mariella whipped past her and walked away, head held high, eyes glimmering with unshed tears. *I will not let that woman ruin my night.* She was going to focus on one thing alone: God.

"Where is she?" Shemiah paced back and forth in the hospital looking for Savannah. A nurse interrupted him with a note. He unfolded the note, scanning it quickly.

> *I took a taxi back to the resort. I know this was a private time of grieving for your family. They are in my prayers. Tell your parents I'm sorry I couldn't stay. We'll talk soon.*
>
> *Savannah*

Shemiah felt his heart drop to his knees. *I know this is a private time of grieving? What was she talking about? She was family.* He folded the note back, stuck it in his pants pocket and rubbed his weary eyes. Maybe it was best that she wasn't still here. Zara's tears of sorrow and quickly turned into shouts of rage. He could still hear her gut wrenching sobs.

"*She killed my son! She killed my son! He told me he was coming down here to straighten things out! Now he's dead! Oh, God, my baby is dead! My only son! Why, God? Why!*"

Shemiah could do nothing in that moment. His parents had looked at him with sympathy, thankful that Savannah had not been able to hear Lysander's mother. They stood transfixed as she had turned to Shemiah, pounding her fists on his chest.

"*She's taken my son! She killed my son! How can you marry her? My baby is dead!*"

Shemiah had stood there like stone, allowing Zara to pound on him, taking the beating, because he felt guilty. *If I hadn't insisted he be removed from the resort, Lysander might still be alive today.* In spite of all their differences these past few months, he had loved his cousin. He needed to sort things out. His father and mother would be taking care of the burial arrangements for Lysander. Shemiah didn't know where he was going to get the strength from, but he would have to go on. Zara's haunting words kept ringing in his mind. *How can you marry her?*

Dinner at Sugar Day

The mood at dinner was decidedly volatile. There were enough tensions in the building to detonate a bomb. Due to dining out, everyone was free to choose their own seating, and they were grateful for it.

"I didn't see Fabritza come down this evening," Giovanni remarked offhandedly.

"I know she was getting ready for dinner when I left," Francheska remarked, sipping her virgin Strawberry daiquiri.

"Oh, you won't be seeing her for a while," Nicholas grinned from ear to ear. "Apparently, her superiors had her watched since she landed. She's been reassigned. They gave her thirty minutes to pack, put her on a private jet to France," Nicholas raised his water glass. "To God be the glory," he toasted his brother.

"Glory to God," Giovanni agreed. He could breathe a little easier knowing he wasn't going to have to watch his back where she was concerned. "Are they sending a replacement?"

"Her superior told me they are bringing in an operative from France. Apparently he was planning to retire but was begged to take this brief stint until we return to the States. Francois."

Francheska choked on a strawberry, coughing until Giovanni had to hit her on the back forcefully. "Geez, Checkers, those drinks are nonalcoholic, right?" he joked.

Francheska glared at him.

"You okay, Chess?" Nicholas looked concerned.

"Fine," Francheska managed to finally get out. She took a long drink of water then. *Francois? Dominic Francois? They absolutely would not do this to me!*

No, they would not. But, I would.

Francheska shook her head. *No, no, no. You and I had a deal. You wouldn't talk to me, and I wouldn't talk to You. I was totally humiliated in France! At least I thought I'd never have to see him again.*

But that is not My plan.

Francheska wanted to shout in frustration. Instead she just sat with a mask of indifference on her face as Giovanni and Nicholas continued their discussion on the merits of French intelligence and mentally willed them to change the subject.

"I don't think I can hold down anything else," Mei-Ling admitted as she wiped the corners of her mouth with her napkin.

Fabian couldn't help wishing he was that napkin. "I'd have to agree with you," he sighed, reining his thoughts in. It was certainly better than focusing on the fact that his sister had gotten herself thrown off their assignment and reassigned to France. Now, Enrique was going to be getting a new roommate, and it was going to be a little tight in the boss's quarters.

"Everything is so beautifully appointed here. I love the open air dining," Mei-Ling closed her eyes, enjoying the scent of ocean-air and the sounds of Calypso setting the mood for a sultry evening.

"Beautiful, yes, but not more captivating than the sight in front of me," Fabian spoke softly.

Mei-Ling blushed at the compliment, but she didn't take Fabian seriously. He was way too handsome to be mooning over anybody, least of all her. Tall, lean, muscular, with piercing gray eyes that dared you to tell a lie, Fabian was way out of her experience.

And her experience was singular. She was done trying to play at being a woman of the world. Her ex-fiancé had been a military officer. They had tried living together, but it had turned out to be the worst mistake of her life. When she'd finally given in to him and consummated their relationship, he lost all respect for her. He had wanted out of the relationship, but she had thought that they could work out their problems. The next thing she knew, she was being questioned, arrested, tortured, and molested. She couldn't prove anything, but she felt sure Daniel Hardingham had been behind her arrest. And so, as handsome and charming as Fabian was, Mei-Ling had no interest in getting involved with anyone who could put her life under a microscope at their whim.

"Do you say that to all the girls you meet?" Mei-Ling looked at him from under her lashes.

Fabian's brow rose at the comment. *Huh.* "I've only had a reason to say it once and I don't say anything I don't mean." The look he gave her was deadly serious.

"Well. Thank you," Mei-Ling cleared her throat. The room seemed suddenly warm. "Excuse me," she stood then and made her way to the restroom, aware that his piercing eyes followed her until she was out of sight.

Giovanni was entering the restroom just as Carlton was leaving.

"Thanks, Giovanni," Carlton grinned from ear to ear.

"For what," Giovanni asked warily.

"Well, I know how busy you've been lately with the "protect and serve" stuff, and well, I've really enjoyed spending time with Naomi. Beautiful girl; sweet, kind, well-"

Giovanni didn't know what had come over him, but before he knew it, he had Carlton two feet off the ground, his hands gripping his collar.

"I will only say this once. Do not talk to, sit next to, walk next to, or even breathe in the fragrance that is Naomi. Don't even say her name. I don't believe a word coming out of your lying, weasel mouth. Because I love God, I will not do to you what my carnal man wants. Your little partner in mischief is gone. If you so much as cause problems for anyone on this trip the Island police will remove you. Are we clear?" Giovanni put Carlton so gently back onto his feet it shook him to his core.

Carlton nodded mutely.

"Good. I'm glad we understand one another."

Carlton scrambled out of the restroom back to his seat. He had been insane to think he could take on a trained former assassin. He breathed a sigh of relief that no one knew how close to death he had just come. He didn't want to think of what would have happened to him had he and Fabritza carried out their plans.

Back at Jamaican Dreams

Savannah took dinner in her hotel room. She knew everyone was at the Sugar Day restaurant, but she just didn't have the heart to go. Besides, she knew they would find out soon enough: Lysander was dead. Shemiah's cousin who had been irrationally infatuated with her was dead. How could she face anyone? She needed time to think, time to plan. Her hotel room phone kept ringing. She knew it was Shemiah, but she couldn't even face him. Seeing him right now would only compound the guilt she felt. *Lord, I need your strength.* She fell to her knees and poured out her heart to the only one who could heal it.

Shemiah decided he would join the others at Sugar Day. Right now, he knew he didn't need to be alone with his thoughts. Seeing Josiah and Angelynn would help him take his mind off the tragedy, at least for a short while. He hoped Savannah was there. He had called her room, hoping he could catch up with her. He had showered and changed at his parent's hotel room and wanted to pick up Savannah so they could ride together. *Lord, please be with my sweetheart. Comfort her,* he prayed, as he headed to Sugar Day. *Turn our mourning into joy once more.*

50

At Sugar Day

"Have you heard anything else from Shemiah?" Elder Worth questioned his son as they were awaiting dessert.

"No, and I'm starting to worry," Josiah frowned. He had been reserving his own feelings on the matter since the morning Bible Study.

Just as Elder Worth was about to encourage his son, he spotted Shemiah wading through the dining room. He waved him over. "He's here, son."

Josiah was the first to leave reach him, leaving his seat with the quick movements of a former athlete. He pulled his best friend into a tight hug.

Shemiah just held on, shutting out their surroundings. He felt a hand on his left shoulder, then another hand on his right shoulder. Still, he felt a gentle reassuring hand on his back. *There was nothing like God's comfort coming from God's children.* He took in the peace, the joy, the love, the hope, that was flowing out of their heart and spirit into his own. He lifted his head then and went to speak the words he didn't want to utter.

Don't utter them. Ask them to pray.

"Let's pray that God will bring life back to Lysander," Shemiah asked.

Josiah nodded in agreement. Those who had come to stand around Shemiah bowed their heads. Those who remained at their tables bowed their heads as Josiah lifted up a simple prayer.

"Lord, you are The Resurrection and The Life. Whoever believes on You should not perish but have everlasting life. We believe on You, Lord. We ask that you bring Lysander fully back to life in everyway. Let him believe on You, Jesus. This is what we ask. Amen."

"Amen," came from the chorus of guests in the Restaurant.

Shemiah felt the peace of God enclose him like a garment. He knew that everything was going to be okay.

Savannah had decided to go down to the hotel kitchens to return her dinnerware when she heard the distinct sound of Indina Newman.

"Hello! Where is everybody? Hey!" Indina ran past her.

"Mrs. Newman!" Savannah ran after her.

She twirled around, clutching her chest. "Oh, Savannah, thank God!" she breathed erratically.

"What's wrong? Where's Shemiah? Is everything okay?" Savannah grabbed her ex-fiancé's mother by the arms.

"I don't know! The doctor called us at our hotel. He said we need to get back to the hospital quickly! Shemiah was going to find you, but obviously he didn't, and oh, we've got to get back! Something's happened, but they won't tell us over the phone!" Indina groaned.

"I'll go with you and we'll call Shemiah on the way," Savannah handed her dinnerware to the receptionist and they ran out to the waiting taxi.

"Isaiah and Zara are already on their way back to the hospital," Indina seemed calmer and in control.

"Let's pray that whatever it is, it's good news," Savannah squeezed Indina.

Leaving Sugar Day

Shemiah was able to grab a bite of appetizer before his cell phone went off. Everyone else was heading back to the resort to unwind before the evening Bible Study session.

"Hello?"

"Shemiah, look, your mom came looking for you at the hotel," Savannah was rushing. Her cell was running out of energy.

"Where are you?" Shemiah was so thankful to hear her voice.

"On our way back to the hospital, so hurry! They told us to come back!"

Shemiah froze.

"Shemiah, are you there?"

He shook himself. "I'm on the way," he ended the call.

Josiah and Angelynn were two of the few who had not headed back to the resort yet. They looked to Shemiah.

"I'm going back to the hospital. Something's happened and it can only be great," he assured them. "Lord willing, I'm going to have a testimony to share tonight," he hugged them both.

"We'll keep praying," Josiah assured him.

"Men ought to always pray," Angelynn chimed in.

Aliya was hanging out in the breezeway of the conference room area, lounging on the couches with a paperback in hand when suddenly she felt like she was being watched. She swung around and nearly smacked Seth right in the head.

"Hey!" he chuckled.

"You nearly scared the Bejesus out of me!" Aliya swatted him with her paperback. "It's not nice to creep up on people.

"You looked so sweet lying there all curled up. I was trying not to disturb you," he reasoned. "Besides, how was I supposed to know you could sense my presence?"

Aliya blushed. "I plead the fifth."

"Um Hmm; that's what I thought," Seth sat next to her. "Looks like we've got about thirty minutes before the start of Bible Study," he noted.

Aliya closed her book, realizing that this would be the perfect opportunity to do a little investigating of her own. "Seth, can I ask you something?"

Seth knew he was in for it. She was not calling him Pastor Davis at least. There was something to be said for that. "Sure," he turned towards her, signaling that she had his full attention.

"What happened to you after I went into that coma?" Aliya's voice was so soft, so quiet that it took him a moment to register what she was asking him.

Seth exhaled a long breath. He was silent for a while before he spoke not sure how he was going to put everything that he felt into words.

Aliya almost thought he wasn't going to answer her at all, that he was going to find an excuse to walk away from the conversation, but he surprised her when he spoke.

"I thought I was going to die if you didn't make it," he confessed. "I looked at my life, my accomplishments, my plans, and realized that if you weren't here to smile at me, to tease me, to annoy me to no end," he grinned, "then there would be no point. I knew then that I loved you, Aliya and that the time for acting as though you didn't matter, well, that game was up," he took her hand in his. "I wouldn't trade knowing you, spending time with you, for anyone else. You are so unique, and special, and full of life and energy, and at times you *are* overwhelming, but I love that about you, too," his lips curved up into a slow smile.

Aliya wanted to throw herself on him and give him the biggest hug of his life, but she wasn't crazy. Seth Davis wasn't ready for such huge doses of Aliya China Peyton. *But he better get ready.*

He took her hand and brought it to his lips, placing a kiss in the palm of her hand. "Does that answer your question?"

Aliya couldn't think beyond the feel of his lips against his palm. "Security, there's a fire in the conference breezeway!"

Aliya snapped out of her reverie as she heard the peals of laughter coming from Augusta, Naomi, and Tatyanna.

She blushed even more, removing her hand from Seth's captivity. "Yes, that was...yes," Aliya answered a bit breathless.

Seth chuckled. "If you keep looking at me like that, there's going to be more than one nuptial on Sunday, China Doll," he stood.

Aliya's mouth was wide open. Seth had *never* called her anything other than her name. She blushed even deeper.

Seth took his finger and tilted her chin to close her mouth. He whispered in her ear. "See you a little later, China Doll."

He left her standing in the breezeway, looking a little bit shocked. *Seth Davis flirting. Who would have thought it?*

Lysander had come to in a brightly lit room with nothing but a sheet covering him. On either side of him lay people who were clearly dead. He looked at the tag on his wrist. *Apparently I was too.*

He had sent one medical personnel screaming from the room. Shortly after that, they had taken him back up to the main floor of the hospital for further examining. He could hear the buzz of one word spreading like an airborne virus: *Miracle.*

Lysander could recall nothing but the crash on the mountain, seeing his mother bent over his body, and his conversation with God. Yes, God. He knew people were not going to believe him, but it didn't matter. He closed his eyes and drifted back into sleep as the doctors conducted their tests. As he drifted back into sleep he went over in his mind the glorious experience of his encounter with Christ.

"Lysander, you've been running for a long time."
　　　"Where am I?"
"With Me,."
　　　"Lord?"
"Why are you running from Me, Lysander?"
　　　"Is that me?"
"Yes."
　　　"Why is my mother here? What's wrong?"
"You're dead."
　　　"I can't be! I can feel! I can speak!"
"You are dead but your spirit lives on."
　　　"I want to go back."
"You don't believe in Life. How can you go back?"
　　　"What do you mean?"
"Do you believe that I am the Resurrection and the Life?"
　　　"Yes."
"Will you live your life like you believe Me?"
　　　"Yes, I will."
"Will you tell others about Me, Your Lord, Jesus Christ?"
　　　"Yes. I will tell others."
"I am reaching into you heart to repair it. I create in you a clean heart and renew a right spirit in you, Lysander.

Lysander remembered a hand clothed in light entering his body, filling him with light. He remembered feeling a love so overwhelming covering him like a garment. He remembered feeling as if he had been jolted awake. He had sat up and smelled the stench of death but had never felt so alive.

　　　"You may enter in about five minutes," Lysander heard a voice above him as he drifted back into sleep.

Shemiah stood holding onto Zara Townsend, tears streaming down their eyes. And not just their eyes but everyone in the waiting room was crying tears of joy and sharing in their miracle. *After being declared clinically dead three hours ago, Lysander Townsend was alive.* The entire medical staff was baffled. They had run test after test, and every vital sign was normal. Even the bruising and swelling that had begun to increase after they had taken Lysander down to the autopsy room had decreased. It was as if he was being healed from the inside out. The doctors had declared it a modern miracle. It would run in the papers tomorrow.

Savannah and Indina hugged each other crying profusely. Isaiah was on the floor bowed in worship to God. It was truly an incredible day.

"Thank you, God! Oh, thank you Lord Jesus!" Shemiah shouted. "Praise God, Hallelujah!" Zara Townsend sang out.

They were finally allowed to see Lysander. He was not unconscious the nurse told them. He was just sleeping and under medication. She turned to them after she had recorded his vital signs.

"Every now and then, he keeps saying the same thing in his sleep," she noted with a smile.

Zara was stroking her son's hair, gazing lovingly at him. "What's that?"

"He keeps saying The Resurrection and The Life," the nurse exited the room.

Savannah hugged Shemiah then.

Isaiah and Indina held each other knowing that God had answered their prayers. He had given Zara back her son.

"Yes, son, Jesus is the Resurrection and the Life," Zara kissed her son's cheek gratefully.

Bible Study

Pastor John Marks was concluding his remarks regarding Wholeness.

"As we think on what we have learned tonight, ask yourself these questions: am I looking for someone to complete me? Am I looking for God to complete me? Am I looking to myself as the answer? Wholeness doesn't come from anyone but the Creator, but God is looking for our participation in the process. Let us pray that as we continue in this time, we will find out who we are relying on to make us whole. Josiah is going to give us our closing announcements and prayer," he ushered him up to the front.

"Father, thank you for this wonderful study time with you; Let us take what we have heard and thoughtfully apply ourselves to know our own hearts and what is in your heart concerning us. Help us discern your will for our lives and our relationships in Jesus name, Amen."

Josiah held up his hand.

"Now, I do have some incredible news. I know that Shemiah and Savannah are on their way back here to the resort but they didn't want me to hold the news any longer. Shemiah's cousin, whom many of you don't know, arrived on yesterday evening. He was sent to another hotel, the driver lost control of the van and the van plunged off the side of the mountain. The driver was DOA but Lysander was taken to the hospital. He regained consciousness once last night but then this afternoon was declared dead," Josiah waited until all of the talked had quieted down.

"But that's not the end. When Shemiah showed up at the restaurant, he was coming to tell us that Lysander was dead, but God told him not to say that. He told him to ask for life. That's when we all prayed. Well, shortly after most of you left headed back here, Shemiah got a call to return to the hospital. When he and the family arrived, a miracle had taken place. Lysander was alive!"

Josiah didn't know if he was going to be able to finish this because everyone was jumping and shouting and praising God.

"Hold up! That's not all! Lysander came back to life three hours after they had declared him dead and tagged him and set him up for autopsy. The whole hospital is in an uproar and the nurses told them that he keeps saying 'The Resurrection and The Life' in his sleep! God is awesome!" Josiah did his own happy dance then.

It was another hour before anyone left the conference room. It didn't take a degree in rocket science or theology to figure out this was a good time to give God praise.

Shemiah and Savannah waved goodbye to Zara, Indina, and Isaiah who were staying at a hotel near the hospital. They were planning to release Lysander tomorrow. Enrique would fly them all back to the States where Lysander would undergo more tests in Hilton Head.

It was time for them to have a heart to heart. Shemiah knew Savannah had been avoiding it, but it needed to be said.

"So, what happened today?" Shemiah put his arm around her, his tone neutral.

"I thought I was going to have to give you your ring back," Savannah stole a glance at him.

Shemiah's brows drew together. "You think that I would have broken off our engagement?"

Savannah threw up her hands. "I didn't know what you thought. I just felt so guilty. If I wouldn't have insisted--"

"But you didn't insist," Shemiah stopped her with a finger to her lips. "If you recall, you said he could stay. I insisted that he leave. If anything, I was to blame," Shemiah scolded himself. "So, don't you go thinking that I am giving you up Savannah Charles-- If it had been God's will to take Lysander, I would have grieved, but I would *not* have given you up. I love my cousin, but I love you more," he kissed her cheek.

51

Day 3 Montego Bay

Everyone was up bright and early for breakfast by the waterfall. The time in Mo Bay was winding down and no one wanted to miss what God was doing. Besides, if truth be told, most of the singles had stayed up late into the night praising God for Lysander's resurrection and sharing stories of how God had worked a miracle in their own lives. It was just like God to bring back a man who not many thought highly of to put a testimony of change in his mouth. What a mighty and awesome God! Lysander had died a sinner, but was raised up speaking the truth of who God was.

"Everyone seems so alert this morning," Jarah who was pushing the twins alongside Dr. Greg Thomas noticed.

"Yep," Greg nodded in agreement. "No stragglers this morning."

"And did you get some sleep last night?" Jarah adjusted the sun canopy of the baby stroller to block out the rays of the sun.

"Oh, I slept like a baby," he grinned. "My roommates on the other hand spent their night on the balcony. Probably why Marco and Jamar are bent over," he chuckled. "They look like they're in need of a cane."

"They needed to be caned keeping me up last night," Kevin muttered. Their room was next to his father's.

"Morning, son," Greg gave him a consoling look.

"Dad, I know you could sleep through anything," Kevin yawned. "I never thought men could talk so much," he shook his head.

"I know. Women are always getting a bad rap for talking too much," she giggled. "Now you know the truth."

Kevin couldn't make out what they were talking about but it had kept them up for a good length of time. Carlton and Pastor Marks had stayed out pretty late in the hotel lobby. He had finally gone to sleep around midnight. "Yeah, well, I'm ready to hear what God is going to say this morning. I say bring it on," he strode on to get some victuals.

Carlton was stoic this morning. After last night's testimony of death and resurrection, he had felt a sense of trepidation over his own life. He was one of the very few people who knew why Lysander had shown up at Jamaican Dreams in the first place after overhearing his argument with Aslan Peyton. Carlton's mind had been fixated on one thought: if God had not brought Lysander back to life, where would he be right now? It was a question that Pastor Marks had been happy to answer for him. Those answers had churned in Carlton's mind making sleep an elusive wish last night. He was almost persuaded that God had a plan even for him.

Jamar and Marco sat near the waterfall this morning. They had found out last night that they had something in common: both of them were fascinated by women who thought they were not suitable for more than friendship. Jamar had even shared with Marco his reluctance to get involved with anyone. Marco had gained a little more respect for the man who appeared to most to be very superficial and carefree, but who was in fact heartbroken and hiding wealth of sensitivity for relationships. Marco had apologized for presuming that Jamar knew nothing about love. He had come to understand that Jamar knew more about love than most of his friends. He had loved deeply and he had lost deeply. Jamar's love or his best friend had never been returned, never fully realized, and with her death, his love had been buried deep, just as sure as his friend's body was lodged six feet under. It was just recently that a tender bud had begun to grow in the place where Jamar had thought his love long buried. Marco could appreciate that. When Jamar had drifted off to sleep, he had written a poem inspired by his story.

"Jamar,"

"Yeah," Jamar had occupied himself skipping pebbles across the small lagoon.

"I uh, I hope you don't mind, but I wrote a poem about your girl. Katarina." Marco knew that some people were sensitive about being the subject of anything.

"Word? I think that's great, man."

"You cool with me writing about it?" Marco wanted to make sure. His friends were few and far between. "I mean, 'cause if you're not, I'll tear it up," he raised the single sheet.

"Nah, man, that's you. That's how you process. I wouldn't ask you to do that," he grinned. "But I would ask you not to title it Katarina."

"Actually, I want to call it six feet deep."

"Let's hear what you got."

Marco cleared his throat.

"Agony and disbelief coursed through my veins
Like blood flow
It was pain
Like I never felt
Love locked inside me
No outlet for what I was feeling
No medicine
You couldn't heal this
Numbness inside me
Your life but a memory
Your love something I

Never had but longed for
My love
Something I always had
But prayed for
A place where I could plant it
It was always
Taken for granted
Obscured by
what you wanted
What you needed
My love
You rather not take
But leave it
And in the end
I found a place to plant it
Where great men end
Where magnificent dreams sleep
Where now you lay
Where my soul weeps
You led my heart on a merry chase
Wish that it
Was held by a paper string
But no
Your grip was stronger than death
My love
More tangible than material things
So here
I hover before your grave
With all my love
That could not save
I took a chance
I played for keeps
But didn't count
On Death to cheat
Waiting for my heart
To bloom again
Waiting for love sown to reap
Praying I can love again
No longer surface
My Love is
Six feet deep,"

Jamar just looked at Marco, tears threatening to fall. He couldn't believe that he had conveyed his heart so eloquently yet kept the memory of Katarina sacred. He shook his head at his friend. "Marco Angelo Arion Bolivar, who *are* you?"

Marco just smiled in his bashful and shrugged his shoulders. "Just a florist, man; Just a florist."

"Good morning, everyone," Vivian Worth chirped. "I'm so glad that everyone was able to come out early and enjoy the breakfast set up outside for us. Isn't this a glorious setting for such a glorious day?"

Vivian was glad to hear an enthusiastic response. "I know everyone is ready to explore the North Coast Marine today and so, I don't intend to keep you long, but I did want to recap first. Who would like to tell us what causes a relationship to flow for them?"

Shemiah was the first to respond. "For me, it's communication. If you can't communicate, then your relationship is dead in the water."

"Chemistry has to be there on both sides," Dr. Gregory Thomas added.

"Compatibility; You have to have similar interests and desire to do things as one," Augusta winked at Enrique.

Vivian smiled. "Communication, Chemistry, Compatibility, Commitment, and Christ are all essential to a great relationship. I am here to talk about a factor that is not the most essential piece but one that out culture gets distracted by. Age," Vivian wiggled her eyebrows causing them to laugh.

"Now, I will preface my comments with the fact that we live in America, therefore child brides are not acceptable, and neither is underage dating," she chuckled. "We are not dealing in extremes," she assured them. "We are dealing with the fact that with Christ as the head, maturity and spiritual equity should be more of a deciding factor in your relationships rather than a number."

Vivian gave them several supporting scriptures and instances of God choosing a mate who was on the same page in faith not age. With examples like Isaac and Rebekah, Ruth and Boaz, Mary and Joseph, it was hard not to see her point.

"Am I saying that God would have you marry someone ten years older or ten years younger than you? No. What I am saying is don't rule God out. Don't judge a person simply by their birth certificate. God appointed the time that we should be born and the place we would live in, the family we would be born into so that we would gain the life experiences we have so that we could become the person you could appreciate and love. That is what I am saying," Vivian bowed gracefully.

Jamar was clapping and giving catcalls and making himself generally embarrassing while Marco was laughing his head off.

Tehinnah narrowed her eyes, shooting daggers that she wished he could feel.

"God is trying to tell you something," Tatyanna sang in her ear as she whisked by.

"Oh, stuff it!" Tehinnah stomped off. She was fed up with people trying to tell her what she should feel. Jamar was silly, immature, and too handsome for his own good. And if he so much as mentioned today's Bible Study to her, he was going overboard at the Marine.

Just Chill

"Today you have the opportunity to go deep sea fishing and catch some rays. We have five charter boats reserved which include bait and tackle. Each boat holds six passengers. Who is up for the travel today?" Zeeland Carr's enthusiasm for fishing was evident. He was bit disappointed that most people wanted to hang around the resort.

"Well, I guess I'll be taking the day off then," he sauntered away, unfazed by the lack of participation.

Aliya shook her head at the singles. "You guys, we are supposed to be exploring," she blew out a frustrated breath.

"Calm down, Aliya," Enrique put his arm around his soon to be sister. "We're having a great time," he assured her along with the chorus of voices. "Everyone's still a little wired from last night." He leaned over to whisper, "besides they may need the rest when they find out a wedding is taking place tomorrow," he teased.

Aliya's eyes grew wide. "That's right. They don't know yet, do they?"

Enrique shook his head. "And you're doing an excellent job with that classified information if I might say so myself," he planted a kiss on her forehead.

Aliya patted herself on the back, all the while thinking that Seth's kiss on her hand had felt nothing like the brotherly kiss from Enrique. *I'll have to think on that later.* "Well, suit yourself. Play golf, pamper yourself, workout, but the Game room is off limits," she warned scanning the pouting faces. "I'm serious," she shook her finger.

Wedding Planning

"So far, everything is going smoothly. Your color selection is beautiful: royal purple, burnt orange, and fuchsia is so island! I love it," Angelynn encouraged Augusta.

"I plan to break the news to Savannah after dinner tonight," Augusta confided. I want her to be my bridesmaid. She's been by me through thick and thin and I couldn't leave her in the dark," Augusta looked to Vivian then. "Mariella is going to be a bridesmaid as well. Enrique and I informed her earlier."

"It's your nuptials, Augusta. You're entitled to have those who are close to you share in your special day," Vivian reminded her.

"How's the counseling going?" Angelynn asked.

"It's going great. I'm going to move in with Enrique, we've talked about assets. We've decided to keep the companies separate. I may even sell my shares to Tatyanna and remain on the board for guidance. Enrique and I are both against a prenup. I know that it is recommended but we are entrusting each other with the rest of our lives so its all or nothing," Augusta confessed. "We both want to start our family as soon as possible," she blushed. "I'm glad we've had counseling. I didn't realize our traditions and values meshed so well until we communicated about it. It's also been great having both our pastors on hand to question us about each other because they know us so well," Augusta flipped through her counseling planner.

"Where will you two worship?" Vivian asked. She knew that Enrique was integral to their praise and worship ministry, but Augusta had her own responsibilities at her church.

"We've decided, with the blessing of our pastors to divide our time between both churches. The first two Sundays we will be at Second Chance. The last two Sundays we will be at New Life. Fifth Sundays we will alternate," Augusta laughed at the disbelieving look on their faces. "We'll try it for the first year. If we feel God pulling us more to one ministry, we have agreed to come back at the end of the year and let them know," Augusta saw more than heard the relief from Vivian and Angelynn.

"What have I missed?" Aliya entered the room with a spring in her step.

"Well, your sister was explaining how she's going to be working out the details of her life with the dashing Enrique," Angelynn made room for Aliya on the couch.

"Oh, cool. So, Auggie, how do you plan to handle the press once it gets out that the Billionaire has married his Sweetie?" Aliya gave her a knowing look.

"I'm still working on that," Augusta tapped her pen thoughtfully against her cheek.

"Well, you've got a little over twenty four hours to figure it out." Vivian Worth announced. "There's nothing you face that prayer can't get you through."

The ladies bowed their heads and submitted Augusta and her plans up to the Lord.

Wedding Counseling

"How are you holding up?" Elder Worth asked Enrique. He had been permitted to use Aslan's private office to meet with Augusta and Enrique.

"I'm doing great," Enrique planted his self in the chair facing his pastor. "I'm a little on edge about the press release that will have to be sent out. My PR people are spastic right now trying to decide if we should release post wedding photos or not," Enrique sighed. "I know how much Augusta wants to keep things under wraps. She's a very private person," he shared.

"That's certainly understandable," Elder Worth folded his hands together. "I'm also sure she's aware though that her life will now be under the scrutiny of the public. I believe that God will give her the grace to handle it."

Enrique leaned forward then. "Pastor, I just want to tell you how much your support has meant to me down through the years and especially this last year. Your faith, your word, your mentoring has been such a blessing to my life," He reached into his blazer's pocket and extended a cashier's check. "I meant to give this to you on the plane, but it slipped my mind. This isn't a personal offering; that's coming of course but this is a donation from EAE Design Group for the church planting and mission work you are doing in Hilton Head."

Elder Worth took the check from him, glancing at the amount, his eyes widening. *One hundred thousand dollars?* "Thank you, son; I appreciate your faith in the integrity of the ministry. This will help us to expedite the building plans for the church and the homeless center." Elder Worth was Second Chance's satellite church, Second Wind and a homeless center, Wings of Love, for the underprivileged in Hilton Head.

Enrique stood then, gripping Elder Worth in a big hug. "Glad the Lord could use me. I look forward to what God is going to do through Augusta and I in the service of the Kingdom." He grinned.

"God has great things in store for you both," he declared. "Keep living holy, keep seeking after God, and there is nothing he will withhold from you," Elder Worth encouraged.

As Enrique exited the office, he lifted up his voice in a melody to God, unaware of Grace and Mercy praising along with him.

52

Late Afternoon

Nicholas, Giovanni, Fabian, Jamar, Noelle, and Marco had just finished a round of golf and had decided they were going to have a Manpower Session in the gym when they rounded the corner and heard a symphony of feminine giggles and a heavy French accent that was decidedly male.

Giovanni eyed Nicholas. "I think the French connection has arrived," he grinned as they rounded the corner but his grin quickly turned into a frown when he saw what was going down.

"What the-" Jamar's eyebrows rose at the sight.

"You've got to be kidding me," Marco stood disbelieving.

In the center of the gym, Mariella, Rosalynn, Ginevieve, and Tehinnah surrounded the newest member of Enrique's security team. It looked like a female welcome wagon. Giovanni stepped forward to make introductions shaking hands with Dominic Francois.

"I'm Giovanni Cartellini; this here is my brother Nicholas, and Fabian Ciccone. You'll be working with us while you're here. Also, this is Jamar, Noelle, and Marco, friends of ours," he added as each man shook Dominic's hand.

"I'm Dominic Francois. The lovely ladies here introduced themselves and made me feel welcome," he flashed them a blindingly gorgeous smile to which the ladies giggled.

Are they under a spell? Giovanni had never seen the ladies so flustered. *Must be the accent; Women always go for the guy with the accent.* "I see you've had a chance to get settled in."

"Yes. Monsieur Peyton assisted me personally during your study time, although I have not located Monsieur Estrada yet," he looked a bit perturbed by the thought.

"We'll be happy to escort you to him. We know exactly where he is," Nicholas interjected, shooting daggers at the man with his eyes.

Dominic stood then, towering over most of them. He had to be at least six-five. He was solidly built, without an ounce of fat. Giovanni had to stop himself from mentally sizing him up.

"Take me to our leader," Dominic joked, causing another outburst of giggles from the ladies. He turned to them and issued a bow. "Excuse me ladies. I look forward to your collective company later," he issued the words like a promise from a long lost love. You could hear the collective sigh as Nicholas, Giovanni, and Fabian followed him out of the gym.

Jamar gagged. "I think I'm going to be ill from all this fawning," he joked.

Noelle and Marco both wore the same look of consternation, their hands folded defensively over their chests.

"Is there a problem?" Ginny looked at Marco pointedly.

"Why would there be a problem? Some of you are just doing what you always do," Jamar strode past them to set up a set of free weights.

"Oh, just admit that you're jealous," Tehinnah went over to confront Jamar. "He was showing us how to operate the equipment."

"In French? And judging by your actions, you looked like you wanted to operate his equipment," Jamar set the bar on the lifting stand.

Ginny, Mariella, and Roz all gasped in shock.

Jamar, so busy grinning at his own remark, was not prepared for the swift slap that felt like a knife cutting across his face.

Tehinnah shook with fury. *I can't believe I just did that.* She turned on her heels and ran out of the gym.

Jamar looked to Noelle and Marco but they just shook their heads. "Okay...so maybe I deserved that?"

Ginny, Mariella, and Rosalynn hurried out to find Tehinnah.

Marco came and stood beside Jamar. "Look, bro. None of us are happy with what we saw. But none of us are crazy enough to put a girl in the flame in front of her friends," Marco chided him.

"Translation: You put Tehinnah on blast, man. That was not cool. You got to talk one to one. You basically called a tart. And I don't mean the dessert kind. You gotta fix this- today. Or it will only fester," Noelle came to stand on the other side of Jamar.

"Look man, I know your story. I know you wouldn't want to hurt Tehinnah, but she did have a point. You *were* jealous and you reacted badly," Marco reasoned.

Jamar laughed at himself. "You're right. I haven't that greedy little goblin in a long time." He looked to both men, appreciating the fact that they wanted him to man up but didn't try to browbeat him into it.

"I'll make sure that I apologize before dinner," he promised. "Just pray that my apology doesn't detonate another bomb."

"Don't worry, Bro. We got you. We'll pray right now that everything goes well because that's what God wants. Peacemaking isn't just possible, its reality."

As Marco and Noelle prayed for Jamar, they sent up their own silent prayers that their own issues would be resolved with the lady in their life.

Introductions

"Dominic, I'm so happy to have you on board our security team, even if it is a brief stint. I've heard a lot about you, how impeccable your record and rate of success is. I'm honored you acquiesced to your superior's wishes," Enrique shook hands with the tall Frenchman.

"I've had an opportunity to study your case and of course Giovanni and Nicholas here have brought me up to speed on the most recent information. I understand congratulations are in order?" Dominic asked.

"Yes. I will be getting married tomorrow night and so far no one has alerted the press for which I am immeasurably grateful." Enrique motioned for everyone to be seated. "Has anyone seen our missing operative?" he asked Fabian.

"She should be here any second now. I believe she took advantage of the spa today," Fabian told Enrique while passing around ginger ale to the team.

Nicholas grinned. "Females,"

"Well, she is entitled to some rest and relaxation," Giovanni defended her.

"*She*," Dominic's smile was somewhat forced.

"Francheska Cartellini, our cousin." Nicholas informed Dominic, watching the play of emotions flash on his face which disappeared quickly.

"Is she an American operative?" Dominic asked his expression schooled into a calm demeanor. *It can't be her.*

"No, Italian. She just finished up an assignment in France. You might know her," Giovanni offered.

Dominic's smile was frozen Nicholas noted. *Bingo.* Before he could fish for more details, there was a knock on the door to the office they were using. Nicholas was closest to the door so he happily opened it to let in his dear sneaky little cousin who didn't tell him she had something going on in France.

"I'm sorry I'm late. My microdermabrasion treatment took for-" Francheska just stood in the doorway looking at an apparition surely of a man she thought she knew. She blinked. He was still there. *Oh, God.* She felt like the bottom was falling out from under her.

"Francheska, I presume?" Dominic took in every sweet and perfect inch of the woman he had known as Marie. A woman he had been in search of. Her superior had been protocol bound to keep her name classified and he had been left at a dead end. He hadn't given her name. Instead he had given him this assignment as a parting gift. *God was good.*

"Hello, Dominic." Francheska moved into the room schooling her features into a determined indifference. "Afternoon, Enrique," she smiled, moving past him further into the room to plant herself into a chair. "So, boys, what's on the agenda for tomorrow?"

While Enrique dove into the security plan for tomorrow, Giovanni and Nicholas looked to each other, reading each others' thought. *No way is she getting out of telling us what happened in France.*

Fabian smiled to himself, fully aware of the simmering tension between Francheska and Dominic. *Saints preserve us.* He prayed the two agents could keep their tempers in check. They needed all hands on deck and no distractions; *Attractive or not.*

Regrets and Repentance

They found Tehinnah by the waterfall sulking and scolding her earlier behavior. Mariella, Roz, and Ginevieve had come to a quick consensus that Mariella should be the one to do most of the talking. Ginny and Roz sat a few feet off to give them some privacy but close enough to support if need be.

"Mind if I join you?" Mariella knelt next to Tehinnah.
"I'm not real good company right now," Tehinnah scowled.
"Want to talk about it?" Mariella offered.
"No much to say. I made a fool of myself back there. I was a total brat."
"It's not like you weren't provoked," Mariella reminded her.
"I've never seen Jamar act so reprehensible. He's usually so laid back," Mariella thought out loud.
"I should have just laughed it off, but no, I had to lose my temper. He's so immature. I just wish he would grow up," Tehinnah tossed a pebble into the waterfall.
"See, that's the thing. You say that he's immature, but I just don't see that side of him. He assists his brother in ministry. He's been a great asset to Alpha, Inc. I even heard him talking about partnership with Tatyanna. He's in school now, but he's been taking extra classes so he can graduate early. Jamar may be young, but he's not immature. I think you see him that way because it's safer," Mariella decided.
Tehinnah turned to look at her then. "Safer? What are you talking about?"
"I'm talking about the fact that you like Jamar. Sure, you flirt a little, but it's nothing serious. I can tell when you like a guy because you don't flirt with him, and when he tries to flirt with *you*, you see it as a sign that he's not serious about you. That's why you're really bothered. Jamar loves to flirt, too. But he only flirts with women who are taken already. The fact that he's flirting with you says a lot. I haven't seen Jamar with any girl, and no, he's not gay," Mariella laughed. "Look, it's safer to say Jamar's immature than it is to say he's what you want but age is an issue for you."
Tehinnah just glared at Mariella.
"Okay, you don't have to admit it right now, but at least admit it to yourself. I personally think you are perfect for each other but that's just my opinion," she giggled as Tehinnah gave her a push.
"I'll take everything you've said into consideration but I plead the fifth. I will apologize though," Tehinnah promised. "I asked God to forgive me, but I need his forgiveness too," she confessed. "I was totally out of line."

Mariella hugged Tehinnah. "I hope I said something that will help you understand Jamar just a little."

"I hope so too," Jamar stood a few feet away.

Tehinnah looked to Mariella who clearly had no idea Jamar was coming over.

"You mind if I sit down?" Jamar waited patiently for her response while Mariella hustled off. He hadn't heard their conversation and wondered just what it was she thought she understood about him. He'd have to pry it out of her later.

"Sure, go ahead." Tehinnah waved him on.

Jamar plopped down next to her. "I figured I'd better offer you the other cheek just in case I put my foot in my mouth again," he gave her a dead serious look.

Tehinnah fell back in laughter.

It was the first time Jamar had heard her laugh at one of his jokes. He was shocked. She had a deep, rich laughter that shook him down to his big toes. He could get used to that sound real easy.

"That's what I mean," Tehinnah wiped her eyes. "Here I am, ready to apologize for hitting you, and you're joking about it," Tehinnah shook her head.

"Hey, the floor's still open—ladies first and all. I've got an apology I need to give as well, so let's just get the ball rollin'," Jamar gave her an amused smile.

"I'm sorry for hitting you. I lost my temper," Tehinnah admitted.

"Only because you love me so much," Jamar told her matter-of-fact.

"Jamar," Tehinnah warned.

"Okay, sorry." He held up his hands then in surrender.

"I was way out of line," Tehinnah continued. "I ask that you forgive me, please," she finished.

"I love the way you said that last word. Could you say it again?" "*Jamar,*" Tehinnah's brows drew together.

"Okay! Sheesh!" he laughed. "No, seriously, though, I forgive you. Would you forgive me for insinuating you were a tart, because I really don't think that about you at all and yes, you were right, I was jealous, but only be-"

"Stop right there." Tehinnah put a finger to his lips. "I forgive you, Jamar, but I'd like to do just one more thing."

Jamar had become speechless the moment her finger had landed on his lips. He nodded his head. *This is a good time to be silent.*

Tehinnah turned his head to look at his cheek. Traces of her handprint were still evident. "I really am sorry I hit you and I hope this will make up for it," she whispered softly as she leaned and placed a kiss on his bruised cheek, her hand brushing past his chin as she released him. She hopped up then. "See you at dinner, Jamar," Tehinnah floated away humming.

Jamar touched his own cheek then and closed his eyes. He had promised himself a long time ago that he would flirt but he would not feel anything for a woman ever again. He should be angry with Tehinnah for toying with his emotions but he couldn't bring himself to feel anything but hope. Hope that he was finally healing and moving forward wherever God would have him to be, whoever God would have him to love.

Pastor John Marks and Columbia Newcomb had decided to go horseback riding after hearing about the trails filled with flowers from The Youngsters as Pastor Marks called them. Pastor Marks was an avid gardener and had designed a botanical wonderland in his own backyard. It was a relaxing pastime for him. He and Columbia decided to stop along the trail for a moment which provided cool shade for the heat.

"Aslan has really got something great here. Folks are going to love this come grand opening," he looked around in approval.

"I'm so thankful I got an opportunity to come along and explore. I don't think I would have done this on my own. If it weren't for the girls, I would have stayed home and done my usual thing." Columbia confided.

"I know just what you mean. The older you get, the more routine things become and you get used to the familiarity and well, you just don't want to rock the boat so to speak," John drew his horse closer to hers. "But, Columbia, I must tell you, I'm so glad you came along and rocked my boat," he spoke gently.

Columbia blushed. "John, I've really enjoyed your company and our time together. You're such a wonderful man and I'm glad you've chosen to share your time with me."

John suddenly felt peace about what he wanted to say to Columbia, so he said it. "I hope you know you have more than my time, Columbia. You have my heart, and if you'll have me, I'd like to share the rest of my life with you. Columbia, would you do me the honor of becoming my wife?"

Columbia was speechless, but only for a moment. "I...Yes, John, I'll marry you."

He reached over to take her hand in his. "You won't leave this island without a ring on your finger. I won't have you going home empty-handed," he raised her hand to his lips and kissed it.

"Pastor Marks, you had better have a good reason for what you just did," Vivian Worth who was walking alongside Elder Worth on the trail called out.

Pastor Marks and Columbia cantered up to meet them.
"I have an excellent reason," he looked to the radiant Columbia. "Columbia has just consented to become my wife."

53

One Hour before Dinner

Savannah was glad that she and Shemiah had been able to make it back to the resort before dinner. They had been gone most of the day seeing to Shemiah's family and Lysander's safe transport. All in all, it had been a day of forgiveness and healing. Savannah truly thanked God for the second chance at life he had given to Lysander. There was no greater joy today than seeing Shemiah lead his cousin back to the Lord, the men weeping together as God knit their hearts and restored their friendship. Lysander had also begged Savannah's forgiveness and let her know he would recall all of his plans and cease his harassment. He even prayed that God would bless their union. Zara Townsend too had asked for her forgiveness. She confessed to Savannah the things she had said at her breaking point. *It was amazing how we as God's people can turn our backs so quickly when tragedy occurs,* Savannah thought to herself.

"Savannah, is that you?" Augusta sang out, padding into the shared space of their suite.

"Hey, lady, how did the Marine trip go today?" Savannah moved toward the closet to look for something nicer to change into for dinner.

"No one went. We mostly just hung out around the resort today and took in the on site amenities. I really haven't seen much of anyone today, which is why I need to speak with you so I'm glad we're alone," Augusta drug Savannah away from the closet and seated her on one of the beds. "You're going to want to be seated for this," she assured her.

Savannah took a deep breath. "Okay, what's going on?"

"Enrique and I got engaged last week," Augusta held up her hand, "not done," she warned. "We got engaged last week but we are getting married tomorrow night. No one knows except my parents, Aliya, and the Pastors and their wives. Now, you can talk," Augusta held her breath.

Savannah's mind was spinning with the implications. "Don't get me wrong, Augusta, I'm crazy excited that you and Enrique are getting married, but why the rush?" Savannah hoped that Augusta trusted that she had only her best interests at heart.

"My father asked us to be married here and I want to honor that. He also wants Enrique to be able to protect me as my husband and end all of this espionage surrounding our relationship. We both agreed. I'd accepted Enrique as my fiancé so I have no problem accepting him as my husband. We've been in what I call Boot camp Marriage counseling since we decided. I've found that we have more in common than I thought," Augusta beamed in excitement. "I would be honored if you'd be my bridesmaid, Savannah."

Savannah nodded in acceptance, feeling the peace of God settling on her friend. "I'd love to, Auggie."

Augusta embraced her friend and prayed for her strength in her relationship with Shemiah, that God would make everything beautiful in his time.

Neither woman saw the angel recording the request and dancing back up into the open heavens on a flame of fire.

Checkmate

Nicholas and Giovanni had waited until everyone had cleared the room before they harassed their baby cousin.

"You want to tell us what that was all about? 'Cause we're not letting you out of this room until you talk." Nicholas told her.

They had been serious.

Francheska tapped her shoe against the desk in the office. "You two can't hold me hostage here all night. They'll be looking for us at dinner. Besides, you have more important things to do than worry about my love life," she rolled her eyes.

"Now we're getting somewhere. How long has this been going on?" Nicholas leaned over her like a criminal interrogator, his arms braced against the desk on either side of her.

"If you don't want to be kicked into the dining room, you might want to back up, *Nicky*," Francheska narrowed her eyes at him.

Nicholas backed away slowly. "Just tell us the truth. We're concerned about you Checkers," Nicholas leaned against the side of the desk.

"Concern is not spelled N-O-S-Y. There's not much to tell. We were deep under cover on a case. I thought he was a criminal. I was his love interest. End of story."

"So you got played by French Intel, huh?" Giovanni was curious as to why.

"How did you find out he was an agent?" Nicholas wondered. That kind of thing was classified.

"I ran across some of the files on the case afterward. They had allowed him to be carted off and taken to jail like he was one of them. I felt stupid really that I hadn't figured it out, "Francheska admitted with a brutal laugh.

"You fell in love with him when you thought he was a criminal didn't you?" Nick knew he had hit the issue right on the head.

Dead silence.

"Wow, Chess," Giovanni stared at his cousin, her features etched in regret. "I'm sorry."

"He's good, then." Nick acknowledged.

"The best they say. He certainly had *me* fooled. I didn't even have to drug him or anything. He said that he wouldn't pressure me to have sex. He respected my religious beliefs," she laughed to herself. "I should have guessed then. Agents can't be involved with agents."

"Did he know you were an agent?" Giovanni wondered.

"He had to know." Nicholas countered.

"So, what happens now?" Giovanni looked to Francheska. "You want us to take him down for hurting you? We'll do it. He's a giant, but we will take him down. Just give us the go ahead."

"Really, Gio," Nick glowered at him.

Francheska shook her head. "No. It's over and done with. I just didn't expect to see him again. I mean it's embarrassing enough that I fell in love with a criminal who's not a criminal but now I actually have to work with him because he's not a criminal, he an agent!" Francheska was nearly screaming.

"Clearly you are so over this guy," Giovanni said with a straight face.

"I agree with you Chess," Nicholas assumed a calm tone. "You are done. Dominic is just a bad memory. Your assignment in France was a total success. You got the bad guys," Nicholas took her hand and pulled her up from her chair. "You go get ready for dinner, Chess. You look great by the way. Love what you're doing with your hair these days," Nick added as he led her to the door. "We'll see you at dinner." He watched Francheska get on the elevator. He could only pray she did not run into Dominic. He closed the door.

"Holy Moley," Giovanni's eyes were outstretched.

"I still want to kick his butt." Nick gritted his teeth.

"Our little Francheska is in love," Giovanni shook himself.

"With a mercenary heartless little Frenchie," Nick reminded him.

"Are you really that clueless?" Giovanni looked at him as though he had clueless taped to his forehead.

"What?" he shrugged.

"He's retiring from Intelligence and this is his last assignment. Why do you think he's really here?" Giovanni waited for the light bulb to come on. "Exactly," he grinned. "Now let's see how Dominic fares at the dinner table with our irate cousin."

Jamar had been waiting for an opportunity to catch Mariella before she went in to dinner. Now was the perfect time.

"Hey, Jamar, you clean up well," Mariella took in his slacks and blazer with his vest and tie, all coordinated.

"And you look gorgeous as always," he took her by the hand and spun her around. "Thank you for talking to Tehinnah earlier today. You didn't have to. I'm going to have to report your good behavior to your cousin," he joked.

"I just told her the truth about you so you can't hide behind your jokes anymore," Mariella teased.

Jamar's heart skipped a beat. "What truth?"

"I just told her that you may be young, but you're far from immature and that you really do like her even though you spend most of your time teasing her," she smiled knowingly.

"It's amazing how much you know about me yet how little you understand about Noelle," he countered.

Mariella leaned back. "Pardon me?"

Jamar folded is arms. "Are you going to deny there is something between you two?"

Mariella narrowed her eyes. "What has he said to you?"

"Absolutely nothing, but I'm not blind. I see the way he looks at you, the way his eyes follow you," Jamar was clearly amused by how flustered she was.

"Whatever. Noelle and I aren't speaking right now. I'm here to learn more about being single and concentrate on developing my spiritual self," Mariella lifted her chin.

"Well, develop away. Nothing wrong with that," Jamar decided to let her off the hook, sensing there was more to the story than she was telling. Looks like God was going to have to work on her heart. "I'll escort you in," Jamar gave her his arm.

"Why thank you, Mr. Maturity," Mariella unleashed a megawatt smile on him as she waltzed into the dining room right past Noelle Marks.

Trip the Light Fantastic

Francheska had decided to take the long route down to the dining hall so she could enjoy the sweeping grand staircase. She had decided that if she was going to face Dominic again, she wanted to look her best. Clothing was one of the many weapons in a woman's artillery. She had decided to style her hair into an upsweep and allow some of her hair to cascade in waves. She wasn't one for a lot of makeup so she had smoothed on some lip gloss, arched her thick eyebrows and threw on her peasant dress with her spiked-heels. She was humming to herself minding her own business and fortifying her mind against thoughts of Dominic Francois.

"You look like a goddess," the voice behind her murmured causing her to lose her bearing on the step.

Dominic caught Francheska, taking in the scent of jasmine that danced around her. He fought to keep from moving in closer to chase the scent. "Careful," he gently helped her to get her bearing. "I didn't mean to startle you."

Francheska was good at playacting. This time would be no different. She would not give him the pleasure of knowing he had affected her in any way. "I'm fine." She continued down the steps, noticing how quickly he moved to keep up with her.

"Can I escort you in to dinner?" Dominic flashed a brilliantly charming smile.

"I'm afraid not," she smiled sympathetically. "You see, I'm not quite sure *who* would be escorting me in. Will it be Carlito Brunelli or Dominic Francois or some *other* persona? Quite frankly, I'm just not in the mood to figure it out," she shrugged her shoulders and left the very handsome, enigmatically charming Dominic Francois staring after her.

"Touché, Francheska." Dominic couldn't help but admire her more for her polite dismissal of his attentions. He wasn't a man who could be so easily dismissed. Francheska would recognize that in time.

Seth was waiting for Aliya in the breezeway. He had asked her to meet him so he could escort her in. Aliya felt just a little euphoric today after her heart to heart with Seth. Seeing him standing there with his sweater vest, dress shirt, and slacks looking model-worthy was doing little strange things to her insides. Aliya felt her stomach flip, then flutter, her nervousness hidden well beneath her bubbly personality. *Why am I acting like this is prom or something? Snap out of it, girl!*

"You look stunning, China Doll," Seth spoke so only she could hear him. He took her hand in his. "I snuck out today after I finished my studies for this evening," he placed a corsage of a red rose on her wrist. "I hope you like it," he gazed into her eyes, allowing her to see all the love he felt for her shining in his own.

Aliya was speechless. Seth Davis was getting very good at silencing the very spastic Aliya Ming Peyton.

"It's lovely," Aliya looked down at her corsage then, "and very thoughtful. Thank you, Seth," Aliya gave him the once over. "You look handsome. I don't think I've ever seen you in a vest before. You're usually in business attire," she commented offhand trying to calm her nerves with small talk.

"You're right," Seth noted, "But don't worry. I plan to make sure we see a lot more of each other after this getaway is over," Seth promised.

"I'll hold you to that promise," Aliya teased as she allowed him to lead her in to dinner.

54

Dinnertime

The mood was decidedly charged as everyone took their seats. Aslan had brought in a Christian Reggae band to play live for them. There was a light-hearted mood amongst the singles. They had been enjoying themselves all day, getting into one scrape or another and now some announcements were forthcoming.

"I trust that everyone has been having a fabulous time here at Jamaican Dreams. I just want to say this now, that you all have become like a second family to me and I would ask that you consider returning in the future. Our doors will be open to you," Aslan waited for the applause to cease before he went on. "Elder Worth has a few announcements that he would like to make before dinner is served," Aslan stepped aside and yielded the floor to Elder Worth.

"The first thing I'd like to do as we wind down this trip is to remind you of our curfews and public displays of affection stipulations for this trip, and as I see some of you are looking guilty, I see that we are all in need of some reminding. If you are married, we ask you keep the PDA to a minimum, engaged couples need to refrain in group settings, and courting and singles need to refrain from all PDA. I hope that is clear. Engaged couples curfew is midnight, courting couples is eleven-thirty, and singles curfew is ten-thirty. That curfew means that after Bible study, you have about thirty minutes to an hour and a half, depending on your situation to make it to your rooms. I will say, that if you are fraternizing with the same sex and the opposite sex is not around, using the hotel lobby up front is fine. Are there any questions?" Elder Worth looked from table to table. "Good, now that we have that squared away, I'd like to introduce our newest engaged couple to you. Please stand," Elder Worth motioned.

Everyone cheered, shouted praises and catcalls as Columbia and Pastor Marks both stood up at their respective tables.

"As you can see, this was definitely an exception to the rule," Elder Worth grinned. "Now, if the rest of you can hold off proposing for just a few more days, that would be great," Elder Worth waited until all the laughter had died down. "The other thing we'd like to inform you of is that there is a wedding taking place here tomorrow night, and you have all been invited," There was plenty of whispering and speculation going on. Elder Worth called them back to attention. "You will have an opportunity to do some shopping in Falmouth tomorrow ladies, so take advantage. The wedding will be our culminating activity for our trip. We will leave out Monday morning at four am, so make sure you pack after your return from Falmouth so you can freely enjoy our culminating activities. What better way to end out Single's retreat than by attending a wedding?" Elder Worth returned to his seat amidst the speculation of who was getting married.

Island Fantasy Table Talk

"Congratulations, Columbia," Angelynn smiled with pleasure at the news. "I'd say that announcement was past due," she winked.

"Hear, hear," Shemiah chuckled, lifting his glass in a toast to Josiah. "Pastor Marks has been looking like he's wanted to propose since he got here."

"So true," Savannah sighed. "I'm so happy for you," Savannah rubbed Columbia's shoulder affectionately.

"It all just happened so beautifully. We'll be picking out an engagement ring tomorrow. The last time I spoke to my girls, they told me that they wouldn't mind me bringing home a father. Well, they got their wish," Columbia was positively glowing. She couldn't help it.

Josiah leaned into his wife and placed a kiss on her cheek. "Angelynn and I will make sure we celebrate on your behalf," he ginned cheekily.

Shemiah and Savannah both made gagging noises at him.

"Hold that down, honey," Angelynn teased. "I tell you, I can't take you anywhere these days."

Columbia was amused by their loving playfulness and looked forward to her own future full of playful moments. *Hold me, Jesus, until that great day!*

Island Carnival Table Talk

"How was your day today?" Trey leaned over to speak with Aurielle. He had spent very little time with her the past few days. He had traveled to the hospital at Shemiah's request to attest to the medical miracle that had taken place. The doctors there had deferred to his expertise in moving patients of trauma with the utmost care. He had tried to get back to the resort as soon as he could to make himself presentable for dinner. Judging by the look on Aurielle's face, he had spent entirely too much time away. *Here I am on vacation and still I find myself at a hospital. How am I ever going to convince her that I'm serious about her?*

"Peaceful," Aurielle decided. "I took advantage of my empty room and got some needed rest," she told him. *After realizing you went off to go play Medicine Man.* Aurielle couldn't say she was all that surprised. Trey was dedicated to his work. It was something she admired about him.

"I missed you today," Trey spoke so only she could hear.

"You had a choice, Trey, and you made it," Aurielle stared ahead.

"What's that supposed to mean?" Trey asked dinnerware midair.

"It means, Trey, that you and I are two ships passing in the night on different schedules," Aurielle finally looked at him, her eyes clouded with pain.

Trey couldn't believe she was just giving up on him. *On them,* He finished his bite of food then graciously placed his dinnerware next to his plate. He wiped his mouth and threw down his napkin. "Excuse us," he nodded to Dr. Thomas, Jarah, Jamar, and Tehinnah, as he grabbed Aurielle by the hand.

"Wha-- where are we going?" Aurielle didn't want to cause a scene so she decided not to put up a struggle.

"Outside," Trey didn't know what he was going to do or say to make her understand his feelings but he had to do *something*. He didn't want to lose Aurielle.

Aurielle had decided they were far enough away from the entrance of the dining room to give him a piece of her mind, when she was pulled forcefully into Trey's arms. He clung to her, his voice filled with agony.

"Please, don't do this to us," Trey shut his eyes tight to keep from releasing all of the pent up emotions he felt just at the thought of Aurielle not being apart of his life. He gently released her and knelt just low enough to look into her eyes as he tilted her chin upward, holding her as if she were the most gossamer of silk. "Aurielle, I love you, so I must tell you the truth.

Aurielle was captivated by his attention. She had not expected this revelation. This wasn't the cool and collected Trey she was used to. He seemed desperate. It was the only word that came to mind. She waited for him to go on.

"My family made a pact with another prestigious family in Trinidad. They engaged me to be married."

"*What?*" Aurielle stepped away from him.

"Hear me out," Trey pleaded. He turned his back then faced her again, his chiseled features etched in frustration. "I've never met her, but my parents feel that I am honor bound to marry her."

"People still do that?" Aurielle wondered aloud.

"Maybe not in America, but yes, other countries still arrange marriages," he shook his head.

"What will you do?" Aurielle studied him. She couldn't believe what she was hearing. This was worse than his workaholic behavior. *This* was a nightmare.

"I'm planning to leave here and catch a flight home to Trinidad where I will explain to my parents that I cannot, in honor marry this girl, because I am in love with someone else," he stepped nearer, pulling a small velvet box out of his pocket, "and if she will have me, I would be honored to marry her in the very near future," he opened the box. "I've kind of been holding on to this for a while. It's a family heirloom that was given to me by my grandfather."

Aurielle covered her mouth with her hands. "I think I'm going to faint," she giggled a little hysterically.

Trey got down on one knee, hoping Elder Worth would understand why he was breaking protocol after he explained the situation. "Then it's a good thing I can revive you," he smiled. "A little mouth to mouth resuscitation never hurt anyone," he teased.

Aurielle stared down at the flawless princess cut diamond, no rock. It had to be at least three carats and on each side sat a ruby and a pearl. It was the most gorgeous ring she had ever laid eyes on. "Are you sure?"

"I have never been surer of anything in my life. Aurielle Foqua, would you do me the express pleasure of becoming my wife in the very near future?" Trey asked his very heart held out to her to receive or reject.

"Yes, I will. I would love to be your wife in the very near future," Aurielle held out her hand as he slipped the ring on her finger.

Trey stood and embraced her once more.

"And replace your mistress," Aurielle warned him.

Trey looked puzzled. "What Mistress?"

"Her name is Workaholic, and she has got to go," Aurielle held him closer.

Pastor Marks had gone out to the restroom and managed to catch the lovebirds at the close of the proposal.

"Another single bites the dust, huh?" He grinned sheepishly.

Trey and Aurielle broke apart like two lovers caught in an illicit affair.

"I can explain," Trey began.

"Don't bother. Just join me tonight in the meeting with Elder Worth after dinner. You can explain then," he chuckled returning to the banquet room.

Island DuJour Table Talk

"Did you see the look on Trey's face?" Aliya leaned over to whisper to Tatyanna.

"It did not look good. I want to go check on them, but I don't want to be nosy," Taty admitted.

"Check on whom?" Kevin asked.

"Trey and Aurielle; haven't you been paying attention?" Ginny looked at Marco. "Even Marco saw what happened at the Island Carnival table."

"But I know what happened," Seth added.

"What?" everyone chimed in simultaneously.

"I believe Trey finally did something with that ring that he's been playing around with since the plane ride over," Seth dropped the bomb so eloquently that no one was prepared for the fallout.

Island Dreams Table Talk

Nicholas, Giovanni, Enrique, and Fabian were all content to eat their food like good little toy soldiers while the girls fellowshipped to their heart's delight. Nicholas and Giovanni had briefed Enrique on the state of the unity within their security team. He had decided to let the relationship matter settle itself. All four men were now watching the smoldering glances that Dominic was sending to the totally oblivious Francheska.

She was either immune to his French charm or she was an excellent playact, Giovanni thought, throwing herself into a frivolous conversation about the best hat for outdoor weather in Jamaica. Giovanni had decided she was the latter. He and Nicholas had decided that Dominic was harmless where Francheska was concerned. After a few discreetly placed calls and reassurances, it seemed the gentleman really *was* interested in their cousin, to the point of pounding the pavement to search her out despite warnings from his superiors which was fascinating information that Giovanni planned to retain in his memory bank. So, now they watched, and dined, and waited for Dominic to make his move and somehow manage to stick his foot in his mouth. *If he hasn't already done so,* Giovanni smirked.

"Have you been enjoying yourself?" Augusta asked Francheska trying to ignore the new agent who kept giving Francheska very passionate looks across the dinner table if she wasn't mistaken.

"I have been surprisingly," Francheska had an idea forming in her mind. It was time to have a little fun with Dominic. "My last assignment was terrible," she glanced out the corner of her eye to see the smoldering look turn to an icy glare. "I mean, not like what I do is fun or anything, but there was this one criminal," she hesitated.

Augusta seemed really into what she had to say. "Go on," she waved her onward.

"Well," Francheska cleared her throat realizing that not just Dominic was listening in. She lowered her voice. "he was really hot and I fell head over heels in love with him," she was barely whispering and trying to hold back her laughter at the table full of men trying to hear the rest of the revelation.

Augusta gasped. "No!"

Francheska nodded her head solemnly and continued on whispering to Augusta. "He was so sweet and kind that I couldn't put together the horrible things I knew he was doing with the person I saw every day for four months. It was really confusing. It broke my heart when they locked him up. Now, I'll never see him again," she sighed.

Augusta stared dreamily off into space. "So romantic, yet, so tragic; Can you find him?" she questioned, an unwitting pawn in Francheska's torture of Dominic.

She stared directly at him then. "No, the man I fell in love with disappeared after he was arrested," she sighed pitifully. "It's like he never existed." She finished, turning her back to Dominic. "So, you see, Augusta, this assignment was a godsend. I can meet new people and leave that painful memory behind. I should have known better than to fall for a thief and a professional liar."

Ouch! Francheska, you're killing the poor guy, Giovanni wanted to rail at his cousin. He gave Dominic a look of apology for his cousin's behavior. In her mind, she was a woman scorned. He just hoped it wouldn't be too late before she realized that she was grinding into dust a man who had intended to offer his heart for the taking.

Dominic was beginning to feel as though taking this assignment had perhaps been the singularly worst decision of his career. *What a way to go out.* Her superior had warned him that she was angry. *Angry wasn't the word to describe Francheska Cartellini. Embittered would be more appropriate.* She had been so sweet during their time together. *So refreshing,* he mused. He wished he had been cast into a better role, but as an operative, you didn't pick or choose; you obeyed or you got out of the game. Now, he truly was confused. Just who was Francheska Cartellini? Was she the sweet, playful innocent or was she the bitter woman sitting before him relishing in his unease and gloating over his humiliation, because, every man at the table knew she was talking about him. He had to find out. Regardless of how much his heart wanted to break free, Dominic was cautious, not careless, and he would guard his heart, like he guarded international secrets: with precision, with diligence, with expert self-control.

Island Carnival Table Talk-Back

"Boy, are you two in for it," Dr. Greg Thomas shook his head.

"You are brave, I must give you that," Kevin leaned back in his chair. "How are going to explain proposing right after *your* Pastor told us all not to," Jamar gave him a pointed look.

"It's a long story," Trey told them.

"A long story; Shoot, it better be a good one," Jarah told him.

Everyone at the table nodded their heads in agreement.

55

Dinner goes on...

Island Masquerade Table Talk

While all the pandemonium surrounding Pastor Mark's engagement ensued as well as the mystery surrounding tomorrow's wedding, this group of guests were ensconced in their own battle of wills. Rosalynn and Mei-Ling were quite at wit's end with Carlton, and Mariella and Noelle were still not speaking. The Island Masquerade table was silent for another evening. This group of diners was thankful that this would be the last night to hold it together for the sake of peace.

Island Dance Table Talk

"I have to warn you now, Elder Worth, that you may have an outbreak on your hands," Pastor Marks patted his comrade's shoulder as he sat down.

"An Outbreak, you say?" Elder Worth had just finished his dessert.

"Yep; another single just bit the dust a few minutes ago. He's coming to speak with you after dinner, so I'm giving you this heads up so you won't forget your Pastor hat when you address him," John warned.

Elder Worth looked like he was about to blow a gasket. "Alright, who is it *now*?"

"Dr. Trey Jones just proposed to Aurielle Foqua. She accepted." John finished off his entrée.

"Look at the bright side dear," Vivian admonished. "These are not singles who have just met on this trip. We have asked them to search themselves, to know what's in their hearts. We can't get upset because they are doing what we asked of them," she reminded him.

"She does have a point," Aslan seemed thoughtful. "Now, some of these singles are still playing games. Some of them need to be taken out to the waterfall and dunked a few times to get their heads on straight. That Carlton fellow, a real cad; he can't seem to stop harassing my niece. I'm inclined to have a word with him if he continues," Aslan's warning cut straight to the point.

"I'm beginning to think we need to have a split Bible Study so we can address some issues," Elder Worth rubbed his chin thoughtfully.

"Sounds good to me," Phet chimed in. She had missed most of the festivities thus far due to arranging her daughter's wedding, but she would get caught up tonight.

After Dinner Mementos

Just an hour until Bible Study and the Single's Getaway was turning into a Couple's Retreat. There was much that needed to be settled in the hearts and minds of the believers. One thing was sure: No one would return to Savannah like they left.

"Hey, Punkin Noodles. Just checkin' in," Columbia could barely make out her daughter's voice.

"Are you having fun?" Rodia asked.

"I am; how are things at the house? How's Delia?" Columbia always worried about her youngest.

"She's fine. She's found a neighborhood girl to play with; Nadia watches out for them. We let them play in the yard," she sighed wistfully. "We sure do miss you, Mom." Rodia's longing for her mother could be felt in every word.

"You miss my cooking," she joked. "Put your sisters on the other line; there's something I want to share with you all," Columbia could hear her other daughters in the background arguing, fidgeting, and fighting over the receiver.

"We're all on the line," Nadia's excitement was palpable.

"Okay. Pastor Marks asked me to marry him," Columbia pulled the phone away from her ear as pandemonium ensued. She could picture them running around the living room, bouncing on the couches and diving over the coffee table. You'd think there was a wild house party underway, but it was just them three.

"What did you say?" They paused in their celebration.

"I said yes," Columbia had to pull the phone away from her ear as the girls continued to scream like banshees, 'We're getting married, we've found a Daddy!'

Columbia knew she would not get another word in so she agreed with them, sent her love and bid them goodnight. Yes, it was a marvelous thought. *We're getting married.*

Elder Worth had admonished Trey Jones to talk fast. After going over Trey's dilemma back home, Elder Worth could understand why the young man had acted in haste, but he certainly would have counseled against proposing tonight. Trey had unadvisedly pitted his bride to be against his family and all they held dear. He prayed that Trey would be able to make amends with his parents, retain his honor, and in due season marry Aurielle, preferably with the blessing of his family. Elder Worth knew that God could take our biggest mishaps and shape them for His glory. *Lord, do it on his behalf, and help Trey to trust you.*

Check Yourself

"What got into you tonight, Chess?" Giovanni folded his hands and looked his cousin over in consternation.

Francheska could not believe that she was being held hostage again. Her cousins had abducted her from her room and brought her back to the personnel office *bodily* for questioning.

"What?" Francheska asked innocently.

"Cut the crap, Checkers," Nick glared at her. "You practically gutted the man tonight. I'm surprised he could still walk away from the table with some of his manhood in tact."

"What do you want me to *say*?" Francheska snapped. "That I'm sorry? I'm not. He deserved it, thinking he could waltz in here and everything would be fine? What did he take me for?" She slammed her fist against the desk, wincing in pain at the sting.

"I think you should be sorry. I think you're going to be sorry," Giovanni warned her.

Francheska narrowed her eyes. "You know why he's really here don't you?"

"I've got a hunch," Giovanni shrugged.

"Since you know so much, let's hear it then," Francheska hopped up on top of the desk.

"It's simple. He loves you." Gio told her straight up.

Francheska laughed wildly. "Like I'm buying that; Okay, Nick, you tell me-why's Frenchie really here?"

"That answer is too simple for you isn't it, Checkers." Nick was deadly serious. Francheska's behavior tonight had hit close to home for his own romantic life that was currently in shambles due to one irritating, interfering brother.

"Well, of *course* it is," Giovanni joined in, "Because if Frenchie came to find his little Chess piece that makes him feel like he's complete and she really does love him too, then she just threw away the best thing that never happened to her—love!" Giovanni threw up his hands.

"Instead, she'll spend the rest her life knowing that the guy she thought didn't exist was right there all along- she was just to bitter to see it," Nicholas finished for his twin.

Francheska's mind was spinning at the implications of what her cousins were implying. If Dominic had indeed taken this assignment so he could reveal his feelings, then she had just squashed any hope of him doing so. Francheska didn't feel so satisfied now. She felt horrible.

God, what have I done?

Linger No More

Fabian had been waiting for the right moment to approach Mei-Ling all day. It had seemed that every time he spotted her, Carlton had been somewhere near observing her. He hadn't wanted a confrontation with him so he had chosen to go another way today. It had been a day full of revelations.

The Savannah crew seemed to be a tight knit group of believers who had their own issues, cares, and concerns, yet still made time for each other and God. It was an interesting mix and Fabian couldn't think of any other culture in the world where this group of people would mix, mingle, fall out, fall in love, and mesh with each other except in the culture of Church. That seemed to be part of the mystery of the Body of Christ. They were people who outside of Christ would certainly rub each other the wrong way, but in Christ they were fitly joined together.

"Hi," Fabian saddled himself across from Mei-Ling on a leather seat.

Mei-Ling looked up, relieved it was Fabian but still a bit apprehensive. Carlton had been trailing her all day, stalking her really. It had made her feel terribly uncomfortable. It was like the guy had missed out on social etiquette the day God was passing it out. "Hello again; I haven't seen you all day," she realized.

"I had to stay away or do something I might have regretted. I saw Carlton trailing you and it sickened me," He admitted.

"I wish you had said something," Mei-Ling smiled at the thought. "I think I may be in need of your services Mr.?"

"Ciccone, Fabian Ciccone," he answered.

"Yes, this stalking thing is very distasteful," Mei-Ling shuddered.

"If you were my lady, you would definitely have my protection," Fabian's words were sure.

Mei-Ling wasn't sure how to answer that statement so she changed the topic. "Did you enjoy dinner?"

Fabian let her escape for now. "It was...quite entertaining although the person who was the subject of entertainment probably was not amused," he thought back.

"No one enjoys being the subject of mockery," Mei-Ling spoke softly.

"I hope you don't think I mock you when I tell you I'd like to visit you once my assignment in Savannah is completed," Fabian helped her to stand.

"No, I don't think that. I simply think you're not ready for the strings that come with the attachment." Mei-Ling eyed him steadily.

"Where ever those strings lead, I can deal," Fabian told her.

Somehow, Mei-Ling believed he meant every word he spoke.

Rosalynn stood in one of the alcoves of the breezeway looking out at the view of the lighted acreage thinking about how much she had enjoyed the trip thus far. Carlton had stopped harassing her but was unfortunately bent on harassing Mei-Ling. She prayed that the Lord would put a stop to it. She could honestly say that she was over her anger at Carlton's revelation. Now she only had pity for him.

"Rosalynn?"

She turned swiftly at the voice that she could point out in her sleep. She gave him a brave smile. "Nicholas, hi," she looked up into his eyes, looking for any sign of wariness. She found none.

"How've you been?" Nicholas leaned against the wall of the alcove.

"I've been well," she managed to say.

"You look beautiful," Nicholas told her in his gruff manner.

Roz smiled demurely. "You clean up pretty good yourself," she complimented him.

"Listen, I know things between us have been kind of distant, but I want you to know that I'm here for you," Nick reminded her. "Are things between you and Carlton any better?"

Rosalynn figured it was time to come clean. "Nick, there's something you should know about Carlton and I. I don't know how to put into elegant terms what I want to tell you, so, I just come to the point. Carlton's not my brother."

Nick was glad he was leaning against the wall of the alcove. "When did you find out?"

"Before we left Savannah," Rosalynn drew in a cleansing breath. "I found out that I was adopted. He knew and he never told me."

Nicholas couldn't believe what he was hearing. Roz must have been devastated. Her parents had never told her. He came to stand behind her, resting his hands gently on her shoulders. "I'm so sorry your parents never told you," he murmured. "I can't even imagine how you must feel," Nick felt glad that Rosalynn had leaned into him for support.

"I'm just happy to know I'm not truly related to Carlton. My parents were great, but I had always felt disconnected from them; now I know why," Rosalynn was glad she had told Nick. Now there were no more secrets between them. "I've even changed my maiden name. It's Godschild now. Carlton has no more holds over me," Rosalynn was speaking more to herself than to Nicholas.

Nicholas kissed the top of head. "That's good news," he whispered.

Rosalynn turned in his arms then. "Here's more good news; I'm ready to move forward with my life and I can't think of any better person to share it with," Roz wrapped her arms around his neck and settled into his embrace.

56

Bible Study Rap Sessions

To the disappointment of some and the surprise of others Elder Worth had decided to split the Men and Women for Bible Study. The men would be hearing from Pastor Seth Davis and Elder Worth. The women would be hearing from Mother Vivian Worth. Guarding Your Heart was the topic of discussion.

Men's Bible Study

"You've got to *guard* your heart. You've got to *lead* your heart. You've got to *train* your heart. The heart is deceitful and who can truly know it but God?" Seth had stepped into his preaching mode. "You have to pray and ask God to show you what's in your heart that's not pure," he paced back and forth.

"The Psalmist penned, 'create in me a clean heart and renew a right spirit' for a reason. If we don't become men after God's own heart, we will find ourselves becoming men after our own carnal pleasures, living hedonistic lifestyles and searching for fulfillment in all of the wrong things, gentlemen." Seth took a moment to let the word of God settle in the hearts of the men.

"Out of our hearts flow the issues of life. Would you pour arsenic into your fountain? Well, when you jump headfirst into a relationship without giving thought to God and his plan for your life that is in essence what you are doing. When you allow your heart to be corrupted by pornography, the only thing that can flow out is impurity, lust, and disrespect for women. When you allow your affections to be distributed from woman to woman, you devalue yourself and your future relationships. When you drink from another man's fountain rather than the one God provided for your refreshment, you stand in danger not just from the consequences of sin, but from missing out on the very plans that God has in store for you." Seth handed the floor over to Elder Worth.

"This being said, gentleman, you need to know that when you don't guard your heart, when your emotions are not in check, when lust begins to take hold of your heart, you begin to act irrationally and outside of the perfect will of God," Elder Worth continued on, noting that several men were jotting down notes.

"When you are no longer thinking with the mind of Christ, but thinking with a certain member of your own body," he waited until the snickers died down, "then you will find yourself giving the ladies attentions they don't want, also known as stalking or harassment. You may find yourself giving in to the lusts of the flesh through heavy petting and fornication, which to those of you who are not familiar with the term is any kind of sex outside of marriage. You may find yourself opening up your emotions through the simple act of flirting. All of these things, some detrimental, some seemingly doing little harm are all signs that you have left your heart unguarded and have let some things in through your experiences, through the process of time, through your relationships that should not be there. Let me make plain for you, gentlemen, that there will be zero tolerance for harassment, sexual or otherwise, and stalking, or heavy petting. You are here for one purpose. If you can't abide by the rules of this trip, then your Pastors will take spiritual disciplinary action," Elder Worth motioned for Seth to come forward to pray for the men.

"Father, we ask that you look on each man present here tonight, and we ask that if there are any unsaved men among us that you save them and bring them into true, abiding faith in You, for they are powerless against temptation without Your salvation, Your Spirit, and Your empowerment through Your Holy Spirit. For those of us who profess your name, we ask that you forgive us. Forgive us for bringing shame upon you name, forgiving us for confusing others with our actions. Lord we ask that you create within us a clean heart and renew the right spirit within us.

Lord, we ask that you help us to get under this flesh, these carnal desires and urges that we have that are natural but need reservation until we are under covenant with our wives, help us to operate in self-control until that appointed time, as single men, and let every married man here drink from his own cistern and rejoice in the wife of his youth. Let her satisfy him always.

Finally Father, we ask for your wisdom, prudence, judgment, and guidance in the things we allow into our heart, cherish in our heart, and hold onto in our heart. Lead us not into temptation, but deliver us from evil. Help us to hear Your Spirit and follow your leading so we will not be taken in by flattering lips or deceitful tongues or beautiful forms. These things we ask in Your Son's name, the Name that alone saves, Jesus."

Seth was not surprised that God had moved on the hearts of the men present. He was surprised to see his brother on his face before God, Pastor Marks leading Dominic Francois in prayer, Elder Worth leading Carlton in the sinner's prayer, and Fabian Ciccone on his knees in prayer with Shemiah and Josiah. He stretched out his own hand over his brother and asked God to shape these men into Mighty Men. There was no telling what God would do through them if they opened their hearts fully to the Master.

Women's Bible Study

Vivian was in her element as she spoke so gently, but reprovingly to the ladies. Mother Worth was no shrinking violet when it came to ministering to women. She just nurtured and loved them right into truth.

"The Word of God says that we must guard our hearts, ladies. Guard, means to protect from harm, to keep watch at, to prevent from escape, to prevent damage, injury, or loss. Most guard positions are on the offensive, not defensive, ladies. When you guard your heart, you don't sit back and wait for things to attack you, or emotions to bombard you, you take initiative to keep your heart pure, your emotions in check, and your mind focused on the things that are true, honest, praiseworthy, and of good report.

We protect our hearts because the issues of life flow out of it. I know most of you here see yourselves as independent and self sufficient, and those concepts have their place. But not when it comes to your heart. Your heart can be damaged, harmed, injured, and suffer loss when you play emotional games. If your heart isn't in a relationship, you should never lead a man to think that it is. Flirting is one of the ways that we as women can play emotional games. If you're not offering a relationship, don't advertise it by flirting.

Let your yes be clear and your no be consistent. In my years of ministry, I have had the unfortunate circumstance of attending the funerals of young women who played dangerous emotional games. If you are unsettled and not at peace about a relationship, let it go until there is peace. Now, let me make this clear: I am not speaking to married ladies, here. If you are in covenant and your life is not in danger, there are some other steps you should be taking before considering separation or divorce.

But ladies, whether we want to admit it or not, we are many times drawn to or are in relationships for different reasons than men are. We are generally more emotional than men and tend to get attached quickly because of this. This is why, ladies, you should not wear your heart on your sleeve. God has no desire to see you come to harm or be taken advantage of. Sharing too much of your heart or sharing your heart too soon in a relationship could cause barriers later. A woman who retains no mystery will soon be history. This doesn't mean you should be secretive or hide past issues. It does mean that you shouldn't be divulging information to just anyone who comes along. They should not hear your life story the first time they meet you.

You, women of God, are treasure, to be searched for and sought out. Treasure hunters don't expect a map pointing directly to the treasure. Where's the fun in that? Treasure hunters operate by studying the object of their desire, studying the clues, and once they find their treasure, they examine it carefully. It may take the treasure hunter years to just unearth the treasure to get to the lock. Ah, but Treasure Plunderers, Pirates are not like that. They take without asking, they may not even take everything, just those things which strike their fancy. They may leave some things behind, throw some things away, sell some things because it brings a better profit than to hold on to it. So, what do you want, ladies? Do you want a Treasure Hunter, someone who knows the value of his find, someone who had done research and study, and knows exactly what he wants, who may have dedicated his entire life to the search of True Treasure, or do you want someone who doesn't know your value, comes and goes at will, uses you for gain, pulls you out for admiration to his friends when its convenient, mishandles you and violates your will? Only you can decide.

You decide who deserves of your heart, your body, your purity. He that finds a wife is finding a good thing and gaining the Lord's favor in the bargain. You have the distinct power of accepting or rejecting a proposal. Don't allow society to fool you into thinking you no longer have the power. You are treasure. You have the treasure. When you know you have diamonds, rubies, and pearls, why would you give yourself to a jeweler who only specializes in Cubic Zirconium? He will be hard pressed to recognize your value. You might find yourself married, but resentful, wishing you had waited for someone who was an expert, who could recognize your value.

Marriage is a holy, sacred estate, not to be entered into lightly, but with careful consideration of the will of God. And yes, hasty or not, God honors marriage between one man and one woman. Many have tried to take a divine institution and fit it to the dictates of civil law. I say, call same sex union a civil union. You can not ordain in earth what God did not ordain in heaven. Writing a law down here does not supersede God's Moral law set before the foundation of the earth. Forgive, me I do go on sometimes," Vivian sighed.

"But marriage is honorable ladies. Once you make that covenant, don't think that temptation will stop knocking at your own door. The Bible tells men to drink from their own cistern. I tell the young ladies in our ministry something similar: if he's not your husband, stop turning on your fountain. It's hard to for another man to drink from another fountain when the waters not turned on," she waited for the ladies to quiet down.

"Adultery is something that destroys not just your marriage, but family foundations. It distorts the image of Christ and the church and implies that God would cheat on his Bride or that His Bride will not be faithful to Him. It sends a damaging message about the Body of Christ, and because the rate of divorce in churches is no different right now than that of the world's I want you to admonish you to say 'I do' one time. Give your consent to marry with prayerful consideration. Make sure it feels right not just for the moment, but for a lifetime."

Angelynn led the ladies in a closing prayer.

"Heavenly Father, we come to you now, asking you to wrap your loving arms around each and every one of us. We come boldly to your throne of grace, asking for your forgiveness. Forgive us, Lord for our sins, individually and collectively. It is against you and you only we have sinned. We ask, Father, that you cleanse us from all unrighteousness and filthiness of flesh and spirit. We ask that you cleanse us from our secret faults. We ask that you blot out our transgressions and purge us from all our iniquities. We ask, Father, that you create within us a clean heart and renew the right spirit inside us. We ask, Father that you deliver us from ourselves, that you heal us from our pasts, that you free us from insecurities and self-destructive tendencies. We ask, Father that you heal the broken hearted here tonight, that you uproot bitterness, malice, wrath, envy, spitefulness, deceitfulness, flattering lips, and lying tongues.

Father, I pray that you make us more beautiful in Your Spirit than we are in form. I pray that you beautify us with salvation. We pray Father, that every woman here give her heart to you fully, commit her life to you. We pray Father, that you fill us again with your Spirit that you baptize us with the Holy Ghost and with fire as you promised. We pray that you would empower us to guard our hearts, to be virtuous women in singlehood and marriage. We pray that every single here would say yes to the right man, Your best choice that You picked out from the foundation of the world. Let every single here, experience Your peace and blessing from that yes. We pray Father that we would walk after and be led by Your Holy Spirit and that we would not walk after the flesh, for it cannot please you. We pray Father that we would not be silly women, carried away by enticing words or by own lusts. We pray Father that we would be wise, discreet, chaste, homemakers, women who lead men to God, women who let the Spirit guide our emotions, women who hear what your Spirit is saying. We pray that we will be able to apply your word in the timing and place and to the people who need to hear it.

Finally Father, we pray for the men in our lives, that they would be all that you have called for and designed for them to be. We pray that would be holy, excellent in spirit, and mighty in You, doing exploits for Your Kingdom advancement. We pray that the men who should not be in our lives and who are not for our good be exposed. Let every plan of the enemy concerning our hearts, be overthrown, dismantled, and brought to nothing. We ask these things in the precious name of Jesus," Angelynn finished. She looked around, not sure when she had dropped to her knees. The power of the Lord fell upon them as they were kneeling and bent over, each woman surrounded by the glory of the Lord, each woman being loved on by The Lover of her soul, the Omnipresent God, able to minister to every woman's heart, yet at the same time, keep the Earth tilted on its axis at the perfect angle to maintain all living things on the planet. *What a Mighty God!*

57

Montego Bay Final Day

Morning Bible Study

"I'm glad to see everyone ready and alert this morning for our study," Angelynn studied the faces of her fellow friends. It seemed that calmness had settled among the group. "I trust that everyone had an enlightening time in the study last night," Angelynn picked up her Bible. "Let us begin."

Several of the singles took turns reading aloud the passage of scripture Angelynn had selected. They had read the story of the woman with the issue of blood who had expended her time, money, and energy, seeking a cure and finding none. She had finally placed her expectation in Jesus and she had sought him out in the press of people, gaining access to the hem of his garment and being healed through her faith in his power.

"I want to talk to you about dealing with your issues," Angelynn laid her Bible carefully down. "If I had a title for what I would share this morning, I would entitle today's lesson, Take Your Issue to the One Who can Heal You. Jesus is our Issue Healer. He can take the most difficult thing that you face and heal it. The woman in the text was dealing with a very real, very tangible issue. She could not hide it. This issue isolated her, shamed her, impoverished her, and left her without hope.

Most of us haven't dealt with an issue this tangible. Some of us have had medical issues, but for the most part the issues we face can be well hidden, emotional issues guarded by our bubbly nature, or our comical gestures. Whatever the issue is, you must bring it to Jesus. He is the only one who can heal it. Just because your issue isn't seen by all doesn't mean that it's not affecting you. It's affecting the way you work, the way you live, the way you embrace or reject others, the way you interact with your spiritual leaders the way you love or withhold love from others.

There are three things that can happen to us when an issue goes unchecked: one, we learn to live with our issue, two, we learn to hide our issue, and three, we confine our lives because of our issue. I can speak from experience. I had an issue, and that issue was suspicion. I was always thinking the worst of whoever I encountered, especially if she was a woman. I had learned to live with my issue, hide my issue, and my life became confined because I got to know very few people because of my issue. I had to come to the point of recognizing it was an issue, and then deciding if I wanted to be free. There are some that don't want to be free of their issue because it draws attention to them, they get sympathy, and at least sympathy is better to them than being overlooked, and they have defined themselves, martyred themselves to their issue. After I decided I wanted to be free, I then had to submit myself to the Issue Healer. One of the biggest problems our society faces is that everyone thinks science and technology is the Issue Healer. God may use those methods, but He alone is The Healer. My challenge to you today, and after we leave Montego Bay is to examine your issues. After all, they aren't hidden to you. Ask yourself; am I like the woman in the text, taking my issues to the wrong people? Am I profiting by holding on to my issue? Do I really want to be set free from it? Consider these things today," Angelynn turned her time over to Mother Worth.

"Let's show some appreciation for all of our presenters during this Getaway," Vivian clapped, her eyes brimming with pride and admiration for her daughter-in-law. "That was very thought provoking, Angelynn. Thank you. Our prayer is that you have been blessed, strengthened, empowered, revitalized, and made better through the Word of God. We pray that you have been making an effort to get to know someone better during this time, strengthen your friendships, and seek forgiveness and reconciliation in the areas that you need to. Just some housekeeping reminders: make sure you pack early because we will be departing at four in the morning. For those of you going to Falmouth, departure is in thirty minutes. Please make sure you leave a tip in your hotel room for our maids as well as an encouraging word on the notepad in your rooms. Pastor Marks is going to give us our closing prayer."

Pastor Marks stepped forward. "Bow your heads, please. Gracious and Most Heavenly Father, we thank you for your mighty acts, your excellent greatness, and most of all, your personal care. You have kept us, watched over us, and protected us. You have allowed us to praise you in the firmament and enjoy the beauty of this earth. We pray Father that the principles we have learned and shared will stay with us, settle in our hearts, that your Word will ever be with us, that your peace will focus us, your grace will ever abound toward us. We pray that everyone here will seek peace and pursue it and that you will keep us this day in your care. We thank you again for raising Lysander to life Lord and showing us that miracles are still apart of your plan for the believer. We ask that you never leave us but go with us, in Jesus' powerful name, Amen.

Everyone departed their separate ways, some to pack, some to prepare for the wedding, some to go shopping in Falmouth, and some to make amends.

Falmouth

Dr. Zeeland Carr was back with his chipper personality to tell Enrique's team a little about the history of Falmouth as they shopped.

"Noted for being one of the Caribbean's best-preserved Georgian towns, Falmouth was founded by Thomas Reid in 1769, and flourished as a market centre and port for forty years at a time when Jamaica was the world's leading sugar produced. It was named after Falmouth in the UK, the birthplace of Sir William Trelawny, the Governor of Jamaica who was instrumental in its establishment," Dr. Carr beamed.

"Is he always this enthusiastic, I wonder?" Dominic looked to Fabian.

"I seriously doubt it. The dude has to have a social life. I hope this isn't it," Fabian chuckled.

Dr. Carr droned on, unaware of his guests disinterest. "The town was meticulously designed from its inception, with wide streets in a regular grid, adequate water supply, and public buildings. A little known fact is that Falmouth had piped water before New York City," Dr. Carr pointed to some historical structures along the way. "During the late eighteenth and early nineteenth centuries, Falmouth was one of the busiest ports in Jamaica, a wealthy town in a wealthy parish with a rich racial mix. This was the heyday of The Sugar Kings," Dr. Carr declared with a theatrical voice. "Within this parish, nearly one hundred plantations were actively manufacturing sugar and rum for export to Britain. Jamaica had become the world's leading sugar producer," Dr. Carr held up his sugar cane he had purchased.

"So who was producing this sugar?" Francheska asked

"I'm glad you asked," Dr. Carr clapped excitedly. "Falmouth became a central hub of the slave trade and the now notorious cross-Atlantic triangular trade, with its economy largely based on slavery. As a result, Falmouth's prosperity as a thriving commercial centre declined after the emancipation of slaves in the British Empire in 1840," Dr. Carr concluded. "The slave trade affected the world, Miss Cartellini. Sadly, other forms of slavery still exist," he shook his head sadly.

As Dr. Carr, walked on ahead, Francheska slowed down so that she could walk alongside Nick and Giovanni. "I'm going to apologize now, so pray me through," She whispered, and then sped ahead, not giving her cousins opportunity to tease her. They were busy anyway keeping the groom away from his bride to be.

"Lord, have mercy on Dominic," Giovanni prayed while his brother seconded his prayer with amen.

Thy King- Dom Come

"You mind if I walk with you?" Francheska had nearly had to run down Dominic, he was so far ahead of the crowd. The Italian Intel referred to it as scouting, searching out the territory ahead of the team to spot good observation points as well as trouble.

"No," Dominic was not in the mood for games today, not after last night's Bible Study. It had been sobering.

Francheska felt nervous and on edge. Dominic's guard was up and she couldn't blame him. They couldn't afford to be distracted so she would make her apologies quickly. "Dominic, I apologize for my behavior yesterday. It was out of line, unprofessional, and hurtful," her voice broke on that last word.

"Apology accepted," he stared straight ahead, not daring to look at her, knowing she would see straight to his heart. He didn't need that.

Francheska swallowed hard. "I meant to humiliate you and it was wrong. I was angry and I lashed out at you because I did like you and then you turned out to be someone else, and I wanted you to feel some of the humiliation I felt," she confessed.

"Who humiliated you?" Dominic frowned.

"It was all over the office. Apparently I was wearing my heart on my sleeve. They thought it was hilarious," her voice was etched with pain.

"I can see why you would be angry. After all, you had no way of knowing how I felt about you," Dominic glanced at her. "How I still feel about you in spite of everything," he laughed mirthlessly.

"You have every right to dislike me. Even I dislike me right now. I really do feel awful if it's any consolation," Francheska sighed.

"I don't dislike you, Francheska." Dominic glanced overhead continuing to scout the area. "We're colleagues. We're on a case. We need to get along, come to a truce," he declared.

Francheska could handle that. "That sounds good to me. I'll work on the humiliation thing. Being made to look like a fool *is* a pet peeve of mine," she warned.

"I am not soon to forget it, Francheska," Dominic's mouth tilted upward almost forming a smile as Francheska grabbed his hand to shake on it.

"You can call me Chess," Francheska gave him a playful shove. "All my friends do," she granted him a mischievous smile.

"Call me Dom," he gave her a reserved smile. *I'd like to call you mine*, he thought to himself. But it was not for this season. As Francheska waltzed back to her cousins, a spring in her step, he couldn't help but feel an urge to do the same, but he caught himself. *Guard, Guard, Guard.* It was his mantra for dealing with Francheska Cartellini.

Heart to Heart

Aliya put her hands to her cheeks. "You look absolutely stunning, Augusta. Enrique is going to be blown away," she breathed out.

"I love the material. It feels so comfortable," Augusta turned. She was wearing a strapless, beaded gown that cascaded in waves of organza that moved freely when she turned. It was flirty and whimsical, and so unlike Augusta that she knew Enrique would be surprised.

Aliya and Savannah were wearing custom made gowns that blended her tropical colors together. Aliya's was strapless and Savannah's and Mariella's gown was one-shouldered. They would carry white calla lilies while Augusta would carry fuchsia and orange calla lilies.

She seated herself so her stylist could begin arranging her hair. Her mother came to sit next to her.

"You look so beautiful, Ming," Phet gazed lovingly at her daughter, taking her by the hand. "I'm so excited about you both. From the time I first welcomed Enrique into our home, I knew he was the one for you," Phet's glimmered with unshed tears. "I'm so happy that you are marrying someone who loves you, respects you, cares for your family; you are going to have a wonderful life together," Phet kissed her cheek.

"Are there any words of advice for the wedding night?" Aliya giggled.

"Leave it to my twin to ask the hard questions," Augusta laughed.

Phet chuckled. "The first time usually hurts but not so much if you relax," she cleared her throat. "But just communicate. If something doesn't feel right, tell him. If something feels wonderful, make sure you tell him that too," Phet blushed. *Some things are never easy to talk about with your children.*

"Mom, you are the best. Liya, stop putting Mom on the spot," She chastised. "You need to start getting dressed. This is not going to be a long ceremony," she reminded her. Elder Worth had decided to turn the officiating over to Pastor Marks. His wife had ordered him to rest.

"Alright, I'm going," Aliya hustled out the door.

Phet turned to Augusta and leaned closer. "Now, here's what I really want you to know about your wedding night."

Going To the Chapel

The Jamaican Dreams Resort Chapel was beautifully appointed and large enough to hold one hundred guests. It had been decorated tastefully in the colors of the wedding with fuchsia calla lilies and white calla lilies for the occasion. Only a few knew who the happy couple was so seating was open. Everyone seated themselves waiting for the festivity to begin.

"This is really nice," Ginny commented as she followed Tehinnah, Columbia, Naomi and Rosalynn down the row. Seated behind them were Jamar, Noelle, and Carlton.
"I agree," Marco smiled as he sat down next to her.
Seated in front of Ginevieve were Kevin, Tatyanna, Greg, Jarah, Trey, and Aurielle.   To the right hand side were Fabian, Dominic, Giovanni, Nicholas, and Francheska. Sitting in front of them were Vivian and Elder Worth, Angelynn with the twins, and Mei-Ling.
"Some of us are going to miss the wedding," Ginny whispered to Marco. She noticed there were still a few of their friends who hadn't made it in yet.
"I think they are about to start," Marco put his finger to his lips.
Pastor Marks strode in from the side door, the Groom's party following him, and everyone gasped; almost everyone. "Surprise," Pastor Marks shot them a huge grin. "Let's celebrate the union of Enrique Estrada and Augusta Ming Peyton," he shouted as everyone stood to their feet, embarrassing Enrique with their hoots and hollers.
Everyone was seated as Enrique, Shemiah, Josiah, and Seth took their places. Then, the chapel door was opened and heads turned as they watched the procession of the bridesmaids. Savannah and Mariella walked so gracefully, floated really down the aisle as an acoustic guitarist played Great Is Thy Faithfulness. Next, Seth stepped down to meet Aliya halfway in the aisle. He bowed; she curtsied and turned to take his arm as he led her up to take her place as maid of honor.
An usher came and rolled out a white runner while two other regally dressed hostesses covered the runner with red roses, so much so, that the runner was overflowing and the pungent smell of freshly cut roses filled the air.
When they looked up, Augusta filled the doorway and no one could keep their eyes from darting back and forth from Augusta's fresh beauty to the groom's entranced gaze.
"She's definitely taken his breath away," Aliya murmured.
"Umm hmm," Savannah agreed, trying hard not to cry.

As the guitarist began to play, to the surprise of many, Enrique began to sing:

"How do you move me? Your grace it soothes me.
Your voice from a distance, keeps me reminiscent,
I don't know why, I won't lie,
You stir my soul, complete my whole;
God chose me to love you,
To have and to hold,
I do know why,
I constantly love you,
And all of the things that you do
Because my love, my love,
You are essentially you;
God chose you for me,
God chose me for you,
You are my love, my love,
I thank my Savior for you." He finished.

There was not a dry eye in the audience. Enrique had written that song but he had sung it only once. He had promised he wouldn't sing it again until their wedding day. He had kept his promise.

58

Call to Worship

"Good evening, and welcome to the ceremony that will unite Enrique and Augusta in marriage. We are gathered here in the sight of God, and in the presence of these witnesses, to join together this man and this woman in holy matrimony; which is an honorable estate, instituted of God. It is therefore, not to be entered into unadvisedly, but reverently, discreetly, and in the fear of God. Into this holy estate these two persons come now to be joined," Pastor Marks began.

"Doubly blessed is the couple which comes to the marriage altar with the approval and blessings of their families and friends. Who has the honor of presenting this woman to be married to this man?" Pastor Marks looked to Aslan and Phet Peyton.

"We do," The Peytons replied. Enrique eager went to hug Aslan and kiss Phet on the cheek causing some laughter from their friends.

Enrique took Augusta's hand in his and guided her carefully up the pulpit steps, Aliya helping her to adjust the train on her gown. "You look absolutely heavenly," Enrique murmured squeezing her hand.

"Enrique and Augusta, the covenant which you are about to make with each other is meant to be a sacred expression of your love for each other. As you pledge your vows to each other, and as you commit your lives to each other, we ask that you do so in all seriousness, and yet with a deep sense of joy; with the deep conviction that you are committing yourselves as God has ordained," Pastor Marks gave them a reassuring smile as he continued, "Hand in Hand you enter this covenant, and hand in hand you step out in faith into the will of God. The hand you freely give to each other is both the strongest and the tenderest part of your body. In your marriage you will need both. Be firm in your faithfulness. Don't loosen your grip on love. Be flexible as you go through transitions and seasons in life. Strength and tenderness, firm commitment and flexibility, make for a strong marriage," Pastor Marks addressed them.

"Also remember that you don't walk this path alone. Don't be afraid to reach out for help when together you face trials," Pastor Marks allowed for the amens to his statement. "Other hands are there: your friends, your family, and the church. To accept an outstretched hand is not an admission of failure, but an act of faith. Most importantly, don't forsake the outstretched arms of the Lord. It is into his hand, the hands of

God in Jesus Christ, that, above all else, we commit this union of husband and wife," Pastor Marks declared.

The Pledge

"Enrique, will you have Augusta to be your lawfully wedded wife, to live together in the covenant of faith, hope, and love according to the intention of God for your lives together in Jesus Christ? Will you listen to her inmost thoughts, to love, to honor, and cherish her, be considerate and tender in your care of her and stand by her faithfully in sickness and in health, and, preferring her above all others, accept full responsibility for her every necessity for as long as you both shall live?" Pastor Marks was deadly serious now.

"I will, I shall, I do," Enrique's voice rang out strong and clear. There would be no mistaking his commitment to this covenant.

Pastor Marks turned to Augusta then.

"Augusta, will you have Enrique to be your lawfully wedded husband, to live together in the covenant of faith, hope, and love according to the intention of God for your lives together in Jesus Christ? Will you listen to his inmost thoughts, to love, to honor, and respect him, be considerate and tender in your care of him and stand by him faithfully in sickness and in health, and, preferring him above all others, accept full responsibility for his every necessity for as long as you both shall live?"

"I will, I shall, I do," Augusta's voice was filled with emotion as she gazed with overwhelming love into the eyes of Enrique.

The Blessing of Rings

"May I have the rings? Let us pray. Father, I ask that you bless the giving and receiving of these rings. May Enrique and Augusta abide in your peace and grow in their knowledge of Your presence through their loving union. May the seamless circle of these rings become the symbol of their endless love and serve to remind them of the holy covenant they have entered into today to be faithful, loving, and kind to each other. Father, may they live in Your grace and be forever true to this union. Amen," Pastor Marks handed Enrique his ring and declared the vow as Enrique followed his lead.

"Augusta, I give you this ring as a symbol of our vows, and with all that I am, and all that I have, I love and honor you. In the name of the Father, and of the Son, and of the Holy Spirit; with this ring, I thee wed. With my body, I thee worship," Enrique slipped the ring on her finger, feeling the weight of God's presence upon him.

Pastor Marks led Augusta in her vow.

"Enrique, I give you this ring as a symbol of our vows, and with all that I am, and all that I have, I love and honor you. In the name of the Father, and of the Son, and of the Holy Spirit; with this ring, I thee wed. With my body, I thee worship." Augusta's voice was strong and clear though she blushed.

The Vow

Enrique felt the peace of God settle over him as he took his vows.
"In the name of Jesus, I Enrique Armande Estrada take you, Augusta Ming Peyton, to be my wife, to have and to hold, from this day forward, for better, for worse, for richer, for poorer, in sickness and in health, to love and to cherish, for as long as we both shall live. This is my solemn vow," he smiled. He was so ready to kiss her, but he held himself in check.

"In the name of Jesus, I Augusta Ming Peyton take you, Enrique Armande Estrada, to be my husband, to have and to hold, from this day forward, for better, for worse, for richer, for poorer, in sickness and in health, to love and to cherish, for as long as we both shall live. This is my solemn vow," she flashed him a blinding grin as he took her hand and led her carefully to light the unity candle.

The Light

Pastor Marks spoke as they returned to the pulpit.
"As you join now in marriage, there is a merging of these two lights into one light. This represents a man shall leaving his father and mother and be joined to his wife to become one flesh. From now on your thoughts shall be for each other rather than your individual selves. Your plans shall be mutual, your joys and sorrows shall be shared alike. You have extinguished your own candles, letting the center candle represent the union of your lives into one flesh. As that one light cannot be divided, neither shall your lives be divided but you will be a testimony of a united Christian home and a united marriage in Christ Jesus, the Light of the World."
Pastor Marks stepped forward.

"For as much as Enrique and Augusta have consented together in holy wedlock, and have witnessed the same before God and these witnesses, and thereto have pledged their faithfulness each to the other, and have pledged the same by the giving and receiving each of a ring, by the authority invested in me as a minister of the Gospel, I now pronounce them husband and wife together, in the name of the Father, and of the Son, and of the Holy Spirit. Those that God has joined together let no man put asunder. Let all people here and everywhere recognize and respect this holy union, now and forever," Pastor Marks turned to Enrique. "And now comes the fun part. Son, you may now kiss your bride," Pastor Marks chuckled.

A Holy Kiss

Enrique wasted no time obeying the Pastor as he gathered his wife in his arms and greeted her with a holy kiss. *Fireworks aren't supposed to be going off yet,* he thought as he fit his lips to the contour of Augusta's savoring the scent, the taste of her.

That's not outside. That's the Fire in your Spirit.

I have given you fire and passion for your wife. You are anointed to love her, cherish her, and care for her. You are empowered to be her husband and fulfill your covenant to the fullest.

Augusta heard a distinct clearing of Pastor Mark's throat as she came to herself blushing. She had totally lost track of where she was. *Wow: Amazing, Incredible, Wonderful. Thank you, God!*

You're welcome. You are anointed to love, bless, guard, honor, and care for your husband. You are empowered to be his wife and fulfill your covenant to the fullest.

"That's what happens when you wait to kiss," Pastor Marks chuckled, "all that pressure leads to a wonderful display. Join with me as we ask God's blessing on this new couple. Eternal Father, Redeemer, we now turn to You and as the first act of this couple in their newly formed union, we ask you to protect their home. May they always turn to You for guidance, for strength, for provision and direction. May they glorify You in the choices they make, in the ministries they involve themselves in, and in all that they do. Use them to draw others to Yourself, and let them stand as a testimony to the world of your faithfulness. We thank you, also, for consecrating this union. By the power of your **Holy Spirit**, pour out the abundance of your blessing upon Enrique and Augusta. We ask your defense from every enemy tactic, trap, plan, device, scheme, or snare. Lead them into all peace. Let their love for each other be a seal upon their hearts, a mantle about their shoulders, and a crown upon their foreheads. Bless them in their work and in their companionship; in their sleeping and in their waking; in their joys and in their trials; in their life and in their death. Bless the fruit of the womb and finally, in your mercy, bring them everlasting peace when that time comes through Jesus Christ our Lord, who with you and the Holy Spirit lives and reigns, one God, for ever and ever. We ask this in Jesus name, The Ultimate Bridegroom, Amen."

59

Fire Works

As everyone exited outside to the reception by the waterfall, Fire Works illuminated the sky. Aslan had arranged for a fireworks show for the outdoor reception. It was Fourth of July weekend for the States and he wanted to bring a bit of that celebration to Jamaica for his daughter.

Augusta was taking the time beforehand to greet the ladies.

"Oh, this was one of the most beautiful weddings I've ever been to," Mei-Ling hugged Augusta carefully, not wanting to get makeup on her gown. "You are positively glowing, cousin!"

"How could she *not*?" Tehinnah teased. "Did you see that kiss? I coulda' I was Moses looking at the burning bush," she laughed.

"Fire Works, girl, Fire Works," Aliya sang as she sped by.

"It was such an intimate wedding. I'm so glad you guys shared your moment with us," Ginevieve was still wiping away tears as she gave Augusta a kiss on the cheek.

"So many people are doing these huge, gaudy, weddings, and its so performance. But tonight, tonight was the real deal. I could feel the love literally emanating from you two. It was surreal," Tatyanna gushed.

"Two of my favorite people tied the knot," Roz held Augusta's hand. "You could have gotten married in a canoe for all I care; I'm just glad I witnessed it. It was amazing. Enrique is such an amazing man and you, my friend are uniquely beautiful. You two deserve each other in the best way," Roz quickly hugged her.

Augusta was overwhelmed by all of the love and support as she feasted her eyes on her husband who was being overtaken with his own crew of well wishers.

"I must say, bro, that was a Top Notch affair back there," Jamar greeted Enrique shoulder to shoulder.

"You made me cry, man. Totally unacceptable," Giovanni grinned. "You know that's Nick's style," he chuckled.

"Watch it, Gio," Nick playfully shoved his twin out of the way to give Enrique an off the ground hug. "It was beautiful, man. The night is only going to get better," he grinned ear to ear.

"Nice wedding," Carlton nodded to him choosing to keep his distance.

Shemiah and Josiah both rushed Enrique lifting him off the ground, onto their shoulders. "Hey!"

The rest of the men joined in with shouts and catcalls. They finally put him back down when Elder Worth called them to order for the blessing of the food.

I Thee Worship

"It was a beautiful night," Augusta tried to make small talk as she entered into the penthouse suite that had been prepared for them.

Aslan had sent them on their way after they had eaten to the wing of the resort that was unoccupied. Their security detail was guarding the wing at each end. They would not be leaving just yet. He and Augusta would spend another day at the family home in Kingston.

"Allow me," Enrique wanted to cherish every moment of this night. He brushed her hair aside, removing the flower in her hair, kissing her temple as he did so. "You smell wonderful," he whispered in her ear.

Augusta felt the rhythm of his voice slide like warm water down into her spirit. "It's jasmine and calla lily. My mother had the Spa prepare it for me," she gasped, surprised by the feel of his lips making a trail from her nape to her left shoulder.

Enrique made a mental note to see if he could have it shipped to the States- By the caseload. He unzipped her slowly, allowing the material to fall away of its own accord. *My Lord.* He turned Augusta in his arms, allowing her to feel the heat of his gaze.

"I keep telling myself. I'm married now. This is not a sin," he joked.

Augusta laughed nervously. "I know what you mean. I've been deprogramming my mind since we started the reception. Weird isn't it?"

Enrique could only nod as she began unbuttoning his dress shirt. He could form no words as she stood before him in all her royal splendor, fearfully and wonderfully made. *Body by God,* he thought to himself.

"I made a promise, Mr. Estrada, and I intend to keep it," she warned.

Enrique allowed her to remove his shirt before impatience kicked in and he began removing clothes like a man on the run. "Which promise?"

Augusta was taking in the fact that her husband was blessed and highly favored. "With my body, I thee worship," the words flowed out on a breathless sigh.

Enrique drew his wife into his embrace. "Who am I to stop you from keeping your word?"

60

Back in Savannah, GA

"How are you holding up?" Tatyanna popped her head into the copy room where Jamar stood, using the copier as a prop for his weary body.

"Pretty good, considering," Jamar yawned. They had touched down at nine this morning and had opened shop at noon to meet customer deadlines with graphics deliveries. Tatyanna was in charge this week due to Augusta's honeymooning.

"Ginny and I are going to Riverstreet Bakery for lunch; want to join us?" She was hoping her sister would join them. She had the day off.

"Thanks for the invite, but sleep is what I need," Jamar yawned again. He was feeling the effects of staying up all night and horse playing with Seth, Noelle, and Kevin. They had played water basketball with the leftover wedding favors. It had been great fun but he was definitely paying the price. Seth, Noelle, and Kevin had taken the day off because they could.

"Alright, well, you can head out once the last delivery truck is back, okay?" Tatyanna felt sorry for him. She knew her fiancé had kept him out all night, not taking into account that he was a college student with responsibilities.

"Thanks, Taty," Jamar yawned again.

Tatyanna shook her head and strolled on down the hallway to her office. *I think Jamar learned his lesson.*

Savannah greeted the students at S.P.I.C.Y. (Second Chance Prep School for Inner City Youth); glad they were ready to get back to work. It was challenging keeping students energetic and excited about their studies during the summer months, especially when their friends were going on vacation, hanging out at the community center, or sleeping in.

"Hi, Miss Van," Delia waved excitedly, as she ran up and latched onto Savannah's hip.

Savannah felt her love radiating from within, her grin a series of spaces and teeth. Delia was a joy to have at the school. "Hi, Dee," She brushed her bangs in place. "It's so good to see you. How are you?"

"I'm spantastical!" Dee giggled looking up at Savannah like she was a human skyscraper.

"Is that another one of your new words?" Savannah teased.

"Yep," Dee nodded with pride. "I think I'm going to be a dictionarian one day," she told her with a serious face.

"A *what*," Savannah gave Delia a puzzled look.

"A dictionarian; a person who studies and works with dictionaries," she added knowingly.

Savannah laughed. "As long as you can define it, I'm sure you'll make sure it becomes a word," Savannah assured her as she walked her to her next class.

Columbia's Classy Cuts

Columbia was back and business was in full swing. Tony had kept things rolling at the shop and along with her daughter's help cleaning the shop, things had run fairly smoothly. Except for Gertrude showing up in her absence; apparently she had given Tony a run for his money. It wasn't until he threatened to call the cops that the woman had decided to split.

"I tell you, Columbia, you need to brace yourself for whatever that woman has planned. She's definitely up to something," Tony warned as he brushed the debris from his client's nape then swung him around, whipping off his cape with one fluid motion. "You're all done, player." Tony collected his money.

Columbia shook her head as she pressed the toddler's hair in front of her. "I'm not worried about Miss Gertrude. God has my back," Columbia declared.

"Yeah, well, you just--" Tony stopped midsentence, pointing at the rock on her hand. "Where did *that* come from?"

Columbia laughed to herself. She had been wondering how long it would take for Tony to notice. "Oh, this," Columbia held up her hand, admiring the two-carat diamond. "I got it from my fiancé," she told him casually, watching his expression go from confusion to comical.

"Stop lying." Tony stood there, his mouth agape in disbelief.

"John and I got engaged two days ago in Montego Bay," Columbia gave him a pointed look, daring him to say something slick.

Tony cracked a grin. "That sly devil," his grin widened.

Columbia gave him a warning look. "I don't think he would appreciate that comment," she lowered her chair so her client could hop down. Her mother would return shortly to pick her up.

Tony shrugged. "It is what it is," he sanitized his tools for the next customer. "I'm happy for you, really I am," he wiped down his station.

"I hear a 'but' coming," Columbia folded her arms in defense. "So let's hear it," she urged him.

"You'll get no flack from me," Tony admitted. "But that doesn't mean you won't get flack," he added.

"Well, I'm not worried about the haters. I love him, my children love him, and whoever has a problem with it, can file their complaints with Jesus. From what I hear, he takes forever to answer those," Columbia shook out her apron.

She and Tony worked in amicable silence, each one thinking about how others would react to her engagement.

Columbia knew whatever their reaction it would not change the truth: God was for them.

A Taste of Savannah Restaurant

"How was your day?" Seth tucked Aliya into her chair and seated himself.

"Pretty busy surprisingly," Aliya stretched her arms. "Savannah and her mom were in today for their final fitting," Aliya shared. "Then Savannah had her final fitting today. Augusta is the last of her bridal party to be fitted, and then I had a couple who are interested in having a lavish twenty-fifth anniversary celebration and they want a matching tux and gown and also I got a call from EAE Design Group about featuring some of my illustrations as greeting cards for a new line they want to market called 'It Girl'," she finish with an exhale of breath.

Seth smiled at the twinkle of excitement in her eyes and the energy that always seemed to permeate her words. He had been trying to figure out how he was going to propose, and it had finally dawned on him how to show her how much he appreciated and loved everything about her. He had wanted to propose during their trip, but he hadn't wanted her to think he was under pressure to do so. He would do it Friday, but he needed a little help from his friends and hers.

"What's that smile on your face about? Seth Davis, you look like you are up to no good," Aliya giggled.

"Trust me, honey, when I tell you it's good. All good," Seth smiled mischievously.

Check-Up

Shemiah stepped into Zara's family room where his cousin was currently propped up recovering. Lysander was staying with his mother until he was fully recovered. Shemiah had gotten off the plane and headed straight for Hilton Head to see his parents and check up on his cousin.

"Ise, man, I didn't expect to see you here," Lysander's voice resonated with strength and vitality.

Shemiah settled himself into his aunt's worn recliner. Zara was known for holding on to furniture past the expiration date, despite the fact that her successful son had tried several times to talk her into getting something up to date. "How're you feeling?"

"I'm alive, I'm breathing, not pushing up daisies; I'd have to say I'm doing pretty good. How did your trip go?"

"Everyone was excited about your resurrection, one of my best friends got married, and I received another outpouring of God's Spirit. I couldn't have asked for a better time. Savannah said to tell you hello, and to mention to you that she's added you to the guest list now that she knows you're not a Wedding Crasher," he joked.

Lysander held up his hands in mock surrender. "Far be it from me to get in the way of what God has joined together," Lysander stated enthusiastically. "Hey, man, I've learned not to box with God," he declared emphatically.

Shemiah took his words in earnest and took that message to heart. He was glad that Lysander's confession and conviction remained strong. He prayed his cousin would move forward and leave no room for returning to the past.

Girl Time

Naomi, Aurielle, and Mariella sat enjoying the breeze and warmth of the sun as they gazed out on the river way. They had stuffed themselves with the delicious strawberry cheesecake from the Riverstreet Bakery. It had taken all three of them to eat one slice so thick was the cheesecake, perfectly topped with glazed strawberries that looked like they came straight from the Promise Land. They rubbed their tummies, giggling at how silly they looked.

"Oh, there should be a law against cheesecake being that good," Mariella licked her lips once more. She could still taste the strawberries.

"I agree, although, I can think of other things there should be a law against," Naomi giggled. "I'm still thinking about that kiss Enrique planted on Augusta. I thought he was going to devour her right there in the pulpit!"

"It was so passionate; one of these days, I'm going to experience that same passion," Aurielle sighed dreamily, admiring her engagement ring.

"Have you set a date yet?" Mariella asked.

"Jeez, girl, we just got engaged!" Aurielle swatted her.

"*Sorry*, I was just asking," Mariella playfully shoved her.

"Who knows, you may be the one tying the knot before me," Aurielle challenged her.

"If she would stop giving Noelle the cold shoulder, maybe," Naomi added.

"Look who's talking," Mariella pointed her finger at Naomi.

"Giovanni and I aren't even courting, much less thinking about getting engaged," Naomi confessed.

"So what's the hold up?" Aurielle wondered.

"Where have you been, Aurielle? Surely you had to know Fabritza Ciccone was practically throwing herself at him the entire trip. Until she disappeared," Mariella smiled knowingly.

"Well, Naomi, then what are you waiting on?" Aurielle questioned.

"I'm waiting on God," Naomi shrugged.

"No, honey, God is waiting on you," Aurielle patted her friend on the shoulder. "Giovanni has already made his feelings known. You've got to do your part or this relationship is going to be stuck on the runway," Aurielle insisted.

"I understand what you're saying, but until God gives me the go ahead, I'm not forcing the issue," Naomi was firm in her conviction. "He's got more important things to worry about right now than courting," Naomi reasoned. *Like a woman scorned and shipped off to another country.*

Mark My Words

Noelle leaned against the kitchen counter observing the domestic scene before him and wishing he inspired just an ounce of that kind of love in Mariella Estrada. *It seems as though hell is going to have a snowy day at the rate things are going between us.* He couldn't help Mariella's issues but he could help his own. Columbia and his father looked happy together, her daughters seemed contented to see their mother happy and were welcoming his father to get involved in their lives. All was as it should be. If he was going to move forward, he had to put behind the notion that all women were conniving, faithless, and evil. Mariella had shown him that wasn't the case. Columbia had shown him that a woman's past didn't have to define her future. *Lord, help my unbelief. I want to deal with my issues. Help me be free of them so that I don't damage these new relationships, this new branch of my family you are grafting in.*

Son, be made whole according to your faith.
Lord, I receive, Noelle prayed.

"I never got a chance to officially congratulate you two," Noelle came and joined everyone at the table for a late lunch.

"Well, thank you, son," Columbia teased him.

Noelle rolled his eyes heavenward. "Lord, please have mercy on me," Noelle groaned playfully.

"This is going to be great," Nadia exclaimed, giving Noelle a great squeeze.

"You're cutting off my cir-cu-la-tion," Noelle managed to choke out.

Rodia ganged up on him too. "Our very own big brother," she sighed, imagining the many ways they could torture him.

Noelle read her thoughts a mile away. "A brother who has his own home which will be completed shortly," he promised, as soon as he could convince Mariella to finish what she started; In more ways than one.

"We could have a slumber party at your house," Dee squealed in youthful delight. "It will be fanterrifical!" she clapped her hands together.

"Fanterrifical? I've studied English and law, and I know that's not a word," Noelle laughed at the sheer genius of it. "What's that school teaching?"

"It's fantastical and terrific put together," Rodia supplied. "It's one of Dee's little quirks; she has many for you to learn."

Nadia gasped as she received revelation of what joining the Marks clan would mean for them. "Rodia,"

"What?" she stared at her twin, wondering what in the world she could be so excited for.

Nadia waved her hands excitedly. "We've g-got another babysitting partner," she stuttered.

Noelle shrugged off the little imps. "Oh, no you don't," he shook his head adamantly. "I see where this is going so I'm jumping ship right now. I'm not about to get stuck babysitting while everyone else goes off to live happily ever after," Noelle gave the twins a look of stern disapproval.

He was doing fine until he felt a little finger poking his kneecap. "Don't you love me, Noel Well? Don't you wanna play with me? I know lots of words and you can help me make them up; you're my big brother and I love you so much, "she stared at him with trust and sincerity and it was all Noelle could do to resist picking her up and setting her in his lap. *Dagnabit-- Sucker punched by a pair of almond shaped eyes and a quite little pout!* Noelle had no doubt about it. Someday, Delia was going to be one little beautiful heartbreaker.

Wise Women

"We are so thankful you two made it back alright," Gram Parker carefully set her tea down on the coffee table in front of her. "So many thing happen these days, what with all these people thinking they're doing God a favor by taking human lives; its all so tragic that so many lives have been cut short in the name of God," Gram seemed to be lost in her own thoughts then.

"We're glad to be back," Marilyn stroked Savannah's hair as she lay curled up in fetal position against her. It felt good to relax and enjoy her daughter's company. "Everything is set, and in order for Saturday," she assured them.

"Good," The women who had been best friends since before their children's birth looked to each other and then to Savannah and Marilyn. "Since you are both getting married within a month of each other, we thought it best to share with you our time-tested, marriage-proven tips for a long and lasting marriage," Gram Parker began.

"These tips will be placed in the hope chest you will receive during your wedding receptions," Gram Tot explained, "but we wanted to share them with you now."

Gram Parker rolled out her scroll. "Tip number one: never go to bed angry. Tip number two: let him leave the toilet seat up; let him sit on the throne the way he needs to, Tip number three: shower together; no explanation necessary, Tip number four: give your offering together, Tip number five: Never let your man walk out the door without these simple words; I love you, I need you, and I look forward to your return you handsome man, you, Tip number six: praise your man in public, disagree in private, Tip number seven: stay in shape and take care with your appearance more than when you were single, Tip number eight: Let him become familiar with your fragrance by avoiding perfumes that cover it, Tip number nine: keep your marriage bed between you, your husband, and God alone, and Tip number ten: pray with and for each other everyday and attend services together whenever possible. Tip number eleven: Remember, an enemy to your husband can never truly be a friend to you, and lastly Tip number twelve: Don't allow any other woman privileges that are reserved for you as his wife alone; he is not a tool to be used, a car to be leased out, or a sword to use as a weapon. He is your husband. Reverence, respect, honor, listen to, pray for, compliment and speak well of him, and his heart will trust in yours and he will have no fears or reservations about your role as the queen of his kingdom and the co-heir and ruler by his side," she finished.

"Let's pray," Gram Tot knelt next to her daughter and grandchild, anointing their heads with oil as she prayed in her heavenly language. She then spoke with understanding. "Father in heaven, Gracious and kind Redeemer, Father of the Eternal Groom, our Kinsman Redeemer, we ask that you look on your dear daughters, Savannah and Marilyn. We ask that you bless their unions that shall take place. We ask that you give them the strength to hold fast to the holy covenant which they have betrothed themselves to. We ask that you fill their preparation, their ceremonies, and their union with Your glory. We asked that You show up. Manifest your presence, Lord and let all who witness and partake of their lives, be assured that you are a Faithful Husband to your people, as they give testimony of this truth through their marriages. We make these requests by the power and authority of your son Jesus Christ. Amen."

The women held onto each other, a ring of love, a circle of generations bound together by the promises of God.

No one was aware of the angel sent to pour out the prayers of the generation before them, anointing them to serve the present generation. No one saw the angel collecting their prayers and reserving them for the generation to come. That angel was curious about that word, Redemption, but it had not been given him to understand. He danced back into heaven on the flame of fire that burned fervently on the altar of prayer they had built.

393

61

July 7

Fabian and Dominic stood like towering oaks as Enrique, Augusta, Nicholas, Giovanni, and Francheska exited the jet, the newlyweds looking refreshed and energized, the security team looking relieved that they were finally on American soil once more. Dominic didn't allow his eyes to stray towards Francheska's slender frame though he was more than tempted to.

"Welcome Home, Mrs. Estrada," Fabian greeted Augusta. His boss had made an excellent choice in a wife. Augusta was discreet, prudent, intelligent, and not to mention beautiful. Fabian thought about Mei-Ling then. They had parted ways regretfully; Mei-Ling giving him her email address and cell number to keep in touch, but no invitation to visit. Fabian was disappointed but not surprised.

"Thank you!" Augusta's eyes sparkled with the glow of matrimony. "You're one of the first to call me that," she shared. Seth had called for Mrs. Estrada while she was overseas and told her of his plans to propose. They were all going out to dinner where they were going to punk Aliya. Enrique had helped by getting his company EAE Design Group to get an early rendering of her card ready. She was to check the card for errors.

"Glad I could be of service to you," Fabian smiled.

Enrique greeted Fabian and Dominic with a firm handshake. "Thank you both for your excellent care while we were overseas. Giovanni and Francheska will oversee my wife's protection while she attends her fitting today with our sister," Enrique smiled when he thought of Aliya, "While Nicholas will join us back at the house. We have much to finalize concerning security reassignments. Thank you, Dom, for making sure Augusta's things were packed up for her so that she could make a quick transition to our home," Enrique truly appreciated an agent who had forethought and efficiency in good measure.

"Not a problem, Mr. Estrada," Dominic assured him. "A satisfied Mademoiselle makes for a happy Mari," he offered. "Mari, is a husband: don't worry, you shall be well versed in French by the time I am gone,"

Enrique chuckled. "Trying to make me trilingual are you?"

"It never hurts to learn French," Augusta whispered in his ear as they were ushered into her wedding gift, a new SUV, "after all, you already have the French kiss down to an art," she murmured.

Enrique had a hard time with any further conversation after that. *Lord, thank you for my Good Thing!*

God, thank you for the courage to be here, Rosalynn prayed, *and please help me to resolve to live in peace.*

"I appreciate your coming," Carlton sat at his kitchen table; his hands clenched together, his face etched with uneasiness.

Rosalynn just stared at him, her face a mask of indifference. She waited patiently for him to get to the point of this requested visit.

"I want to express to you that I am sorry for the way I have acted towards you," he began, "I deliberately hurt you in an effort to control you and as a result, I lost the only sister I've ever known. I'm not proud of my actions. I honestly believed that Nicholas was up to no good, and I can't say I like the guy, but he does care for you," his frown turned into a quick smile, gone before it could settle. "That much is clear," he admitted.

Rosalynn felt some of the tension leave her body. "Well, I accept your apology but the feelings of humiliation and deception are still with me. I don't hate you, Carlton, and I don't wish you harm; I just don't trust you anymore," Roz, stood then to rid herself of her nervous energy. "You have to understand, that for a long time you were my esteem; when you lost weight, I won; when you became a champion weight lifter, I did too: when you became world renowned for your fitness and body sculpting techniques, I basked in the same spotlight. Why? Because you were my brother. I was so proud of you. I was so excited the day you told me you were moving here. I pumped up the entire church community about how great you were. Together, I thought to myself, we are unstoppable—the church isn't going to know what hit them!" Roz turned to face him then, letting him see her tears that had been flowing as she poured out her feelings. "Then, little by little, you began taking that sunshine, that spotlight away from me. The weight jokes, the offhand comments about y ability to do things independently, the depth of your sincerity that no one could possibly interested in me. Suddenly the brother I had idolized like a Wonder of the World became a pillar of salt," Roz sat down to face him once more. "I was devastated. When you told me the truth, you snatched the rug from under me, Carlton, for the greater truth was revealed: you had never cared for me in the way I had always cared for you. I was never the sister you were proud of; I was the sister you pitied, because you knew I was living vicariously through your success. Once I started experiencing and achieving success on my own, the game was up. You needed me to feed your ego just as much as I needed you to feed my self-esteem. It was simply unhealthy and I am glad that it came to an end, though I'm not happy about how it came to an end." Roz stared into his eyes, now welled with tears and realized that Carlton Rhodes had finally come to the end of himself. "My question to you, Carlton, is where will we go from here? I can't go back to being that needy, overweight, insecure girl; you can't go back to being that muscle-bound, egotistical, self-important guy. We're not family, we owe each other nothing but cordial communication."

"I'll take cordial any day over never speaking again," Carlton conceded. "And, Rosalynn, I will work to build back the trust I destroyed."

"Let's pray and ask God to help us keep working at this relationship," Rosalynn took her hand in his, and for the first time in a long while, she felt renewed hope.

Ginny was pouring over some outstanding accounts at the secretary's computer when the bell overhead rang signaling entry into Alpha, Inc. She had sensed Marco's presence before she even looked up.

"Delivery for Ms. Ginevieve Dubois," Marco had been none too pleased with the gentleman who had called in the delivery, refusing to give his name.

Ginny looked up in surprise. "From *who?*" she questioned warily.
"The sender chose to remain anonymous," Marco's brow furrowed together. *Just how many other admirers did she have?*

Ginny took the card thinking it was a joke. *Maybe Marco is trying to wind me around his finger.* She read the card puzzled. "Are you pulling my leg?"

Marco's perfect lips formed a frown of epic proportions. "I thought you were pretty clear on where we stand. I would not risk getting cut off from you completely by disrespecting your wishes," he reminded her.

"I have no idea who sent them, but since you arranged them so beautifully, I'll keep them," she gave him a sweet smile.

Marco grinned like the besotted man he was and went on his way thinking the delivery had been worth his trouble after all.

Jamar sat at his desk and admired his own genius. Marco and Ginny were meant for each other. They just needed a little help realizing it. He would send Ginny a mysterious bouquet from a secret admirer every once in a while from Marco's shop. Marco had decided that he was going to see Ginny only when necessary. Jamar would make necessary happen quite a bit until it was too late for them to realize it. *I do love playing matchmaker,* mused. Jamar had decided that until he could find happiness of his own, he'd use his time making his friends happy. He hoped.

Mariella was surprised to find Noelle Marks waiting for her outside her home. He stood as she entered the gates, meeting her halfway.

"This is certainly different: what brings you by?" Naomi walked past him up the steps to her door.

"Hear me out first, before you send me packing," Noelle took some of bags off her hands. She had gone shopping for a newlywed gift and wanted to give it to Enrique and Augusta later when they met up for the Celebratory dinner at the new French restaurant Manifique.

Mariella ushered him in, taking time to unload her things while he settled into the quaint living room she shared with Naomi. "Have a seat; I'll be there in a moment," she informed him.

Noelle sat on the cozy loveseat, taking in his eclectic surroundings. He noticed a framed picture of Mariella and Naomi and was struck by how uncannily alike they looked. His eyes wandered over the mock mantelpiece where pictures of Mariella in Costa Rica with her father sat. There were also several pictures of her with children. Noelle could picture her in his mind's eye with their children. She would love. She would—

"So, to what do I owe this official visit?" Mariella sat down opposite him, taking in his anxious body language.

Noelle got down on one knee.

Mariella rolled her eyes and stood up. "Don't even think about it," she walked away and then paced back to stand in front of him.

"What do you think you're doing?" Mariella set her mouth into a disapproving frown.

"I've come to ask you back. I've come to ask you to finish what you started, Mariella." Noelle was confused by her obvious annoyance.

"Oh."

Then it dawned on him. "What did you think I was doing?"

Mariella waved her hand in a silly gesture. "Oh, nothing; anyway, we both know it's not a good idea for me to come back to work for you," she added.

"God seems to think it's a good idea. He seems to think you and I are a good idea; and I'm inclined to believe Him," Noelle stood slowly.

"And trust me when I tell you that when I propose, it will demonstrate how much I value you as the woman who will compliment me in life and ministry," Noelle moved to the door, "so you can run all you want, Mariella, but this is a fair warning: What I want, I pursue; what I pursue, I pursue relentlessly; what I gain, I cherish forever." Noelle reached for the door and opened it, turning to look her way one more time. "I look forward to the sweet victory of winning you over," he flashed a handsome and lethal grin.

As he closed the door, Mariella wondered if she should have just agreed to work for him. Then, she heard the Voice of God.

Anything worth having is worth the patience. Let patience have its perfect work. Stand still and see the surrender of Noelle Marks. He will not win you until he wins Me.

Chance Encounter

Tehinnah stepped into her favorite pastry shop to pick up her blueberry cheesecake. She had a love-hate relationship with cheesecake: she loved what it did to her taste buds but hated what it did to her waistline. She saw her blueberry cheesecake waiting for her on the counter, freshly made. She had made friends with baker upon arriving to the city and he was great about having her supply of cheesecake when she called ahead ready and waiting. She had already cut out a piece and raised it to her lips when he heard a choking sound behind her. She turned to see what the problem was, blueberry already staining her lips.

"Why are you eating my cheesecake?" Jamar managed to choke out. He had just paid for it and told the cashier he'd be right back. He stared in disbelief at Tehinnah Adams devouring a slice of *his* cheesecake as if all was right with the world.

Tehinnah shook her head. "This is my cheesecake. I ordered it hours ago. The baker always leaves it out on the counter for me. Nobody in these parts orders blueberry cheesecake," she laughed off his offence.

"Wrong. Blueberry Cheesecake is one of my favorite. I bought this one because the cashier told me it was the last one being made for the day," Jamar added.

"For me," Tehinnah argued.

"Where's your receipt?" Jamar held his own up in the air in challenge.

"I was going to pay when I got here," she stomped her foot as Jamar sidled over and swiped the uneaten portion of the pie off the counter. "Hope you enjoyed that slice," he taunted, "'cause that's all you'll be getting," he promised.

Tehinnah realized he was right: someone hadn't communicated and now she was out of her comfort food unless she did something drastic. "Wait!" she grabbed his arm.

Jamar turned slowly and looked down at her firm grip on his arm. "I hope you're not about to mug me over cheesecake," he chided her.

Tehinnah gave him her sweetest smile. "Surely you wouldn't think of leaving a lady standing here with expectations of drinking coffee and eating cheesecake without the hope of getting another slice would you?"

This girl is good, Jamar thought to himself. "What incentive do I have to offer you another slice? I mean, it's not as if we're seeing each other; I mean, if that were the case, I wouldn't hesitate, but, seeing as we're nothing of the sort, then..." he let his words trail off, seeing how far he would have to go to get a response out of her.

"Jamar," Tehinnah moved towards him slowly, looking him in the eyes as she came chest to chest, her right hand curved upward to his head, stroking his hair. "I thought we were done playing games," she leaned in her lips a hairsbreadth away from his. "But I guess not," she turned and spun away.

Jamar stood there a full five minutes before he realized Tehinnah had given him an almost-kiss and left him standing with his hand still outstretched to hold a cheesecake that was on its way home with her. *I've been sucker- punched.*

Celebratory Dinner at Manifique!

It was the eve of her mother's wedding and one month before her own nuptials and Savannah could hardly contain her excitement. Marilyn was being treated to a WOW Shower by the Mother's Board at Second Chance, an event for women over forty who were either re-marrying or marrying for the first time. Marilyn had insisted Savannah spend time with her younger friends rather then attend with her. She had blushed at the thought of her daughter hearing the older women roast her which they were bound to do as the showered her with 'WOW', Words of Wisdom. Savannah was just grateful that tomorrow her parents would be married! She still stood in awe and wonder at how God had reunited them, healed them, and ordained an awesome future for them. There was talk of them moving to Hilton Head to help establish Second Wind, the satellite church for Second Chance. Savannah knew she would hate to see her parents move, but it wouldn't be too far away. They had a purpose and calling just as much as she did and she respected that. The dinner tonight was just a small gathering of the crew from Montego Bay; not everyone could attend on short notice, but Savannah knew that something big was about to go down. She could feel it.

Mariella, Naomi, Seth, Aliya, Enrique, Augusta, Savannah, Shemiah, Nicholas, Giovanni, Francheska, Tatyanna, Kevin, Jamar, Marco, Aurielle, Josiah, Angelynn, and Ginevieve had all gathered to welcome Enrique and Augusta back from Montego Bay. What did not know, was that this gathering was a front. Seth had masterminded the whole thing along with his partners in sneaky, Enrique and Augusta. The French cuisine had been delicious and exquisitely prepared. Conversation was rolling smoothly and Aliya and Enrique were having a lively discussion about her designs being used as greeting cards for his company.

"As a matter of fact, I brought a sample with me," Enrique reached into his inside coat pocket. "This one is fresh off the press," he held it up so everyone could see.

Aliya was bubbling over with joy. "You sure do move fast on an idea," she noted.

Enrique handed her the card while Seth excused himself. "Here, why don't you read it out loud? It's got a great inscription. You can keep as a memento for your first 'It Girl' series cards.

Aliya read the outside of the card.

"You're the 'It Girl'
Of My Dreams"

"That's so sweet," Aliya opened the card.

"I'd love to spend the rest of our lives,
Greeting you every morning,
As the 'It Girl' of my Reality.

Aliya China Peyton
Will you do me the honor
Of accepting my hand in marriage?

From your 'I Do' Man,
Seth Davis"

Aliya wasn't the only one stunned. She turned to see Seth on one knee. Enrique had taken out his guitar and was playing the melody to one of her favorite songs. *The one I've waited for. The one I've prayed for. The one that I dreamed about; the one I can't live without. The one I been hoping for; All in God's time,* Aliya heard the words in her head, as she saw the love of God shining in the eyes of Seth Davis. Love for her.

Seth opened the wooden chest he was holding in his hand, no larger than an index card. He opened it, thanking Enrique for insisting on offering his security.

Aliya gasped as she looked into the box. At that moment, she fell. She fell deeply in love with the serious, complex, gentle, strong, tender, man kneeling before her. He *got* her. He understood her, what moved her heart.

"We have this treasure in earthen vessels that the power we possess can be recognized as God's and not our own. Aliya, when I first met you, I saw you as this box, a bit rustic, unpolished. It wasn't until I got to know you that I saw you the way God sees you; as a priceless treasure. Inside of this box are seed pearls for the hope I have that you will design a beautiful dress to display in all its glory for our wedding day.

Sitting on the bed of pearls is the diamond I hope that you will wear as a symbol of my love and a down payment on the I Do I want to declare on our wedding day," Seth spoke with such passion that most of the restaurant was on its feet listening, the customers holding their breath to hear what the petite woman would say.

Aliya felt as though her heart was seized with such emotion that it would explode. She nodded. "Seth, I will gladly wear your ring as a symbol of your love; I will marry you," Aliya laughed and cried as the customer's cheers and applause filled the air like the charged atmosphere of a winning touchdown at a stadium. As she held out her hand, Seth slipped the ring on her finger, and just like that, Aliya China Peyton, stepped into a new season.

"We got her good didn't we, honey?" Enrique was warmed to his toes as he watched Seth and Aliya hold hands and lean into each other to speak privately.

"I'm glad you thought to hire a videographer to capture the memory for them and my parents," Augusta kissed her husband in appreciation. "They are going to love it."

"I always knew Seth had it in him to be romantic," Enrique mused. "He just needed to be inspired by the right woman," he said thoughtfully.

"What are you two going on about over here?" Shemiah gave Enrique their hand snap of a greeting.

"Oh, Enrique was gloating over how he finally duped Aliya by helping Seth plot his proposal," Augusta leaned in to Enrique, enjoying the feel of holding him close.

"So that's how he did it," Jamar had wondered. "I had no clue; I mean I know he's been busy, but I thought it was sermon preparation or something," Jamar nodded. "It's good to see my brother finally putting an end to his misery," he chuckled.

"May you should take notes," Marco taunted him as he passed by.
"Yeah," Shemiah had entered the conversation then. "What's going on with you and Tehinnah?

Jamar knew when it was time to beat a hasty retreat. "You know, I really should get going. Bedtime and all that good stuff," he hurried off leaving Shemiah puzzled.

"Don't think too hard over it, Ise," Enrique stared after him. "We all have our own emotional timetable."

"True words," Marco agreed as he wondered what had really set Jamar off.

Lord, heal every hurt.

62

Second Chance at love

Saturday morning dawned bright and clear; it was the perfect day for an outdoor wedding. Marilyn had decided she wanted her ceremony held in the gazebo of the outdoor courtyard at Second Chance. She hadn't wanted fanfare. The only thing that mattered to her was having the people she loved most by her side to share in her intimate moment. As she stood at the altar pledging her vows to Andre Charles, she thanked God for this moment. In just a few minutes, she would be Mrs. Andre Charles, and her dream that had been deferred through disobedience, stubbornness, and pride would finally come to fruition by God's grace. *Thank you God for second chances*, she smiled to herself. Elder Worth's voice rang out loud and clear.

"For as much as Marilyn and Andre have consented together in holy wedlock, and have witnessed the same before God and these witnesses, and thereto have pledged their faithfulness each to the other, and have pledged the same by the giving and receiving of rings, by the authority invested in me as a minister of the Gospel according to the laws of the State of Georgia, I pronounce that they are husband and wife together, in the name of the Father, and of the Son, and of the Holy Spirit. Those that God has joined together let no man put asunder.
Let this holy union be respected, admired, and blessed now and forever. Amen," Elder Worth placed his hands on both Marilyn and Andre.

"Join me in prayer for this couple," he instructed his son to come forward with his anointing oil, placing a small bit into each of their palms and instructing them to join hands together.

"Lord, we thank you for sanctifying and setting this marriage apart. By the power of your Holy Spirit, let your blessings be upon them. I ask, Lord that you give them all that pertains to life and godliness and that their heavenly reality would match their earthly existence. We ask you to cover their marriage, their life, their livelihood, their home with your blood. May they always show each other forgiveness, mercy, love, trust, and care; May they always turn to each other for marital comfort and to you for guidance, strength, and hope. May they please you in the choices they make, in the ministries they involve themselves in, and in every endeavor. Use them to draw others to yourself, to do kingdom exploits and be a living example of the love you have for the believer. We ask this in Jesus name, Amen," Elder Worth gave Andre a big smile. "Now, sir, you may kiss the bride."

Savannah, Shemiah, Gram Parker, and Gram Tot, along with Vivian and Josiah, applauded wildly as Marilyn Robinson became Marilyn Charles. *Finally,* Savannah's spirit leapt for joy.

Reboot My Heart

Aurielle was home on break grabbing a quick lunch when she heard her doorbell ring. She was always annoyed with door-to-door salesmen and she simply had no time to be persuaded to buy something she didn't need. *Obviously they don't understand that an unanswered door means go away,* Aurielle reasoned as she stomped to the door, yanking it open with attitude.

"Wha--"

"Hey," Trey Jones chuckled. "I hope I'm not the reason you're angry because I've got great news."

Aurielle was so happy to see him; she threw herself on him, hugging him tight. "Trey," she sighed.

Trey returned her enthusiasm relishing the feel of Aurielle in his arms. He stepped back, aware that he was feeling more than brotherly towards her. "Do you have a few minutes?" Trey recognized her work attire.

"Just a few," she led him into the kitchen. "You talk, I'll eat; then I'll ask questions," she got out her condiments and began moving at breakneck speed whipping up a sandwich while Trey spoke.

"I met with my parents and told them everything about you," his eyes lit up just thinking about his conversation. "and before I could finish, my father just stopped me and told me I should marry you," he shook his head in wonder. "I asked him about the arranged marriage and he explained that the girl had run off with some musician to Europe, embarrassing her parents. The last they had heard, she was expecting his child," Trey shared.

"Well, that had to be disappointing to your parents as well," Aurielle spoke in between bites.

"My father told me that he had always hoped that I would marry for love. The arranged marriage was a contingent option," Trey explained. "I told him that I had come to inform them you and I were indeed planning to marry and my mother just lost it," he grinned. "All in all, I'm glad I went and faced the issue head on," he stood then, and joined her at the counter, leaning over to wipe a mustache of mustard away. "You are worth fighting for, Aurielle."

Aurielle grinned widely, thinking she was one of the most favored women in the world. "I really appreciate you, Trey. Your support from the first you met me has been more than I could ask for," She had stretched her arms around his neck, her hands resting on his nape.

"If you keep looking at me like that, we're going to be eloping, not planning a wedding," he laughed.

"No way, young man; Elder Worth would string you by your toes," she giggled.

As Trey walked her outside and gave her a kiss on the cheek, he looked forward to many more days just like this one.

"Hello, Noey," a smooth voice cooed behind Noelle as he was busy at his secretary's desk looking for a file.

Noelle hadn't recognized the voice; he hadn't heard it in so long. But he would recognize that condescending nickname anywhere. He braced himself and schooled his facial expression into a mask of calm as he turned to face her.

"Hello, Fiona."

"Fiona?" Fiona Oppenheim strolled around his richly appointed office taking in Noelle's décor. "You used to call me mother," she pouted.

"You used to be one. Mother is just too maternal a word for," he added, noting that his mother was still as beautiful as ever thanks to her cosmetic surgeon of a husband. "What are you doing here in Po-dunky little Georgia? You couldn't get away fast enough," he reminded her. "Has your husband fallen on hard times?" he prodded.

"We're...separated," Fiona spat out rather stiffly.

Noelle raised his brows.

"He's completely irrational!" she threw up her hands in defense. "He's frozen all my accounts," she complained.

"Because you are a shopaholic," Noelle reminded her.

"He's reviewed my call log," she huffed.

"Because you are a serial adulterer," he was trying to hold his peace. "And prone to flaunting your men," Noelle shrugged.

Fiona paced back and forth. "I never should have left John in the first place," she finally stopped pacing, looking to him in misery. "Your father was the only man I ever really loved," she spoke softly.

"He was the only man who ever put up with your antics, you mean," Noelle folded his arms in defense.

"You've got to help me win him back," she pleaded.

Noelle stared at her in shock. "Win him back? Are you out of your *mind*?"

Fiona tugged on her son's arm, surprised when he shook her away. "Noelle, I need your support," Fiona begged. "I'm down to ten thousand dollars," she confessed. "I left California because well, Joseph, he's...its over," she hedged, not wanting to give too much information too soon.

Noelle gave his mother a look so cold, it nearly froze her. He came to stand toe to toe with her. "Let me make myself abundantly clear, Mother. I will not help you in any way or assist you in scheming your way back into my father's heart. As a matter of fact, I'm going to recommend that he run for his life."

Fiona slapped Noelle so hard, his ears began to ring. Or maybe that was her screeching he heard as she made her way out of his office, overturning furniture as she went. Fiona was good for making scenes, but one could never get her to stay around to witness the affects of living life like a walking tornado, destroying everything and everyone in her wake leaving them to pick up the broken pieces and try to rebuild their lives. As Noelle rubbed his aching jaw, he realized that Fiona had given him the key to resolving his own issues. *Lord, forgive me for grouping all women into the category of walking tornado.* Fiona was clearly in a class all her own.

Saturday Night at Kevin's

Kevin had decided to cook for Tatyanna and he had invited a few of his friends over to join them in playing a few games. Tatyanna had mentioned it to her sister who was all for joining them. She was looking to get to more acquainted with the people in the city. What she didn't know was that Kevin was cooking up a plan. He was so tired of hearing Tehinnah fawn over Jamar Davis in his absence, yet totally ignoring him or treating him with disdain in his presence. It was time to throw them in the pot of proximity and see what the Lord would do. Tehinnah could be a bit brash in personality but she was a really sweet girl. If only she was inclined to show Jamar her good side. Kevin had invited his partner Ameer; Tatyanna had invited Ginny and Jamar; Jamar had invited Marco. No one was prepared for the fallout of the fellowship.

"You didn't tell me he would be here," Tehinnah complained to Tatyanna as she helped her put quiche on trays in the kitchen.

"You didn't ask; besides, you talk about him all the time anyway," Tatyanna gave her a knowing look. "Maybe you should try talking to him."

Tehinnah shook her head adamantly. "He probably doesn't want to see me after last night."

"Wait. You guys hung out?" Tatyanna was surprised.

"No," Tehinnah shared with her about the bakery incident.

"He probably wants to strangle you," Tatyanna struggled to hold in her laughter. "Poor Jamar; no wonder he grimaced when he saw you," Tatyanna thought aloud.

"Whatever," Tehinnah spun out of the kitchen with the tray directly into Jamar.

"Careful," he warned. "I'd have thought you a little more graceful than this considering how you ran off with my cheesecake," he chided. "You owe me," pointed. "And I intend to collect," he promised as he walked past her and headed to the living room.

Tehinnah set the tray down onto the table in front of Ginny who was supposed to be socializing but had her nose buried in her latest romantic fantasy.

"Girl, put that book down," Tehinnah snatched it out of her hands.

"My *page*," Ginny whined, snatching the novel back. "I'm putting it away. Right after I finish this last paragraph," she reasoned.

Jamar and Marco came to hijack the quiche and load up their plates with nachos.

"Whatcha' reading," Jamar asked curious. It was not unusual to see Ginny reading during her breaks at Alpha, Inc.

Ginny was eager to tell him. "It's actually a new author. She's really good," she breathed excitedly. "Carmo Arion," she flipped the cover over.

"Are you okay?" Tehinnah patted Marco on the back.

"Something got stuck in my throat for a minute there," Marco brushed off the incident refusing to meet Jamar's eyes. *She's reading my novel!*

"She's a great writer," Ginny gushed.

"How do you know it's a girl?" Jamar threw out, watching his friend squirm.

Ginny looked in the back of the novel but there was no picture. "You know, that's strange; there's no picture," she shrugged. "I think it's a girl," she decided. "No man could be this intuitive."

That's what you think. We can be full of surprises, Marco wanted to tell her, but refrained from saying anything, yanking Jamar back into the living room before he said anything else to blow his cover. It was obvious he had figured out that he was Carmo Arion. *Lord, keep his tongue from revealing it*, Marco prayed.

Jamar was none too happy to find Tehinnah in deep conversation with Kevin's Savannah partner, Ameer Hanif. He was a new believer, having converted to the Faith from Islam. Kevin had asked the men to pray for him because he was facing persecution and death threats from some of his radicalized family members. He had recently decided to join Second Chance and had been attending the Foundations class to learn the basics of Faith. Jamar could see that he was intrigued with whatever Tehinnah had to say to him. She had not spoken to him all evening, and after the stunt she had pulled last night, he knew for certain she would not. It would be up to him to offer the olive branch. If she took it, it would be a miracle.

"What's got you so distracted tonight?" Kevin had sidled up to Jamar, reading the scowl on his face as displeasure.

"She hasn't spoken to me once." Jamar grumbled.

"Well, at least she isn't antagonizing you; I'd say that's growth." Kevin offered.

"She owes me," Jamar spoke to no one in particular. "And she's afraid of what the payment is going to be," he realized.

"With that look on your face, I'd be concerned too," Kevin chuckled. "Unless that look has to do more with the fact that someone else is claiming her attention," he grinned.

Jamar glared at him.

"Hey," Kevin threw his hands up, "I'm just saying," he nodded to his partner. "Ameer is a great guy who's ambitious, determined, faithful, and not afraid to go after what he wants," Kevin confided looking at his partner. "It looks like he wants to get to know Tehinnah better," he deduced.

Jamar's fists had clenched so tightly, it took him a moment to realize it. "Tehinnah's entitled to see whoever she wants," Jamar ground out.

Kevin nodded in agreement. "You're a great man, Jamar. You can stand here and watch another man fawn over the woman you're interested in. I have to say, I just couldn't be that cool about it," he patted him on the back.

Jamar watched Kevin saunter away all the while thinking he felt anything but cool.

Nicholas Cartellini was nervous. *Lord, help me not to be anxious for anything, even this moment,* Nicholas prayed. He had asked Roz to meet him and Giovanni and Naomi for dinner tonight. She had sounded different, almost distracted when he had called her earlier. He brushed aside the uneasiness and let the peace of God rule his heart. He put his cares into the Father's hand.

"Are you as nervous as I am?" Gio laughed at himself. He was acting like a teenager on his first date, all giddy and clumsy. He'd spilled two glasses of water. The waiter had to move them to another table before the ladies who were arriving together had come in.

Both brothers rose when they spotted the two being ushered towards their table, taking the opportunity to pull out their chairs so they could be seated.

"Hello, ladies," Nicholas was the first to greet them. "Glad you both could make it," he tucked Roz's chair in.

The ladies greeted them simultaneously. They had shared an interesting car ride, Rosalynn regaling Naomi with Nicholas' antics, keeping her in stitches on the way to dinner. Naomi sharing her misgivings about starting a relationship with Giovanni, due to all the drama surrounding Fabritza Ciccone's dismissal; they had prayed for each other and declared that if God wanted to make them sisters then it would happen.

"How was Kingston?" Roz accepted her drink from their waiter.

"It was great; we got a little bit of exercise in; Augusta's mom is a bit of an adventurer," Giovanni remembered fondly.

"Yeah, I couldn't believe her stamina," Nicholas corroborated.

"I hope to look that good at her age," Rosalynn sipped her tea.

"You look beautiful and I know you'll only grow more beautiful with time," Nicholas encouraged her.

"I know what you mean, Rosalynn. It's important as we get older to discipline our eating habits even the more. Those days of pizza in the middle of the night are long gone for me," she smiled wistfully.

"You maintain your figure well," Giovanni wiggled his eyebrows playfully.

Naomi rolled her eyes heavenward at the remark. "Flattery will get you nowhere," she reminded him.

"Flattery is when you elevate someone to a standard they haven't met; you, Naomi, meet all of my standards for perfection," Giovanni leaned over; speaking so only she could hear.

Rosalynn noticed the flush that had come over Naomi's face.

"Gio, stop teasing Naomi," Roz grinned at Naomi's silent thank you.

"We just got here."

The foursome shared their analysis of the trip to Montego Bay, thanking God that no one had been injured, people had been blessed, and that almost everyone had gained something positive from the trip. Rosalynn had shared her story of reconciliation with Carlton, and everyone had marveled that the trip had blessed them in unexpected ways. Roz finally felt free to pursue her relationship, Giovanni was freed from the cloying presence of Fabritza, and Carlton had repented and made amends. It was encouraging to know God was still making good on his promises. As they left the dinner and headed for home, Nick and Gio couldn't wait to see what God would do in the services on tomorrow. Naomi and Roz reflected upon the same thing as they made their way home.

63

Church on Fire

Savannah was a quiet city on a Sunday morning, with couples strolling through the eloquently appointed city squares to reach their respective churches, enjoy a morning run, or have coffee in one of the quaint cafes. This was not the case in Second Chance, Fresh Fire, or New Life where the believers were going forth in worship, seeking God for change, refreshing, and understanding of His Word. No, the picture inside the churches was no quiet stroll but a outward display of the unquenchable fire and passion they had to live for God, to serve God, and to do the works of God. The Singles of Second Chance, Fresh Fire, and New Life would be handing out lunches to the needy after service. They had taken time away from their own hectic lives; now, it was time to return to doing the work of the ministry.

Fresh Fire

"God is more than willing to meet your needs today; He is willing to exceed your expectation today if you will put your faith and trust in Him today. Many of you are too busy examining God rather than expecting God. When you expect God to act on your behalf instead of trying to figure out how God will act on your behalf, great things can happen," Seth declared coming from behind his pulpit and stepping close to the altar. "My prayer for you is that your prayers will reach heaven; they will reach heaven and then return to the earth to water the ground you've sowing in," Seth walked down into the aisle of the church. "I want your heavenly reality to manifest in your earthly existence. The promises of God are yes, and in Him amen. We have to believe God as we pray, that He is present, He is working in the now to heal us, deliver us, bless us, sanctify us; Enoch believed God so much in his now, that God pulled him into his heavenly reality. Don't you want God to pull you into that reality because you believe Him right now? That your faith is so full, your present can't contain it and it has to spill over into your future?" Seth hopped forward with excitement, running up the aisle. "I don't want to end this present life and get to heaven only to have God tell me, 'enter in Son; this is who you are, but let me show you who you could have been, what you could have accomplished for the Kingdom with the power I've placed in you," Seth finished. "I want everyone who will join me at the altar today, to come and recommit to following the plan of God; Recommit to being steadfast in prayer, in fasting, in the study of God's Word, in faithfulness." Seth stood at the altar, inviting them to come, pleased that Aliya who was visiting with him today joined him at the altar along with several college students. As Seth prayed, he thanked God that every

409

member would receive the Holy Spirit and the fire that Jesus promised to baptize them with.

New Life

Columbia Newcomb and her daughters had come to visit Pastor Marks in service today with her pastor's blessing. He had been surprised to look up and see her. He had called her forth to introduce her as his fiancé and it had taken several minutes to bring the congregation back into some semblance of calm. John had been surprised at how enthused his members had been, some shouting, 'about time'. Their encouragement had lit an extra fervency in him this morning.

"Jesus came to baptize us with the Holy Ghost and with fire! I've come to tell you today that the Fire works! It worked for the apostles, it worked for the early church fathers, and it still works today. If you have an issue, the Holy Ghost will point you to the Healer, If you have a situation you feel like you can't get out of, the Holy Ghost will show you the way to escape, if you have any doubts about Jesus, the Holy Ghost will reveal His ways to you. If you need power to live right and say no to temptation on a daily basis, the Holy Ghost will give you the power to say no to the devil and to say yes to God," Pastor Marks paused in his speech as he spotted Fiona, his ex-wife in the congregation. He shook off the distracting thoughts that wanted to bombard him. "If you need help keeping your mind on Jesus, the Holy Ghost will point you to the good, the honest, the just things to think on," he motioned for his son to join him at the altar.

"I challenge you today. If you need God to become the Lord and Savior of your life, come forward and receive Him. If you say to yourself, 'Lord, I am saved, but I've been struggling to live consistently for you', come, let us pray for you that you might receive the Holy Ghost. He is a gift that comes into a life that has been surrendered. He will only come if you ask. The Holy Ghost will not reside in you against your will. If you are ready to make that decision today, come," he beckoned.

As the people moved forward to receive salvation, some to pray for God's Spirit to fill them, Fiona was making her way out of the sanctuary. She had heard enough. *So, John was engaged, now, was he?* Fiona didn't remember Noelle mentioning anything about it. Nevertheless, she would have to re-strategize how to win him back. He looked more handsome than she remembered. It would take some time but Fiona was determined to have John Marks back in her life. It had been a mistake to leave him. She was free to pursue John without any attachments. She would give full attention to him this time; until she got what she wanted. After all, she had something more than just words to convince him.

Ordination Sunday at Second Chance

Savannah, Shemiah, Angelynn, Enrique, and Augusta as well as the faithful members of Second Chance were all on hand to witness a long awaited moment: the ordination Josiah Edward Worth to the office of Pastor. He would serve as Senior Pastor of Second Chance, releasing his father to establish Second Wind in Hilton Head. It was an emotional moment for many, watching the boy they had known return home to serve his father in ministry and now today, he would receive the mantle to take Second Chance to the next season.

Savannah handed Angelynn tissue as she tried to hold her own back. Her best guy friend would now be her leader. She knew that though they were friends, his leadership and commissioning as the shepherd of her soul would take precedence. She could appreciate and respect his leadership because she had seen his honesty and integrity lived out from how he loved his wife and cared for his children to how he treated everyone who entered the doors of Second Chance as if they mattered to him, not just as another pew warmer, but as an individual who was valuable to God, and therefore valuable to him.

Vows of Ordination

"Before God and this congregation you are called upon to answer in all truthfulness the questions I now ask you. Do you believe that you are truly called to be an ordained minister in the church of Jesus Christ and with the help of God to serve faithfully in the fulfillment of the responsibilities of this ministry as senior pastor?" Elder Worth asked Josiah.

"I do, God being my helper," Josiah's fervor was evident.

"Do you promise to be faithful in prayer, fasting, and in the reading of the scriptures and through study to deepen your knowledge of divine truth and human experience, whereby you may make full proof of your ministry and feed the people with knowledge and understanding?"

"I do, God being my helper."

"Will you seek to bring others into an acceptance of the cost and joy of discipleship, and through faithful teaching lead them into a full understanding of Christian commitment and Kingdom expansion?"

"I will, God being my helper."

"Will you have a loving concern for all people and give yourself to minister impartially to them without regard to race, creed, gender, or lifestyle? Will you pull out of the fire those who need fervent rescue?"

"I will, God being my helper," Josiah felt the presence of God overshadow him.

"Will you endeavor to uphold the integrity of the church and to seek that unity in which all churches will manifest the one Lord, one faith, one hope and one baptism?" Elder Worth's eyes were filled with tears as he neared the completion of his son's vows.

"I will, God being my helper."

"Will you give yourself to the denomination in which you are being ordained and in so far as possible serve its causes and seek to enlarge its witness at home and abroad?

"I will, God being my helper," Josiah affirmed one last time, thanking God for this moment. He had not entered in lightly into this calling.

Elder Worth turned to the congregation then. "People of God, you have heard the commitment made by Josiah Edward Worth III. What is your desire?" he stared into the faces of his congregation, some happy, some calm, but all affirming.

"He has proven he is worthy! In the name of Christ and relying on God's grace, let us ordain him," The congregation spoke with one voice.

"Will you give her your full support in this ministry? Will you give your support to Josiah Edward Worth as your Senior Pastor, and those serving under his direction?"

"Relying on God's grace, we will," the congregation spoke with clarity and confidence.

"Then let us acknowledge and confirm this ordination by the laying on of hands in prayer," Elder Worth motioned his son to kneel as he took his shofar filled with oil and poured it upon his head. Josiah wore his father's old pastoral garment, and as he poured the oil, it flowed onto the robe. "As we pray, I ask that you point your hands toward my son, your Senior Pastor.

Josiah was overwhelmed by the presence of God as the congregation and his father lifted up their voices in the commissioning of his leadership. He could feel the unity of the church, their love coupled with the love of God, pouring over him in waves. It was an incredible moment and he would strive to live everyday worthy of this calling.

I will make you a Pastor after my own heart. Fear not, for I am with thee. As I was with Moses, with Joshua, with your father, so will I be with you.

USO~ United Singles Outreach

"This is really fun," Aliya spoke softly to Seth as she leaned over and grabbed more lunches to pass down military style to the inner city community of Savannah. The singles had decided to end their retreat by coming back to the city to give back in a tangible way. They had decided the Singles of their respective churches would unite and serve the local community through outreach on a quarterly basis. Augusta and Columbia had coordinated the outreach side of the trip. Aliya had focused on the planning of the Getaway. It was a great combination: Singles Getaway – Singles Giveback.

"I'm enjoying myself too," Seth agreed, watching the faces of the children light up when they realized they had candy and toys in their lunch packs. "Thanks for coming to visit this morning. I'm glad your pastor agreed to release you," he teased. Seth had a great time at the close of service introducing Aliya as his fiancé.

"Pastor Marks seems a little euphoric right now," Aliya giggled. He was manning the bouncing station with Columbia. "I heard the church went wild with the news that he's engaged," Aliya sighed. "He's such a great man; I'm so glad the Lord has blessed him to find love once again."

"I know what you mean," Noelle sauntered over to them joining in the conversation. He was done putting together lunches so he had a minute to catch up before he took over as DJ for Shemiah and Savannah. "I never thought my father would love again after all he's been through. I'm asking you to pray though: my mother showed up yesterday at my office and then she showed up at service today. Let's just say its not a good thing," Noelle shared.

"Well let's lift her up to the Lord right now; whatever reason she returned to the city won't matter once God gets a hold of her," he assured him.

As they lifted Fiona in prayer, God inclined his ear to hear them.

Celebratory Dinner

"I'd like to thank all of you for your support today. It meant a lot to look out and see your faces," Josiah stood up to address his close friends; Shemiah, Savannah, Enrique, Augusta, Jamar, Seth, Aliya, and his closest friend and companion Angelynn. Jarah and Dr. Greg Thomas had taken the twins for the evening. He had shared lunch with his parents after service while the singles had participated in the outreach. "I'm so thankful that I have friends like you; friends who have been there for me, who have prayed with me, who have shared your hopes with me, who have kept my secrets," he chuckled looking to his wife. "Angelynn, I couldn't be the man I am today without your love and support. I'm so glad you didn't complain or gripe, or give me a hard time when I asked you to stand by my side in ministry," he leaned down to kiss her. "I love you," he gazed into her eyes, eliciting sighs from the ladies and throat clearing from the men. "I got a bit carried away," Josiah grinned as Angelynn stood then to toast her husband.

"I'd like to say, thank you as well; I know this meant a lot to Josiah, and I can tell you that I am honored to stand by his side in ministry. He's prayed consistently and fervently that he would be in the will of God, he's covered our house with prayer, and he's just led a life before God that I can admire," Angelynn gave Josiah a tender look, raising her glass of sparkling pomegranate. "To righteousness, peace, and joy in the Holy Ghost, as we embark upon this service of Pastoring God's flock," she toasted her husband.

Everyone settled into companionable conversation during dinner, and the teasing ensued; from Enrique and Augusta to the upcoming nuptials of Savannah and Shemiah, everyone was in good spirits. Nicholas, Giovanni, Fabian, Dominic, and Francheska seated at their own table not far from Enrique and Augusta, and were engaged in their own discussion.

"I have to say I quite enjoyed myself today at the park with the kids. It was just great to get out there and play some touch football," Giovanni was still hyped up.

"It would have been great had you actually let the *kids* touch the football," Francheska smirked.

"We did let them run with the ball," Nicholas defended his brother.

"You ran with the children under your arm," Fabian laughed. "That doesn't count," he added.

"I thought it trés mignon," Dominic murmured.

"You would think it was cute," Francheska, who knew a little French, chided him. "I think there were two big kids out in the field today," she decided.

The security team bonded over dinner, recalling their most intense moments protecting the lives of others. Josiah's inner circle bonded over their most intense encounters with God. It was an evening that would be remembered long after they departed from the restaurant.

Fire Works

Andre and Marilyn Charles stood out on the yacht they had rented for their honeymoon in Hilton Head. The waters were slightly choppy, just like Andre liked them. They had headed out of town after the ordination service because they had not wanted to miss Josiah's installation as Senior Pastor. They had discussed plans for the future on the drive up; He and Marilyn would live in the home he had bought; they would remain in Savannah and help assist Pastor Worth on the weekends with Second Wind Ministries in Hilton Head, staying with Shemiah's parents. Elder Worth had a strong membership of two hundred who had been driving to Second Chance to attend services. They had been overjoyed at the news that by next year, Second Wind would be opening its doors and dedicating its new sanctuary. Savannah would enjoy the blessing of living under her parent's household for a month but wedding bells were just around the corner.

Marilyn wrapped her arms around her husband, the love of her life and leaned into him, enjoying the feeling of safety, security, and peace that she found in his arms.

"I'm so thankful you said yes," Andre spoke into her ear, sending a shiver down her spine. "I love you so much," Andre kissed her forehead, her eyes, the ridge of her nose, resting his lips upon hers." He had nearly fainted today at the altar. It was nearly thirty years since he had kissed her. It had felt like the very first time, heady and wonderful.

Marilyn kissed him with all the passion, love, and pent-up desire that had been reserved for him alone. The fourth of July was long past, but Marilyn could have sworn she heard fireworks as Andre guided her below deck.

The Lord makes everything beautiful in his time, she smiled to herself. *And his timing is perfectly right!*

64

Showers of Blessings

Thursday, August 6

Two more days! Savannah felt ready to jump out of her skin. She had written Mrs. Savannah Newman more times than she could count, doodling on napkins, stationary, dry erase boards; even her screen saver was sporting her new name. Savannah had been on edge the past month, especially as Josiah had met with her and Shemiah for their last counseling session in July and had ordered them to refrain from embracing for the last month and to fast and pray. He called it sanctifying the marital tie and strengthening their relationships with the Lord; Savannah had called it pure torture. She hadn't realized how much she had begun to depend upon Shemiah's Latte Letters of love, on his texts and phone calls, on his regular deliveries of flowers, on his dropping by her office unexpectedly to bring lunch or take her out until he had to refrain. Savannah readied herself for her Sisterhood Soiree. Angelynn had offered her home for the shower. Savannah could not wait to see what Augusta and Aliya had planned; everything had been hush-hush. *Lord knows when those two get together, something funny is bound to happen!*

Shemiah had been feeling the building excitement as well. As they worshipped together on the Praise and Worship team, as they attended Bible Study far too aware of Savannah seated by his side, as he went about his day, his longing for his intended grew until the ache within him was more than soul-deep. It went to the very core of his spirit. *Lord, this is just an inking of you feel for us, Your Bride, every day you are away from us. You withhold from celebrating until we are with you once again where we were predestinated to be.*

Now, you understand. This consecration was not to punish you but to allow you to see how very much I long for fellowship, for communion with My Bride. I long for the day when she will enter the Marriage supper and we will feast together.

Even so, come Lord Jesus, Shemiah felt the words reverberate through him. He had barely made it through the wedding rehearsal and dinner last week. Now, tonight, his fellow friends were throwing him a Brotherhood Bash at Seth's beach house. He was two days from ending his bachelor days and he was counting the minutes until he said 'I Do'.

Brotherhood Bash

The bash was in full swing down at Seth's Tybee Island beach house. Shemiah had been roasted thoroughly about his relationship with Savannah from the first time they had met (she stole his parking space) to the time she had plowed into the passenger side of his truck (the test of true love). He was pleased Lysander had been able to come down a few days early to attend the event. He seemed in good spirits and great health. Every man who had impacted Shemiah's life in some way was there; even Savannah's father had teased him, printing out one of his Latte Letters for Savannah and reading a line or two. Shemiah was glad that he was a dark brother, or his cheeks would have been as red as cherries. Now, they were challenging him to test his Wedding Day readiness with a Garter Pulling contest. Jamar had borrowed a mannequin for him to test out his skills. Shemiah had to pull the garter off the mannequin's leg with his teeth- blindfolded.

"I hope you understand that there is no way you're getting a look at my Savannah's thigh, so I will *not* be performing this routine at the reception," they all laughed at Shemiah's promise. "Here goes," he knelt down and through many trials and errors finally managed to get the garter off. "No one better be videotaping," he warned. "If I see this on the Internet, I'm coming after you," he vowed.

The men enjoyed themselves until midnight, laughing, talking, and finally praying God's blessing on Shemiah, each man laying their hands on him to bless him, each single man sowing financially into good ground for their own future. The married men had collectively purchased him an engraved luggage and personal grooming set, along with some hilarious night wear inside the luggage.

"You guys are on point and I love each one of you. Thank you for your prayers for endurance," he chuckled. "I'm not going to go there," he shook his head.

Though most of the gentlemen had left for the evening, Shemiah had remained, listening to his best man, Josiah, recount wonderful tales of his first year of marriage. Shemiah prayed that his first year would be filled with everything that was good.

Sisterhood Soiree

Pin the bowtie on the groom? Savannah shook her head. Not only did they want her to do it, they wanted her to do it blindfolded with more than one groom on the wall. They had blown up a picture of Shemiah along with two other random pictures so there were three grooms represented. They were only allowed to yell 'hot' if she was close to her target. She had thirty seconds to accomplish her goal. If she did not meet it, she had to read a Latte letter. Savannah would rather fight the fires of a blazing inferno than share one of her letters.

"Ten...nine...eight...seven...six..." Aliya counted down to the screams of hot as Savannah managed to pin on the bowtie with three seconds to spare.

"Geez, that was close," Savannah wiped her brow as the ladies applauded her efforts. She was led over to her chair as her 'Fire and Ise' themed party continued. It was gift time. Savannah cringed to think what was in those boxes.

"Now's not the time to be shy," Marilyn told her daughter. "Go on, open them," she handed Savannah the first gift.

Savannah opened the gift to oohs and ahhs. She lifted up the negligee that seemed to be missing quite a few things. Savannah's face was screwed up in puzzlement.

"That, my dear, is called an 'easy access' garment," Mother Worth explained.

"There's not much to it; what's the point of putting it on?" Savannah couldn't help but notice the ensuing laughter. She felt so inexperienced but she wasn't embarrassed by it.

"The point is to allow him to take it off," Augusta giggled, clearly not out of her honeymoon state. She had shared with Savannah after the rehearsal dinner that the honeymoon never had to end.

"Whatever happened to naked and not ashamed?" Savannah wondered out loud sending the women into more peals of laughter.

As Marilyn wiped her eyes from overflowing mirth, she knew she would have to have a heart to heart with her powerful, anointed, yet endearingly innocent Savannah Evangeline.

August 7 Revelations

Columbia's Classy Cuts

Friday was always a busy day for Columbia. Many people took Friday off to prepare to go out of town, to attend funerals and weddings on the weekend and they wanted to look their best; that's where she came in. Columbia was a Master stylist and had a good reputation in the city for excellence in healthy hair care, prompt service, reasonable prices, and stringent sanitation practices. She served a variety of clientele; from the poor to the politician. Her skills were diverse, caring for all types of hair. It was no surprise then, to see the very lavishly dressed woman enter her facility, her nose pointed in the air, a look of haughty disdain etched onto her delicate features.

"Can I help you?" Columbia had just finished sanitizing her station and was preparing for her next client.

"Maybe," Fiona took in Columbia motherly figure, her casual dress that wreaked of blue collar nobody to her. She studied her in silence. "I just came to...view my competition, though judging by the looks of you really is no competition," she allowed her soft words to slice like a blade through flesh.

Columbia felt the verbal attack like an unexpected blow to the stomach. *What in the world?* The woman continued on.

"I can see John must have been down on his luck, how he must have pitied you; but to allow you to trick him into engagement? Well, I'm glad I've returned to claim my rightful place," Fiona gave a mirthless laugh.

Columbia could feel her temper rising as this woman stood in her shop, daring to insult her, daring to discredit what God was doing between her and John. "Just what right do you have to tell me anything?" Columbia demanded.

"Well, I have every right; I'm his wife," Fiona gave her a superior look.

"You must be joking; John is divorced; has been for years now," Columbia countered.

"Wrong; John thinks he's been divorced. I never filed the papers," she grinned evilly. "And I have no intentions of doing so," she warned.

"Get out," Columbia could barely speak, her voice breaking, her heart praying it wasn't true.

"I'm sorry to disappoint you, but John is mine. Once he realizes we never divorced, he'll take me back, and you will be but a unfortunate memory," Fiona promised as she turned swiftly on her heels leaving Columbia reeling from shock.

Coffee Break

Nicholas and Dominic were taking a break while the rest of the team watched Enrique, Shemiah, Josiah, and Seth try on their tuxes for the nuptials tomorrow. Nicholas had to give it to France; they had sent one of their best. Dom had already foiled two more attempts on Enrique's life before they had even reached their operatives in the States. He was good at what he did and Nick wondered about his dedication, yet his upcoming retirement from the field.

"Can I ask you something personal?" Nick sipped his coffee, waiting for Dominic to give him the go ahead.

"Go ahead," Dominic kept his eyes fixed on the shop across the street.

"You're extremely good at what you do—your superiors sing your praises. I've even heard talk of them wanting to elevate you to the head of French Intel; so why retire?" he was puzzled.

"I'm looking to change my life path," He shared.

"How long you been in this?" Nick was curious to know.

"Fourteen years. I started when I was twenty," he added.

"I'm impressed. It usually takes about twenty years just to be trusted in this industry," Nick admitted.

"This trust has cost me too much," Dominic stared as if he were somewhere else entirely. "I lost my wife and my unborn child two years ago tomorrow as a matter of fact," he delivered the revelation with no fanfare, but Nick was deeply affected nevertheless. "She was an agent; someone informed on her; she was carrying my child. She would have been close to two years old now," Dominic shrugged. "I'm still working on forgiving her for not telling me; her mother knew. Marguerite didn't want to tell me because she knew I would demand she be taken off the case." Dominic's piercing blue eyes looked into Nick's, seeing his fears, seeing his compassion. "I'm not in need of pity. I'm just in need of a change of course, so I'd appreciate you keeping this information to yourself." Dom turned away then.

Nicholas wasn't sure there were any words that could truly soothe Dominic's loss. "I'm here if you just need to process," he patted him on the shoulder briefly.

As they rose to join the others Dominic thanked God for that point of contact. It had been a long time since he had felt connected in a real way; even longer with another woman. *Guard, guard, guard*, Dom reminded himself.

65

August 7

Literary Obsession

Ginevieve was so caught up in the storyline of Carmo Arion's novel that she hadn't heard the bell overhead ring.

Marco was arranging the flowers for the wedding and he had to meet with Augusta to go over the floral design and receive payment. He was also standing in the lobby of Alpha, Inc. with another mysterious delivery for Ginny. The caller had asked him to write the most ridiculous drivel. *You are a fount of beauty,* Marco thought angrily. *I could do much better than that.*

He had tried to wait patiently until she noticed him in the lobby, but he realized she was reading. "Delivery for Ginevieve Dubois," he spoke with his official voice, trying not to laugh when Ginny nearly flipped her chair over, her book flying out of her hand, landing at his feet.

"You could have at least warned me," Ginny gave him a cross look.

"It's not my fault you didn't hear that extremely loud gong," he pointed to the bell overhead, then scooped up the novel she had been reading. *His.* "Didn't you finish reading this?"

Ginny nodded excitedly. "I did but it was so good, I'm reading it again from beginning to end," she added, turning to her desk to hand him a newspaper article. "I also read this yesterday; apparently someone has leaked that the author is indeed male which made me want to read it again," she confessed. "This is actually my third time through. I think it's going to be a classic and I can't wait for his next novel," Ginny sighed. "He's such a great writer; his words come alive on the page, and you just get lost in his story," her words came out on a breath.

Marco was starting to get jealous of this guy. He had painted himself into a corner: if he told her he was Carmo Arion, it could jeopardize his anonymity and his father would certainly come calling. Marco had built a quiet, peaceful existence for himself in Savannah, and he wanted to keep it that way. Besides, if she couldn't accept all of him, there was no hope for a future between them anyway.

"Well, these are for you," he shoved the bouquet towards her, frustrated at himself. "Your admirer again," he added stiffly.

Ginny saw his attitude change and she almost fulfilled the fiery redhead theory just then as he shoved the arrangement at her. "Thank you," she smiled sweetly. Then she gushed exaggeratedly over the worst piece of poetry she had read in a while just to annoy him.

Marco shook his head at her antics as he went to meet Augusta. *Lord, help me to hold my peace. And let me not strangle my agent.*

Mark My Words

John was reading over his upcoming sermon notes in his study when he heard his doorbell ringing. He rose up quickly to answer the door, believing Columbia must have finished up early today. He was not at all expecting to see Fiona on his doorstep since it had been over a month since he had last seen her.

"Are you going to just stare at me, or are you going to invite in?" Fiona planted a hand on her barely there hip.

"Staring sounds like a good idea," John folded his arms defensively. "Come to get a better look? Did you expect to see me broken?" He chastised her.

"Before you dismiss me, you might want to hear me out," she suggested sarcastically.

"Not here," John had no intention of letting Fiona into his sanctuary.

He followed her a few miles to a local café where they were quickly seated and served.

"Let's have it," he sat back, a look of suspicion in his eyes.

"I don't know how to say this, so I'll just come right out with it," she paused for effect. "I'm still Fiona Marks."

John reared back in his seat. "What are you saying?"

Fiona leaned forward allowing him a view of her surgically enhanced cleavage. "I'm saying, honey, that we never got divorced; we're still married."

John shook his head, no. "I saw those papers; you signed them."

Fiona agreed. "I did. But I never sent them. It was Joseph who pointed out to me that I was still married. His attorney discovered it," Fiona snapped.

"So, here I am, husband dear," she batted her eyes, unaware that John was completely unaffected by her.

"Divorce or not, you're no wife of mine; I will consider us separated until I can figure this out," John rubbed the back of his nape.

"Oh, I've got it all taken care of. I told that little hairdresser that I wasn't going anywhere. We're not divorcing John. I'm here to stay.

John Marks realized his mistake in coming with her to the café. "Think what you will, Fiona, but this isn't over. You released me years ago, and if I have to take this to court, it's bound to get messy for you," he warned. "You received a settlement from me that you may have to return.

"That's okay," Fiona countered in a brittle laugh. It may get messy for me, but as a Pastor, it's going to be damaging for you," she promised as she walked out leaving John Marks with a bitter taste in his mouth.

Reaping the Whirlwind

Fabian Ciccone was getting ready for dinner out with Francheska, Dominic, and Enrique and Augusta when he got the call.

"Falcon here," Fabian took the call he recognized as Italian Intel.

"Bad news, Falcon," his superior sounded distressed. "They've got Maltese. The French trafficking ring traded her to a ring in Beijing. I don't know we're going to infiltrate. My sources there tell me its nearly impossible," he sighed.

Fabian sank to his knees, his worst fear coming to pass. "Send me in," he spoke with determination. There was no way he was going to leave this to the hands of some neophyte. Someone had already screwed up.

"We'll see what we can--"

"No, you'll send me in. You know what Maltese means to me." He almost revealed too much.

"Fine; we'll send you in with Dominic. Tell him to prepare to shift gears," he declared and hung up.

Fabian readied himself for dinner. He and Dominic would prepare to leave on Monday. He held his emotions in check wondering, *Fabritza, what did you get yourself into?* He blamed himself for not curtailing his sister's behavior and impetuous nature. He prayed for her safety and hoped he would find her whole in every way. He would rely on the Lord to help him ferret out her location and anoint him to defeat the adversary.

Conquering All

Columbia had decided to meet John for dinner alone rather than bringing the girls along. She wanted to prepare herself for any potential fallouts and revelations and she didn't want her children involved.

He stood as she entered the restaurant and strode toward him. Her eyes took in everything about him; from the cut of his blazer, to the well polished shoes he wore to the strained look in his eyes. *He's seen Fiona today as well.* Columbia was a very cut to the point straight forward woman and tonight would be no different.

"Is it true, John?" Columbia sat across from him, holding herself with the composure and grace of a queen; something Fiona with all her polish had never managed to achieve.

John had spent the past few hours meeting with Noelle and pouring over records. Fiona had been telling the truth: they were still married; but they did not have to stay that way. Noelle warned him of the damage it could do to his reputation and ministry. Pastor Marks would have a ministry meeting in the place of his normal Bible Study this coming week to inform his congregation of the events unfolding. Then, he would ask for their prayers that God's will be done.

Fiona had proven herself an unrepentant serial adulterer. He had found peace in prayer today and believed that God would release him. He had not found happiness with Columba only to have it dashed to pieces.

"It is true, but it's complicated," John admitted, helping her into her seat.

Columbia allowed him to seat her. "I hope you can explain because I'm confused; I thought you divorced years ago," she stated.

John allowed the waitress to take their beverage orders before he answered. "She never filed the papers. She forgot to," he confided.

"So, it's just a matter of filing the paperwork, then?" Columbia looked so hopeful.

John hated to dash the look of expectancy in her eyes; a look that expected this would all be over with the motion of a pen across paper. "If only it were that simple; Fiona, for whatever reason has gotten it into her head that she wants to remain married," he shared, wincing at the look on Columbia's face.

"Oh, There's plenty of reasons to want to be married to a wonderful, loving, forgiving, kind, intelligent, prosperous, handsome man of the cloth," Columbia found herself making light of the situation to keep from drowning in despair. She looked down at her engagement ring. "I can't wear this in all good conscience," she looked at John in regret.

John drew the line then, taking her hand in his. "You're not taking that off, Columbia. I made a promise to you and I am a man of my Word; we have to trust that God is going to work this out. Fiona broke covenant with me; she agreed to end it; I am no longer bound to her in that respect. If I have to fight her in court I will. Her signature on those papers means that she didn't contest the divorce; she signed the papers and collected the settlement. She has no true hold over me, naturally and certainly not in spirit; my heart belongs to you, Columbia," he squeezed her hand, raising it to his lips.

"I guess we're going to have to make sure our armor is on tight then," her grasp tightened within his.

As they ate dinner, Columbia shared with him her hopes for their blended family and John felt at peace once more. *Lord, thank you for quieting our hearts. Do what only you can do!*

Good Friends, Good Times

"Feels good to be off duty together," Nick smiled at Giovanni. They had been invited over to Trey's home to hang out seeing as all the others were out handling final preparations for the wedding tomorrow. A wedding they were happy to see take place. *Finally!* Nick chuckled to himself. He had observed Shemiah and Savannah's courtship mainly from the periphery, but he had seen them struggle together, endure their hardships, celebrate each other, and respect the boundaries their leaders had put in place. He knew his time would come eventually but for now, he admired Shemiah immensely. It was something when a man that powerful in God and in the marketplace could put himself under the authority and direction of another.

"Yes, it does," Giovanni kicked back taking a stab at the chili, cheese, and guacamole dip Aurielle and Mariella had prepared. They were getting ready to watch a new Christian film out about a farmer turned preacher.

Aurielle sat down next to Mariella on the love seat, both ladies wrapping their feet underneath them. "So, how are things going at the Estrada compound?"

Mariella had heard about the recent plots uncovered and dismantled. "I'm glad that my cousin has security; I used to think he just liked having an entourage; now I realize how serious it is," she confessed.

"Well, unfortunately things are going to get more intense and we're going to have to tighten back up; Fabian and Dominic have been moved to another assignment and will be headed out come Monday. I ask you to pray for Fabian especially because it involves his sister," Giovanni expressed in as serious a manner as he could without divulging too much information.

"I'm sorry to hear that," Aurielle could only imagine what Fabian must be feeling; they were twins after all.

"Hey, why the gloomy look?" Roz and Naomi stepped into the family room surprising everyone, especially the Cartellini brothers.

Giovanni and Nicholas had greeted the women they were enamored with while recounting their security issue in brief detail. Trey had entered then, hearing the disheartening news.

"There's no better time like the present to lift her up as well as Fabian and Dominic. They are going to need the wisdom of God to infiltrate that ring, dismantle it, and return to the United States safely," he declared.

As they joined in prayer, it struck Mariella how very vital unity was in the Body of Christ. The enemy was after them all and there was no room or time for foolishness or petty disagreements. They only had time for fellowship in the Lord, development in the Word, and empowerment in the Spirit to do Kingdom works.

66

August 8 ~Tying the Knot

Savannah enjoyed an intimate Bridal Brunch with her mother, Vivian Worth, her Grams, Aliya, Augusta, and Angelynn. She would spend an hour before her wedding with her father, who wanted to pray for her and speak over her as a wife-to-be. Savannah quieted her thoughts allowing her heart's prayer to go out to the Lord.

Lord, I am so grateful for this day. I know I've been impatient at times, and I haven't understood some of the sacrifices, some of the restrictions you've asked of me, but I thank you for everything. I thank you for showing me how I needed to change, how I needed to embrace growth, how I needed to put my confidence in your love. All of these wonderful women you have placed in my life to be friends, to be vessels of honor, to be examples, to be iron sharpening iron, and Lord knows, I needed to be sharpened. Lord, help me as I go through this day to not get frustrated or anxious about anything but to really trust You to bring me through this wonderful day in righteousness, in peace, and in joy in the Holy Spirit. Touch Shemiah's heart and mind, and let him have great peace today because he keeps your law. I love you Lord, and I'm so glad you have made me apart of Your Bride, not just today, but apart of the Body of Christ, forever.

I do all things well; I loved you before you knew Me. I love you with an everlasting love. I love you because I created you. I called you good. I loved you before you could realize you needed my love; I loved you before you could do wrong; I will cause you to draw near to me today, to experience the joy of My union with you.

The voice of God was more than a comfort to Savannah. It was her life source. Savannah prayed that she would never lose sight of the importance of her relationship with God.

Men's Manna Session

"Now, Lord we ask that you fill Shemiah with peace as he prepares himself to become one today; shower down your favor and blessing, anointing and power, righteousness and strength; be all that he needs for this day, in Jesus' name," the groomsmen who had attended the breakfast responded with a resounding amen.

Shemiah felt ready to take on the mantle of marriage; there was an excitement on the inside ready to pour out. He was ready to embark on the journey into the holy and sacred covenant of marriage, and in doing so, better understand that unsolved mystery to the world; Christ and the church.

Ceremony of Praise

Savannah had chosen a small bridal party by modern day standards but many friends and fellow congregants had come out to see Shemiah Isaiah Newman pledge his life to Savannah Evangeline Charles. Over a thousand people had showed up for the wedding, but less than fifty would be attending the private reception. Shemiah had secured the church fellowship hall to treat the rest of the visitors with a light appetizer. They would stay for roughly thirty minutes to greet those who would not be joining the private reception. Then Shemiah would whisk Savannah away in their limo, blindfold her and fly her to Coral Gables for the private reception in their vacation home, a home he had purchased from Enrique last year.

The sanctuary was charged with the Spirit of God and the positive energy of the people as the Bridal party entered. The ladies gowns were strapless, A-line dresses, an iridescent pearl pink and champagne color, and their white roses contrasting nicely against their floor length gowns. The gentle men wore black tuxedos with custom made bow ties and vest the same color as the bridesmaids' dresses. Aliya had outdone herself with the simple yet elegant designs. Already women were searching their wedding programs for more information.

Josiah escorted Angelynn in as the first Matron of Honor and Best Man, leading her to her place in the pulpit. He went to stand beside Shemiah who looked calm and relaxed as the ceremony proceeded. Enrique and Augusta were next, the glow of marital bliss still upon them; they received some sighs of their own as Enrique led his wife to her place, kissed her cheek and took his own place next to Josiah as the second Best man. Next, Seth Davis and Aliya entered to the murmurs of those surprised to notice she too, was wearing a ring. A buzz of excitement went through the ladies that Aliya had finally accepted the Lord's will for her life. As Seth led her up the stairs, he lifted her hand and brought it to his lips. He placed a red rose among her white ones and then took his place as the last Best Man.

Savannah's Bridesmaids were Rosalynn, Tatyanna, and Naomi, escorted respectively by Jamar, Kevin, and Trey, their floor length strapless gowns an iridescent champagne color that seemed to radiate in the low lighting of the sanctuary. Delia, Columbia's daughter, served as flower girl, laying down pink roses. It was now time for the entrance of the Bride.

Speechless

The doors to the church swung open and Savannah clung to her father's arm. He had prayed over her, blessed her, spoke to her womb and declared it to bring forth life, and prayed for the husband and home that it be united and tied together by the three-fold cord of faithfulness, hope, and love, and the Father, Son, and Holy Spirit.

Savannah was so lovely in that moment; she left the congregation stunned into silence as she seemed to float down the aisle, her dress hand sewn with several diamonds sewn into the bodice among pearls, her dress deepening from pure white to pearl pink near her train, her hem embroidered with Proverbs eighteen and twenty two in the finest thread. Her father had spared no expense to see that Savannah have whatever she desired.

Her bouquet, the dark pink Mini Calla Lily had large, trumpet-shaped blooms that rested upon long, smooth stems. Symbolizing magnificent beauty, the Calla Lily was truly representative of the Bride who stood before the congregation. It had taken Shemiah several moments to recover and collect his bride.

Melding Lives

"In addition to the Candle Lighting, the Bride and Groom have chosen to use two different colors of sand, one red for the blood covering, one white for the holy covenant of marriage, also representing their two individual lives," Elder Worth informed the congregation. "As you join now in marriage, there is a merging of these two sands into one sand; this is what the Lord meant when He said, "On this account a man shall leave his father and mother and be joined to his wife and the two shall be one flesh." As you each take a vase of sand and together pour the sand into the center vase, you will let the center vase, the new colored sand represent the union of your lives into one flesh. As this sand cannot be divided, neither shall your lives be divided exemplify a home that is blessed by Christ, letting the legacy of your natural and spiritual seed number more than the sands of the earth," Elder Worth led them in the furtherance of the ceremony.

As the first act of their covenant together after performing their vows, Shemiah and Savannah took communion and Elder Worth laid his hands on them and prayed for them as Enrique played The Lord's Prayer on acoustic guitar. There was a holy hush that fell over the congregation as the last note resounded through the sanctuary.

God was present, God was pleased and that was all Savannah needed to know as she felt the presence of the King of Glory. It took the Matrons of Honor and the Best Men to help the couple to their feet as the glory of the Lord descended on the house, even Elder Worth had to pause for the glory of the Lord to minister to the congregation.

Prayerful Pronouncement

Elder Worth had nearly lost himself in worship before he remembered there were a few more necessary steps to the ceremony. *Lord, thank you for your power! Help me to bear this weight as I conclude.*

"For as much as Shemiah Isaiah Newman and Savannah Evangeline Charles have consented together in holy wedlock, and have witnessed the same before God and these witnesses, and thereto have pledged their everlasting faithfulness each to the other, and have pledged the same by the giving and receiving each of covenant rings, by the authority invested in me, I pronounce that they are husband and wife together, in the name of the Father, and of the Son, and of the Holy Spirit. Let all people here and everywhere recognize and respect this holy union, now and forever. For what God has joined together, let no man put asunder," Elder Worth stepped back. "Shemiah, you may, with reverence, kiss your bride," he beamed.

Shemiah wasted no time drawing Savannah into his embrace but he took his time planting his lips on hers, savoring their first true kiss, mouth to mouth, heart to heart. He felt the foundation beneath him shake as she wrapped her arms around his neck, returning the kiss with a measure of her own passion she had been sanctifying for just this moment. To the cheers of the congregation they slowly drew apart and joined hands as Elder Worth sealed their wedding with a closing prayer.

"I'm going to ask the parents of this couple to come forward to lay your hands upon them to confer the blessings of your generations upon them and their seed," Elder Worth waited as Isaiah assisted Indina Newman to the pulpit, and Andre assisted Marilyn.

"This is no light thing this couple has entered into, especially with the calling upon their lives. Let us pray," Elder Worth, along with both sets of parents laid hands on Savannah and Shemiah.

"Join with me as we ask God's blessing on Shemiah and Savannah Newman. Eternal Father, Matchless Savior, we ask that as the first act of this couple in their newly formed union, we ask you to bind every generational curse from proceeding into this new union. We ask that you release the generational blessings into this new union. We ask that the prayers of their righteous generations be answered in their lifetime as they store up prayers for the generations after them. We ask you to protect their home, protect their assets, their communities they serve, work, and recreate in. May they always turn to you for direction, for strength, for provision and hope. May they glorify you in the choices they make, in the ministries they involve themselves in and the marketplaces they work in. Use them to draw others to yourself, and let them stand as reconcilers of men and women back to you. Let them always love each other and you and bind them together with Agape love. We ask this in Jesus precious name, Amen.

Clueless

"Where are you taking me?" Savannah teased. She had been trying to figure it out for the last hour. The Bridal Party was with her, but no was saying a word, giggling instead.

"Honey, this is the first test of your faith," Shemiah chuckled. "You've got believe I know where I'm going," Shemiah whispered in her ear as the pilot announced that every one prepare for landing, Savannah grew more excited.

"We're flying?" Savannah couldn't believe she hadn't noticed they were in a plane. She had been overwhelmed during the brief church reception by all the well wishing, and flower showering she had received in the church fellowship hall. Shemiah had not allowed her feet to touch the ground, loading her into the limousine, and now apparently onto a plane. "Who's here?" she wondered.

"Everybody," they all shouted. They were trying to stay quiet because no one wanted to spoil the surprise.

Savannah recognized every voice. Before she could ask any further questions, she was lifted and carried down the steps. She held on, containing her excitement and wondering just when her husband had become a mastermind Wedding Planner.

Love Unveiled

They were finally here, Shemiah thought to himself, as he set Savannah on her feet and motioned for everyone to form a circle around her as he undid her blindfold.

"Surprise!" her private reception guests shouted.

"Savannah, welcome to your reception at 333 Coral Way, our new vacation home here in Coral Gables, Florida," Shemiah's own heart flipped over as Savannah placed her hands over her mouth in complete surprise.

The home, just minutes away from the financial district, shopping and some of the best beaches Miami had to offer, the home was six bedrooms, three baths, with a sun room, formal dining room, a fire place, a Spanish tiled roof and stone driveway which sat back from the road. Valued at over two million, Enrique had practically given his friend the property.

Savannah looked around at all the familiar faces as they went in; her bridal party along with Greg and Kevin Thomas, Lysander and Zara Townsend, Columbia and her daughters, the Cartellini brothers, Francheska, Fabian, and Dominic, Mariella, Ginny, Aurielle, Marco, Jamar, Vivian, Tehinnah, along with their respective families were there. The reception was held in the formal dining room. As everyone went to be seated, Savannah pulled her husband into the personal library.

Before he could say a word, Savannah kissed her husband soundly and thoroughly before she released him, staggering a little herself, a cute grin plastered on her face. "Thank you, Ise," Savannah's gift was waiting for him back in Savannah. She kissed him again. "My gift is back at home; I didn't know you were planning to abduct me," she teased.

Shemiah allowed her to see the heat in his eyes, the love that was now stirred and awakened. "You, Princess Sugar and Spice, are the entire gift I need right now," he kissed her neck, her bare shoulder, the top of the swell of her breast. "And I plan to take my time unwrapping my gift," he promised, kissing her once more and finding it really hard to come up for air.

Toasts

"I'd just like to say that I wish you all the best, Shemiah; you and Savannah have really been a road map for Augusta and me," Enrique confided. "To hold on to God, how to let go of self; how to preserve our sanity while we waited on God to mold us, so that we could merge and become one; Thank you," Enrique toasted.

"Ise, you have been like a brother to me, Savannah, a sister, and I'm just glad that you two became a family unit. You're both very loving people, and it's so great to see that in this day and age. You love each other but you love God more passionately than most. May your quiver be full and may your house be filled with joy always," Josiah toasted.

"Shemiah, you and I met through Savannah, but God bonded our hearts. I'm so glad that Savannah has met her match in all ways. I pray that your love for each other grow stronger everyday," Seth toasted.

Teasing

"Savannah, wow, here we are; when I first met you, I hated you, now I realize that without your love, your patience with me, Josiah and I wouldn't be where we are today. Thank you for opening your heart to me and allowing me the grace to be forgiven and see the beautiful, gifted woman you are; I love you, "Angelynn hugged Savannah, wiping her eyes and handing the mike over to the twins who leaned on each other for support.

"You're all grown up now," Aliya began. "Both of you; Savannah, you helped me to really evaluate myself, to grow comfortable with my own skin, to develop my talents; for that I am grateful; Shemiah you have been like a tower of strength, a listening ear, the voice of reason when I needed and I know others here share the same sentiment. We love you both," Aliya hugged Savannah carefully.

"What can I say, Van? You look incredibly gorgeous but that has more to do with what's inside you. I'm so happy God gave you Shemiah. You both compliment each other so well. I'm glad God gave you a praying man," she teased. "And most of all, I'm glad that you're married!" she allowed the laughter to flow before she went on. "You kept us on pins and needles for a while, but through the power of prayer, you came through; besides, Shemiah was going to elope if you held off for one more day," she joked. "Love you, girl," Augusta squeezed her tight.

Everyone got their chance to toast them and it was just what Savannah had wanted; A night of celebration.

Jetting Back

Dominic played with the garter he had caught tonight. After the look of shock had crossed her face, the catcher of the bouquet had sat stiffly while he had taken the piece of lace and tied it around her arm at Shemiah's suggestion. It was hard enough on him that Francheska had caught the bouquet, but to place a garter on her thigh? That was just asking for cold showers and sleepless nights. He had thanked God for Shemiah's quick thinking observing their gazes of embarrassment. He hadn't been able to look Francheska in the eye after that. Nick had given him a consoling pat on the back. Come Monday morning, he would be on his way to Beijing. Dominic disliked unfinished business. He had found what he was looking for, only to have to let it go. He prayed it was but for a short season. Wherever she went after this assignment, he would find her. *Francheska Cartellini had set his heart aflame.* He wasn't planning to put out the fire.

Francheska allowed her eyes to close for just a moment, savoring the hour of rest until they reached the city. She had a dream Dominic leaned near and whispered in French, 'je ne vais pas vous oublier ou de votre beauté'. *I will never forget you or your beauty*; she translated as she settled deeper into sleep. What she had failed to realize as he placed his jacket over her for warmth, was that she hadn't dreamed those words at all.

The flight went smoothly and as everyone returned to their own homes, Savannah and Shemiah settled into their vacation home to experience church love the way God intended; one man, one woman, united as one flesh.

Epilogue

Couples Sunday

Everyone was surprised to see Savannah and Shemiah during Second Chance's Sunday morning service. As his wedding present, Enrique had offered to fly them back in to services and return them to their love nest in Coral Gables. They had happily welcomed the invitation, wanting to begin their first Sunday of marital bliss in services together.

As Pastor Josiah Worth brought his initial Pastoral message, 'Love on Fire' to a close, he asked the engaged and married couples to come forth.

"We want you to get a good look at these couples. We believe in the sanctity of marriage and the process of godly courtship. Marriage is not just for you; marriage is for ministry. When you join together, you become a visible representation of Christ and His Bride. You either demonstrate God is faithful to His Bride or you demonstrate God is unfaithful to His Bride," he motioned for the couples to come closer. "I want the married couples to hug each other at the altar here and I want to do something different; Married couples as a seal today, I want you to greet your spouses with a holy kiss; engaged men, I want you to kiss your intended's hand," Josiah instructed.

"Now, let's give God a praise for every marriage in this ministry, that it will be filled with love, joy, peace, prosperity, fidelity, and longevity," he shouted.

Shemiah and Savannah lifted their hands together on one accord at the altar, praising God together and thanking Him for putting them together, in love, in purpose, in ministry.

It was a blessing to worship alongside their family and friends, to trust God to meet their needs, resolve their life's problems, and give them the counsel they needed for daily living. That was the beauty of the Christian walk; it wasn't without struggles, it wasn't without persecution; but with God, life was more than bearable. It was blessed beyond measure.

Together Shemiah and Savannah would do exploits for the Kingdom of God as they lived the Word along with their community of believers: one faith, one hope, one Lord, one church unified in the love of God.

Questions for Personal Reflection or Book Club Discussion

1. What do you feel is the overall theme of this story?
2. What are the underlying themes?
3. Do you hear God as clearly as some of the characters in the novel?
4. What character(s) do you identify with the most? Why?
5. What are some of the issues that you could see reflected in your own life?
6. Did you find yourself reading a situation that you have personally encountered but discovered a different way to approach? Explain.
7. Which character (s) frustrated you? Why?
8. How do you think incorporating the scriptures into our daily conversation and lifestyle will affect the way we think and live?
9. What situation, if any, did you think was unrealistic? Why?
10. Do you think the characters matured in their walk with God as the novel progressed?
11. What scriptures spoke to you personally? Write them down and reflect upon them.
12. Which characters do you think experienced the most radical change?
13. What does this book convey to you about God's providence in our lives?
14. Do you feel as though God is concerned about your everyday affairs, issues, or dilemmas?
15. What does this book convey to you about the need to forgive?
16. What does this novel convey to you about the need to be whole before entering into a relationship with the opposite sex?
17. What role do our friends play in accountability? Our pastors?
18. What concepts about relationships had you not considered until reading this novel?
19. Which couple's relationship most impressed you? Which single?
20. What relationship in the story is close to your ideal?

Growth Stimulators

Take some time to serve someone without expecting something in return
Take some time to reconcile with those who have hurt you
Take some time to deal with the unfinished business in your life
Take some time to share the word in your community/workplace
Take some time to fellowship with your local church body outside of the four walls

Shantae A. Charles, founder of GOD Ideas, LLC. , is an educator, psalmist, licensed evangelist, poet, artistic creator, danseuse and children's advocate. For the past ten years, Shantae has been touching lives daily and reaching the future and currently serves as a Teacher/Advisor for a gender-specific program. She serves as Christian Education Coach for her church and serves under the dynamic leadership of Pastors Gerald and Judy Mandrell at Life Changers Church of God in Christ in Tallahassee, FL (www.lifechangerscogic.com).

Shantae holds a B.S. in Art Education with an emphasis on graphic design and child psychology. She lives in Tallahassee, Florida with her husband Robert Charles, President and CEO of ROC Studios International, where she serves and helps to meet his vision as Vice President.

Her philosophy for life is summed up in these words: "For Christ I live and for Christ I die." Her favorite quote is St. Francis of Assisi's impassioned words: "Preach the Gospel at all times and if necessary use words." Shantae is a multifaceted gift of God, and she gives all credit to God knowing that she can do nothing without His Son Jesus Christ who strengthens her.

To write Shantae or to contact her for speaking engagements, workshop facilitating, graphic design, or artistic commissions **email her at:** churchlove333@yahoo.com **or visit her websites godideasllc.com** shantaecharles.com spiritualauthenticchange.com

Church Love Fans

I would like to thank you, the reader for journeying with me into the heart of Savannah with all of the characters. Some of you felt like they were your very own friends. It has given me great joy to contribute to the up building of the believer through the ministry of writing. I could have not done this without prayer and fasting and the constant support I received through emails, texts, internet postings. I'm honored that some of you have posted me as your favorite author among many well known ones.

I have been humbled by stories of marriage, engagement, giving love another chance, forgiving others, marriages being kept in tact all because of the choice to be obedient in writing. These testimonies have kept the purpose of why I write ever before me: to change lives for the cause of Christ.

There is one last journey into the heart of Savannah, which I am working on through the Church Love Series with Church Love Book 4. However I will be shifting focus this year to releasing my CD Project and non-fiction Book of Wisdom, Holy Ghost Quotes in 2011.

I ask that you pray with me as my husband and I seek to fulfill the Kingdom Mandate on our lives through service in our local church and community. It is our desire to mentor, teach, and empower others in whatever God has called them to do.

Words cannot express how much your support of this project has meant. I pray that the words in this series will continue to resonate as you seek peace with others and intimacy with God. I pray that as you love fallen people in a dying world, that the saving grace of Christ will keep your compassion alive. Remember, God always answers the righteous!

Shantae A. Charles

Special Thanks

Special thanks to my husband who allowed me to work all night several times. To Marilyn Griffith and Sharon Ewell Foster who gave feedback, encouragement, and shared wisdom with up and coming authors during the SistaFaith Conference. Also, thanks to fellow authors Tremayne Moore, Michael Beckford, for their extra push to get Church Love completed. I would also like to thank Anita Wholuba for her awesome editing skills along with Marsha McCoy. I would like to thank my Teen Team (Patrecia & Laterria) who made sure the story would interest the younger believers. Last, but not least, I thank Jesus Christ, my Lord and Savior who placed me on a spiritual consecration during this writing, for without him, none of this would have been remotely possible.

Personal Reflections
John 13:35

The relationship I'm in now is

_____

_____

_____

_____

One thing I would change about my past relationships is

_____

_____

_____

_____

One thing I need to improve about my own relationship is

_____

_____

_____

_____

My best friendship is with _____

_____

_____

FAQ: What's the Difference?

Single- unattached to anyone; can be single by choice, by calling (eunuchs), by birth (some people have certain birth defects and choose to remain single.

Dating- seeing another person of the opposite sex for the express purpose of enjoyment; there is no purpose beyond the immediate; there are no intentions towards marriage

Courtship- seeing another person of the opposite sex for the express purpose of consideration for marriage; the purpose is deciding suitability for permanent commitment; intentions are towards marriage; there is usually some pastoral counsel/advising here

Engagement- committed to person of the opposite sex and intention is marriage; counseling advised through this period of at least 6 months. **Note**- You should not plan a wedding **during** engagement; they should be **two separate events**, with time dedicated respectfully to each.

Marriage- a covenant relationship ordained and originated by God between one man and one woman. Not to be entered into lightly, but reverently, and with the express **intent** of remaining together until death do you part.

Now Available:

Church Love 1: Second Chance   **Church Love 2: Fresh Fire**